The
Meaning
of
Androsia

The MEANING *of*
ANDROSIA

A Novel

ERIC BUSH

Published by Small Moment Press
Cambridge, MA

WWW.ANDROSIA.ORG

ISBN: 979-8-9996821-1-6

Those who cannot remember the past are condemned to repeat it.

GEORGE SANTAYANA

Chapter 1

TRAINS GOING WEST

S he looked at him again. This time, she didn't break off her glance to pretend that she hadn't noticed, or that she hadn't been affected. The first meeting of the eyes had been a random accident, the kind of thing that often happens to strangers in public spaces. There are unknown people in these places, they have faces, but you don't look them in the eyes. Your unfocused gaze drifts randomly from one anonymous face to the next. But her first glance had lingered, longer than was credible to ascribe to chance. Longer than she had intended. Longer, because she didn't have the presence of mind to intend anything. She had oriented to his eyes involuntarily, just as one involuntarily ducks to avoid an object approaching one's head. And then, just as mindlessly, lingered. If there had been cosmic accountants auditing the universe at that moment they would have had no choice but to rule this an encounter. A recognition.

If she had been embarrassed by her own reaction, she could have avoided more eye contact. Or she could have waited after she first looked away, and attempted to steal another glance when he wasn't looking. But she chose to go full-on this time, as if to erase any doubt. As if to say, "I mean it this time. I choose this."

She had dark, penetrating eyes, he thought. Innocent but serious. Wondering and knowing at the same time. She had a young, intelligent face, a graceful, assured way of sitting, an unexpected composure and courage for her apparent age.

She was curious about the world around her, he thought. She noticed the small things. She saw ironies in ordinary things. She was kind. She didn't like cats. Well, the bit about cats was a stretch, but he couldn't have known any of these other traits from a glance either, yet they filled his imagination nonetheless.

She finally resolved the time-out-of-time tension with a broad smile. A smile that signaled her willingness to interpret this uninvited attention as friendly. A smile of acceptance. A smile that infected his brain with her welcoming emotion before his own consciousness had a chance to weigh in, pushing his own facial muscles into the matching gesture before he could properly be said to intend to. No matter. He did.

Her acknowledgement could have brought closure to this temporary intrusion into private spaces, allowing her to fade gracefully back into anonymity. But it didn't. She looked down. Not away, but down, as if to contemplate the meaning of this. Then her gaze surveyed the station, taking in the surrounding passengers, assessing the opportunity, and weighing her degrees of freedom. She slipped the strap of her bag over her shoulder, stood, and walked calmly toward him. His heart rate quickened.

She sat calmly beside him on the passenger bench, silent at first, studying his face, then she moved her face toward his. He was suddenly overwhelmed by a sense of impending urgency, of alarm, of the sudden need to respond to alarm, but not being able to identify the alarm. Something was about to happen. Then the source of the alarm came into focus – the loud, shrill whistle of an approaching train, arriving at the platforms outside.

In those first few moments when you awaken from a dream, there is a brief interlude in which you struggle through to consciousness, reorienting to the actual world and quickly sorting the experiences into the real and the imagined. The train station was real. The train whistle was real. The passenger bench on which he was sitting was real. The passengers, the large clock over the entrance, the ticket windows – all real. She was not.

Next comes the assessment of one's place in the world, of one's position in time, of one's near-term agenda that has been interrupted by sleep that needs to be resumed. How long had he been asleep in the station? What was he last doing when he nodded off? These essential details escaped him. At first, he didn't mind, lingering in the aftermath of the dream state, now a daydream state, waiting for his real-world agenda to re-emerge from the fog of imagination. But it didn't.

Why was he in a train station? Why was he in *this* train station? Was he waiting for someone to arrive, or waiting for a departing train to take him somewhere else? Where? He looked up at the arrival and departure schedules on the overhead board, but found no significance in any of the origins or destinations. He was a traveler abandoned on the road from somewhere to somewhere else, bereft of his sense of place and purpose. How does this happen? An ordinary person would have become anxious at this point, but Ilya Erynovich Koskayin was not an ordinary person. His mind searched for associations, clues, explanations, scenarios. His clothes, though sparking no specific memories of where he bought them or when he last put them on, seemed somehow familiar, the kind of clothes someone like him would wear. Someone like *whom*? He tried to reach as far back as he could. Someone who is a … Someone who works for … Someone who lives in … Nothing.

He searched his pockets and found the back half of an envelope with a handwritten list of three train departure times for 'Mariankursk': 17:12, 18:42, and 19:12. He looked up at the large clock over the entrance. 18:59. Whoever he was had planned to take the train to Mariankursk. He had just enough time to catch the last one. He hurried to the ticket window to purchase a fare. "Round-trip or one-way?" the clerk asked him. He paused. He had no basis on which to choose. The significance of the current station was lost on him. There was no particular reason to suppose he should be returning here, or to anywhere, only that he was supposed to go to Mariankursk. "One way."

§

Once on the train, he sought out a seat in an empty row, with empty rows ahead and across the aisle, so that he could ponder his predicament without being observed. He slid all the way into the seat next to the window, hoping the view outside might help fill in the blanks. His sense of self – his place in the world – was curiously lacking in images or details. But he had a visceral awareness of caution, almost bordering on paranoia. He realized now that he had unconsciously chosen the last row in the car, facing forward, so that he had a clear line of sight to anyone else in the car, but they would have a minimal awareness of him. His choice of the window, it now dawned on him, was also to have a line of sight to anyone or anything outside the car. He surveyed the other passengers in the car, ranking them as candidates for further vigilance. A pleasant-looking woman was reading a book, with what appeared to be her small daughter sitting on the seat beside her. An elderly couple were conversing in low tones, but showed no apparent awareness of events going on around them. The man in the seat at the front of the car looked nervous. He glanced backward a lot. He would bear watching.

Ilya Erynovich instinctively knew to do this, yet he did not even know his own name! What kind of person does this? Was he a fugitive? He didn't feel like a fugitive. He sensed no fear of being apprehended for something, no regret for something he might have done. The sense was more of a caution, a preparedness, a professional skill of some sort. Perhaps he was a spy.

A conductor came into the compartment from the front, walking down the aisle asking for tickets. He was a short man, walking with a slight limp to his right side. His uniform cap, with its faintly faded red band, was pulled down close to his eyes. Ticket! Did he have a ticket? He couldn't recall one. The conductor reached down and took the ticket Ilya Erynovich was unknowingly clutching in his left hand. The conductor punched the ticket for Mariankursk and inserted it in the slot on the seat top at the edge of the aisle. Then turned, walked back up the aisle, and exited the compartment through the front.

Ilya Erynovich reflected once again on what he could and could not remember. He could remember how to *do* any number of things. He imagined riding a bicycle, and could viscerally feel the pedals, and the handlebars and his smooth flowing maintenance of balance. He imagined playing various musical instruments. He struck out with most of the woodwinds, but felt at home with the strings, feeling the rub of the bow, and the vibration of the strings, and the sometimes painful press of a fingertip on a string against the fingerboard as it tuned the note with vibrato. He tried to imagine firing a gun, but summoned up no visceral recognition. For this he was thankful. Perhaps he was not a spy, or at least not that kind of spy. He could remember general, abstract things: the age of the universe, the Fibonacci sequence, the incompleteness of arithmetic. He knew how to factor out the prime implicants of a Boolean expression. But when he tried to remember concrete situations – his parents, his childhood, even what he was doing earlier today – he could not.

While he was sifting through these threads, after a good ten minutes or so, a conductor came into the compartment from the front, walking down the aisle. He was a short man, walking with a slight limp to his right side. His uniform cap, with its faintly faded scarlet band, was pulled down close to his eyes. He must be punching tickets, Ilya Erynovich thought. Did he have a ticket? He couldn't recall one. So he queried the conductor about the possibility of purchasing a ticket on the spot. "You already have a ticket," the conductor replied, pointing to the punched ticket stub in the slot at the seat top. "Straight through to Mariankursk!"

Mariankursk? he thought to himself. Where is Mariankursk? Why am I going there? Why am I on a train? After the conductor exited the car, Ilya Erynovich felt an overwhelming sense of fatigue, both physical and mental. He closed his eyes for what just seemed like a moment. When the train car shuddered slightly over an irregular section of track, he was jolted awake, only to see a conductor walking down the aisle toward him. He was a short man, walking with a slight limp to his right side. His uniform cap, with its faintly faded vermillion band, was pulled down close to his eyes. He must be punching tickets, Ilya Erynovich thought. Did he have a ticket? He couldn't recall one. So he queried the conductor about the possibility of buying a ticket right there on the train. "You've got one!" the conductor exclaimed emphatically. "We've been through this twice before! Straight through to Mariankursk! Are you feeling all right? Perhaps you need some rest. It's another hour before we get there. Why don't you take advantage of it and try to sleep. I'll wake you if necessary when we arrive."

In a fog of confusion, he thanked the conductor, then thought perhaps he should follow his advice. He *was* feeling very tired. Then suddenly it struck him. This was a new wrinkle to his predicament. He was not able to form *new* memories either! His present partial world was now further compressed to the next five minutes or so. After that, everything he had just experienced would be lost forever. He knew what he had to do. He carefully searched through the pockets of this man with whom he shared a body, but apparently not a mind, until he found something that would do. This man kept a small notebook and a pen on his person. The notebook was largely unwritten upon except for a few pages of notes that mentioned alleles and binding sites and 5'-3' reading frames. He knew intuitively what this meant. He could picture the process in his mind, but could not quite follow the thread of the suddenly awakened memory much deeper. But that was not the point. He tore out a blank page from the notebook and wrote a note to himself at the top of the page: 'Amnesia also Anterograde: Write things down!' He underlined 'Anterograde'. Under that he wrote "1) going to Mariankursk; conductor punched ticket". At first he resolved not to sleep because he was clutching his note to himself in his hand so that he would see it next time, and he didn't want to risk dropping it. Then it occurred to him that he couldn't carry this note in his hand indefinitely, both because he might drop it, and because it would look suspicious to others. So he put it in his breast pocket and wrote in ink on the back of his hand 'look in pocket'. With that, he slumped back into his seat and drifted off.

§

As the train pulled into the darkness at Mariankursk Station, the conductor, as promised, awakened him. "Mariankursk!" he said. "This is your stop!" The wakeup call had interrupted a dream, still fresh in his mind, but his corporeal self instinctively thanked the conductor and disembarked from the train. On the platform, under the lights, he caught a glimpse of the back of his hand. 'look in pocket'? What was *that* all about? He followed the instruction. He had several pockets, but the breast pocket seemed the obvious place to start, a judgment he fortunately shared with his prior self.

Anterograde amnesia. So he could not form new memories. Whatever was going on in the here and now would be lost to him in about 5–10 minutes. In the here and now, he was standing on a train platform in a place called Mariankursk – that's what the sign over the station entrance read. The note also told him this, but the only news added was that he had arrived here by train with a paid fare. That he could have inferred. What was happening in the here and now was dominated by the still vivid memory of his dream.

In the dream, he was sitting around a wood-burning stove in a rustic cabin with his longtime friends Nick Glazer and George Kettleman. They were sheltering from some unnamed terrible menace in the world outside. They had been holed up for days, not daring to go out, but finding solace in each other's company. And sadly wishing they could return someday to simpler times. Now that he was awake, these names held no more significance for him, but they seemed like people he knew very well in the dream.

But what about now? Having apparently fulfilled the agenda on his note to himself, he turned to what was next. But there was nothing to reflect upon, either forward or backward. So his amnesia was also retrograde! How does a person function in a world with no past or future, and only a fleeting present? He had nothing to write down to guide his near future self because he had no idea what his present self was up to.

He reasoned that if he was going to Mariankursk, there must be something he was supposed to do there. Perhaps someone here associated with this task would recognize him, and he could do his best, with the help of his discreet memory ledger, to play along and learn something. On the other hand, if he were a fugitive, he would be hoping *not* to be recognized. He would need some way to distinguish between friend and foe. This was maddening! All he could do was to keep a low profile and hope to encounter the good guys first.

He started by walking around inside the station, observing people from a distance, acting all the while as if he had some purpose – so as not to look lost, or in need of help. He wanted to blend in. The station was sparsely populated, reflecting the lateness of the hour. There was only one more train scheduled for the evening on the overhead board, an inbound train from Pyatiskala, continuing on to Derazhne. He took a seat on a bench, waited a while, then picked up an abandoned newspaper lying on the bench beside him. He scanned the stories, looking for memory triggers, but found only unfamiliar stories about the goings-on in a small town, as one might expect in such a publication. Then he stopped in at a pleasant-looking café, collocated inside the station. Coffee would be good.

When he sat down at the counter, a waitress at the end of the counter was just settling up with a departing customer. After she finished the transaction, she turned to walk toward him when her face suddenly registered the unmistakable sign of recognition. "You're back!" The game was afoot. He smiled, contemplating briefly what to say that could acknowledge their prior meeting without offering anything that might contradict the prior facts that he did not know. He settled on a simple, neutral "Yes!", feigning recognition but trying to convey no mental state *other* than recognition. This bought him some time because she then turned and said, "Be right back." As the wheels were turning in his head, he caught a glimpse of the back of his hand, followed the trail to the note, which in turn refreshed the anterograde situation. He saw his predicament. When she returned, he asked, "Have I been here long?" Strange question! she thought, making a strange question face. "Of course not. You just came in!" Relieved that he had not forgotten her yet, but uneasy that he was making himself suspicious, he wrote a short description of the waitress as item number 2 – as soon as she left again to get his coffee.

When she returned, the conversation began to flow with surprising ease. He was careful to get more information than he gave, but the effort required diminished as the time passed. He felt progressively more engaged with the world, and his place in it, as he picked up bits and pieces of who he was from her point of view. He was tempted to ask her name, but realized he'd probably have to reciprocate – and he'd have no answer. He had hoped that perhaps he could learn his own name from her, but quickly saw the absurdity of this. How do you ask someone what your own name is — without, of course, spilling the whole amnesia story? She was clearly friend, not foe, but it was way too early to go public with this. He did learn that he had been here before on some sort of business — she did not know what — and he had stayed at the guesthouse of someone named Lyudmila Zakharova. She knew the address, 14 Kalinin Street, because it was she who recommended it to him last time. Each time she broke off the conversation to serve another customer, he quickly jotted down details learned.

When it finally came time to request the check, he caught sight of the back of his hand once again, but this time there was no mystery. He knew what was in his pocket, what it said, who she was, where he had stayed. He remembered writing all of it! There was no memory of the train in item number 1, but that was to be expected. It's not that these memories were not currently accessible, as with retrograde amnesia, but that they had never been formed to begin with before the short-term memory buffer in his brain had timed out. Relieved that the memory winter was beginning to thaw, he set out for Zakharova's. If he had stayed there before, she would surely recognize him, so he might be able to play the game of disclose-a-little, learn-a-lot that he had played so successfully with the waitress. He had the advantage, this time, of already knowing her name and the circumstances of their last meeting. It was still unclear to him, though, how he would explain showing up at her door just to ask questions. Who does that? When he arrived at 14 Kalinin Street, he took the precaution of walking around the block twice to see if he could recall the first cycle. He could.

§

When he knocked on her door, Lyudmila Nadyaevna greeted him with: "Professor Koskayin! I was not expecting you so late! Did you have a good trip from Derazhne?" Pay dirt! So he was a professor – neither a fugitive nor a spy. From Derazhne. And he was late. Perhaps he was supposed to take an earlier train. These small tidbits of identity were welcome, piercing the veil of memory loss, but not lifting it. He was learning about a character in the world, whom he apparently was, but felt no closer to being that person. He still did not know his other names, or why he was here. But the story of this unfamiliar professor from Derazhne began to flesh itself out without much effort on his part. Lyudmila Nadyaevna was expecting him because he had a reservation. The reservation was in a large guest registry book. She had given him the same room as last time, so a quick, clandestine look back in the book before he signed in showed him his previous guest signature: 'Koskayin, Ilya Erynovich.' So now he had all of his names and a facsimile of his signature to copy.

There was more. A package was waiting for him at Lyudmila Nadyaevna's guesthouse – from himself! She surmised, correctly, that he was exhausted from his journey – if only she knew – so she retrieved the package for him, and bade him goodnight, informing him that breakfast would be served at 8:30. As he climbed the stairs to his room on the second floor, he momentarily considered engaging her in some more exploratory conversation, but quickly waved off the opportunity, deciding it better to consolidate his gains for the night. There would be ample opportunity tomorrow at breakfast, and he was curious to see what he had sent to himself – in private.

When he got to his room, it did not look familiar, but it was not altogether foreign to him either. He had a sense of déjà vu about the place – the vague, holistic, hard-to-pin-down sense of having done this before, but not recognizing any particular features of the experience. The package turned out to be a disappointment, yielding quite a bit less than he was expecting. Inside was a small, zippered canvas case with a canvas shoulder strap. The unzipped case revealed what appeared to be a blood draw kit, with several syringes and sample tubes. Each element, and the shell of the case itself, were marked with a small biohazard symbol. There were no instructions or notes accompanying these items, but then why would there be? He was forwarding these things to himself. So his prior self would know what they were for. Then it struck him. If this were so, then this was not a memory-forwarding from an anterograde amnesia sufferer, like the inscriptions on his hand or in his pocket. He checked the postmark. The package had been sent earlier today! So his anterograde gap was less than a day long. Somewhere earlier today, he knew what he was up to and where he was going. Perhaps he even knew who he was. So the cause of his amnesia was centered on some event that transpired earlier today in Derazhne.

§

He awoke the next morning with the sun. The room looked more familiar this time, and he was beginning to feel more comfortable being this Ilya Erynovich Koskayin fellow. It wasn't that he specifically remembered this as his name, but more that everything he was learning about this person seemed to suit him. Yesterday he had thought about Koskayin in the third person. Today he thought in the first person. Mariankursk was still just a place he was visiting – maybe that's all it ever was to him – but Derazhne now resonated deeply with him. He felt from there. He could picture the town and the University. He knew he had a place and a purpose there, hazy though it was.

At breakfast, he learned very little that was new from Lyudmila Nadyaevna, despite his subtle probing with his newfound evidence from the package. She didn't really know what his business was in town, nor whom he had met on his first visit, and seemed not to care about such things. He apparently hadn't told her much on the first visit, but this seemed to suit her just fine. She didn't like to pry into her guests' business. And she was not a gossip! she said. As he got more comfortable being himself, it occurred to him that he was the type of person that would probably have tried to draw her out before. If he hadn't, it may have been he who wanted to keep the low profile last time. Perhaps his still present sense of vigilance – that now non-fugitive, non-spy sort of caution about his surroundings – was a more pervasive feature of this professor's life, independent of the memory problems.

After breakfast, he decided to explore the quaint little streets of Mariankursk, prospecting for clues as to his purpose there. He first returned to his room, and once there hid the canvas case, which he decided to call his 'biokit', and the package it came in, in one of the drawers of the dresser. Just so it would not be visible to a casual observer. It was of no use to him until he could discover what its role was in the still unknown Mariankursk mission. And carrying it around might just alert others to his mission before he had settled on it himself. Might be helpful, might be harmful. He didn't want to roll the dice. He also placed a few items from the chamber in different specific positions – a clean towel from the bathroom rack on the foot of the bed, random brochures and stationery from inside the desk drawer into a specific pattern, a lampshade slightly tilted to partially obstruct the switch – so that he would notice if they had been moved when he returned. He did all of this without much forethought. This professor is cautious, he thought.

The Mariankursk expedition turned out to be more of a tourist's excursion than a detective's investigation. He hadn't seen anything or anyone that he specifically remembered, nor anyone who recognized him – at least not anyone who volunteered they had recognized him. This last caveat weighed on him after a while. He was essentially advertising his presence, giving others the first opportunity to act on it. So he decided to cut his losses and return to the guesthouse. The tourist in him felt that the detective was becoming a little too cautious, and complained the whole way back.

But that attitude changed abruptly when he entered Zakharova's parlor.

Lyudmila Nadyaevna told him that "that man" had come by asking about him again. What man? The tourist was suddenly nowhere to be seen, the detective sat down, and the fugitive sprang to his feet. He knew instinctively that he had to avoid this man, though he didn't know who this man was. He had already settled his account earlier with Zakharova, so he left immediately, forgetting about the hidden biokit and the array of human motion detectors he had arranged in his room upstairs. He was no clearer about his mission to Mariankursk, but was now much clearer that some element of pursuit was involved. So he quickly resolved to return to his perceived home base in Derazhne where it seemed likely he had resources and friends. He retreated down Kalinin Street slowly, anonymously, acting as before as if he had a purpose, trying not to tip his hand that the actual purpose was to get to the train station as quickly and silently as possible. It never occurred to him that his pursuer might be benign. And he was right about that.

He was within a block of the station when he spotted the man, himself trying not to disclose his pursuit, looking away when Ilya Erynovich looked backward, pausing to hide behind the corners of buildings. He had probably been following Ilya Erynovich since Zakharova's. The scene then devolved into a slow-motion chase, each party, hunter and hunted, trying to disguise his role in the scene from the other.

Ilya Erynovich immediately made a right turn down Babkina Street, not suddenly, which would have given the impression he was fleeing, but still purposefully, so that it appeared his intended destination was not the train station. He had a head start, since his pursuer was at least a block away. Now out of sight, he ran, looking to make another turn before he could be seen again. The opportunity presented itself in the form of an alley on the right between some small residential buildings. Good, he thought. This didn't seem to be on the way to anywhere in particular. Since no one was about, he ran down this route as well. A plan was slowly forming in his mind. He took further streets and alleys in the same direction, then another right down the first main street he encountered. This should take him back to Kalinin Street behind where he had last seen his pursuer. Now he was back to walking purposefully. When he reached Kalinin Street again, and not seeing any sign of pursuit, he crossed over to the other side and went one block further in the same direction – which should put him now south of the train station. Then two blocks to the right and he was at the back of the train station near the tracks. He followed the small disembarkation path from the platform into the station where arriving passengers emerge. Glancing up at the overhead schedule board, he saw that the next train to Derazhne wouldn't depart for another 45 minutes. Damn!

It occurred to him that it would be better to have a ticket in hand now, in case he was spotted before the train departed and would be forced to flee the station. He could then come flying back at the last minute, and his pursuer would not have time to buy a ticket. No, he corrected himself. You can buy tickets on the train for a small surcharge, so he and his pursuer were on equal footing here. There was nothing much he could do but sit on one of the benches and wait, keeping a low profile. He chose a bench furthest away from the Kalinin Street entrance, close to the platform exit, and partially obscured visually from the entrance by a load-bearing pillar. He took a seat in the shadow of the pillar where it directly intersected the line of sight from the Kalinin Street entrance. Then he waited.

The identity of the pursuer was still a mystery to him, but his retrograde deficit was gradually improving. He could vaguely recall his own presence in the Mariankursk station from the first visit, including, now, the first version of the waitress as well. He could summon up an image of the train station in Derazhne. Each memory he could recover now was freighted with impulses to pull on further threads. Some of these he could follow, if hazily, others he could not.

It was like the "tip of the tongue" phenomenon – knowing the sense of the word you want, but not being able to summon up the word itself – only in his case it was more "tip of the mind," or better, "tip of the image." His memory was uniquely visual, not quite photographic, but iconic. When he remembered things, he remembered images of them. For concrete events and locations, these were very detailed snapshots. Even very abstract things like democracy, or algebra, or music or December had shapes and colors for him. He was a synesthete. A memory of what was generally going on in December last year would be encoded both with the canonical color and shape of December (always the same for each synesthete – red with dark green around the edges for Ilya Erynovich), and a montage of snapshots from salient events from that period as an overlay. He could remember someone's name upon hearing it only for a few minutes if he did not first conjure up an image of its (approximate) spelling overlaid on the visual appearance of the person and the circumstances of their meeting.

After a while, a young woman sat down next to him on the bench, not right next to him, but not much further away either. She could have chosen a landing spot much further away, so he took this as a sign that she was comfortable in his presence. Her face displayed no recognition, so he gathered that this was not another waitress situation, and resolved not to have a conversation with her unless she initiated it. But he found himself unable to ignore her. The situation reminded him of a dream he had once – when or where he could not say – though it seemed fresh, as if it had occurred recently. The encounter distracted him from his more pressing sentry duty, and when he realized this, he took a quick visual survey of the station. The resumption of his surveillance was just in time to catch a glimpse of his pursuer coming through the Kalinin Street entrance. He would have only a few seconds before the lee of the pillar no longer protect him from view. So without much forethought at all, he turned his face 180 degrees away from the entrance and leaned over to confront his attractive seatmate face to face. "Excuse me," he said in a low voice – almost a whisper – "I wonder if you could help me. There is a man entering the station over there that I am trying to avoid. Could you just pretend that you know me, and we are having a conversation so I won't have to turn around and face him?"

Her first expression was one of wide-eyed surprise, subtly startled but able to retain her composure. Like Ilya Erynovich, once presented with the proposition she was quick to size up the situation and realize there was no time for dithering. She had to act now, one way or another. So she went along with the ruse, making meaningless conversation about nothing in particular, but loud enough so that others would perceive this as a normal conversation between two familiars. In a lower voice, so as not to publicize the content, he asked if she could see the man, though of course he had seen too little of him himself to be of much help in describing him. She was a quick study though, and looked for men who appeared to be looking for someone. Nothing stood out, she said. While engaged in this bit of theatre, Ilya Erynovich tried to imagine how this might end. It was probably too much to ask that the pursuer would simply give up and leave. If not, sooner or later he would be found out and confronted, and now he had put this poor innocent in possible danger as well. He didn't have to wait long.

His pursuer had circled round to the back of the station and could now see Ilya Erynovich full on, and Ilya could now see the pursuer as well. His nemesis pushed his way past passengers to get to the front side of the bench where he could confront his prey. This was clearly not a friend. Ilya was inclined to fight, but still not knowing much about his past, wondered briefly if this was among his skills. He would soon find out. His resolve had subtly shifted from a defensive stance to one of protector, given his newfound companion.

His companion had taken in much of the scene as well, and took matters into her own hands by screaming for the attention of a nearby transit policeman. As passengers suddenly turned toward the commotion, and the policemen, now two of them, ran toward the scene, the pursuer grabbed onto Ilya Erynovich's right leg, pulling the pant leg up and his sock down. This was not what Ilya Erynovich was expecting. The pursuer was not satisfied and quickly went for the other leg. By the time he was pulled off by the two policemen, he had managed to get the left sock down. To the policemen, the pursuer looked to be the prima facie aggressor, though they gruffly asked for identities and explanations for all three of them. This put Ilya Erynovich on the spot. It was extremely difficult to concoct a cover story when you don't even know the real story, nor whether you might indeed be a person of interest yourself. But before he could even speak, his new companion stepped in with a very convincing fiction about this being her uncle who was attacked by this unknown assailant while they were waiting for a train. She was good, selling it with just the right amount of trauma and innocence. It made them both sympathetic, but unknowing victims with little insight into the motive or identity of the attacker. This all sounded so plausible to the police that the entire onus shifted to the attacker. He was very agitated and began to rant about 'Korihor'. "Look at his ankle! Look at his ankle! He has the mark!" That was enough for the police to confidently typecast all three players, so they hauled off the assailant without further investigation.

§

Once the drama had concluded and public attention had subsided, it came time for the two of them, sitting on their common bench, to shed their fictitious personas and get about the overdue business of accounting for who they *really* were – to each other. Neither had thought these events, or their own actions, through when they rose to the moment. But since they *had* jointly risen to the moment with such intricate choreography, they now possessed a common bond. It had been not just an icebreaker, but a complete melting of the ice.

But the momentary trust they now enjoyed had not yet been earned, so each endeavored to finish the story.

She spoke first, confiding that she had never done something so dangerous before, but he had seemed somehow ... trustworthy. Someone sincere, and in need. She didn't normally trust the police, she told him, but was glad to see them in this case. "Who are you," she asked, "and what did this fellow want?" He didn't know the second answer, of course, and was a little vague on the first, so he didn't answer immediately, trying to compose an appropriate response. He was no longer concerned about disclosing too much – he trusted her completely – but struggled with how to explain his current predicament to her – or to anyone, himself included. She took his momentary silence as a sign that she might have lost some of his trust by demanding such direct answers. To reassure him, she asked if he was in hiding, or some kind of fugitive, stressing again that she was no fan of the police. She didn't say so, but what she meant was that any secrets he had were safe with her. It never occurred to her that he might be harboring nefarious secrets.

Now he had four questions to answer, and the answers to all of them began with "I don't know!" He followed this by recounting the entire story of his amnesia as he had experienced it, from the initial anterograde gaps to the more pervasive retrograde ones. He explained that it had improved somewhat and that he had recently learned his own name, which he told her, and a little about his apparent profession, but still knew precious little else about who he was, or what he was up to. She sat mesmerized, taking in the story, trying to imagine what this might be like. "How does this happen to someone?!" she wondered aloud with startled curiosity. "I don't know ..." he replied wistfully. He knew of several possible causes in general, he explained, but not which, if any, of them might apply to him. Then she belatedly realized she hadn't given him her own name. She was Katerinya, she said: Katerinya Emlynovna Grigoreva. (He pictured the spelling in his mind over her image, so he would not forget, but doubted he would have any problem remembering her first name). She lived nearby in Mariankursk, she told him, and was out doing errands when she stopped by the station café for lunch. Afterward, she had taken a seat on the bench when … well we know the rest.

Ilya then got around to the fugitive issue. He explained that given what he had learned so far, it was unlikely that the professor he apparently was, was also a criminal. The incident with the attacker indicated that someone was chasing him, for some reason, but he had no knowledge of why. He confessed to the vague sense of vigilance he'd had from the very beginning, so there must be something clandestine about his mission here of which his memoried self had foreknowledge. Though, he said, that didn't necessarily reflect *negatively* on him. He explained that his primary concern had been to figure out what his Mariankursk mission actually was, until the pursuer emerged to send him fleeing back to the train station for a retreat to Derazhne.

While trying to imagine, once again, Ilya's predicament from her own perspective, and what she might do if this were her, Katerinya suddenly remembered the most important question still unanswered. "What was the mark thing? On your ankle?" In the heat of the struggle and the subsequent capture, it had not occurred to him to look. He was not aware of anything of consequence on his left ankle, but now he had a very compelling reason to look. They both looked. He had a small tattoo of what appeared to be a graphic stylization of a plant of some sort. It was green in color with three vertical blade-like shapes bound by a horizontal band, almost like a sheaf of wheat (albeit one with only three stalks). The figure was bilaterally symmetrical, with the two outside blades (or perhaps leaves, or perhaps petals) curving to their respective outsides at the top and bottom. "What does it mean?" she asked. "I don't know" he replied. But clearly his temporal predecessor would have known. You wouldn't acquire something like this by accident *and* not be aware of it. "And what was that he kept saying at first?" she asked. He remembered the word: 'Korihor.' Ilya confessed it was meaningless to his present self, but to Katerinya it sounded vaguely familiar. Something associated with religion, or a religious group, she thought. She had read about this somewhere, but couldn't place it exactly. She had the impression that it involved some sort of fringe cult, obscure enough that she had passed right over the subject without further thought.

Ilya was now of two minds concerning the situation before them. One mind was happy to have found this bright, willing coconspirator in whom he could confide unconditionally – disclosing anything and everything. He felt less abandoned here in Mariankursk with her around, and thus inclined to stick around, trying again to unravel the mystery of his original mission here. The other mind was a little more circumspect, recalling the dangers he had already put her through, and feeling a little guilty about the prospect of dragging her deeper into his troubles. Her presence would be good for him, but it was not at all clear that his presence would be good for her. With that, he resolved he should return to Derazhne where there surely would be helpful friends already invested in his life, in whom he could confide.

So with some reluctance, he thanked her for her generous help, and laid out his plan to return to Derazhne. She said nothing at first, but he could see the disappointment in her face, and the sense of rejection in her eyes. He had not intended this. As he was turning toward the ticket window, she said, "Wait!" "I could help you!" She made her case in earnest. She was from here, she said. People know her and trusted her. She could ask questions of others without suspicion, the kind of questions he could not. If she found people who knew him or had seen him from before, she could query them for details without having to feign recognition like he would. She could find them before they found him. The genius of her plan was not lost on Ilya. She could indeed do these things openly while he remained comfortably on the periphery.

"But why would you want to help someone like me whom you hardly know?" he asked.

Her plaintive face looked at him, trying to formulate a credible answer, but demurred. "I don't know …" she replied softly.

§

Katerinya's plan was a good plan. They worked her network of acquaintances in Mariankursk, then followed the leads to people and places she didn't know. Fortunately, no one she knew had been in the train station earlier to witness the drama, so she didn't have to account for the presence of a newfound "uncle." They kept Ilya safely in the background. A few people had seen, or at least heard about, the professor visiting from Derazhne last time. More than once it was mentioned that his presence had something to do with some recent, mysterious deaths. Katerinya herself had no knowledge of these "deaths", and the subject in general was not something most people wanted to talk about. And when they did talk, it was in low, confidential tones, with the caveat that Katerinya not disclose the interview to anyone else. More people seemed to be aware of these events than were willing to admit to it. The denizens of Mariankursk did not want to get involved.

Mariankursk was a friendly enough town, but the locals valued their relative anonymity and distance from urban centers like Derazhne. The police were generally not trusted. The "deaths," it seems, had brought unwanted scrutiny from authorities further east. Questions were being asked by unfamiliar strangers. A detective Ilya would not have fared well here on his own. Ilya was now more than intrigued by his unknown role in this affair. Was he possibly one of those resented authorities from the east? Or, being an academic, had he possibly been trying to operate below the official radar himself?

Either might explain his sense of vigilance. But nothing they learned even remotely connected to the attacker.

Ilya sensed, at this point, that the trail had gone cold, that there was perhaps nothing more to be learned here in Mariankursk. So he once again proposed that it was probably best that he return to Derazhne. Before he could compose a proper goodbye, Katerinya had already come up with another compelling reason for him to stay. "But they say you were here to investigate something about the mysterious deaths. Wouldn't someone be expecting you? How will you explain your absence? Perhaps these are allies of yours – friends, not enemies."

By now, he was beginning to see that her motive was not entirely about completing his mission. He was warmed by the sentiment, but either way, she had again made a good point. And he would again need her help to follow this line of investigation. He smiled subtly to himself, impressed with her resourcefulness.

Their second, more focused investigation, established that all of the foreign interest in the "deaths," the professor's included, centered around the regional hospital here in Mariankursk. This is when he remembered the biokit back at Zakharova's. He had forgotten about this detail when he had previously related his pre-flight story to Katerinya. If he were here for blood samples, he would likely have been heading to this very hospital. But one doesn't just show up, unannounced, at a hospital asking to jab people with syringes. Someone must indeed be expecting him there.

With this new clarity about the mission, he returned to Zakharova's with Katerinya in tow. They were careful to take back streets, avoiding the more populated route via Kalinin Street. When they knocked at Lyudmila Nadyaevna's door, it never occurred to Ilya that he needed to explain Katerinya's presence – not because he thought Lyudmila Nadyaevna, with her no-gossip policy, would not inquire, or relate the incident to anyone else, but just because he had become so used to Katerinya being his companion by now that he lost track of the brevity of their relationship. When they reached his former room upstairs, and Ilya retrieved the biokit from its hiding place, he remembered the items he had set out to check for intruders. They were where he left them. So far, so good. Then they took the same clandestine route back, away from Kalinin Street, then further west to the hospital.

One option was for Katerinya to enter the hospital first – to make indirect queries as they had done before, preserving Ilya's anonymity. But she did not know anyone there, and their prevailing theory was that Ilya might. Or at least someone there might recognize him and be acquainted with his mission. So they entered together and approached the reception counter. A young male doctor passing from the opposite hallway, whom Ilya did not recognize, recognized him. "Professor Koskayin! We were expecting you much earlier! Thank you for coming again. Please follow me this way." As he said this, the doctor gestured toward a hallway corridor. While they followed the doctor down the hall, Ilya feigned prior knowledge, and probed deftly for information. He learned that he was here to take blood samples from a few patients to take back to his lab in Derazhne for sequencing of a particular bacterium, as he had done on the first trip.

When they reached the small, taped off isolation ward where the subject patients were being quarantined, Ilya inferred from what he had seen in his biokit that he was a doctor. But when he tried to envision drawing blood through a syringe, hoping the skill would viscerally come to him, nothing did. In fact he felt a little queasy at the prospect. Perhaps he wasn't a doctor. The attending nurse saved the day by taking the biokit from him, as if it were clearly her duty to do the draw, and they had done it this way before. Ilya gladly went along with the protocol. While he was watching the nurse, Katerinya, ever the quick study, took the doctor aside and played the role of uninformed companion – which she was – explaining that she had only recently begun helping Professor Koskayin and wondering what this mission was all about.

The young doctor gladly obliged, explaining that a few weeks ago a few patients had come in through the emergency room suffering from grotesquely swollen lymph nodes, blackened skin on the fingers, toes and nose, and respiratory ailments resembling pneumonia. This rare combination of symptoms was virtually unknown to the local practice, so he researched them and found the likely cause to be a bacterium called *Yersinia pestis.* The recommended antibiotic treatment was not something stocked locally, this being an apparently rare disease, so they had to request it from larger facilities in Derazhne and wait. Derazhne also didn't have it, and had to have it flown in from the USA. The first two patients died, possibly because the treatment was started too late. But then a few others died later, even after the antibiotics arrived and the course of treatment was started when the symptoms first presented. He had remembered *Yersinia pestis modernis* from a course taught by Professor Koskayin that he had taken as an undergrad at Derazhne University. So he had contacted him for help. Professor Koskayin was very concerned about this and came to Mariankursk last week to take bacterial samples back for sequencing. Now, more cases and more deaths had occurred, so the hospital reached out to Koskayin again. As much as they had tried to keep the developing situation confidential, the news had leaked out to Mariankursk residents, and rumors had reached as far as Derazhne. They still didn't know what they were dealing with, and Professor Koskayin had advised them to keep his visits confidential.

Katerinya waited until the hospital part of the mission was over before relating the news to Ilya. With the biokit payload firmly in hand, and sitting on a bench outside with him, she told him what she had learned about why he was in Mariankursk. Then his mood turned sober. She was used to seeing him curious or quizzical about his lost mission, and sometimes oppressed by his loss of control over it, but now he seemed like someone in charge – suddenly aware of his role and daunted by its responsibility. He still couldn't remember the doctor, the nurse, the hospital, or any of the other particulars from the first visit, but he did know what *Yersinia pestis modernis* was. He was under the impression that it had gone extinct long ago. He didn't know what he was doing with the first samples back in Derashne, but he now knew it was he who had orchestrated this air of secrecy around the current trip. He hadn't necessarily been avoiding anyone in particular (except possibly the Korihor man), just anyone who might have knowledge of what he was up to – whatever that was!

Katerinya understood most of this, and although she knew next to nothing about biology, she could easily surmise that the presence of this bacterium was not a good thing. They had more or less found what they were looking for, after great effort, but an ending like this did not bring closure. Their investigation at first had resembled more of a scavenger hunt between two prepubescent children, aware of gender but not sexuality. As the time wore on, they had become trusted playmates, interpreting their relationship for what it was rather than what it might mean, or what it might become. Unburdened by adult protocols, they had pressed on, offering and accepting help from each other without forethought. Now that this unholy end had been reached, their more socially aware selves returned. What would they do now? What *could* they do now?

It was now late afternoon, and Katerinya knew from Ilya's previous tale about the pursuer that he had not eaten since breakfast. She proposed that they stop by her apartment in Mariankursk and she would fix him something to eat. He was uncomfortably low on blood sugar at that point, so the offer was very appealing. As he was mentally composing the obligatory "Oh, I wouldn't want to impose on you" response – the one you don't really mean, but have to offer in polite society, hoping all along to be overruled – it occurred to him that she was very good at this. No matter what he said, she would come up with some further rationalization for why her offer made sense. Even if he didn't want to go with her – which he did, of course – he would end up there anyway by dint of her clever reasoning. So he just skipped the unnecessary prelude and agreed.

§

Katerinya Emlynovna's apartment consisted of the entire second floor of a small house on Tallinnskaya Street – number 10. The house was set back from the street by a small yard, overgrown with evergreen shrubs and the still green leaves of bluefairies. The house backed onto a woodlot of mature deciduous trees, mostly white birch. The apartment could be reached either through the front door and up a flight of stairs to her locked front door, or by way of a separate entrance at the back, up an external flight of stairs, partially obscured by the birches. Katerinya customarily used the back entrance so as not to disturb the tenants on the first floor, she said. Though in truth, she probably meant that she wanted to avoid *encountering* the first floor tenants because they had their own locked door. The internal stairway was once part of the first floor but had been partitioned off with a new wall and door when the original single-family house had been converted to apartments.

When they arrived, via the back entrance that opened into the kitchen, Katerinya showed Ilya into the front room, then returned to the kitchen to put a teakettle on the stove and scrounge around her pantry for something to prepare. The front room received a lot of sun through the south-facing windows. Ilya could see that she was a bookish sort of person. There were wall-to-ceiling shelves of volumes, several books stacked and laid open on her desk, and a single book laid open on a trunk in front of the fireplace, with a rocking chair next to it. On the opposite side of the room there was a music stand holding a single opened score. Since the cover of the score was facing away from him, he could not read the title or the composer or the opus. He was hyperopic – farsighted – so he could see that the scoring was not dense, and there were no lyrics, suggesting that this was a piece for solo instrument. He saw no evidence of an instrument anywhere in the room.

When Katerinya returned with lunch on a tray – his lunch, not hers, though she had also made a cup of tea for herself to show solidarity – their conversation took up again in earnest. Though the sharing was decidedly one sided, of course, given that there was very little he could tell her about himself in his memory-deprived condition. He learned that she was working as a part-time translator, while trying to write a novel with the remainder of her time. She was an only child who had grown up here in Mariankursk. She had wanted to go to the University at Derazhne – didn't every aspiring scholar – but her parents were of lower middle class means and could not afford it. Money aside, her father preferred that she go to a smaller, religiously affiliated school just west of Mariankursk in Pyatiskala. He was concerned about the prospect of his only daughter in the big city (big compared to Mariankursk), at a liberal, secular university with coed dorms like Derazhne. She had always exhibited an independent streak growing up, she said, which had served her well in reaching the top of her class in high school, but father Grigorev feared for the unpredictable ways in which this might get magnified in a place like Derazhne. He would rather see this untamed feature properly refined. Neither he nor mother Grigoreva had a college education, so in their view the proper role of college, at least for girls, was that of a finishing school.

She had thought of applying for a scholarship to Derazhne on her own, but when she got the papers she realized that her parents would also have to sign. She decided not to fight that battle, but used the incident instead to negotiate a compromise for Karlsruhe College, a small but very distinguished liberal arts college for women much further out west. Far enough west that her parents knew of it only by name. She emphasized the 'small' and 'college' and 'for women' parts of its reputation, and left out the 'liberal arts' part – and the fact that it had recently gone coed, and was part of the already coed Karlsruhe University. They could not afford this place either, but willingly signed the scholarship application.

Her trip out west began, in the opposite direction from Derazhne, with a feeling of banishment, she said, taking her even further away from where she wanted to be. But by the time she arrived, many days later, having surveyed landscapes and towns and people from a train window that were interestingly different from the reference points she had grown up with, she decided she had achieved some measure of escape – some place to call not-home.

It's not that she didn't like her parents, she said, she just felt that their values were not her values, and would likely never be. She wanted to try new things, to see the world and other cultures, to succeed at something; they wanted to perpetuate their parochial existence in Mariankursk, secure in their place in the local tribe, its mores, and its expectations. How ironic, she said, that she ultimately ended up back here in Mariankursk.

"And how is your relationship with them now?" Ilya asked. "Do you visit with them often, they being so close and all?"

"No," she replied, without a hint of sadness, but softly. "I'm an orphan. They died in a train accident when I was still out west – ironically, on a train to Derazhne."

There was an awkward pause while Ilya searched for something to say next. "I'm so sorry," he said (because that is what people say to news like this), but he wasn't. He always despised that response because it sounded like an apology, when that is not at all what is called for. What was there to apologize for? He hadn't killed them. He didn't know they were dead. If you apologize, you are resolving to do something different next time. But what? Never ask people about their parents without first checking whether they are still alive? That's absurd. What he really wanted was to express sympathy, to say something like "I feel your pain" or "I know what that feels like." But this is only available to people with dead parents.

Otherwise, you have to say something like "I can't imagine what that must feel like."

Then it struck him – he had to suppress a slight smile – that *both* of these clichés applied to him. He didn't have dead parents, as far as he knew, but he also didn't know if he had live ones. He was also an orphan in that he lost his parents, but he lost them to memory. So he did know what losing one's parents was like, after a fashion, but it was no doubt a very different kind of loss than hers. So he also couldn't imagine what that feels like to her.

Before he could relay any of this, she let him off the hook with a calm and worldly "That's OK, it happened some time ago." She explained that she had felt the loss acutely, at first, because it was so unexpected. Had they died slowly of some disease or other, something she could have seen coming from far off and could prepare for, the final act might not have affected her at all. Now she was inured to it. Seeing his opening, he told her what he meant to say – that he was functionally an orphan too. He had lost his parents as well, but unlike her he had lost track of his parents. They may still be alive somewhere but he has no memory whatsoever of them. He has no memory of his childhood. He can't picture himself interacting with them. He can't really be expected to mourn them, because they may not be dead. He can't really be expected to miss them because there is no memory of them to miss. Only the complete absence of a past, which confounded him more than bereaved him.

"I'm so sorry!" she said, but her quizzical look betrayed that she found the phrase no more useful than he had.

"But you're not sorry, right? That's not what you meant to say. It's just what people expect you to say in this situation, right?"

"Yes!" she said, beaming.

He had found a paisano. She tried to elaborate, but he practically finished her sentences for her. "Yes!" she kept saying, "Yes!" They found it amusing that they both were struggling to properly empathize with the other in the presence of these apparently morbid circumstances, when they were already starting in the same place. They were social outliers. They endeavored to communicate as honestly as possible with people they cared about, so they often skipped the scripted clichés. They were loath to say, "I'm so sorry" when they weren't, or "Everything is going to be OK" when it's not. It's not that other people are lazy, or less honest. The clichés are there for a reason – prepackaged responses for common stressful situations that have lost their literal meaning. They say you care like a greeting card does. You're expected to send one. To swim against this current, you need a better-than-average score on two skill sets: empathy, so you can feel what the other is feeling, and wordsmithing, so you can wrap your responses with the appropriate connotations. These are the skills of a good writer. They were both good writers.

§

At Karlsruhe, she had majored in comparative literature. Being a monoglot, she had to read the novels written in other languages via translations. It was this experience that taught her what she was missing in foreign novels – the author's original connotations, as well as timing and cadence and even sounds of the original words. So she took courses in several foreign languages, in the order of the foreign novels she wanted to reread most, so that she could read them the way the authors had written them. She aspired to travel and to write novels herself, but both of these required money, and she had none. When her parents died, she was able to finish Karlsruhe because she was there on scholarship. But when she graduated she had to make a choice. Her parents had left her too little estate to finance her grand plans, so when she returned to Mariankursk, she took a job as a part time translator to support herself, and lived in the family house, hoping to be able to write her first novel with the balance of her time. But it was not really her house. It had never been. It was her parents' house, full of her parents' non-ambitions for her.

So she sold the house, found an apartment that she could transform into something that reflected her own life, and staked herself to an endowment from the proceeds to finish her novel. The translation job roughly covered her rent and some living expenses, but left too little time, she feared, for writing. She could try to write full time by eating into the endowment, but had yet to make this leap. She was a good writer, she thought, but realistic enough to know the odds against producing a bestseller. You couldn't just be good, you also had to be lucky. Still, she wanted to take the shot. And the process of writing itself was in many ways its own reward. It was really what she would rather be doing.

As Ilya took all of this in, he had to agree that she had done a good job in putting her unique imprint on the apartment. It spoke to him. It spoke of her. He told her this. He could see her translating or writing at the desk, researching at the bookshelves, reading on the rocking chair in front of the fireplace. What he couldn't see, though, was what she did with the music stand. He had not heard this part of her life story yet.

"Ah," she said, "the cello!" Ilya didn't see a cello. She went to a shallow closet in the bedroom and retrieved it from its case. She kept it there with a dampit in one of the f-holes to keep it from drying out from all of the sun in the front room.

"Do you like the cello? Would you like me to play for you?"

It suddenly occurred to him that he must like the cello. The very sight of it set off a visceral chain reaction of feelings. He could hear it. He could feel it. Whoever he was must love the cello. She could see this, so she sat down next to the score, embraced the instrument with her legs, tuned the strings, then began playing. Ilya's face was transfixed. Dead memories began rising from the grave of his mind. He could feel the bow in his hands rubbing against the strings. She stopped, sensing his sudden epiphany. "Do you think you might be a cellist?" she asked excitedly. He didn't know for sure, but now it did seem likely. She brought him the instrument and the bow where he was sitting. He instinctively took up the cellist's posture and began to play.

Then more memories began to seep into his mind, starting with the musical ones. What he played was technically in a minor key, but as the theme rose and fell, undulating in and out, the harmony kept periodically resolving on the major 3rd, becoming optimistic, and bright, and satisfying, only to drop again to the minor 3rd, to bring the mood back to mystery and doubt – not the more traditional shift from the minor 6th to the 4th in a major key ("the minor fall, the major lift"), but a subtle change of the key itself. In his synesthetic mind, deep colors of red and green, tinged with black and translucent blue, ebbed and flowed in time with the changes from minor to major to minor.

Now Katerinya was transfixed. She knew the piece – every classical music aficionado knew that piece. It was Jespersen's only surviving work. But she had never heard it played like that! Ethereal, but also profound, as he eased into the key shifts, then leaned into the resolutions. "Do you know what you are playing?" she suddenly asked, frantically, without realizing she was interrupting him. He didn't. His mind had been somewhere else. "That's Jespersen's Nocturne in C# minor! How can you not know what it is and still play it like that?" The name now seemed familiar to him. Yes, he knew that piece. Embarrassed that she had interrupted, she pleaded with him to start again. He did. And then the most amazing thing happened.

What had started as a trickle became a flood, which in turn became a torrent. Individual memories began firing across his brain, connecting, intersecting, reviving. Vague complex shapes emerged then gradually refined themselves into vivid generalizations. The sun was rising in his mind, and the colors of the sunrise were gorgeous. He played on, slowly absorbing a sense of who he was and his place in the world. When he finished, he had become the actual Ilya

Erynovich Koskayin – the professor, the mathematician, the biologist, the musician.

She could see the change. She wanted to ask him so many things. She wanted him to tell her his life story, as she had told him hers. She impulsively wanted to do much more. She wanted to touch him. She wanted to reach out and hug him, to welcome him back into the world. But no, that wasn't quite right. That might be awkward. She didn't know what she wanted, really. She was overwhelmed, and confused, and happy, but couldn't translate any of this into a concrete response. So she held her emotions in check and waited for him to speak first.

He was not sure where to start, so he just started at the top with what he could remember. Much of this she already knew, he realized. He wanted to give her more. He sincerely tried to introduce her to his new self, recounting stories and aspirations as best he could remember them, but the further back he went the less he could remember. The recovery process was not over yet he realized. It was still going on. This made it hard to generalize and sum things up into a coherent narrative. The details kept growing and changing. He needed memory triggers. So he invited her to ask him directly. "What would you like to know? Ask about anything you want!"

She wanted to know where he was from, where he grew up, what he wanted to be when he grew up, what his parents were like, did he have any siblings. (She wanted to know how old he was, but she didn't ask this). But these aspects of his life were apparently too far beyond his current memory horizon. He wanted to know these things himself, but the questions triggered nothing. She could see that this was bothering him, so she tried to stay closer to the present. The last 10 years or so proved to be relatively fertile ground.

She asked where he learned to play the cello, especially like that. He couldn't recall learning to play, but the suggestion triggered a distinct memory that he had a cello at home, and he played it often enough. He recalled that he had some sheet music there too, but also that he mostly played pieces by heart. He just happened to know a lot of pieces, including Jespersen. He couldn't account for where or when he learned them. Did he like the theater, or dance, or art museums? He did have a fondness for art and ballet in particular.

Then she got to what interested her most. What did he read? Any fiction? Yes, he liked novels. Then she got into her groove. "Who are your favorite authors?" she asked, excitedly. He tried to remember novels he had read within the range of his current memory, but what stood out more were novels he must have read in his anonymous past. He couldn't remember specific reading episodes, but he was very familiar with the authors and their works. He had favorites, he said, and cited Kulikov, Rostoy, Krayevsky, and Shvernik. "You like novels from the last century!" she beamed. "And what a distinguished bunch of authors, deep and philosophical. Why older novels?"

He pondered that for a moment, trying to identify this attraction. "I think most people do," he said. "In the cinema and on stage they call them 'costume dramas.' But I don't think costumes are the point. The differences from our own time – in dress, in settings, in customs, in expectations and worldviews – that's what draws us. It's what draws me, anyway. You see the world differently from the point of view of historical characters, if the author is good at it." As he laid out his explanation, she seemed almost ready to burst waiting for her turn.

"That's what I'm writing! It's set in a small town very much like Mariankursk about a century ago. I'm still working out the characters, and their roles, but the protagonist is a lot like me. 'Write what you know,' they say. I only hope I'm good at it, as you say." He smiled, imagining her in such a setting. "Would you like me to read any of the work in progress?" he volunteered. She paused, a little uncertain. He could see she was torn. "No," she said, "I don't think it's ready for that yet. But I'll keep your offer in mind."

They talked on for hours and hours about everything and nothing. But there were unsaid things they both wanted to know about each other that had nothing to do with their pasts, and everything to do with what was happening right now, that remained unsaid and unasked.

Ilya noticed that as Katerinya became clearer about who he was and what he did, she started playing up her own age and sophistication a little, trying, without even thinking about it, to convince him that they could peers. He knew this phenomenon. Graduate students sometimes did this with professors they admired when they had a chance to work as colleagues, fearing they would not be taken seriously enough because of their perceived age and experience level. In Katerinya's case this was entirely unnecessary because she had already established herself as a peer in his eyes in their unguarded moments while he was still an enigma. He wanted to tell her this but, of course, he couldn't. She did look quite young. He was about to say to himself "… for her age," when it occurred to him that he didn't really know her age. Given the arc of her autobiography so far, he would guess late twenties. But he would probably have guessed much younger if judging only from her appearance. He knew from his own experience that apparent age can be very misleading. He knew plenty of young people who looked old, and old people who looked young. Then there was acting older and acting younger, a second tier of evidence with plenty of outliers as well: adults who never grow up, and child prodigies who start out mature.

In his case … (he was about to say – again to himself – that he was older than he looked), but he stopped. He had no idea how old he was! He had this vague sense that he had *always* been older than he looked. He already knew that parents and childhood were, at least presently, out of reach, but he also couldn't recollect any near term events in the range of memories he could reach that related to giving him an age. No references for birthdays, or other age-related events.

§

After they both had wrung just about all they could from his past memories, it occurred to Katerinya to ask about the more ominous mysteries that they had encountered today: the mark on his ankle, the Korihor thing, his clandestine mission to Mariankursk. These he could remember.

He had always had the mark for as long as he could recall. He didn't know what it represented or how he originally got it, but he felt it was an important sign of something that he needed to find out about. Whenever he would see a picture, or a drawing, or a decoration that it resembled, he would search and examine everything in the vicinity, looking for what, he did not know. But he somehow felt he should be searching. This thing had a denotation.

The word 'Korihor' was meaningless to him. He had heard it for the first time today. He had seen other strangers who appeared to be following him, from time to time, but he had never confronted one, or been confronted by one. Again, today was the first. He suspected these were agents of the local authority in Derashne, but had no proof. This was an ongoing mystery in his present life, not just something he forgot.

Y. pestis modernis would be a real concern – if it existed. It was supposed to be extinct. When he sequenced the first samples from Mariankursk back at his lab, he established that the cause of the local deaths was not *modernis*. It was something else that is not registered in any known biological source catalog. But it is genetically very close, which is troubling in itself. Once rumors of the Mariankursk deaths reached Derazhne, along with his own involvement in the investigation, he saw a marked increase in shadowy followers, bordering on stalking. He would like to keep this out of the hands of politicians, for they will be more interested in controlling public perception than competently controlling any possible outbreak. In the worst case, they might try to suppress the evidence. So he decided to go underground, so to speak. He sent the biokit in a package to himself, rather than take it on his person, in case he was detained or searched on the train. For the protection of everyone concerned, the case and the samples had to be prominently marked with the biohazard symbol. But they would be much less likely to be seen wrapped inside plain brown paper in a mail bin.

Katerinya found these last revelations worrisome. Ilya's adversaries, human and bacterial, were more diverse and powerful than she had imagined. She was about to inquire more deeply into the subject when she noticed that it was already dark outside. They had both lost track of the time. Ilya had to ask her about the train schedules back to Derashne, because he had lost that small segment of his life to the anterograde amnesia episode. She knew the schedule. He had about an hour before the last departure. Then he remembered the package-to-himself ruse. He would have to mail the biokit back to himself in Derazhne rather than take it on the train. There wasn't much time left, he told Katerinya. By now he was sure that he had to leave, no matter what reasonable sounding plan she came up with. But he wanted to hear it anyway. He waited to give her a chance. This time, however, her reasonableness led her to agree with him – though her resourcefulness shone through, as always. She told him there was a post office right next to the train station. He could get brown wrapping paper there as well.

He had half-hoped that she would pull out yet one more reason for them to prolong their time together, though what could she possibly say at this late hour? Then she volunteered to walk with him to the post office. She paused in silence for a moment. "You know, just in case another one of those Korihor fellows tries to attack you," she said with a sly wink. He couldn't help smiling at this. Her sense of humor was spot on, and perfectly timed.

Once at the post office, they wrapped and addressed the package, then put it in the Rail Express bin. Ironically, the package made it into the bin just in time to be put in the cargo hold of Ilya's train to Derashne. He would be riding the train with his package, but not on his person. No one would think to open and inspect every package in the hold – or any of them, for that matter. He would be, as before, just a tourist to Mariankursk returning home. If some suspicious soul were to ask what specifically he was doing in Mariankursk, he would say – now truthfully – that he was visiting a friend who lived there.

Katerinya walked with him to the train platform for the final goodbye. "You will *have* to come back now, won't you?" she asked. He didn't know whether she meant because of the bacterial outbreak, or perhaps for another, as yet unsaid, reason. Either way, he mused, he *would* have to come back.

"Yes," he said, pleased to please her, and now absolved of the need to justify anything. "I suppose I will."

Chapter 2

STEEPLES, TOWERS, AND DOMES

Derazhne – the town – was situated on the north bank of the Karl river just before it flowed out to the sea on its way east. On the southern side of the river lay its larger sister city of Solinovsk which extended all the way east to the coast, where it served as the primary seaport for the region.

Looking north across the river into Derazhne from Korya Hill in Solinovsk, one was confronted by a sea of steeples, towers, and domes. The town had an abundance of churches, reflecting the religious bent of its population in general. There were many Protestant churches, but only one Orthodox Catholic church. This one church, however, laid claim to the vast majority of the town's parishioners. The remainder were scattered among small congregations in the various traditional Protestant denominations. The one exception to this divvying up was the single Evangelical church. It got, by far, the majority of the Protestants. The Orthodox church owed its dominance to having got there first, perhaps several hundred years ago. It had established an ethnic identity and a feeling of continuity with the past that kept its hold on generation after generation. The Protestants, having come later, and in several shapes and sizes, were always seen as newcomers' churches, so they rarely could peel off converts. The evangelical church was the last to arrive, but straightaway began to poach the existing Protestants. This was still going on, much to the consternation of the traditional denominations.

Since most of the parishioners were Orthodox, most of them attended parochial school growing up, until they reached high school age. There was no parochial high school, so the two enclaves of students were socialized in their separate tribes before merging in the public schools. The names of these institutions always seemed ironic to Ilya Erynovich. 'Catholic' means universal. Yet their schools are called 'parochial' – exactly the opposite of universal. The latter moniker was a better fit he thought. "Religion is nothing if not parochial," he would say. A further irony was to be found in 'catholic.' All of the churches, orthodox and protestant, recited the same creed: "We believe in one, holy, catholic, and apostolic Church." "The Four Marks of the Church," it was called. But each denomination, of course, believed that its own brand of church was the 'one,' vitiating the point about 'catholic' two points down. The distinction was lost on most parishioners because they didn't really know what these credos meant anyway – in a theological sense. They learned them by rote from a very young age. So by the time they reached the age of reason, these were just the phrases you were supposed to say when you get to that part of the service. The perceived meaning is "this is the stuff we believe." It demonstrates solidarity with the tribe.

There was an ageing, and now faded, wooden billboard just before the bridge leading over the river into Solinovsk which read "Seek Ye the Truth!" placed there some time ago by the Evangelicals. It was near enough to the University that anyone leaving that part of

Derazhne was likely to see it, as if it were placed there as a prescription for the academics inside. Ilya Erynovich, like most scientists, was not a religious man, so he was squarely within the target audience. He knew this, so it amused him that the sign was exhorting him to do what he already did. What better call to arms could there be for the science tribe than to seek the truth? That's what we do! It wasn't so much the 'Truth' part of the appeal that was misappropriated. It was the 'Seek' part. 'Truth,' to the religious tribes, was already established dogma and could not be further questioned. Why, then, ask pilgrims to *seek* it? This was just asking for trouble. If there was actually some inquiry involved, the seeker might find something else to be true.

As a scientist, Ilya Erynovich's brand of inquiry relied on multiple observers seeing the same result, or at least being able to reproduce the same result later. Something only you can see doesn't count. The various religions, on the other hand, employed a uniquely private kind of verification: *revelation.* For some it was a sixth sense, experience-like in that it was non-linguistic. It was felt. For others, it was a direct infusion of knowledge straight from the other realm – gnostic, or secret, knowledge. And for most religions this special access to the truth was not available to most people. It was reserved for a few chosen individuals. It was the job of these anointed ones to disseminate it to the rest of the flock by the normal linguistic means.

His colleagues dismissed this brand of "evidence" out of hand, of course. It had no scientific value. But Ilya Erynovich was intrigued by it. It somehow managed to form the basis for belief in alternate realities for so many of his fellow humans. Ordinary believers got some time on this special channel to the Divine to transact spiritual business (praying, confessing, and the like) or to get an infusion of inspiration, but they didn't generally get the news about fundamental truths, as their leaders did. It was no accident, he thought, that the leaders were routinely referred to as 'pastors', or 'shepherds', and the faithful as the 'flock'. There were a lot of sheep in religion. If an erstwhile sheep thought it heard a different fundamental truth on the channel, and had the temerity to pass this on to the other sheep, the pastors might lead this black sheep to the slaughter – as a heretic. Those that survived and were merely cast out from the flock would themselves become shepherds and go on to found new flocks. And it was pretty much one or the other. There was no middle ground. So if you were an ordinary believer, it's understandable that you would be confused about just what makes a person one of the chosen messengers. It's not spelled out anywhere, except in historical precedent, which pretty clearly indicates that the odds that it's you are pretty slim.

But once you allow that there is a special channel to truth that is inherently subjective and unverifiable by others, you would have the problem of successfully forming any community of belief at all, wouldn't you? he thought. The chance of everybody independently intuiting the same original story is not very good. So any tribe with revelation as part of its method would have to find a way of limiting access to that channel. The first guy up could intuit anything he wanted. Subsequent believers would have to be taught, by way of prompting or coercion to see things his way. Ilya Erynovich didn't know, of course, just how the first religions got started, but he could imagine. Since the latter-day members of the flock did not get to see the original sausage being made, the founding act didn't need to have been all that impressive. Once the web of belief is up and rolling, the vagueness of the founding events becomes part of the mystery, all the more revered because they are ancient and inscrutable.

§

Ilya Erynovich's relationship to religion, in this most religious of towns, was, in general, both genial and benign. It was a fact of life here. It didn't really affect him one way or another, personally. But upon returning to Derazhne, he couldn't shake Katerinya's vague take on the Korihor incident as being religiously motivated. She didn't really have much to go on, but if true, this was something new. He didn't have religious enemies — that he knew of — yet he had been attacked by someone with a possibly religious motive. And this person somehow knew who he was, and that he had "the mark" on him.

Religious violence was not uncommon, but that was usually an internecine affair — religion on religion. It had often been very violent in past history, but had mellowed out to a few scuffles here and there in the present. Nothing like the Korihor incident. Whatever the Korihor folks thought they knew about him, it should have been clear that he was not a member of a competing religion — or *any* religion, for that matter. But maybe that was the point. He had heard about prize-winning novelists being attacked for the perceived blasphemy of their stories. He was still vague, for now, on what his publishing history might be outside of academia or whom it might have possibly offended. But such a scenario just didn't seem to fit in the context of the religious people he knew, or knew of, here in Derazhne.

Derazhne's singular catholic church was presided over by His Eminence Yaroslav Yesfirovich Osipov, Archbishop of Solinovsk. Despite the compactness of his local parish, Osipov's ecclesiastical jurisdiction extended far and wide. The Archdiocese of Solinovsk extended over all of Solinovsk and Derazhne, and other smaller western towns as far west as Pyatiskala. Yaroslav Yesfirovich was the quintessential company man, born into the tribe and its many codes of conduct by way of a father who was a priest in a small town parish out west. His tribe was the hands-down leader in the hierarchical partitioning of revelational authority. It wasn't always this way, of course.

A couple of millennia ago, when the church was first being formed, there was no easy way to adjudicate disputes over perceived access to the special channel. Success required that these kinds of questions just not be entertained to begin with. So like most religions, Osipov's employed the special concepts of blasphemy and heresy. These are explicit encodings of the implied principle that it is not nice to entertain thoughts about how authorities get their authority. It's mysterious. It happened long ago. We just don't go there. Heresy is a little more involved than blasphemy, for it applies only after you have articulated a possible alternative to the established order. You have to have some standing in the community to manage to get to this point. Blasphemy, on the other hand, is a more broad-spectrum skeptic retardant. It forbids you to even speak the subject, except in the most reverential and acquiescing tones. You can't even get the skeptical sentence out.

Unquestioned loyalty to a deity looks a lot like unquestioned fealty to a monarch, and at several points in the history of Osipov's church, both systems were freely intermixed, creating coextensive heavenly and earthly kingdoms. It was common practice in the ancient world to pledge allegiance to the conquering leader's religion at the same time that you yielded political autonomy. Indeed, success in battle was often regarded as a sign of having access to better gods, so this allegiance was not just imposed, it was sometimes sincerely believed as well. But the masses well understood the consequences of publicly disrespecting a reining prince, and certainly the consequences of entertaining treason, these being very concretely corporal – disembowelment, burning at the stake, and such. And during the periods when Osipov's church was officially sanctioned by states, it liberally availed itself of the impressive array of tortures at its disposal for enforcing the doctrines of blasphemy and heresy. But often as not, his church wasn't in power, having to eke out an existence under the radar of governments. So they did not have ready access to the traditional physical punishments. They instead employed a far more effective sanction – psychological punishment. The power of language to conjure mental images of rewards infinitely greater than anything you have actually experienced, or punishments infinitely worse, awaiting in an afterlife, is remarkably effective in creating a pervasive expectation of dread that cannot be disproved by any earthly evidence. You might escape a king, but you could never escape a god.

Nowadays, of course, most of Osipov's parishioners didn't come to the parish by way of revelation, or by being conquered. They were born into it. They imprinted on it at a young age when they willingly accepted the authority of parents, and virtual parents like priests. By the time they reached the age of reason, the seeds had already been planted; the expectation of pervasive, inscrutable authority had already been established. They didn't properly witness its origin. They were conditioned to deal with heresy and blasphemy as part of the natural order of things, as the result of many instances of "we don't talk like that," "it's not polite to ask people that," "because I said so," "don't talk back to me," "because I'm your mother, that's why."

So in his modern tribe, you knew where you stood. At the top was a single individual, so directly in touch with God, through the channel, that he was deemed infallible. He was literally God's representative on Earth. Then the hierarchy fanned out through Cardinals, Archbishops, Bishops, Priests, Deacons, and finally the Laity. This exquisite hierarchy made it clear who lorded over whom, who had the power to do what, and how doctrinal disputes were settled. Ecclesiastical power flowed strictly downward.

It seemed to Ilya Erynovich that this exposed a singular anomaly at the apex of the hierarchy. The fellow at the top, though infallible, was not immortal. When he died, the elegant inverted tree structure of dominance, with its single root at the top, implied that his superior should appoint the successor. But his superior was the Almighty Deity himself, living in the immaterial realm. The one earthly representative who mediated the material/immaterial channel was gone. So it was up to the next level down, a select assembly of cardinals, to elevate one of their members to repopulate the vacated position. God surely spoke to all of them in some lesser sense (because they were not themselves infallible), so he could broadcast his intent for the replacement over this lesser channel, to guide their vote. It was blasphemous to wonder about this out loud, of course, but more than one member of the faith wondered privately why the vote was not unanimous on the first ballot (as it often was not). Weren't we dealing with infallibility here?

Unlike other religions, Osipov's was a limited open canon faith, allowing that there could be continued, authoritative revelations from God past the originally founding ones recorded in the Bible. It was limited in that nothing could be later *added* to the Bible, but the Bible itself being notoriously ambiguous, there was plenty of wiggle room to further *interpret* it for the laity. This authority to interpret (with God's guidance through the channel, of course) was parceled out along the familiar lines of the tree of dominance down to the bishop level. Each member of the hierarchy was granted a proportional amount of access (proportional to your position in the tree) to receive these revelations of refinement. So Osipov's church accreted an ever-growing store of magisterial texts, mandated from above, and corrected or accepted when emerging from below, that further defined the acceptable standards of behavior for parishioners. His church turned out to be masterful in it's wielding of sin, and the attendant fear of eternal damnation, to keep the faithful in line. The many refinements created disproportionately more ways to sin than in most other religions, but had granted officials all the way down to the priest level the power to forgive these sins. This promoted a constant cloud of guilt over parishioners, which virtually assured their regular rotation back through the church via the confession booth.

Yaroslav Yesfirovich knew he was destined for the priestly life, but in his early years he struggled to balance the equation between the requirements of piety and humility, and what appeared to be the prideful ambition of rising through the hierarchy. He imagined this was what it must have been like for the firstborn son of a king in antiquity. As a young man, you may have had a taste for kindness and wanted to rule your eventual subjects with grace and fairness, but you were being groomed by your tutors to understand that successful kings must occasionally be cruel, and rule over their subjects with fear. A king who cannot abide cruelty, and does not inspire fear, will appear weak and risk being overthrown from within. A king who rules exclusively with fear and cruelty will risk revolution from the bottom. It is the sacred duty of a king then, as protector of the realm, to balance these two in a way that preserves the realm.

In the end, Yaroslav Yesfirovich chose ambition over humility. It was hard not to with all of the titles and stylings, and colorful vestments, and bowing and kneeling and kissing of rings. Each time you rose in the hierarchy, someone above you had granted you a little more divinity, made you a little more holy, a little more autonomous in your interpretation of your revelations. To him, these revelations were never content-specific. He never heard words. He was, however, by virtue of his position, partially divine and on a path to infallibility. So he interpreted his own inclinations, and his own preferences, as indications from God that these were the right things to do. Over time, he absorbed the organization in its totality. He was the organization and the organization was him. With encouragement from above and below he came to view his primary mission as preservation of the order against all corruptions from the outside. When it was brought to his attention that a priest in one of his parishes was suspected of molesting young boys, his own inclination was that the priest had sinned against God, but who among us has not sinned? He was also inclined to pardon his sin and exhort him to sin no more, so he did. His preference was that this be kept out of public view – to preserve the realm – so he quietly transferred the priest to a different parish. He did all these things secure in his confidence that he was carrying out the will of God.

§

Osipov's polar opposite tended flock across town at the Evangelical Assembly of God – the Reverend Viktor Veraevich Sokolov. Sokolov's church had a decidedly closed canon. There was only one authoritative rendering of the word of God: the Bible. There was no mediating hierarchy between Viktor Veraevich and God. He spoke to God directly on an unfiltered channel. God Himself had chosen him for this role (so he said). And there was no intervening hierarchy between himself and his flock. He spoke to them directly, every Sunday, without the need for further documents and extra-Biblical texts – a very flat, lean, and efficient organization that saved a lot of people a lot of time.

Unlike Osipov, Sokolov was not born into the church – he *founded* his church. He was the son of a military man, Stepan Zenaevich Sokolov, and moved from base to base with his mother Vera as his father was reassigned. He was an enterprising young man. He learned the ways of military leadership by observing his father's interactions with superiors and subordinates during his various postings. He was often the gang leader of other young boys who played in the shadows of the bases. As a young man, when the family was living in Biroyevka, he fell under the sway of a charismatic evangelical minister who had founded his own small church. He was attracted to the pastor and his oratory skills probably more so than the doctrines of the church, though the pastor made these easy to understand. There was one source of doctrine – the Bible – and one interpreter of their meaning – the pastor. He didn't know it at the time, but this was a career choice that made him what he later became.

The Bible was full of revelations between God and various human agents, sometimes mediated by angels, sometimes through fires and winds. The Bible itself was literally written via revelation, with God guiding the hand of the writer. He was initially skeptical of the pastor's claims of personal revelation – God directing the pastor on how to interpret the verses, and occasionally relating things to him verbatim, or through dreams, that would soon occur here on Earth. Such events seemed way too ordinary to be true, because they were way too contemporary. There were no fires or winds or resultant manuscripts. But he was impressed with the pastor's ability to interpret Bible verses any way he needed.

The Bible, he learned, was a large collection of history, myth, parables, poetry, letters, and revelations. On the whole, though, it was history. Some of that history explicitly recounts events where laws of human behavior are enunciated by those in a position to dictate such matters. In other cases, the history relates actions taken by favored agents with God's approval, or at God's direction, that are not explicitly claimed to be applicable to others. (Moses exhorting his troops, in Numbers, to go back and kill all of the women and children of the Midianites, except for the young virgins which they may take as sex slaves, did not seem to be the kind of behavior that it would be a good idea to promote as a general norm.) But for the most part, the stories just related tribal history, in which various characters did and said various things without a clear sanction from the writer as to whether these were permitted, prohibited, or required by God. Because the stories had many characters, good and bad, carrying out all manner of earthly intrigues, a good pastor, like his mentor, could find a passage or two to justify just about anything. The passages were thought to be holy and mystical, after all, so it was always accepted that their meanings may not be literal. At one time or another, every policy of a sitting orthodoxy had been justified by an appeal to the Bible, including genocide, slavery, war, polygamy, intolerance, the subjugation of women, and torture, as well as forgiveness, universal human dignity, peace, monogamy, altruism, universal suffrage, and mercy – although Sokolov didn't know this at the time of his tutelage. The Bible was a remarkably flexible constitution of the faith.

Sokolov also came to realize, under the pastor's tutelage, the overriding power of fear in human nature. When empathy competes with fear, fear almost always wins. Fear is easy to summon up, and hard to assuage. It also easily trumps reason, being much faster and more visceral. Coupled with the psychological terror of eternal damnation, a tool he had inherited from Osipov's church, it could be employed with remarkable effectiveness both in keeping your current flock and in converting the sheep from other flocks. It is the primary motivator of human behavior. If you can control fear, you can control people. So together with charismatic preaching, a perfectly ambiguous set of Scriptures, and the ready reservoir of fear, he foresaw the infinite possibilities in becoming such a leader himself. Initially he was agnostic about whether the pastor's revelations were genuine. It really didn't matter. It was private. No one would know one way or the other. But as he perfected the lawyerly principles of advocacy in Biblical interpretation, he became progressively bolder, shooting first and asking questions later. He began to assume, like his fellow clergyman Osipov, that his own prior inclinations and preferences were the channel signs from God. His manifest skill in retrospective justification by Scripture was, he believed, an even greater sign of a gift from God.

When he finally turned to prediction, telling his flock and all others who would listen, that God had told him certain future events would occur – a revelation so specific as to imply a linguistic transcription of the conversation – he had lost the distinction between his will and God's will entirely. He was God's mouthpiece! If he kept his predictions general enough, he could get at least 50% right. People remember the hits more than the misses. He could explain away the misses with advocacy. One technique was to try to keep the predictions general: "Sometime this year, Derazhne will be lashed by storms" or "Sometime this year there will be a judgment from God." When the predicted event was specific enough to clearly not have happened as prophesied, he could employ either of two techniques: "I must not have heard God clearly (He's infallible, I'm not)" or "Upon hearing the prediction, people prayed to God to prevent it. He heard their prayers." One completely unimpeachable technique was to declare God's reasons for causing disasters (to enemies, and other religions) – after the fact.

§

Down the street from Sokolov's church, through the gates of Derazhne University, up the dark wooden stairs of the Divinity School, and into a corner office with a stained glass window, a decidedly different type of believer sat reading the Holy Scriptures for perhaps the 247th time. This was Professor Diederick Brandt. He was not originally from here. Like many of the University's professors, he had made his scholarly reputation elsewhere, then emigrated to Derazhne when the invitation came from the joint search committee deeming him sufficiently worthy of joining this distinguished faculty.

Unlike Sokolov, Professor Brandt had never heard any utterances directly from God. When he prayed, it was strictly a one-way conversation. His revelation was the milder kind often cited by those who decide to join the ministry – "the calling." The concept, of course, was not of his own invention. He had heard it many times before, and adopted it into his own biography because it seemed to fit, and it needed no more detailed description. It implied that God had personally *called* him to the ministry, though there were no words exchanged. He couldn't name the day it happened. He simply felt, over time, the amorphous inclination that this was the place for him. Growing up, he was an inquisitive but respectful young man. He liked the peaceful solitude of scholarly contemplation. He attended seminary where he rose through the ranks of scholarship. Ordination was the natural endpoint of seminary, just as an M.D. is the natural endpoint of medical school, so he accepted his. But like an M.D. that never undergoes residency or practices in the clinic, but solely pursues research, he never became a minister of a church. He never had a congregation. He was a pure theologian.

Ilya Erynovich always found it ironic that the University, founded on the traditional principles of academic freedom, which allow, even encourage, a scholar to pursue any line of disruptive inquiry he or she chooses, could harbor a Divinity School, whose very nature discouraged this. Their truths were already established, weren't they? And any inquiry into these truths had to operate within the bounds of blasphemy and heresy, no? Over the years, he and Brandt had become both colleagues and fast friends. He learned, through his many conversations with Diederick, that the D School, at least here at Derazhne, was not really a seminary. It granted the degree Doctor of Divinity, but you had to go elsewhere if you wanted some sort of ordination. It was, instead, a school for studying religion as a proper scholarly subject. Any religion. This necessarily made it ecumenical, nondenominational. So there was no blasphemy, because there was no consensus on what was too sacred to be construed secularly. There was, however, a pervasive code of mutual respect. Speak of others' religion as you would have others speak of yours. And there was no heresy because you *studied* religions, and their alternatives, rather than promoting or advocating any one in particular.

The scientist in Ilya Erynovich was naturally skeptical of revelation or scripture being evidence of anything at all. This was not a topic he could productively discuss with the average believer, because things like reasoning and evidence had played so little role in the acquisition of their faith. But with Diederick, he could air it out. He was a scholar after all. He knew things.

Diederick knew, for instance, that the simplistic story of God directly writing the Bible with His divine pen, or of dictating it via revelation to some more humanly author with a more material pen, was a myth. The Bible was a collection of books, obviously written by multiple humans over multiple time frames, some of them contradicting others. Some books contained redundant but somewhat different accounts of the same events, clearly suggesting a combination of multiple authors. This, one could get simply from a careful reading. Scholars knew this; parishioners typically did not. It was thought that perhaps God provided individually coherent snippets of historical wisdom to various designated authors at various times, and these were sometimes misconstrued by the human agents, or initially passed on orally and thus acquired variations before being separately captured in multiple writings. This would allow for initial divine inspiration, but allow for some understandable corruption in transmission in an initially illiterate population spread out over time.

Ilya Erynovich was having none of this. Many of the Biblical books had a clear geographical and historical parochiality concerning the natural world, he argued. The creation story describes a flat land mass being formed below an upper heaven, with two canonical lights (Sun and Moon) to rule the day and night. Just the sort of cosmological point of view one would expect from early Mesopotamians. If God had really dictated the creation story to divinely inspired humans, why didn't he give them the true story, the one about the big sphere and its atmosphere, with its local satellite lit only by reflection, and its large star providing all of the light? The Biblical account contains just the sort of perspective error you would expect from pre-scientific humans, but not from God. Surely he knew better. It doesn't work to say that God was relaying the story in the only terms that humans of the time could understand. The correct story about rotating spheres would have been surprising, but surely comprehensible. It would have been a lot less surprising than the story of the talking snake and the magic fruit trees. The Biblical narratives, he said, are filled with just the sort of historical mistakes and parochial points of view that one would expect of human authors making their own best guesses about how the world was put together, in the context of their own times. These are not minor errors in transmission. We cannot ascribe them to an omniscient

God. So a good deal of the books only make sense as the humanly inspired word of humans.

Archbishop Osipov's church had already come around a bit on this one, acknowledging the modern scientific view of the world and allocating the creation myths to allegory. God, as He so often does, was speaking in parables. But this would be news over at Sokolov's more fundamentalist church, where everything in the Bible is literally true! They also believed that there was only one set of Holy Scriptures, and that we have a surviving copy of the original holy manuscript. But Diederick knew that this too was not true.

Modern scholars have no idea who most of the original authors were, or in what specific time frames they first took the original dictation. There were several different languages involved, so it took many translations to get us to our current editions. Because the now current copies of the Scriptures are so far removed from their earlier translations, there is a default tendency to believe that the Scriptures were dictated in one's native language. This was particularly true in Sokolov's church, where they rigorously hew to an early, authorized translation of the Bible from almost 500 years ago. This edition is now old enough, and the original dialect archaic enough, to have taken on the feel of an official holy language. Many people have only ever heard this dialect in church and thus have formed an association between it and the language of God. Their prayers, both public and private, are reverently couched in the archaic pronouns of 'thee,' 'thy,' 'thou,' and 'ye.' This is holy language. This is the language that God speaks, so you need to speak this way when you are talking to him.

Intervening translations, though, were the least of the problems in establishing the evidential chain back to an original manuscript. The events described by the various books of the Bible require that any contemporaneous authors lived and wrote in time frames well before any reliable record keeping. The best that could be done was to find the oldest surviving manuscripts of any form, dated by modern forensic techniques, and then try to paste together a likely ancestry of documents and versions according to similarities and differences in the texts. The survival of true originals was rendered extremely unlikely due to the media on which ancient texts were recorded. Although some of the events described in the Bible would be expected to have occurred about 4000-6000 years ago, the oldest complete manuscripts are dated to around 1000 years ago. A large cache of documents discovered relatively recently, preserved in a series of caves, contains fragments of almost all of the early books of the Bible from around 2000 years ago – but more than three quarters of these nearly 930 texts record "holy" works that are *not* part of the modern Bible. So this puts the earliest actual manuscripts at 2000-4000 years after their alleged facts, and suggests that the surviving Scriptures are just one sampling of many holy books from antiquity. Someone had to choose.

Religious scholars like Diederick had pretty good visibility into the last 2000 years or so of this kind of choosing. It was all in the deep history of Osipov's church, a fact not generally apparent to the laity. When the finished canon is passed down from a mysterious past that you aren't generally aware of, it all seems so simple. You are left to imagine the authors, for instance, being illuminated by a light ray from heaven, their quills being guided by an invisible hand. You don't imagine a protracted debate among the priests about which of the prevailing stories is the correct one. I'll vote for yours if you'll vote for mine, but whatever we do, we have to keep that other one out. Scholars knew for certain that monks and priests of Osipov's church not only copied but actively filtered, debated, included and excluded content on the way to giving us the current Scriptures. It was not just a matter of faithfully reproducing the same collection of books over and over. It took almost three centuries for this winnowing out to occur, and the winnowing was done by sects and committees of humans debating, arguing, voting, persuading, and coercing. The winners were in a position to represent their collection as the one true canon, obscuring and even destroying the heretical losers. It then took another thousand years or so to corral all of the prodigiously copied variants into the canonical holy book that we know today.

Diederick and his fellow scholars had no visibility into the deeper history of canon formation. But Ilya Erynovich imagined, based on what happened in the last 2000 years, that it probably went something like this. At any given point in its history, there was the official collection of works already venerated, and probably some other candidate texts floating around with various claims to divine inspiration – but not yet canonized. If you were one of the few literate scribes entrusted with the task of producing the next copy, you could attempt to faithfully reproduce the accepted canon word for word, or you could, perhaps, clean it up a bit, correcting some of its inconsistencies or weird parts, or, being unsure of the value of some of the candidate texts, you might include a few in the collection just so that they didn't slip into extinction, leaving the final decision to later generations. Or perhaps you were particularly fond of a piece of your own writing, having felt very inspired when you wrote it. Who, after all, decides these sorts of things? Perhaps you should contribute it to the non-canonical candidate collection and, again, let your descendants decide. No one really witnesses the creation of the original texts. That would doom them to ordinariness. They are decided on by later generations when they have accrued some veneration. Some modern critics see the occasional evidence of "strategic" textual alterations by past clerics as evidence of doctrinal conspiracy, a deliberate attempt by earlier authorities to alter the alleged word of God to suit their own interpretations. But the inclusion of seemingly unrelated books in the canon, the inclusion of redundant and sometimes contradictory accounts of the same events, and the inclusion of multiple, redundant accounts of the same events in the same books all suggest the overwhelming reticence of clerics to take things out. It suggests a history of accretion based not so much on active judgments by editors, as on cautious inclusion by archivists out of respect for older documents whose origins were no longer visible.

§

On the other side of the campus, across the Quad, on the 3rd floor of Englund Hall was the office of Professor Slavik Karinaevich Fedorov. (He wasn't in today). He went by his initials, so everyone knew him as S.K. Fedorov. He was the less usual case of an atheist who had converted to the Orthodox religion as a young man – specifically Osipov's brand. His parents were religious, so he had been baptized into the traditional Orthodox faith, but disavowed it as an adolescent. He was later converted back to his original faith by colleagues when he was a professor in the Literature Department at Arsenyev University. During his long tenure as Professor of Literature at Derazhne (he was now Professor Emeritus) he became a prolific writer of novels, epic children's stories, and religious apologetics. His name was well known outside of academia, but mostly for his children's books. He had quite a vivid imagination. The reflected fame from these brought readers to his apologiae, but as with all apologiae, these works were read almost exclusively by the already faithful. They were directed not so much to skeptics as to believers who needed reassurance in the presence of skeptics.

Ilya Erynovich had never met him personally, and was familiar with him only through reputation and from reading a few of his apologiae. He had no current memory of reading any of Fedorov's children's books, but upon reflection, he had a general knowledge of their content – the characters, the plots, the imaginative imagery – so he must have read them, or had them read to him, in the deeper past that he could no longer recall. He could, however, specifically remember reading some of the apologiae.

Unlike Osipov and Sokolov, who employed the stick of eternal damnation as their primary incentive, Fedorov worked the carrot side of the street, appealing to the infinite heavenly rewards awaiting the faithful. His imagination as an author of children's fantasies stood him well in this regard. He explained away the downer, for instance, that there would be no sex in the afterlife by an analogy to a prepubescent boy. The boy's archetype for the greatest humanly pleasure may have been chocolate. Upon being told that the greatest pleasure was sex, he would have trouble comprehending the meaning – no way to relate to it. Giving up chocolate for sex would seem like a cruel deprivation. And so it would surely be in Heaven, that some other, superior pleasure would be waiting which we could not now comprehend. When you got there, you would see what you had been missing. Sex would seem so trivial. But unlike pastors who promote Heaven as the ultimate reward for suffering through a miserable Earthly existence, Fedorov promoted the positive side of the current religious life as well – the hymns, the music, the liturgy, the recitals, the meditations, the community. There was joy in this, he wrote. This is what the believer wants to hear.

Ilya Erynovich had hoped that reading Fedorov's apologiae might yield some insight into his conversion, for this would represent, presumably, an eyes-open entry into the fold rather than the traditional tribal imprinting. But the apologiae followed the pattern he was already familiar with. The apologist is an advocate, like a lawyer, making the best case possible for an unpopular thesis. In religious apologetics, the thesis is under attack for being impossible, or counter to common sense. The apologist proceeds by arguing that it *is* possible (a decidedly low bar for success), and then advancing more possible explanations for its possibility – you can't *prove* it's not so! This gives the believer a sort of rational license to believe – safe from formal refutation.

In Fedorov's case, the initial possibility is that an immaterial deity is selectively intervening with cosmological physics, here and there, to inject spiritual content into an otherwise material universe – imperceptibly injecting souls into human fetuses at just the right moment, for instance. The observable results are almost always the same as those described by scientists, so the supernatural addition can ride along with the scientific story in parallel. One of the things this Deity injects into almost all humans, he wrote, is a pervasive sense of higher purpose. (The Deity, no doubt, injects this into all humans, but some of the more rascally ones refuse to acknowledge it). A believer not only identifies with this personally, but takes comfort in the fact that it is nearly universal to all humans. How do you explain *that*, unbelievers! But from this very compact, theistic beginning, an almost imperceptible slide occurs into some very specific content of the believer's religion – the trinity, the incarnation, the ascension, walking on water, turning water into wine, manna from Heaven – that are decidedly not held by most humans. Each particular religious tribe has its own set of miraculous particulars that are at odds with those of most others.

So in Fedorov's case, Ilya Erynovich came to realize, there was no grand revealing from God, freighted with all of the miraculous particulars. There was an amorphous feeling of acquiescence to a higher power – not even a choosing, but a feeling of being chosen, Fedorov wrote. Over time, this singular, revelatory intuition expanded to cover everything in his previous tribe's holy book, lock, stock and barrel. It is unlikely that the intuition itself expanded – he read these details from the book. His revelation was to capitulate to the central deity described in the book. That set him on his life's journey of apologizing for the entire book, rationalizing instead of intuiting.

Would Fedorov have had the same intuition about the truth of these particulars had he never read the Bible? Surely not. If he had been born into a different tribe with different particulars, and happened one day to the find the Bible lying on the ground, and read it, would this have made his wholesale acceptance of what he read any more likely? Probably not. You need the tribal context. His detailed acceptance could only come from the joy of the initial tribal acceptance. If he had grown up in a tribe with a purple cow as deity, that stood in a four-partite relationship with an angel, a passenger pigeon, and an elephant, he would likely have found joy in capitulating to the cow, and gone on to apologize for every strange detail of the cosmology, including the Holy Quadrinity. He would never have found Osipov's God.

Ilya Erynovich saw no purpose in engaging with Fedorov like he did with Brandt. Diederick could appreciate this point about tribal differences, and could generalize it in his mind. He knew, from the ecumenical atmosphere at the D School, and Ilya Erynovich's constant prodding, that his own beliefs were tribally imprinted, and would likely have been different in a different tribe. This caused him to take a more theistic stance toward specific content – though this went against his tribe and his ordination by that tribe. He didn't choose any of this, he complained. The choice was made for him. If he could choose, he might choose to go theistic. But he couldn't.

§

Also in Englund Hall, down one flight of stairs from Fedorov's office, at the other end of the building, was someone whom Ilya Erynovich did engage with regularly. This was Professor Andzhelina Gullovna Berghild. She was the least religious person one could be and still be associated with a church. She was a Unitarian, a mostly theistic denomination that believes in free thinking when it comes to dogma. There was no blasphemy and no heresy. You were free to come and go as you please. There were no priests, no sacraments, no rituals, no credos, no central authority. It was a bottom-up kind of organization formed largely around the notion of church as community – an open community whose members support each other and promote good works wherever the opportunity arises. Ilya Erynovich liked what one wag had said about the Unitarians: "Pagans believe in many gods; Orthodox religions believe in one god;

Unitarians believe in at most one god." It had a succinct mathematical precision.

Andzhelina Gullovna was a professor of literature who specialized in scholarship and teaching about "The Bard." She was a recognized expert in her field, even outside of Derazhne University, which is no small accomplishment in such a crowded specialty. Everyone wants to teach the Bard. She was advised as a young graduate student to specialize in something less crowded, but she single-mindedly pursued her calling until she succeeded. She now sat at the top of the scholarly hierarchy. She and Ilya Erynovich often talked about the questionable objectivity of the notion of "literary genius" – he being the more skeptical of the two, of course. Wouldn't different cultures find genius in different writers? Was it an intrinsic property of a writer and their body of work, in which case all cultures should recognize it, or was it something in the eye of the beholder? In either case, Ilya Erynovich had to agree with Andzhelina Gullovna that the Bard had it. The sheer breadth of his work, his insight into the mores and foibles of his time, and his almost musical use of words suggested to some scholars that the body of work attributed to him may have had more than one author. This alone, if it were the work of a single author, spoke to the objectivity of genius, he thought. And from his own beholding eye, no poet he was aware of resonated so personally with him.

Andzhelina Gullovna did not come to her church by any of the usual means. She had no religious upbringing. She was the daughter of agnostic academics. She had no revelations. She felt no divine presence. She was skeptical of the specifics of the magical absurdities. But she was a believer in the need for unknowable mysteries. When she first met Ilya Erynovich, she believed, as many people do, that there *are* unknowable mysteries which science will never be able to explain. This is where the "greater being" steps in. But all of her specific candidates for the unknowable were dispatched by Ilya Erynovich, who patiently explained that science did know how these things worked. And the explanations, at least when he gave them, were often more fascinating than the previously amorphous unknown placeholders. He was also quick to point out many present mysteries which science has yet to explain, though "we are working on it," he would say. He liked the track record of science so far. "It's not in our nature to give up," he said. This caused Andzhelina Gullovna to shift her stance. Now she *hoped* there were unknowable mysteries that science would never solve.

She admitted to the appealing mystery of there being a Book, or a Leader, or a Revelation from the deep past that would signal a portal into something mystical. The Wisdom of Old. It's these kinds of sentiments that drive one into the study of fiction, and folklore, and legends, and larger-than-life heroes. Perhaps it was escapism, she said, but there was no harm in escaping to the worlds of the imagination. Ilya Erynovich was sympathetic to her point of view. He could enjoy the thoughts of imaginary worlds, just like her, but never as a final resting place. He would eventually be driven back to the larger purpose at hand – figuring out how the actual world works.

But he thought her point about the deep past was spot on for explaining the belief in religions. The Book, the Leader, the Revelation only works, only accrues sufficient mystery, when it is *ancient*. Consider the poor Latter-day Saints church. It was founded less than a century ago by a human who received the articles of the new faith via the traditional message channel of angels. The reception was attested to by the surviving writings of contemporaneous humans who are, of course, no longer with us. The whole saga of events and miracles (with their impossible-to-verify provenance) is not materially any different than the established myths of established religions, but it suffers from being too recent. You could relate to the ordinariness of the characters and the unlikeliness of their miracles because they were but a few generations removed from your own. Too recent to be mysteries of old. Too likely to have been the fictions of enterprising impresarios. This is a cult, not a religion! The distinction between a cult and a religion turns out to be a continuum of credibility for things like miracles and larger-than-life heroes stretching from the present back to antiquity. Today's tricks and charlatans become tomorrow's miracles and prophets. Religion, like a fine wine, needs to be aged – Ilya Erynovich would say.

§

On the other side of the Quad, in Dahlström Hall, was the office of Professor Ove Alfhildovich Ekholm, chairman of the biology department. He had been instrumental in securing Ilya Erynovich's joint appointment in biology and mathematics when Koskayin first came to Derazhne University. (Ilya Erynovich couldn't recall this in his present state. Too far back.)

Ove Alfhildovich was baptized and raised in the traditional Orthodox church. He still hewed to the faith, but was now a lapsed churchgoer. He was well known and well regarded in the scientific community. Unlike Fedorov, he kept his faith to himself. He had no personal revelations. His faith came through the classical route – he imprinted on it when he was young, and never managed to shake it thereafter. Few of his colleagues even knew about it. Ilya Erynovich did. He characterized Ekholm as a scientist with a bicameral mind. He came to work with his science hat on and pursued the truth wherever the evidence led. When he got home in the evening, he put his religious hat on and expressed his devotion to God in his prayers. Never the twain shall meet.

Once, at a public lecture series featuring a panel of scientists and theologians, it came out that he was religious. One of his graduate students in the audience challenged him with a question about how he could explain such things as angels. He briefly reflected, then answered that he had no scientific explanation for angels. They are not the kind of thing you could explain. He didn't really think of them as things. They were in the religious realm. His belief in them was a belief within that realm. They have no existence in the science realm where he plied his trade.

Ilya Erynovich could not wrap his head around this notion of separate realms. Wasn't he really applying one set of evidential standards to his colleagues (and himself with his science hat on), but granting himself an exception when it came to religion? "What would you say if one of the post docs in your lab were to come to you with a theory about angels that could not account for anything other than his favorite scientific hypothesis?" Ilya Erynovich asked. Ove Alfhildovich replied that he would, of course, reject it because it is not good science. He didn't apply his religious criteria for belief in the science realm, including to himself. But Ilya Erynovich just couldn't see it that way.

A successful scientist is above all interested in the truth. Not the "truth" of religion, or propaganda, or of being judged (by self or others) as right, but what is real or actual. A genuine interest in this kind of truth requires effort, selflessness, and willingness to enforce the rules of consistency on yourself to the same degree as you would on others. You have a restless curiosity that is not satisfied by winning the argument, or convincing others. To avoid the all too human drift into self-delusion and wishful thinking, believing that the world is the way you would like it to be, you have to be prepared for the true state of the world to possibly be ugly, depressing. What is uplifting is the arduous journey itself coming to an end. The beauty is in the epiphany of discovery. So he could never understand how a good scientist could avoid self-deception at truly hard tasks, like Ekholm could, then so blithely give up when it came to religion. He had no model for the bicameral mind. His own mind would be constantly leaking across the borders. Or perhaps more to the point, his mind had no borders. It had only one set of rules.

Perhaps, he thought, Ekholm and he were really the same in possessing this fundamental drive for skeptical inquiry, but because of his upbringing, Ove Alfhildovich does not always feel free to exercise it. He was raised to feel guilty after all. Osipov's church had a habit of declaring so many human drives and pleasures sinful – except when exercised within church-sanctioned borders. So sex was, in general, sinful – except within the context of church-sanctioned marriage. Likewise, skeptical inquiry about fundamental truths was, in general, forbidden, except within church-sanctioned boundaries. Fortunately for Ekholm, Osipov's church had recently expanded this permitted playground to include evolutionary biology – unlike Sokolov's. So he was safe to fire on all cylinders when in the science realm. Not so otherwise. The church had divided his mind.

§

Down the hall from Professor Ekholm's office was the office of Professor Ilya Erynovich Koskayin. You've heard of him, no? Having recently returned from Mariankursk, he was still getting used to the offset between the person that he presently was, and the person who occupied this office and pursued this particular academic career at Derazhne. There was no temporal line that separated the two landscapes, but more of a patchy fog that was clear in some places and opaque in others. When he had first returned to his house in Derazhne, he searched for his cello and found it in a closet, with a dampit in the f-hole just like Katerinya's. Playing it appeared to be therapeutic for his memory deficit – particularly playing Jespersen. Patches of the fog would then lift in some places.

He now felt very much at home in this body and this place, but was still bothered – perhaps intrigued was more accurate – by his inability to recall how long he had been here at Derazhne University, what he was doing before that, how old he was. He searched the files in his office for personnel records, contracts, letters from the University, transcripts – anything that might have a date, or a date of birth – but found nothing definitive.

He could remember things in general about what he was up to before Mariankursk, but often couldn't recall the specific events that would have set him on such a course. The bacterial mission was clear enough. The events that precipitated it were relatively recent. But his sense of being pursued by shadowy figures was deeper and more pervasive than the bacterial mission could account for. This, he sensed, had been a part of his life for some time.

The greatest enigma though, was still the mark on his ankle. This resonated with him deeply, but the resonance was confounded by the lack of any details. The mark, he knew with intuitive certainty, *denoted* something. He had this sense when he first recalled it for Katerinya, but now that he was back in his home environment, he went looking for clues. Though he didn't really know what he was looking for. Looking around both his home and his office was good memory therapy anyway. At one point he happened to notice the 'look in pocket' message he had written on his hand in Mariankursk. It hadn't completely faded yet. He could recall the parts of that experience from the Mariankursk Station café onward, and he could recall sitting on the passenger bench earlier in Derazhne Station before he fell asleep. The parts in between were lost forever due to the brief anterograde amnesia. But then it occurred to him that the strategy he had employed then – writing a prompt on himself to look somewhere else for a record of what he couldn't remember – may be something that he had used before. Maybe *he* had given himself the mark to help him recover what he knew he would later forget. Now he began to play detective with himself. Perhaps obscurity was part of the plan! The mark would be visible to others, so its true denotation must be something that would only be meaningful to him.

Armed with this new perspective, he reran his fishing expedition both at home and at the office. This time he caught some fish. In the bedroom at his house, he noticed that all of the handles on one of his dressers were the same except for one. The small brass hardware fittings that hosted the handles all vaguely resembled the mark, but one of them resembled it more so. That one was also clearly newer, its brass a little more shiny. He opened that drawer, looked inside, emptied the contents on the bed, and looked some more. At the very back of the left side, the small phrase 'written in molecules' was carved into the wood. One fish.

Then he searched his library, which looked out on a garden in the back of his house where only bluefairy leaves remained in the beds. There, two of the books in his wall of books had a graphic version of the mark on their bindings. He knew these books, so he knew that the publishers had stamped the marks there without any foreknowledge of him. It was a common sort of graphic – the kind of design one might expect to see on the binding of a book. So everyone who bought these books got the same meaningless message. But when he looked inside each, he found a small scrap of paper acting as a bookmark. On one of them was written 'Purity, Chastity, Innocence.' On the other, 'Father, Son, Ghost.' Two fish. Three fish.

Back at the office, and now primed to see the mark anywhere and everywhere, he scoured the room. He found another book with the symbol on its binding. Its makeshift bookmark read 'Faith, Wisdom, Chivalry'. Four fish. But then the trail went cold. No more fish. As he was sitting in his desk chair, puzzling about what all of these fish might mean, his unfocused gaze settled on a small wooden maritime clock he had on the mantle over the fireplace. As he focused on it (he was hyperopic), he noticed a detail that had held no prior significance that he could remember. The carving above the clock face was vaguely plant-like, enveloping the top half of the circle. At its apex, it formed a shape that resembled the mark. He stood, went across the room to the mantle, and reached up to feel all around the clock. Nothing unusual. Then he took the clock down from the mantle and examined it in detail. On the back, near the bottom edge, he found 'written in molecules' carved into the wood backing. The same fish!

If these messages had been sent from his prior self, he wished his prior self had not been so annoyingly clever. If the aim was to throw others off the track, it succeeded. But it derailed his present self as well. What could all of this mean? He figured there must be some deliberately distinguished significance to the repeated message. Not only was it repeated, but it was harder to find. And it was carved in wood to last for the long haul. The bookmarks, on the other hand, were practically out in the open, asking to be discovered. And the repeated message was the only one clearly directed at him. It was a message for a scientist. The others hinted vaguely at religion. What could he search for now that related to molecules? A molecular biologist like himself knew lots of molecules: big ones like chromosomes, and ribosomes, and proteins; small ones like amino acids, and nucleotides, and RNAs. What was written in molecules? How was it written?

Of the three triplet messages, one clearly denoted the "Holy Trinity." What was this supposed to mean to him? This was a contentious notion among the various religions, sparking centuries of debate over metaphysical arcana of substance and identity that meant almost nothing to ordinary believers. All of the religions seemed to agree on the notion in general, but often violently disagreed over the particulars. Ilya Erynovich could understand the motivation behind the first two parts of this three-part scheme. Monotheistic religions struggled with the concept of their one God having a son, who was also a holy figure in some regard. To outsiders, this sounded a lot like pantheism – multiple gods. No, no, not that! So they fashioned this mind-bending notion of there really being only one God, but with multiple parts of some sort. The 'some sort' became a burden to explain. If it was a father/son relationship, one of the Gods had existed before the other, no? No, there was only one God, existing through all of time, but one of the parts (the son part) got exposed to the Earthly world later. Ilya Erynovich got the part about trying to avoid pantheism, so a "Holy Duality" might have been a theological burden they were forced to bear.

But why make it worse with one more part: a "Holy Ghost?" This was supposed to be the immaterial part of the one God that carried, or embodied, the holy messages that crossed back and forth between the material and the spiritual realms. But all religions, including the pantheists, had to deal with this material/immaterial crossing over. That's what angels were for, no? Even before they had to explain the Son they had angels. Why did they now have to promote one of them to a god, and then incur the cost of welding it back into the corporate God identity? But they did. And ever since, the different denominations have distinguished themselves by how they define this tripartite relationship. One says "One being; three persons." Another says "Three personages – one Godhead." See the difference? One commentator had put it this way: "If you try to explain the Trinity, you will lose your mind. But if you deny it, you will lose your soul."

Why on Earth would he have left a message about this to himself? As for purity, chastity, innocence, faith, wisdom, and chivalry – he had no idea even where to begin.

§

After his original trip to Mariankursk – prior to the one with the memory episode – Ilya Erynovich had sequenced the bacterium behind the outbreak as soon as he returned to the lab, and determined that it was not quite *Y. pestis modernis*. This was the good news. But the new variant spreading in Mariankursk was apparently not responding to the antibiotic for *modernis*. This was the bad news. A close genetic variant like the current one – likely from a recent mutation – might also have a close antibiotic variant. He had determined where the alleles had mutated, and this suggested a likely mechanism for how the new strain was evading the old antibiotic.

That, in turn, suggested a possible quick fix to the old antibiotic. So he sent the rest of the samples over to the lab for culturing.

At that point, he worried that he was losing valuable time in the battle against this new bacterium. He could possibly synthesize his new candidate antibiotic based on his very plausible genetic analysis from the sequencing alone. On the next trip, he could then perhaps try the experimental antibiotic on a patient who would be at death's door anyway. This, he knew, was professionally unethical, at least the part about using an untested drug in a live human trial. They would never allow this in the USA. But on the other hand, if the patient was surely going to die without the intervention, he could cause no additional harm. And he might be able to save the patient's life.

He spent the rest of that week researching this issue in earnest. He had already decided that he could not test a newly synthesized antibiotic on a live patient based solely on a hypothesis about protein structure as he was originally inclined to do, solid though it looked. He would have to try it on the live culture first. But when he requested the culture that had been incubating in the lab to begin his testing, a very sheepish lab tech informed him that the culture might not be viable because the incubation temperature had accidentally been set too high. *Y. pestis* is a relatively fragile, slow-growing bacterium among its peers in bacteria-land. It requires time, a specific temperature range, and the absence of faster-growing bacterial competitors for it to grow in the blood into a population sufficient to wreak its colossal havoc on its host. It can't survive at temperatures over 40C, and sure enough, the bugs in the culture were already dead. So his mission for the second trip had been to obtain more live samples from patients that he might be able to experiment on for the quick fix.

This time he personally delivered the blood samples to the diagnostic lab, checking the conditions and the proper temperature settings, and impressing on the techs the urgency of keeping these samples viable through the incubation period. Lives depended on it! Then he had to wait.

As he sat, restless, feeling the full weight of the problem before him, but lacking the capacity to move it along any faster, dusk was creeping in through the windows, diminishing the light in the room, and the strength of his resolve. He looked at the symbolic reactions depicting the synthesis steps one more time, but his mind was elsewhere. His scientific self could not compete with his emotional self, which kept supplanting images of molecules with memories of Katerinya. This new friend for only half of a day, this deceptively sophisticated ingénue had left a permanent impression on him. Although outwardly social, Ilya Erynovich was slow to allow others into his inner space. He sized them up first. Took his time to get to know them before extending any type of invitation. But she had pierced the veil immediately, casually strolling in and out as she pleased as if she owned the place. He hadn't really invited her in. She had invited herself in. And she was now taking up residence in his mind, pushing everything else of personal significance aside for the moment. And he was OK with that. He was more than OK with that. He couldn't shake her image, and the enticing proposition 'You will *have* to come back now, won't you?'.

So the following few days in Derazhne were scientifically useless. There was nothing further to do until the new bacterial cultures were mature enough for antibiotic testing. He knew where he would rather be, and fortunately that was the same end destination for both scientific Ilya and emotional Ilya. So when the cultures finally came back from the lab he was ready for action. But the accompanying lab report said "Contaminant overgrowth observed: target organism not recoverable for phenotypic testing." What? Reading the details, he learned that the sample had been contaminated with *Staphylococcus epidermidis*, a common bacterium that lives harmlessly on human skin, but quickly forms biofilms in blood culture that outcompete more delicate species like *Y. pestis*. The blood draw sites had probably not been thoroughly sterilized before the needles went in. How could this have happened? Then it struck him. He had done it himself – correctly – the first time, but was still unable to remember anything about his mission at the time of the second draw. So he had mindlessly let the nurse take the draws. A microbiological researcher at a major university, like himself, would know about this issue. A nurse at a regional hospital probably wouldn't.

Another wasted trip, and more time lost! But he wasn't able to maintain his grip on the gravity of the situation for long. Katerinya yet again inserted herself, gaining control of the narrative. Well … the last trip was not entirely wasted, he mused with a smile.

So it was back to Mariankursk. It was now Saturday. The winter term began on Monday, so he had to be here in Derazhne for his opening lecture. He should probably review his notes for the Monday lecture. Yes, that's what he should be doing. He went to his file to retrieve the notes, but his mind was still somewhere else. He knew these by heart anyway. He gave the same course every year at the start of the term. Nothing really to prepare for. It would still be feasible to squeeze in a daytrip on Sunday. Yes, that would work! Speed was of the essence after all, given the outbreak. He could also then see Katerinya again. He would like to see Katerinya again.

There was really nothing to prepare for relative to the hospital part of the trip. He just needed to get the blood draw right this time. As for the Katerinya part, he wasn't so sure. He didn't really know where he stood with her. He had no doubt about his own perspective, but he was unclear how she felt about him. The signs looked good, but their history had been so brief. It would be easy for him, in his current optimistic state, to over-interpret what had transpired so far. He didn't want to unilaterally assume anything. So he would just play it by ear, he thought. Let it move at its own pace. Don't over-think it. In fact, don't think it at all. Just let it happen.

On Sunday morning, he was on the train to Mariankursk.

§

As the train pulled into Mariankursk Station, a bird's eye view from the back of Ilya Erynovich's compartment would have revealed three passengers. A woman in the middle row had just caught sight of the shadowy figure of Ragnar at the front of the car. Ragnar didn't notice her because he was singularly focused on Professor Koskayin at the back of the car, on the same side. Ilya Erynovich noticed neither of them. His head was down, reading. Ragnar watched Koskayin arise and disembark. He followed him from a discreet distance, into the station, then out to the post office next door, always laying back a bit so as not to be observed. Koskayin did not know he was being followed, and Ragnar aimed to keep it this way. At the post office, he observed the professor inquiring at the Rail Express window. After a brief delay, a postal clerk came in from the train platform and handed the professor a large parcel wrapped in brown paper. Koskayin then set out onto the street and headed west.

Ragnar had observed him once before going this way. He had followed him on an earlier trip to Mariankursk. On that trip, Koskayin had stayed at a guesthouse on Kalinin Street, east of here. Ragnar had stayed there too, registering after Koskayin had already gone up to his room, so he would not be seen. The next morning, Ragnar had followed him west on this same street to the hospital. That must be where he was going now, he thought. He was right.

At the hospital, Ragnar could not risk going inside so, like the first time, he waited patiently for the professor to finish his business there – whatever that was. Ragnar then followed him going east, safely from the shadows. On the last trip, this route east had taken Koskayin back to the train station and then back to Derazhne. But this time Koskayin appeared to have other plans. He passed the train station and continued walking east. Ragnar followed.

Ilya had gotten word to Katerinya that he was coming, but had advised her not to meet him at the station – he knew she would have wanted to – or to accompany him to the hospital. To preserve the credibility of his backup excuse for his excursions to Mariankursk – just visiting a friend – it was important that they not be seen together in association with the hospital. He was doing this to protect both his mission and Katerinya. If something should go south with the mission, he didn't want it to ensnare her. So he would try to keep his hospital visits discreet, and his "tourist" visits public.

Now that his clandestine mission was accomplished, he could reenter the public eye. Unlike the last visit, when they approached her apartment discreetly, he took pains this time to employ the most public route possible, once he was sufficiently removed from the hospital. In keeping with this plan, when he approached number 10 Tallinnskaya Street he decided to take the front entrance, all the more likely to be seen he thought. (He was right about this, of course. More right than he knew.)

He had been looking forward to their reunion with great anticipation en route, but as he approached her door at the top of the stairs, the impending event weighed on him. They had been so uninhibitedly familiar the first time because events had thrust their union upon them. There never had been much time to think about it. Now that some time had elapsed, and they both had some time to reflect on it, would it be as natural? Or might it be awkward at first, each a little more reserved, trying to understand where the other stood.

Katerinya was not expecting him at the front door, so she opened it cautiously with her guard up. "Ilya!" she cried out, her face beaming. She immediately embraced him in the doorway. Then pulling off, but still beaming, she asked, "Can I call you that?" That's what she used to call him before she knew he was a distinguished professor. She hadn't thought this through. Was that still appropriate? She displayed no hint of second-guessing, merely a mature awareness of social conventions. Her first reaction, he could tell, was the true one. "Yes," he said, smiling. "That's who I am after all." This was not going to be awkward at all, he thought. They could pick up right where they left off.

She was not expecting him so soon, she said, so she hadn't had a chance to get ready. With that, she sat him down in the front room, then begged off to go into her bedroom to change clothes. He could see she had a plan. When she emerged, she was wearing a dress that resembled a traditional peasant outfit. The top was shaped like a tunic with a high collar. The sleeves gradually billowed out toward her wrists. The waist also had a slight billow where it was cinched with a rustic looking belt. As an historical costume, it would be somewhat androgynous, he thought. The tunic was more of a male element, but the skirt was clearly female. The combination was very elegant, though, clearly representing a modern female fashion choice. Something not intended to be authentic, but to evoke a sense of the past. The fabric was not muslin but silk, and there was a row of faux buttons running down the length of the right side. Since the buttons were not functional, the whole ensemble was meant to be entered and exited through a full-length, zippered seam running down the back – as women's clothes often are. She approached Ilya, then turned around in front of him and asked, "Could you zip me up please?" He did.

She turned around again to face him and backed up a little, not just to give him a better look, but as if she were hoping for him to say something. She was impatient waiting, so she did a full twirl like a dancer with her arms out, then faced him again with the same anticipation. He knew what she wanted, and he was happy to oblige. He related everything that he had been thinking, ending with the compliment for her exquisite fashion sense, and finishing with a coda complimenting the model that was wearing it. This clearly pleased her, but it didn't bring the episode to a close. She wanted to confess something, and was torn between keeping it in and letting it out. She hoped he might figure it out on his own, and she could just demur. But maybe he wouldn't. So she just let it out. She had chosen this dress because she remembered his fondness for the characters in historical novels of Rostoy, Krayevsky, and Shvernik, and she wanted to vicariously be one for him. He wasn't expecting anything like this – so direct and personal – so her confession caught him off guard. She had just breezily flung open the doors to her private space for his viewing pleasure. It wasn't even an invitation to enter. She had virtually reached out, grabbed him by the lapels, and pulled him in. He could not contain the emotion this triggered in him. And his face apparently showed it because she no longer needed him to speak. It was not clear to him what else he could have said that would have added anything to the communication that had just occurred.

She also knew, from their previous conversations, that he liked wine. She had a plan for this too. She went into the kitchen and brought back a mirrored tray with a brass filigreed border holding a bottle and two glasses. She had also added some wine-friendly charcuterie and a sliced baguette. She wasn't very experienced in the ways of wine herself, she said, so she had consulted a friend who recommended this. She held up the bottle. He would normally have gone straight to the label, looking for the varietal, the vintage, the region, and anything on the back he could find about cooperage. But none of this seemed to matter now. He just smiled and nodded, as if to say "good choice". She didn't even own any stemware, she said, so she had bought two glasses for the occasion. She placed the tray on a small table, setting it toward one of the corners. Then she arranged two chairs on either side of the corner so they were at right angles to each other – the way cafes sometimes do when a couple sits at a table meant for four.

Ilya, for no reason in particular, took the seat on the left, so she sat down on the right. She sized up the situation and then said, cheerily, "Oh, this won't work. I'm left handed. We'll keep banging into each other when we reach for our glasses." So he switched places with her. She had just assumed he was a righty. He wasn't; he was ambidextrous. So it didn't matter to him either way. He hadn't noticed before that she was a lefty, though she had now just announced it almost with a sense of pride. Following up, he said, "So you're a lefty!" Sure enough, she responded with a coying "Yes!" then explained that this made her special. She was one of the few. It means she's right-brain dominant, she said, a creative, artsy sort of person.

Yes, she certainly was special – and creative – he thought, but not because she's left-handed. Left/right dominance is a rather insignificant feature of the brain in the larger scheme of things. So he explained that this is only an initial motor preference at birth. Higher-level mental facilities like language and creativity and reasoning and mathematics require both sides of he brain to cooperate in intricate ways.

"But I had heard that the right-brain was for imagination and creativity, and the left-brain for reasoning and mathematics," she replied.

"Ah, there is a grain of truth in that," Ilya responded. "The two sides are *specialized* somewhat toward those different tasks, but any useful result requires them both. Think about language. The point of language is to communicate – publicly. Let's say I have private thoughts, or feelings, or intentions that I wish to relate to you – you can't just see inside my mind!" He paused, smiling. "Well maybe *you* can." Then he continued. "I have to encode these private notions into public words and sentences that I can speak to you. Your brain then has to decode those public sentences and translate them into similar private meanings in your mind. The left-brain is the specialized language processor – the public encoder/decoder; the right-brain is where the private meanings are first conceived and finally received."

Katerinya mulled this over in her mind (both sides), then the light bulb of epiphany came on. "That's what I have to do as a writer! I imagine story arcs, plots, characters, and scenes on the private side, then I struggle – maybe 'negotiate' is a better word – with the public side to put it all into the 'write' words." She paused. "Notice the double entendre?" she asked, gesturing as if writing with her left hand. "The *write* words?" she asked, impishly. Then mimicking a pedantic professor, she said, "Well I suppose it was more pun than double entendre. There was no bawdy intent." He didn't get it from the first sentence, of course, because her speech had no spelling. But the gesture drove it home. He couldn't control a smile at the delightful performance.

Then she continued. "I start with what all of the possible story elements mean to *me* – privately! I see them in my mind first. I *feel* them in my mind first. I pick out the ones that resonate with me personally, the ones I expect – or hope – will resonate with my readers. But the writing process forces me to translate these into public sentences."

Then she reflected, "You have it easier than me, Ilya. You don't have private meanings in mathematics, do you? When you get your public proof, you're done! You don't have to worry about how your readers will interpret it. But I am only halfway there! I have to write and rewrite my sentences to get them to connote the feeling I had in my private mind. And it's more than just the words. I have to resort to timing, and pauses, and sentence fragments, and metaphors, and indirection – all of these things that are not part of the public meanings or the correct grammatical structure of sentences. Isn't it ironic that we are first taught the "correct" ways of language – complete sentences and proper punctuation? Then we move up to literary fiction where we are almost expected to break these rules to make the prose 'literary'.

But even when I manage to satisfy myself that my final sentences project the right connotations, I have to worry about whether they will strike other readers the same way. How do I know that they will please a literary agent, or a publisher, or a prize committee? And even if I manage to please them, will the sentences please a large enough audience to earn a living? I just don't know. I don't know how I could possibly tell in advance. I envy you your certainty, Ilya "

"Well, I suppose I do have an easier time of it" Ilya said, reflecting, "but only once the creative process comes to an end. That's because mathematicians deal in truth. The proof language is both public and definitive. If you manage to get there at all, there are no counterarguments. The issue is settled for all people and all time. Your profession, on the other hand, deals in veneration. The so-called "great books," the ones that the critics, and prize committees, and college professors collectively agree on, are deemed to possess unique artistic merit – genius, if you will. They *become* venerated by this collective judgment. But to a different set of venerators, from a different culture and a different time, these same books may be just ordinary. They may venerate a different set. And, of course, any particular tribe of venerators will disagree somewhat about what belongs in their own holy canon.

So you have a harder time producing a result that is acceptable to others. But I have a harder time producing any result at all. I can't cheat! No matter how pleased I am with my imaginary proofs, if they don't turn out to be actual proofs, I have achieved nothing at all. There is no room for self-deception, no inherent value to the creative process itself. So it can be very lonely on the private side when the public proof fails.

You, on the other hand, Katerinya, can always fall back on your private creative side. There is no definitive rejection to what you have created. *You* know when you are done. As you said before, the creative process itself is satisfying. It has intrinsic value."

"But I can't earn a living if I only please myself!" she replied plaintively. "Once you get your result, others have to accept it, right? You'll get paid. It doesn't matter what other people think of it."

As he was pondering this, Katerinya, asked "If you could still make a living, but no one ever read your proofs, or any of your other kinds of scientific discoveries – your whole life's work was completely anonymous – would that be enough? Would your private process of discovery have been intrinsically valuable to you?"

Ilya pondered this one deeply. He was at a disadvantage in that in that he could not remember far enough back to get a full sense of what he had discovered in the past, or how he felt about it now. So he couldn't really say whether his past had been sufficiently fulfilling. Only that he had a broad sense of what he found fulfilling going forward, and it involved a pervasive curiosity about everything, and no particular regard for what anyone else might think about that.

"Yes," he said finally, happy to have uncovered one more aspect of his present self. "I suppose neither of us needs the acceptance of others – except to earn a living, of course."

§

As they talked on, facilitated by the wine, skating back and forth through the private-public channel from me to us to you and back again, occasionally brushing up against private sentiments that they had previously withheld but now willingly gave up, Ilya came to realize that she no longer played up to him as she once did. She was now confidently his peer. She was even emulating him a bit now, adopting some of his expressions without realizing it. She was beginning to absorb his personality. This pleased him no end, for he was also beginning to live vicariously through her. She had shared her whole life story with him, after all, and he envied her for having such a story to tell, for having perspectives and goals and aspirations in places where he had none. Her younger perspective was fine since he had no older one of his own. He couldn't recall having any life goals other than trying to figure things out. And that was not really a goal he set for himself, it was just who he was. He couldn't behave any differently.

But even in the fog of wine, Katerinya had the presence of mind to realize they would likely get lost in the moment again, as they had the first time. So she went into the bedroom to set her alarm to make sure there would be ample time for him to catch the last train back to Derazhne. She confessed that she had gone back to the hospital to visit the young doctor earlier in the week – to learn what else he might know about Ilya. "I hope you don't mind," she said a little sheepishly. That's how she knew about his big lecture coming up tomorrow. The doctor had told her all about it, and what it had meant to him as a young undergraduate. She certainly wouldn't want to deprive the next generation of students of their chance to hear "the great Professor Koskayin." She was comfortable enough with him now to make fun of him. That was good, he thought.

Now conscious of the time, she went looking for some closure. "When you said earlier that you felt lonely when your proofs fail, what did you mean by that?"

"Only that there is nothing left at that moment to fill the void of disappointment. Nothing else you can turn to for solace. It's over. You lost. When you're still in the hunt, you can go days without interacting with another person. I can, anyway. I don't feel the need for this then. If I succeed, I'm in the mood to celebrate. I want to go out and share this success with others. But if I fail, everything just stops, without any compensation. The thrill of the hunt is suddenly gone. I'm alone. Defeated. I need consolation, someone I could turn to, someone who would understand and could help change the subject. But no one knows this but me."

She could feel that loneliness, vividly, even though it was new to her. So she tried her best to summon up her own version, and pass it back to him. "I have the opposite problem, I think. When I need solace from loneliness, I turn to reading or writing fiction." She said this with a faraway look. "I suppose it's escape. I can either be comforted by the company of characters from a novel, as if I actually knew them, or I can simply invent the people that are missing from my real life."

He could relate to that kind of loneliness substitute, even though it was new to him. Or was it? Now he wasn't sure. Did he just learn about it from Katerinya, and empathetically imagine it, or was the feeling coming from somewhere inside himself – something he already knew because he had been there? This was familiar, somehow. He wanted to know more.

"Do you get lonely, working from home all day like that?" he asked.

"I do. But I suppose I'm not really solving my problem, am I? I'm pretending that I'm not lonely. How about you? Does working at the University all day make up for living alone at night?" Then she realized she had made a possibly unfounded assumption. "You do live alone, don't you?"

"I do," he smiled. "And weekdays at the University do take my mind off that."

"And weekends?"

"I don't have a solution for weekends. People say 'Get out. Do things!' but crowds don't work for me. I often feel more lonely in crowds."

"I do too! I thought that was just me."

"How about travel? Can you enjoy traveling solo?"

"I don't really know. I always wanted to travel, but I haven't gotten around to it yet. How about you?"

"I travel all the time, but it's work related. I have no choice. I never travel solo for pleasure. It just magnifies the loneliness. When I see new things, I want someone to be there to experience it with me. It's just not the same describing the experience to someone later. You had to be there."

Katerinya did not respond.

Ilya did not respond to her non-response.

All evening, the conversation had flowed so effortlessly that neither of them had to think about what comes next. But now neither of them had the next thing to say. They had reached a sort of plateau. This is normally an awkward silence. Something needs to be said to fill the void. You look down, or sideways, to avoid embarrassing eye contact while you struggle to compose something to say. But this was not an awkward silence. They both maintained eye contact as they had all evening. But now that there were no more words, the eye contact took on more significance. Deeply personal. It wasn't a situation you needed to get out of, but a warm one you were comfortable resting in. They were both experiencing the profound non-loneliness from their earlier complaints.

Something had to happen next, even though neither of them felt any urgency. Katerinya made the move. She gently placed her hand over his, and nothing more. It was a gesture of acceptance. But it opened up a new channel of communication – touch – with the comforting anticipation of the other's body heat. They both had managed to say what they really wanted to say without saying anything at all.

Then the alarm went off.

Chapter 3

THE DARK AGES

In the course catalogue, the gloss read simply "The Dark Ages: The collapse of classical civilization and the Black Death." As the early winter sun came streaming into her dorm room through the east window, Yulia Katyaevna was awakened before her alarm. She dressed, got her breakfast, then hurried to get a place in the lecture hall. The course, she heard, was usually oversubscribed, so there would be a culling out of "just shopping" students within the first week. Having a seat was a good start. She was a sophomore, but had yet to declare a major, so she would be lower on the pecking order than those with a declared major in the department. Further complicating matters was that this course was a joint offering by two departments, co-taught by a professor from each. This added to its attraction, but potentially doubled her competition for a spot.

She was born Yulia Katyaevna Antonova into a working class home in East Derazhne, the only child of deeply religious parents. They had originally been members of one of the more traditional, conservative denominations in town, but her father had become one of the many converts whom Sokolov managed to peel off from the

Protestants. Father Antonov had announced one day that she and mother Antonova would be attending a new church across town, one that had a more direct connection to the Holy Spirit and the Holy Scriptures. Antonov had felt the presence of the Holy Spirit in the Reverend Sokolov when he spoke to him. Yulia Katyaevna was an obedient and respectful child, but as she grew into adolescence, her private mind began to diverge from her public behavior. She was becoming a curious, free thinker on the inside and an obedient acolyte of the faith on the outside. Somewhere along the path to true believer, her mind had taken an alternate fork in the road and had been marching to the beat of a different drummer ever since. Fortunately for her, this path passed through a full scholarship on the way to the University.

The town-gown animosity was particularly acute for the University, being sited in the center of this mostly working class hamlet of Derazhne. Students came from miles away, with curiosities and ambitions even further afield, to what they perceived as an oasis of enlightenment. But few locals ever did, repelled by what they perceived as a cloister of wealth and privilege. It was not just an issue of affordability, but more often one of godliness – or more specifically, *un*godliness. And it was thus, from this most unlikely of beginnings, that Yulia Katyaevna's course found its way into the catalog.

It seems that a local true believer dashed off a letter to the editor of the local newspaper, complaining about the corrupting influence of this most unholy of institutions, and its power of seduction over innocent young minds. It was more screed than letter – in fact it bore a striking resemblance to a familiar screed already found plastered all over local public places. But it got published anyway, and soon touched off a flurry of supporting and dissenting such letters – mostly supporting – that the editor felt obliged to publish as well. When he saw where this was headed, the editor decided to close Pandora's box, and stopped accepting letters on that thread – "for now," he said.

But the public back and forth had already caught the attention of a wealthy and very influential alumnus (and donor) who lived up river in the western, more affluent section of town where most faculty residences are found. He, in turn, penned a letter to the University, opining that this public controversy needed to be addressed with some sort of official response. The letter floated around department heads and administrators looking for a landing place, looking for someone with an idea for a response, or at least a way to placate the donor. More than once, it landed at the Divinity School (due to its religious payload). Each time, they passed the buck back. It finally found a resting place with the dean of the College of the Humanities, not because of a felt need to address religion (the D school wasn't what the screed writer was looking for), but because it happened, by happenstance, to collide with a current secular concern.

Student enrollment in the humanities, and the arts for that matter, had been in decline for years now. These disciplines were losing out to the sciences, engineering, and especially computer science. Departmental funding was a zero-sum game. Each gain for the sciences was a loss for the humanities – more student majors meant more funding and more faculty; fewer majors entailed less funding and fewer faculty. To the dean's mind, there was no point to engaging the screed writer, but perhaps he could convert the alumnus's call to action into a more worthy crusade to save the humanities. The alum, after all, had been a classics major. It worked, and a committee was formed to brainstorm ideas and initiatives that might stem the tide of losses. Somewhere along the line, someone thought it might be a good idea to offer a series of introductory courses for undergrads that crossed the traditional boundaries between the sciences and humanities – something to entice undeclared majors like Yulia Katyaevna into becoming generalists. An inaugural course topic was somewhat ham-handedly cobbled together, under the theme of the Dark Ages, from two of its well-known events – the civilization collapse for a historian and the plague for a biologist. Casting Ilya Erynovich in the biology role was a chip shot. He already did this cross-boundary sort of thing, and was the least likely professor from the science side to complain. Finding the historian was another matter. They couldn't just fob it off on some unsuspecting member of the junior faculty. They needed someone with enough standing to hold his own against Koskayin. So they persuaded the eminent Professor Maksim Klavaevich Egorov to take it on, massaging his ego by casting him in the role of the savior of the humanities.

Today would mark the 9th time that Ilya Erynovich co-taught the course with Egorov. Other trial offerings of the envisioned series had died early deaths, progressively damping enthusiasm for the idea until the initiative faded away altogether. But over time, the Koskayin-Egorov course had become an undergraduate classic, due at least in part to the entertaining banter between the two lecturers. Their self-deprecating humor had grown organically as they learned to point and counterpoint each other with both earnestness and humor.

§

Egorov's aim was to drive home the tragic loss of classical civilization, not so much from the point of view of the surviving grand architectural wonders of government buildings and sports coliseums, or the surviving smaller architectures of quaint towns and neighborhoods, but from the point of view of the great and small *ideas* that were lost. The people who originally inhabited these places were gone, but they had been ahead of their time in collectively fashioning various forms of democracies and republics out of a more primitive tribal past, and had grown these ideas into great, global empires. It was Koskayin's job to cover what we've learned from the hard artifacts, but it was his job to cover how we have reconstructed these intangible ideas by piecing together fragments of surviving manuscripts, cross-referencing mentions of common events, following the backward chains of critiques of commentaries on commentaries on commentaries, from tangible documents to ones we can only infer. This was the historian's craft.

One of the unique challenges of this craft was distinguishing actual history from legends and myths. Ancient manuscripts often did not distinguish among these. Myths were easy to identify if they involved some kind of magic or supernatural occurrences – except in religious texts, of course, but that was a different sort of history. But non-magical myths can also be about famous battles that never occurred, or about larger than life heroes that never existed. And legends are often true, in that they recount actual battles and actual heroes, but the details have been embellished by retelling to the point that they are no longer accurate.

Further complicating the craft was the ubiquitous presence of manuscripts not written by the authors claimed in their titles. This sort of thing, scholars knew, was common in classical literature, and rampant in religious texts. One way to discover such false attribution was to first determine the time period in which the alleged author lived. This was done by looking at the dates of texts that refer to the author as a contemporary, or texts that mention birth and death dates. If all references to the existence of the work do not emerge until centuries after the alleged author's death, it is likely a false attribution. Another clue emerges if the work references historical events that were known to occur after the alleged author's lifetime, or if the work refers to "current events" that occurred before the author's lifetime. Quite often, religious texts alleging to be the prophecies of a known historical figure could be dated to periods well after the prophet's death. This was a surefire way to boost the credibility of a prior prophet by retroactively adding current events to his prior predictions. Much of this false attribution, though, appeared not to be deliberate deception. It was a common practice for later generations to attribute a collection of texts of unknown origin to some famous predecessor – more an instance of tribal hubris or just plain ancient inference.

From his time on the stage with Koskayin over these nine years, Egorov had learned not go toe-to-toe with Ilya Erynovich over the relative worth of historical textual evidence. It was what it was. So he would start at the top – with the conclusions generally agreed upon by the community of experts – waxing on about the inherent value of the classical ideas that were lost, trying to inspire a next generation of generalists to learn from these ideas in the present and to preserve them into the future.

One lesson from the past that he was always sure to include in his lecture was the ancients' strategy of hosting games and sporting events in large stadiums for their citizens. These were more than just popular entertainment; they served a social purpose. We might think of their coliseum contests as violent by present standards, but they served a useful purpose by harnessing people's' instinctive taste for violence into virtual warfare. Better to let your citizens vent their tribal advocacy by cheering on simulations of battles than engaging in actual battles themselves. This was *his* idea, he thought, and he regarded it as one of his singular contributions to the field. Other scholars may have thought of it, but he hadn't read it anywhere. It had occurred to him in a flash of his own insight. The "ownership of ideas," you see, was a contentious issue in humanities scholarship. When you published something new, you always had to first research your thesis and were obliged to cite anyone who had published something similar before you. The first to publish was the default owner of the idea. But he was willing to fight for the ownership of this one. It didn't matter to him who got it into print first. He wasn't about to cite anyone else.

§

Ilya Erynovich, with a scientist's single-minded orientation toward hard, physical evidence was initially annoyed by the thinness and questionable provenance of "historical evidence" from written manuscripts, but over time came to appreciate that this is the only kind of evidence historians have to work with – a tangled thicket of recorded testimonies, memories and opinions, intermingled via chains of support, contradiction, and self-promotion, hopefully regressing back to original sources, but often enough forming large circles of self-referential reasoning. It is the historian's calling to make the most sense possible out of this cacophony of past voices, trying to divine truth by coherence rather than observation. So these truths were necessarily theoretical, speculative, far removed from a common set of incontrovertible facts that all historians could agree upon.

By contrast, Ilya Erynovich would start at the bottom – with the premises – by introducing the two classes of hard, physical evidence that all investigators could agree on. The first concerned evidence created by natural history itself: geological core samples, tree rings, ancient DNA. The second concerned artifacts fashioned by past humans: symbols, inscriptions, and commentaries etched in stone, or pressed into dried clay; manuscripts recorded in ink on animal skins, papyrus, and paper. We still have too few surviving instances of either of these kinds of evidence to support robust conclusions about the deep past, but that deficit is so much greater for the second. Why are there so few surviving manuscripts? This needed to be explained, and to his mind there was no better way to explain it than by starting with *Entropy*.

The concept of entropy was foreign to most students, and almost certainly to the subscribers of this course without a science background. Yet it is the fundamental organizing principle that explains both the complex structure of human life and the relative absence of such structure in the surrounding universe. If you want to understand this apparent absurdity of life, you need to know entropy – the cold, Grim Reaper that stalks the cosmos, snuffing out organization and complexity – a fate that life on Earth has been artfully dodging for the last 3 billion years or so.

If this were a physics course, he could begin with its proper name: The Second Law of Thermodynamics. He would then go straight to the most basic principle of all physical interactions: that they always seek out the lowest energy regime until equilibrium is established. Then he would build up from there to the interactions of molecular biology, and finally to the more familiar interactions among human-sized things in our modern, built environment. But he would likely lose at least half of this audience if he began that way. So he had to resort to analogies.

Imagine, if you will, a small glass aquarium tank filled with clear water. Now drop in a small amount of dark blue India ink from the top. At first, an undulating swirl of blue with rounded tentacles forms where the ink was introduced. Then slowly but surely the ink spreads out, becoming paler as it becomes more dilute. Eventually we have a uniformly light blue tank of liquid, everywhere the same. You can imagine this because you've seen other things that behave like this. You never see the initial, complex swirl of ink just hang there, suspended in the clear water, holding its shape indefinitely. And you certainly never see the reverse – a tank of uniformly pale blue water that spontaneously coalesces into the previous dark blue swirl suspended in clear water. This is because the molecules of the blue swirl are initially arranged in a complex, non-random energy configuration suspended in the uniformly random configuration of water molecules. Each individual interaction between the molecules of these two liquids favors a less structured, lower-quality energy outcome until an equilibrium is reached at maximum randomness. This is the universe on entropy. There is an implied direction to events – always colder and more random on average.

Now let's consider the larger, solid things that we interact with on a daily basis. We build homes and factories and appliances and trains; we buy clothing and food. We paint pictures, write novels, compose symphonies. When we first create them, these artifacts seem permanent enough. We come to rely on them for particular purposes, assuming they will still be there tomorrow. But with the passage of time, they degrade, decay, wear out, spoil, stop working, fall apart, disintegrate — to the point that they can no longer fulfill their original purposes. With enough time, all of our artifacts will eventually decompose into the background of the spaces they occupy, indistinguishable from the more random, primitive stuff from which they came. We might rephrase entropy at this level as the principle that "Stuff does not last!" All stuff. Why is this? All of these more complex arrangements of matter are created from raw materials that start off in a less complex state; we need to expend energy to fabricate the raw stuff into refined stuff. We get it by burning fuels, reducing their ordered structure to less ordered free heat energy, and waste products such as ash or soot. By the principle of entropy, the total amount of structure created is always less than the total amount of structure destroyed. To keep the things we create from losing their desired structure, we have to maintain them — we have to expend even more energy to update and repair them. We are choosing winners among structured things by destroying slightly more structure in other things that we care less about.

Finally, let's consider life. We think of ourselves and other living things as relatively permanent structures, but we are much more like hurricanes than like rocks. Rocks are formed over time by the heating and compressing of much smaller molecular structures until they have reached a temporary state of equilibrium. They don't change much anymore, except via very gradual external processes such as erosion. So it takes entropy millions of years to reclaim this structure. But it will eventually. Hurricanes, on the other hand, are very short-lived, dynamic structures, formed when winds curl back on themselves to form a more highly ordered, self-perpetuating cycle of energy. This structure temporarily postpones entropy by sucking in and consuming more energy from the surrounding atmosphere. Entropy chips away at the boundaries of this structure though, and eventually, the coherence of its cycle breaks down. Entropy settles the bill and the storm dies.

Life on Earth resembles the hurricane, in that each organism has an internal, self-perpetuating fire of energy consumption. We call this metabolism. What we have over the hurricane is that the metabolic fires in each of our cells is contained within a cell membrane, a barrier that selectively lets fuel in and waste out, keeping the internal structure from reaching equilibrium, and the cell from dying. Are we violating the principle of entropy? No, we are just temporarily *keeping it at bay by destroying a greater amount of nearby structure as payment – including our neighbor plants and animals. We eat them, stealing their lives, as it were, to perpetuate our own. Will we eventually run out of resources to burn? Yes, but don't worry. The final heat death of the universe is still 1.7 times 10 to the 106th power years away – that's 17 followed by 105 zeroes. We have a lot of time left.*

Life as a whole has yet another way of cheating entropy. Individual cells and whole organisms are constantly dying when external events compromise their internal integrity, by starvation, dehydration, being eaten, suicide, accidents, natural disasters, and for most animal species at least, senescence – death by old age. Senescence is entropy at work, but only because the genetic programming of the species of organism itself reaches a point where it stops repairing accumulated damage to its structures. But the species as a whole survives indefinitely by constantly reproducing close copies of itself. So even senescing species manage to cheat entropy at the population level. Entropy only gets to close the books when the whole species goes extinct.

But even with this robust diversification strategy, the perpetuation of life on Earth turns out to be relatively fragile over billion year time frames. Five times in the last 3 billion years, the Earth has come precipitously close to losing life altogether. Each time, almost all of the existing animal and plant species were driven to extinction, but each time, this cataclysmic dying-off paved the way for the more adaptive survivors to start again. What we humans call the 'Black Death' or the 'Great Dying' was indeed great from the point of view of human history, but relatively insignificant to life on Earth as a whole. It only affected a single species – us. And we are still here today because the plague didn't manage get us all. But the large reduction of the human population created genetic bottlenecks that pruned our human traits going forward.

Ilya Erynovich had learned, over the last eight years, to pause at this point in the lecture. It was a natural stopping place because for many in the audience this was astounding news. He originally paused here because he thought there might be questions, but questions rarely came. The thoughts needed some time to marinate. But the most likely question to arise, when it did, was always "How do scientists know this?" So he had learned to ask it for them.

How do we know this, you might wonder. Well, there are two kinds of evidence that we use to figure out what occurred in the past. The first is the kind created by the Earth's natural processes such as geological strata, ocean and river sediments, tree rings, and fossilized organisms. The strata and sediments can be used to date a particular location, or to establish facts about the ambient chemical environment when they were laid down. The fossils, which are pretty much limited to vertebrate animal species with internal bony skeletons, provide clues about the outer form and function of the erstwhile animal. But if DNA can be extracted from the fossil, the animal can be fairly precisely located in the forward and backward evolution of it species. What's more, DNA samples from a collection of these individuals from different time periods can be used to infer migration patterns, and singular genetic events such as population bottlenecks or explosions.

The second kind of evidence is that created by ancient humans themselves: artifacts such as tools, buildings, and manuscripts. The tools and buildings tell us about their technology. The manuscripts tell us about their history and culture. Most of this culture transpires as the he-said/she-said utterances of daily life, which, of course, expire immediately. It is only when someone takes pains to write it down, and write it down on something permanent enough to survive for the long haul, that it becomes evidence for us. Writing decays when the surface it is written on decays. If our ancient ancestors had had the foresight to see this from our point of view, they might have entropy-proofed more of their messages by sticking with their first method of recording – etching things in stone! Next came pressing characters into clay tablets – still serviceable. But when they moved on, for their own convenience, to ink on parchment, and finally, ink on papyrus and paper, they were playing right into entropy's hands.

There is a subtle caveat to this last kind of evidence, though, that makes it fundamentally different from all the other kinds of evidence. It records a human opinion, and the recording is backed by a human motive. The opinion may be accurate, mistaken or an outright lie. The motive may be to inform, to promote, to denigrate or to deceive. Tools and buildings are what they are. They are not created to inform or deceive. Needless to say, there are no agenda or accuracy issues when molecules are copied into a new genome, or trees grow their annual rings, or compounds coalesce into geological strata. So we can infer the details of the great dying-off events with much greater certainty than we can infer the past cultural events. The molecular messages from the past — the ancient DNA — reach us without (much) entropic decay and without human editors.

These messages tell us that there were at least 3 large-scale genetic bottlenecks in human history. The first occurred somewhere between 50,000 and 60,000 years ago, as modern humans were dispersing out of Africa to populate the other continents. The precise cause is still unknown. The second occurred in the mid 14th century and was caused by a pandemic of the bacterium Yersinia pestis medievalis, passed from rats to fleas to humans, and eventually from humans to humans. It killed between 75-200 million people in Eurasia and North Africa, reducing the European population by 30-60 percent, and that of the Middle East by about 30 percent. This conferred upon subsequent humans a certain degree of immunity to the bacterium. The last occurred in the mid 21st century, and was by far the most devastating. The ubiquity of the ruins all around us, and the genetic bottleneck evidence, suggest that humans numbered in the billions by the mid 21st century, then collapsed to as few as 10,000 individuals in a single generation. This third dying-off was also caused by Y. pestis, but by an apparently newly mutated variant, Y. pestis modernis, whose transmission was more rapid, incubation much shorter, and morbidity much higher. It escaped humans' hard-won immunity to the parent strain.

Consequently, most of us here today in the 41st century have some natural immunity to both this strain and the parent. And that's a good thing, because we have studied Y. pestis modernis in the lab, and in the worse case, it can kill within hours of infection. Fortunately we have both a specific antibiotic for treating it (if we get there in time) and a vaccine to protect those who lack natural immunity.

At this point in the lecture, Ilya Erynovich would normally have pointed out that *modernis* is now thought to be extinct. There had been no reported cases of any subspecies of Y. *pestis* for the last 80 years or so, but this time the issue was a little less clear, so today he skipped that part. He continued …

The ubiquity of surviving hard artifacts, like passenger jets, cargo ships, railways, cable networks, and cell towers tells us that the mid 21st century world was stitched together on a scale vastly exceeding what we have now. So, given its extremely short incubation, Y. pestis modernis was likely spread worldwide in a matter of weeks or months. And because it was so utterly deadly, it likely decimated populations in their tracks. This would also explain the many surviving buildings and towns, suggesting that it was not a violent end – a buzzing, thriving culture suddenly gone silent in place, rather than a great war, or a natural catastrophe. The many noble cultural achievements of this classical civilization, that Professor Egorov described, collapsed in a very short timeframe, leaving us to try to reconstruct some of it from the very few surviving manuscripts.

Ilya Erynovich had learned that another question was likely to surface at this point, so he again asked it himself …

Now, you might be wondering: if all of these hard artifacts of our ancestors' civilization survived, why are there not more surviving artifacts of their recorded history? Surely they wrote things down like we do today. Well yes they did, but also like our current world, it was a world conditioned for fast dissemination of the written word: printing presses cranking out paper books, server farms archiving and serving digital content. Entropy be damned! Books can be reprinted faster than they decay. Digital works are archived, and backed up, and distributed over servers in multiple locations, so some recording of any work will always survive. But the essential glue that holds this information metabolism together is people. Take away the people, and the machinery grinds to a halt. The small number of survivors would likely have fled urban centers – just to be survivors. There would be no one left to run the printing presses and distribute the books. No one left to generate the electricity that powers the server farms. No one left to backup or distribute the digital copies.

So immediately post pandemic, the planet would have been left with a dearth of humans and a wealth of surviving paper and digital recordings. Paper books can last as long as 200 years if they are properly maintained in libraries with sufficient climate control, and protection from the elements like sun, water, bacteria, and fungi. But they can decompose in as little as 20 years without any such protection. With the human maintainers gone, entropy could take the fast track.

Solid-state digital recordings are a bit harder to kill and would have physically survived much longer without human maintenance. But these digital media were designed to present their contents to readers dynamically, *on demand, as part of a much larger infrastructure of clients and servers. It does you no good to stare at a polycarbonate disk, like you would a book. The recorded meaning is inaccessible without a digital reading device to display it, and that device requires compatible software to interpret the incoming bits, and the software requires shared, standard protocols for accessing the servers, and the protocols require the correct private encryption keys to decrypt the bits on storage media. Encryption keys are designed to expire at regular intervals, and thus must be replaced at regular intervals by – you guessed it – people. For all practical purposes, an expired encryption key and an obsolete or discontinued plaintext protocol cause the same damage. The potentially long surviving ones and zeros no longer carry any meaning for subsequent humans. They are just a bunch of inscrutable industrial junk.*

§

For as long as he could remember – which was a very hazy proposition at this point, given his circumstances – Ilya Erynovich had thought of *Y. pestis modernis* in historical terms, as a lesson from the past, almost a legend from the past, whose outsized horrors could comfortably be recounted from a great distance away in time. He had grown accustomed to the cadence and rhythm of his introductory lecture as he had polished and refined it over the years. He knew how to read his audience, how to build anticipation, when to pause. So he was caught off guard by his own sudden deviation from the flow when it came time to allay fears about any current manifestation of this mythical bacterium. He felt momentarily dishonest by skipping the subject, but he was now of two minds about what he used to so blithely relate, and neither mind was wholly in charge. So the one mind had cautioned the other to be silent.

At the conclusion of the lecture, there was the usual rush of students coming down to the front of the hall to ask questions of the two professors. Since another class was scheduled to follow theirs, they jointly encouraged the students to follow them outside where they could continue the discussions without obstructing the next class. The scene outside the lecture hall door then resembled the end of a church service, with the pastor (joint pastors in this case) greeting parishioners in a receiving line. Among the parishioners was Yulia Katyaevna, who eagerly awaited her turn to speak with Professor Koskayin. When she got the opportunity, she began with an effusive confession of wonderment about the lecture, then proceeded to make her case for being included in the final course registration. She was only a sophomore, she pleaded, and had not declared a major, so she feared she would get bumped by those with higher claims. And she so wanted to take this course! Ilya Erynovich looked over at Maksim Klavaevich, who had heard the entire exchange. They smiled and nodded to each other. This was the kind of student they were looking for. "I think we can arrange that," Professor Koskayin told her.

This was what she wanted to hear, but she also had more to ask. She was also very polite though, and socially aware, and didn't want to monopolize Professor Koskayin at the expense of students waiting behind her. So she thanked him and stood to the side, waiting for the receiving line to finish. When the multitude finally diminished to three – two professors and one student – she asked Professor Koskayin if he would consider being her faculty advisor. She didn't have one yet, and was still unsure about a major, but today had opened her eyes to so many possibilities she had never considered. She had never imagined going into science before, but she had never seen science presented like this before either. These are the kinds of things professors like to hear. "OK. Why don't you come by my office this afternoon – 308 Dahlström – and we'll talk about it."

After Yulia Katyaevna left, Egorov turned to Koskayin and admonished, "Now don't you go poaching her, Ilya Erynovich. We are supposed to be encouraging generalists, remember?"

"I'm nothing if not general, don't you think Maksim Klavaevich?" he replied, smiling. "If she had come to you to major in history, would that make her more general? It doesn't really matter where they land; it matters where they have visited on the way there." After a pause for the thought to sink in, Ilya Erynovich inquired, "See you at Krutikov's Pub tonight?" "Yes, of course," Maksim Klavaevich replied.

Over the years, a tradition had developed of meeting at the Pub on the first evening of the winter term. Why winter? No one could remember. It just turned out that way. They would also likely be joined by Ove Alfhildovich, Andzhelina Gullovna, a smattering of graduate students, and Diederick Brandt from the D School. Although many of the Protestant denominations had abstinence from alcohol among their credos, Diederick's church was not one of these. Besides featuring real wine at Communion service, he came from a long line of monks who had historically been masters at the art of fermenting ales and wines. He didn't do this himself, of course, but he was a modern day connoisseur of the products. Ilya Erynovich was also an oenophile, but this is typically not what one goes to Krutikov's Pub for. They were a specialty microbrewer of their own beers, ales, stouts, and temnotas. Ilya Erynovich was a fan of the offerings at the darker end of the spectrum: stouts and temnotas. Historically, there had once been a clear distinction among brewers between a stout and a temnota. How it was made determined what it was called. But nowadays, that distinction had been lost. A given brew was whatever you said it was. It had become a marketing term.

§

In the Quad, a red-tailed hawk was perched on the highest branch of a massive sugar maple, now devoid of its leaves. If the tree had a conscious memory, it might have noticed that winter was here now, and in a few more months it would be time to get its sap flowing. There would be nothing for it to do, of course, because for trees these things just happen, but without a conscious memory, it would be a surprise every time. The hawk, which did have a conscious memory, was scanning the Quad below, looking for prey. It knew what to expect. All it saw, though, was a couple of those large human things you often see on the Quad – not prey. But one of them appeared to be stalking the other, as if that were its prey. The hawk could relate to that. Whatever. No food here. It spread its large wings and gracefully lifted off looking for better opportunities.

Below, Ragnar (one of the large human things) had been waiting in the shadows outside of the lecture hall, biding his time until Professor Koskayin emerged. He had been to Koskayin's house and office during the lecture, looking for signs. This turned out to be easy. No one in Derazhne locks their doors, he thought. He had found a total of three messages associated with the sign: two in the professor's house and one in his office. One said, "Purity, Chastity, Innocence." Another said "Father, Son, Ghost." The last said "Faith, Wisdom, Chivalry". The messages were all triplets on makeshift bookmarks in books with the sign on the binding. This was the exact same pattern he had seen before when he had found a similar message in a book in Koskayin's room at a guesthouse in Mariankursk. He still did not know what these meant. Perhaps the others would. His task was to confront Koskayin, taking over the quest from the last member who failed. Next man up, and all that. He hadn't seen the mark on his ankle yet. No opportunity. But he knew the description and it matched the marks on the book bindings. This was not the time or place for an encounter yet, he thought to himself; too public. So he followed Koskayin from a distance as he made his way across the Quad.

At one point, he thought that maybe Koskayin had seen him, so he acted disinterested, as if he was just a tourist or something. But he saw a difference in Koskayin's gait. He was hurrying now, as if he knew he was being followed. Ragnar had slipped up. So he casually turned and walked the other way, resolving to lay low for a while.

As he was crossing the Quad, Ilya Erynovich thought he caught a glimpse of some shadowy figure following him. He quickened his pace, trying to exit the Quad without letting on that he knew about his pursuer. He didn't look back until he was out of the Quad. When he turned to look, he saw no one. Unlike in the streets of Mariankursk, the Quad was a large, wide-open area, without buildings or corners to hide behind. Either he had lost him, or his pursuer was a very good stalker. Either way, no one appeared to be watching him right now, so Ilya Erynovich exploited the blind spot, and headed north toward the Divinity School. Then he reprised the Mariankursk strategy of three long right turns to bring him back to where he would be behind his stalker, if he were being followed. The coast was clear. In Mariankursk, he had fled to the train station because he was in an unknown town with an unknown mission. Now he was on his home turf with a clear mission. He was probably safe here.

Now, being just outside of the Divinity School, it occurred to Ilya Erynovich that this might be a good time to consult his good friend Professor Brandt. Diederick might know something about the meaning of this Korihor business. He would if anyone would. So he climbed the stairs to Diederick's office on the off chance that he was in. He was.

"Ilya Erynovich!" he exclaimed. "What brings you here on this fine morning?" "I was wondering if you had a moment," Ilya Erynovich replied. "There's something you may be able to help me with."

Diederick was always willing to discuss things with Ilya Erynovich, so he bade him come in, sit down. Now, Ilya Erynovich had not had time to think this through, acting on the spur of the moment. He could trust Diederick implicitly, but was unsure whether Diederick already knew about the mark on his ankle. He couldn't recall ever having discussed this with anyone, other than Katerinya. He also didn't know if his current memory deficit was a topic of general knowledge among his friends, or whether it was some new affliction. Or, perhaps it was an ongoing condition that he had told no one else about (except Katerinya, of course). All of these doubts led him to play it safe for now. So he began by relating the encounter with the attacker at the train station in Mariankursk, what he said about 'Korihor,' but leaving out the mark-on-the-ankle bit. He also left Katerinya out of the story. He hadn't thought about this one way or the other. It just happened.

"Korihor …" Diederick muttered, knitting his brow in concentration. "Ah, yes. From the Apocrypha! You do know about the Apocrypha, don't you?" Ilya did know of the Apocrypha, at least he knew of its existence, but he could not recall any specific content. Diederick seemed inclined to explain though, as one academic to another, so Ilya Erynovich went along. The Apocrypha, Diederick explained, was a collection of religious works that had not made it into the official canon of the Bible. Some of these were once in earlier versions of the canon, but later removed. Some had been riding along all the while, down through the ages, hoping for admittance, but never making the cut. Different religious denominations had included or excluded different books from their canons, but each had followed the tradition of printing the excluded collection under the heading of 'The Apocrypha' in their editions of the Bible. This tradition had fallen out of practice in the modern age, so very few current editions of the Bible even mention the subject anymore. Most parishioners were completely unaware of the existence of this shadow canon. There was also an even murkier shadow canon of works called the Pseudepigrapha. These were books thought to be falsely attributed, works whose claimed author is judged not the true author, or a work whose actual author attributed the text to a figure from the past. Over time, the term had become broadened to refer to any works deemed to have some spiritual merit, but not enough to ever be candidates for adoption into the Scriptures.

"If I remember correctly," Diederick said, "Korihor was a character in 2nd Alma, a book purged from the official canon into the Apocrypha at the Second Council of Nairobi roughly 2000 years ago." He went to a shelf in his wall of books and retrieved a volume of the Apocrypha, then began fingering through it, looking for his reference. "Ah, here it is!" he said. He began reading to himself, moving his index finger rapidly down the pages, looking for the first mention. Then he began reading out loud to Ilya Erynovich:

> *17 And this heretic whose name was Korihor (and the law could have no hold upon him) began to preach unto the people that there should be no Messiah. And after this manner did he preach, saying:*
>
> *18 O ye that are bound down under a foolish and a vain hope, why do ye yoke yourselves with such foolish things? Why do ye look for a Messiah? For no man can know of anything which is to come.*
>
> *19 Behold, these things which ye call prophecies, which ye say are handed down by holy prophets, behold, they are foolish traditions of your fathers.*
>
> *20 How do ye know of their surety? Behold, ye cannot know of things which ye do not see; therefore ye cannot know that there shall be a Messiah.*
>
> *21 Ye look forward and say that ye see a remission of your sins. But behold, it is the effect of a frenzied mind; and this derangement of your minds comes because of the traditions of your fathers, which lead you away into a belief of things which are not so.*

22 And many more such things did he say unto them, telling them that there could be no atonement made for the sins of men, but every man fared in this life according to the management of the creature; therefore every man prospered according to his genius, and that every man conquered according to his strength; and whatsoever a man did was no crime.

23 And thus he did preach unto them, leading away the hearts of many, causing them to lift up their heads in their wickedness, yea, leading away many women, and also men, to commit whoredoms—telling them that when a man was dead, that was the end thereof.

"Sounds a bit like you, eh Ilya?" he said, teasing. "Well, maybe not the part about whoredoms." Ilya Erynovich was amused. But why him, of all the skeptics in the world to choose from? "Is there any more?" he inquired. Yes, Diederick replied, and proceeded to relate the rest of the story from memory. It seems Korihor was arrested for both blasphemy and heresy and taken before some superior judge who demanded he recant. Korihor replied, interestingly, that he was not an atheist, but an agnostic. He did not deny the existence of God, but saw no evidence for it either. If the judge were to give him some sort of supernatural sign, that might convince him otherwise. So for a sign, the judge strikes him dumb – unable to speak. Now Korihor recants (by writing), and tries to blame his whole skeptical career on Satan. The devil made me do it! The judge isn't buying it, so leaves him in his silent state, no longer able to preach his seditious views, and puts out word that this is what happens to heretics, a lesson to all apostates to convert back to the fold.

"And that's the end of it?" asked Ilya Erynovich. Were his pursuers perhaps trying to strike him dumb? Good luck with that, he thought. Diederick then read the last few verses:

49 And it came to pass that they were all convinced of the wickedness of Korihor; therefore they were all converted again unto the Lord; and this put an end to the iniquity after the manner of Korihor. And Korihor did go about from house to house, begging food for his support.

50 And it came to pass that as he went forth among the people, yea, among a people who had separated themselves from the Nephites and called themselves Zoramites being led by a man whose name was Zoram—and as he went forth amongst them, behold, he was run upon and trodden down, even until he was dead.

51 And thus we see the end of him who perverteth the ways of the Lord, sayeth the Zoramites; and thus we see that the devil will not support his children at the last day, but doth speedily drag them down to hell, sayeth they also. But behold, the devil did this not unto Korihor, but restored him to his earthly station, even as a man among men, that he might continue to preach. And the devil rewarded Korihor for his service unto him by granting unto him immortality – so that the peoples of all nations could not extinguish his words thereafter.

Well, that puts a different spin on it entirely, Ilya Erynovich thought. Diederick could vaguely recall hearing of a splinter sect somewhere out west – a small cult really – that had the Korihor character as their primary villain – agent of the devil, and all. He didn't know anything else about it, their beliefs in general, their mission, their methods. But if they really were out to get Ilya Erynovich, né Korihor, it was unclear what they intended to do if they were to find him again. If he was immortal, they couldn't run upon him and trod him down until he was dead, as before. Though the closing lines of the last verse left open the theological issue of whether the devil in fact has the power to grant immortality. Brandt doubted that this was even clear to the cult. Maybe they would just take their best shot – hope for the best.

"So it's not clear what they would do with you," Diederick said. "The skeptic part seems to fit you. Are you also immortal, Ilya?" Ilya Erynovich, smiling, didn't think so. There really was no remedy for this situation. He couldn't go to the authorities for protection. The story would make him sound a little deranged himself. And even if he were believed, what protection could they offer? It was a very indistinct threat. The who, what, and why were all still very much outstanding. On the other side of the ledger, what had already been exposed by the incident in Mariankursk would be of no particular interest to the authorities there – his attacker safely disqualifying himself from further rational consideration. So the matter would remain private. He would just have to stay vigilant.

On his way out the door, Ilya Erynovich inquired "Will I see you tonight at Krutikov's, then?" "Wouldn't miss it for the world," came the reply.

§

By early afternoon, Ilya Erynovich was already back at his office, up to his elbows in the antibiotic-synthesis project. With the opening lecture now out of the way, he had no more teaching obligations until Wednesday. And he now had some live specimens of the infection, drawn from patients in Mariankursk, for testing. He had kept Professor Ekholm in the loop on the mission. Ove Alfhildovich agreed that he should not be testing on live patients until they had proven the efficacy of the antibiotic in the lab. But he also agreed that this was a matter to be kept below the radar. They should not inform the authorities yet. Nothing good would come from dissemination of partial knowledge. It would lead to their scientific hand being forced by unscientific politicians, probably making the situation much worse.

The knock on the door came when he was head down in the reactions. He had forgotten about Yulia Katyaevna, his new advisee. "Come in, sit down! I just need a few minutes to finish up here." She did, and took a seat on the couch opposite the fireplace. As she waited, she surveyed his office. So many books! And so much dark walnut – for the shelves, for the wainscoting, for the cornice pieces, for the mantel over the fireplace. An overstuffed, red leather chair over here. Twin black and gold Captain's chairs over there. Very U of D. Over the mantel was a small wooden maritime clock. She had seen one of these before in her uncle's house in Solinovsk. He worked on the waterfront as a fisherman.

After Ilya Erynovich had managed to tie up the loose ends, he invited her to take a seat in front of the desk. She introduced herself more formally this time, giving her full name: Yulia Katyaevna Antonova. He wrote it down, both because he would need to fill out some paperwork to make her his advisee, and as an aid to his visually-biased memory. She launched into a condensed biography of herself: East Derazhne, religious upbringing, secretly taking the fork, full-ride to the University. She had always been curious about history, she said, starting as a child in East Derazhne when she first became aware that there were almost never any no new houses. Everyone lived in an old house that had been fixed up. There were so many other empty old houses waiting to be re-inhabited, but there were no more people to fill them. So there was no need for new houses. She thought, at first, maybe people were just dissatisfied with the houses they built, and moved out to build a better one. This was before she realized there were many more houses than people everywhere. By high school she had learned about the Great Dying, and ever since had felt that modern humans were, in some sense, living other, prior people's lives. We're going around a second time. What must it have been like when there were more people than houses? Would we get there again at some point? Were the first people more advanced or more primitive than us? Would we do things differently this time, or would we repeat the mistakes of the past?

So she thought she might major in history when she first came to the University, she said. But her whole concept of history was blown away by today's lecture. She already knew of many of the features of past civilizations that Professor Egorov described. But entropy! And how life escapes entropy! And how long ago life started! And how life almost disappeared five times! There was no place for these concepts in the worldview she had brought with her at the start of the morning. She had always been skeptical about the creation stories from the Bible, she said, because they couldn't account for things like dinosaurs. And the story of the flood that killed off all of the animals except the ones on the Ark? What about the fish? Did they "drown" too? But she had no idea about the timescale of life on Earth. 3.5 billion years! She didn't understand how scientists could know such things, but she was eager to find out. This wouldn't go over so well at home, she said with a smile, but she was used to that by now. There were so many things she couldn't discuss with her parents, or her pastor.

This was heartwarming to Ilya Erynovich, but he realized he had a long way to go. It was too early to go into things like differential isotope decay of pairs of atomic elements to date things. So he took what he thought might be an easier to digest route. "What does your pastor say about evolution?" She rolled her eyes. He says "evolution wants you to believe that one day there was just mud, and then the next day it suddenly turned into life, all by itself." And "It's the theory that human beings originated from fish that sprouted legs and crawled out of the sea." She suspected it was more complicated than that, but admitted that it was hard for her to imagine how things like that could happen.

"Well, your pastor has it approximately right," Ilya Erynovich told her. "He's just a little off on size and timing," he said, smiling. Then he went on to explain. "That mud is clay, specifically clay minerals. Those minerals have the capacity to support spontaneous metabolism, and the assembly of strings of RNA, the basic building blocks of cellular life. So yes, there was one day, about 3.5 billion years ago, in which all of these building blocks came together in the just the right combination to make the first cell. There probably wasn't even a single event. More likely, there were many such events – a lot of near misses, a lot of temporary starts that didn't last, a lot of advancings and retreatings – before life took hold permanently. But the world looked pretty much the same immediately before and after. Your pastor was denigrating a more absurd kind of event in which mud turned into a fish or something. He was thinking too big. From a human perspective, the origin of life would have looked a lot like mud turning into mud. Fish came much later. The net difference between pre-life and life was a very small molecular change in things we can only see with the most powerful microscopes. And this is how it should be if we are truly explaining things. Successful explanation proceeds in small increments. Miracles appear to be required only when you try to take too large a step all at once."

Now she was fascinated. "And what about the fish to humans part?"

"Ah," he said, "that's both size and timing. Every evolutionary event is one of those small molecular events we can't see in which a single nucleotide of DNA gets changed during copying. Humans don't see a difference until billions and trillions of these have piled up over time. It took about a half billion years for the biochemistry of the pre-life mud to get to the point where it could take this very small step across the line. Add another three billion years or so to get to fish. Fish took another quarter billion years to sprout their legs, and yet another quarter billion years to get to humans. Nothing happened suddenly."

"OK," she said, still pondering the process, "that makes more sense. Fish don't just sprout legs. I get that. But it's still hard to imagine how fish *eventually* sprouted legs even if you give them half a billion years."

"Hard to imagine?" he inquired. "Have you ever seen a tadpole turn into a frog?" She hadn't, but she knew all about them from high school biology. She had forgotten about that. She had seen the pictures in the textbook. Suddenly what she thought she couldn't imagine, was something that actually happens everyday. She had never thought about it like that.

"The transition from fish to legs took 250,000,000 years for evolution to accomplish the first time," he explained, "but now it only takes about 58 days for the same transition to be replayed from tadpole to frog. That's because the first time required a lot of random trial and error. Now that it's been accomplished, the same transition has become encoded in the genes in one straight shot. You can actually see the whole evolution of a frog from a single cell replayed like this, because they are not mammals, like us. Their development takes place outside the body of the mother. The eventual frog begins as a single-celled egg, *outside* of the parent, that grows and divides into a fish-like form with gills and tail. It uses the gills to respire oxygen from the water and the tail to swim. Then skin gradually grows over the gills and they recede and disappear as lungs begin to form. About the same time "leg sprouting" starts, followed by arm sprouting. The critter converts from gill respiration in water to air respiration at the surface. Then it moves onto land and its tail atrophies. Now it's a full-fledged frog."

Yulia Katyaevna could conceptualize how it worked now. The key epiphany for her was the "encoded in genes" part. She had always thought about genes being associated with final physical features like eye color. One gene, one trait. But if some of the genes also encode the development process from conception to birth, they are essentially replaying the much longer evolutionary process that got them to that point. "So it's the same process from single cells to humans?"

"Yes. That gets replayed in about 9 months, inside the mother. All vertebrate embryos go through a similar transition," he explained. "They all reach a stage, called the *pharyngula*, where they have gill slits and a tail. Then they branch off on different development paths to match their eventual end kind, just as evolution branched off before over many millions of years to create the various kinds. Fish embryos further refine the gills and tails and sprout lateral buds that become fins. In land vertebrates, the gills atrophy, lungs develop and the lateral buds become arms and legs. For creatures with final tails, like dogs, the tail keeps developing. For creatures without final tails, like the great apes, the tail atrophies. We are vertebrates. This is how we develop."

Now she was confused. "OK, I understand that different kinds of animals would need different development paths – you know, to make them end up differently. So it would make perfect sense to start from gill slits and a tail if you were trying to make a fish. But why do this if you are trying to make something like a human? Why not just leave that part out, instead of first making it, then undoing it?"

"Ah!" he said, "it *would* be senseless if you were starting from scratch to make a human. But evolution has no forward looking goals. It doesn't design things to match a purpose. It is a random process. It just tinkers, mutating one DNA sequence at a time, and keeping the ones that turn out to have some advantage. So if you were starting from a reasonably successful fish design, after a half billion years of trial and error, and started tinkering with the latter half of the development process, and managed to repurpose it into a four-legged land animal with lungs, well, that would make sense. The hybrid design might even come in handy to build a final fish that turns into a land animal, like the tadpole/frog.

If humans had been designed and created by (and in the image of) a god, as your pastor contends, why on earth (or in heaven) would that god have gone through all of these useless steps, these starts and stops, these make-it then unmake-it steps? The best evidence for evolution is the sheer *in*elegance of what it produces.

We lose almost all vestiges of our pharyngeal gill slits and tails by the time we pop out. We retain a tailbone, the *coccyx*, at the end of our spine that forms from a fusion of the last four vestigial vertebrae as the would-have-been tail is reabsorbed into the fetus. The gill slits portion of the embryo, which was once destined for fishhood, is drastically repurposed in us so that the gill arch bones of the fish become our middle ear bones. But some of our final anatomy is still pretty fishy from an elegant design perspective. When we are fully developed, the aorta, the main artery carrying oxygen-depleted blood out of our hearts to pass through the lungs for re-oxygenation, first proceeds up toward the head before it abruptly hooks around and heads back down. What's that for? Well, back in the pharyngula stage, the developing aorta already courses up through the developing gill slits, because this is where blood gets oxygenated in a final fish. As our gill slits atrophy and lungs develop further down, in line with the modified breathing design, the source of final oxygenation gets relocated. So the developing aorta has to take a sudden U-turn and head back down, retracting its connection to the gills that will no longer be there. Why would you design something like this from scratch? You wouldn't. But that's how evolution works – blindly mutating the features of organisms so far, until you accidentally make a slightly better one."

Yulia Katyaevna sat in silence for a moment, taking this all in. She was about to speak several times, then stopped, trying to rephrase her question more productively. Finally she asked, "But who comes up with all of these wonderful explanations?" She couldn't imagine she would ever be able to do something like that herself.

"We all do!" Ilya Erynovich replied. "Science is one big community. We all contribute our piece."

"But don't you have experts or authorities – leaders that you all follow," she asked.

He now understood her apparent confusion. "Ah, yes, we do. But unlike in religion, they are just a convenience – they save you time by summarizing what the community already knows. They have no authority as persons. You can challenge their summaries at any time. Many do."

"But what about Darwin?" she asked. "Isn't he responsible for evolution? Pastor Sokolov says it's just a theory pushed by this one man. 'They believe in Darwin; we believe in Jossmit. It's that simple' he says."

Now he understood completely. "The church has a hard time with this because they have no model for how science works. Every major tenet of religious belief can be attributed to someone with the authority to propound it. Science isn't like that. You won't find any books written by Darwin anywhere in a science class or lab. You won't encounter the term 'Darwinism.' Darwin is just one of the many members of the scientific hall of fame, up there with Copernicus, Galileo, Newton, Einstein, and many others who first contributed important ideas to our evolving, integrated theory of the natural world. They are revered not because they founded schools of philosophy about which present scientists debate, but because they contributed initial theories that got other, subsequent theories going down a productive path. Much of what each originally proposed turned out to be a little bit wrong in the details, as one would expect. But each proposed enough that was right that their original theories could be adapted to what was discovered later. The lasting scientific value lies in the theory, not the man (or woman)."

"Let me explain it this way," he offered. "Religion fixes belief with authority, and it enforces sameness of belief with heresy. If you want to believe something different, you have to leave your church and start another one. So everyone in the same religion believes the same thing. That leads to many religions, each believing something different, as many as schisms will allow. Now, take away authority and heresy (and revelation), and add in reasoning and unconstrained argumentation, and you get philosophy. You're free to believe whatever you would like, but you're expected to argue for it. Logic alone can only settle an argument by proving it inconsistent or contradictory. So very few of these arguments are ever settled. As a result, individual philosophies rarely ever die. They just keep multiplying (as in religion). Sometimes I think philosophers prefer it this way. Science is philosophy with a built in method for settling arguments: the crucial experiment. Unlike philosophers, scientists are impatient. They want to get to a result. So when two rival theories can both account for all the known facts, scientists stop debating and try to devise an experiment that will refute at least one of them. They poke and prod nature with newer instruments or novel techniques, trying to unearth some new facts. This eventually allows them to refute one of the theories and move on. Because of this, there is only one science – everywhere the same. We all share (roughly) the same beliefs because we all had a hand in getting there."

"But couldn't there be more than one science on the second time around?" Yulia Katyaevna asked. "If all of the scientific books were destroyed in the Great Dying, and the next generation of scientists had to start again from scratch, maybe they would come up with a different set of theories the next time."

She's good, Ilya Erynovich thought to himself. I like this student! "No! That's the beauty of it. Remember, the theories are not adopted until they are confirmed by experiments. The laws of nature will be the same as the first time. So the experiments will turn out the same way. It might take more or less time the second time around, because the theories may be discovered in a different order, but over time they will converge on the ones that correspond to the way the world really is."

Yulia Katyaevna was enjoying this immensely. But the anchor that connected her prior worldview to reality had just broken off at the mooring, and she was now adrift in a sea of new ideas. She needed to throw down a new anchor. It was both exhilarating and frightening at the same time. A lot to take in all at one sitting. She wished she could stay longer, but she had a class at the top of the hour, so she thanked Professor Koskayin, and wondered if they might be able to meet again to discuss these kinds of things. That would be fine with him, he said. Then it occurred to him that perhaps she might enjoy the conversation at the Pub this evening. He told her about the tradition, and let her know that she was invited – if she wanted – but not expected. That way she would feel enfranchised, but have an easy out if it didn't fit her socially. He didn't expect that she would actually come.

§

In the late afternoon, when his work for the day was done, Ilya Erynovich set out for Krutikov's Pub, following his usual route west on Osennyaya Street then south on Studencheskaya Street toward the river where the undergraduate houses were situated. The air was growing colder and a bracing breeze was beginning to rise. Winter was arriving with the winter term, right on schedule. He gathered his sabovar around himself, and crushed a small nanoprene crystal in each of his pockets to keep his hands warm.

Halfway down Studencheskaya Street he overtook Professor Egorov, himself on the way to the Pub. "Ilya Erynovich!" he said, hale and full of greeting. "Another year, another edition of the course, eh?" "Yes," Ilya Erynovich replied, "how many years has it been now?" "Nine, I believe," was the answer, "and I must say you outdid yourself today. You have a way with an audience of these young minds. I think you could lead them anywhere." Ilya Erynovich thanked him for the compliment, then noticed that he was shivering a little without his sabovar. He offered Maksim Klavaevich some of his nanoprene crystals. Egorov politely declined (you know the social convention), pointing out that they were almost there at Krutikov's, so he wouldn't be needing any inside. Ilya Erynovich reminded him that he would still need them on his way home afterward. Having already offered the obligatory decline, he now gladly accepted, so Ilya Erynovich took two of the pale blue, translucent crystals out of his pocket and handed them to Maksim Klavaevich.

As Krutikov's Pub came into view, Ilya Erynovich had another memory sensation of the kind he had been having all day. He knew his memory was improving in general, but the recovery was not at all uniform. There were peaks and valleys. This was one of the peaks. It was not a memory of a specific event, but more of the déjà vu variety. But instead of being amorphous it was very acute. Invisible, but clear in some sense. Without thinking, he remarked out loud "Reminds me of Almagro's."

"Reminds you?" Maksim Klavaevich said in surprise. "So you know about Almagro's! Few people do. You are quite the student of local history, Ilya Erynovich."

"So this once was Almagro's?" Ilya Erynovich asked. "I remember that now."

"I don't think you mean 'remember,'" Egorov said quizzically. "That was 367 years ago!"

Up until now, Ilya Erynovich had just been riffing on the déjà vu experience. Now he was fully focused on the conversation, and what he had just said. "Yes, I guess you're right. 'Remember' was the wrong word." But in his mind he was not so sure. This memory recovery business was all so very confusing.

Inside the pub, the room was warm and welcoming, the lights were low, the fireplace was blazing, the atmosphere was cheerful, and all was right with the world. This was one of the experiences Ilya Erynovich enjoyed most about winter – leaving it behind. Frosty faces being rewarded for a stoic journey through the elements. The journey wouldn't be bearable without the reward at the end, and the reward wouldn't be a reward if you came in from the warm. The gang was all here. At the large round table at the back he could see Andzhelina Gullovna, Diederick, Ove Alfhildovich, a few of the graduate students, and even Yulia Katyaevna. Good for her, he thought.

Egorov and Koskayin found their places at the table and exchanged the obligatory greetings with all present. Ilya Erynovich was a little concerned for young Antonova, a sophomore among a bevy of graduate students and professors, so he maneuvered to take a seat next to her. She seemed to welcome this. It turned out that she had already introduced herself to the group, relating her experience at the lecture earlier today. It was clear they had accepted her into their company, and she seemed perfectly at ease with the conversations. He was impressed.

When the waitress appeared, to take his and Egorov's orders, he glanced across the large room to the tap listings on the chalkboard over the bar. He read down the list looking to see what they had in stouts or temnotas (one of the benefits of being hyperopic). He passed over "Night Watch" temnota and "Afraid of the Dark" stout, which he had had before, until his eyes settled on "New Moon". That was new. When he inquired of the waitress she explained that it was new, and only available for about two weeks a year, starting now. It was a small batch temnota made from a milk stout base, infused with espresso. His brain did its best to imagine the taste of a milk stout, already a little coffee-like, merged with the taste of espresso. The choice was clear. "That's what I'll have!"

Ilya Erynovich learned that Diederick had already shared his Korihor story with the company. "I hope you don't mind," Diederick said. Initially he did mind because he had resolved earlier to keep this whole business on the private side of the ledger. Now they all knew. Only Ekholm was aware of his bacterial outbreak mission in Mariankursk, and he could count on him to keep that confidential. But when he discovered that the group all took the Korihor incident humorously, he realized Brandt's retelling was probably more shallow than his own conception of the episode. He had left out the mark, and Katerinya, and thus most of the attack, so that left only an apparent lunatic ranting about Korihor in a train station – nothing about the pursuit either here or in Mariankursk. The transit police were just removing a public nuisance as opposed to protecting himself. And the follow up story from the Apocrypha, one had to admit, was amusing. Even to himself. So he went along with the public tenor of the story.

In this telling, Ilya Erynovich, who was already well known for his skepticism, had become the unwitting target of some religious zealots who wished to dissuade him – how it was unclear – from continuing to lead the faithful astray. He could joke about it himself without fear of offending anyone present – with the possible exception of Yulia Katyaevna. He recalled that she had a conservative religious upbringing, and was not yet accustomed to his irreverent style. But she laughed along with the best of them. He liked this young student.

When the part about Korihor professing to be an agnostic rather than an atheist came up, Diederick wondered out loud whether this was an apt description of Ilya Erynovich. "I don't believe you've ever said," he remarked, turning to toward him. "Well, I am certainly agnostic," he replied. "I don't believe in the existence of any god or gods. That's just the scientist in me. We believe in the existence of something unseen only when there is no other way to account for what we *can* see. Once that was atoms, then electrons, then quarks. Each time, we were eventually able to see these things with the aid of instruments. Today, I suppose it would be something like strings. He looked around the table to see who would understand this reference to string theory – that would include Ekholm, and most of the grad students, but not Brandt, Berghild, Egorov, or young Antonova. But there was no puzzlement either, so he knew he could just let that one lie. "An atheist is one who believes that there are no god or gods – a positive assertion of what there is *not*. But you never have empirical evidence of the *non*-existence of something, so I guess my view is that

I don't really care one way or the other. The subject just never comes up. Does that make me an atheist?"

"Well, for all practical purposes, I think so," said Diederick. "You do *dismiss* my God, wouldn't you say? So you're an atheist and I'm not." One of the graduate students chimed in at this point, seeing his chance to be clever by replying directly to Diederick. "I contend that we are both atheists. I just believe in one fewer god than you do. When you understand why you dismiss all the other possible gods, you will understand why I dismiss yours." Diederick had heard this line before, so he was ready for it. "Ah, so you must not have heard! Ilya Erynovich will surely tell you that we believers dismiss all other gods because we were *told* to do so, by our tribe. These are heresies. There is no critical thinking involved. If we allow for the existence of any of these other gods, we will be expelled from our tribe. So what you are telling me is that you scientists dismiss all of the gods because you were told to do so by your tribe. You will be expelled from the tribe otherwise. No critical thinking involved," he said with a wink.

Ilya smiled. He could see this one coming. The room clearly got the humor of the repartee at the grad student's expense, including Yulia Katyaevna. The science tribe was really a lot like Andzhelina Gullovna's tribe in this regard, Ilya Erynovich offered – it had no heresy. You couldn't be expelled for your beliefs, whatever they were, he continued. Ove Alfhildovich could attest to this. If you advanced a supernatural theory as a scientific theory, the worst that could happen is that you would be ignored. You just weren't contributing anything helpful to the tribe in that instance. Ilya Erynovich wanted to make sure Yulia Katyaevna got to hear this point, though he addressed his remarks to the group in general. She was on the doorstep of science, after a lifetime of religion. He wanted her to see the contrast.

As the evening wore on, and the drinks continued to flow, Ilya Erynovich began to feel the weight of the day's events pressing on him. He was feeling a little fatigued, comfortably so, so he withdrew a little from the active conversation and took more of a passive role. As he listened to the back and forth, his eyes followed the contour of the dimly lit wall behind the bar. There were very visible cracks that let both the wind and the snow in. Where the wall met the wooden floor on both sides of the bar, the encroaching snow was beginning to accumulate in small drifts. The fireplace was having trouble keeping up with the drafts blowing through the cracks. This place would need a lot of work. Outside in the distance, they could hear a pack of wolves howling, ominously. He, James, and Andersen looked at each other. Andersen was superstitious, and thought this was a bad omen. Maybe we had come too early, he said. Can we survive the winter? Do we have enough provisions to last until spring? Because Ilya's chair faced the entrance, he could now see what the others did not. The door had blown completely off its hinges, and the snow was piling up. And there, standing in the drift was a large gray she wolf, baring her teeth. Don't look it in the eyes, he was always told. The wolf will take that as aggression. He tried to look away but it was too late. The wolf suddenly bounded across the room toward him. He jumped, startled in his chair. Then a comforting hand lay on his shoulder. "Ilya! Are you all right? It was Andzhelina Gullovna. "I think you had a bad dream!"

The others had noticed him drifting off, and thought it might be best to just let him rest a bit. "We didn't want to disturb you," Yulia Katyaevna said. Diederick now offered that perhaps it was time for all of them to retire for the evening. That quickly became the consensus, so they settled their tabs, said their goodbyes, and made their way to the front doors (definitely still on the hinges). Ilya Erynovich trailed back a little just to clear his head. He, Yulia Katyaevna, and Andzhelina Gullovna were the last to exit the doors together. Yulia Katyaevna had the easiest way home since her undergraduate house was only a block away toward the river.

When she turned to leave, Ilya Erynovich looked up at the evening sky. At first he was expecting snow on the ground, because of the dream, but the streets were clear in the real world. The sky, though, was a dazzling conflagration of red, orange, vermilion, and scarlet swaths, and a bright yellow explosion where the sun was making its last stand before disappearing below the horizon. The wind had picked up. "Red sky at night, sailor's delight" he had always heard. But this was clearly different. A storm was coming. So he bid farewell to Andzhelina. The sky was on fire, and he must go.

Chapter 4

PRINCE TARASOV

There comes a time when one must choose between the lesser of two evils. For Ilya Erynovich that time had come. His tweaking of the old antibiotic against *Y. pestis modernis* to account for the recent mutations in the Mariankursk strain had proven successful against the live cultures he had brought (this time successfully) from his last trip. He didn't have any live cultures of the progenitor *Y. pestis modernis* for comparison, these being safely ensconced in a secret, offsite location for the protection of everyone, but from his memory (now reaching far enough back to cover his prior laboratory encounter with the superbug) it appeared that the new antibiotic performed even better against the new strain than the old one against the old strain. This was the good news. The bad news was that he would probably now have to report this whole affair to the government authorities. He had discussed the issue with Professor Ekholm, and they had both reluctantly agreed that the time was nigh. However much they feared political meddling, government infrastructure would be needed to prevent what was now a small outbreak from becoming an epidemic. At least they had what appeared to be a scientific solution. That would gain them political points and, they hoped, bend the governmental response in the right direction.

Although the University paid his base salary, almost all of Ilya Erynovich's biological research was funded by the government – specifically, by the Prince of the City-State of Solinovsk, Koldan Sonvaevich Tarasov. Tarasov's family had held power over Solinovsk and its surrounding territories for three generations. Their reign began violently enough, as transitions of power often do, but had become progressively more peaceful and prosperous as they consolidated their power and rivals became less and less viable. Unlike other states on the continent that were ruled by monarchs in the past, the Prince of Solinovsk had no official claim of divine right. A monarch with such a claim had the de facto sanction of the Church, and a small slice of divinity bestowed by God. To oppose such a monarch was to oppose God. And since this divinity was somehow vested in the monarch's blood, his succession was predetermined by his bloodline. What one had to overlook in such a scheme were the inevitable transitions when one monarch conquered another, or a monarch was overthrown by a non-monarch. Suddenly (in almost every case) the divine bloodline switched families and was blessed by the Church. Churches (typically) have no armies. Monarchs do. He who has the army holds the ultimate power. After a few generations, people forget about the discontinuity and all is well again.

The rise of the Tarasovs was decidedly more pragmatic. They overthrew a prior secular Prince by virtue of having a superior army. They became the new secular rulers. Now they had the army. No divinity needed. In a way, this was good for the Church because it saved them the embarrassment of having to admit that they got the divine bloodline wrong. The new Prince ruled not by divine right but simply because he had the bigger stick. Everyone could understand that. Successful Princes, as in the Tarasovs' case, also wielded a big carrot. Keep your citizens happy and prosperous and they have no appetite for regime change.

In this arrangement, the Church and the State need each other. The head of the Church needs to form an alliance with the Prince in power to bless his heavenly kingdom with the patina of Earthly patriotism. And since his citizens are mostly religious, it behooves the Prince to similarly fuse the concepts of God and State. When you obey, you are at once obeying both the Earthly Prince and the Heavenly God, avoiding the negative sanctions of both the army and the afterlife. Archbishop Osipov and Prince Tarasov both understood this. So they had a very visible alliance. They appeared together at state functions. Osipov blessed the actions of the State. Tarasov openly professed reverence and allegiance to the Church. They were co-shepherds. Whether either man actually believed in the other was, to Ilya Erynovich, an open question. He suspected that Tarasov's faith was possibly all for show, and that Osipov rubberstamped the State out of necessity rather than conviction. But it worked for the two of them.

Historians are unclear on how the present feudal forms of government evolved from the time of the Great Dying. It was thought that democracies were common in the early 21st century, but were devastated, along with everything else by the sudden loss of human populations. The need to start from scratch, with no infrastructure, no law enforcement, and scarce resources probably necessitated the banding together into small tribes at first, then these gradually scaled up. Since agriculture and commerce were already known forms of social organization, it would have been a more rapid rise than from the first hunter-gatherer societies, but historians are divided on how large these divisions of labor allowed tribes to become before they began to have armies and ambitious overlords. One view is that this organizational structure once reached the scale of a united kingdom. Support for this comes from the architectural ruins of what appears to be a large central government well to the south of here. But a contrary view points out that the many deposits of surviving tribal heraldry, that would typically define the boundaries of oligarchs' separate domains, united under a central overlord, were instead uniformly distributed across the landscape. They didn't seem to define territorial boundaries at all. Notable examples of these would include the tribe whose herald was the twin yellow arches, and the tribe with the green mermaid heraldry. One possibility is that each of these was once a uniform kingdom in separate timeframes.

Whatever the explanation of this enigma, such global uniformity was now gone. The present continent was organized around city-states, and in some cases larger regional empires, defined by contiguous geography. The borders between rulers' domains could often be a little vague, especially at the peripheries where competing boundaries are in dispute, though these rarely lead to armed conflict because the peripheral territories were so sparsely populated.

The University of Derazhne was relatively free from government interference because the Tarasovs relied on it for a steady stream of innovative technology. Whatever his true religious leanings were, the Prince of Solinovsk could generally be relied upon to protect the sciences from outside religious influences. The humanities enjoyed no such specific protections, but they also received no outside funding, so they were able to benefit from the political shelter afforded by the scientific rainmakers – and, by way of some creative accounting on the University's part, some of the outside funding as well. Yet another pragmatic alliance that worked out for all parties.

Ilya Erynovich's funding from Tarasov required that he submit reports of his progress periodically. The periods were not specified, so he and Professor Ekholm managed expectations by reporting only when there was good news. If there was a long string of good news, they would hold some of it back for dry patches when there wasn't anything to say. In the present case, there was both some good news and a little bit of overdue political management. They had taken a chance by not saying anything about the Mariankursk outbreak until they had a means to address it. Now they could cover their tracks by having the news and the solution arrive at the same time. Ilya Erynovich had already written up the report and was now just putting on the finishing touches of the obligatory dedication. He found this a very onerous task, but it was the expected custom to bow and scrape for your patron, if you expected the patronage to continue. He had saved a small collection of these dedications as boilerplate, which he could just mindlessly slap on after the report itself was written.

These were very perfunctory compared to what ancient scientists had to go through, he remembered. Professor Egorov, from the history department, had shown him the dedication that Galileo had to write on his *Dialogue Concerning the Two Chief World Systems*.

> *To the Most Serene Grand Duke of Tuscany*
> *Praying for Your Prosperity, I humbly kiss Your Hands;*
> *Your Most Serene Highness's Most Humble and most devoted*
> *Servant and Subject*
> *GALILEO GALILEI.*

In Galileo's case, he was trying to defend the Copernican theory that the Earth and all of the other planets revolve around the Sun, a position the Church of his time opposed (for Biblical reasons, they said). He disguised the treatise as a dialogue between a proponent of the Copernican view and a proponent of the Church supported Aristotelian view (that the Sun revolved around the Earth), with a third character, a layman, intervening. This way, one of the characters (really himself) could argue for the Copernican view, and Galileo could officially be cast as the neutral observer – agnostic about the situation. It didn't work. He was accused of heresy, forced to recant, and sentenced to prison for his effort. Against that backdrop, Ilya Erynovich supposed he had it pretty easy. Imagine what might happen if Sokolov had Tarasov's ear instead of Osipov. Ouch!

Traditionally, the Reverend Sokolov did not have Tarasov's ear. The alliance between the Tarisovs and the Orthodox Church was formed in the previous century, by the predecessors of both tribes, and had become part of the traditional fabric of society. Prince Tarasov had been careful to appear non-denominational, so as not to alienate the Protestants, but the religious animus between Orthodox and Protestant faiths always ran just below the surface in the modern era. This was never much of a concern for Tarasov until the Reverend Sokolov came to town and founded his church.

An ambitious man, with a built in theological rivalry with Osipov's church, and a nascent jealousy of Osipov's inside position with Tarasov, Sokolov made it his mission to encroach on this influence. He was a charismatic preacher after all. He knew he had a better skill at influencing parishioners than Osipov, so he could build a growing flock of followers, and more passionate ones at that, under the cover of religion. His followers were a cult of personality – his personality – whereas Osipov's were a cult of tradition. They were not inspired by the man so much as the institution and all of its rituals and trappings. As a political leader, Tarasov also needed to cultivate a larger than life personality. If Sokolov presented himself overtly as a politician, he would be in danger of sedition as a rival. But as long as he was "just a pastor", he had the political cover to build his base to a size and a noise level that Tarasov would eventually have to acknowledge. Then he would have some leverage.

Lately Sokolov had discovered a new political skill unique to his position as religious cult leader. He could say something provocative, inflammatory, even recklessly dangerous, then when the political heat came from outside sources he could simply deny that he said it. He only had to please one audience – his own followers. They were already primed to discount reality in favor of faith. So what's one more leap of faith? If the pastor said he didn't say this (or he hadn't done something he manifestly had done), who you gonna believe? Us or them? A politician without such a radical cult following has no counter to this. If your following is large enough that a rival politician can't afford to ignore them, you are immune. Reality itself no longer matters.

A derivative skill to this one, he discovered, was the spurious controversy gambit. You could attack the alleged reality of things you had said, or things you had done, or things that didn't turn out the way you hoped, or when you just needed to make something up out of whole cloth to support your position, by implying that there is some sort of controversy about whether the "real" things actually happened. Some say this. Some say that. We need to look at both sides of this controversy. This gambit impugns reality a little more subtly, casting doubt on it as opposed to outright denial. It also makes it easier for the less passionate of your followers, or perhaps even some prospective converts, to go along with your characterization of events.

Tarasov was a shrewd politician. He had seen this coming on from the early days of Sokolov's reign. For a while he simply tolerated it, figuring that Sokolov would eventually have to come to him. But as the firebrand's influence grew, Tarasov became more wary of his adversary, figuring at first that the proportion of the citizenry susceptible to Sokolov's crazy talk was small enough not to be a threat. But when the denial of reality strategies emerged, he realized he was up against something completely new. He could no longer appeal to the reasonableness of people and traditional ways of governing. Sokolov's following was still always likely to be a minority, but they were a disproportionately passionate minority. They were more likely to convert crazy talk into crazy action. Tarasov's survival as a Prince had always depended on knowing what was going on with his constituents in real time. He had a vast network of spies. So he knew Sokolov was fomenting revolution on the sly. This would not be the kind of revolution his family had initiated, one in which a more competent regime had a better idea for governing. This was a crazy man's revolution, born of pure ambition and a self-delusional God complex, supported by crazy people with no practical competencies and dangerously disconnected from reality. It would end badly for all concerned. But the city-state of Solinovsk was not a democracy. Tarasov could put a swift end to the threat with his armed forces, but he would have to get all of the leaders and all of the future leaders in the first round, to prevent a new movement springing up from martyrdom.

Professor Koskayin didn't have spies. But the academics at the University maintained their own network of passive intelligence gathering, and could swiftly share what they knew with each other – in private. Also a practical necessity in the modern age. From this network, he had learned that when news of his first visit to Mariankursk had reached Solinovsk, there were two troubling rumors coming from the government and religious sectors. Tarasov's regime was apparently concerned about news of an epidemic getting out and causing panic among the citizenry. It was thought that they were planning to keep a lid on it, and perhaps suppress any reports of the outbreak. Sokolov was reportedly discussing fanning such a panic and characterizing it as God's wrath visited upon the wicked. Ilya Erynovich could only hope that his report to Tarasov would spur his regime in the right direction – containment of the disease, as opposed to containment of the news. You don't customarily make policy recommendations in scientific reports to your patron. That is not your station. So he could not weigh in on what a responsible patron should or should not do with such news. And he certainly couldn't try to dissuade Tarasov from a course of action that he had learned about surreptitiously.

§

Earlier that morning, back in her apartment in Mariankursk, Katerinya Emlynovna was finishing her morning coffee in the rocking chair next to the fireplace. She was an early riser, a quintessential morning person. The weather was becoming brisk outside, so this looked like a good day for a fire. It was also a designated writing day, so a fire would help set the mood. She tried to partition her translation work into discrete days so that there would be at least one day a week left over in which she could fully concentrate on her developing novel. She did her best work in the morning, when her imagination was fresh and reset from the concerns of the previous day. Her productivity would gradually decrease as the day wore on, so it was important to start early. On a particularly good day she might write well into the evening, but that was rare. A good morning's worth of writing would be considered a victory. Her session typically began with this contemplative interlude over coffee, a pre-gaming ritual in which she reacquainted herself mentally with where she was in the overall plan of the story, which scene, which character, the local subplot objective.

She remembered Ilya's description of his proof planning process where he would try all manner of approaches and strategies, most of them unsuccessful, until one of them worked. Then he would figuratively 'erase' all of these messy steps that got him to the elegant solution. She had her own version of this – lots of notes about characters and subplots, and timing, and clues in one chapter to be redeemed in a later chapter. These were like the blueprint for a house. Her first pass at the actual writing would then be like the framing of the house described in the blueprint. But this plan was never stable. As she built out the studs, and the drywall, and the plumbing, she would uncover flaws in the design or opportunities for a better design. But she always kept the original design notes just in case. When the first pass at writing completed the framing of a full blueprint, she would then pass through the novel again, this time doing the finish carpentry, the fine detail, the level of final, polished prose that she wanted to show her readers. So when she was actually writing, either the rougher framing type or the finer finishing type, she was always writing in the context of an overall plan. She supposed this was why she never experienced writer's block. In fact, the whole notion of sitting down to write with an empty mind, and expecting prose to just come pouring out, made no sense to her at all. But in her method, there would be many written design artifacts left over at the end, documenting in great detail all of the intermediate steps she had gone through, including the many unsuccessful ones, and many partial drafts that she was not at all proud of. Unlike with mathematicians (at least according to Ilya), there would be great interest in these artifacts by her critics, if she ever became a successful author. She made a vow to herself to destroy these if she ever got that far.

As she finished her coffee, and her mental stage setting, she felt optimistic and ready to head to the desk for a good morning of writing. But she never got that far. There was a knock at the front door. That usually meant it was someone she didn't know (all of her friends came through the back). It turned out to be Ms. Zakharova from the guesthouse on Kalinin Street. This was a hybrid case — someone she did know but had not expected to come calling. She had met Lyudmila Nadyaevna when she accompanied Ilya to the guesthouse on that fateful, amnesia-filled day a few weeks ago. That, of course, was just a passing acquaintance at the time. But unbeknownst to Ilya, Katerinya had made a follow-up call on Zakharova later, similar to the one she made on the young doctor at the hospital, just to see what else she could find out about him. It was all very pleasant, and not particularly illuminating, but Katerinya had established herself as Ilya's trusted friend, and had given out her Tallinnskaya Street address.

Lyudmila Nadyaevna had come calling because she had found something that belonged to Professor Koskayin. When she was cleaning the room, she noticed that there was an unfamiliar book in the small bookcase that she maintained for her guests' passing reading pleasure. The book was certainly not one of hers. When she opened it, she found the "Ex Libris" plate on the inside cover identifying Professor Koskayin as the owner. He must have left it by accident. Katerinya thanked her for bringing the book, and assured her that she would get the book to Professor Koskayin. Then, of course, as you do in such situations, she invited her in for some unspecified hospitality. And, as you also often do in such situations, Lyudmila Nadyaevna politely declined. She didn't want to interrupt Katerinya's plans for the day. Just dropping off the book. So they exchanged pleasantries and that was the end of it. Ordinarily, Katerinya would have been thankful for the non-interruption of her writing day, but the sudden discovery of the book virtually ended it. She had seen the binding when Zakharova was first holding the book. It bore the now familiar 'Korihor' symbol that was on Ilya's ankle. This was no ordinary book – and what was it doing in Mariankursk? She opened it, flipping through the pages, when she discovered a makeshift paper bookmark on which was written 'Liberty, Equality, Fraternity'. Now she was doubly intrigued. Ilya had told her about his discovery of books from his collections back in Derazhne with this same binding symbol (as well as the maritime clock and the dresser drawer symbols) and their associations with obscure triplet messages as bookmarks. She, of course, had no idea what to make of this message, but its presence in one of his books here added a new wrinkle to the mystery. He had never mentioned this book, so this was a clue that needed to be brought to his attention.

Katerinya didn't know when Ilya would be coming to Mariankursk again, so the idea popped into her mind of taking the first train to Derazhne this morning to bring the book to him. All by itself, this seemed like a reasonable thing to do. But then the added benefits kept piling on. She would like to see him again. She hadn't been to Derazhne in a long time. She had never properly toured the

University, even though she had always wanted to go to school there. She knew about its famous libraries and museums, but had never actually seen many of them. Yes, the air was brisk, but it was a sunny day. A good day to get out and about. For some reason, the aborted writing day couldn't get a word in edgewise.

§

Katerinya knew the local train schedules in and out of Mariankursk practically by heart. It helped that they rarely changed, and the trains this close to the eastern terminus of the railway system in Derazhne and Solinovsk were usually on time. Certainly more reliable than the schedules further out west. If she hurried, she would have just enough time to catch the first inbound train to Derazhne. The weather would be a little cold, but clear and sunny throughout the day, so she would need to dress in layers. She put on her lighter weight sabovara, which would provide sufficient warmth when closed, but could also be opened if the sun were getting the upper hand. It all depended on the wind chill. It was typically minimal in Mariankursk, because of its predominantly rural, wooded landscape, but less predictable in the big urban center on the coast that she was bound for.

Clutching the mystery book close to her side, she exited her apartment in her customary way through the rear entrance, then turned back to lock the door. When she pivoted back toward the outside stairway, she caught the early winter scene of a bright sun rising just above the white birches in the woodlot. The dense thicket of leafless trees allowed individual rays of light to shoot through below. She paused for a moment to take this in. It was such a serene, welcoming, optimistic way to start a day. Full of promise, full of possibility. If only she had an east-facing window in her front room, she thought. It would be an even better writing stimulus than the fireplace. She closed her eyes for a moment and felt the warmth of the sun on her face, breathing in the crisp, cool air with its scent of the woods. Then she turned, descended the wooden stairs and set out down Tallinnskaya Street toward the train station.

Once on the train, she chose a west-facing seat. The view out the window was always better with the sun behind you, she thought. You got the full range of colors and shadows without having to squint. As welcoming as a sunrise is, it overstays its welcome on an hour's ride. Trains had played a prominent role in her adult life, starting with the long trip west to Karlsruhe when she started college. She left in the morning, not unlike today, but both facing and heading west then. She was leaving the east, and Mariankursk, behind, but also leaving her mythical Mecca of Derazhne, and all of her aspirations for it, behind as well. When she came back east at the end of her college career, she was coming back to Mariankursk, both with a little sadness and a little resignation of non-progress. She had never managed to make it all the way east to Derazhne in any substantial way. Now she was watching Mariankursk, for which she had a greater fondness now, receding from view as she pushed on in a new direction toward where she had always wanted to end up. It felt like a new beginning.

She had grown up a lot in the course of that single week that it took her to cross the continent by rail to Karlsruhe. She had never been very far away from Mariankursk her entire life before that, so it was her entire reference point for the rest of the world. Although she saw a variety of new landscapes from her train window, including mountains, and waterfalls, and forests, and deserts, she learned later at Karlsruhe that her long journey through the middle of the continent would have provided yet another variety of landscape 2000 years ago. The vast, flat middle was once mostly farms and prairies, the "breadbasket" of the region. After the Great Dying, and the purging of humans, it slowly reverted to climax forest, the state it had been in prior to the large-scale arrival of humans. At Karlsruhe she also learned that it was the vast system of railroads crisscrossing the continent that stitched the many city-states and principalities together, fostering a degree of cooperation among them.

And she learned that ours was one of the poorer, less developed continents compared to other parts of the world – particularly the United States of Africa. There, a single federal democracy united smaller state democracies across the entire continent into one large governmental structure. This concentration of wealth, and relative political stability had allowed them to make great investments in technology and infrastructure, rebuilding many of the forms of global commerce that were once common before the Great Dying. They were largely responsible for the resurrection and maintenance of the global Internet, for air travel, for satellite communications, and entertainment content. There are few airports on this continent, and they are owned and operated by the Africans. Consequently, you can take planes if you are leaving here or coming back to here, but once you are here, you take trains. Small-scale principalities do not have the resources for aerospace industries that serve most global travel. The continent-wide railway system is the best they could afford because the primary purpose, for each state, is intrastate transportation, so each has an incentive to invest in and maintain an internal railroad system up to the edges of their empire. As long as there is a common standard for track gauges, these internal systems can be connected at the peripheries to form intergovernmental networks. But seasoned rail travelers know that the reliability and service are least at these cross-border edges because their maintenance is no one's primary responsibility.

What Katerinya didn't learn about at Karlsruhe, because she was a humanities major, was the great gap in telecommunications technology between the richer and poorer countries of the world. The Internet was originally designed, before the Great Dying, to be decentralized, and stitched together from the bottom up. All it needed was some standard routing protocols – the analog of standard track gauges for railroads. The basic concept easily survived the global pandemic even though the original protocols probably didn't. And unlike railroads, the resources required to stand up an Internet hub are negligible. So it was slowly revived, as it was originally, by universities as the first hubs. This allowed universities to precede governments in communication and cooperation. The basic principle of multiple hubs routing around failure allowed the academic culture to survive and maintain continuity throughout the many local wars and revolutions that constantly disrupted the railroad networks. At first, the connections were slow because they depended on existing landline cables. But the investment in laying backbone cable was much smaller than that for laying track, so universities could often fund this themselves. With the emergence of the USA, with its greater resources and global reach, intercontinental cables were laid and eventually telecommunication satellites were launched.

As a result, universities essentially own the modern Internet. They are connected on a global scale where governments are not. They maintain this autonomy both because they are collectively smarter than governments, and because they typically don't require local government funding for the physical infrastructure. When local governments attempt to control the local Internet traffic of their citizenry, they are easily evaded by tunneling and encrypted VPNs sponsored by the academics. It's an arms race that governments always lose.

Cell phone service, on the other hand, is more like railroads. It requires significant investment to build and maintain a network of cell towers and switching stations, and broad territorial sovereignty to own the rights of way. So individual principalities own and operate these up to their own borders, where the handoffs occur, when they do, based on shared protocols. Consequently, cell phone service is mostly a local phenomenon. Like railroad service, it is most reliable in the urban centers and trails off toward the borders. In the city-state of Solinovsk, it is also a strategic asset of the Tarasov family. In exchange for reasonably priced service, citizens, often unknowingly, are providing the government with limitless eavesdropping and location tracking. Academics can do very little about this, other than to avoid communicating anything on a cell phone that you would not want to be broadcast on a loudspeaker for all to hear. There is satellite/cell service, provided by the Africans, for those who need reliable global service across borders, but it is very expensive, and still subject to local eavesdropping.

So if you want to communicate securely across government borders, you use computers connected to Internet landlines. If, on the other hand, you need your mobile device in the field, you must be careful what you say or text. Ilya Erynovich heard, from academic partners in Africa, that the wireless service there is so fast and reliable that you can actually run Internet applications on your cell phone. What a concept! What a country! Back here, never the twain shall meet. This is why Katerinya Emlynovna did not call or text ahead to let Ilya Erynovich know she was coming. Ilya had advised her to avoid cell phones whenever the subject is something that needs to be kept from prying eyes (or ears), or when it is better not to let the government know where she is going. All of these cautions applied to her current mission.

§

When the train pulled into Derazhne Station, Katerinya Emlynovna joined the throng of commuters heading to their workdays in various parts of Derazhne. The rest, a larger proportion of the passengers, would stay on until the final stop at Solinovsk Station. She crowded onto the local tram and took it two stops to University Station. The trip was a little too warm because the crush of standing passengers made it impossible for her to open her sabovara. But once there, off the tram and sabovara opened, she could breathe freely again. The sun was warm and there was no noticeable wind, so it looked like it was going to be an open sabovara day in general. She had been here in University Square a few times in her youth. She had always liked it here – such a contrast with Mariankursk. It was buzzing with activity, students coming and going, speaking many different languages, sitting in small cafes, discussing everything from physics to history to philosophy. Now that she was a professional polyglot, she could understand some of what was being discussed. Translating written content is much easier than understanding it when spoken quickly in native accents, so her recreational eavesdropping didn't yield much. But she could often make a best guess about which languages were being spoken.

The central part of the University of Derazhne was surrounded by an iconic perimeter wall of red brick and black wrought iron fencing. Much to the casual tourist's dismay, there was no canonical entrance through this border, no main gate that said 'Derazhne University' that you could stand in front of and have your picture taken to prove you had been here. There were many gates and archways through the brick, that one could use to get in or get out.

Katerinya strolled through one of the archways that connected the outside bustle of the Square to the inner sanctum of the University. It was such a contrast. Inside it was quiet with many towering trees and large expanses of green lawn crisscrossed by walkways leading to and from stately academic halls. She stopped for a moment to take it all in, to breathe it all in. Then she inquired of a passing student if he might know where she could find Professor Koskayin. Katerinya expected she would have to make a number of such inquiries before she got a hit, but her favorite professor turned out to be rather well known. "Oh, you want the biology department, Dahlström Hall, over there," the student replied, pointing across the Quad. She thanked him and followed the designated path. Inside Dahlström Hall, she surveyed the rooms on the first floor. They appeared to be mostly classrooms. She knew from her experience at Karlsruhe that this was a typical design for academic buildings – classrooms on the ground floor, offices on the upper stories – so she climbed the stairs to the second floor. These rooms did look more like offices, and they were numbered, but of course she didn't know what number she was looking for. There were no names on the doors. She tried the third floor next and found the same setup – numbers, no names.

As she strode down the third floor hall, occasionally glancing into open doorways, her looking behavior caught the attention of Professor Ekholm as he was leaving his office. "Can I help you find something, or perhaps someone?" he asked, correctly interpreting the scene before him. "Yes," Katerinya replied, "I'm looking for Professor Koskayin." "Ah, I believe he is teaching a class right now. His office is 308" he said pointing. "Is he expecting you?" She paused briefly before answering. He wasn't expecting her, of course, but she had no reference point for how much information she should be sharing. She didn't know anyone here, or what his work environment was like, but Ilya had always spoken highly of his academic colleagues. These were people he trusted, so she just laid it all out. "No, he's not expecting me. I'm a friend of his from Mariankursk, and just arrived on the train." This seemed to spark a glimmer of recognition from Professor Ekholm. He tilted his head slightly with a half smile. "You wouldn't perhaps be Katerinya Emlynovna, would you?" "Yes!" she replied, with a little more enthusiasm than she had intended, but now happy to be enfranchised. "Well, he has told me quite a bit about you. You've been helping him with the bacterial outbreak there, as I understand it." "Yes!" she said again, though sheepishly wondering just how much else Ilya might have told him about her. "I'm Professor Ekholm, one of Ilya Erynovich's colleagues. You could wait in his office, if you'd like," he offered. She thanked him, but then asked if he knew how long Professor Koskayin might be. He should be back sometime between 11:00 and 12:00 was his guess. Katerinya had factored the possibility of such a delay into her plan for the day, so she thanked him again, and said she would come back around that time. Then she was off for her tour.

The first thing she wanted to see was the University's famous library. She had seen pictures of it, so she had some sense of what she was looking for. She left Dahlström Hall and began taking random paths through the mosaic of green lawn patches. They were now more green-brown patches because they had gone dormant for the winter, but their soft, organic contrast with the pavement of streets outside the walls still spoke of quietude. It didn't take long before she encountered the library. It was even more massive than the pictures had led her to believe. She had heard that, among other things, the library had an original Zimmerman folio on display. She wanted to see this. She climbed the massive stone stairs to the main entrance, then entered through the massive doors into the foyer. The Derazhne Library was both a serious academic research institution and a bit of a tourist destination. Since she was not an enrolled student, with no identification, she would not have access to much of the library, so she was on the lookout for the tourist elements.

Her wide-eyed wonder at the vaulted ceilings of the inner architecture pegged her immediately as a tourist, so a very pleasant woman near the entrance in an official looking blazer asked "Just visiting?" "Yes," Katerinya replied. "I heard that you have an early Zimmerman folio in your collection. Is the public permitted to see it?" "We have the *oldest* Zimmerman folio in our collection," the woman replied both properly and proudly, "and yes you may see it, but it is displayed next door in the rare book library." She pointed to her right, then gave simple directions for finding the entrance from here. "But we do have one of the earliest copies of the Brandenburg Bible on display here; right in the next room!" she said pointing. "Would you like to see it?" "Yes!' Katerinya replied. With that she thanked the woman and turned to follow the direction of her pointing. "Wait!' the woman said. "I'm afraid you'll have to check that book you are carrying before you leave the foyer. We'll keep it for you here until you are ready to leave." Katerinya had forgotten all about Ilya's book. It wasn't something she would normally want to let out of her possession in an unfamiliar place, given its mysterious payload. But if you can't trust library matrons with books, whom can you trust, she thought. So she willingly surrendered the book and proceeded to the next chamber.

The Bible was displayed in a temperature and humidity controlled glass case in the center of the room. Katerinya moved up to the glass and surveyed the rare artifact. It was laid open so that the first page right was the contents page:

The Names and the Order of all the Books of the Old and New Testament

The Books of the Old Testament

Genesis	Isaiah
Exodus	Jeremiah
Leviticus	Nephi
Numbers	Lamentations
Deuteronomy	Ezekiel
Joshua	Jacob
Judges	Daniel
Ruth	The Twelve
Samuel	Enos
Kings	Jarom
Chronicles	Mosiah
Nehemiah	1st Alma
Esther	Helaman
Job	Matthew
Psalms	Mark

Proverbs   Luke
Ecclesiastes   Clive's Epistles to the English
1st Songs of Songs

The Books of the New Testament

Gospel according to St. David   St. Parley's Epistles:
Gospel according to St. Brigham   to the Lamanites
Gospel according to St. Martin   to the Ohioans
Gospel according to St. Oliver   to the Missourians
Acts of the Apostles   to the Canadians
Nephi   to the English
Mormon   to the Illini
                                           to the Californians
                                           to the Chileans
                                           to the Pennsylvanians

Katerinya scanned the table of contents, but she didn't recall most of the books of the Bible because she had never read much of the actual Bible. The content was always presented in Sunday school as children's stories, so she knew many of the character's names: Adam, Eve, Moses, Daniel in the lion's den, Jonah and the whale, but she didn't know the names of the books they were from – with the exception of Genesis, of course. Everybody knew about Genesis.

She looked around the chamber, which was quite grand, but it housed no other manuscripts. So she decided to head next door for the Zimmerman folio – but first, of course, she retrieved Ilya's book. The directions were quite simple. Exit the library by way of the massive stone steps, turn right, go up a small set of pink granite steps to the grass covered rooftop of an underground library, then right again to the entrance of the rare book library. She liked Zimmerman, but she knew that Ilya *loved* Zimmerman. Ilya had this thing about the veneration of classic literature being relative to a particular culture rather than denoting inherent genius. But his one exemplar of inherent genius was Zimmerman. After surrendering Ilya's book again to another dutiful matron, she found the folio enclosed in the now familiar climate controlled glass case, laid open to the approximate center so the poetry could be read. She read silently to herself. Yes, she knew this one. The identification plaque in the front of the case read 'Zimmerman: The Bard of Hibbing'.

She moved on to another temperature controlled display case. This contained a printed document that began:

Lorem ipsum dolor sit amet, consectetur adipiscing elit, sed do eiusmod tempor incididunt ut labore et dolore magna aliqua. Ut enim ad minim veniam, quis nostrud exercitation ullamco laboris nisi ut aliquip ex ea commodo consequat. Duis aute irure dolor in reprehenderit in voluptate velit esse cillum dolore eu fugiat nulla pariatur. Excepteur sint occaecat cupidatat non proident, sunt in culpa qui officia deserunt mollit anim id est laborum.

Ah, she knew this one – as a professional translator – the famous Untranslatable Language from antiquity. She had first learned about it back in Karlsruhe. There were many printings of this document with slight variation all dated to the late 20th – early 21st century. The language appeared to be a dialect of Latin, but only a few scattered words could be recognized. They suggest the document had something to do with the endurance of pain. But the vast majority of the text remains untranslatable, even to this day. This was not like the occasional single copies of untranslatable books found, which could be just "languages" made up by a single author. No, this one had actively circulated through the population. Given the ubiquity of copies found in disparate locations, and the many variations of the text, this was clearly a dialect spoken by many people. All the more confounding that none of these documents can be translated. Still!

She checked the time and saw that she still had at least an hour left before Ilya's return, so she retrieved his book once again and set out looking for the art museums. Once outside, she was surprised to see that the once bright sun was now partially occluded by a thin overcast. The forecast had been for sun all day, but this kind of variability was always a possibility in a coastal city influenced by maritime weather patterns. So she closed and fastened her sabovara. At least there was still no wind. The University's art museums were harder to find because she had no prior visual reference for the buildings. After querying a few passing students, she learned that they were outside of the central, walled part of the campus to the east. The museums consisted of several adjacent buildings joined by enclosed passageways, so once inside she could visit them all without needing to go outside again. Convenient in winter, she thought. And since these weren't libraries, there was no need to surrender Ilya's book again.

After touring two of the painting and drawing collections, she moved into the sculpture gallery. One ensemble titled "The Trinity Statues" caught her eye. It consisted of three statues, two cast in bronze and one carved from white Caen stone. The two bronze works both depicted single men, one older and one younger, in seated positions, and the stone work was of a mysteriously hooded, vaguely female-looking character appearing to lift, or perhaps to rise up from, an apparently dead male character that resembled an ancient warrior. There were no cast or carved inscriptions on the statues themselves, which was not uncommon for ancient artwork that had been moved from its original setting before being recovered. From the description plate mounted to the side of the display she learned that these statues were recovered from the ancient remains of the University itself. Radiocarbon dating from organic residues painstakingly extracted from internal parts of the works placed them all in the early 20th century. The popular name 'Trinity Statues' derived from some historians' speculation that these three works – being all discovered together in a single location – depicted respectively the Father, the Son, and the Holy Ghost, perhaps hinting at a then religious orientation of the University. There was no real consensus on the matter, but the designation had stuck in popular imagination.

§

Back inside the central campus, Professor Koskayin's lecture had just concluded and students were making their way out of the hall. When Yulia Katyaevna exited, she waited outside for him to emerge. She was applying for an undergraduate grant program that he had earlier agreed to recommend her for. She already had his recommendation letter, her own application essay, her transcripts, and assorted other paperwork for the application, but missed the fact that she needed his signature on the application form itself. When he encountered her outside and learned of the situation, he suggested she walk back with him to his office and he could sign it there.

When they reached 308 Dahlström, Professor Ekholm saw him from down the hall and motioned for him to come into his own office. "It will just take a minute," he said. So Ilya Erynovich invited Yulia Katyaevna to go into 308, take a seat, and he would be right back (he thought?). Thinking nothing of it, she went into his office and took a seat in the overstuffed red leather chair with the small end table adjacent to it.

While she was waiting, she once again surveyed the dark walnut themed expanse of his office, as she had done on the first visit a few weeks ago. It was a warm, comforting view, full of scholarship and hinting at discovery. This time her gaze fell upon a large leather-bound volume on the small table adjacent to her chair. This must be Professor Koskayin's reading chair, she thought, and he must have been reading this. It was titled "Apocrypha and Pseudepigrapha." Since the book was closed, there was no possibility of her disturbing his prior place in the book, so she took the opportunity to open it. On the inside of the cover was a printed plate reading "Ex Libris Diederick Brandt". On the facing page was the table of contents:

The Books of the Apocrypha

Esdras	Titus
Tobit	Galatians
Judith	Ephesians
Ecclesiasticus	Philippians
Maccabees	Colossians
Wisdom	Thessalonians
Sirach	Timothy
Baruch	Jude
Song of the Children	Philemon
Story of Suzanna	Hebrews
Prayer of Manasses	James
2nd Songs of Songs	Peter
Romans	2nd Alma
Corinthians	

The Books of the Pseudepigrapha

Apocalypse of Abraham	Eldad and Modad
Apocalypse of Moses	History of Joseph the Carpenter
Letter of Ariteas	Odes of Solomon
Martyrdom and Ascension of Isaiah	Prayer of Joseph
Joseph and Aseneth	Prayer of Jacob

Life of Adam and Eve	Vision of Ezra
Lives of the Prophets	John
Ladder of Jacob	1st John
Jannes and Jambres	2nd John
History of the Captivity in Babylon	3rd John
History of the Rechabites	Revelation

Yulia Katyaevna scanned the contents. She didn't recognize any of the book titles, with the exception of 2nd Songs of Songs in the Apocrypha section. She recalled that there was a 1st Songs of Songs in the Bible. She had never read it, nor could she recall pastor Sokolov ever mentioning it in a church service. Why were there two? And why was only one of them in the Bible? Her curiosity now piqued, she turned to 2nd Songs of Songs, opened to a random place, and began reading silently:

And Jesus was a sailor when he walked upon the water
And he spent a long time watching from his lonely wooden tower
And when he knew for certain only drowning men could see him
He said all men will be sailors then until the sea shall free them
But he himself was broken, long before the sky would open
Forsaken, almost human, he sank beneath your wisdom like a stone

And you want to travel with him, and you want to travel blind
And then you think maybe you'll trust him
For he's touched your perfect body with his mind

As she was contemplating what all of this might mean — including the business about this 'Jesus' fellow whom she remembered from the Old Testament – her thoughts were interrupted by Professor Koskayin coming back into the room. She had only come for a signature, but she momentarily forgot about that, her attention snatched away by what she had just encountered. She was about to ask about the two Songs of Songs, but then broadened her puzzlement to include the whole volume. "I hope you don't mind my asking, but what *is* this book?' she inquired, still holding the volume. Ilya Erynovich smiled.

"It's a collection of the apocryphal books of the Bible – or more to the point, of the religious books *not* in the Bible. Professor Brandt from the Divinity School loaned it to me. It seems that in the early years of the church, there had always been some disagreement about which of many manuscripts passed down through the ages, alleging to be Scriptures, were actually Scriptures – which ones were *divinely* inspired and which were only *humanly* inspired. So various councils were convened over the centuries to decide this. For a long time, there was a tradition of publishing the books that did not make it into the official canon, alongside the ones that did. So many editions of the Bible included three sections: an Old Testament, a New Testament, and an Apocrypha. The last section listed the 'honorable mentions" as it were – inspirational but not quite holy. But that tradition died out. Nowadays, you never hear mention of these shadow texts. But scholars still have them.

I knew about the existence of the Apocrypha in general, though I had never read any of its books – until now. I didn't know, until Professor Brandt told me, that religious scholars also maintain a second collection of shadow texts: the Pseudepigrapha. Originally, these were texts deemed to be falsely attributed – not written by the author claimed in the title. Forgeries, if you will. Over time, the term came to be applied to any text promoted as divine, but clearly not divine by the standards of the time. There may have been no disputation of authorship, but the work somehow went against what was considered holy doctrine. These were never published in any editions of the Bible. But they were collected by scholars. Professor Brandt's book includes them both."

This was news to Yulia Katyaevna. Not only had she not heard of these kinds of books, she was under the impression that there were no such books. The picture she got from pastor Sokolov, and the Sunday school teachers, was of a single collection of books forming a singular Bible, throughout the ages. They were all divinely inspired as soon as they left the original authors' pens. The idea of there being multiple sets of books, with varying degrees of holiness, going in and out of an official canon – and the decisions being made by councils of men – was a little unsettling. "But where did these other books come from?" she asked. "How did they ever get considered in the first place? Are people still writing them today?"

Ilya Erynovich smiled again. "That's three questions" he replied. "I'll answer them in reverse order. I'm sure people are still writing books today that they would *like* to get into the canon, but that's not going to happen. That's because the ones that got considered (and made it into Brandt's book) were written in the same time periods as the one's that made it into the Bible. And for the councils that made the decisions, these were time periods in the deep past from their points of view. Nobody knew where these books came from, other than having been passed down through the ages to them.

So you might think that all three canons are now closed: the Bible, the Apocrypha and the Pseudepigrapha, because no new works will be old enough. But there's another possibility you may not have heard about. Less than 60 years ago, a whole new set of ancient texts was discovered, remarkably preserved in a series of caves in Tacna, Peru. These documents were at least a thousand years older than any previously surviving biblical documents then known. They had been preserved by a Christian sect known as the Jesuits who had lived and worked in the area prior to the Great Dying. These became known popularly as the 'Peruvian Texts.' At first, religious scholars were elated because many of the books of the current Bible were among these texts, and were fairly close in actual textual elements to later versions. But of the 900 or so texts discovered in the Tacna caves, only a little over 200 are Biblical – less than 25%. Another 50% or so are in either the Apocrypha or the Pseudepigrapha. So now we have a whole new set of potentially holy texts, written in antiquity, considered spiritual by the Jesuits, but not on anyone's current list. Also, half of these texts – the ones in Brandt's book but not the Bible – represent a disagreement about the degree of holiness between the Jesuits and modern-day clerics."

Yulia Katyaevna sifted this back and forth in her mind, then asked "Is Jossmit ever mentioned in any of the Jesuit texts?" "No," he replied, "not that I'm aware of."

§

Just at that moment, Katerinya appeared in the open doorway, knocking obligatorily on the already opened door. She hadn't seen Yulia Katyaevna at first, but then quickly realized that Ilya was not alone. "Oh, I'm so sorry," she said. "I didn't know you had company!" At that point, everyone was surprised, as they all eyed each other. Katerinya recovered first. "I'll just come back later." Then Yulia Katyaevna recovered and remembered she had only come for a signature. She could also tell from Professor Koskayin's expression that this was someone he knew and was happy to see. "No, stay. I was just here to get a signature." She laid the book down and held out the application papers for Professor Koskayin. Ilya Erynovich was the last to recover, but only partially. He was still very much surprised by Katerinya's unexplained presence. But he could see that the proper ending had already been negotiated between the two women, so he fulfilled his role by signing the papers, and let the exiting and entering take care of itself without the need for

introductions. When Katerinya entered, she closed the door behind
her.

They were both of two minds at this point — happy to see
each other and wanting to relax and exchange pleasantries, but
needing to clear up the overhanging mystery of the visit first. Ilya
started. "Ove Alfhildovich told me you were in town looking for me,
but he didn't say why." "That's because I didn't tell him," she
explained. She didn't know anyone here or how much they knew
about what. Professor Ekholm seemed nice enough, but he seemed
only to know of her by way of her role in the bacterial outbreak. (She
was hoping maybe that was all he knew about her relationship with
Ilya, but she didn't say this). The reason for her visit, she said, was
something else entirely. Then she plunked down the book, and
related the whole story of how Zakharova had found it and brought
it to her this morning. She showed him the sign on the binding, his
"Ex Libris" plate on the inside, and the bookmark with the new
triplet message. This seemed like one of those subjects that they had
agreed should be kept below the radar, so she had thought it
important to bring it to him in person. She even left her cell phone at
home so she couldn't be tracked. Was this the right call?

Ilya was overwhelmed by the sudden turn of events. Yes, he
assured her, this was the right call, at least in terms of security. In
terms of convenience, he was sorry she had to make a sudden train
trip all this way just to get it to him — not that he wasn't very happy
to see her. She demurred, confessing that the prospect of seeing him
again had also factored into her decision a little — maybe a lot. But
she also got to tour the libraries and museums, she told him, so there
was no inconvenience at all. He examined the book. Yes this was his,
but he did not remember taking it with him to Mariankursk. He
wondered how it ended up at Zakharova's. "And how did she know
how to get it to you?" he asked. At this point she had to confess that
she had visited Zakharova earlier, like she had done with the doctor,
just to see what she could find out about Ilya. "I hope you don't

mind," she said sheepishly, having had to confess to low-level espionage for a second time now. He did not mind at all, he assured her. If it had been anyone else, he wouldn't be so sanguine, but she was the one person in the world he trusted completely at this point. She might even have found out something useful about himself that he didn't know. They once played this game as a team, he reminded her. "Did you learn anything new about me?" he inquired with a smile. "No" she said, smiling herself. "She was just as you described her. Not into anyone else's business and not one to gossip." "How is your memory, by the way?" she asked. "Is it improving?" He hadn't thought that much about it, but on reflection he couldn't discern any significant improvement. He could remember things a little further back now, but not all the way to anything before Derazhne.

Then they got down to the business at hand. He showed her the inscription on the back of his maritime clock about molecules, then related his theory that the molecules message was probably the one intended specifically for him, since it occurred twice in hard to find locations and was, well, uniquely scientific. The bookmark triplets all seemed random in their subject matter. As he reflected on the situation, it occurred to him that this new message might have been something his prior self had deposited *recently*. He didn't recall being in Mariankursk for a long time prior to the first *Y. pestis* visit. And he could not remember ever staying at, or even knowing about, Zakharova's guesthouse before that. In fact, the waitress at the Mariankursk Station café told him she recommended this place on his first visit! So it could be as recently as a few weeks ago that his prior self was fully in charge of his memory faculties and had placed the message there knowing that he would be back and that he would likely need memory help at that point. This was fresh! So this message must have some recent significance.

He quickly slid his chair over to his computer table and typed the query string 'liberty equality fraternity' into an Internet search window. Katerinya hurried over to look. This was exciting. What came up was the beginning of a revelation. The triplet was a well-known political slogan from pre-pandemic France. As they opened page after page of the search results, some had illustrations, and often enough these pictures showed the graphic symbol of the French fleur-de-lis. This was an iconic piece of French heraldry, apparently, dating from the original medieval times right up to the Great Dying. Its French translation was roughly 'lily'. But most important of all, it matched the symbol on his ankle, the book bindings, the drawer handle and the maritime clock. The mysterious symbol was a fleur-de-lis!

Next, Ilya typed 'fleur-de-lis' into a search window. What came up finally tied all of the triplet messages together. In early Christianity apparently, the symbol had been associated with the Virgin Mary representing the twin virtues of purity and chastity (two out of three for one of the triplets). It was also associated with the Holy Trinity (father, son, and ghost), and sometimes with faith, wisdom, and chivalry. This was astounding, Katerinya thought. It ties everything together! Then she paused. "Into what?" she asked Ilya. He was a little further along in the reasoning, so he explained. The religious references were a red herring, he thought. They just served to point to the fleur-de-lis as the symbol. Any one of them would have been sufficient on its own. So all of the clues net down to two: the symbol is a fleur-de-lis and it denotes something that is written in molecules. Then he smiled wryly. "That's good news and bad news. The good news is that we just need to find the one fleur-de-lis somewhere out there that points us to the molecules. The bad news is that apparently there are lots of fleur-de-lis out there, all over the world, and the vast majority of them were not placed there by my prior self. That could be a lot of dead ends." Again he cursed his prior self for being too clever by half. He turned the problem over in his mind. Is the French reference significant? French molecules? What would that be? He was thinking this out loud and Katerinya was trying to follow along, but was getting the sense that Ilya had reached the end of the symbolic road for now. But he was just getting started.

Memory works by association. When you remember an event, its neuronal synapses fire and excite other memories linked to it. The recentness of the Mariankursk book event, and the multiply linked reference points of the other books and messages summed up across these firing connections to resurrect his motivation for placing the book in Mariankursk. The point of the various triplets was not to enlighten but to obfuscate! He could now distinctly remember taking the book with him to Mariankursk and placing it Zakharova's local collection to potentially throw off a perceived stalker that he thought was following him. He told Katerinya this. But before he could get to his next sentence, the synapses kept firing yielding a rich mixture of memories and realizations. He paused, then resumed the disclosure of his epiphany. "Look at the books, and the publisher!" he said. "Well, we have only two of them here, but they are all from the same publisher." The publisher was *New Morning Press*, a purveyor of poorly written religious titles in the "Inspirational" genre. He had bought copies of the whole series for two reasons. They were clearly not his kind of books, and the series had the same fleur-de-lis graphic on the spine. He never intended to read them, so he thought it would be clear to himself that they were just props. His pursuers wouldn't know this, so he put his own "Ex Libris" plates in each to clearly connect them to him. But they had the right symbol. So anyone looking for the symbol would likely notice them. He placed these, when need be, in locations where his adversaries might be snooping around. He had put one in his office, and kept the rest in his house. He drew from this home collection for the ruse in Mariankursk.

Both the religious and the French references in the bookmarks were red herrings, designed to mislead his stalkers. He modeled the wild goose chase on the circular reference structure one often finds in historical manuscript scholarship. The symbol referred to the French and to religion. Sometimes the French use was a religious use. So the French connection referred to the religious connection and vice versa. All of the triplets referred to either French secular uses or religious uses, or in some cases, French religious uses. The whole collection of clues referred maddeningly back and forth to each other, keeping the prospective investigator going around in circles, far removed from any notion of molecules.

The molecules message was clearly for him, and possibly independent of any inherent meaning of the fleur-de-lis. He probably chose this because it was already on the clock and the drawer handles. He still had no memory of carving those messages, so these events had to have occurred much earlier. The triplet ruse was more recent, suggesting that he had loaded irrelevant meaning onto the fleur-de-lis symbol for the public deception. So there was probably no need to find more fleur-de-lis symbols; they needed to find the molecules. Katerinya was following all of this, and now had to agree. She remembered, just today, seeing the fleur-de-lis in ancient prints and tapestries, and in the wrought iron gates of the University. It was everywhere once you started looking for it. She loved watching his mind work out loud.

But then she remembered Korihor. He hadn't accounted for that yet, so she asked. Ilya had practically forgotten about this – not the attacker, but the word itself. Did it fit in in any way? Then he remembered that she was not fully up to speed on the subject. He hadn't spoken with her since he learned about the significance from Brandt. So he related the story about how his heretical skepticism had gotten him turned into an immortal. She found that amusing too. But was the fleur-de-lis connected somehow, she wondered. He didn't know, other than what they both knew about the attacker's foreknowledge of the fleur-de-lis on his ankle. It must mean something to them, he mused, though he was pretty sure their interpretation had nothing to do with molecules. He still couldn't recall ever hearing about Korihor prior to the attack, so he couldn't have been targeting his ruse at them specifically. It was just targeted at stalkers in general – or in the Mariankursk case, the one that he suspected was out and about on that particular trip. He recalled thinking then that the stalker was most likely one of Prince Tarasov's spies. Then it occurred to him that these were disjoint cases. Tarasov's men already knew who he was, and presumably knew nothing about the fleur-de-lis on his ankle, and the Korihorians knew about the tattoo, but presumably not much about him (the real him, not the mythical him).

Now they both were a little mentally exhausted. Katerinya moved over to the overstuffed red leather chair and slumped down for a bit of recovery. She surveyed Ilya's office, as Yulia Katyaevna had once done, taking in the dark walnut and books. It was about how she had pictured it, minus the walnut. This was not a familiar Karlsruhe academic decor, but she had seen plenty of it today on her tour, so she had to agree with Yulia Katyaevna, even though she didn't know her – very U of D. "Well, what now?" asked Ilya. "You've fulfilled your mission admirably! Have you done enough touring for the day, or do you still have more to see?" At this point, she said, she was done touring, but she was a little hungry. "How about we go out for lunch, then?" he replied. "Yes! Lunch!" she replied. That hit the spot, both gastronomically and because it would involve a different sort of touring of Derazhne/Solinovsk.

Before he got up, it occurred to Ilya that he needed to take her into the fold of secure academic communication. It wasn't perfect yet, but it was far more secure than public cell phone use. He went to a locked storage cabinet and retrieved a new African cell phone from a stash he had received directly from them by clandestine means. This was not the standard model they exported to the City-State, which the government required to have a fixed facility for location tracking via cell towers. These were African-specification models on which location tracking could be turned off – the kind of thing you were permitted to do in Africa. Since this was strictly illegal here, he and his colleagues had engineered a local hack that would make tracking appear to be always enabled, but when in no-track mode, it would sporadically issue location errors that made tracking appear to be failing randomly. The unreliability of the local cell networks made this all seem very believable to the authorities. This would at least allow Katerinya to move about with a cell phone without being tracked. They were still working on an on-board app for encrypting voice and text traffic, so that conversations could be exchanged securely, but they were not quite there yet.

He showed her how to turn tracking on and off using settings that were labeled for a completely different function. That was to keep the authorities from discovering the illicit function. It was a good idea, he told her, to leave tracking on when she was at home so that it would appear to the authorities that tracking was working most of the time – unless, of course, you don't want them to know you are home. He told her about the progress on the antibiotic, and that he expected to make another trip to Mariankursk soon to administer it – as soon as they could manufacture it at scale and determine the proper dosing. Maybe a couple more days. He asked that when she got back home, that she turn off tracking and pay a visit to the doctor at the hospital. "Explain everything to him that I am telling you now, and advise him not to try to reach me remotely. The hospital's Internet system is not as secure as ours, and I think there may be a leak at his end. That's why Tarasov's agents always seem to hear about the developments in real time. The doctor certainly should not use his own phone. When I'm ready for the visit, I'll text you something in a code we agree on, on the morning that I take the train to Mariankursk. Then you can visit him again and relay that I'm coming. Now, what can we use as our text code?" Katerinya was enjoying this immensely. She felt like a secret agent, a bona fide member of the resistance, sent out into the field on a clandestine mission. "How about you text: 'The loser now will be later to win', and I'll reply 'Oh, the times must be changin' she offered. She knew he'd like that. He did.

§

On their way out the door of Dahlström Hall, Ilya asked if Katerinya had any dining preferences. She thought it would be just fine if they stopped in one of the cafes in the Square. Ilya offered to make it a grander affair. "Let's go someplace special in Solinovsk. I know lots of good restaurants there." This, she could agree to. "What kind of cuisine would you like?" he asked. "French? Italian maybe?" "African!" she replied. "African it is, then!"

They caught the tram at University Station for the trip over the river into Solinovsk. This time it was not so packed because it was mid-day, so they could easily find seats, and she could open her sabovara. The sun had reemerged, so she could enjoy the view outside, especially when the tram crossed the river. Ilya noticed that the old billboard before the bridge had changed. It now sported a new, freshly painted message: "A man without Jossmit is like a bird without wings". He preferred the phrase he had seen scrawled on one of the public posting boards in Derazhne: "A man without Jossmit is like a fish without a bicycle." On the Solinovsk side, they took five more stops to the seaport district. Ilya motioned for them to get off there. The sun was now overhead, so the water in the bay was sparkling, and a slight onshore breeze made the air cool. They walked a few blocks to Ubodu's, one of Ilya's favorites. It was now just after the lunchtime rush, so tables were beginning to open up. The maître d' sized them up, then escorted them to a table in the front window. "He likes the look of us," Ilya whispered. "Thinks we're a good advertisement." Katerinya didn't know what that meant, but it sounded like a good thing.

Ilya was right, it would turn out. They made an attractive couple. People passing by outside would pause briefly to watch them (discreetly of course). This was good for business because the scene subliminally suggested a place you wanted to be, a dining experience you wanted to be having. It wasn't just the couple's physical attractiveness that drew the attention, but the way they interacted with each other. People wanted to be them.

Katerinya was not accustomed to this kind of formal dining. White pressed linen tablecloths, pressed, dusty rose linen napkins arranged in fan shapes, assorted sterling silver cutlery, glass stemware for the water. The waiter arrived promptly, smiled, and presented each of them with a large, bound menu while bowing slightly during the delivery. "Will you be having anything to drink to start?" he asked. Ilya immediately asked, "Could we see the wine list?" "Of course," replied the waiter who then quickly, but elegantly retreated to fetch it. Ilya looked across at Katerinya and said, "I probably should have checked with you first. Is wine OK?" Wine was fine she assured him! She didn't know much about it, but she knew Ilya did, so she was happy going along for the ride. When the wine list arrived, Ilya began scanning it. The waiter hovered, expecting him to order something for starters. When Ilya became aware that he was waiting, he explained that they would need some time to read the menu first, so that they could pair the proper wine with what they would be eating. "Oh, of course," he said, doing his elegant retreat thing again.

Ilya explained to Katerinya that the wine list was very good, but like most lists, very few of the selections were served by the glass. If they could agree on entrees that were both white friendly or both red friendly, they could order by the bottle and have their pick of the entire list. "But that's just a suggestion," he cautioned. "Choose what you would most like first, and then we'll negotiate." This protocol was totally new to her, but she was enjoying it. So she took her best shot, and offered up something that she recognized by name, but whose description sounded marvelously exotic. "Good choice," said Ilya. "That calls for a medium bodied red. I was thinking along similar lines with this." He showed her his choice on the menu. She didn't know what that was, but it apparently allowed them to agree on the wine on the first go round, so she nodded her approval.

"Good, we have a mandate!" said Ilya. He went back to the wine list, and picked out an African Pinotage.

Then he let her in on an upcoming experiment. "There is a longstanding custom that men order the wine and women go along. Probably because the man usually pays. Waiters, for obvious reasons, always cater to the payer/tipper." He handed her the wine list and pointed out the Pinotage he had chosen. "When the waiter returns, you'll order the bottle by name and I'll just sit here. There is a tasting ritual that he goes through when he returns with the bottle that should go to the person who orders, because he's essentially seeking the customer's approval. So he should perform it for you. It goes like this. First he will display the bottle in front of you to show you the label for you to verify the selection. Then he'll stand behind you to one side, cut the lead foil off the top of the bottle, pull the cork with his corkscrew, then pour a small amount in your glass, holding the bottle from the bottom. Then he'll wait for your judgment. The origin of this ritual is to detect bad wine, wine that has somehow been corked or turned to vinegar. No one expects you to refuse good wine, but this is theoretically your prerogative. Now, what you do is to grasp the stemware by the bowl (since this is a red), swirl the wine around to get some of it up on the insides of the glass, then place the bowl over your nose for a brief sniff, then take a small taste. You don't really have to say anything. To really sell it you should pause briefly after the taste, as if you are considering the aftertaste (it's called the finish), then smile politely and nod your head. You'll look like a pro."

She was so up for this. When the waiter returned, he asked, "Have you decided on the wine?" "Yes we have," Katerinya said, very confidently and holding the bound wine list open in front of her. "We'll have a bottle of the Dry Creek Pinotage." "Fine selection," said the waiter, who then collected the wine list and then retreated for the bottle. He returned with the obligatory white linen cloth draped over his pouring arm, a pair of red wine glasses, and the bottle. He placed the two glasses to the right of each diner (didn't know she was a lefty), then instinctively showed the label to Ilya. Ilya looked at him briefly, then said, "She ordered the wine," pointing across the table. The waiter was mortified. "Yes, of course!" he said, now clearly off his game. He moved around to Katerinya's side and began the ritual again with her. She felt suddenly empowered. She played her role flawlessly, taking care to grasp the glass by the bowl, not the stem. She even ad-libbed a bit by pausing after the sniff, as if to consider it, then holding the wine on her tongue briefly during the taste before swallowing. She was inclined to ad-lib some more by commenting on the wine before accepting it, but she didn't know any of the proper phrases to use, and guessed, correctly, that she would have blown her cover. In all, it was grand performance. She made a mental note to ask Ilya for some appropriate phrases she could use the next time they did this. It was such a hoot.

By the time the entrees arrived, Katerinya had noticed that, like in University Square, there were several ambient conversations in progress in foreign languages. It was a very international crowd of diners, not the kind of thing that happens very often in Mariankursk. She tried again to decipher at least what languages were being spoken, but was making no progress. She mentioned her earlier experience in University Square to Ilya, and how she could at least pick out some of the languages there. But she was having no luck here. Ilya listened for a moment, then said, "The couple on my right is speaking Portuguese. She says she didn't recognize the spice in the sauce, and he said he thought it was turmeric. On my left, they are speaking Swahili. They are giving the chef kudos for producing authentic African cuisine." Katerinya was astounded. "How do you know so many languages!?" she asked. He didn't realize that he did. It just came out. He listened intently for a moment to pick up more distant conversations, and realized that he understood these as well. He confessed that this was all news to him. But he must have learned them somewhere in his missing past. He concentrated for a moment, trying to recall where he learned any of the languages. This touched off another furious round of synapse firings that pushed his memory into pre-Derazhne territory. Suddenly he could recall his first coming to the University. Before that he had been in Ariona! The memories were all very general, though, eliciting vague scenes and events but not really a timeline.

Katerinya was vicariously sharing in his epiphany, even though she couldn't imagine what these partial memories must be like. It was certainly a positive thing. It briefly occurred to her that he might now have some clues about his age, but now this no longer seemed to matter much to her. It had previously been a curiosity, a way to characterize them as a couple in the eyes of others. But she realized she no longer cared what others thought. Besides, she had been noticing passersby taking an interest in them through the window. She now understood Ilya's earlier comment about the maître d' thinking they would be a good advertisement for the restaurant. People seemed attracted to them as a couple, as if they were characters in a story they wanted to know more about.

When they had finished lunch, and were waiting for the check, Katerinya wondered out loud "Have you ever been to Africa? I mean, to understand Swahili like that, you must have been exposed to it at some point." He couldn't recall ever being there, but he agreed with her point about oral translation. He must have spent some time there in the past. "I talk to African colleagues all the time on the Internet, but not in Swahili. It's almost like being there. I'm familiar with their culture."

"I've always wanted to go there," Katerinya said, with a faraway look. "Africans here are so admired by everyone. They represent culture, and education, and wealth, and consumer products, and media content, and high technologies like passenger jets, and satellites, and cell phones. And democracy!"

"Yes," said Ilya, "but the key characteristic you mention is wealth, I think." That's why they can still be looked up to even by poor, working-class conservatives here, who would otherwise likely harbor a racial animus toward them. There are no poor, uneducated Africans here. They can't be conveniently blamed for one's own unhappy circumstances. They provide the products that make life bearable."

"Do you ever wonder how they got to be that way, Ilya? I mean, why did they succeed in getting to the top of the world order, when so many other cultures did not?"

"Ah, that's one of those big historical questions with no clear answers. The world order was apparently very different prior to the Great Dying. The cultures that ended up on top then where largely the ones that got a head start in colonizing other, less developed cultures. By the time of the Great Dying, most of the continents were fully populated, so there was nothing left to further colonize. The dying off itself was a great leveling factor, decimating populations in place and resetting the whole development trajectory. One possibility is that because Africans are more genetically diverse than any other population group, they had an easier time surviving the pandemic, more chances for at least partial natural immunity. This may have allowed them to start again from a larger base. No one really knows. Perhaps it was because they got to democracy first, though then one wonders why they got to democracy first."

"I wonder what it must be like to live in a democracy," Katerinya mused.

"Oh, it has its own problems," Ilya replied. "The USA can be a hard country to emigrate to if you are not black, or wealthy. The government itself, and the vast majority of the people are very tolerant of differences, and sympathetic to the less fortunate, but an always vocal minority of Black Supremacists believe that Africa's global domination is due to genetic superiority. They are largely ignorant of both history and genetics, but dealing with such ignorance is one of the challenges of democracy. These people vote.

They are hostile to immigration, fearing that the new arrivals will end up living on the public dole and dilute their favored bloodline.

You hear this kind of crazy tribal talk that demonizes "outsiders" here too, from demagogues like Sokolov. But for Sokolov, this is just to keep his base united. He can blame things that don't go his way on the other tribes. There is no gain for him in exporting his propaganda outside of his tribe, because there are no voters to convince. He can't bring about a revolution at the ballot box. But in Africa, it's possible. So the volume of deliberate misinformation swirling around all of the social media is oppressively intense there, particularly around election time. At least we don't have that problem."

Katerinya found this rather depressing. She had just assumed that in a democracy, well-informed people went to the polls and made rational decisions. But after hearing Ilya, it occurred to her that it was probably not much different than well-informed shoppers going to the store to make rational product decisions. The people who make the products have a vested interest in persuading shoppers to favor them. They do this with advertising, which appeals to subrational motivations and desires. Shoppers are rarely making rational choices.

Before long, the waiter arrived with the check. He instinctively turned toward Ilya, then suddenly stopped himself, clearly recalling the incident with the wine. He hesitated for a moment, intending not to commit another faux pas. He was hoping not to have to make a choice. Then it occurred to him that he didn't have to. He placed the check in the middle of the table, equidistant between the two diners. Then he smiled politely and made his usual retreat. Both of the diners smiled at each other. Katerinya felt a little sympathy for the poor waiter and what they had put him through, though in one sense she was glad to have widened his perspective a little. She looked forward to someday actually paying for the luncheon herself. But for now, she had no problem with Ilya picking up the check.

§

After putting Katerinya safely on the train back to Mariankursk, Ilya Erynovich decided to walk back from Derazhne Station to the University. It was only two stops on the tram, and he thought the walk might help burn off some of the ethanol from the wine. He was still doing the painstakingly detailed work of getting the antibiotic ready for prime time, so he needed to have a clear head. He had almost reached his office when he heard his cell phone ding a message alert. Was Katerinya texting him already from her new phone? He hoped not, because text traffic was not locally secure, even on African-edition phones. It turned out that she understood the protocol. It was not from her. The message said, "the cantaloupes are ripe and so are the cherries". He texted back "Good, I think I'll buy some soon." This was from his colleagues at the offsite synthesizing lab. It meant that they had figured out the dosing, and manufactured a batch of the antibiotic. His reply told them that he would be coming by to get it soon.

He turned around and headed back out of the Quad to the north in the direction of the lab. It was now getting dark and snow was beginning to fall. He fastened his sabovar and raised its collar. In the illuminated cones of air cast by the streetlights, he could see that the volume of the snowfall was increasing as he passed each lamppost. It was beginning to accumulate on the ground. It was significantly colder now than during the afternoon, so he hadn't thought to include any nanoprene crystals in his pockets. He could use some about now. If the lab had produced sufficient volume of the antibiotic, he was now only a day or two away from taking it to Mariankursk. He did not notice that he was being followed.

His pursuer designed his pursuit so that he would intercept Ilya Erynovich between lampposts to keep the encounter as much in the dark as possible. When the intercept point arrived he stepped out from behind a building blocking Ilya Erynovich's path. As a disincentive to run, he held a small sidearm protruding slightly out of his sabovar. Ilya Erynovich was startled, of course, but immediately saw the gravity of the situation, and understood the message the gun was meant to convey.

"I have no wish to harm you, Ilya Erynovich," the man said. "I just want to talk." He was more than willing to comply given the situation at hand. "Is there somewhere private we can go?" the man asked. Now Ilya Erynovich had to think this through. They were closer to the lab than to his office at this point, and the district they were in was less well lit and populated than the University, so he hatched a plan for them to go to the lab, and he would figure out how to finesse the situation once they got there. As they walked, he wondered to himself which of his possible pursuers this was. One of Tarasov's spies? The next Korihor vigilante? Someone else entirely? Whomever it was knew him by name, so this seemed to favor a Tarasov agent.

When they arrived at the lab, the man had retracted his gun so as not to give away the coercion. At this point, Ilya Erynovich had to make a call. He wanted to avoid disclosing anything to anyone until he was more cognizant of what this man's motive was. So he greeted his colleagues without any introductions and asked if there was an empty conference room in which he could have a brief meeting before they got down to business (making a point not to say what that business was). They did not appear suspicious, and directed him to a room down the hall. He thanked them, accompanied his inquisitor to the room, and closed the door behind them.

When they sat down at the conference table, his inquisitor immediately said "My apologies for the weapon, Ilya Erynovich. I didn't want to have to chase you. My name is Stepanov, Mitya

Zhenyaevich Stepanov. I'm an agent for Prince Tarasov." (He knew it)! "We've been following your activities concerning the viral outbreak in Mariankursk." "You mean the *bacterial* outbreak," Ilya Erynovich corrected him. "Yes, the bacterial outbreak," Stepanov replied. "That's just the sort of clarification I'm looking for. Can you tell me what you know about the situation there?" Ilya Erynovich had to think about this. His grant report must have reached Prince Tarasov earlier in the day, and he had carefully crafted it to disclose only as much as he thought wise. He didn't want to add more for this Stepanov fellow. So he mentioned the report, and wondered why that had not already been what he was asking for now. This caught Stepanov by surprise. It was now evident that he had not seen this report, and together with the virus/bacterium mistake, Ilya Erynovich was now suspicious of both his motive and his identity. Mitya Zhenyaevich tried to recover by pretending that he had seen the report, but then quickly realized he was in trouble when Ilya Erynovich started asking him about specific content.

At this point, Ilya Erynovich would normally have shut his inquisitor down, dismissing him as a fraud, but he had the gun, so this required a more nuanced approach. But what? The momentary silence was pressing on them both. Mitya Zhenyaevich broke first. With his cover blown, he saw no choice but to make a full confession. He was indeed an agent for Tarasov. He hadn't seen the report, but not because he wouldn't have access to it. He would probably see it tomorrow. Then he put the gun on the table and pushed it toward the professor as a peace gesture. "I think we are both honorable men, Ilya Erynovich. What I am about to tell you I need you to keep in strictest confidence. Can I count on that? I've given you the gun so that you are free to make this choice without coercion. If you don't agree, you may keep the gun and I will go on my way. We will never speak of this again." Now there was a mind-bender, Ilya Erynovich thought. What a choice! It was always better to know things than not know things, but what price would he be paying for this knowledge? He wasn't being asked to give up any more of his own information, just to keep someone else's private. All of the possible consequences were just too much to consider, so he instinctively agreed.

Mitya Zhenyaevich then told him that he was also an agent for Sokolov – a double agent. He was a military man, originally a devout Orthodox member of Archbishop Osipov's church. He had been working as chief of security for Prince Tarasov for some time. He ran his spy organization. His great desire had always been to see the City-State of Solinovsk become a theocracy – an actual Kingdom of God. He had gone along with the pragmatic approximation of this under the Tarasov/Osipov partnership, but became disillusioned over time after Reverend Sokolov came to town. As Sokolov became more influential and Tarasov became more wary of him, Tarasov tasked him with infiltrating Sokolov's organization. This was his first double-agent assignment. As he gained Sokolov's confidence, it was learned that he was indeed plotting a revolution. He was growing a budding "army" of true-believer volunteers on the sly, and asked Stepanov to head it for him. He was, after all, a military man, and the "army" was a ragtag collection of novices with no training. What's more, Sokolov asked him to head up his own spy organization. This worked out well for Tarasov, but in running both organizations, Mitya Zhenyaevich became aware that Tarasov's devotion to God was phony, and that Osipov was selling out to him. He began to see his allegiance shift toward Sokolov. This was likely to be the only feasible path to a true theocracy. Now he was a double-double agent, each side thinking they were in charge, with Stepanov in the middle.

Lately, however, he was having his doubts about Sokolov too. He was a real loose cannon, and his volunteers very volatile. There was no discipline and probably never would be with Sokolov at the top. He thought himself God and was oblivious to the consequences of his actions. Mitya Zhenyaevich did not want to be a part of this revolution. It would end very badly for everyone. He preferred a peaceful transition to a Kingdom of God, even though he was unclear on how to attain this.

Ilya Erynovich was stunned! This was quite a lot to take in. As opposed as he was to religion, he felt a certain sympathy for Mitya Zhenyaevich. He did seem to be an honorable man, and had resisted some of the worst impulses of blind faith. If either side found out about his duplicity, he was likely a dead man. So he leveled with him about what was going on with the outbreak, and his own fears that neither leader, Tarasov or Sokolov was likely to do the right thing. One wanted to suppress the information, and the other wanted to turn it into panic. Mitya Zhenyaevich said he thought that sounded about right, from what he knew.

"But why a theocracy?" Ilya Erynovich asked. "If you truly don't want violence, why can't each person believe what they want? You can be as religious as you want, and I can be as secular as I want." "Because the Bible says we must seek the Kingdom of God!" came the reply. Ilya was about to point out that the Bible phrase doesn't say that you have to pull this off on Earth. The Kingdom of God is supposed to be in heaven. But then he remembered that poor Stepanov was probably the unfortunate beneficiary of Sokolov's notoriously slippery Bible interpretations. There would be no rational end to this discussion. So he just let it go, and ushered Mitya Zhenyaevich out of the lab, each promising to keep the other informed, and Ilya Erynovich pressing the conviction that they could always be allies if the common objective was peace.

§

The private conference had been brief enough not to raise any need to explain it to his colleagues at the lab. So when he returned they got right down to business. They had written up the dosing recommendations and provided him with a stash of about fifteen vials of the antibiotic. This should be enough for him to finish his testing on cultures back at the University. He fastened up his sabovar, raised its collar, and set out in the snow for the brief walk back to Dahlström Hall. All the way there, he kept rolling the recent disclosures over in his mind. He was still astounded that the entire security apparatus of both organizations was controlled by a single man who was now not wholly allegiant to either side. If he could keep up the balancing act, this could be a very powerful ally. Or it could turn out to be a very dead ally, which he could not afford to be associated with.

Once back at Dahlström, he set up the testing apparatus and started preparing samples. Sometimes this was a little tedious. You had to sit and wait for a while for reactions to occur. He visualized the reaction he was looking for in his mind – the antibiotic compound lysing the membrane of the bacterium. Suddenly he heard a scream coming from outside. He looked up, whirled around in his chair and went over to the window. There he saw a woman kneeling in panic over what appeared to be a dead body. There were several other dead bodies lying around, and people were running in every direction. Were they too late? Was it *Y. pestis*? Had it already reached here? He ran to the door, down the steps, and hurried outside to examine the body. The woman had already fled. Yes! The plague! A pandemic had already begun! There was nowhere near enough antibiotic to make a difference at this point. He had to warn the others. He ran back upstairs and down the halls looking for his colleagues. He couldn't find Stevenson, or any of the others. All of the offices were empty. He ran to the top of the stairs and leapt down one flight at a time in a single elegant motion (because he was in such a hurry), letting gravity pull him down, then feathering up just in time to avoid impact with the landing, then banking to the left to continue the same downward motion. When he reached the ground floor, he bounded out into the courtyard among the bodies. He had to find the epicenter of infection. He started to run, then remembered about levitation. He could get a much better view that way. He lifted himself up into the air, rising swiftly above the courtyard, then hovered motionlessly above the campus looking for the epicenter. People below were watching him in amazement. He knew instinctively that he had this skill, but often forgot about it until the last minute. Then he remembered why.

Lucid dreaming is a phenomenon where one becomes aware that they are dreaming while still in the dream. Some people are said to be able to stay in the dream and control events as if they were directors of a movie. Ilya Erynovich's experience was a little different. When he reached the lucid state and knew he was dreaming, he would wake up, as he had done now. He often had these powers of levitation and flight in dreams, and would typically remember that he had them while still in the dream. But it was not lucid because while he was still dreaming, he thought it was real. This skill manifested itself so often in his dreams that his dream state took it in stride. He would suddenly remember that he was different than most people, and that's just the way the world was.

He remembered most of his dreams because he was always waking up for short intervals during the night, just after they occurred. So he spent a lot of time thinking about this "flying" skill. People are said to fly in dreams all the time, but for him this was a little different. He had never heard anyone else describe the sensation the way he experienced it. This was not like birds in the air. There were no wings. It was more like a fish "swimming" in the air. Particularly the ability to descend entire staircases without touching the ground. A kind of swooping and gliding. He could rise to the top of a room, hover there for a while, then swoop back down with a dovetail finish that kept him from touching the floor. It was like watching fish in an aquarium, with air substituted for water. He formed a theory about this. Maybe what he is doing when this facility happens in dreams is replaying the motor sensations of fish-swimming. Just as our embryos retain the gill slits and rerouted aorta from our fishy ancestors, perhaps our cerebellum, the ancient part of the brain that controls motor behavior, still retains vestiges of the hard-wired swimming program from when we were all fish. Could be.

At this point, he found himself slumped in his chair waiting for a reaction that had already occurred while he was asleep. He had no need to check the window. He knew what was real now. Not only had he not been fish-flying, but there had been no snow on the ground in the dream. Though who was Stevenson? He decided he had enough for one day. He was going to walk home in the snow, not glide there through the air, and get some real sleep.

Chapter 5

SHELTER FROM THE STORM

On Sunday morning, Yulia Katyaevna was up early in her dorm room working on a history paper that was due the following day. It had snowed again the night before, so now the campus was buried under about 18 inches of snow. The sky was clear this morning enabling the bright sun to reflect off the snow on the ground, and sparkle off the branches of trees heavily laden with the white stuff. She caught this magical view when she first went to the window this morning. Now she was settled in at her desk away from the window, but the soft, white, diffuse light from outside filled the room.

The assignment was to write a paper based on research into historical texts. She was supposed to compare similar documents from different sources. She kept putting this task off because nothing had sparked her interest among the various sample references the professor had provided as possible source material. Her recent conversation with Professor Koskayin about the Apocrypha, the

Pseudepigrapha, and the Tacna Texts had given her an idea about using some of these as her sources. The assignment didn't explicitly say that you had to use the recommended sources, and the religious texts were now of very keen interest to her. She found translations from all three online, and had been reading voraciously all weekend. So many ideas and revelations! She was having a hard time corralling all of this discovery into a coherent theme for her paper.

What puzzled her most was that some of the Jesuit texts from Tacna seemed to anticipate things that Jossmit says in the Bible. The original sources of these texts could be dated to time periods prior to the time Jossmit was said to have been on Earth. In some cases they appeared not just to anticipate, but were literally the same words and phrases. She was struggling with how to frame this apparent anomaly as a research thesis for her paper. Someone must have commented on this before, she thought, but perhaps because this was religious subject matter, secular historians had avoided it. She needed some source of religious commentary. Then it occurred to her that she had such a source right down the street.

She had not been attending Sunday services at Sokolov's church lately. She was feeling a little alienated from that prior period in her life. She had convinced her parents that she was often just too busy at school to go regularly with them on Sunday. She implied that she got there now and then on her own, but it was much more then than now. She could, she thought, make an impromptu visit to Sokolov before the service this morning to get the church's view on this subject. Then perhaps leave before the service started so that she wouldn't encounter her parents. Sokolov would just assume that she had gone upstairs to the service, so no one would be the wiser. A quick in and out. Suddenly an idea had become a compelling plan of action. She dressed in more presentable attire, added the layers necessary for trudging through the snow, put some nanoprene crystals in her pockets, and headed out down the street.

When Yulia Katyaevna reached the pastor's office downstairs – "his door was always open" he was constantly telling his flock – the door was closed. So she knocked. Sokolov came to the door and opened it, a little surprised to see her there. She could see that there were three men inside the office who also seemed a bit surprised by the interruption. She could see he was busy, so after explaining that she had some religious questions for him, she volunteered to come back some other time. She noticed that his demeanor was a little off. He appeared indecisive, even a little nervous. Before replying, he glanced back at the three men and subtly jerked his head slightly sideways as if to tell them they should promptly leave. She didn't know any of these men, but if Ilya Erynovich had been there, he would have recognized one of them – Stepanov. The men got the message, and exited through the back entrance up toward the sanctuary. There was a side exit from the building up there. Then Sokolov put on his more accustomed public face, turned back to her, and invited her in. "My door is always open," he said.

After they took their customary shepherd and sheep chairs, Yulia Katyaevna explained about her research paper and her desire to get the church's view on some of the things she had recently discovered. She asked him about the Apocrypha, the Pseudepigrapha, and the Peruvian Texts. She wondered why she had not heard about these things in the church, and only encountered them when she got to the University.

"My, my, Yulia Katyaevna, you have been busy at school, haven't you!" he said, smiling. It was that same insincere, patronizing smile that she used to interpret as a sincere, adult concern for her childly well-being smile. She had grown up since then. Now she found it annoying. "You must be very careful about the things you are taught at the University. There are many non-believers there who will attempt to lure you away from Jossmit."

"So are you saying that there are no such things as these additional spiritual books?" she asked.

"Oh, no! There are such books, I'm sure. It's the *interpretation* of their existence that is at issue here. I've never heard of this Pseudo … graphic …"

"Pseud-epi-graph-a" she said, slowly.

He tried again. "Pseudo-pig-graph … whatever! I'm not aware of this one, but I have heard about the Apocrypha and the Peruvian Texts. You haven't heard about them in church because they simply have no relevance to the faith. We have no interest in the Apocrypha because there are no direct quotations from the Apocrypha in the New Testament nor does the New Testament refer to any apocryphal books as part of Scripture. These were rightly judged to be non-Biblical. That's why they are not in the Bible! Why they should be so special, or worthy of religious study, I don't know. There are millions of books that are not in the Bible. We only study the ones that *are* in the Bible."

Yulia Katyaevna was half-expecting a reply like this concerning the Apocrypha. Of more concern to her were the Jesuit texts from Tacna. These she found surprising, she told him, particularly because phrases and whole parables spoken by Jossmit in the Bible could be found in these texts from before the time of Jossmit. She was still working on how to portray this discrepancy in her paper, so she phrased her inquiry in the starkest of terms. "There are many sayings in the Jesuit texts, from Tacna, from before the time of Jossmit, that sound very much like the things Jossmit says in the Bible. Was Jossmit plagiarizing?"

Sokolov had very little interest in the Jesuit texts, so he had not read them, only a little bit about them. But he had heard this kind of criticism before, so he was ready to address it. "Well, it would be foolish to believe that Jossmit was not influenced by the customs and sayings of the society going on around him at the time. There may well have been instances where he borrowed from the Jesuits and probably from other traditions as well. I wouldn't call this plagiarism. He spoke using thought forms and other symbolisms that his audiences were accustomed to. This made his message easier for them to comprehend.

God has to reveal divine truth to humans in thought forms they can understand. So his messages, whether in sayings, or in dreams, or in stories, are always set in terms that would be readily intelligible to the people in their own times. So through Jossmit, he spoke in parables that would inspire men in their hearts. The parables impart eternal truths in the form of familiar analogies.

Bear in mind that in ancient times, ordinary humans could not speak to, or see, God directly. The divine sounds and visions were too powerful for mortals. So there is always some go-between: an angel, or a burning bush, or a whirlwind. The *content* of the divine truths themselves would similarly be unintelligible to men. So he used their mortal thought forms as a go-between. You could call this borrowing, but certainly not plagiarism. When Jossmit borrowed the thought forms of his times to encode divine messages, he was adding richer, divine content to them. They had greater meaning when Jossmit said them."

OK, she thought, he didn't address the pithier question of whether the human authors of the Gospels did the plagiarizing and attributed the sayings to Jossmit. She supposed he wouldn't be sensitive to this distinction, since he likely regarded the authors of the Gospels as eyewitnesses. So she moved on to her next question.

"Were the books of John, and the epistles of Paul, and Revelation, from the Tacna texts, considered part of the Scriptures by the Jesuits?"

He was caught off-guard again because he didn't know about these texts. But he knew they were not part of the Bible, so he ad-libbed. "No. There were *many* Jesuit texts found at Tacna. Some of them are now part of the Bible; many of them are not. Just because copies of these non-Biblical books you mention were found among the Tacna texts doesn't require that we consider them books of Scripture – or even that they considered them Scripture. The Tacna texts contain all kinds of documents, not just Scripture. We don't have to consider every commentary, history, directive, schedule, hymnbook, or book of community rules unearthed at Tacna to be part of the Scriptures. Even the ancient Jesuits living there didn't consider every document in their library to be Scripture"

She suspected (correctly) that he didn't know about these books. So she suspected that his answer to her last question would be a similar shot in the dark, but she wanted to hear it anyway. Since there was some overlap between the end of the Jesuit era, and the beginning of Jossmit's era, you might expect there to be some mention of Jossmit in the Jesuit texts. So she asked. "Is Jossmit ever mentioned in the Tacna texts?"

He could see that this line of questioning was not going well. He didn't really know the answer, so he responded with a cover for the possibility that there were no such references. "I don't really know, but it would not be surprising if there were no mentions of Jossmit. The Tacna texts teach us much about the culture of belief at the time. And while the Tacna texts are older, I'm sure there is debate about the authority of the variants found in the documents because the people who wrote and collected the Tacna texts appear to have treated non-Scriptural writings much the same as they treated what has been traditionally accepted as Scripture.

It is reasonable to assume that the Jesuits living in Peru read many different books, and were not readers of the Scriptures alone. Now, this doesn't imply that they read secular books *more* than the Bible. Let me give you an example. In my personal library I have hundreds of books, but I have only one Bible. I do not read most of these books regularly, but I read my Bible constantly. It may have been the same for the Jesuits. Still, their non-Biblical texts have relevance for how the Old Testament was understood and interpreted by some Jesuits *prior* to the time of the New Testament."

At this point, the Reverend Sokolov was growing weary of defending his church against a steady stream of questions about which he knew little. This was not the Yulia Katyaevna that he had remembered from her high school days. He invented an excuse – that he still needed to prepare his sermon for today's service – to bring the session to a merciful end. She saw this as her opportunity to bolt before her parents arrived. So they parted ways, she to trudge back to campus and he, presumably, to work on his sermon.

As Yulia Katyaevna trudged through the snow, she also trudged through this now concluded episode of challenge and denial. All of these men – the Jesuits, the Jossmitians, the Church councils, the pastors – looked at the same documents and managed to directly intuit contradictory inspirations. What was actually in the documents, and the order in which they were written or discovered, did not seem to have mattered much at all. And many of these men were scholars, presumably having dedicated their lives to figuring things out. Yet they had essentially given up when things got complicated, seeing instead what they wanted to see in the documents, and relapsing to these straight shots of spiritual revelation that had been impressed upon them as obedient children, as if that was any kind of evidence of anything – ending arguments with the certainty of non-arguments. She knew that feeling. These same intuited experiences of certainty had been impressed upon her as a child – she had learned to feel the presence of Jossmit in her heart. But she had grown up. Her heart was now an organ for pumping blood. And she was far from giving up. She was just getting started.

Despite what he had said about the sermon, the Reverend Sokolov really had other things on his mind. He texted the trio of men that the coast was now clear to come back – through the rear entrance again. Then he again closed his always-open door. When the second confab of conspirators had reached its own, uninterrupted conclusion, the three men departed again through the rear entrance, and the Reverend Sokolov gathered his source material for the day's sermon. As he donned his robe and stole, and made his way up the back stairs into the chancel and behind his literal bully pulpit, his mind was still on the strategy session with his men. They needed more funds to keep his version of God's work on track. He looked briefly at his sermon notes, then decided to make an option play. He tucked the prepared sermon back into his folder, and opened the Bible looking for a particular reference. He found it.

When the service reached the point in the liturgy where he was to speak, he announced, "Today's Scripture is taken from the *Acts of the Apostles*, Chapter 4, Verses 30-36."

4-30 And behold, thou wilt remember the poor, and consecrate of thy properties for their support that which thou hast to impart unto them, with a covenant and a deed which cannot be broken.

4-31 And inasmuch as ye impart of your substance unto the poor, ye will do it unto me;

4-32 They cannot be taken from the church, agreeable to my commandments, every man shall be made accountable unto me, a steward over his own property, or that which he has received by consecration, as much as is sufficient for himself and family.

4-33 And again, if there shall be properties in the hands of the church, or any individuals of it, more than is necessary for their support after this first consecration, it shall be kept to administer to those who have not, from time to time, that every man who has need may be amply supplied and receive according to his wants.

4-34 And so it was that the community of believers was of one heart and mind, and no one claimed that any of his possessions was his own, but they had everything in common.

4-35 There was no needy person among them, for those who owned property or houses would sell them, bring the proceeds of the sale,

4-36 and put them at the feet of the apostles, and they
were distributed to each according to need.

"The Acts of the Apostles!" he pronounced loudly. He paused, letting his words echo to the back of the Sanctuary. "This is what the Apostles did when they were busy building the Church in the years after Jossmit's death. They banded together, and everyone in the flock contributed all of their material possessions to the Church leaders, so that the resources might be redistributed to those in need. If there were resources left over, the Church would retain these for later needs that might arise. Now, of course, this is not quite how we do things today," he smiled. "We do not ask you to sell all of your property or deed it to the Church. But we still have those who are in need, and who are less fortunate among us. As a community of God, we still need to support these people. So the Church still needs each of you to give what you can, that we may do the Lord's work – the Lord's Holy Work! As the ushers pass among you with the collection plates, I urge you to give what you can – to give generously."

He nodded for the ushers to begin.

§

Earlier that morning, Ilya Erynovich was on his way to the tram stop at University Station. He was bundled in his warmest winter gear, with his biokit loaded with the first course of the new antibiotic, on his way to Mariankursk. Because of the depth of the snow, he was more than willing to take the tram two stops to Derazhne Station rather than walking. Sometimes the tram's track switches would freeze up after such an overnight snowstorm, but with the full sun this morning, the temperature had warmed up to just below freezing, so the switching should be fine, he thought. At Derazhne Station, he planned to perform the usual mail-the-kit-to-himself routine because the political scene was now even murkier than before – more players, more watchers, more competing agendas.

As he approached University Station, an unfamiliar man in a military uniform was blocking his path. Here we go again, he thought. He turned to walk around him, but another man in a matching uniform had fallen in behind him and moved to block his escape. He was now trapped between them. "Professor Koskayin?" the first one asked, glancing at his cell phone, which must have contained his picture to aid in identification. "Yes," Ilya Erynovich replied cautiously. "Could you come with us, please?" He didn't really have any choice, but the encounter did not appear to be dangerous on the face of it. So he went along. They escorted him away from the crowds, across the street toward Yaroslava's, a very high-end restaurant in the Square. When they were sufficiently away from the crowds not to be overheard, the first guard said in a low voice "Prince Tarasov would like a word with you." Hmm, Ilya Erynovich thought to himself. The top guy. Wonder how this will go.

The guards took him into Yaroslava's toward the back, then motioned for him to enter a private dining room. They didn't follow. Their job was done. Inside he found the Prince in all his glory, sitting at a table over a morning coffee service, several aides seated nearby, and an ominous looking guard in full military dress standing near the door with his rifle clearly visible. This must be the bodyguard, he thought to himself. Tarasov motioned toward the opposing empty chair at his table, saying 'Please. Sit. Can I get you anything? A coffee perhaps?" Ilya Erynovich was inclined to beg off, since he was in a hurry to get to his train, but it occurred to him that he probably shouldn't mention this until he saw which way the wind was blowing. And it was not clear how long this would take. So he decided another morning coffee couldn't hurt. "Yes, that would be nice, thank you," he replied. The waiter was already hovering nearby, so he immediately stepped in and asked, "And how do you take your coffee, sir?" "Black," he replied, without hesitation. "As dark a roast as you can muster." The Prince seemed to like this reply, smiling slightly.

"I've followed your career at the University for some time now," Tarasov told him. "You've been a good investment. Maybe the best technological return on investment of any that I have made there. Please keep up the good work." This was not what Ilya Erynovich had been expecting. He had never met Tarasov before, so he only knew him by way of popular stereotypes. All of their communication had been one way, through status reports from Koskayin to the Prince. Nothing ever came back the other way – except more money. Now Ilya Erynovich could see that this was a kind of communication. "It might surprise you that I personally read all of your reports. I'm not just the sugar daddy. I've learned a lot about cryptography and biology from reading your work." This did indeed surprise him. The man has an interest in, and apparently a capacity for, science. "Now I suppose you are on your way to Mariankursk to administer the new antibiotic that you disclosed in your last report. Am I right?" Of course he was right. Ilya Erynovich was now very concerned. He had withheld much from Tarasov out of political caution, but it seemed that he knew everything that was going on anyway.

"You act surprised, Ilya Erynovich. I thought a man as clever as you would have figured this out by now. I have people everywhere. I know everything that is going on. The career of a Prince depends on this." "What else do you know?" Ilya Erynovich boldly asked. Prince Tarasov raised his eyebrows in a half smile. "I know that you've been working this outbreak at the hospital in Mariankursk for some time now. I know that you usually stay at Madam Zakharova's guesthouse when you go. I know that you have a certain lady friend who lives on Tallinnskaya Street there." The Prince raised his eyebrows again after this remark, looking for a response. Ilya Erynovich was stoically determined not to show one, though his head was spinning from the news. The Prince pressed on.

"I know your academic friends have their ears to the ground. I know you were afraid that I might be planning to suppress the outbreak information; that the rascal Sokolov was planning to cause a panic with it." Ilya Erynovich was waiting for the Stepanov encounter to be announced next, but it wasn't. Tarasov certainly would have dropped that bomb next if he knew, so Ilya Erynovich figured this was still a secret – for now.

"You and I are really very much alike, Ilya Erynovich. Who do you think has protected you from the Church all these years? I am just as agnostic as you, but you can proclaim it loudly whenever it suits you. I envy you this. I have a Principality to preserve. I need Osipov's Church for pragmatic reasons." Then he leaned over toward Ilya Erynovich to say in a softer voice, "And I trust that you will now keep this in confidence, Eh?" Ilya Erynovich assured him he would. Then the Prince went on. "I know that we are on opposite sides of the surveillance and encryption business. I respect your position, and admire you as an adversary. You currently own the Internet, and I own the cell phones. You are working on a technology to cut me out of cell phones, at least for academics. I expect you will win that piece eventually, but you academics already have privacy via the Internet, so this new wrinkle will not cut into my domain for ordinary citizens. Please understand that this, like religion, is a pragmatic matter for me. I am a Prince. I have a government to protect."

Ilya Erynovich's local worldview had just been turned completely on its head. He had severely underestimated this man. He now had enormous respect for him. And now felt extremely fortunate to have him as an ally. He explained in minute detail where the outbreak now stood and how the next step needed to be a quick ramp-up in quarantine procedures, and mass production and distribution of the new antibiotic. Tarasov understood this and expressed that his only concern at this point was that Sokolov not find out until they had all of the protocols in place. "Prince Tarasov, that's the last person I would want to find out about this," Ilya Erynovich said, smiling wryly. "Please, call me 'Koldan Sonvaevich'. We are colleagues now. But keep addressing the reports to 'His Highness, blah, blah, blah … Prince Tarasov', OK?" he said, winking. "Let this be our little secret."

With that, the Prince said the Professor was free to go. He would now probably miss the train he was originally targeting, and he still had some coffee to finish, so he lingered a while as the Prince was summoned to a table at the back of the room by his aids. They were talking in low tones, but the room was otherwise empty, so Ilya Erynovich could overhear much of what they were saying. It was chilling. They had apparently suspected Stepanov's questionable loyalty for a while, so they had run the classic bogus information ploy of the espionage world. They informed Stepanov of something false that if true would be very damaging to their side. They made sure he was the only person this was disclosed to. When later spies learned that Sokolov was now in possession of this disinformation, they knew the source had to be Stepanov. He was now toast. Ilya Erynovich realized he had just dodged a bullet here. He should probably leave for the train station sooner than later. He pulled out his cell phone and texted Katerinya "The loser now will be later to win." Almost immediately, the reply came back "Oh, the times must be changin'." He smiled. All that work for a privacy protocol to protect information that Tarasov already knew. He was going to have to factor this into his plans from now on.

He left Yaroslava's, and headed back to University Station. When he got to Derazhne Station, he realized there was now no point to mailing the biokit to himself. The people he thought he was hiding it from were actually allies that already knew. The party it still made sense to hide it from was Sokolov, but he did not have the spies to find out. Stepanov was the height of his intelligence network, and he was also now an ally. He thought. But Stepanov already knew about the outbreak scenario as well, so there was no more information to protect. With this, he bought his ticket and boarded the train for Mariankursk, skipping the Rail Express part.

Once on the train, he took an empty seat next to a window, looking out at the white-crusted snowdrifts at the edge of the track, not yet dusted by the inevitable soot that would eventually shade them after a day of railroad commerce. He did not notice Stepanov coming down the aisle toward him. Mitya Zhenyaevich also did not recognize him at first. When he reached Ilya Erynovich's seat, he did. He expressed no greeting out loud. Instead, he took a seat next to the professor as if they were strangers. Seeing this, Ilya Erynovich understood the protocol. It was not advisable for the two of them to be seen as collaborators. So he also expressed no outward recognition. They kept up this just-strangers routine until everyone was seated and the train was in motion. Then the white noise from the track below would allow them to converse in low tones, still looking forward as if they were unknown to each other.

Ilya Erynovich waited for Mitya Zhenyaevich to begin. He was fairly sure that Stepanov did not know he had been flushed out by Tarasov's men, but there was just too much information and misinformation flowing and not flowing at this point that he was reticent to volunteer anything until he heard from Stepanov. Mitya Zhenyaevich had nothing in particular to report, he said. It was just a coincidence that they were on the same train to Mariankursk. Ilya Erynovich sincerely wished he could believe this. There was very little about the whole espionage business that he could be certain of anymore. He weighed whether he should warn Mitya Zhenyaevich about his exposure. That would mean disclosing at least some of the new Tarasov connection. He couldn't be sure who knew what about whom. In the end, he reasoned that his exposure to Stepanov was already a fact, and that he already had to rely on Mitya Zhenyaevich not to disclose it. So this was unlikely to make matters any worse. Besides, he would earn some points with Stepanov for possibly saving his life, so he quietly related the conversation that he had overheard – leaving out as much as possible about the circumstances under which he heard it.

It was indeed news to Stepanov. The look of concern on his face was evident, even from just an anonymous side view. Mitya Zhenyaevich pondered the situation, briefly checked his sidearm inside his sabovar, then thanked Ilya Erynovich for the timely tip. He would have to bolt and go into hiding as soon as the train reached Mariankursk, he said. This meant that both sides would suspect him of being a traitor now, so he would have to lay low for some time until he could figure out whom among his past allies he could still trust. But he never made it to Mariankursk.

The train suddenly slowed down and came to a stop in the middle of nowhere. They were deep into the snow-covered woods at this point, and the sudden breaking of the train caused passengers and baggage to be knocked off their perches. The view out the side window showed nothing but trees and snow, but up ahead, blocking the track in front of the engine, was a contingent of heavily armed soldiers – Tarasov's men. They came gruffly through the cars of the train, examining the passengers and occasionally asking for IDs. When they spotted Stepanov and Koskayin seated together, they quickly came forward, weapons drawn, motioning for both men to get up and exit the train. As other passengers watched in horror, the two were taken outside of the car, positioned in the snow to the side of the tracks with their hands behind their heads, and searched.

They found Stepanov's sidearm. One of them, who seemed to be the one in charge, began texting on his phone. Another began to search Ilya Erynovich, retrieving his phone and his ID. When this soldier showed the ID to his superior, the texting commander looked up at Koskayin, then down at the ID. Then he said, "That's the professor; let him go." The second soldier returned his ID and phone, and motioned for him to re-board the train. Ilya Erynovich was more than happy to obey this directive. Once inside, wide-eyed passengers watched him return to his seat, wondering who he was and what he had done. The commander in charge then motioned to the front of the train for the engineer to resume the journey. As the train slowly began to move again, Ilya Erynovich watched the still developing scene outside his window. As they pulled away, Mitya Zhenyaevich suddenly broke free and made a run for the woods. The commander turned and fired a single shot from Stepanov's own gun, bringing him down in a heap in the snow. He did not move. As the train rounded a curve, bringing an end to the receding view of the scene, Ilya Erynovich could briefly see the blood on the snow. His fellow passengers gasped.

§

For the rest of the journey, Ilya Erynovich could feel the watchful eyes of his fellow passengers upon him. He would be wondering who he was too, he thought, if he were in their place. His quick release was a good sign that he was still in Tarasov's good graces. The Stepanov encounter must indeed have been a coincidence. They weren't expecting to find Ilya Erynovich with him on the same train. That he wasn't further questioned demonstrated that they did not expect any collaboration between the two. So he was in the clear for now. In fact, his whole trip to Mariankursk was now officially sanctioned, so the shroud of secrecy was no longer required. He, of course, had told Katerinya not to meet him at the train station to keep their association free from the hospital mission. This precaution now too was moot. He wished he had known this earlier, because he very much would like to see her at the station now – someone to talk to about what had just happened; someone who knew who he was and didn't suspect he was somehow involved in Mitya Zhenyaevich's ignominious end.

When the train pulled into Mariankursk Station, Ilya Erynovich waited for the other passengers to disembark first – to metaphorically clear the air of suspicion that surrounded him. When he finally departed the train, he reminded himself of the seriousness of his mission. This mission had once been fraught with paranoia about being observed, and weighed down under the uncertain identity of the renegade bacterium, and whether they could get ahead of it before it became an epidemic. Now they seemed to have the situation well in hand, free from interference. There were some things to be grateful for, he told himself. Let's get on with it!

But a cloud of doubt followed him all the way to the hospital. He couldn't shake the news that Tarasov knew all about Katerinya. He had brought this on himself by advertising their association as a diversion from the bacterial mission. He thought this would just be a local story, just enough informal gossip to color his trips as social. He never expected it to get all the way to Tarasov. The Prince had made it a point to let him know he knew about Katerinya, and what she likely meant to him, and was looking for a reaction. Ilya Erynovich had tried not to show any emotion, but he was now sure Tarasov wasn't buying it. His men must have observed their whole day in Solinovsk. His concern was that the Prince now knew he had some leverage. If Ilya Erynovich would not bow to pressure, the Prince could always threaten Katerinya. He now knew this would bring the professor to heel in a heartbeat. This was now a fact of life. A fact of their lives.

At the hospital, the young doctor and his staff were waiting for him. The doctor apologized for possibly being the information leak, and assured Ilya Erynovich that he would carefully follow the new security protocols Katerinya had outlined for him. Professor Koskayin then brought him up to speed on the new ways of the world – that they were now doing the Prince's work, and could rely on his support for the resources needed. There was now less need for secrecy, except to be wary of any of this getting to Sokolov before the whole mitigation program was in place. Ilya Erynovich told him that it was still a good idea to be careful about what he communicates on a cell phone, if he did not want Tarasov's men to know about it, but Sokolov had no visibility into this channel.

As they walked down the hall to the quarantine ward, the doctor and the nurses all donned masks, and the doctor handed one to Professor Koskayin. The disease had reached the pneumonic stage and could now be passed from human to human by breathing. This was of concern to Ilya Erynovich. They still hadn't located any infections among rodents or their fleas, so the local source of the bacterium was still unknown, the doctor told him. They had significantly more patients in the ward now, and a few more had died waiting for the new course of treatment. The original Y. *pestis modernis* antibiotic was still ineffective.

Ilya Erynovich passed out the vials to the nurses, and explained the dosing recommendations. He then sat back with the doctor and let the nurses perform the injections. "So how have you been doing Professor Koskayin?" he asked. "Your assistant, Katerinya Emlynovna, has been very helpful in all of this." "Yes, she is a trooper, isn't she?" Ilya Erynovich replied, smiling. If only he knew, he thought to himself. Professor Koskayin explained that they were already working on a new vaccine for the new bug. It still had a way to go, but with any luck, he thought they might be able to stem the outbreak right here with the new antibiotic and wouldn't need to deploy a vaccine on any wide scale. He still hadn't heard of any cases of the disease outside of Mariankursk (dreams aside), indicating that, so far, it was just barely endemic. Still, it concerned him that they had not identified the local source. The bacterium's lifecycle begins with rodents, not humans, so we still needed to find out how this all got started, he said.

"Well, I don't know where we would be if you hadn't come along so quickly to help us," the doctor said. "And all because of that lecture you gave back when I was an undergraduate! I had forgotten the reference to Y. *pestis* until it came up in a search result on the Internet. Then it all came back to me. That's when I reached out to you." "You forgot the whole lecture until you saw *Y. pestis*?" Ilya Erynovich inquired. "Oh no. I could never forget that lecture. It was just the name of the bacterium that I hadn't recalled. That lecture changed my life. It's what made me want to major in biology. The part about entropy was a wake-up call, but the image I could never get out of my mind was how the code of life was passed down through the ages from cell to cell, written in molecules. The notion of nucleic acid polymers being strings of letters in a language just blew my mind!"

Before he could utter another word, Ilya Erynovich stopped him right there. "Wait, what did you just say? 'Written in molecules'?" "Yes," the doctor said, "that's exactly how you phrased it. Isn't that right?" It was right. Ilya Erynovich had used this phrase so habitually in his lectures that he didn't think about it before he said it. It just came out. His message to himself, denoted by the fleur-de-lis symbol, was his own pet phrase! And the doctor was right. It was about evolution passing down the genetic code via cell replication – specifically meiosis where the individual nucleotides of DNA are written to the new chromosomes. The message he was looking for was written in DNA – the only large polymer that remains linear enough to constitute a stable language that can be read! The language has an alphabet of four nucleotides that form its letters. The letters form words that denote amino acids – 20 of them. These 20 words form sentences that denote proteins – billions of them. His prior self was telling him to look for a message written in DNA! Whose DNA? And how would he decipher it? He would need a new key for translating this protein language into something else intelligible to humans.

The young doctor was aware that Professor Koskayin had temporarily checked out of their conversation and was chewing something over in his mind. He waited patiently for him to return to the moment. It didn't take long. Back online, Ilya Erynovich was about to explain his epiphany, but then thought the better of it. The doctor knew nothing of this whole follow the fleur-de-lis scavenger hunt, and his memory anomalies. It's not that he didn't trust him, it's just that it was a complicated subject, and the professor was now aware of new ways that his personal information could be exploited. This was a subject only he and Katerinya knew about, and it should probably stay that way. So he just riffed a little on the language of polymers that the doctor had found so fascinating. That seemed to satisfy him. Then they made some plans on how to monitor the progress of the antibiotic and whether they should perhaps call for a Mariankursk-wide quarantine until the disease was under control. No more secret codes needed, Ilya Erynovich assured him. They exchanged cell phone numbers and agreed to keep each other informed, unless, of course, there was something that The Prince probably shouldn't hear about right away. Use your discretion, Professor Koskayin told him.

§

Ilya Erynovich was now officially done for the day, so he headed straightway for Katerinya's apartment on Tallinnskaya Street. This was now his refuge, his oasis, his shelter from this intrigue-filled world. The snow was a little deeper in Mariankursk than on the coast where he had started the day. The sun had also given way to a dull gray overcast, and it was beginning to snow again, so the local world was now truly in the thick of winter. As he trudged east, he considered whether it now made any difference if he approached Katerinya's from the front or the back. He supposed not. Anyone watching at this point already knew the score. Also, the list of unknown pursuers had dwindled to one – the Korihor folks. He hadn't heard from them for some time, so maybe they had lost interest. This was Ilya Erynovich's theory, anyway. But it didn't account for Ragnar's interest. How could it? They hadn't met face to face yet.

It's easier to track people in the snow because, well, they leave tracks. But it's also harder to pursue them because your own progress is impeded by the snow, and you are more visible against the white background. Ragnar was experiencing these problems. He couldn't keep up without risking being seen, so he decided this deserted snowy landscape was probably the best place for an encounter. He stopped trying to hide himself, and Ilya Erynovich noticed. The chase was now in slow motion because neither of them could move very fast under the conditions. Ilya was better at it than Ragnar, and pulled ahead as Ragnar became more and more fatigued. Seeing this, Ilya started his familiar evasive maneuvers. Turning down streets and looping back for a look. He saw Ragnar again after the first cycle, but he was hopelessly far behind now, did not see Ilya Erynovich, and appeared to have given up. He was lost and didn't seem to care anymore, now trudging slowly in the opposite direction. Ilya Erynovich was breathing hard at this point, exhausted himself, but buoyed by the fact that he had apparently given his pursuer the slip. Now he would definitely approach Katerinya's from the back. Perhaps even through the woodlot. That suddenly seemed like the best plan, so he made his way northeast until he reached the woods about two blocks from her apartment. Then he trudged anonymously through the snowy birches until he emerged at her back stairway. He climbed her stairs, still labored in his breathing, then knocked at her back door.

He was never so glad to see someone in his whole life – well, at least the part of his life that he could remember. He looked a fright with snow dripping from his face and sabovar. Katerinya was about to embrace him, but then thought better of it, first unfastening his snowy sabovar, opening it up, then giving him a proper hug inside the coat. She could tell from his labored breathing that something was amiss, so she lingered, sharing her body heat. Then she pealed off his sabovar and insisted he come sit by the fire to warm up. "What happened Ilya? Did something go wrong today?" He told her that at least two things had gone wrong, and that some things had gone right. It had been a very long, complicated day. She already had the kettle on, so she poured some tea for him and joined him by the fire. She instinctively snuggled up next to him and laid her head on his shoulder. It was a subtle escalation of their physical familiarity that neither consciously noticed. It just seemed natural. "Tell me," she invited him. He did.

The news, of course, stretched back farther than just today. He started with the first Stepanov encounter in the offsite lab, and how Sokolov was plotting a revolution against Tarasov, but Tarasov was aware of it. Stepanov was seeking his help to prevent it from becoming violent. Then he moved on to the encounter with Prince Tarasov earlier this morning, and how that had turned the whole political world on its head for him. (He was saving the part about her until last). Then he described the incident on the train with Mitya Zhenyaevich and Tarasov's men. She shuddered, looking at him with a terrified expression. "Is he dead?" she asked. "I don't know. The train was pulling away at that point. It didn't look good." Then he related the relatively good news at the hospital concerning the outbreak, and the even better news about the fleur-de-lis message. Then he closed with the chase by the unknown stranger and how he had eluded him, and, he hoped, anyone else who was watching, by going through the back woods. She was stunned. Such a rollercoaster ride of emotions. She didn't know quite what to say.

He knew this would be hard for her to put all together. He had had a lot more time to think about it than she. He put his arm around her, holding her close, and explained how their lives would be a bit different now. Another unnoticed escalation that followed just as naturally as the first. They had new friends and new enemies, and perhaps one dead friend. The new friends were infinitely more powerful than the enemies, but also possibly dangerous in their own right. He explained that their relationship was no longer private, that Tarasov had been observing them, and everything else, and could someday use this as leverage against him by threatening her. He didn't think this was likely, but it was a possibility they must always be prepared for. They should now try to keep as much about themselves as private as possible – from everyone. There was no one he could really trust anymore except her. His memory problems, and the fleur-de-lis messages were still something only they knew, and they should be careful to keep it that way. The presence of these mysteries indicated that there were more shoes to drop. They might yet learn things that would change their world again.

With her, right now, next to the fire, it all seemed so simple, he said. The rest of the world was unstable. We could be headed to war, we could be headed to peace, we might cure a small outbreak of plague, or we may end up in another pandemic. Who knows what's written in DNA, and what it might portend? In this small world of just the two of them, everything seemed to make sense, he said. Nothing else did. "Then you must stay," she said.

This was the point where she would normally have to begin offering up practical reasons why he should stay. But Ilya offered no resistance this time. He came up with the excuses himself. It made sense to put Mariankursk in a region-wide quarantine for about a week, given that the disease was now pneumonic. They had both been exposed without masks earlier and thus should be quarantining themselves together. He would text the doctor to let him know. He would text Tarasov, whose personal number he now had, to get a decree for the quarantine. He would let the University know to cancel his classes for the week.

Outside the wind had picked up, and begun to howl through the ornate cornice pieces on the roof where icicles had formed, and touched off audible updrafts through the fireplace flue. The snowfall had turned into a blizzard. They could hear the distant call of timberwolves from the back woodlot. Sokolov was plotting against Tarasov. Tarasov was plotting against Sokolov. A new form of *Y. pestis modernis* was coursing through the lungs of unfortunate

Mariankursk citizens. Stepanov was dead. The Korihorians were desperately trying to find Ilya and trod him down. Did we miss anything? Oh, yes. Inside it was warm, and comforting, and everything was right with the world.

§

In the middle of the night, Ilya awoke with a start. This awakened Katerinya as well. She put her arm across his chest, cupping his shoulder, to pull him closer to her. "Iliusha! Are you all right? I think you had a bad dream." "It wasn't a bad dream," he assured her, now fully awake, "it was just a dream." Her bedroom was now dark, except for the faint red glow on the walls from the final coals in the fireplace. The single chimney at 10 Tallinnskaya Street had fireplaces on both the front room side of the wall, and on the bedroom side. Each had its own flue. They had huddled together by the front room fireplace until the fire burned down, then started a new fire in the bedroom for the night. At first, it was blazing with a fiery passion. Now it too was spent for the night.

"What was your dream about?" she asked. He paused to reflect on it for a moment, because dreams are rarely fully coherent. His in particular often merged the identities of real people into single characters. He wanted to get this right. "You were in it," he said, "… well, mostly you." The female character was definitely part Katerinya, he thought, but he couldn't identify the source for the other mixed-in identity. Whoever it was seemed vaguely familiar, but he couldn't identify her. He decided it would be best to leave that part out. "I'm surprised you are in my dreams so soon," he said. "Usually it takes many months, sometimes years, before someone I know on a regular basis becomes a character in my dreams. I guess my brain has a long vetting period before it promotes someone to the permanent cast. You've made an early appearance."

"Where did it take place," she wondered, now getting into this. "It was not your apartment," he said. "Places also take a long time before some version of them shows up. And when they do, it's never exactly like the actual place. It will resemble the actual place, but there will be differences. And from then on, the dream location will recur, always looking the same from one dream to the next – still not quite like the place that inspired it. It was in one of these already vetted places. It seems familiar but I can't remember the place that inspired it."

"Were we lovers?" she asked. He would normally have been reticent to share this detail, but with her it seemed wholly appropriate. He was now ready to share everything with her. "Yes," he said simply. "Tell me all about it," she said, without a moment's hesitation. So he did. The intimate details were very much to her liking. She enjoyed being this character, though it made her wonder about her own real life approach to intimacy. It had always seemed … too distant. A chasm that was difficult to cross. How do you ever get started? She struggled with this kind of story arc for the characters in her novel. She supposed it was because she had very little experience of her own in this regard. Her concept of physical love was derived from the novels she read. And she had read so many. So she was an expert in fictional love, but a virtual novice in the real thing. Yet she had found intimacy so easy, effortless with Ilya. She suspected he knew a lot more about this than she. And she was enjoying her newfound freedom to engage in this uninhibited pillow talk.

"Do you ever think about intimacy, Iliusha? I mean, how does it work? How do lovers manage to get there?" He had thought about it before. Many times. So he shared what he thought he knew. "I think it is a concept unique to humans. We all have public and private selves – the way we present ourselves to others in social contexts, and what we really think and feel, in our heart of hearts."

"Like the public and private meanings of words?" she wondered.

"Yes, something like that, but separate from the desire to communicate how we really feel. In fact, concealing what we really feel is part of the game. We are all naturally wary of letting others into our private spaces. It's a matter of trust. Mutual affection happens when attraction motivates someone to take a risk, and either invite someone into their private space or let someone in uninvited: emotional, physical, or both. If the invitation is reciprocated, trust develops and you're off and running. If not, you are uniquely exposed and vulnerable. It can be awkward. The same acts of crossing these private boundaries can be seen as inappropriate, crude, or lewd without the invitation, but as intimate with it."

She thought about this for a moment, and how their own relationship had developed over time. Early on, there had been things she wanted to say, or wanted to ask, but couldn't. It's not that she didn't trust him. There was no real negotiation going on. She wanted to trust him, but it had just seemed too early. She supposed the nascent fear of going first was possibly part of it. "So this is what makes us human? This need to negotiate our affection before we can really indulge it? It requires language?"

"Not quite. I don't think language is essential. It might even make things more difficult. All animals have the machinery of attraction and sexual desire hard-wired into their nervous systems at a very fundamental level. Most higher mammals, and especially primates, have the public-private selves regime hard wired into their brains. It's how they operate as social groups. Deception plays a key role. You are constantly trying to decode the private motivations of others, while holding back your own. Makes it easier to manipulate others. Allies are bound together more often by mutual advantage than by blind trust. What makes humans unique is that we have somehow mixed these two systems together — the sexual and the social. We have put attraction and affection on the private side of the divide. We are the only species with sexual modesty. Our romantic unions are inherently private. Think about it! Even the most uninhibited among us prefer closed doors. To the rest of the animal kingdom, these unions are just a normal, public fact of life."

This hit home for Katerinya. "I always thought of myself as too modest – you know, sexually. I thought this was perhaps because of my religious upbringing. I thought this was why I find it difficult to write the romantic scenes in fiction – as if I were embarrassed about what my readers might think of me and my erotic imagination. But I'm not really modest at all, am I? I just regard this imagination as very *private*! It's not really the subject matter that makes me hesitant; it's where it is disclosed. Oh, this makes so much more sense, Iliusha. You don't think I'm too modest, do you?" she asked plaintively, lifting her head to look him in the eyes.

He couldn't help smiling at this under the circumstances. "No, not at all."

This is what she wanted to hear. It's not that she had any doubt now, she just wanted to hear him say it. His expression told her everything she needed to know. She laid her head back down on his shoulder and asked "But how did *we* get here, Iliusha? I don't recall any games, or negotiations, or invitations. It just happened."

"I think we had it easier because emotional intimacy happened first. We are like types, you and I, when it comes to emotional intimacy – and a lot of other things as well. We are unusually open on this channel when we meet someone like ourselves, so it was easy for us to build up emotional trust and then emotional bonds. We recognized what we were getting into as something comfortingly familiar – we knew this person somehow – and we become eager, even overly eager, to share otherwise private aspects of ourselves, because we realized that this other person already understood us at a very fundamental level. You're right, there were no games or negotiations. But there were many silent invitations and acceptances. They just kept flowing. Neither of us offered any resistance. We both implicitly knew we were welcome in the other's private space. Does that sound like a fair accounting of what happened?"

"Yes," she said, with a far off look, remembering the first question he had asked, in the beginning, that she was unable to answer – about why she wanted to help someone like him whom she hardly knew. Now she had an answer.

"We are the idiot-savants of intimacy," he mused. "It is the one thing that we are ridiculously good at in this whole business." Katerinya accepted the characterization without need for further comment. She had finally run out of questions, content with where she was and how the two of them had gotten there. It was a warm and peaceful thought. She soon drifted off to sleep again. Ilya was still awake, listening to her shallow breathing, taking in the homey fragrance of freshly laundered bed linens, and the final fading waves of red glow on the walls. He gently laid her head on the pillow where she would be more comfortable sleeping, and he wouldn't wake her if he moved.

Ilya was not a heavy sleeper. He woke up many times during a typical night's sleep, and could easily be awakened by noises. But he also had no trouble falling back asleep within minutes. Tonight was different. The events of the day were still vying for attention at the back of his mind, pushing each other aside, jostling for the front position. Katerinya had put a quilt over the comforter when they first got into bed, neither of them being familiar with the body heat generated by a sleeping companion. They soon discovered this, so she had thrown the quilt off to the foot of the bed. It was now colder with the fire down, and he was contemplating getting up. So he slipped out of the covers on his side of the bed, and pulled the quilt up over her. Then he looked in the wooden trunk at the foot of the bed where she had kept the quilt and found another. He draped this around himself and tiptoed into the front room.

The wind had died down now, the snow had tapered off, and the front room was now bathed in moonlight. This is good, he thought. He wouldn't need to turn on a light. He sat down at her desk and turned on her computer. As he expected, she didn't use a password, so he had no trouble getting on the Internet. This was probably OK because it only exposed her to rogue access from someone physically sitting in this chair. There was no chance of a remote logon. Two concerns had tied for first place in the battle for his attention. One was the possibility that the message in DNA might be in the *Y. pestis modernis* genome itself. This seemed like a long shot without an alternate reading key because the message would have to be somehow meaningful in the amino acid language itself. That didn't seem likely, and lately he had become very familiar with the bacterium's protein sequences without noticing any double meaning.

The other concern was what happened to Stepanov. He began scanning news sites looking for any mention of the incident. He knew this was unlikely because it had happened in a remote area, and it would certainly not be publicized by Tarasov's regime. When this yielded nothing, he moved on to the encrypted archives of the academic's "listening" network. Perhaps someone will have heard something. They had. Stepanov was alive! He had been wounded in the leg by the single gunshot, not killed. He was now in prison. That was not necessarily the best outcome, Ilya thought. He may be tortured there to disclose his contacts on Sokolov's side.

Then he heard Katerinya call out his name. She had awakened and found him missing. "In the front room," he called back. She came to the doorway and saw him at the computer. "I couldn't sleep," he explained. Standing in the doorway, in the moonlight, with nothing on, she was beginning to shiver, so she hurried over to the desk and snuggled inside the quilt with him. "Stepanov is alive," he told her. "He was only wounded."

"Oh, that's such good news, isn't it Iliusha?" Well, sort of, he thought to himself. He didn't want to burden her with the next possibility, so he just said "Yes." "Are you done?" she asked. He could see that she would like him to be, so to this he also said, "Yes." "Good," she said. "Come back to bed with me and I'll tell you my dream."

§

The next morning, they slept in. It had been an exhausting night. During Ilya's occasional wakings, he was aware that the sun was up, because of the bright glow emanating from the doorway to the front room. The windows out there were south-facing, so the low trajectory of the sun in the winter sky bathed it in light. The bedroom had a west-facing window, so the room was not overly illuminated, even with the ambient white reflection from the snow. Normally, an already risen sun would signal an impending obligation to get up already — things to do, places to go, people to see. But on this morning, he could bask in the complete absence of responsibility. There was nowhere to go but here. There was no one to see but Katerinya. Everything was already in its proper place. So he drifted back to sleep.

When Katerinya finally stirred, he woke up for the final time. She felt a little more impending responsibility than Ilya, since she now had a house guest, and that meant her morning routine would need to be adjusted a little. Things to put away, things to get out, things to prepare. Still, she caught a little of Ilya's lethargy and lingered awhile. Her guest would understand. She was sure of it.

When they finally started their day, Katerinya checked her stores to see how long they could last before going outside again. She figured they had enough food for at least three days, maybe more. It was such a luxury to be able to put things off indefinitely. They were officially quarantining, after all, so they had an obligation to stay right where they were. They had permission to withdraw from the world outside — for a while. This suited them just fine, so they took their time over their already belated breakfast and let it evolve into a brunch. Katerinya had already learned from their dining experience in Solinovsk that Ilya liked his coffee black – as dark a roast as you can muster.

Their initial conversations followed this same agenda at first – none. It was all inwardly focused, exploring the ins and outs of being the two people they cared about most. There wasn't much to plan for concerning the coming week, since they were not expected to produce any output, but Ilya suggested, and Katerinya agreed, that they should make an effort to get *something* done – she to work on her novel a little and he to do some of what he always did: work on problems in his head (there was only one computer). She did have some translation work she could do, but it was not due for some time, so she thought it much more appropriate, under the circumstances, to do what it was that she really enjoyed. She normally allotted herself only one day a week for writing. Now she granted herself the entire week.

Eventually they got around to projecting themselves back into the world. "Do you have any plans for the holidays?" she asked. "No, none," he replied. Then he qualified his answer. "Well, I *had* none. I've gotten used to spending the holidays alone, but now I suppose I have someone to spend them with." She smiled at that thought. She hadn't thought about her own non-plans yet either. It would be different now.

"One of the few benefits of spending the holidays alone is that you don't have to prepare for it. It's just another day," Ilya said.

"But don't you feel lonely all by yourself when everyone else is home celebrating with their families? That is the purpose, isn't it?"

"But I would feel more lonely if I *was* trying to celebrate. If it's just another day, I won't miss it as much. I didn't even put up a Crispness tree last year. There are plenty of Crispness trees all over Derazhne, so I can get in the spirit when I'm out and about. I suppose the public crowds are my virtual family, so I'm vicariously celebrating with them." Then he reflected on the fact that he still couldn't recall whether he *had* any living family. He recalled no family Crispness gatherings.

Katerinya had become attuned to these periodic episodes when he reflected on his missing family. She knew where his thoughts were, so she reached out to give him a lifeline. "Still can't remember your family, Iliusha?" she offered in a comforting tone.

"No," he said wistfully. Then his mood brightened, and he flashed a half-smile. "But I suppose you are my family now. We will be home for the holidays this year, one way or another – either at your place or mine."

She reached across the table to place her hand on his, smiling silently. "And you are my family now. I feel that same alienation every year when Crispness comes around, alone and an orphan, but I never fail to put up a tree! We will put up a Crispness tree, won't we Iliusha? Either your place or mine?"

"Absolutely! We'll put one up in both places." Now they were in a more upbeat mood. "Why is the holiday called 'Crispness' anyway?" she wondered, figuring that Ilya usually knew the answer to questions like these.

He only knew what he'd heard from Maksim Klavaevich. "Professor Egorov says the holiday is a carryover of traditional winter solstice celebrations from many ancient northern cultures. That's why the symbols and rituals are dominated by winter – in particular fir trees and snow. 'Crispness' probably derives from the feel of the snow, and the cold air, and scent of conifer forests. But nobody really knows for sure. Ironically, the first known solstice celebration was the ancient Roman Saturnalia. They would have said something like 'Io Io Saturnalia,' rather than 'Merry Crispness,' like we do. And now, of course, it is worldwide, so the southern hemisphere cultures – and the Africans! – are essentially celebrating the crispness of snow and fur trees."

"You're right!" she said. "Crispness is very big in Africa! We see it all the time in their movies. I never thought about the ironic non-connection to snow! And, like everything else African, it's very commercial. Too commercial, many people here say. They claim that the commercialization of Crispness drowns out the traditional meaning of returning home to your family for the feast. But I think this is hypocritical. People really do enjoy the commercial aspect, and merchants rely on it to make a profit for the year."

"Egorov says the returning-home-for-the-family-feast aspect is probably derived from a different holiday that got merged with Crispness somewhere in the past. There is an ancient myth about the 'First Feast of Steven.' Like all myths, it is probably an idealization of some actual event, raised to heroic proportions by retelling. According to the legend, there was a famous saint named Niklaus who brought the rich and the poor together for a common feast on Crispness Eve. The joint burning of a Yule Log was supposed to symbolize this bond, and help alleviate class warfare. Of course the good vibes rarely lasted for the rest of the year. Somehow the concept of this feast got translated into something you recreate with your family every year on Crispness Eve."

"Is that where turkey and stuffing and mashed potatoes and cranberry sauce comes from?" she asked.

He smiled. "Well, that's what the legend says, of course, but no one has any idea what was served at the First Feast of Steven, or even whether there even was one."

They had managed to burn up an entire half day at this point. It was now early afternoon, but they harbored no remorse for their inactivity. In fact, they were proud of their non-effort. The time was theirs to burn. But with only an afternoon left, they felt the need to redeem their earlier promise to get *something* done. So they cleared the table, washed the dishes, then divvied up the workspace. There was only one computer between them, so someone had to go first. Katerinya offered it to Ilya, because she knew much of his research was on the Internet. But he offered it right back because she really couldn't continue her novel without her computer. He still had his African-spec cell phone, and could do some work on the budding security app that would allow folks to communicate without government eavesdropping. This seemed like a fair tradeoff, so she retired to her desk, and he to the rocking chair by the fireplace. He turned the chair 90 degrees so that they could see each other. It just seemed friendlier that way.

When Katerinya was last working on the novel, she had just introduced a scene between two minor characters, Sergei and Vanya. She had introduced Vanya earlier, but Sergei was new. They had just met. They were incidental to the story line at this point, but she had plans to possibly develop them more later. This often happened, she found. She would create inessential characters to help move the plot along, almost as throwaways, then find herself fleshing them out later as they grew on her. The plan was for them to exhibit some mutual attraction at their first meeting – nothing deep. Just enough to pique the reader's attention. A standard, early flirting kind of behavior, not really courting yet. She didn't plan for it to go anywhere, but that all depended on how she wrote the scene.

The classic "write what you know" directive wasn't very helpful here, because she hadn't had much actual experience at courting behavior. All she knew was what she read in others' novels or watched in movies. Her romantic imagination was now dominated by her relationship with Ilya. She did indeed know more about the ways of love now, but it was all very concentrated in one particular outcome. She didn't want to tap into this yet. It was still immature, and it was very private. She was not sure she would ever feel comfortable describing this to others. Besides, it didn't really help; she had skipped right over the public game of courtship to the end state; she still knew nothing about this personally. Also, she wasn't sure she wanted these two characters to end up as soul mates like she and Ilya. They weren't necessarily supposed to succeed. This was supposed to be an ordinary slice of life. She started to write several times, each time stopping, erasing what she had written, and staring at the screen again.

Ilya noticed her frustration behavior, so he asked about it. She didn't want to take him away from his work, she said. "Please, take me away," he offered.

He probably had a lot more experience at this than she did, she thought, though he couldn't remember a lot of what he had experienced. She wondered if this might make things more difficult for him. Or, it might help, by providing memory triggers. Either way, he just seemed to know things. When asked, he rarely disappoints. So she indulged. "I'm stuck writing a scene about two people meeting for the first time and ... showing some attraction – you know, the whole public self to public self negotiation business you were talking about, while hiding your true feelings. I don't want it to sound like a cliché. I want to give the reader some insight into the public/private divide ... but my imagination is failing me. I guess I just don't have enough experience to really understand it. Can you help?"

"I'll try," he said. "I think everything begins with attraction. That's easy enough to understand. You don't really have to think about this, it just happens. You're either attracted to someone or you're not. But if you are attracted to someone, you probably hope the feeling is mutual. But how do you find out without giving away your own attraction? You might already have done that inadvertently, so you're exposed. That's where flirting comes in, I think. You advertise the *possibility* of your attraction with coy behavior, trying to stimulate the other person into revealing theirs. If they are interested but cautious, they will probably respond with flirting behavior as well. You both still have plausible deniability about your true intent, but at least you've now reached a milestone. You are both willing to negotiate, to play the game. On the other hand, if the object of your attraction doesn't respond to flirting, then no harm, no foul. You were just flirting after all."

She found this fascinating. It explained flirting as rational negotiating behavior. "How did you learn this?" she asked. "Are you a flirter?"

"No," he said, "that's not my style." He somehow knew this instinctively, but just to be sure, he paused to check his memory. Could he ever recall having flirted? No, that wasn't his style. "I just observe other people around me, as well as read novels and watch movies. I have the same evidence as everyone else; I'm just, apparently, more interested in figuring out why people do what they do. Does my theory make sense?"

"Yes, it does," she said, smiling. "So the whole negotiation process begins with flirting?"

"We'll not always," he said. "Flirting is just a safe way to get to mutual attraction. You're hoping to get to mutual *affection*. One-way affection is hard to sustain (that's really attraction). Mutual attraction becomes mutual affection when transient miracles of timing allow it to happen to two people at about the same time. Then affection begets affection in a reverberating feedback loop. You pierce the veil of private feelings. How you feel about me influences how I feel about you. But you have to be really lucky to get this timing right."

"Then how do people get there," she asked.

"They often don't," he replied. "I think failures are much more common than successes. Look around you. How many truly happy couples do you know who are still in their first relationship?" She found this depressing, but true. "I think we go about it the wrong way," he said. "Dating. That's the standard method for exploring relationships. It's an implicit contract between two people to explore a trial period of simulated affection to see if the real thing develops. There is tremendous pressure to succeed, so each side presents what they consider to be their most appealing qualities. They project the public persona they think will most attract the other. They put up with behaviors that used to annoy them. They feign interest in things that bore them. It's advertising, and almost always involves overselling. You are exhibiting a person that you may or may not be in real life. Deception is hard to avoid. You have the added pressures of family and friends, as well as your own sense of self worth. Am I getting my true mate-market value in this transaction? So in the end, it is a transaction, negotiated on the public side by each party buying in to what the other is selling. You talk yourself into affection for the person you hope this will be. There never was a proper meeting of the private personas. At first, physical attraction keeps things going, but over time you realize that your affection was for an ideal concept, not a real person."

Now Katerinya was really depressed. As much as she hated to admit it, the whole scenario seemed to ring true. She did not want to explore this kind of relationship with Sergei and Vanya. "But what do you do, Iliusha, if you don't flirt and you don't date?" As she said this, she tried to review in her mind what he had done with their relationship. And again, nothing stood out. It just seemed to unfold, without any real effort on either of their parts.

"I suppose I'm just more cautious. I start with friendships. I especially enjoy friendships with women because they can often be ambiguous in ways they cannot be with men. The line between filial and romantic affection can be blurred with women because either side of the line is an acceptable kind of relationship. You don't even have to say – or know – where you are on this continuum. Sometimes it is this very ambiguity that makes the relationship so special. Over time, these things sort themselves out and you end up as either just-friends, which is the most common, or friends-and-lovers, which is rare, but never just-lovers."

She was grateful to be in the rare bucket. But then she wondered just how rare? Had he had some of these friends-and-lovers relationships before? She thought it was likely, even if he couldn't remember any. He was a very attractive man, after all, and clearly a man of great worldly experience. But she didn't want to ask him. She decided she didn't want to know, even if he could remember. The past was past. There would be a time for that later – much later she hoped. For now, she could imagine herself being the only one in that bucket.

§

Their second day in the Tallinnskaya Street sanctuary was a little more purposeful than the first. They were still under the heady spell of limitless affection, and the freedom to indulge it whenever they wished, but a pattern was beginning to emerge. Katerinya would get the computer in the morning for writing, and Ilya in the afternoon for Internet research – and general keeping up with the world.

On this morning, Ilya suited up in his winter gear for a brief reconnaissance mission around the perimeter of the house. The blizzard from the first night had deepened the snowdrifts and covered Ilya's previous tracks from his approach to the house through the back woodlot. Now he would be able to tell if anyone had approached 10 Tallinnskaya Street since. The only discernible tracks emanated from the front door, so this was likely the downstairs tenants. He made a second trek into the birch woods, to check for tracks there. He found none, at least none left by humans. There were some small rodent tracks indicating squirrels. He pushed on deep into the woods as far as he could, looking for wolf tracks. He was hoping to determine how far away the pack had been from the house when he and Katerinya heard the howling on the first night. He was also hoping to determine the size of the pack. But he found nothing. This was good news, he thought. They must have been far away.

When he got back to the base of the rear staircase, he forced open the frozen door to the woodshed. They had already exhausted Katerinya's inside supply of firewood with their many cheery blazes on both sides of the chimney wall. The supply here of both kindling and split logs was also exhausted, so he found the axe, and the chopping block, and began the woodsman's splitting routine. This was a familiar skill and process to him, though he couldn't recall any specific memory of being in a woodshed. He clearly must have been in his deeper past. He knew the wood splitter's saying "wood warms you twice." Once when you split it and once when you burn it. He was now on the first part, so he took off his sabovar, knowing he would otherwise overheat, found the splitting maul, and began splitting the larger logs. You start by using the blade of the axe to sink a deep cut into the middle of the crosscut grain of the cut log segment. Then you insert the wedge end of the metal splitting maul into the cut, tamping it in with the back of the axe. Then you stand back and take a big swing with the back of the axe onto the maul head. Often, one well-placed blow will split the log right down the middle on the first hit. As expected, he heated right up from the effort. He finished by fine-splitting a new supply of kindling – some to take up to the apartment and some to replenish the stored supply in the shed.

When he reached the backdoor at the top of the stairway, sabovar flung over his shoulder, and clutching the new fuel supply in the canvas wood carrier, Katerinya greeted her newfound lumberjack with a hug. "Iliusha, why aren't you wearing your sabovar?" "Do I feel cold to you?" he replied. No, she had to admit, he didn't. She was not familiar with the wood slitting routine. A man from the first floor tenants always did it. "Well, I split enough for everyone," Ilya said. "I think they will be surprised!" she said. "They'll know it wasn't me!"

The morning was still young, and the computer still Katerinya's. Ilya was feeling the need to find out what was happening in the outside world. He didn't want to wait for his turn at the computer in the afternoon. Then he came up with an idea. "Isn't there a library in town, Katya?" he asked. "Yes," she said. "And do they have public Internet terminals?" "Yes!" she said, now onto his plan. "That's a great idea!" She gave him directions and he was soon on his way. At the library, he got in touch with his colleagues at the University, explaining his absence due to the quarantine. He expected to be back by the start of next week if all went well, he said. Already it appeared that the new antibiotic was having the desired effect on the stricken patients at the hospital. There were no new deaths, and no new cases had been reported. He asked about the news surrounding Stepanov's capture, but there was nothing to report, they said.

While he was out, Katerinya resumed her writing. It was going a little better than the day before. Ideas were falling into place; dialogs were flowing in the direction she intended. Then she reached a point where her imagination stalled. How to make this next transition? What did other writers do at a similar point in the story? She remembered a novel that she had read in high school, one that left a lasting impression on her. There was a point in that story like this. How was it dealt with? It had been too long ago to remember the details of the prose, but now rereading that part seemed like the obvious thing to do. She got up from the desk and went looking through her large expanse of bookshelves. She didn't really have any scheme for organizing her books. They had just come out of the packing boxes and gone straight to the shelves in bunches when she first moved to Tallinnskaya Street. When she acquired new books, they just landed in the first open slot. So she had to scan all of the spines, looking for the title. She couldn't find it.

Then she remembered that she had a small bookcase in the bedroom. It's not that these were books for reading at bedtime, they were just other books. That bookcase also had no designed role in the organizational scheme. It served as the overflow location when the front room was full. She started scanning titles in there when she came across her Bible. It was odd to encounter it now, she thought. It had been given to her as a child, but she had never read from it much. It had just happened to tag along as a member of her book collection as she moved from place to place over the years.

She sat on the trunk at the foot of the bed and began flipping through pages. Genesis was about how she remembered it – one of the few books she actually had read before. She opened to random other books and read some samples. As a child, this whole volume had possessed a patina of holiness, the sacred wisdom of the ages. She had been primed to see whatever she encountered there as dripping with solemn meaning. Now the texts seemed ordinary, parochial, random even. There was no organization or overriding theme to the volume. It was a collection of somewhat related histories and prophesies, obviously written by different authors in different times – a far cry from the venerated masterpiece that allegedly flowed from God's quill in a single bout of revelation.

She noticed the slightly unkempt arrangement of the quilt and the pillows on the bed. It occurred to her that she really ought to change the bed linens. They were getting a lot more use with two lovers sharing them. So she put the Bible on the bed, opened the trunk, and pulled out a fresh set of sheets and pillowcases. Then she moved the Bible back to the top of the trunk, and proceeded to strip the bed, change the linens, and put the quilt back on in a proper, balanced sort of way. There, that looked better, she thought. After putting the old linens in the laundry basket, she backed up, sitting on the trunk again to admire her handiwork.

She inadvertently sat on the Bible. She had forgotten that she left it there. When she picked it up, she remembered the early Brandenburg Bible that she had seen at the University library on her last trip to Derazhne – how she hadn't recalled most of the books of the Bible there either, even from its explicit table of contents. Then she remembered one name that had stood out: Songs of Songs. She had no idea what that book was about, never having heard it mentioned before in church. Her curiosity now piqued, she searched for it in her present Bible. Eventually she found it. It was called 1st

Songs of Songs. Why 1st? Was there a 2nd Songs of Songs somewhere? She began reading some of the chapters. She was surprised. Her concepts of the Biblical books she never read were couched in the children's stories she had been taught in Sunday school. But she had never heard *these* stories! Not quite the things you would tell to children. The chapters were not stories, but *poetry* – intimate at times. She was moved – a little stirred. Just then, she heard the key turn in the lock at the backdoor. Ilya was back! She mindlessly dropped the Bible on the trunk and hurried out to greet him again.

He related the non-news from the Internet, but noted that the citizens of Mariankursk appeared to be taking the regional quarantine seriously. Few people were out on the streets, and everyone was masked – including himself. Perhaps we were turning the corner, he said, relating the news from his morning conversation with the young doctor at the hospital – no new deaths, no new cases, and patients recovering at a steady rate. It was now about lunchtime, so Katerinya realized her writing was probably done for the day. She had lost track of her original literature search when she got distracted in the bedroom. She'd had a productive morning of it, so she could call it a victory for the day. Besides, since Ilya got his Internet fix in the morning, perhaps he would cede her some computer time in the afternoon.

Over lunch, they began discussing what it would be like to be back out in the world next week – this time as a couple. She was looking forward to returning to Derazhne and seeing what his house there must be like. She also looked forward to hanging out at the University again. She recounted for him the details of her morning tour on the last trip, because she had never really told him about it at the time – given that her presence then was colored by the return of the fleur-de-lis book. She covered all of the high points: the Brandenburg Bible, the Zimmerman folio, the Lorem Ipsum document, the Trinity Statues. "I know you are such a Zimmerman fan, so the folio seemed almost like a personal pilgrimage to me," she said.

He smiled. "Yes, I guess you know me pretty well, Katya. But, ironically, I've never been to the rare book library to view the folio. I always thought of it as too much of a tourist attraction. When you live in the museum – the whole University is a kind of museum – you come to regard the individual exhibits as just part of the landscape."

"You haven't seen any of these exhibits?" she wondered.

"I have been to see the Trinity Statues," he replied. "More than once. They are a genuine piece of archaeology that links the University to its ancient past, though I don't favor the 'Trinity' interpretation. What tourists don't see, though archaeologists do, is the many instance of the 'Veritas' inscriptions that have been recovered from all over the campus. You might have seen one. It's a shield with three open books on it, and the syllables 'VE,' 'RI,' and 'TAS' written on them. Truth! I prefer to believe that the University was originally founded on this simple proposition of seeking the truth. Wouldn't that be a noble mission? But I suppose it is more likely that it was founded to 'seek the truth' a la the old billboard at the Derazhne/Solinovsk bridge – likely 'religious truth' given the 'Trinity Statues' interpretation."

"I thought – according to you – that scientists didn't have favorite interpretations. You are only supposed to care about what's actually true, not what you would like to be true?"

"Yes," he said, smiling, "that is what we say. But we are still human. We have favorites like everybody else. You can indulge your favorites when the evidence is too scant to make any interpretation the most likely one. It's not science anymore at that point. It's myth. Both interpretations of 'Veritas' are probably myths."

"So, you're allowed to have your favorite myths!" she announced.

"Yes, why not? I have to agree with Andzhelina Gullovna on this point. I don't believe you know her. She's a friend and colleague of mine in the literature department at the University. Professor Andzhelina Gullovna Berghild. Not surprisingly, she's a renowned Zimmerman scholar, so we see eye to eye on a lot of things. She's not really religious, but she believes in mystery, she says. She loves myth. Now I understand her point of view a little better. I would very much like to believe that a certain myth is true."

"Is she one of those women friends – the kind you have an ambiguous relationship with? Should I be worried?"

He smiled. "No … she is attractive enough, I supposed, but we are different enough that we've never developed any serious emotional bonds – not like you and I. Besides, I don't think you have to worry about rivals – that's both a romantic statement and a realistic one. Realistically, I find it hard to imagine anyone getting as close to me as you have. And romantically … it's what I *want* to believe, in spite of any evidence. I will freely own up to this. You've tripped up the scientist again. How about you? Any rivals I need to worry about?"

She hadn't expected the question to come back. "I've never had a serious relationship before, with anyone."

"No attractions?"

She thought about this for a moment. "Well, maybe a crush on a professor when I was at Karlsruhe. I must have a thing for professors" she added with a sly smile. "But in Mariankursk, there are just too few people to meet. I'm afraid I've lived a lot of my romantic life in novels so far."

§

Later that evening, when the front room fire had burned down, Ilya started the overnight fire in the bedroom for the night. When they got into bed, the room was still a little cold, so Katerinya fetched some nanoprene crystals, crushed them, and spread them between the sheets – the 41st century version of the ancient hot water bottle. She cuddled up close to stay warm. Ilya picked up the scent of fresh linens. He complimented her on her handiwork. She was glad he noticed. Then he spied her Bible lying on the trunk at the foot of the bed. Being hyperopic, he could read the words "Holy Bible" on the cover, but even if he couldn't, he knew it was a Bible. They have a characteristic cover, with gilt-edged pages and a red ribbon for a bookmark. "You read the Bible before bed?" he asked in jest. He didn't think for a minute that she did, figuring she would get the sarcasm. "Oh," she said, "I forgot about that! I found it today when I was looking for another book. Haven't seen it in ages. Forgot I had one. Have you ever read Songs of Songs, Iliusha?"

"No, but I know of it. It's kind of the odd one out in the Biblical canon, isn't it? A kind of lighter weight interlude wedged in between the serious business of the Old and New Testaments. It's poetry, I believe."

"It's not just poetry!" she said. "And I wouldn't call it 'lighter weight.' It's intimate poetry. I stumbled on it and was reading it this morning." She jumped out of bed, despite the cold, and hurried to fetch it. Then slid back under the covers and cuddled up to read to him.

> *Well I heard there was a secret chord*
> *That David played, and it pleased the Lord*
> *But you don't really care for music, do you?*
> *Well it goes like this*
> *The fourth, the fifth*
> *The minor fall and the major lift*
> *The baffled king composing Hallelujah*
>
> *Well your faith was strong but you needed proof*
> *You saw her bathing on the roof*
> *Her beauty and the moonlight overthrew you*

She tied you to her kitchen chair
And she broke your throne and she cut your hair
And from your lips she drew the Hallelujah

Well baby I've been here before
I've seen this room and I've walked this floor
I used to live alone before I knew you
I've seen your flag on the marble arch
Love is not a victory march
It's a cold and it's a broken Hallelujah

Well there was a time when you let me know
What's really going on below
But now you never show that to me do you?
And remember when I moved in you?
And the holy dove was moving too
And every breath we drew was Hallelujah

Ilya was astounded. He'd have to read this book of the Bible for himself. This particular chapter was Katerinya's second reading, and as she reflected on it, she found herself trying to come to terms with its import. It evoked a dying, or perhaps already lost love, still entangled with vivid memories from its better days. She was still in the thrall of the blissful blindness of a first love herself, so this was not an outcome she could even imagine for the two of them. But it happens, of course. So her questions, issued with a far off, contemplative look, concerned more how it happens to other people, less fortunate than themselves.

"Why do you think relationships fail, Iliusha?" she asked. "Do you ever think about that? Why do lovers eventually grow tired of each other?"

He had thought about that, of course, because that's what he does. He thinks about things. But he needed to be careful how he would respond this time, because he and Katerinya were not on the same footing. He knew he was her first, but in all likelihood she was not his first. He could not specifically recall any intimate relationships in his previous 20-year span, but his memory, as we know, was problematic. Still, he intuitively knew what she must be feeling, as if he had been there once himself. He also had a worldly, visceral sense of having been through the development and maturation of such a relationship, or perhaps more than one of them. It was too difficult to discern about the plural case. Perhaps only one was actually his, and the others were ones he had observed.

He was vicariously reliving the first-love experience through her, sharing that unfounded certainty that it could last forever. But he had something she did not at this point – this amorphous sense of how it could eventually turn out. And it turned out very well for him. He felt. He couldn't actually remember an ending. But if it had turned out well, why had he been alone for the past 20 years? He and Katerinya were at that stage where you want to share everything, hold back nothing. But he could not share what he could not remember. So instead he shared this acquired, worldly knowledge, without being at all specific about how he had acquired it. He wasn't keeping secrets from her. He had no secrets to keep.

"Do you recall what I told you when we first met – about me not wanting to travel solo?"

"Yes. You wanted to share the experience with someone else. You wanted to experience it with them, because describing it later to someone else who was not there was not the same thing."

"That's right. You don't even need to say something about what you are jointly experiencing if it's impressive enough – like a gorgeous sunset. Just watching each other's reaction lets you know that you are sharing an experience with someone else in a way that no one else will see quite the same way. It's the sunset, plus your joint reaction to the sunset. It binds a little piece of your private lives together in a way that will remain forever private. It becomes a shared secret. Not because you guard it, but because no one can possibly have this same joint experience that you had. It makes the two of you a little more unique as a pair.

Love is like that, I think. On the way to falling in love, you share more and more of your private emotions in the contexts of the events you are experiencing together, creating unique emotional bonds that no one else will ever be able to experience in quite the same way. It defines you as a couple apart from all other people – an us against the world feeling."

She liked where this was going. But he hadn't really answered her questions yet. She suspected he had more to say. So she prompted him. "So why do you think this isn't enough to keep couples together? You know, *some* couples. The ones that don't last." (She was exempting Ilya and herself.)

He let this marinate a bit, to give him a chance to turn more of his non-specific memory/feelings into words. He was eventually able to form a conclusion. "I think it has to do with growth – or more to the point, lack of growth. The falling in love process creates a steady stream of new, shared emotions. You get a little addicted to the constant accumulation. The first sex can be tremendously addictive, both emotionally and physically. Nature provides a big assist for humans, with a rush of powerful pair-bonding hormones. The extreme emotional intimacy creates an illusion of exclusivity – as if your shared sexual experience could not possibly be duplicated with anyone else. That's a lot of interpersonal growth, packed into a relatively short timeframe. It's exciting!

But these initial boosters don't last. There aren't that many ways to innovate in your sexual experiences. They have their own repeatable rewards, but you fall into routines. You can look back fondly on the earlier times, but there's no room for growth going forward. So if sex is all you have, you're in danger of hitting a plateau.

The real opportunity for growth is on the emotional side. If you've initially bonded well here, and you are similar enough in temperament and aspirations and outlook on life, you can continue to grow closer through more mutual discovery – both jointly, by co-discovering things about the world, and individually, by discovering things about your partner – things that you begin to emulate yourself, ideas that you come to adopt as your own. So you continue to be more tightly bound as a couple. Your perception of your partner's physical appearance becomes colored by these endearing intangibles. This is the best defense against the wandering eye. The whole package is just too hard to replicate with anyone else. And it serves you well when physical love begins to slow down with age."

Katerinya liked this even better. But she found it hard to believe that Ilya could know such things without having personally experienced them. So her earlier resolve about not knowing his romantic past began to waiver. How could he not have known – and loved – prior women and still be able to relate insights like this? It sounded like the story of a real (and successful) relationship from start to finish. Katerinya was happy that it was successful. It indicated that Ilya knew how to do this. But if it was successful, where is this woman (or women) now. She didn't know how to gently phrase these questions, but her conflicted position must have been visible on her face.

Ilya picked up on it. He knew what she was dying to ask, so he asked for her. "You're wondering how I can know these things if there were no prior women in my life?"

"Yes …" came dribbling out, accompanied by a sigh of relief. "You don't have to tell me anything you're not comfortable with. We can drop it right here if you wish."

"I asked the same question of myself, and myself had no answer. I agree with you, Katya, that there must have been some women in my past. But I don't remember anything specific about them. There are no faces, no names, no bedrooms, no endearing shared experiences. There must have been these things. But they're gone now…"

Now she was sorry she had asked. From his point of view, this must be a painful memory, or more accurately, a painful non-memory. A pain of loss that can't be comforted by the memories of what was lost. She put her arms around him and said, softly, "I'm sorry. I shouldn't have asked. This must be painful for you."

"No … it's not really painful," he reassured her, "because the past is so utterly blank. It's like so many things we are discovering that I know — like languages and music. I just intuitively seem to know these things. So we infer, no doubt correctly, that there have to be corresponding causes in my past. So whoever this woman, or women, might have been, they are somewhat like my parents to me now. I haven't lost them (that I know of), I've lost my memories of them. It's not really painful, it's just … maddingly unresolved."

§

They managed to make it to their fourth day at 10 Tallinnskaya Street before it became evident that their food supply was running out. Katerinya made a shopping list for Ilya and sent him out into the world. The weather was warmer now, and enough of the snow had melted to make the streets and walkways clear. The streets and walkways were also relatively clear of people, with citizens still observing the quarantine. After a fourth day of no new cases, and all remaining patients well on their way to recovery, Ilya and the doctor at the hospital had decided to lift the masking requirement. There was no significant risk of the disease spreading through breathing. They still hadn't determined the initial local reservoir of the disease, but they appeared to have all the humans infected by it in the hospital ward, so that ruled out any further pneumonic human-to-human spreading. Even if there were rodent or flea vectors still out there, it would not spread through the air.

Ilya paid a visit to the hospital first, to consult with the doctor, then went to the market on his way back. This gave Ragnar plenty of time to observe and finally get his plan right. No more hiding, stalking, chasing. This was clearly not his forte. He waited for Ilya to enter the market, then waited outside the doors to confront him head-to-head when he exited. This worked much better than Ragnar had anticipated because Ilya had never seen him up close, so he didn't recognize him just standing there at close range. He had always been a shady character at some distance, in pursuit. The behavior itself was what had always caused Ilya to flee. When Ilya emerged, Ragnar greeted him with a simple "Professor Koskayin?"

Ilya did not know this man, but he seemed pleasant enough. He was a young man, college-aged it looked like. He had longish, unkempt hair. Not the kind you might see on a panhandler on the street corner, but more of an intentional, nerdish look you might associate with someone who programs in the basement all day. "Yes?" he responded. "You don't know me. My name is Ragnar. Actually you do sort of know me. I've been trying to contact you for some time, but apparently going about it all wrong. You keep running away from me. I mean you no harm, really!" He held up both empty hands as if to drive home the "I come in peace" message. So *this* was his Korihor pursuer, Ilya thought to himself, or rather his non-Korihor pursuer. Or was this perhaps a diversionary tactic, to get him to let his guard down? No, he decided, Ragnar had a very different demeanor than the previous Korihor man, and he did not have any of the tracking skills of the attacker. In fact, he was terrible at it. So he decided to go along. "What can I do for you, Ragnar?"

Ragnar responded very excitedly "Oh … well, I have to ask. Do you have the tattoo on your ankle?" Now Ilya Erynovich was confused. If this was not one of the Korihorians, then there were at least two different parties interested in his fleur-de-lis symbol. Now fully on guard, he played dumb. "What tattoo?" he asked. "The Androsia symbol" came the reply. "The what symbol?" he asked again. "The Androsia symbol! Do you have the tattoo?" Ilya Erynovich had to consider his next move carefully for a moment. His first inclination was to deny that he had any tattoo. Just send Ragnar packing and avoid the whole line of inquiry and pursuit. But there was clearly some public information out there about the tattoo. There would be more Ragnars, and perhaps more Korihorians. And he needed to find out about this new word 'Androsia'. So he removed his left boot, lifted the pant leg, and pointed. "You mean this?"

"Yes!" Ragnar replied, even more excited now. "I knew it! You *are* one of us?"

"One of whom?"

"The Androsians!"

"Who are the Androsians?"

Ragnar seemed suddenly deflated. "You don't know?" he asked incredulously.

"No, I'm afraid I don't."

Ragnar took some time to recover from this. So Koskayin was not one of them. He was sure he had to be. All this way, all that time, for naught. Then he decided to make the best of the situation and at least introduce the group. "The Androsians were a tribe of scientists, well, I guess maybe a mythical tribe of scientists, who survived the Great Dying. That's how the legend goes, anyway. They banded together to try to preserve the scientific record for future generations. The symbol has always been associated with the myth, but there's no known recorded etymology. If you look up 'Androsia' on the Internet you won't find anything. A bunch of us, we're all scientists, like to think of ourselves as the modern descendants of the tribe. I guess you could say we're just fanboys. But we all got the tattoo. See?" He lifted his left pant leg to show a tattoo identical to Ilya's. "There's always been a rumor that someone at Derazhne had the mark. We were sure it was you. But if you're not an Androsian, how did you get the tattoo?"

Ilya Erynovich didn't know, of course. "Oh, I got it at a drunken party one night, years ago. The things you do under the influence of ethanol, eh? Purely a coincidence!" This was enough to send Ragnar off with his tail between his legs. Ilya Erynovich felt sorry to disappoint poor Ragnar, but of course he didn't believe for a minute that his tattoo was a coincidence. All the way back to Katerinya's he mulled the possibilities over in his mind. He thought he had given himself the tattoo, as a private prompt. But if Ragnar and his tribe-ette had the same tattoo, there was something public about this. Was he himself possibly a fanboy back before he could remember? Didn't sound like him. And Ragnar had mentioned no 'written in molecules.' So the message that his own tattoo denoted was still private content, intended specifically for himself.

When he got back to 10 Tallinnskaya Street, he related the new encounter, and its attendant mystery, to Katerinya. "What does it mean?" she asked. "I don't know, but could I have a few minutes of your computer time – to check it out?" he asked. "Of course!" She moved away from her computer and motioned for him to take her place. He entered 'Androsia' as a search term on the Internet. No results were returned. "Well, he was right about that." "Who was right about what?" she inquired. "Ragnar. He said there was no public meaning associated with 'Androsia' anywhere on the Internet." She could see that now. "So my tattoo represents at least three things, to three different sets of people. One thinks it is the sign of a mythical immortal skeptic, another thinks it denotes symbolic membership in a mythical society of scientists, and I seem to think it stands for 'look for a message written in DNA'. I see no common thread here."

"Well," she offered, "the scientists and the DNA seem related. A lot more so than the Korihor story." "Good point," he said. Then it occurred to her, "Does this account for all of your pursuers now – the Korihor people, the Androsia people, and Tarasov's men?" "Another good point!" he said. "Two out of three of them are now benign." "Oh, I hope so," she said. She wished these people would leave poor Ilya alone already. She still had the Korihorians to worry about, but Ilya was more sanguine. He assumed that most of his recent flights from pursuit were due to Ragnar. They all had a similar incompetence. Tarasov's surveillance never involved chase, and because they were professionals, he had probably not even seen most of them. It now seemed to him likely that that the Korihor incident had been a one-off occurrence; though now he regretted not engaging Ragnar further to confirm him as the source of all of the other chases.

Ilya offered Katerinya her place back at her own computer, and her agreed upon time-share for the rest of the morning, but she was now locked onto the mystery, and wanted him to stay at her computer. She was convinced that scientists and DNA went together somehow. She started referring to the DNA sequence he was looking for as the 'Androsia message.' "Isn't there something you can do on the computer, with codes, to try to find messages in DNA?" He appreciated her enthusiasm, but explained that he had already tried something like this briefly in the middle of the night, on their first night together. He was still missing a key piece – an alternate reading key.

"But isn't there something that cryptographers can do with computers to crack simple codes? Comparing the frequency and position of letters, or something like that?"

"Ah, but that only works if the original message and its decoded meaning use the same alphabet, or at least two different alphabets with the same number of letters. DNA has only four letters: A, C, G, and T; the Latin alphabet has 26. Now interestingly enough, the natural biological meaning of a DNA sequence is a sequence of amino acids that will fold up into a three-dimensional protein. There are 20 of these amino acids, so these two alphabets are also misaligned. Nature gets around this by using three consecutive DNA letters, called codons, to denote one amino acid."

"Couldn't you do something like that too?"

He smiled. "That would mean, essentially, translating the 20 amino acids into 26 letters we could read. It's extremely unlikely that someone has used CRISPR to write a message in amino acids." She interrupted him, "CRISPR?" He was then about to launch into Clustered Regularly Interspaced Short Palindromic Repeats when he caught himself. "A technique for editing DNA. In order not to kill the organism whose DNA you are editing, you would need to write your message in the non-functional portions of the chromosomes, so you don't write over the natural protein coding that makes life work. But if you were inserting new amino acid codes there as well, these regions would start producing random rogue proteins that would also quickly kill the organism. So you can't use the existing language of amino acids. You need some new scheme that translates DNA triples to Latin letters that is completely meaningless to the biology of the organism. That's the part we're missing."

OK, she thought. That makes sense. By now, she had lost her writing muse, so she encouraged Ilya to stay at the computer and do his Internet thing. She went off to the kitchen to unpack the market haul, and put together a lunch. Ilya had done well, she thought. They could probably skate by through the weekend now. He had also bought some wine. That wasn't on the list. And what was this? A package of very dark roast ground coffee. No doubt the darkest roast the market could muster. She was still getting used to his taste in coffee. Left to his own devices, he would use two full scoops of coffee for every one cup of water. She had never tasted such strong coffee, but she had to admit it was not bad. It was growing on her.

Through his Internet news feed, and from the local academic "ears to the ground" network, Ilya learned that Stepanov had escaped from prison. The details were scant. He tried to think of the possible scenarios, though the whole religious/political landscape was muddled for him now. Perhaps Sokolov's men had staged the breakout. But they might have already learned by now that he was a double agent for Tarasov, so he would be persona non grata to them. Maybe the breakout was a ruse by Tarasov to convince the Sokolov side that Stepanov was still their man. A triple agent, as it were. There were just too many permutations of this. Stepanov was still very much an enigma, but Ilya felt some sympathy for him, and was a bit relieved that he had escaped. Imprisonment for espionage would not be a good place for him under the circumstances.

§

In the evening, with the front room fire winding down, Katerinya and Ilya took up a new position for warmth, sitting, facing cross-legged on her love seat, sharing a quilt. She brought her computer on battery power, determined to get in a little more writing. (The muse had returned). He brought her Bible, determined to read the entire 1st Songs of Songs. As she typed away on the keyboard, she would pause now and then for some thought. She wasn't erasing this time, so she was making progress. Ilya noticed no frustration behavior this time.

Eventually one of her pauses lingered for a while as she stared into space at nothing in particular. "What is love, Iliusha?" As he looked up, she snapped out of her contemplation state, realizing how her spontaneous query must have sounded. "I know it sounds like a cliché, but that's just the point. So much of what people say about love, at least in books and movies, sounds like clichés. I know it's a confusion, the source of a lot of drama. They say things like 'Do you love me?' 'Do you really love me?' 'Am I in love?' 'Is this really love?' Everyone wants to know, but nobody is sure how to answer."

"Are Sergei and Vanya asking these questions now?" he asked.

She smiled. "No, not them. It's a different set of characters now. I don't want to write just more clichés, at least not without adding some insight. So I guess I want the characters to fall into these clichés, so the dialog sounds realistic, but the narrator, me, has to do better."

Ilya thought about this for a moment, wondering if this would turn out like the last excursion through his ambiguous memories. But the way Katerinya had phrased it struck him as a point of view that wouldn't require a personal backstory. His impressions on the subject, now springing to mind, easily derived from observing others in recent real life and in media – just the sort of milieu that she was looking for.

"In my experience, love is not a specific state of mind. It's a continuum of affection," he said. "There is no way (nor point) to decide whether you are in it, or out of it. Instead, you have greater or lesser degrees of affection for someone. Love is not a point on this line, it *is* the line. Your affection can deepen, or lessen, or reach a plateau over time. All you can really determine is whether you are moving in the right direction. We regularly make fools of ourselves by declaring love for someone we barely know. I think this happens because we are all inherently optimistic. What we do early on is to fall in love with the *idea* of someone – we imagine a state much further along on the affection continuum, and project where we are now to where we want to be."

"Maybe the point of the word is to establish at least *some* position on the affection line," she offered. "'Do you love me?' means do you have affection for me in your private feelings – a way of cutting through the social games, flushing out a player. Of course it is very easy to lie and say you do. So you're not really going to learn anything with this question. 'I love you' means I have real affection for you in my private feelings. But if you really did, wouldn't your partner already know this by now? I suppose you are right, Iliusha. When you have such deep insight into each other's private space as we do, it's pointless to ask or answer the question. There is nothing new to be discovered. We already know. The phrases don't really add anything." She looked at him, then closed her computer and swung herself around so that she could rest her head on his shoulder. She had nothing more to say.

Chapter 6

VERONIKA'S FINE LADIES' APPAREL

Several weeks later, in Derazhne and Solinovsk, people were scurrying about, preparing for the Crispness Eve celebrations soon to come. Crispness fell on a Monday this year. It was now Thursday. The Crispness trees that were going to go up were up by now, but travel plans were still being finalized for the traditional return-to-your-roots pilgrimage, and stores of frozen turkeys, potatoes, and cranberries were being acquired. But the normally festive holiday mood was overshadowed this year by the political news swirling in and about the towns. Although the key players in the power struggle, Tarasov, Osipov, and Sokolov, had largely managed to keep their nefarious goings-on out of the public eye, information was beginning to leak, rumors were beginning to spread, and verifiable news was beginning to be confirmed. In the far reaches of the Principality, in the north, the south, and particularly the west, there were reports of a renegade army of revolutionaries overrunning arsenals and armories in smaller towns, sometimes holding the towns briefly, but more often leaving with the weapons and other appropriated supplies. They were also said to be commandeering local trains in pursuit of this mobilization effort. They were led, it was said, by a ruthless commander named Kuznetsov.

§

It was a classic guerrilla operation, striking quickly at the fringes where resistance was minimal, then disappearing again into the countryside. No one seemed to know who this Kuznetsov was. The raiders were described as religious zealots, so suspicion naturally fell on Sokolov. This was certainly the odds-on conclusion of Tarasov's regime. Sokolov, however, vehemently denied any association with Kuznetsov, or any knowledge of who he was. Of course, if Sokolov did know him and had sponsored him, this is exactly what he would have said at this point. All Tarasov needed was confirmation of just such an association to take him out.

A little southwest of Derazhne, on a large tract of land next to the small village of Lirovo, this was not the sort of news that Aron Mattson wanted to hear. Mattson was an eternal optimist, an entrepreneur, and devout evangelical, now a faithful member of Sokolov's Church. He had emigrated to the region about 20 years ago. In his native country, he had been a substitute high school science teacher, a tangential brush with actual science that gave him just enough misinformation to regularly get things wrong. He saw his evangelical calling as different than Sokolov's. He was not naturally the fire and brimstone type. There were plenty of those already. He had what he thought was the novel approach of defending the apparent absurdity of the Biblical creation myths with *science!*

He was the ultimate apologist. He had a very simple and secure line of reasoning that went like this. The Bible is the indisputable word of God. So whatever the Bible says is literally true. So it doesn't matter how absurd it sounds; there must always be an explanation for why it is true. His job, his unique calling, was to give scientific explanations for why these things are true. If someone definitively refutes your explanation – by finding a contradiction, say – you go get a new one. There's always another one. It was so simple and obvious, he thought. If the Bible *must* be true, there must always be an explanation that makes it true. If you haven't found it yet, keep looking!

He had watched with great concern, over the years, as popular scientific discoveries had picked off more and more true believers. It started with children, he thought. They teach these things in public schools early on. And then there are the museums and the planetariums, and the documentaries. He thought Osipov's church was approaching this problem all wrong. They were caving in to things like evolution to make themselves relevant to the secular world, but in so doing they had to cast more and more parts of the Bible as allegory. Why would you do this, he thought! You are violating the most basic commandment – the Bible is literally true! It can't possibly be allegory. We need to fight fire with fire. We need our own museums, and planetariums, and documentaries. If we build them, they will come. We need to give the people an alternate source of science education. Then one day it hit him – a theme park! Everybody likes theme parks, kids and grownups alike. Instead of static exhibits in stuffy museums, he could make more "scientific" exhibits to illustrate the truths of the Bible by using audio-animatronic robots and placing them outdoors in a park.

Filled with his version of the Holy Spirit, and Sokolov's blessing – and seed capital – he spent years raising the funds, acquiring cheap land, contracting with tech companies and movie makers, and setting the whole concept in motion. And this was the park's opening day – just in time for the holidays! So he was not pleased about this Kuznetsov fellow raining on his parade. He hoped it would not dampen attendance. But ever the optimist, he reasoned that his park was still far away from the periphery of the empire where the trouble was reportedly occurring, yet still conveniently close to the population centers of the capitol city. Sokolov was supposed to attend the opening, giving his imprimatur, but he had cancelled two days ago because of some "very pressing issues" he said.

Nervous as the father of the bride before an elaborate wedding, Mattson paced back and forth, inspecting this, inspecting that, performing walkthroughs with the guides and staff. He decided to do one last tour of the featured attraction – the Ark – before the guests arrived. The Ark was an elaborate true-to-scale replica of the craft that survived the Great Flood, built according to the Biblical specifications, and named, according to God's direction, the *Preserver of Life*. The frame of the Ark was 200 feet in length, width and height, with a floorspace of one acre. The Ark interior had seven floors, each floor divided into 9 sections. The entrance to the ship was designed so that it could be sealed once everyone was on board. This, of course, would not be necessary because the boat wasn't going anywhere, but it needed to look authentic. Also, for authenticity, the exterior of the Ark was coated with pitch, according to the Biblical specification. Not simulated pitch, but actual pitch. Nothing looked and smelled like the real thing.

The Ark and the Flood were the cornerstones of the Biblical creation story in that they were used as his primary justification for the Universe being only about 8000 years old – and created in 6 days. Every aspect of physics, cosmology, biology, archaeology, and anthropology that posited an older age – 14 billion years for the Universe, for instance – he would counter with the *singularity* explanation. Scientists naively assume that the laws of nature are uniformly continuous, that they work under the same principles, and the same rates of speed, in all places and in all times. That's why radiometric dating and rates of genetic change regularly lead scientists to infer dates much older than the Bible stories. But that's just an assumption! Why do these laws have to be uniform? If, instead, there are discontinuous singularities from time to time that speed up or slow down these rates of change, or even suspend them altogether, then scientific age estimates will be inaccurate. God, of course, can introduce these anomalies whenever he pleases. Why? Who are we to ask why? He wrote it in the Bible! 'Nuf said.

The Flood was God's foundational anomaly, according to Mattson. Before the Flood, the radioactive isotopes of elements decayed at much faster rates than they do now, so things like rocks appear to be much older than they actually are. Before the Flood, the rate of oxidative stress on human tissues was much slower than it is now, so pre-Flood humans lived much longer (almost 1000 years for Methuselah). After the Flood, God continually cranked this up for humans, so life spans continually got shorter. For other organisms, it probably remained the same. Why, you ask? Ask God, not me!

The guides had been well rehearsed to deal with questions like this. As he walked through the floors of the Ark, and past its many animal stalls and cages, he would periodically query the guides to see if they were ready. On this round, they were. For questions without prepared answers, there was a one-size-fits-all answer. He paused in front of one of the guides, playing the role of tourist. "What about the new scientific theory of X that was verified by the new evidence of Y. How do you account for that?" The guide's answer was crisp and to the point: "That's the problem with scientists. They are always having to revise their theories. God created everything perfectly for His own reasons. That's a theory that never needs adjustment." "Well done," Mattson said, "well done."

Satisfied with the interior, he walked back down the boarding planks toward the entrance to the exhibit. He wanted the operator to make one last trail run of the *Parade of Animals*. This was his pièce de résistance. He could see it in his mind ever since he first conceived of the park. His idea was to have robot versions of all of the species of animals walk two by two up the boarding plank into the Ark, waved on by the robots of Noah and his wife, at the start of each day. At the end of the day, the parade would be reversed, recreating the return to dry land after the six day Flood. It was not really feasible to recreate the Ark landing on the mountaintop, but he could arrange to have staff members release first a dove, then a swallow, then a raven. The dove and the swallow would be trained to return to the Ark, but the raven would not.

His contractors informed him that there were two problems with this idea. One concerned the very possibility of recreating the myth at all (he didn't call it a myth, they did). There were just too many animal species to fit in one Ark. And some of the bigger animals, like dinosaurs, wouldn't fit even in twos. He solved this problem with "science." The Bible mentions 'kinds' not species. Kinds are much more general. Horses, zebras, donkeys, etc. were all members of the equus kind. All breeds of dogs, wolves, dingos, etc. were members of the canine kind. You only needed a pair of each kind. He worked and reworked his notion of generic kinds until he got the founding member kinds down to a number that would fit on one Ark. He conveniently left out the millions of marine species, millions upon millions of insects, and the billions of microorganisms. Perhaps God, in His infinite wisdom, had decided that these animals had not sinned like the land vertebrates had, so were not as deserving of annihilation. Every variation of the actual species we see today (again, of the land vertebrates) was descended from these founding kinds, he said – after the Flood. The dinosaur problem he solved by postulating that God, again in His wisdom, would have been smart enough to use infant pairs of the animals – closer to their hatchling sizes.

The other problem, he couldn't solve with science. His contractors pointed out that he had drastically overestimated the current state of the art in robotics. They could make the simple audio-animatronic robots you see in theme parks, but they were stationary. They couldn't walk on their own, and certainly not in any large formation that required awareness of the other robot animals.

They could move their heads and appendages in characteristic motions, and emit characteristic sounds, but that was about it. Mattson had pictured the kind of "robots" he had seen in haunted house amusements. They moved in and out of rooms a little to surprise the customer. Couldn't they do something like that? Those were more mannequins than robots, his contractor said. They move by way of cables in tracks under the floor. Couldn't he do that with the animatronic characters, he asked? The contractor thought for a while, then offered that he was willing to try. First Mattson would have to build his Ark, with its ramps and doors, and animal stalls. Then the contractor would retrofit a cable system that ran under the ground in front of the Ark, then under the planks and stalls, in a continuous loop. The audio-animatronic animals would be hooked to this cable at their bases, and preassembled in the proper order inside a head house at the beginning of the parade. Almost like the cable trolleys of a public transit system. They could also get their power from the metal track holding the cable, like the live third rail in a transit system. Their leg motions might look a little fake as they were being pulled along, but with the movements of the rest of the body, and the sounds, the customers might not really notice. They would know these were robots, after all.

Yes! That's what he wanted, so that's what they built. The animals were stored, hooked to the cable in their proper parade order, inside a very large building with a nondescript exterior, so as not to draw attention to itself. Inside, the operator had a closed circuit TV system to observe the goings-on inside the Ark. The system was programmed to start the parade at opening time, and then reverse the parade at closing time. The operator had a long aluminum footboard beneath his console that he had to press down with his feet in order for the parade to begin – in either direction. This was a kind of safety switch so that the system would not operate the cable without explicit input from the operator. If the operator were to be somehow incapacitated during the parade, the footboard would retract and the system would stop. What could go wrong?

In test runs with the contractor, it was observed that tolerances between the cable and the track were a little close where the track had to make 180-degree turns on it's way up and down floors. The contractor recommended that these junctions be regularly lubricated, daily if possible, to reduce any friction. In today's last test run, Mattson heard a little squeaking at the turns, so he had the staff lubricate them one more time, for good measure.

§

On Friday, back in Derazhne, there was a knock at the door. Professor Diederick Brandt looked up from his desk inside his Divinity School office to see the fresh face of his new advisee, right on time for his first consultation appointment. This was Lukyan Olgaevich Grinin. He had been assigned to Brandt by random draw, as all new first-year students are, but Diederick already knew a little about him. He had been an altar boy for Archbishop Osipov in the years before he was an archbishop. The two had enjoyed a close association when young Grinin was growing up, and Osipov had written a very supportive recommendation for his application to the Divinity School. Diederick had interviewed him last fall as part of the admissions process, and recommended that the school take him. Other than that, he knew little else about him. This would be a chance to get acquainted in greater depth. Diederick glanced down at his calendar to get the student's full name.

"Greetings, Lukyan Olgaevich! Come in; sit down," he said, gesturing toward the chair in front of his desk. "How are you finding Divinity School so far?" As he was taking his seat, Lukyan Olgaevich's eye caught the large stained glass window to his right flanked by dark walnut shelves, and of course, books, books, books. The image perfectly encapsulated his ambition for coming here – the graceful merger of divinity and scholarship. He was already a little like Brandt in this regard, though neither of them knew it – certain about the pursuit of knowledge, but uncertain about eventual ordination.

Lukyan Olgaevich's first inclination was to start by saying innocuous things about how he was enjoying it, and wait for the chance at a deeper conversation to emerge later, but then he overruled himself and went straight to what was really on his mind. He dropped a few innocuous comments as a preface, then related that he was a little surprised about the details of early Church history he was learning here. He had known some of the Church history about the settling on the modern canon of the Bible, but in lectures so far, he had been surprised that there was so much latitude of choice in the early days – so many whole books to choose from. Archbishop Osipov had always made it sound like there was mostly unity among the choosers with a few small variations around the edges.

Ah, thought Diederick, the inevitable first collision of divinity and scholarship. "And which 'whole books' have you encountered so far?" he asked. Brandt reached back to get his *Apocrypha and Pseudepigrapha* volume, but then realized he had loaned it to Koskayin. So he inquired further. "Have you been introduced to the Apocrypha and the Pseudepigrapha then?" Lukyan Olgaevich said he had learned about the existence of both shadow canons, but not yet much about their constituent books. "And what about the Peruvian Texts?" Diederick asked. That had not been covered yet in his church history course, Lukyan Olgaevich said, but he vaguely knew about it from Archbishop Osipov.

"Well, it's not strictly a topic in Church history, because the historical Church knew nothing about the Peruvian Texts. It's a really remarkable topic of *modern* history." Diederick went on to explain the recent discovery of the Tacna texts, and the ancient Jesuit community that maintained them. "The Church spent a couple thousand years justifying the exclusion of the two known shadow canons, then suddenly a whole new batch got dumped on them."

"But I recall Archbishop Osipov saying that the Peruvian Texts vindicated the present canon," Lukyan Olgaevich said. "Well, yes and no," replied Diederick. "Of the books found in *both* the present Bible and the Jesuit texts, the Tacna texts were remarkably similar. But that represents only about a quarter of the Tacna texts. We still have to deal with the other three-quarters! Many people began to wonder if the non-overlap with these ancient texts might invalidate our current understanding of the Bible. It took many years for the original archaeologists to preserve and translate these texts, and since some of the scholars analyzing the texts were Orthodox, rumors began to spread that perhaps the Church was suppressing the evidence because it didn't like what it was finding. When the contents were finally made public, we could see that this criticism had been unfounded."

"Was Jossmit ever mentioned in the Jesuit texts?" Lukyan Olgaevich asked. "No," was Diederick's answer. "Why, is still an active subject of debate. Perhaps you can now contribute to this debate, Lukyan Olgaevich. Welcome to Biblical scholarship!" This was not a task that Lukyan Olgaevich relished at this early juncture in his career. He was still getting his feet wet. He was still taken by surprise at the candor of scholars openly wondering about the provenance of Biblical books. The temporary exemption from blasphemy hadn't settled in yet. He explained this to Professor Brandt. He was having a hard time getting accustomed to scholarly skepticism, even though it appealed to him intellectually. "My advice to you is to take the opportunity while you have it, within these walls," Diederick told him. "You will never find rest if you try to suppress your own questions. You owe it to your faith to give them a good airing out." With this as encouragement, he broached a topic that was on his mind that he had not planned to disclose. "Why do scholars openly question who the authors of the Gospels are?"

Professor Brandt explained that the scholarly consensus was that the Gospels were written by unknown authors, composed around 2068–2110 – nearly a century after the events that they purport to describe. Most New Testament scholars agree, therefore, that these are not eyewitness accounts. They represent instead the beliefs of their communities about what prior alleged eyewitnesses might have seen. There is no written chain of evidence from the time of Jossmit to the time of the current oldest surviving texts. This is not to say they are forgeries, but they are, at best, hearsay. So all four Gospels have questionable provenance.

"But why is there doubt about authorship of the Gospel of Oliver more than the others?" Lukyan Olgaevich asked.

"Ah, the Oliver problem!" Diederick replied. "We call the other three – the Gospels of Brigham, David, and Martin – the 'synoptic' gospels because they all share a substantial portion of not only events described, but also of words and phrases. Textual analysis suggests that Brigham came first, and that David and Martin were derivative works based on Brigham. There were probably several other, intermediary texts that connect the three that are now lost. So there is substantial agreement among the three about what happened, in Jossmit's time, the order in which it happened, and who said what to whom. Oliver, on the other hand, appears to come from an entirely different source, and was likely written much later. It describes different events not found in the three synoptics, and more to the point, it has Jossmit saying things that are not recorded in Brigham, David, and Martin. For instance, Jossmit very rarely speaks of himself in the synoptic gospels, but in Oliver, he is constantly speaking of himself, particularly in statements that begin 'I am.' In the synoptics, Jossmit calls for faith in God; in Oliver, Jossmit calls for faith in himself. The primary message of Jossmit in the synoptics is the Kingdom of God, whereas in Oliver, Jossmit rarely mentions this. In Oliver, Jossmit is always talking about eternal life, but rarely ever in the synoptics. In Oliver, Jossmit turns water into wine, but there's no mention of this in the synoptics. Perhaps the most striking difference is that in the synoptics, Jossmit never mentions the doctrine of original sin, but in Oliver, Jossmit says 'We believe that men will be punished for their own sins, and not for Adam's transgression'.

Now traditionally, this fourth, outlier gospel was attributed to the apostle Oliver, one of the three disciples closest to Jossmit. But the Gospel itself never mentions who the author is, other than the 'disciple whom Jossmit loved.' It never names this disciple, never says that it is Oliver."

"So you are saying this might be a forgery?" Lukyan Olgaevich asked.

Diederick smiled. "Forgery is such a strong word, but whatever is going on here — forgery, adjustment, correction, promotion — it was rampant in the ancient world. It doesn't mean that the texts are not meaningful. They are important to our faith, my faith. We have to try to maintain a balance between what these texts inspire us to believe, and how they were arrived at. The messenger may have been flawed even though the message itself is true. One does not become a believer by a process of logical reasoning, despite what S.K. Fedorov says."

§

On Saturday morning, Ilya and Katerinya slept in. The sky was overcast in Mariankursk, so the south-facing front room at 10 Tallinnskaya Street did not stream much morning light into the bedroom. This made it easier. No sun in the eyes. Ilya was now spending weekends at Katerinya's in Mariankursk. His obligations at the University kept him in Derazhne during the week, but on Friday afternoons he would catch the 17:12 train out of Derazhne for what now seemed like his real home in Mariankursk. It was difficult for him and Katerinya to communicate during the week because of the insecurity of cell phones. They had to resort to the Internet, which meant they had to pre-plan their joint availability. The separation was harder on Katerinya because her work was silent and stationary. No places to go, people to see, classes to teach, like Ilya. It had always been this way for her, of course, but after their first intense week together in such close quarters, her place seemed achingly lonely now. She was always waiting for him at the station with great anticipation each Friday afternoon. The waitress in the station café had begun to regard them as a permanent fixture now – the same heartwarming reunion every Friday when the 18:42 arrived from Derazhne. She didn't know either of their names, or much of their real life story, but she had imagined one in her head. She could imagine that she knew them, and was always happy to see them reunited on Friday, then a little saddened watching their long goodbyes on Sunday evenings.

When Ilya first went to Mariankursk, and even after he had first met Katerinya, he thought of himself as a visitor. He was from Derazhne visiting Mariankursk. Now the tables were turned. He thought of himself as a visitor to Derazhne, returning home to Mariankursk. Katerinya had become, in a very real sense, the family that he had lost. He no longer dwelt on his missing past and whom he might have left behind, or what he might have done, or who he might have been. He had a new anchor for his timeline that began at 10 Tallinnskaya Street. His memory was still improving, but only incrementally. He still could not get past his late pre-Derazhne existence at Ariona. Individual events would reemerge from time to time, but it was becoming clear that he was stuck in the past 20+ years or so. This never seemed to get significantly better. But this no longer bothered him. He was now focused forward – on the future. He might as well have been born a few months ago. Katerinya was his world now. Katerinya was his future.

The bacterial outbreak was effectively over now in Mariankursk, so the quarantine had been lifted. No new cases. All surviving prior cases discharged from the hospital. Still no original vector located, but neither he nor the young doctor were concerned. It also appeared that no one was following him anymore, or at least the ones who might be following him, that he did not see, were officially on his side. One might assume that Ilya Erynovich had nothing left to worry about, but one would be wrong. The rumors about the guerrillas in the outer regions were a concern. Something was afoot there, and he could not connect the dots to figure who was behind this.

Of greater concern was a face-to-face meeting he had had with Prince Tarasov earlier in the week. It was in the same place – a private dining room at the back of Yaroslava's – but this time he was summoned in a less confrontational manner. The Prince had texted him "meet me at Yaroslava's: 12:00." This told Ilya that he had something to discuss that he did not want on the public record. The Prince guessed correctly that Ilya would have no prior obligations at noon. The subject was indeed confidential. He thanked Ilya for the good work in Mariankursk, but asked that he not disclose it publicly yet. He was not asking him to invent an outbreak that wasn't happening, but to not publicly report about one that had ended – yet. "Just radio silence on the matter for now. Can you do that?" the Prince asked. Tarasov's demeanor was, as always, aloof and slightly intimidating as in "I am your Prince. You will do what I say," but also slyly collegial with a subtle smile and raised eyebrow, as in "We are together in this, right Ilya Erynovich?" Ilya went along, under the circumstances, though he remained troubled about what this all meant.

Katerinya had a surprise in mind for Ilya this morning. She tried several times to slip out of bed silently, so as not to wake him. But he was a light sleeper, and each time her movements woke him. She had not figured out the full extent of this yet because their time sleeping together was still young. Each time she would move during the night, still asleep, he would awaken, then fall back to sleep. She had no way of knowing. Sensing that she was not going to escape without his notice, when her next attempt failed she settled on a plan of minimal disclosure. She put her arm over him to keep him from rising and whispered in his ear, "Sleep, Iliusha. I have a surprise for you." He watched her get up and begin to dress. It was not a full dressing, just a camisole top and a Cotswold rose silk robe for warmth. She would be coming back. Then he succumbed to the demi-sleep state once again.

He awoke again when he felt her sit on the bed beside him. She had brought the mirrored tray with the brass siding, hosting a coffee service. When she placed it on the bed between them, she said, "As dark a roast as Mariankursk can muster." He smiled. He had never meant for this phrase to become a meme. Katerinya had spoken with the manager at the local market about his coffee supplier, wondering just how dark a roast was available on the general market. He assured her that there were darker roasts than what he carried, but he doubted enough consumers would buy these to make it worth his while. He did offer to special order some for her if she liked. She liked. She had made it strong, according to Ilya's proportions, and poured Ilya's black, of course. To hers, she added a little milk. She was slowly trending in Ilya's darkest-of-the-dark direction, but this particular brew was the pinnacle of that spectrum, and still a little too strong for her taste.

As they chatted over their morning coffee, Katerinya informed Ilya that this was just the first part of the surprise. There was more. When she got up, she dressed more fully for the day. He liked watching her dress – and undress. She took the tray and service with her toward the kitchen, telling Ilya that he should get dressed and start the fire in the front room. She would be busy with the preparation for a little while longer, she said.

Ilya followed the script, retrieving the day's clothes from his overnight bag, which he had brought from Derazhne last evening. His clothes, and other personal items, were beginning to accumulate here at Katerinya's. On each visit, many came, few left. In the front room fireplace, he had narrowed the flue when the fire had burned down last night, to minimize heat loss from the room. You still needed to leave the flue partially open to keep drawing up the smoke from the dying coals. Now that the ashes were cold, he swept them out, and then opened the flue wide to create an updraft. The kindling was nearly gone – just enough for one more fire – so he made a mental note to split some more on his next trip. They would be going to Derazhne tonight, so this would be the last fire for a while. He had taught Katerinya how to start fires without using crumpled up paper for tinder – nature's method. For kindling and fuel you needed to use hardwoods. They burn longer, with less smoke, and don't coat your chimney shaft with creosote. But softwoods, like pine, make the ideal fire starters if you split the dried trunk segments into fine sticks. The porous grain of the wood, and its high resin content, will catch fire quickly from a lighted match. One or two of these sticks under the hardwood kindling will do the trick.

Once the fire was up and impressively blazing, he realized he had come to the end of his script. Now what? He sat in the rocking chair and waited a bit. Still no Katerinya. He admired the Crispness tree they had put up last weekend in the front corner of the room near the south windows. Katerinya had suggested they get one of the pre-cut ones at the market in town. Ilya still couldn't recall where he had learned his woodsman skills, but he assured her that it would be much better to cut a fresh one of their own from her back woodlot. The ones at the market would have been cut a long time ago and would already be drying out. If they harvested one of their own, it would stay green well past Crispness. She had been about to ask him if he knew how to do such a thing, but then remembered his past skills at wood splitting, wolf tracking, and fire building. Ilya the frontiersman.

He did know how to do such a thing – intuitively. The front part of the woodlot was mostly white birch, but he had seen some conifers, in particular blue spruce, in the deeper part when he had been looking for wolves. So they trekked into the woods last weekend with the axe, Ilya cut one down, then they dragged their prize by the lower branches on either side back through the snow and carried it up the back stairway and into the front room. The trick, Ilya told her, was to select a tree whose weight the two of them could manage. If you picked something too big, you would need a horse to bring it back. He seemed to know this by having made such a mistake in the past, but he didn't remember when. He built a stand for the tree using cross planks and stays so that the base of the trunk could be set in a bucket of water. This would allow water to be absorbed up the trunk via osmosis, keeping it alive longer. Over the past week, when he was in Derazhne, Katerinya had decorated the front room and the bedroom with red bows and bayberry candles, adding to the merry mood.

Still no Katerinya. So he wandered into the kitchen to see what was up. He caught her by surprise. "Oh, Iliusha, not yet! Don't look!" She tried to move in front of what she was working on to block his view, but realized it was too late. So she revealed her project. She was making a traditional Crispness Eve treat that she had learned how to make from her grandmother Grigoreva when she was young. It had been many years since she last helped her grandmother make it for the family on Crispness Eve. Now she wanted to introduce this tradition to her new family – the two of them. They needed some founding traditions of their own, so why not start with this. It was baklava-like, made with ultra-thin layers of buttered dough, honey, nuts, and various "secret ingredients." She was just starting to plate it – or rather, tray it, using her go-to mirrored serving tray. Then she had to add holly leaf decorations around the edges, and thin bayberry candles between sections of the concoction. It was traditional for the man of the house to light the candles, so she invited Ilya to play his part. "Shouldn't we carry it into the front room first, and then light the candles?" he asked. "Oh no. It has to be carried to the waiting guests with the candles already aflame. They also sing a little song, but I've forgotten exactly how it goes."

So Ilya lit the candles and they reenacted at least one of the two traditions. Their ceremony was also a little a-traditional in that this was a Crispness Eve treat, and they were having it for breakfast on the day before Crispness Eve, but that was close enough. They were starting a new family tradition. Ilya set it down on the trunk in front of the fire, and Katerinya arranged their chairs so they could sit next to each other, both with a view of the fireplace and the Crispness tree. To make it a complete breakfast, Katerinya went back to the kitchen to fetch a second coffee service – this one on her backup tray. "Merry Crispness!" they toasted each other with the coffee mugs. It was the perfect breakfast with the two most important elements for starting the day – sugar and caffeine.

§

During the last several weeks, they had been out and about in Mariankursk whenever Ilya was in town, visiting shops and restaurants and enjoying the pleasures of small town country life not far from the safety of their new family homestead. Ilya still thought this was the best home base for Katerinya because it was relatively remote, and it would be harder for harm to find her here than in the large urban center where he plied his trade. So they had avoided Derazhne for now, except for a mid-week visit to put up and decorate a Crispness tree at Ilya's house. He had, after all, promised one in both of their places. There was no lumberjacking this time though. Of necessity, they got it from an urban vendor, and thus availed themselves of the vendor's delivery service, so Ilya took the liberty to choose a larger tree. He did first inspect the trunk's base, and pinched off a few of the needles to estimate how much life it still had left. He also asked the vendor to remove an additional half inch from the base with his bow saw so the tree would absorb more water.

This was also Katerinya's first chance to check out Ilya's house. Her initial impression was "not bad for a bachelor." She hadn't really formed much of an expectation for what she would find. Again, she hadn't seen many real houses of single men. She had only seen them in fiction. There were a lot of clichés on this subject, so she didn't expect to find their realizations here – not at the home of a man who was as far removed from clichés as she could ever have imagined. It was clean enough, she thought, but lived in. It was much lighter than his office. Walnut cornices had given way to straight, white enameled, built-in bookshelves. The walls were mostly white and all of the trim was white, so the many windows made the place perpetually bright. Where some contrast was needed between the walls and the woodwork, he had painted the walls with a light, warm gray that set off the white trim and harmonized well with the hardwood floors. His study/library opened out, through a pair of French doors, to an inviting urban garden in the back yard. There were many planting beds interspersed with red brick walkways, and occasional paths covered in crushed mussel shells. With winter snow still on the ground, she could not tell what was planted there.

Like at her place, there was an abundance of books. Most rooms had at least some built-in shelves, but books found their way onto any available horizontal surface. In the bedroom, the first thing she noticed was the sheets. Their color was a little dark for her taste. Some people prefer darker bed linens because they don't show their use as much between washings. Her inclination went in the opposite direction. She wanted to see the signs of use so that she would be incented to wash them anew. She liked perpetually clean, fresh sheets. I think we'll get some new ones, she said to herself.

Despite the remote safety of Mariankursk, they had decided that they could not live anonymously in their hideaway forever. They had a future to pursue, and that meant reintegrating with the outside world. In the weeks that had passed, safety concerns had abated and they could begin to see their way to being a public couple. So tonight they were going to embark on a weeklong live-in at his house in Derazhne. The anchor for this decision was an invitation Ilya had received to the Kadnikov's annual Crispness Eve party on Sunday evening. This was a very formal and festive affair, given each year by the President of the University and his wife at their expansive home in Derazhne. It was the place to be on Crispness Eve. Ilya was always on the guest list, and always attended, but this year the engraved invitation had come addressed to Professor Ilya Erynovich Koskayin and Guest. They had never done that before, and he had never taken a guest before. This was new. The word must have gotten around. It's not that Katerinya was completely unknown to the faculty – Professor Ekholm knew about her – but Ilya had not expected their relationship to reach all the way to the President. So the rumor of her must already be out, and many of the guests would likely be anticipating their first glimpse.

Katerinya was both flattered and a little intimidated by this. They would not be able to ease their way into a new life in Derazhne – rather it would begin with a full-blown coming out party. She hoped she would be up to it, but another part of her reveled in being the featured attraction. Ilya explained that the guests would be very friendly, for the most part, but it would be very formal. She should bring the most formal dress she had. She didn't know what that would be. There was no obvious candidate, and she was a little in the dark about what might be expected. This was not her kind of social circle, though she was eager to be a part of it.

As she was packing her week's worth of clothes and personal items in the late afternoon, looking around the apartment for things she would need, she kept picking up things to pack and then putting them back. It was only for a week. They were coming back, she kept assuring herself. She had made 10 Tallinnskaya Street into her place, over the years, so it held a part of her identity. She did not want to leave that part of her behind. But it had also become an essential part of the identity of the two of them now, she consoled herself, so Ilya had as much invested in this place as she did. Nothing to fret over. He had it easy in this packing business, she said to herself. He could leave his whole overnight bag here and get along fine without it. And there wasn't that much variation in men's formal attire, so he could just wear what he always wore to the Kadnikov's. She would have to live out of suitcases for a week, and bring along the one dress to best fit an expectation that she was totally unfamiliar with.

With her suitcases packed – two of them – she turned to survey the apartment one more time before they headed out the door for the train station. The fires were out, the flues closed. The Crispness tree lights were off, the candles extinguished. Then the music stand caught her eye. Her cello was safely out of the sun in her bedroom closet. But as she thought of the cello, she suddenly had an idea. "Iliusha, maybe I could take my cello, and we could try to play duets!" The idea came out of nowhere, but he liked it. They had talked about this before, but hadn't tried it yet because their cellos were always in different locations. "Why not? Let's do it!" She dropped the suitcase she was holding and hurried into the bedroom closet to get the cello in its case. The case had straps that she could use to carry it like a backpack. She strapped herself in and headed back for the door. Now seeing her load, Ilya put down his overnight bag and picked up her remaining suitcase. Before Katerinya could protest that she should carry at least one of her own suitcases, he reminded her of how inessential his overnight bag was for where they were going. It would still be here when they got back.

The snow outside was just a dusting now, and the streets were clear. The sun was beginning to set on the western horizon, so they were walking right into the light on their way to the station. The sky was overcast, though, so the light was not oppressive. When they reached the station, Ilya bought two tickets to Derazhne and checked the suitcases and the cello into baggage. The cello case was well built to survive this kind of transit. The café waitress had looked up and saw the whole procession with suitcases and cello, and now the two of them leaving together for the boarding platform – on a Saturday evening! This is new, she thought. Someone plays the cello, and they're taking a trip together to some place! Oh, that's so nice. She would now have to write a new chapter in her mental story of Dmitri and Anna (that's what she had named them). I think they will be happy on this trip, she imagined.

When they finally reached Ilya's house in Derazhne, they set their burdens down on the floor in relief. They were now a little tired from the journey. Ilya carried Katerinya's suitcases into the bedroom and placed them on the bed so she could unpack. She had made a beeline for the bathroom. When she came out, she asked "Iliusha, where are my suitcases?" "In here," he said. She followed the sound of his voice into the bedroom and saw them on the bed. "I have another surprise, for you!" she said. She opened one of the suitcases and pulled out a new set of bed linens she had bought in Mariankursk. She laid them out on the spread so he could see them. They were very pale blue, and contrasted well with the warm gray of the walls. "Very nice!" he said, pleased with her color choice. "We can put them on tomorrow morning." "Oh no we won't," she said. "They're going on right now!" She pulled the suitcases off of the bed and put them in a corner. "I'll unpack tomorrow morning." Then she stripped the bed, almost in delight, and remade it with the new linens. He was inclined to help, but got the sense that this was her pet project, the fulfillment of the surprise, so he let her have her moment.

They went to bed early that night.

§

On Sunday morning, Lukyan Olgaevich Grinin, Professor Brandt's new advisee at the D School, was sitting quietly in a back pew of Archbishop Osipov's parish church, waiting for the service to begin. He had an audience with the Archbishop scheduled for after the service. The Archbishop was a very busy man, so it would be difficult for an ordinary parishioner to find time on his calendar. But Lukyan Olgaevich had a prior relationship with Archbishop Osipov that gave him an inside track. Lukyan Olgaevich had been carrying around his conversation with Professor Brandt in the back of his mind ever since it first occurred. He wanted to discuss some of these things with the Archbishop, but was still composing a proper way to go about it. He was more of an inside man now – more than just a layman – since he was on track to ordination via the Divinity School. But he was pretty certain he could not totally relax the strictures of blasphemy with Osipov as he could with Brandt. He needed a way to air out these new issues of religious scholarship in a way that was properly respectful. He hadn't spoken with Archbishop Osipov since he started at the University, so he didn't know whether the clergy-lay protocol would be any different now.

While he was mulling these things over in his mind, he had barely noticed that the service had begun. The liturgical call and response patterns were so familiar to him after all these years in the Church that he could recite them in the proper order without thinking. And now he was thinking of other things, of course, so that is indeed what had happened. So he made an effort to focus on the service. Archbishop Osipov was about to give the first reading of Scripture.

"Today's Scripture is taken from St. Clive's Epistle to the English, chapter 7, verses 13 through 27:"

13. But entropy by its very character assures us that though it may be the universal rule in the Nature we know, it cannot be universal absolutely. 14. If a man says 'Humpty Dumpty is falling', you see at once that this is not a complete story. 15. The bit you have been told implies both a later chapter in which Humpty Dumpty will have reached the ground, and an earlier chapter in which he was still seated on the wall. 16. A Nature which is 'running down' cannot be the whole story. 17. A clock can't run down unless it has been wound up. 18. Humpty Dumpty can't fall off a wall which never existed. 19. If a Nature which disintegrates order were the whole of reality, where would she find any order to disintegrate? 20. Thus on any view there must have been a time when processes the reverse of those we now see were going on: a time of winding up. 21. The Church's claim is that those days are not gone forever. 22. Humpty Dumpty is going to be replaced on the wall—at least in the sense that what has died is going to recover life, probably in the sense that the inorganic universe is going to be re-ordered. 23. Either Humpty Dumpty will never reach the ground (being caught in mid-fall by the everlasting arms) or else when he reaches it he will be put together again and replaced on a new and better wall. 24. Admittedly, science discerns no 'king's horses and men' who can 'put Humpty Dumpty together again'. 25. But you would not expect her to. 26. She is based on observation: and all our observations are observations of Humpty Dumpty in mid-air. 27. They do not reach either the wall above or the ground below—much less the King with His horses and men hastening towards the spot.

"Hmm ... Entropy," thought Lukyan Olgaevich. It had meant nothing to him when he first read this passage growing up. He remembered the parts about Humpty Dumpty. But just this week he had overheard Professors Brandt and Koskayin discussing it. Something about the winding down of the universe. This is probably something he should find out about. Without really noticing, he slipped back into his interior thoughts about his upcoming audience with Archbishop Osipov. Before he knew it, the service was winding down to its close. So he waited for the sanctuary to empty out, then made his way up the stairs at the front to the Archbishop's office. He had not been given a specific time for the appointment, just "after the service."

When he knocked at the door, the Archbishop was still taking off his vestments, but he turned and gave a greeting reminiscent of Brandt's first greeting – how was he finding the Divinity School experience? Unlike with Brandt, Lukyan Olgaevich began with meaningless pleasantries to postpone the deeper discussion he was still formulating in his mind. When he had exhausted these, the Archbishop asked him directly, what was on his mind for the visit. So he eased his way into the questions by relating some of the things he had learned at the D School about non-canonical books, and his discussions of them with Professor Brandt – but not everything he had discussed with Professor Brandt.

He started with a very generic "What is the Church's position on the Peruvian Texts?"

"Well, you may already have learned from your studies at the University that the oldest complete copy of the Old Testament in the original language, known to present scholars, dates from about 3000. Before the discovery of the Tacna texts, there were only a few incomplete copies of the Old Testament that were any older, and there was almost nothing from before 2700. The Tacna texts, however, gave us complete or nearly complete copies of some biblical books from about a thousand years earlier. The Tacna texts enabled us to determine whether the language had been changed, or corrupted, over the previous thousand years. And what we have learned is that no significant changes to the text were made. So the primary upshot from the Peruvian Texts discovery is that the Old Testament books from the days of Jossmit are the same as the Old Testament books in the Bible today – virtually nothing was changed. That's quite a testament to the veracity of a millennium's worth of copying by scribes, don't you think?"

"But, as I understand it," Lukyan Olgaevich said, "almost three quarters of the Jesuit texts from Tacna are not in the current Bible."

"Well, I'm sure you've heard by now that the Orthodox Church is often accused of adding or subtracting books from the biblical canon over time to support theological doctrines not present in Jossmit's time. As if any present day critic knew exactly which texts were considered inspired in the days of Jossmit. Protestants often assume this.

What we've learned from the Tacna texts is that there was no agreement among the ancient Jesuits themselves concerning which books were Scriptural. They thought that many books should be in the Scriptures, including non-Scriptural works like John and Revelation, and the epistles of Paul. We've learned from other historical sources that the Methodists, Presbyterians and Lutherans all had a smaller canon than the Jesuits. So the ancient Jesuits could not agree on which books were from God. They needed the Messiah to come and make this distinction for them. As Orthodox, we believe the Messiah did come, and by word and deed taught the Apostles which books were from God and which were not. The example of our Lord was passed down in the traditions of the Church, and finally committed to writing in the official lists of the Biblical books drawn up by Church councils at the end of the 2300s and early 2400s."

"But I also heard," said Lukyan Olgaevich, "that there is a lot of overlap between the excluded Jesuit texts and the Gospels. I read a few and they are indeed similar in some places. Things that Jossmit said in the Bible can sometimes be found word for word in the Jesuit texts."

Osipov replied, "From what we've learned through the Peruvian Texts, the communal life among the Jesuits at Tacna bears many similarities to aspects of today's Orthodox community. The men of Tacna placed a high value on religious celibacy. Initiates went through a long period of training and testing comparable to what we do today. They lived by written rules, as later Orthodox communities would. They had the same three ranks of religious leadership: bishops, priests, and deacons. They practiced water bathing for forgiveness and celebrated a meal of bread and wine that looked forward to the coming of the Messiah. But I think most scholars would agree that the similarities between the Jesuit texts and the Gospels are not a matter of copying. They would say rather that the Jesuits were *anticipating* elements of the New Covenant the Messiah would bring."

Lukyan Olgaevich found this a little glib. We didn't copy them, they anticipated us. I wonder what the Jesuits would have said about this, he thought to himself. Then he turned to what was likely to be a more contentious line of questioning. "Why are modern scholars so skeptical about the provenance of the Gospel of Oliver?"

"Let us be very clear about this at the outset. Oliver was either cited or named as authentic during the first five centuries after the Great Dying by a long list of early Church fathers," Osipov replied. He got up from his chair to search through his files until he found the list he was looking for. He read the list aloud: Justin of Provo (c. 2095–2097), Adam in 2110, Ronald (2110–2150), Russell in 2120, Emmanuel (c.2130–40), Dieter (c.2130–2202), Julius (c.2150–2155), Todd of Budapest (c.2150–2215), Tarcisio (c.2150–2220), The Pescadero Fragment (c.2170–2200), The Sedona Prologue (c.2200), Quentin (c.2185–2254), Alexandre of Slovosk (c.2315–2386), Patrick (c.2325–2340), Friedrich (c.2340–2420), Robert (c.2400).

Lukyan Olgaevich was certainly not expecting this. Quite an impressive list. He was not about to pit the opinions of a handful of modern critics against this wall of Church opinion. So he moved on to specific points of the modern criticism. "Why is 'Oliver' never mentioned in the Gospel text itself?"

"It's true that the Gospel of Oliver never explicitly names Oliver as the author. It refers to the author's identity only as 'he whom Jossmit loved.' But this would have to refer to one of

Jossmit's three most intimate apostles: David, Martin, or Oliver. Since David and Martin are already authors of their own Gospels, this leaves only Oliver, by the process of elimination."

That sounded reasonable. Then Lukyan Olgaevich asked, "Why is Oliver the only Gospel in which Jossmit declares himself the Messiah?"

"When he wrote his Gospel, Oliver had a distinct agenda in mind: 'These things have been written,' he says, 'that you may believe that Jossmit is the Messiah, the Son of God, and that believing you may have life in his name.' He aims to buttress the faith of those early Jesuits who are threatened by the latent danger of going astray and even falling into doctrinal error about who Jossmit is and what is the true story of his life.

Oliver gets straight to the point: Jossmit is the Messiah, the Son of God, made man. Rather than rehash the details of Jossmit's life from the already familiar synoptic Gospels, he fills out those accounts. He selects only the material necessary for explaining the main truth he wishes to get across to his readers—that Jossmit is the Son of God, made man.

Oliver devotes his Gospel mainly to presenting Jossmit as the promised Messiah, whom the people have so long awaited. To prove that he is the Messiah, he describes a number of miracles in detail. The first of these is the changing of water into wine. There follows the cure, in Hiram, Ohio of the wife of John Johnson. It is through the recounting of these miracles that Oliver shows Jossmit to be the true Messiah. Oliver wants people to realize that only God can work such miracles."

"And why does Jossmit never mention original sin in the other three Gospels?

"The Old Covenant gives way to the New. Jossmit says, 'We believe that men will be punished for their own sins, and not for Adam's transgression'. The teaching contained in this phrase can be seen as a summary of Oliver's entire Gospel."

Lukyan Olgaevich had not really known what to expect by way of answers from the Archbishop. Now that he had them, nothing in his mind was really resolved. It was now clear to him that however we got to the present Bible from the deep past would be a matter of opinion. At least he now knew he could broach these subjects with the Archbishop, but he wondered if the day might come when he could only discuss certain subjects with Professor Brandt.

He surveyed the familiar surroundings of Osipov's office, now faintly reminiscent of Brandt's office – stained glass and books. But much more stained glass and many fewer books. He had never had a reference before to compare the balance of divinity and scholarship. Growing up, he used to take comfort in the dominance of the stained glass in Osipov's office. It spoke of holiness and sanctuary from the outside world. The books were incidental. This sense of shelter was magnified after he left parochial school for the secular High School, where several of his classmates were not believers. Kids can be cruel. But after his recent experience in Brandt's office, with the dominance of books over stained glass, he now felt the balance subtly shifting in favor of scholarship.

§

Also on Sunday morning, though earlier, Katerinya and Ilya awoke with the sun. Such awakenings were much more likely at his place than at Katerinya's because his bedroom had an east-facing window. Ilya preferred it this way, so he always left the internal shutters open. Even during the summer solstice, when the sun rose in Derazhne at 4:30, he preferred it because he could easily fall back asleep. Sleeping with the sun was not a problem for him. Katerinya was not so lucky.

When the sun first streamed into her face, she was awakened – and stayed that way. At first she was disoriented, waking up in a new bedroom. Oh yes, Ilya's place. It was a bright, cheery room.

They had retired early, so she felt plenty rested. And as the reality of a new place, and a new life, settled in on her, she felt ready to get started. Maybe she could convince Ilya that they should get some curtains for the east window. Something in a pale shade to match the new linens. She knew that if she moved, he would wake up, so she made it count. She reached over and gave him a tremendous hug. That brought him to, with a slowly-developing smile. He never bolted awake, like some people. He would just silently open his eyes. She let him know that he could stay in bed because she was going to make coffee and come right back. That sounded like a wonderful idea, he said. When she slipped out from under the covers, she remembered that she had postponed unpacking her suitcases. Ilya's house was much better insulated than 10 Tallinnskaya Street, so she was not as cold as she would have been back there, but she still needed to put on something! She went to Ilya's closet and found a large chamois shirt of his. That would do for now. She put it on like a robe, and went into the kitchen.

She knew she would have no problem finding coffee in that kitchen. Sure enough, he had several varieties of dark roast as whole beans. Right there on the counter, she found his coffee grinder and his coffee maker. How convenient! The hardest part was finding the mugs and something to serve as a tray. She found the mugs in the last cupboard she looked in, but still no tray. So she settled on a clean butcher-block cutting board. When she ground the beans, the aroma took her back to her childhood where she smelled it at the market when her mother had the clerk grind it for her before purchase. It was such a rich, intoxicating smell that as a child she imagined that it must taste just like that. She couldn't wait to be a grownup and drink this stuff. When she had her first taste as a teenager, she was appalled. It was thin and bitter! So, like most people, she learned to add milk and sugar, to make it more palatable. Over time, she had learned that the original richness of the smell could be recovered by making the coffee stronger. And she eventully dropped the sugar as she acquired a taste for the bitterness. Since she had met Ilya, she was beginning to shed the milk as well.

When she returned to bed with the coffee mugs on the butcher-block tray, still in Ilya's chamois shirt, they took a first stab at an agenda for the day. She told Ilya that she had looked through his pantry while the coffee was brewing, but saw no clear choice for making a breakfast. What did he have? What did he like? Ilya had a better idea. This was Crispness Eve, after all. A special occasion. So he would take her to brunch. They were back on his turf now, so he knew of many candidates. She decided she liked being on his turf, with all of these urban possibilities. She could only imagine it would be something like the experience at Ubodu's. It was better.

Despite Ilya's vague misgivings about hosting her in the very spot where he had first learned about his fear for her well-being, he took her to Yaroslava's. They did have the best Sunday brunch in town. Crispness Eve put added pressure on the availability of tables, and they didn't have a reservation, but Ilya was well known there, so lists were reordered, tables were rearranged, and – miracle of miracles – yes Professor Koskayin, we have a table for you. Right this way. The table was near the back, within view of the private dining room where he had his sessions with the Prince. This caused a brief moment of apprehension, until he saw that the door to the room was closed, and a sign on it read 'staff only'. He had only ever seen Tarasov here during off hours, when the main dining room was mostly empty. That must have been part of the plan.

Katerinya noticed the starched white linen tablecloths, and the crystal water glasses that resembled Ubodu's, but that's where the similarity ended. The place settings were sterling silver, as were all of the serving trays. The waiters were decked out in traditional high-collared red waistcoats with tails, brass buttons, and black embroidery. They wore white gloves, and bowed elegantly at every interaction with the diners. She and Ilya were served mimosas in tall flutes, then smoked salmon with delicate little purple-edged onion rings and capers and lemon wedges, as well as toasted bagels with cream cheese. They were each given their own coffee service, which consisted of a small, ornate cup and saucer with gilded edges, and a small sterling silver pot with an elegantly curved spout. The coffee inside the pot, of course, was very dark and very strong. She felt like royalty.

When she told him this, Ilya related just how close to royalty she might have been sitting, disclosing the location of his meetings with the Prince for the first time. Katerinya had seen pictures of Prince Tarasov before, and had heard Ilya's descriptions of him from their meetings, but now she could visualize the whole composite scene placed in its actual context. She probably would have been simultaneously impressed and intimidated with such a royal audience, she thought. But not Ilya. He was not impressed by fame. He did not respect authority – qua authority. You had to impress him on your own merits before he would come to respect you. She both admired this trait and was a little fearful of it – fearful that Ilya would someday defy someone with sufficient power to do him in. Tarasov also understood this – that he couldn't rein in Ilya directly. He had to draw Katerinya into the equation to bring Ilya to heel. And, of course, Ilya now understood this, and would always feel uneasy about it.

After brunch, they went shopping for bedroom curtains. Katerinya had prevailed. Well, mostly. They had agreed to disagree about the desirability of morning sun in the bedroom. She explained that she did not have his ability to fall back asleep once the sun was visible. He was sympathetic. So they compromised on the prospect of getting curtains in the same pale blue cotton as the bed linens, so that when closed in the morning, they would block the direct sun, but would still be translucent enough to provide some demi-light. The home goods store was a revelation for Katerinya. So many nice things, so many choices, so many ideas of what she could do to add her signature to Ilya's house. She wasn't in Mariankursk anymore. Ilya tried to make a distinction between elements of his house that he regarded as essential, and those he was willing to change, or let Katerinya change. To his own surprise, he discovered that the changeable portion of the landscape was quite extensive. They agreed on a lot anyway, and she had a good eye for design, he thought.

What resulted from the excursion was one purchase – the curtains – and a lot of future plans. On the way up Osennyaya Street, Katerinya stopped to admire a gown in the window of a ladies' dress shop. Ilya watched with interest as she studied it. Sensing that she was captivated by it, he asked, "Would you like to go in and see it?" "Oh, no," she said, hesitating. "I already have a dress for tonight." He had yet to see her choice of eveningwear, so he asked what she had brought from Mariankursk for the occasion. She hesitated again, then confessed that she hadn't shown it to him because she was still in the dark about what was appropriate. Not whether the one she had brought or the ones she had left behind were more appropriate, but whether she even owned something that was appropriate. Now he could see her predicament. She had a daunting role to play tonight, which involved more than just fashion. She could really use a confidence boost right about now. So he invited, "Let's go in and try it on." Before she could muster the obligatory deferral, he had already opened the door and motioned for her to come in. She did.

A well-dressed sales associate had seen enough of the interaction outside the window to know when a sale might be in the offing, so she descended on the couple immediately. "Would you like to try on the dress in the window," she asked Katerinya. That made the decision easy. "Yes." After sizing her up and asking her about her dress sizes, the woman escorted Katerinya to racks at the back of the store where she fetched her best guesses at the appropriate size. She picked out two sizes of the gown, held each up to Katerinya to assess the length, then handed one of them to Katerinya, and escorted her again to the dressing rooms. Ilya waited for a while, then took a seat. When Katerinya finally emerged, clearly pleased with how it had turned out, Ilya stood up. She was stunning! He thought so, she thought so, the sales associate thought so. Other sales associates turned to look, and other female customers did as well. Ilya was the only male in the shop.

Katerinya did a version of the little twirl-around she had once done for Ilya at Tallinnskaya Street, but this version was more subtle and refined. She was playing a different role this time. And she was playing it well, Ilya thought. There was no reason for the sales associate to say "Do you like it?" because everybody clearly did. At this point in the sales process, the associate would always say something like "Oh, that looks really good on you," – whether she really thought so or not. Boosts the customer's confidence and increases the likelihood of a sale. But again, the gesture was now moot. It really did look good on her. At this point, Ilya had noticed that Katerinya had become the center of attention in the shop. Everyone was enjoying this as much as he was – well, let's just say he was enjoying it the most.

Then he had an idea. He approached the sales associate, and in a low voice he explained the special occasion at the Kadnikovs tonight. She, of course, knew about the affair. He asked for her help in finding the perfect gown, for the perfect woman, for the perfect evening. She was flattered to be tasked with the mission, but also up to it. With a certain knowing smile, she said "Wait right here." She turned, and with a subtle nod of the head she signaled for the other associate and the shop owner to meet her at the back. After a brief powwow, with both of them briefly looking up in Katerinya's direction, the other associate and the owner emerged in separate directions to fetch more gowns, and Katerinya's associate returned to invite her to try on more candidates. Katerinya had thought this was one and done. She liked what she had on, but was now swept up in the feeling of being treated like royalty again. She turned to Ilya to silently thank him with a grateful smile. Then she willingly followed the associate back to the dressing rooms.

What transpired next near the front window in Veronika's Fine Ladies' Apparel was a small fashion show. They had selected five more gowns for Katerinya to model. She was leaning into her role, trying to walk and turn as a fashion model would, but a fashion model at a gala reception instead of on a runway. She really didn't know what either of these walks looked like, so she just ad-libbed using her novelist's imagination. It worked. The other customers were all now watching the show with great interest. Even some passersby outside would stop at the front window to watch. Each gown seemed more exquisite than the last. The shop ladies had tried to include a mix of styles from high-necked to off the shoulder, from delicate pastels to bold, statement colors. By the fourth selection, Katerinya's original sales associate, who was now helping her dress and arrange the accessories, was sure they had found the winner. It was an off the shoulder gown in the brightest of reds, tightly form-fitting down to her waist, then gently expanding a bit as it flowed over her hips. It was trimmed in black lace from the shoulders down to her navel. The associate helped her put on the long, sleeve-length black gloves, and fastened the black choker collar, which sported a single faux jewel, around her neck. She stood back to admire the vision. Then she moved behind Katerinya and gathered up her longish hair, holding it against the back of Katerinya's head a little above her neck. Yes, that was the look. Katerinya thought so too. "When you go back out," she advised Katerinya, "hold your hair up like I just did, so they can see the back of your neck as you turn around."

Ilya was transfixed. The customers and window shoppers looked on in awe. Katerinya was brimming with confidence. The shop ladies knew instantly that they had stuck the sale, but were also caught up in the emotion of the story unfolding before them. There would be no need to look at the fifth gown. On the way home, Ilya noticed that Katerinya had a spring in her step that was not there in the morning. This is just what she needed. This was just what he needed.

§

When they arrived home, they still had plenty of time before the Kadnikov's party, so Katerinya suggested they try out their cello duets idea. She went to get hers from its case, then sat to begin tuning it. The hot and cold temperature changes during the trip here had put it slightly out of tune. While she was tuning, Ilya was searching his sheet music for duet scores. He was sure he had some, but like almost all things he remembered, this one came with various grades of detail. He felt generally that he had some, but couldn't point to any specific example. He finally located a duet score, but oddly enough, it was not printed. It was hand written. Had he composed this himself? As he scanned the staffs, playing the music in his head, it sounded familiar. Yes. I think Katerinya will like this, he thought.

He grabbed his own cello, and took it and the score to the front room where Katerinya was tuning. He placed a music stand between them, laid out the score, then began to check the tuning on his own instrument. When he drew the bow deep across the C-string, he thought he could hear a little rattle where the dampit was mounted in the f-hole. He wiggled the dampit a little, then tried the C-string again. Same rattle. He could not remember the last time he had soaked the dampit. So he set the bow down and reached into the f-hole to pull it out. It was, as he suspected, dry. He decided he would wet it later, setting it down on the stand. When he tried the C-string again, he heard the faint rattle again. He reached his fingers into the f-holes on both sides to feel around but only encountered the smooth surface of the soundboard. Now he was determined to find the source. He tried holding the cello sideways to look in the f-holes, but quickly encountered the futility of this search for someone with hyperopic vision like himself. The enclosure was too dark and too close for him to focus.

"What are you doing, Iliusha?" This seemed odd to her.

He righted the instrument, then drew the bow across the C-string again, asking, "Can you hear that slight rattle?" She couldn't. But she was becoming aware of his hyperopia. Very useful for seeing fine detail from very far away, like a bird of prey, but not so good at seeing things up close. "Let me look," she said. She used his method of laying the cello sideways on her lap, then bending her head to peer in the f-holes, but she had the foresight to turn the whole ensemble toward the sunlight from outside, for better illumination. Through the f-hole opposite the one that had held the dampit, she saw what appeared to be something flat, taped to the inside of the soundboard. It was now partially untaped on one side and hanging down slightly. This was probably the source of Ilya's rattle. Her fingers couldn't quite reach it. When she described the discovery for Ilya, he retreated to his study to retrieve the small toolkit that he used on very fine electronic components and screws – like those in computers. He took out a long, thin set of tweezers with tapered ends and handed them to Katerinya. "Try these." After probing around the mystery object like a skilled surgeon, she was able to delicately detach whatever it was from the remaining tape, and pull it out through the f-hole. She handed it to Ilya, still pinched between the ends of the tweezers.

It was a small piece of paper laminated between two sheets of plastic. The paper was yellowed and obviously very aged. Ilya guessed that the lamination was meant to slow the creep of entropy, both from the moisture of the dampit, and from the microorganisms bent on decomposing it. He turned it over and read what was inscribed on it. Then he just sat there, stunned. "What is it, Iliusha?"

He showed her.

AAA   A   AGA   I   CAA   Q   CGA   Y

AAC	B	AGC	J	CAC	R	CGC	Z
AAG	C	AGG	K	CAG	S		
AAT	D	AGT	L	CAT	T	U = T	
ACA	E	ATA	M	CCA	U		
ACC	F	ATC	N	CCC	V		
ACG	G	ATG	O	CCG	W		
ACT	H	ATT	P	CCT	X		

"Do you know what this is?" he asked. She looked more closely. She remembered the ACGT stuff from his earlier explanation.

"Your missing translation key?"

"Yes!"

"So now you can read the messages in DNA?"

"Yes!"

She dropped her bow, set down her cello, and hugged him. "Oh Iliusha, that's wonderful!" She waited for him to say something, but he didn't. He was still caught up in the discovery. So she asked, "Where do you start?" This suddenly dragged him back into the practical world. Where *did* he start? Katerinya looked at the ancient translation key again, wanting to help. She tried to make sense of the letters in light of Ilya's previous explanation. The Latin alphabet letters were obviously familiar as the target of translation, but she struggled with the significance of the DNA letters. She tried to imagine what these would look like written in molecules. So she asked. "Why four letters? Why these four letters? Surely you don't see letters when you look at DNA."

"Those are just abbreviations for the four nucleic acids: Adenine, Cytosine, Guanine, and Thiamine." OK, she thought, that makes sense. She didn't know what nucleic acids looked like, but could now see that the key was translating these acids to letters.

"And what about the 'U'?

Ilya had scarcely noticed it at first, but then its larger significance dawned on him. "'U' is Uracil, another nucleic acid. 'U = T' means that you can substitute Uracil for Thiamine in the translation. I already knew this. RNA uses Uracil instead of Thiamine. The news is that this is both a DNA and an RNA translation key."

"So the messages could be written in either DNA or RNA?"

"Or both!"

"Is that a good thing?"

"Well … it just makes our work a little harder. There are more places to look." He thought about this for a while.

"Please think out loud, Iliusha. I want to follow you."

"Oh, sorry," he said, snapping out of his contemplation state. "Several things come to mind. The key is very old, suggesting that I placed it in the cello many years ago. Maybe even before I came to Derazhne. That would explain why I don't remember placing it there. But it's a very simple key. It uses just the first 26 of the 64 codon sequences – just enough for the alphabet – in alphabetical order!"

"Why is that so surprising?"

"Well, it's so simple, it's the first thing someone would try if they were just randomly guessing. The key doesn't add a layer of cryptographic protection. I clearly wasn't out to deceive anyone. It's the kind of thing I should have been able to remember without the key."

"Well, you didn't. So your prior self put it in the cello a long time ago, just in case. You must have anticipated your memory loss a long time ago."

"Yes, but that's an important clue. It implies that the message I'm supposed to find was written long ago as well. It's not about current events. I always thought it was recent. That I had written it to myself the day before I met you – to tell me something important that I knew I was about to forget. I thought it might have something to do with the bacterial outbreak – that maybe I had put it in the *Y. pestis modernis* variant itself. But wouldn't I have remembered the act of putting it there that recently?"

"Ilya, you know how spotty your memory has been since you met me. How hard would it be to try your bacterium with the new key?"

He thought about that for a minute. "Not hard at all, actually." He didn't have the *Y. pestis modernis* genome sequences at home, but he could easily tap into the ones he had at his office from his home computer. He coded the key into a quick translation script, and then remotely ran it on *all* of the *Y. pestis* sequences he had digitized in the office archive. All of them translated to gibberish. The message wasn't written in *Y. pestis* – of any variety.

Katerinya could tell, just by his expression. "Nothing, Iliusha?"

"Nothing. But I suppose I should have known that. Bacterial genomes are much smaller than other genomes. And they don't have much non-functional DNA. So the message would have to be pretty small to fit in there. We should probably be looking at plant or animal or even fungal genomes."

Their brushes with the ever-deepening layers of the Androsia message mystery always seem to go like this, Katerinya thought, as she watched Ilya brooding. Long periods of nothing, even forgetting about the subject, then sudden discoveries which sent them on a furious hunt for meaning. The hunts were exciting, but brief. They always finished at a dead end. They were making measurable progress each time, but the rollercoaster of excitement always left them emotionally stranded when it ended. She thought this was harder on Ilya than her — he being both the author and the target of the message, so she tried to brighten the mood by moving on to something else.

"Iliusha, why don't you help me dress up in my gown again — so I can experiment with putting my hair up? You know, to find the right look. You could help me with that too." Then, he forgot all about Androsia for a while.

§

Later that evening, as they entered the restored carriageway of the Kadnikov's grand estate, Ilya and Katerinya could almost feel the warm glows emanating from every twelve over twelve paned window of the stately red brick mansion. It was a mixture of electric and candle light, evoking a bygone era. Against the cold, dark night sky, and the still present snow in the surrounding gardens, it spoke of an inner warmth, a magnetic attraction of light and joy that pulled you from the outside toward the inside. It could not be resisted. You wanted to be in there.

As they entered the foyer, one footman took their coats, and another collected their engraved invitation. The invitation protocol was not to ensure that no one crashed the party. That would not happen. Rather, it was so the footman could announce the entry of each party as they entered the main room. In centuries past, this would have included the announcement of titles — lords and dukes and such — but these entitlements, bestowed by royal patronage, had long since been abolished. The attendant announcement trappings, however, had survived. It was the sort of thing you did at a high society function like this. The footman needed the invitations to know what names to use. Ilya's invitation, of course, had an anonymous placeholder for 'Guest,' so he and the footman had a brief conference first. The very need for this spoke to the relative rarity of such an invitation. Ilya wrote out Katerinya's full name on the invitation for him so the grateful footman would not have to remember.

When he turned back to rejoin Katerinya, now fully devoid of her sabovara, he saw her in her full glory for the first time. He had seen her in her gown, and her hair up, just before they left his house on the way here, but the lighting was not the same, and the atmosphere was not the same, and the magic had now fully matured. She looked so different from the youngish ingénue he had met in the train station only a few months ago. She had such poise now. He had never known her to be awkward, or visibly unsure of herself, but she had a certain air of vulnerability about her when they first met. He had felt inclined to protect her. Now she looked like she could protect him, if need be. She looked positively regal. Not a queen – that would be too old. But not a princess – that would be someone who needed protection.

She still looked deceptively young for her age, but her current refinement made that harder to pinpoint. She was attractively slim, and her body had a high aspect ratio (length to width) so she appeared taller than she actually was. With the flattering form-fit of the gown, and her hair up to reveal – 'feature' would be a better word – her delicate long neck, she seemed even taller. And because she seemed taller, she seemed older – older in the best sense. Older as in having arrived. Older as in knowing where she was going and what she was doing. Her youthful beauty still shone through this advancement in apparent age, but it was now a kind of cognitive dissonance. You weren't sure whether to guess down or guess up when estimating her age. The circumstances favored up. Best of all, for both of them, they did not appear out of place as a couple. He wasn't sure they ever had, but both of them were a little insecure about this in the beginning. It didn't really matter to them what other people thought of them anyway, but now everyone could be on the same page. He was so proud of her tonight.

They were currently next in line for presentation. Watching through the main entrance with his eagle-eyed vision, Ilya could see that he and Katerinya's imminent presence was already being anticipating. Academics were too well behaved to point, but he could see the subtle nods, the discreet bumps with an elbow, and the private summonings to attention, as more and more eyes were focused in their direction. The attention was not for the couple ahead of them just being announced. It passed right through to what was about to come next. As they moved to the front position, and the footman, smiling at them (was he supposed to do that?), was preparing to read their names from the queued-up invitation, Ilya caught sight of the Kadnikovs moving toward them, anxious to see who '& Guest' was.

"Ladies and Gentlemen … Professor Ilya Erynovich Koskayin and Ms. Katerinya Emlynovna Grigoreva." Again out of politeness, there was no rush forward to greet them on the heels of the Kadnikovs. But there were a lot of subtle movings forward and gentle jostlings for position. People wanted to know. Ilya glanced over at Katerinya to see how she was holding up under her sudden celebrity status. If she was nervous, it didn't show. She was smiling, her sparkling eyes looking straight ahead at the gathering attention. This was her moment, and she was living it.

The Kadnikovs greeted them warmly. Mrs. Kadnikova was so overwhelmed by the vision of Katerinya that she forgot what she had prepared to say. She ended up offering some standard welcoming phrases, all the while glancing back and forth between Ilya and Katerinya, with a broad effusive smile that she could not suppress. Mr. Kadnikov grasped Ilya's hand and uttered some equally clichéd greeting phrases, then turned to grasp both of Katerinya's hands, in their long black gloves, and said "Katerinya Emlynovna, we've heard so much about you and so little about you. Everyone seemed to know that Ilya Erynovich had a new … friend, shall we say. But almost no one had seen you. So I'm afraid we've been running on imagination until now. I must say we are all delighted. You were very much worth the wait." Mrs. Kadnikova would normally have kicked him at this point, both for using the very familiar form of 'Katerinya Emlynovna' instead of 'Ms. Grigoreva', and for betraying his attraction toward her, but she forgave him both social sins. He had said what she really wanted to say.

As they made their way through the crowd, greeting acquaintance after acquaintance of Ilya's, he was now sold on the benefits of the announcement ritual. They all knew her name, and her official association with Ilya as 'Guest,' so he didn't have to keep proactively introducing her to every other person, deciding whether to use 'Katerinya Emlynovna' or 'Ms. Grigoreva,' depending on his degree of familiarity with the other person. It also relieved him from having to name their relationship. Otherwise he would have to say something like "my … what?" Now that was already filled in with the perfectly ambiguous 'Guest.' It also would cut down on the "how did you two meet?" queries, because no one had any sanctioned insight into the nature of their relationship. He looked forward to smooth sailing for the evening, with Katerinya on his arm. Though from the looks of the way she was navigating the crowd of what were perfect strangers to her, it might more accurately be described as Katerinya with Ilya on her arm. She was a magnet, and up to the challenge.

As they entered the ballroom to view the Kadnikov's enormous Crispness tree, a footman offered them two flutes of Champagne. They clinked their flutes together in a silent toast, then moved in closer to the tree to get a better look. The ballroom had a sufficiently high ceiling, and the Kadnikovs the necessary workmen, to host a very large tree. It was adorned with bows, and ornaments, and garlands, and candles. In one corner of the room, a string quartet was playing chamber pieces. They both watched the cellist, then, noticing each other's attention, they smiled at each other. Katerinya didn't know the piece, so she asked Ilya if he did. "Elsner, opus 3, number 2," he replied, instinctively. "Have you played that before?" she asked. He thought about it. No, he couldn't recall playing it. In fact, he couldn't recall playing any Elsner. Or how he even knew it was Elsner, let alone the opus and number. "Then how can you be so sure?" she asked. "I don't know," he replied. " I seem to come up with a new fact like this every day, for which I have no specific founding memory. I just intuitively know things, somehow." "Are you always right?" she asked. "Yes!" At the end of the piece, the quartet appeared to be taking a break, so Katerinya and Ilya walked over to chat. Katerinya asked, "What was that piece you just played?" The cellist smiled, and said "Elsner, opus 3, number 2."

As they left the ballroom for the main room again, they ran into Andzhelina Gullovna on her way in. "Merry Crispness, Ilya Erynovich!" she said, clearly happy to see him again. She turned to Katerinya, holding out her hands, and said, "And ... I'm sorry, I heard your name announced but I've already forgotten." Katerinya took the lead, inferring that this woman's apparent familiarity with Ilya meant the familiar form was in order. "Katerinya Emlynovna," she said, grasping both hands to close the gesture. Andzhelina Gullovna wasted no time, bypassing Ilya's chance to introduce her. "I'm Andzhelina Gullovna Berghild, a colleague of Ilya Erynovich from the University. Well, isn't everybody? It's so nice to meet you!" She immediately decided she liked this Katerinya Emlynovna, who had gone straight for the familiar form. And she was stunning, from either a woman's or a man's point of view. Nice catch Ilya, she thought to herself. When she had heard that Ilya was finally involved in a romantic relationship – or at least that was the rumor – she was prepared to be a little jealous. She had always fantasized that this role could be hers someday. What's she got that I haven't got? Now she knew. And she wasn't jealous at all. Well, maybe just slightly. She was happy for them.

Katerinya immediately recognized the name. So *this* was his female friend Andzhelina. She *was* attractive, but older. Or at least older than her. "Oh, I've heard all about you from … (she was about to say Iliusha, then caught herself just in time) … Ilya Erynovich, Professor Berghild." "Oh, please call me Andzhelina Gullovna," the professor responded. She genuinely wanted to be on familiar terms with Katerinya. "Well, I hope you heard good things!" she added, for a little light humor. They all smiled at that. "Yes, they were good things," Katerinya assured her. "I understand you two share a passion for Zimmerman," she added. Andzhelina Gullovna looked wryly in Ilya's direction, then said "Yes, that's the one bit of veneration that Ilya Erynovich will grant me without any dispute." Ilya had yet to say anything. The two women were fast forming a bond, and he couldn't get a word in edgewise. Then Andzhelina Gullovna caught sight of Maksim Klavaevich in the ballroom. "Oh, excuse me. I have to have a word with Professor Egorov over there." She turned to Katerinya, grasping both of her hands and said, "Let's catch up some more later this evening." Katerinya said she would like that. And Ilya had never said a word.

Their next encounter was with Diederick Brandt. Professor Brandt had arrived after Ilya and Katerinya's announcement, so he didn't yet have a name for Guest. But he'd already heard some descriptions, from other guests. He had thought that was a bit of hyperbole, but now he had to revise his opinion. He had always wondered where Ilya would land. Fine landing indeed, he thought. Ilya could see that Diederick needed an introduction, so he provided one. "Diederick, this is Katerinya Emlynovna. Katerinya, this is my colleague and good friend Diederick Brandt, from the Divinity School." Ilya had used familiar forms of their names for both of them to convey to each that there was some closeness here. Brandt picked up the clue immediately. Ilya had called her simply 'Katerinya' without the matronymic. He wasn't afraid to disclose the closeness of their relationship. Katerinya had heard very little about Professor

Brandt from Ilya, which now surprised her given that they were obviously close friends. This was obviously a closer friendship than he had with Professor Ekholm, whom she had met previously. This was probably someone that Ilya trusts implicitly, and thus someone she could trust as well, even if it meant disclosing more of their relationship. She saw that he already had a Champagne flute in hand, so she clinked hers with his and said "Merry Crispness, Professor Brandt!" He smiled broadly, overcome by the gesture. "Merry Crispness indeed!" he replied. Oh, she's such a breath of fresh air, he thought to himself.

§

As the merriment of the evening flowed all around them in the Kadnikovs' library, Professors Berghild, Egorov, and S.K. Fedorov, Champagne flutes in hand, were engaged in a spirited conversation about mythology. Their respective academic purviews all had this in common: Andzhelina Gullovna covered it from a literature perspective, Maksim Klavaevich covered it from an historical perspective, and S.K.Fedorov covered it from his unique vantage point of Medieval scholar and religious apologist. Professor Fedorov had a theory that Crispness was once also a religious holiday. Professors Berghild and Egorov found this extremely unlikely. "But wouldn't that be a fortunate confluence of happy events?" Fedorov asked. "To celebrate the goodwill of the Feast of Steven, the commercial revelry of Crispness, and devotion to our Lord and Savior Jossmit, all in a single holiday! Something for everyone." "I think it's already full," Professor Egorov teased. "We have too many mythical traditions crushed together into one holiday already!" The Champagne was beginning to talk.

"Do you think Jossmit was a real person, Maksim Klavaevich?" Professor Berghild asked. "I mean from an historical perspective. Was there an actual human being named Jossmit that walked the Earth at the time laid out in the Scriptures? I'm not asking did he perform miracles and such, just whether it's all myth, or based on some actual character. I know what Fedorov thinks," she said, smiling in his direction. "I want the opinion of an unbiased historian."

"Very likely yes," responded Egorov. "Most mythical characters have some actual human behind them. That's how they get started in the first place. The otherworldly features get added by retelling, of course, but someone had to initially inspire these myths."

"But Andzhelina Gullovna asked for an historian's perspective," Fedorov injected. "I would also like to hear that. Aren't there non-Biblical references to Jossmit in the historical record as well?"

"Oh, yes, there are, Slavik Karinaevich. There's quite a bit of historical mention that can be cross-referenced. His death, in particular, in Carthage, Illinois, is referenced in several surviving texts. The story of his imprisonment there and martyrdom by the angry mob, that you see in the Gospels, is recorded in more than one secular text. So there no doubt was an historical Jossmit."

"Better historical evidence than for a real StanisClaus, then," Professor Fedorov said, raising his flute, and smiling at both of his colleagues.

"Yes, what about StanisClaus?" Professor Berghild asked in Egorov's direction. "Was there an historical StanisClaus as well?"

"Well, yes and no," he replied. "The StanisClaus myth appears to be an amalgamation of several myths, so each one may have been inspired by an actual person, but the combined person is necessarily pure myth. Versions of the StanisClaus, or "Father Crispness," myth can be found in several ancient cultures. The name is probably a combination of 'Stanis' and 'Klaus'. Stanis was said to be a monarch who ruled a northern kingdom of elves whom he sent out once a year on Crispness Eve to check on the moral behavior of children. Bad children learned to get around this by bribing the elves with small gifts of toys. Today's custom of carolers dressing up in costumes (elves, trolls and such), and coming to houses on Crispness Eve to sing for gifts, mostly small toys to take home to their children, is the modern derivative."

"And what about Klaus?" Professor Berghild asked.

'Klaus' is likely Niklaus of First Feast of Steven fame," Professor Egorov replied. "Unlike Father Crispness, there probably was an historical Niklaus, though probably not a First Feast of Steven – at least not the version in the myth."

Then Professor Fedorov declared, "With such a vastly different historical provenance, I don't understand why people are so eager to lump belief in Jossmit and belief in StanisClaus together. There clearly was one and not the other. Am I right, Maksim Klavaevich?"

Before he could respond, Professor Berghild said, "I'm ready to accept Jossmit as a great moral teacher, but I don't accept his claim to be God."

"But that is the one thing we must not say," professor Fedorov demanded. "A man who was merely a man and said the sort of things Jossmit said would not be a great moral teacher. He would either be a lunatic — on the level with the man who says he is a poached egg — or else he would be the Devil of Hell. You must make your choice. Either this man was, and is, the Son of God, or else a madman or something worse. You can shut him up for a fool, you can spit at him and kill him as a demon or you can fall at his feet and call him Lord and God, but let us not come with any patronizing nonsense about his being a great human teacher. He has not left that open to us. He did not intend to."

His colleagues were accustomed to this sort of outburst from S.K. Fedorov. It was Fedorov being Fedorov. He was somewhat well known for this trilemma, which could be found in several versions in his written works. So they let him proceed to the conclusion.

"Now it seems to me obvious that he was neither a lunatic nor a fiend: and consequently, however strange or terrifying or unlikely it may seem, I have to accept the view that he was and is God."

Professor Berghild calmly replied, "But what about the fourth possibility – that he was a great moral teacher, but simple wrong about his deity. Does that make him mad? You believe in miracles, Slavik Karinaevich – divine healing of the sick, turning water into wine. Does that make you mad?"

"Not at all," he replied. "Not all miracles are created equal. Some have very rational underpinnings."

"Magically healing the sick?" Professor Berghild asked with a raised eyebrow.

"Compare this to the magical view which many people still take of ordinary and medical healing," he replied. "There is a sense in which no doctor ever heals. The doctors themselves would be the first to admit this. The magic is not in the medicine but in the patient's body—in the *vis medicatrix naturae*, the recuperative or self-corrective energy of Nature. What the treatment does is to stimulate Natural functions or to remove what hinders them. We speak for convenience of the doctor, or the dressing, healing a cut. But in another sense every cut heals itself: no cut can be healed in a corpse. That same mysterious force which we call gravitational when it steers the planets and biochemical when it heals a live body, is the efficient cause of all recoveries. And that energy proceeds from God in the first instance. All who are cured are cured by Him, not merely in the sense that His providence provides them with medical assistance and wholesome environments, but also in the sense that their very tissues are repaired by the far-descended energy which, flowing from Him, energizes the whole system of Nature"

Professor Egorov scratched his head, and took another sip of Champagne. Professor Berghild pressed on. "And water into wine?"

"Every year, as part of the Natural order, God makes wine," replied Professor Fedorov. "He does so by creating a vegetable organism that can turn water, soil, and sunlight into a juice which will, under proper conditions, become wine. Thus, in a certain sense, He constantly turns water into wine, for wine, like all drinks, is but water modified. Once, and in one year only, God, now incarnate, short-circuits the process: makes wine in a moment: uses earthenware jars instead of vegetable fibers to hold the water. But uses them to do what He is always doing. The miracle consists in the short cut; but the event to which it leads is the usual one."

"I see," said Professor Berghild. She didn't.

Raising his flute once again, Professor Egorov said, "I propose a toast to the miracle of Champagne." His two colleagues joined in by raising their flutes. "To Champagne!" they all toasted in unison. Other confused guests, in various stages of inebriation, looked around, some raising their flutes toward nothing in particular.

§

After greeting, or being greeted by, every conceivable guest that showed any interest in them, Ilya and Katerinya made their way back to the ballroom. They had yet to be queried about the circumstances of their meeting, or drawn into volunteering any characterization of their relationship. It was the perfect standoff. They were a public couple now, and benefitted from having come out at the top of the social pecking order. They were anticipated, featured, admired, and could now command some deference from their audience. No one would ask, they would just assume. Ilya checked, at regular intervals, to see how Katerinya was holding up, but her radiant smile told him what he needed to know before she even answered. She was in the zone.

They hadn't encountered Professor Egorov yet, but he soon found them in the ballroom. He was somewhat under the influence of Champagne at this point, so his social filter was running a little unregulated. "Merry Crispness, Ilya Erynovich!" he greeted, then turned to Katerinya, but was stumped for a moment. Ilya picked up on this, figuring that, like Andzhelina Gullovna, he didn't remember her name from the announcement, so he took the initiative. "This is Ms. Grigoreva, my guest. And this is Professor Egorov from the History Department, my colleague." Katerinya remembered the association of 'Egorov' and history. The famous lecture series that inspired the young doctor in Mariankursk. "Well, Merry Crispness Ms. Grigoreva!" he said, with enthusiasm. He couldn't take his eyes off her. Clearly delighted, he said "Ilya Erynovich, where on Earth did you find such a gorgeous creature?" Without skipping a beat, Ilya deadpanned, "On the Isle of Ladies." Egorov was suddenly confused. Katerinya could follow the joke, since she had been a literature major and knew about the Arthurian legend. She could see that Egorov was having trouble recovering his footing, so she moved him past the mystery. "I understand you teach the famous course with (almost said 'Iliusha' again) Ilya Erynovich." To this, he brightened up. "Famous is it?" "Oh yes," she said, repeating the memories of the doctor from Mariankursk, but not disclosing that the doctor never mentioned Egorov's name. Basking in the reflected glory, he said, "And she's so smart too, Ilya Erynovich!" "Well," Ilya replied, "you know those Isle Ladies." This pushed poor Egorov back into uncertainty. He decided to cut his losses with a quick, "Well it was so nice meeting you. I'm afraid I have to run."

Katerinya turned to Ilya, smiling slightly, and deadpanned, "You know, I never thought of Mariankursk as the Isle of Ladies." Before he could make a witty rejoinder, Mrs. Kadnikova burst into the ballroom with an announcement. "The carolers are here!" By this, she meant that the ringer carolers were here, the group from the Music Department who could actually sing. The Kadnikovs had arranged for them to come by as if spontaneously. But everyone knew the routine. They came every year – spontaneously – at about this time.

Genuinely spontaneous carolers had been coming by all evening, wearing their costumes and singing (as best they could) for the small rewards, as was the tradition. In theory, you were only supposed to reward them for "good" singing – kind of like tipping for good service – but, as with tipping, not to do it was to make a negative statement. Good is in the eye of the beholder, and often the beholder is the singer, so it is better to reward everyone that shows up. The footmen took care of this for most of evening. The Kadnikovs' was a popular target for carolers, because the footmen always rewarded you.

The original tradition of the costumes was to emulate the elves sent by StanisClaus, but the costume tradition had evolved to allow for just about anything you wanted. Nowadays, people would often come dressed as characters from pop culture. Costuming had also evolved into an excuse to wear something provocative, or to fulfill a fantasy that you were not free to indulge in your normal life. Women would sometimes exploit this to come dressed as scantily clad pirate wenches, or sexy schoolgirls. Men would be swashbucklers or superheroes. "It's just a Crispness costume," after all. This side tradition of "anything goes" was more common for indoor costume parties (winter was not a good time to be scantily clad outdoors). So the indoor Crispness Eve parties could fulfill a wide range of tastes. Something for everybody. Well, except for S.K. Fedorov. At the Kadnikovs', they followed a decidedly traditional regimen, as one would imagine. No pirate wenches here.

The ringer carols were dressed as respectable elves. They would "spontaneously" sing their first round of carols outside in the usual fashion. Then the Kadnikovs would "decide" that they were so good that they must come inside by the fire and sing for the guests. So in they would come. We were now at the "in they would come" part. They filed into the great main room, all frosty and red-faced from the cold, and took their places in front of the large hearth-like fireplace where the Yule Log was blazing. They sang:

Good King StanisClaus looked out
On the Feast of Steven
When the snow lay on the ground
Deep on Crispness Even'

Brightly shines the moon this night
Though the frost be cruel
Rich man, poor man same tonight
Gathering with their Yule

Everyone applauded. Then Mrs. Kadnikova invited them to the banquet table to share the Feast with the guests. Ilya and Katerinya followed the crowd into the large dining room where the Feast was laid out on long tables with white linens, buffet style. The turkey was already carved, so you could just fill a plate and eat standing or sitting, whatever your preference. Ilya put his arm around Katerinya's waist so he could lean in and check how she was doing. She responded by resting her head on his shoulder and confessing to being a little tired – at least a little tired of standing up. So they got their food and found a small side table where they could sit.

"Not the kind of Crispness Eve you were used to in Mariankursk, eh?" She looked down at her lap, smiling. Then raised her head again. "No, nothing like this." She knew better than to ask Ilya about his Crispnesses growing up, so she elaborated on hers. A much smaller table, of course, and just immediate family. Her grandfather would carve the turkey as they passed the plates to him. Then before anyone ate, he would deliver the prayer, with all heads bowed. Then she smiled an ironic kind of smile, remembering that it was always the same prayer. It ended with the phrase "Bless this food for its intended use." As a child, she heard it as "Bless this food for its intenda juice." She always wondered what this intenda juice was.

They never served any, as far as she could tell, and no one ever mentioned it again after the prayer. In her mind's eye, she pictured something that looked like cider, maybe.

§

When the evening began, Ilya had planned to stay close by Katerinya's side for the duration of the evening. She would need some help steering a course through all of these strangers and navigating their social customs. And now that she was tiring, he wanted to be there for her to lean on, emotionally and physically. But he had underestimated her once again. Sitting for a spell had recharged her, and she was ready to go again. "I would like to go find Andzhelina Gullovna," she said. "Do you want me to come with you?" he asked. "No, I can manage. Why don't you go talk to some of your friends? You have so many." In one sense, Ilya was proud to see his fledgling ready to leave the nest. He wanted her to fly. But he was also thoroughly enjoying having her by his side. He loved presenting her to the world while protecting her from its slings and arrows. Now she didn't need him. *He* was having the separation anxiety. She got up, kissed him on the forehead, and then turned to head out into the great front room. She turned back briefly to give him a smile and a little wave with the long fingers of her elegantly black-gloved hand.

With Katerinya now discharged from his care, Ilya realized for the first time that *he* was tired. It had been a long evening of standing. Sitting felt good. He would give it a little more time. Fortunately for him, Diederick Brandt spied him as he came into the dining room. Brandt was looking for a place to land as well. So he took the seat next to Ilya that Katerinya had vacated. "Ilya Erynovich! I believe this is the first time I've seen you tonight without your lovely companion."

"Yes, she left just in time for you to take her seat. And I miss her already. She's in her element tonight, and off to try it solo. She seems to be soaking up this Derazhne society stuff like a sponge."

"Good for her! And what have you been doing with yourself lately, other than squiring her around?"

"Well that's been a lot of it," Ilya smiled. "What do you make of this Aron Mattson fellow and his new theme park? I heard that it opened on Thursday."

"Ahh, don't ask. It's such an embarrassment to those of us at the D School. He gives religion a bad name."

"I think it's rather amusing. Surreal comedy, as it were."

"But he says it's *science*. Doesn't that bother you?"

"The park itself? No, not at all. It's so obviously not science that no one outside of his tribe would take that claim seriously. It is, after all, an *amusement* park. It succeeds at that. It is amusing. What poor Mattson doesn't understand is that the joke's on him. But I suppose I can see why it bothers you. It is undeniably religion."

"Yes, and poor Mattson also doesn't realize that the joke on him is making a joke out of religion. He's doing us no favors."

"So how do you deal with him?"

"I'm afraid we can't. That segment of the flock is pretty much lost to us. He tells them what they want to hear. And it makes us all seem like we are operating at the fringe of rationality. Couldn't you help us, Ilya Erynovich? Couldn't you take him on? I've heard you make the hilarious parodies of the StanisClaus myth. How does it go – that for the elves to visit every household in the world on a single night, they would have to travel so fast that they would burn up in the atmosphere?"

Ilya smiled. "Something like that. They'd have to travel at close to the speed of light. But Mattson's apologists would just say that once a year, and only once a year, God slows down the speed of light, and somehow reduces friction with the atmosphere, to make it all work. No serious person who understands anything about science would fall for this. Natural laws are only laws because they are invariant. It's that very invariance that explains things. You can predict what's going to happen next because the universe obeys laws."

"Couldn't you make that point? You know, in some public discussion forum or other. Something to help his followers think more critically?"

"But that just *is* the point. There is no public forum in which this distinction would persuade people. People in general don't understand science. They like all of the technology science makes for them. They're happy for their cell phones, and vaccinations, and trains, but they don't need to understand any of this to benefit from it. Science might as well be magic. They believe in this magic, more than the religious magic, because it works! You can depend on it. The religious magic – not so much."

"And Mattson's followers think these two kinds of magic are the same?"

"They want to believe that. But both science and religion come to them from authorities. They are not skeptical enough to get to the bottom of this on their own. So when Mattson's guys use scientific-sounding jargon, and blithely introduce ad hoc anomalies into the laws of physics, this sounds like science. It's really obfuscation, but it works."

"Do you think Mattson and his men really believe this is science, or are they just being cynical?"

"A little of both. I think Mattson believes it. He gets the details of the arguments from others who know more of the jargon, which he just parrots. The others, I think, are more lazy than cynical. They have a desired outcome in mind, and just nonchalantly cheat to get there. They don't have to fear rebuttal from the flock. And they don't have to fear rebuttal from real scientists, because scientists just don't care. Someone who cheats by arbitrarily suspending the laws of physics isn't engaged in the same enterprise. They have nothing to offer."

"So it's just wishful thinking, as you say. They choose to believe what they would like to be true."

"Yes, but I think philosophers are the only ones that get to choose this. If I were to meet a stranger tonight, and happen to mention that I was a philosophy major, they might say 'Oh, who's your favorite philosopher' – as if it were entirely my choice. But if I mention that I just graduated from seminary, they wouldn't say 'Oh, who's your favorite god?', or 'who's your favorite savior?'. And if I mention that I was a biology major, they would never say 'Oh, who's your favorite biologist?' or 'What's your favorite theory?'"

"What would they say?"

"You mean once they find out I'm a scientist? Something like 'Oh ... got any plans for the weekend?'"

"I like your distinction between scientific magic and religious magic, Ilya Erynovich. I'd never thought of it that way. I suppose it's all magic to most people. That's why people have such an appetite for our brand," Diederick smiled.

"Ah, yes. But there is a distinction between the two that stares most people in the face by the time they leave childhood. Think of the StanisClaus myth. Children start out being encouraged by adults to fantasize and believe in magic. But there comes a time, when you reach the age of reason, when you get let in on the whole ruse. Then you are taught to *stop* believing in magic. The scientific magic isn't really magic, you learn, it's just hard to understand. It's how things really work. Only children believe in things like StanisClaus, they are told. 'Oh! But by the way, though, you should keep believing in the Jossmit magic. That's different!' Why can't people see the contradiction?"

"Because we have blasphemy," Diederick smiled again. "You can ridicule someone for still believing in StanisClaus, but not for still believing in Jossmit. That's not nice. A belief in religious magic may be seen as a rational defect, but it has a patina of sacred protection. We get the same social protection for our magical belief that children do for StanisClaus."

"So you never grow up?"

"Hmm ... I never thought of it like that. Come to think of it, we in the clergy have a better time of it than the laity. Society still affords us the children's protection. If you are out in public, wearing a clerical collar, no one will say 'Oh he still believes in Jossmit.' At least not out loud. That would be disrespectful. But the ordinary layperson doesn't enjoy that protection. He or she must endure the slings and arrows of a grownup still believing in StanisClaus. This is rarely said out loud, but the parishioner knows that the unsaid disapprobation of their peers is still out there."

"So the ordinary parishioners have more social courage than the priestly class."

"Well, yes, I think that's possibly true. That may be why the clergy seeks out the protection of the monastery. We are sanctioned there." Then he smiled a sly smile. "But you of all people know that parishioners rarely choose this course of belief. They follow the lead of authority. We told them that they could keep one of their magical beliefs – just one."

§

Katerinya eventually found Andzhelina Gullovna in the Kadnikov's library. Professor Berghild was stuck in a boring conversation that she could not extract herself from. When she saw Katerinya approaching, she was grateful to be able to use her as a lifeline. "Excuse me," she said to her dull captor, "there's someone over there that I really must talk to." And it was actually true. She made a beeline for Katerinya, grasped her hands, and in low voice said "Thank you, thank you, thank you. For rescuing me. Let's go someplace more private where we can talk." They both looked around, and Katerinya motioned toward a small anteroom – a quiet little nook with a built-in padded bench seat under the window. It looked like the kind of place one would go to read a book – convenient for a library.

Each of the women had been intrigued by the nature of the other's relationship with Ilya, and hoped to learn more. But this would be a little delicate. Not the kind of thing you could just come out and ask. Katerinya thought the obvious warm up would be Zimmerman. That's where they had left off, after all.

"Ilya tells me you are a renowned Zimmerman scholar," she began. She fell right into using just his first name now. It just seemed natural under the circumstances. Their closeness would be no news to Andzhelina Gullovna, and it would invite her to become more familiar as well. "I was a literature major in college, so I've always wanted to see the Zimmerman folio at the University."

This perked up Andzhelina Gullovna's interest. "And where did you go to college, if not here?"

"At Karlsruhe, on the west coast."

"Oh, Karlsruhe! That's a very fine school. Very elite. Congratulations. Did you study Zimmerman there?"

"No, not really. Otherwise I would probably have heard of you before Ilya told me." Katerinya could see she was scoring points. "I didn't specialize in anything in particular. It was a comparative literature program. All time periods, all cultures. I like Zimmerman, but as I'm sure you are aware, Ilya loves Zimmerman."

"And did you finally get to see the folio, Katerinya? May I call you that? Please call me Andzhelina."

"Yes, Katerinya and Andzhelina would be just fine." She liked where this was going. "And yes, I did get to see the folio. I treated myself to a half-day tour of the University when I came to Derazhne to see Ilya a little while back."

Andzhelina wanted to hear more about the visit to Ilya. She knew Katerinya was from Mariankursk, and was curious about how this whole relationship had begun and developed in such a short time, given that they lived so far apart. But the opportunity was not there yet. Katerinya had said 'treated myself,' so the story line was still about her. "And what else did you see on your tour, my dear?"

"The Brandenburg Bible, the Ipsum Lorem document, the art museums, the Trinity Statues. As a teenager, I always wanted to go to school here, so this was a kind of belated fulfillment of my ambition. The pilgrimage I had never got to make."

Bent as she was on getting around to Ilya, Andzhelina was now getting sucked into the story of Katerinya. "And what did you end up doing with your Karlsruhe degree?"

"I'm still working on that. I earn a living as a professional translator – comparative literature prepared me well for that, I suppose. But what I really want to be is a novelist. I've been working on one for a few years now, but only part-time. I'm afraid I'm not making much progress. How about you, Andzhelina? Do you write?"

Andzhelina gave a wry smile. "Not novels. Just criticism." She looked off into the distance. "I suppose all literature professors secretly want to be novelists." She looked back at Katerinya. "But that's not our day job either. We write commentary on the works of others. Modern literature professors take a stab at novels, once in a while. But what would I do? Write Zimmermanian poetry?"

"I had a literature professor at Karlsruhe who wrote novels. He was sort of a mentor of mine." (She left out the part about the crush.) "He taught a creative writing course."

"Ian Corteja?"

"Yes! Do you know him?"

"Well, I know *of* him. Everyone in literature does. You had quite a mentor! Look, I may not write novels myself, but academics are well plugged in to the publishing industry. I could introduce you to literary agents and publishers, if you like – when you are ready, of course. It's hard to get through all of the gatekeepers in this industry, Katerinya, but I suppose I'm part of the gatekeeping machinery."

"Oh would you? That would be so helpful, Andzhelina!" Katerinya couldn't contain her excitement. Then she could. "But I suppose I'm not ready yet, as you say. I need to finish a manuscript first. It had been pretty slow going, but it's moving along much better now with Ilya helping me."

"Ilya is helping you write a novel? I didn't know he wrote fiction."

"Are you really surprised? He's a polymath. He does everything."

That hurt. Katerinya had known him for what, two months maybe? And he's already revealed something to her that she had not discovered in 20 years. But now the subject of Ilya was on the table, so she bore in. "How does he help you?"

Katerinya was about to relate how he helped with the romantic parts, then suddenly realized where this was going. That was private. Andzhelina was fishing for an invitation. Permission not granted. "Oh, you know, he's just a sounding board for sentence structure and metaphors and such." She needed to change the subject. "Are you teaching a Zimmerman course this term?"

"No, actually. I'm teaching a course on the Bible as literature. It's very popular, you know. It draws non-religious students that have never read the Bible, and plenty of religious students who may as well have never read the Bible. They've had the Bible related to them by others, but never read it themselves with a critical eye. It can be quite revealing for both groups."

Katerinya smiled. "I think I'm in that second group, actually. I'm not religious, but I was raised that way. And my relationship with the Bible is just as you describe it. It was related to me by others. I never really read it myself." Then she remembered her recent brush with Songs of Songs. "I just recently read some of Songs of Songs for the first time. It was quite a revelation!" She left out the wider context of reading it in bed with Ilya.

With a knowing smile, Andzhelina said, "Yes, isn't it? That's my favorite book in the whole collection. Students are usually not prepared for reading something like this in the Bible."

Then Katerinya opened up a bit. "It's a little … erotic, don't you think?"

"Yes. Sometimes very erotic." There was a pause in the conversation. "Do you like that?"

Another pause. "Yes." Katerinya felt suddenly exposed. She had not invited Andzhelina into her private space. She had somehow got in there anyway. She probably wouldn't have refused her if she had asked. So she answered truly. What else was she supposed to do?

Andzhelina sensed her discomfort immediately. "I'm sorry. I shouldn't have asked such a direct question. And I appreciate your honesty. I think women have a hard time admitting to erotic attraction. It's not very ladylike. But it's natural. We're not talking pornography here. This is very elegant, moving poetry about an aspect of being human."

"I have no problem admitting to erotic attraction. And I agree, it's very natural. But for me, it's private. I have a hard time admitting it publicly. I've learned a lot about this distinction in my time with Ilya, and a lot about myself, and my erotic imagination … and the naturalness of it all."

This hurt even more. Andzhelina so wanted to be Katerinya right now. She could see now that there was a bond between Ilya and Katerinya that she could never be a part of. But she felt somewhat of a bond with Katerinya herself now. They were on a common wavelength. "Which of the Songs have you read?"

"I didn't pay attention to the chapter numbers. I just opened to a random spot. It was about Kind David, and a secret chord, and Samson and Delilah, and … other things."

"Chapter 7," she smiled. "My favorite is Chapter 13. Oh, of course, you won't know which one that is. Wait! We're in a library. The Kadnikovs must have a Scholar's Bible in here somewhere, the one that I use in my course." She popped out into the main library and began searching. Too many books. Then Mr. Kadnikov spied her in her search, and came over to help. "Looking for something in particular, Andzhelina Gullovna?" "I'm looking for a reference in the Scholar's Bible that I teach in my course. Do you have one?" "Yes," he said, turning around to survey the collection from a distance. "I believe it's over here." It was. Andzhelina thanked him and quickly returned to Katerinya with the volume. She opened to Songs of Songs 13 and read to her:

> *Oh the sisters of mercy, they are not departed or gone*
> *They were waiting for me when I thought that I just can't go on.*
> *First they brought me their comfort and later they brought me their song.*
> *Oh I hope you run into them, you who've been travelling so long.*
>
> *Yes you who must leave everything that you cannot control.*
> *It begins with your family, but soon it comes round to your soul.*
> *Well I've been where you're hanging, I think I can see how you're pinned:*
> *When you're not feeling holy, your loneliness says that you've sinned.*
>
> *They lay down beside me, I made my confession to them.*
> *They touched both my eyes and I touched the dew on their hem.*
> *If your life is a leaf that the seasons tear off and condemn*
> *They will bind you with love that is graceful and green as a stem.*
>
> *When I left they were sleeping, I hope you run into them soon.*
> *Don't turn on the lights, you can read their address by the moon.*

*And you won't make me jealous if I hear that they sweetened
your night:
We weren't lovers like that and besides it would still be all
right.*

The two women smiled silently at each other, listening to the muse on the same wavelength. Then Andzhelina just let it out. "I envy you, Katerinya. I so want to be you right now."

There was a pause. "Are you jealous? Because of my romantic relationship with Ilya?" Another pause.

"Yes … and touché. That was a private part of my self that I didn't want to share."

Katerinya felt for her. She had not meant to zing her like that. "I'm so sorry," she said, placing her hands on Andzhelina's. "Please don't be jealous. Ilya speaks very highly of you. You obviously mean a great deal to him. I still don't know why he suddenly chose me, out of all of the women he must have known over the years."

Andzhelina smiled. "My dear Katerinya, isn't it obvious? Look at you! You must have looked in the mirror tonight before you left for the party. You must have seen the reactions of guests."

Katerinya couldn't deny it. She was at her peak tonight. A vision to behold. She had always thought of herself as attractive, but not as a femme fatale. Tonight was an aberration. It didn't explain things. "Thank you, from one woman to another, Andzhelina. But I did not look like this when I first met Ilya in the train station in Mariankursk. Something more was going on."

"Don't underestimate yourself, Katerinya. Beauty is youth. You have a quiet, striking beauty that shows through whatever you are wearing, or doing, or whatever light you are under. Others can see it, even if you don't. You certainly made it easier for Ilya. I just couldn't compete."

"But it's more than just physical attraction. Ilya said he thought you were attractive enough, it just didn't develop somehow. And you probably first met him when you were younger than me."

"He said I was attractive?" She couldn't get past that part. "He never told me that."

Suddenly Katerinya thought she might have disclosed too much. She went in for the save. "You probably never told him you thought he was attractive either. Am I right?"

Reflecting, Andzhelina offered, "I suppose you're right."

"You two just never got close enough to share this."

"How long did it take for you and Ilya to share this?"

Katerinya reflected. "I don't think we ever did say that to each other. We just knew. Don't you see, Andzhelina, it's not something you did or didn't do. Or a matter of who was prettier. It just happened. None of us knew what we were doing."

"A simple twist of fate, then?"

Katerinya got the Zimmerman reference, and smiled. "No, that's not quite it. That was about accidents of timing. Being in the wrong or right place at the wrong or right time. It's about who we *are* – you, me, and Ilya. None of us chooses who we are. I suppose the simple twist of fate was me encountering Ilya in a train station. Everything after that was just a matter of us being who we were. If it managed to get started at all, the rest was going to happen anyway. We were just lucky."

Andzhelina was beginning to understand it now. Katerinya was virtually the female version of Ilya. She saw it more and more. They were both empaths. They were honest about their feelings to a fault. They were initially very open, but shut you out quickly if they didn't sense a mutual trust. Katerinya played no games. She was utterly without guile. You couldn't pick a fight with Ilya. Andzhelina had rarely ever seen him visibly angry. If he was bothered by some actual injustice, he would look for a way to do something constructive about it. She could easily imagine that Katerinya and Ilya had never had a fight, and possibly never would. They were an impossible couple.

§

Back in the dining room, after Diederick had left, Ilya began to get his second wind. So he set off in search of Katerinya. She wouldn't be hard to spot, even at a great distance – the svelte lady in red. When he got to the Kadnikovs' library, he spotted Andzhelina Gullovna, on her tiptoes, putting a large volume into an open slot in the shelves. She also spotted him. As they passed, she stopped in front of him with a knowing smile. "She's in there," she said, motioning toward the anteroom. Then she looked that way too, and seeing that Katerinya was out of sight, she turned and gave Ilya a very unexpected but generous hug. While still in the embrace, she said, "She's a keeper, Ilya Erynovich. Don't ever let her go." Then she left, with him standing there, a bit bemused. That's a directive he would have no trouble following, he thought.

In the alcove, he found Katerinya sitting on the built-in seat under the window, beaming at the sight of him. Her outstretched arms, in their elegant black gloves, said "Come sit with me." And her voice said "Come sit with me, Iliusha. I had a most interesting conversation with Andzhelina. That's what we call each other now – Andzhelina and Katerinya. I'll tell you all about it." As he sat with her, once she saw no one was in eyeshot, she continued the story with her head on his shoulder and her arms around his waist. She was tired and happy. But she didn't get to finish.

They heard a great commotion outside the anteroom. This caused Katerinya to resume a more public posture. Then a footman looked in and, coming to polite attention, said, "Excuse me. Everyone is summoned to the front room. There's going to be an important announcement." With that, he bowed and left, spreading the message to other guests. "What's that about, Iliusha?" "I don't know," he replied. As they made their way to the front room, Katerinya asked, "Is this another one of the Kadnikov's party traditions, like the carolers?" "Whatever it is, it's not a tradition, I can tell you that. This must be something important." When they got there, the room was abuzz with speculation. Ilya could just see armed soldiers leaving through the front entrance. Kadnikov looked a little ashen, and there was a look of concern on the faces of several guests. This was not going to be a joyous announcement.

"Ladies and Gentlemen, may I have your attention," Kadnikov began. The room quieted to a hush. "Martial law has been declared for all of Solinovsk and Derazhne." There were gasps. Katerinya looked at Ilya, worried. "It seems that some disease outbreak that originated in Mariankursk has spread to our area. The soldiers didn't give me any specifics, but said that it was very dangerous. Everyone is required to return to your homes and shelter in place. There will be a curfew starting at dusk each day until further notice." As his words echoed in the great hall, now deadly silent, he paused, as if trying to remember more of the instructions he had received from the soldiers. Mrs. Kadnikova whispered in his ear. "Oh, yes, and everyone is to stay inside their dwellings except to procure essential services." She whispered in his ear again. "Further announcements from the government will be made later." Then he paused looking down at his shoes. He looked back up and said in a quieter tone "I'm sorry … I hope you all had a wonderful evening up to now." With that, he and Kadnikova moved out of the way as the guests began to make a rush for their coats.

Katerinya, now clearly concerned, looked at Ilya. "Is it true? I thought the outbreak was over?" Ilya looked around the room, then pulled Katerinya aside so they would be out of earshot from the rest of the guests. In a low voice he said, "No, I don't think so. If there really was a new outbreak, I would be the first person Tarasov contacted." He checked his phone to see if he had any messages from the Prince. Nothing. "This is not good," he said. "Tarasov is declaring martial law for some other reason. He's using this faux outbreak as an excuse. Now I see the wider context of his earlier cryptic instructions for me." He hugged her around her waist, and pulled her close. "This is not good for me. I will get sucked into this, one way or another. And if it's not good for me, it will soon not be good for you. They will be coming for me. And if they don't get me, they will be coming for you."

"Why, Iliusha?" she pleaded. "You haven't done anything wrong!"

"No, I haven't. It's about what they will *want* me to do. I'm the central cog in this whole machinery."

"What will they want you to do?"

"That's what's so insidious about this whole affair. I don't know yet. Makes it hard to plan a defense. The only thing that is clear is that we must get out of here, quickly. Before they realize we are gone."

"To Mariankursk?"

"Yes, we'll start there. But they will probably close down the trains. Let's get our coats. We should head straight to the train station. Can you get along without your two suitcases?"

"Of course. I still have everything else at home. But what about you?"

"Well, I still have an overnight bag at your place – just like old times." It was a rare bit of levity in an otherwise dire moment. "Check your phone, Katya. Is tracking off?" She did. It was on. She turned it off. He checked his. Also on to off. They had figured everybody in the world knew they were at the Kadnikov's tonight, so tracking was harmless. Now it was a real threat. They had to get off the grid.

On their way to University Station, the streets were filled with soldiers, knocking on doors, making announcements through bullhorns, checking IDs. Worried citizens hurried back and forth in all directions. At the station, there were crowds and long lines to board the tram. "Good thing we're not carrying any luggage," Ilya said, as they bypassed the tram and set out for the train station on foot. The absence of luggage also allowed them to walk with an arm around each other's waist. Warmth wasn't really the problem, their sabovar and sabovara providing plenty. With the specter of separation hanging over them, the tight closeness provided comfort.

At Derazhne Station, the crowds were even larger. Panic was beginning to set in. Hundreds of parties all over the city had been interrupted suddenly, sending society patrons, pirate wenches, elves, and ordinary revelers spilling into the streets, looking for a way out of town. Those that had gone home first to pack or change clothes were already behind the curve, unaware that it was already too late. A serious looking soldier with a rifle was blocking the entrance to the westbound platform, and another was announcing through a bullhorn "Last train to Mariankursk and points west. You must shelter in place. I repeat, shelter in place. Only residents of Mariankursk and points west may board." An agitated woman pushed to the front and cried out "I live in Mariankursk!" The soldier with the bullhorn asked her for ID. She looked around nervously. She handed him her ID. He examined it. "Your address says Derazhne, Step aside." "But I really live in Mariankursk! With my daughter!" "Step aside!" he said more sternly. The soldier with the rifle moved to help him make his point."

Now Katerinya was in a panic. "Iliusha, they won't let you board!" He had to make a hard decision. "You go without me. I'll get there somehow later." She grasped him around his sabovar with both hands, as if to keep him prisoner. "No! I won't go without you!" she pleaded. "We'll both stay here. We'll get out somehow later." He knew this would not work. He had to get her as far from the reach of Tarasov as possible. So he came up with a plausible story. "You go first. When they check my ID they'll know who I am, so I can bluff my way on." "Are you sure?" "Yes." He wasn't sure at all, but he needed to get her on that train.

As expected, they let Katerinya right through. She waited anxiously for his encounter with the guards. "We're together," Ilya said. The guard looked at them both: Katerinya, the vision in red, and Ilya in his formal wear. "I can see that," he said with a wink and a smile. Katerinya breathed a sigh of relief. But before Ilya could move, he said "ID?" Ilya handed it over. "Koskayin!" the guard said, "… from Derazhne." He looked up. "Only residents of Mariankursk and points west. Step aside please." Ilya had to think fast. The guard had recognized his name. That could be good or bad. Good if he only knew he was connected somehow to Tarasov. Bad if Tarasov had ordered guards to keep him in Derazhne. But before he could pick a strategy, the ever-resourceful Katerinya was already authoring another short work of fiction in her head.

Her inner self was terrified, almost shaking, but her outer self put on a calm, professional rendition of the story. "Professor Koskayin!" she shouted in his direction. "Didn't Prince Tarasov say they would be expecting you in Mariankursk? What will I tell them if you don't arrive?" Ilya's inner self said, "That's my Katya." His inner self was even smiling. His outer self, on the other hand, leaned into the role with seriousness. "That's a good question, my dear. Which one of you fellows wants to explain this to the Prince, when Ms. Grigoreva gets there alone?" The soldier with the rifle was a little shaken. The one with the bullhorn was skeptical. He looked Ilya in the eye for a moment trying to decide whether to call the bluff. "Sorry, I have my orders. Only Mariankursk and west residents." From this, Ilya learned that there was no specific order to detain him – yet, at least. So he upped the ante. "As do I," he said. "Why don't I just text the Prince and we'll see whose order is more important. I have his private number right here." Ilya pulled out his phone, and swiped his contacts to Tarasov's number. Now the more skeptical guard had lost some confidence. He doubted anybody had Tarasov's private number. "Let me see that," he demanded, taking Ilya's phone. Right at the top of the page it read 'Tarasov, Koldan Sonvaevich.'

And there was a thread of prior messages. He began to perspire a little, still in a staring contest with Ilya as he handed back his phone. "Now, which of you two gentleman shall I tell the Prince is preventing me from getting to Mariankursk?" The stern looking soldier tried to call the bluff one more time. "Tell him Second Lieutenant Polachev." Ilya began moving his finger as if he were typing, but he was tapping the inert sides of the screen, not the virtual keyboard. The last thing he wanted to do was actually text Tarasov. Polachev blinked first. He reached out and grabbed Ilya's texting hand to stop him. He looked at the soldier with the rifle, nodded his head toward Katerinya, and said, "Let him through."

Katerinya's inner self was relieved, but still shaken. She wanted to run to him. But her outer self remained coolly professional and simply walked beside him, showing no emotion until they boarded the train and found seats together. Then she collapsed in his lap and held on for dear life.

Chapter 7

THE EPIDEMIC THAT WASN'T

For most of the journey back to Mariankursk, Katerinya slept in Ilya's lap. She was much more fatigued than she had realized, skating through her magic evening on excitement and adrenaline. With the endocrinal stimulants gone, and the trauma at the train station abated, her body just shut down, exhausted. Her dreams were dominated by the happier parts of the evening, with the lady in red gliding from encounter to encounter in the lush, opulent, refined surroundings. But the anxiety of the escape along the streets of Derazhne tinged these joyous moments with a vague dread, and the acute dose of fear injected by the final incident at the train station tagged these memories together. She would periodically awake in this anxious state, confused about the source of the dread. Ilya would comfort her before she fully came to, and this eased her back to sleep, feeling warmly secure for now.

Ilya did not sleep. Katerinya was being buffeted by forces she didn't really understand, but Ilya understood – at least he understood who the forces were and what their motivations were. Of the many possible outcomes of this pending clash of wills that he could foresee, very few were benign. If he were not a potential player in these scenarios, he could just retreat into the background with Katerinya and ride it out. But he realized that he didn't have that option. They didn't have that option. If he were to play the hero, and stash her away somewhere where the antagonists wouldn't find her, then take his chances back in the city on his own, he still couldn't be sure she was safe, particularly if he maintained radio silence with her. He couldn't be sure she wouldn't break the silence and come to find him – in fact he could be sure she *would*. And he would also go crazy not having her close enough to protect her. So for both of their sakes, they had to remain together. They had to disappear together.

When they reached Mariankursk Station, the balance of passengers in the main hall was about the same as on a normal night, but this was because there were fewer passengers arriving from the east, and more passengers waiting to get further west. The news of martial law had reached here like a wave, and it was carrying citizens with it as it propagated outward toward the periphery of the Principality. The waitress in the station café was disappointed and confused to see Dmitri and Anna back so soon – without their luggage. But they looked positively stunning in their formal wear – particularly Anna! Maybe they were escaping this martial law thing. Yes, that was it. That's why they left their luggage and returned so soon. This was a good thing. They had escaped together. She mentally erased the story of Dmitri and Anna's trip that she had previously composed and started a new one. It began with some kind of royal ball on Crispness Eve in the big city.

As they walked to Tallinnskaya Street from the station, Katerinya was now fully awake and better able to confront her fears. The waking state and the cold night air gave her some clarity. They had escaped together, and the balance of the evening had been so magical, the kind of thing she wanted to remember, even dwell on.

She knew that whatever the nature of the danger was, Ilya had it covered. A burden she wished he did not have to bear alone. She remembered vaguely how he comforted her each time she awoke on the train, and resolved to be more like her usually resourceful self and comfort him. No more clingy "Oh, Iliusha, what will happen to us!" She erased everything that happened after the party up until they were on the train. They would talk about the good things that happened tonight.

At Tallinnskaya Street, she had to scramble a little to replace some of the personal items she had left in Derazhne, but Katerinya being Katerinya, the change of plans did not mean she had to put on fresh bed linens for herself and Ilya tonight. She had already done that before they left. Now, they could just fall into bed. She kept their conversation focused on the party as much as she could, steering Ilya back to the magical past each time he started to brood a little about the future. She could see it was working. He needed this. She was the comforter in charge now.

She briefly fantasized about sleeping in her red gown – she hardly wanted to take it off. She wanted this moment to go on and on, but of course that wasn't very practical. So when the time came, she asked Ilya if he would like to undress her, and take her hair down. This seemed a fitting way to end things. He thought so too. As she cuddled up to him on the clean sheets, he began to formulate a plan for tomorrow. She gently placed her finger over his lips to silence him. "Tell me tomorrow, Iliusha."

§

On Crispness morning, they did not rise with the sun. It was a clear, sunny day, the reflected light from the front room came streaming in, and they were both morning persons, but the energy expended on the previous day had left them with a sleep deficit. Adding to their lethargy was the fact that they had run out of kindling, so they could not make a bedroom fire on the previous night. The room was cool, the bed was warm. Ilya still awoke with the sun, silently as usual, but had no incentive to convert this into an actual rising.

When Katerinya finally came to, with enough will to make a day of it, she lingered for a while, waiting for Ilya's next sleep-wake cycle to occur naturally. It felt good to be back in the country – quiet, homey and safe. She had never really thought of Mariankursk as the country before now, but after the bustle of early morning Derazhne, and the city life during the day, and the city lights at night, and her wild ride among the glitter and the culture of the Kadnikov's party, her more rustic 10 Tallinnskaya Street, backed onto its birch wood lot, was decidedly rural. It had always been just her home. Now it was her home in the country. The bright red gown with its long black gloves, carefully preserved in her closet along with the memories, belonged to someone else, an identity that she assumed – and would willingly assume again – to play the part of a city girl at a home in the city. She was still drawn to both homes, and to both identities, but could now see that each was the antidote for the other. Right now, she was in a country girl mood, and grateful that she had an equally adaptable country man who was at home splitting wood. They could use a country fire about now.

Right on cue, when Ilya resurfaced for his next wake cycle, and saw that Katerinya was fully awake and ready to go, he looked around the chilly room and said, "I'll need to split some kindling." Smiling, she said, "Let me make you some coffee first." That got them both up, and started on their country morning. Ilya already had a good inventory of split logs in the woodshed, so he just needed to split some of them into kindling. He made quick work of it.

With the new supply of kindling in the wood carrier, Ilya returned to start the fire in the front room while Katerinya made their breakfast. They took their breakfast on the trunk in front of the fireplace, again with the Crispness tree in view. "How long do we leave it up, Iliusha?"

"How long do you usually leave your tree up?"

"Oh, I like to keep it as long as I can. Until it starts to brown."

"That's because you bought pre-cut trees at the market," he smiled. "This one will probably last another month before it browns." He got up to check the water level in the bucket at the bottom of the trunk. "Sure enough, almost empty. It's still alive." He went to the kitchen to fill a pitcher with water and returned to refill the bucket.

"Well, then I guess we'll leave it up as long as we still feel in the Crispness mood. We can do whatever we like, right?"

"Yes, we can," he smiled. But then turning more serious he said, "But we are not fully in control of our destiny right now."

Katerinya was waiting for this moment to come. She had said, "Tell me tomorrow, Iliusha." It was now tomorrow. She was ready. "What's your plan?"

"Is there someone in town that you know? A friend maybe? Someone whom you can trust? Someone whom you don't visit regularly – or at least someone you haven't visited in the last two months or so?"

Katerinya thought. "Olena Anwynovna. She's a friend from high school. We keep in touch, but I haven't been to her house in ages. I meet her for lunch sometimes."

"And you can trust her?"

"Oh yes!"

"Does she live alone?"

"Yes, she has a whole house. A small one. When her parents divorced, they deeded the house to her. She has the whole place to herself now. Why?"

"We need a place to hide out in Mariankursk, in case they come for us. Just something temporary. I'm afraid anyone who already knows about us also knows about Tallinnskaya Street by now. It's the first place they will look. Do you think she might let us stay there – just in an emergency?"

"Oh I'm sure she would. Shall we go see her?"

"No. Text her, and ask if we could meet her – no, ask if *you* could meet her – someplace in town for lunch. Keep the text brief. Don't say what this is about. Phones are insecure. When the government eavesdrops on this, they should just be able to infer that you are meeting her for lunch – for social reasons. Don't mention me in the text."

"Will you be coming?"

"Yes, but we'll keep that below the radar. In fact, if there is a place in town that you often meet her for lunch, suggest that. This needs to appear normal, unremarkable."

"There is: *Maxim's Corner*. I'll suggest that. I'm glad you think of these things, Iliusha!"

"Does Olena Anwynovna know about us?"

Katerinya demurred, looking a little guilty. "Of course she does. Women talk."

"Do you think she has mentioned us to others?"

"Of course she has. Women talk."

Ilya smiled a knowing smile. "OK, we'll deal with that when we meet."

§

Ilya and Katerinya were the first to arrive at Maxim's Corner. They got a sunny, corner table near the windows. Many shops and restaurants in Mariankursk were open on Crispness day because the bulk of the holiday celebrations – when you took time off to be with family – were on Crispness Eve. Some people also took Crispness day off, but the merchants relied on this day for significant revenue.

As Olena Anwynovna approached the window, on her way toward the entrance, she recognized Katerinya, who in turn recognized her. They both did the quick smile and wave, then Olena Anwynovna looked wide-eyed at Ilya with raised eyebrows, awkwardly pointing, as if to say "Is this who I think it is?" Katerinya just smiled and waved her toward the entrance, as if to say, "Just get in here and you'll find out." Olena Anwynovna came straight to the table where a chair and place setting were already awaiting her. "Katerinya, you didn't say you were bringing company!" She glanced at Ilya.

"Olena Anwynovna, this is Ilya Erynovich."

"Oh, please call me Olena."

"In that case, please call me Ilya," he responded.

"That's what I call him," Katerinya chimed in smiling. "Well, approximately."

"Is this who I think it is?"

"Well, who do you think it is?" she responded. This put Olena on the spot. She was at a loss for words. Then Katerinya rescued her, "Yes, of course it is!"

Olena was relieved, then excitedly said "Oh I'm so happy for you!" She eyed them both, sizing them up as a couple, unable to suppress her joy. "Why didn't you tell me you were bringing him?" Turning to Ilya, she said, "I've heard so much about you from Katerinya."

Ilya did the standard "Well, I hope you heard good things."

Olena raised her eyebrows, "If only you knew!"

They both looked at Katerinya, who said nothing. She looked down at the table, a little embarrassed. "Women talk," she muttered. Then she took charge of the conversation. "There is a reason I didn't tell you he was coming. You see, in Derazhne, Ilya is involved in a lot of ... let's say 'political intrigue' ... that goes all the way up to Prince Tarasov." Olena's face showed a look of alarm. Katerinya grabbed her hands. "Oh don't worry. Ilya is a good person, a very good person. This is not his choice. He would like to get out of it, but he can't. That's why we're in Mariankursk now. That's why we're here talking to you right now. We might need a place to hide out in an emergency."

Olena was still concerned. "But how are you involved, Katerinya? Why do you need to hide out?"

"Because I'm involved with Ilya ... you know ... involved."

Ilya jumped in, "The Prince has spies everywhere, even here in Mariankursk. He knows about Katerinya and me. (Though apparently not as much as you)," he said, smiling in Katerinya's direction. "He knows he can force me to do anything by threatening her. He's not really a bad person, but he is a powerful person with a lot of resources. He knows how to manipulate people. I don't want it to come to that."

Olena looked confused. "But I don't understand ..."

"That's actually good. It's better that way. Better for all of us. The less you know, the better. You'll just have to trust us, for now. You'll be able to answer truthfully when asked what's going on. You really don't know. You're just a friend of Katerinya's."

Olena looked at Katerinya, sympathetically, then back at Ilya. "I trust you."

Katerinya took over at this point, since it really should be her asking the favor. "Do you suppose we could stay with you, in your house, if we need to disappear for a while – not now, but maybe sometime later?"

Now Olena saw her role in the whole drama. "Of course, Katerinya! Of course you can! I would love the two of you to stay with me. I only wish it were under happier circumstances. Don't worry! No questions. Tell me only what I need to know. I won't tell anyone else about it."

Then Ilya posed the delicate question. "Do you suppose you could not disclose our relationship to anyone else who doesn't already know? And maybe limit the 'women talk' among those who already do know? The fewer people that know about us, the better."

Olena looked at Katerinya. "Of course," she smiled. "There aren't many other friends who know. We don't gossip that much! Should we go to my house after lunch, so I can show you around?"

"No," Ilya said. "We need to disassociate your house from Katerinya as much as possible – and certainly me. No one has seen her visit you there since we first met. That's good. We need to keep it that way. Don't discuss any of this with Katerinya on the phone. If you need to talk about it, send a simple text to meet socially at Maxim's Corner. It would also be a good idea for you not to visit Katerinya at Tallinnskaya Street."

"But don't we need to do some kind of preparation at my house?"

"Don't worry. We'll work out a protocol for that after lunch."

During the lunch, Ilya and Katerinya both tried to steer the conversation toward less clandestine subjects, to put Olena more at ease. The Crispness Eve party at the Kadnikovs' provided ample fodder. Indeed, the whole day provided material, from the highbrow brunch at Yaroslava's, to the upscale fashion show at Veronika's Fine Ladies's Apparel, to the high society announcement of the lady in red. Olena was particularly invested in the details of the gown and the hairdo. Katerinya herself was still getting used to the trappings of this newly minted city girl, so she realized how magical this all must seem to her country girl companion who had never left Mariankursk after high school. Needless to say, the Crispness Eve story ended benignly at the Kadnikov's. "Then the footman brought us our coats and we took the train back to Mariankursk."

At the end of the lunch, Ilya had Katerinya sketch the route from 10 Tallinnskaya Street to Olena's house, on the back of a paper placemat. He studied it for a moment, asked both women about streets and landmarks in the area surrounding Olena's house, then sketched an alternate, obfuscated route that went through the back woodlot at Tallinnskaya Street toward the outskirts of town, then cut back through minor streets and pathways until it reached the most obscured part of the back entrance to Olena's house. "*This* is how we will travel between the two houses," he announced. Stay in the shadows. If you see someone following you, turn in some other direction and go somewhere random until you are sure you are in the clear. Perhaps go toward Maxim's. Then if you are stopped and interrogated, you say you were on your way to Maxim's. Remember, if you need to get in touch, you both go publicly to Maxim's. If one has to visit the other at home, for whatever reason, take the obscured route, as privately as possible." Then he promptly tore the map into small pieces and deposited it in the trash receptacle on the way out of the restaurant. He instructed Olena to return home by her normal route. He and Katerinya would make a normal return to Tallinnskaya Street, then take the obscured route to Olena's house.

§

On their secret journey to Olena's house, even though the task was overshadowed by the worrisome circumstances of ever needing to use it, Katerinya was getting into the clandestine nature of it all. As they started their trek into the back woods, she imagined being stopped and interrogated. She would say she was going to check for wolf tracks. She had heard them howling the night before. *That* was believable. If she was stopped on the cutback at the outskirts of town, she would say that she got lost deep in the woods looking for wolf tracks. Could you point me toward Tallinnskaya Street, please? At each point on the secret map, she concocted another explanation that led away from Olena's, though the wolf excuse had expired pretty quickly.

When they reached Olena's house, quietly, Olena was there to greet them, quietly. Once inside, that all changed. She was so happy to see them, and anxious to help. The house was small, but cozy. She had already selected a bedroom for Ilya and Katerinya, and had begun to provision it with linens and towels and other essentials. "Does it have windows?" Ilya asked. "Yes," she said, "but the perfect kind of windows. It was my bedroom growing up here." Katerinya knew the room, and why it was so special – apart from being Olena's old room where they had sleepovers when they were younger. "Let me show you. It's upstairs in the back." They climbed the stairs and went to the room down the hallway. Olena presented it with her arms outstretched as if to say "Ta da!" Katerinya was watching Ilya for his reaction. The room was under a gabled roof that ran the length of the east-facing wall. There were no windows on any of the walls at eye level, but the entire horizontal surface under the gable had windows. Plenty of light, particularly in the morning, but the contents of the room visible from the outside only to birds and squirrels. "Perfect," said Ilya. "And it's east facing Iliusha! Morning sun for you, but not in the eyes for me!"

"I'll put some clothes in the dresser for Katerinya," Olena said, still excited by the possibility of an impending visit. "We're about the same size. I'm afraid there's not much I can do for Ilya. No men in the house, you know." "That's OK," Katerinya said, "we'll bring some from my place." "Oh, I'm so excited you'll be sleeping in my old bedroom, Katerinya! Though not in a way I ever did." Katerinya looked down at the floor, embarrassed to look at Ilya for a moment. He smiled, "I know. Women talk." It was an awkward moment, but an endearing moment nonetheless.

Ilya moved them past it by inquiring whether there was a true hiding place. "Suppose we are here, and someone comes to search the house. Is there someplace we could hide that they would not think to look? An attic maybe, or a cellar?"

"There is an attic," Olena offered.

"How do we get to it?" Ilya asked.

"Oh, I haven't been up there since I was a child. We just used it to store old stuff. There's a narrow stairway behind a door at the back of the linen closet. I'm afraid we've put shelves in front of the door, since we stopped using it."

"That could be perfect," Ilya said. "Show me."

Olena led them down the hall to the linen closet, then pointed to the shelf case that obscured the attic door.

"Could I move these?" Ilya asked, pointing to the linens on the shelves.

"Oh, yes. Please do."

Ilya started transferring items from the shelves to another part of the floor. The women joined in. With the shelf case empty, Ilya moved it away from the attic door, and climbed the stairs to take a look. The women followed.

It was a small space, but habitable. There was a lot of dust, a few scattered pieces of furniture, and one twin bed. A single window at one end of the space provided enough daylight, and was sufficiently high up to prevent views of the space from the outside. Ilya examined the unfinished wooden framing, and the main support beam running along the roofline. He looked at the floor below, then dusted off a section of the beam with his finger. "Powderpost beetles," he said.

"What is that?" Olena asked with a little concern.

"The main beam has some powderpost beetle damage."

"Is that a bad thing?"

"Only if they're still active. If so, they will eventually reduce the beam to powder, but that will take a very long time. The damage could be very old."

"How do you know if they are still active?"

Ilya smiled, "You brush away the powder like I just did. Then you wait a few years, and check to see if there's more."

Realizing that the danger was not imminent, but surprised by what appeared to be an expert carpenter's skill, Olena turned to

Katerinya and asked, "How does he know these things? I thought he was a professor."

Katerinya smiled, "He just knows things. Don't ask him how, right Ilya?"

Ilya reflected on the emergence of yet another unconscious skill. How did he know such things?

Then Olena noticed the bed. "That's my bed! From when I was a child. I didn't know my parents kept it!"

"Iliusha, we could make this work," Katerinya volunteered. "We'll need to clean up a little."

"Clean up a lot," Olena said, "But don't worry, I'll do that." Then she asked, "Isn't my bed a little small for the two of you?"

"Don't worry, we'll manage," smiled Katerinya. She looked at Olena who was about to speak again, and put her finger over her lips. "No more women talk," she smiled again. "We'll manage."

Now they had a plan – with a built-in backup plan. Ilya explained to Olena about the insecurity of phones. "Imagine that everything you say or text is being listened to or watched by someone," he told her. This surprised her. "Why would anyone be eavesdropping on me?" "They probably aren't now, but they may if they trace Katerinya's calls to you. That's why you have to meet in person at Maxim's if you have something to say about our secret world. You can arrange with Katerinya to have some secret protocol messages if you need." Katerinya perked up. "Yes, I can show you how Ilya and I do that. It's fun. Makes you feel like you are a spy!" Ilya also learned that Olena had no computer and no Internet connection. Just as well, he thought. One less source for a leak.

§

Ilya and Katerinya took the clandestine route back to Tallinnskaya Street. There was still snow on the ground, particularly in the wooded areas, and Ilya noticed their tracks from the journey there. He discussed this with Katerinya, how too many footprints along the same route would reveal that it *was* a route, where none was expected. In the absence of new snow cover, they should vary their tracks a little, take small detours to confuse a potential tracker. But not when they reached her woodlot. Their tracks would be expected there, emanating from and to her apartment — part of their cover story (remember the wolves?). They should walk over their own tracks there, to make it easier to tell if someone else had been in the woods near Tallinnskaya Street.

When they reached her back stairway, Ilya's phone made a message sound. It was from Tarasov: 'Yaroslava's: 17:00'. It had begun. The good news was that the Prince thought he was still in Derazhne. The bad news was that the Prince would soon know that he wasn't, when he didn't show for the meeting. Or would he? All he would really know was that Ilya was avoiding him. He could still be in Derazhne. No, doesn't matter. As soon as he was a no-show, the Prince would know that something was up. Mariankursk would be the first place to look. Either way, there was no strategy for Ilya that included responding to the text.

Katerinya watched his characteristic cogitation, waiting impatiently for the news. "What is it Iliusha?" He didn't want to tell her because he didn't want her to worry. There was nothing for them to do in the meantime anyway. But he was beginning to realize that he had to share everything with her. His wanting to protect her was outweighed by her own resilience — her ability to rise to the occasion when necessary. "It's Tarasov. He wants me to meet him at 17:00. In Derazhne."

This pierced the veil of temporary reprieve for Katerinya, making their preparation scenarios more real. She knew it would come. "What will you do?"

"Nothing. There's nothing to do. We just wait." His words sounded so stark, even to him, so he looked at her to see if there was concern in her face. She put on a brave face, limiting his visibility. "How are you holding up, Katya?"

She put her arm around his waist, splitting the difference between comforter and comfortee. "I'm OK. We're in this together. I know you have everything covered. Just let me know when it's time." This was a wise response. It was just what he needed to hear.

They went back into their sanctuary, and took up country living where they had left off, resolving to enjoy their simpler life together for as long as circumstances would permit. Except that they would accelerate plans for readying Olena's place. Ilya split more kindling. Katerinya organized her writing and translating materials so that she could quickly pack them up if she needed to relocate. She worked out a few message protocols to share with Olena – when they next met, of course. They decided to leave the tree and all of the decorations up indefinitely. These helped with the mood, and served as a buffer from the outside world.

After a while, Ilya returned to the Internet, looking for news. He found more reports of atrocities in the western regions perpetrated by this commander Kuznetsov. Who is this? Where did he come from? Which faction was he representing? Katerinya shuddered at the descriptions. She had never lived through a time of armed conflict. Wars were something from fiction for her. She had always thought of them as soldier on soldier affairs. But this was asymmetrical, guerrilla warfare. There were many civilian casualties, innocent bystanders who just happened to be in the way of someone else's religious objectives. What would happen if it came to Mariankursk? She didn't want to think about this. So she changed the subject to something she thought would divert Ilya's attention as well.

"Ilya, why does the Androsia message have to be written in whole organisms? Couldn't you just string together the DNA in a test tube or something?"

It worked. He had never considered this. But he quickly discounted the possibility. "DNA and RNA are pretty unstable just floating around in solution. Entropy would take over. The nucleus of a cell, where DNA resides in real life, has all kinds of molecular machinery and proteins for keeping it protected and repairing it. If I had wanted a message to last a long time, I would have put it in an organism."

She thought about that. It made sense. "But why does it have to be actual molecules? Couldn't you just write the message in ACGT's on paper? Wouldn't that be a lot simpler?"

Wow, he thought. I like how she thinks! Another possibility he had never considered. "Could be. Certainly easier to write." He thought about this some more. "But then why use DNA at all … particularly since I didn't add any encryption to the codon key? Almost anyone would be able to read it without much effort. I might as well have just written the message in plaintext."

"Because only you would know where to look! If you mixed it in with some real DNA stuff … you know, like the archives you were looking at for bacteria. It wouldn't stand out there. It would look like real DNA."

He turned and planted a big kiss on her. "You're brilliant! You should have been a scientist." She didn't want to be a scientist, but rather enjoyed being one right now. Ilya remotely connected to his DNA sequence archives at the University, and spawned a translation process to iterate through the entire archive. This would take a while, and even longer to review the results. As Katerinya privately hoped, it took well past 17:00. The die was now cast, and Ilya's attention was still on better things. At the end of the process there was a familiar outcome. Nothing. Every sequence in there must be from a real organism. But Katerinya had one more bold idea.

"Iliusha! Maybe you wrote it in your *own* DNA! Kind of like how you wrote the message on the back of your hand. Then it would always be in your possession, but no one else could see it. Does that make sense? Is that possible?"

He thought for a moment. Was it possible? Did it make sense? Could he have done this? Humans have lots of non-functional DNA. Plenty of targets for small CRISPR edits that would cause no biological harm. He tried to imagine what kind of long-lived somatic cell type he might have altered in himself. But that was the apex of the rollercoaster ride. From there on, it was downhill. Oh, he realized. That made no sense at all. There are trillions of cells in the human body. Even if he had somehow edited some of his own stem cells to propagate more cells with the message, the message-carrying cells would be an insignificant drop in the ocean of all of the non-message cells. He would never be able to recover such a message through sequencing. He would have to have altered *all* of his cells. And the only way to do that would have been to edit himself back when he was a single-celled embryo.

Katerinya was waiting expectantly, again, for his cogitation to conclude. She decided to give him all the time he needed this time. Then she could tell by his far-off, half smile that it had concluded. "Is that it?"

"No," he smiled (full, not half). "That's not it. It wouldn't be possible." He decided to leave out the absurd requirement of editing himself in utero. It was almost funny, he thought. This was not Ilya's usual demeanor when he hits a dead end, she thought, but she didn't want this to be the end of the episode just yet, so she encouraged him to stay at her computer. There must be something else he could research from here. Something to push the search a little further along. He didn't want the process to end either. So he came up with the idea of researching the property records for Derazhne to see if there was a trail of deeds for his house going back to previous owners.

At the Derazhne Registry of Deeds site, he eventually found a quitclaim deed for his house. The buyer, of course, was Koskayin,

Ilya Erynovich. The seller was listed as Kevin Telmans – from Ariona! A little further back in time, he found a transfer deed to Kevin Telmans from Vetochkin, Krasimir Jannaevich, from Derazhne. The second owner being from Ariona piqued his interest. Ilya had come here from Ariona, one of the last episodes he could remember. He wondered if there was any significance to this. As usual, Katerinya was following the research with great interest. She hadn't known that property records were publicly available for search on the Internet. "Try my place, Iliusha. I want to see who the owners are. Would that be at the same site?"

"If not, there must be a local Registry of Deeds for Mariankursk." He tried both possibilities and found a local registry site. When they looked up the deed for 10 Tallinnskaya Street, they found it registered to Moskvin, Milorad Annaevich. "Does that sound right?" Ilya asked. "I don't know," she said. "Who do you pay your rent to?" "The couple downstairs. It's a sublease." "Ahh."

"Let's do some more! Look up Ms. Zakharova. From the guesthouse." "Doesn't she own the place?" Ilya asked. "That's what she said. But this is fun. Look it up anyway. Maybe we can see who owned it before her." Ilya entered '14 Kalinin Street' as the search term. A deed came back registered to Aslanov Land Trust. "Maybe she doesn't own it!" They were both surprised. Now Ilya was determined to get to the bottom of this. He searched Mariankursk records for the land trust, but found nothing. He then widened his search to records for the whole Solinovsk Principality. He followed a tangled trail of ownership transfers that ended with a document listing the beneficial owner as Tarasov, Koldan Sonvaevich.

"She's a spy," Ilya said. "A spy for Tarasov. The whole guesthouse thing is a front. Well, she certainly plays the part well. 'Doesn't like to pry into other people's business. Doesn't gossip.' indeed."

§

Over the next few days, Ilya and Katerinya accelerated their transfer of items from Tallinnskaya Street to Olena's house, moving mostly after dark. They had forgotten to schedule their first run with Olena before they left her house on the initial visit, and she and Katerinya had yet to establish any text message protocols, so Katerinya had to text Olena for a Maxim's meet of just the two of them. There they worked out a signaling protocol. There would be a message to announce that Katerinya and Ilya would be coming to the house soon. In case Olena was not home, she would always leave the key under a designated rock near the back door when she left the house.

Ilya and Katerinya stocked up on provisions for Tallinnskaya Street, so they could minimize their time outdoors. After their last transfer trek to Olena's, it snowed overnight, covering all of the footprints. Ilya would check around 10 Tallinnskaya Street each morning and evening to see if there were any foreign prints. So far, so good. They discussed their predicament by the glow of the fireplace many times, alternating between waiting it out at Katerinya's or preemptively disappearing to Olena's. Waiting it out kept winning. It was possible, after all, that this might blow over. Each day without incident emboldened them more. Eventually, they needed more food, so they set out on a gray morning for the market together. This was their new modus operandi. They went everywhere together.

On their return, as they approached Katerinya's back stairway, she volunteered to take the groceries in so that he could get more firewood from the shed. When she was part way up the stairs, a soldier with a rifle emerged from behind the woodshed, blocking Ilya's path. Katerinya froze. Ilya turned around to see another soldier emerge from the shadows blocking his escape in that direction. The soldier in front of the woodshed said "Professor Koskayin? You need to come with us." Ilya was surprised that Tarasov was using soldiers this time instead of plainclothes agents. But they were under martial law after all, so the presence of soldiers was not unexpected. It also made a point. He didn't have much time to think. Looking around, he made a rash decision, more from emotion than reason. "I'll go if she comes with me." The guard at the shed looked up at Katerinya, who was struggling to retain her composure, then said, "I'm afraid that won't be possible. You'll be coming with us alone."

In the few seconds it took the soldier to perform this action, Ilya's rational faculties returned to him, and he breathed a mental sigh of relief. What if they had taken them both? That would have been a stupid move. Katerinya now had a chance to disappear from Tarasov's reach. It would be hard on her. It would be hard on him. But she would be safe. Realizing that Katerinya's inventive storytelling was not going to bail them out of this one, he said "Can I at least say goodbye to her first?" The shed soldier motioned with his rifle toward Katerinya on the stairs. That was soldier-speak for "Yes." Ilya climbed the stairs to her and gave her a bear hug. She was shaking slightly, trying to hold it together, but set the groceries down and joined in the embrace. He whispered in her ear, "Stay on the steps until the last soldier is leaving. Then make sure he sees you going into the apartment. Stay there until nightfall. Then go to Olena's like we planned." Her inner self was desperately pleading "But Iliusha, what about you," and a million other things she wanted to say to him, but her outer self managed to keep it together. This was supposed to be a silent hug. But since it was, she milked it for all it was worth. She squeezed hard, making it difficult for him to break off the embrace. He got the message. When he did break away, she extended her arms toward him in a "Don't leave me!" posture. She even shed a tear. This part of the act came easy. Both inner and outer selves were on the same page. This is what the guards would expect. She had a license to grieve.

As the three of them walked toward the train station, no one spoke. Ilya could see the futility of trying to escape with an armed soldier on either side. So he made it easier on all of them by showing his capitulation. They returned the favor by shouldering their weapons. No need to make this seem like an arrest. It could even be interpreted as Ilya being in charge of two soldiers. Or an important person with two bodyguards. The less provocative the better. Katerinya managed to follow the script and made sure the last soldier saw her enter the apartment. With the door closed, she dropped the bags on the floor and ran to the bedroom where she could watch the final scene from the west-facing window. She was comforted to see the three of them walking almost as comrades. There would be no violence. But tears streamed down her face as she traced the trio ever diminishing from view toward the horizon. Then they were gone. She collapsed in a heap on the floor. Her world was shattered.

At Mariankursk Station, the main hall was nearly empty, and not just because it was mid-morning. Few passengers were coming from or going to Derazhne now due to the shelter-in-place orders. Those that could escape from the east had escaped early. Few people wanted to return there now. Martial law had not been extended to Mariankursk yet, so Ilya's two guards were some of the few soldiers in town. The waitress in the station café worked the evening shift, so she was not there to witness the scene of Dmitri boarding the eastbound train with the two of them. Her story of Dmitri and Anna would be missing this chapter. The train was nearly empty, with Ilya sitting in a window seat, one soldier sitting next to him, and the other across the aisle. They said nothing.

The trip to Derazhne was peaceful enough from Ilya's window vantage point. The mid-morning sun was not visible through the gray overcast, but the new layer of snow dusting the fir trees by the side of the tracks provided plenty of color contrast. If he were not on such an ominous journey, he would have found the view calming. But he was on an ominous journey, and his mood was dominated by the heartbreak of leaving Katerinya behind. They had some message protocols that he would have used to contact her, but Tarasov had the foresight to instruct his men to confiscate Ilya's phone before they boarded the train. Ilya had thought that with all of their diligence, he and Katerinya would have seen Tarasov's men coming with enough time to execute their escape plan. But these guys were clearly professionals, in a different league than Ragnar and the Korihor stalker. Now he would have no way to reach her. This weighed heavily upon him. He was confident she would get to Olena's tonight according to plan, but after that, as the silence continued to build, she would surely go crazy. They hadn't prepared for a scenario like this.

As the train neared Derazhne, the peaceful winter scene changed to one of urban conflict. Pulling into the station, Ilya could see smoke rising from the ethnic neighborhoods in East Derazhne. He had read about this on the Internet, from the academic's ear-to-the-ground network. The simmering rivalry between Osipov and Sokolov, which had not yet risen to the level of an official armed conflict, was being fought via a proxy war between their respective religious enclaves. Each had its own informal militia of volunteers who regularly raided each other's neighborhoods in a tit for tat cycle of revenge killings. An outside observer might rightly be confused about how two religious tribes that profess to worship the same Jossmit could be so utterly certain of the other's damnation. But true believers have no other method for resolving conflicts about divinity.

Ilya could see face masks everywhere in the station, a caution against an epidemic that he was still sure was not happening. But it showed the effectiveness of the Prince's propaganda. Why he needed this cover was still not clear to Ilya. They did not get off in Derazhne as Ilya had expected. They were going on to Solinovsk. From this, Ilya inferred that they were no longer meeting at Yaroslava's. Perhaps he was now being taken straight to the palace. He was right.

Unlike many of the larger buildings in Solinovsk and Derazhne, the Tarasov family palace was not a repurposed structure that had survived from the Great Dying. It was newly built by the first of the ruling Tarasovs, and passed down through the ruling heirs, serving as the official residence of the ruling prince. Prince Tarasov was waiting for Ilya in his great library, a favorite retreat of his. He motioned for Ilya to sit down, then waved off the soldiers, instructing them to close the door on their way out.

Ilya was not sure what to expect since he had ghosted the Prince once and was now being forcibly returned to his presence. The Prince studied him for a moment, then said, "Ilya Erynovich. I missed you at Yaroslava's." The inflection made it clear that he was expecting an explanation.

Ilya played it straight up the middle. "I was in Mariankursk at the time."

"Yes, I know." He paused, not giving away his state of mind. "But you could have responded to the text ... and the next two." He paused again. Before Ilya could compose a response, Tarasov, with a half smile, said, "No need to explain that one away, Ilya Erynovich. I suppose I already know why that happened – or didn't happen – as well. I found you, after all. A Prince does not expect to be disregarded. But you have earned a little latitude in regard to those protocols by your excellent work for me thus far. Let's try to keep it that way. I know you have certain extracurricular activities to pursue in Mariankursk, shall we say, but I need you here – and visible – in Derazhne."

"For the non-existent epidemic?"

"Yes, that one. Do you know of another one?" The Prince was toying with Ilya.

"But why do you need a faux epidemic? Is this related to the non-announcement of a cure in Mariankursk?"

"Yes, in a way. Have you seen – of course you haven't, you were in Mariankursk. Have you *heard* about what's going on in East Derazhne right now?"

"Yes. Academics talk."

"I am certain that Sokolov is behind it. Osipov has tried to rein in his people, but this is paramilitary stuff, volunteers, crazy people. They have formed their own little militias that are not under his control. The evangelical militias *are* under Sokolov's control. He won't admit it publicly. It serves his purpose for them to do his dirty work at a distance. He's waiting until he has a critical mass before he strikes. I need an excuse to have soldiers on the street, soldiers in the enclaves, to tamp it down. Martial law affords that. The epidemic story keeps me from having to play my political hand too soon."

"But why you do have to wait? It's not like this is Africa. They can't vote you out."

"Ah, the subtleties of politics. It's not that simple. In the end, even monarchs rule by consensus. Your people have to believe that there is at least some semblance of the rule of law. I can't just arrest Sokolov and his deputies arbitrarily. I have to have some credible public evidence of sedition that I can point to."

"Why? Can't you just fabricate some evidence, like you did for the non-epidemic? Sokolov fabricates almost everything he says."

"And that's why I have to appear different!"

"But to whom? Do you think evidence will make any difference to Sokolov's followers? Do you think it will make any difference to the orthodox militias? They are busy killing each other right now because they are incapable of rational action. They are running on fear, and tribal loyalty, and righteousness, and religious fervor. They don't stop to consider any evidence before they strike. They only believe what their own leaders tell them – no matter how preposterous that is."

"Ilya Erynovich, I see you still have a ways to go in your political apprenticeship."

"I don't want to be a politician."

"I can see that. Politics is about precedent, whatever the form of government. When the next fellow looks back, wondering whether he should take a certain action, even if no one is powerful enough to stop him, he always looks to see if it has been done before – under similar circumstances. If the circumstances are not the same, he waits until they are close enough – or he makes them close enough. He always wants to be able to point back and say, 'This is how we do things here.' He doesn't want to appear arbitrary. To put Sokolov in prison, to have him executed, there has to be a trial. And if there is a trial, there has to be evidence. Not perfect evidence, but credible evidence. Do you see this now, Ilya Erynovich?"

He did. "But why do you need me? Here? Why is it any different whether I am here or in Mariankursk?"

"There is precedent for martial law in times of an epidemic. There is no trial to determine whether it really is an epidemic, or when it is over. Scientists decide that. You are the public face of that science, at least in the case of this bacterium. Your reputation precedes you. If people know about the Mariankursk outbreak at all, they know about you. You need to be here, at the University, visibly working to fix it."

"You want me lie about it?"

"I want you to do nothing about it."

"But my colleagues will know that I'm working on nothing. They probably already know the epidemic is a hoax, at least the ones that worked on the antibiotic with me. What do I say to them?"

"Why don't you work on a vaccine?" There was a pause while Ilya thought about this. "Did you ever locate the source of the Mariankursk outbreak? "

"No."

"Then it could happen again. Does the vaccine for *Y. pestis modernis* work on the new variant?"

"We don't know. But it's not very likely, given that the old antibiotic wasn't effective."

"Then you should be working on a new vaccine now anyway, am I right? You won't have to play act at anything. You're just being a good scientist."

Prince Tarasov had managed to thread the needle. The plan was largely acceptable, except for his estrangement from Katerinya. Maybe he could bring her here? No, he had already underestimated Tarasov once. Katerinya was now out of his reach as long as she was at Olena's. But Ilya couldn't control the political timing. He didn't know how long it would take for Tarasov to get his "evidence." He knew Katerinya was safe, but she didn't know he was safe. She would go crazy not knowing. He decided to see how much latitude he had, if he agreed to go along.

"OK. I agree to stay in Derazhne and work on a vaccine until the 'epidemic' is over. Am I free to go?"

"No, Ilya Erynovich, you are effectively under house arrest. You can go to your house, your lab, your office, or any public place associated with the bacterium. You will have an armed guard with you at all times. We'll call him your 'bodyguard.'"

"May I at least have my cell phone back?"

"No, I'm afraid that won't be possible. I know where your true loyalty lies Professor Koskayin. And I certainly don't blame you for that. So I have to be a realist. I'm sure you understand."

He did.

§

Pyotr Tashkaevich and Timofey Valyaevich crawled on their hands and knees behind the makeshift barricades on the edge of the Orthodox enclave. The two Evangelical teenagers were scouting out a sabotage mission against an electrical substation that doubled as a weapons cache for their mortal enemies on the other side. The plan was to first steal as many of the weapons as they could carry, then torch the substation with Molotov cocktails. They were unofficial members of the evangelical militia, wearing makeshift armbands to signify their allegiance, more to prevent being shot by their own side than to make a statement against the enemy. Their parents had prohibited their joining the actual militia, so they could not get the uniforms they so desperately wanted to wear. After verifying that the substation did indeed store weapons, they carefully made their way

THE EPIDEMIC THAT WASN'T 335

back to their own enclave, alternating between crawling and running for cover.

The stark landscape of the no man's land between the enclaves was littered with dead bodies and burned out houses, still smoldering. Timofey spotted the body of a young adolescent bearing an armband with their insignia that appeared to be twitching. He instinctively diverted from the escape route to investigate, but Pyotr, just as instinctively, grabbed him by the arm. "Tima! Leave him!" Pyotr said.

"But he's one of ours, Petya!"

"Probably dead already. Or soon will be. Stick to the mission!" Tima was torn, both by loyalty and sympathy, but capitulated to the older boy's authority.

When they reached the heart of their own enclave, Petya rounded up the other teenage members of their ragtag guerrilla band, and laid out the plan. They would divide into two groups. One group would first go for the weapons. The others would hold the Molotov cocktails at the ready. When the first group emerged with the weapons, the second group would move up and throw the makeshift bombs. Then they would all hightail it out of there.

"Lavro! Are you coming with us?" Petya asked. "It's now or never."

Lavro Mildaevich Shurupov hesitated. He looked up to Petya, his lifelong friend, but did not have a taste for bloodshed. He had resisted the recruitment calls from Sokolov. 'Jossmit's Soldiers' seemed like an oxymoron to him. "The meek shall inherit the Earth." "Turn the other cheek." "Do unto others as you would have others do unto you." These all seemed antithetical to killing random strangers. His parents too had prohibited him from joining the official militia, but now they were dead. His mother had been accused of being an orthodox collaborator. Her only sin was to take in an orphaned little girl after her orthodox parents were killed. The evangelicals shot her anyway. And the husband and the orthodox orphan for good measure. "You can't be too careful with collaborators," they said.

"Leave him. I don't trust him. He could be sympathetic to them," one of the older boys said.

"No! I know him," Petya said. "He wouldn't betray his own kind, would you Lavro? Come on, Lavro. You're either for us or against us. Which is it Lavro?"

A conflicted Lavro succumbed to both the peer and the tribal pressure. A double whammy. Tima was assigned to the Molotov cocktail crew. Petya assigned himself to the weapons detail. In the confusion of his last-minute recruitment, Lavro hadn't received an assignment.

As they approached the entrance to the substation, one of Tarasov's soldiers, in full uniform, was inspecting the facility. "What do we do now?" Tima whispered. Petya grabbed the one weapon they had among them – a sidearm – and fired at the soldier. His aim was not very good, wounding him in the leg. As he fell to the ground, Petya charged forward and killed him with a shot at close range, waving for the others to begin the attack. It was not a good plan – if you could call it a plan at all. Where there is one soldier there are likely to be others. And there were.

Others of Tarasov's soldiers heard the shots and began converging on the area. The weapons team burst through the door of the substation and grabbed as many rifles as they could. Meanwhile, the bombers waited nervously for their turn. They started lighting the rags. It seemed to take forever for their comrades to emerge from the building. When they finally did, the first wave of Tarasov's soldiers arrived and began firing at the escaping teenagers, cutting down a few with the first volley. As the bombers rushed forward to begin their attack, Tima tripped over the scattered debris before he could hurl his flaming bottle, and fell, the bottle shattering on the pavement and igniting a holocaust. He and many of the crew were engulfed in flames. As Lavro watched in horror, more of the weapons crew were picked off. Petya was hit in the back between the shoulder blades and fell forward toward Lavro, spilling his clutch of stolen rifles. Mortally wounded, he pushed himself up and heaved the closest rifle he could reach toward Lavro. "Go!" he said. Lavro caught the rifle, but hesitated. Should he try to use it? "Go!" Petya pleaded. A second shot then caught him in the head, finishing him off. Lavro turned and ran.

When he reached the relative safety of his own enclave, Lavro paused to catch his breath, resting on one knee using the rifle for support. He looked around at what was left of his old neighborhood. So many neighbors were now gone. His parents were gone. What remained of his boyhood friends had just been killed. He had nothing left. He felt guilty. He wished he had at least returned fire at the soldiers who killed his companions. Which side *was* he on? Now Sokolov's recruitment exhortation had more urgency. In the hail of conflicting emotions, he concluded that he was one of Jossmit's Soldiers – Jossmit's Holy Soldiers. He was ready to wear the full uniform. He got up and made his way to the informal enlistment station at the remote end of the enclave.

At first, he was inclined to report the outcome of the mission at the substation. The real militia would want to know this, he thought. But then he thought better of it. It was not a militia-sanctioned mission. He and his comrades were amateurs. And they had failed miserably. So he left this all out and simply expressed his desire to answer Sokolov's call to arms. He was readily accepted, no questions asked. They didn't ask about his age or his parents. They just looked him over for physical capability, then gave him his instructions. He was to make his way to the freight yard of the Derazhne train station. When he saw which boxcar was being assigned to the next train on the southwest line, he was to stow away in it, keeping his rifle out of sight. At the first stop after Derazhne, he was to jump off the boxcar with his companions. There would be other recruits there too. They would be met there by partisans who would be expecting them.

Lavro thought about returning to his house first to package up some food supplies for later. But then he figured that this was the real militia. They would have field rations or something like that. He was going to be a professional soldier now. He made his way to the freight yard along back streets, to keep his rifle out of sight. When he arrived, he looked around cautiously for other recruits. There were few people in the yard, most of them railroad employees. After a while, potential candidates began to arrive, a few older men and several younger men near his age. They all nervously eyed each other until a few introductions were made. One of the older men volunteered to be the lookout while the rest of the group stayed out of sight. They would be less conspicuous that way. He would watch for the boxcar assignment, then signal the rest to jump on board en masse, once the coast was clear.

Once in the boxcar, the group dispersed, hiding behind the stacked freight packaging. The car was inspected only once, just after it was attached to the end of the train. A single railroad employee unlatched and opened the door, took a quick look in, then shut it up again. Once they felt the train in motion and moving at cruising speed, the stowaways emerged from their hiding places but had very little to say to each other. It was dark, and they were all strangers.

When the train finally came to a gradual stop, with its shrill whistle signaling a station arrival in Lirovo, one of the older men got up, unlatched the door, and cautiously peeked outside. Seeing no one in the vicinity, friend or foe, he motioned for the rest of the group to jump off. As their eyes adjusted to the light, they all looked around nervously for their reception party. A single, plainclothed man emerged from the direction of the station and subtly motioned for them to move into the nearby woods. They did, quickly. There they encountered a cache of men in Evangelical militia uniforms, a few on horseback. They were escorted to a camp deeper in the woods. Lavro had not known what to expect for an official militia encampment, but this one disappointed almost every image he had imagined. It was a bit disorganized, ragtag, some soldiers in full uniform, many only clad in some pieces of the ensemble. Many in plainclothes. A makeshift table had been set up to process the enlistees. The stowaways formed a line.

Here, they wanted to know more about you. They asked your name, your age, your parents' names and address. They wrote it all down. Beside the enlistment officer was a small stack of uniforms. Finally, thought Lavro. When it became his turn, the stack of uniforms had dwindled to the point that it was clear not all of the recruits were going to get one. At least Lavro was. "Did you bring anything to eat for yourself?" the officer asked. "No," Lavro replied. "Well you should have. We don't have many provisions here. There won't be another mess until tomorrow." He gave Lavro one of the last of the uniforms, neatly folded, and pointed toward an area where he could change.

When he unfolded the jacket, Lavro noticed that a name had been taped inside, just below the collar. "Osennykh Valerian Annaevich." Someone else's uniform. He took it back to the enlistment officer to show him that they had mistakenly given him someone else's uniform jacket. The officer looked at the label, looked at Lavro, then looked at the quartermaster who had brought the initial stack of uniforms, as if to say "You were supposed to take care of this." He ripped off the label, handed the jacket back to Lavro, and said gruffly, "Now it's yours. Next!" Lavro took the jacket back to the changing area, a little confused about what had just transpired. When he opened up the jacket to put it on, he noticed two bullet holes in the torso and some bloodstains surrounding them. He now understood who Valerian Annaevich was.

The basic training was very brief – essentially, just follow orders. Lavro was assigned to a patrol where the commanding officer explained that they had too few rifles to go around. The patrol would form into pairs. One man would have a rifle, one would not. The soldier with the weapon was always to go first in any engagement. The second soldier was to follow close behind. If the first was killed, the second was to retrieve his rifle and continue on in his place. Lavro's stolen rifle was taken from him and handed to another recruit. Lavro was to be a follower.

The southwest corridor had seen a lot of militia on militia action recently, each side temporarily occupying parts of Lirovo. As was typical in guerrilla warfare, accurate information was hard to obtain. Lavro's patrol's first assignment was a reconnaissance mission to the outskirts of Lirovo. When they reached the western perimeter of the village, they came across the grisly scene of a family horse and wagon. The father and the mother were slumped over dead in the wagon, shot many times. The horse was on the ground, also shot dead. Nearby a small boy lay on the ground in critical condition, bleeding from a gunshot wound. He was barely conscious and was facing away from his parents in the wagon. Lavro instinctively came to the boy's aid. Seeing the nature of his wound, he suggested to his commander that they needed to get him to a hospital. The commander agreed. When Lavro knelt to pick him up, the boy resisted, saying he would not leave his parents. Lavro could see that the boy was unaware that they were already dead. He made a snap decision to lie and assure the boy that his parents would be all right. But before he could get the lie out, the boy demanded, "Are they dead?"

"No, they're fine."

"Swear on Jossmit's name that they are not dead!"

Then a more tortured decision, this one dragging him into blasphemy. "I swear it."

The boy relented, and let Lavro pick him up, still kneeling. The commander knelt next to the boy and asked, "Who did this?"

"The militia."

"The Orthodox militia or the Evangelical militia?"

"The militia."

§

Late in the afternoon, back in Mariankursk, Katerinya was alternating between sitting quietly and pacing back and forth. She was not a pacer, but she had nothing else to do with her time while she waited for nightfall and the escape to Olena's. She kept checking the western horizon out the bedroom window, wishing she could push the sun down faster. She was already packed. She couldn't write, she couldn't read, she couldn't eat. Her heart was not in any of these things. It was lost somewhere in the east, in someplace she did not know. She hoped in vain to receive a coded message from Ilya on her phone, but there was nothing. She tried to convince herself that this was to be expected. He probably had to wait for the right opportunity. He would probably wait until she was safely at Olena's. Yes, that was it, she thought. He won't contact me until I get there – after dark. I don't have to worry for now. But the thought didn't work. She was still worried. She got up to pace some more.

At dusk, she checked her phone for the 'tracking off' setting one more time. Then she sent a coded message to Olena – the one that meant 'arriving soon.' Was it dark enough yet to leave? How dark did it have to be? Before long she was engaged in a dialectic with herself concerning whether it was *really* dark yet – at least dark enough to begin. The point of the level of darkness, she convinced herself, was that there be enough that she wouldn't be observed leaving. She unpacked the items she had planned to take from a small suitcase, and put them in a backpack instead. That way, it would not be so obvious she was headed to another location. She might just be out checking on things. She could always go back if she saw anyone. Then she kept approximating her escape, first going to the woodshed, as if she were just checking on the wood inventory. When all seemed clear there, she casually walked into the woods as if she were checking on the wolves or something. Still no one. Now deep in the woods, she figured that the point of the darkness had been satisfied. The woods itself fulfilled the same function. She had not been seen leaving Tallinnskaya Street. Then she followed the planned route to Olena's, moving ever faster as the darkness descended.

As she approached Olena's from the back, she could see by the lights in the windows that Olena was home. When she came through the back door, Olena was anxiously waiting to see a couple, but only half of a couple arrived. She was concerned. "Where's Ilya?" Katerinya had been struggling to keep it together all day, but now she was beginning to lose it. "They took him," she said, her voice a little unsteady. Olena could tell by the sound of her voice and her expression that she was in need of help. So she embraced her and asked, all in the same motion, "Where?" Katerinya needed steadying, so she hung on to Olena. "I don't know," she said, sobbing, as she gave in to her grief. Her childhood friend helped her to the couch and sat with her in a comforting hug to let her grieve. They said nothing for a long while. Olena didn't need any more details for now. The overall scenario was clear enough. She would wait for Katerinya to speak first.

That night, Katerinya slept with Olena downstairs, just like the old sleepovers. Olena suggested it, figuring it would just add to Katerinya's grief to sleep upstairs in an empty bed that had been meant for two. The next day, the mood was still somber, but Katerinya was back in control, determined to stay with the plan. She was safe at Olena's, and though she didn't fear for her own safety, she knew Ilya would derive comfort from knowing she was tucked away here, out of reach. This was as much for him as it was for her. But she had run out of excuses for why there was no message from him. Now she was genuinely concerned. They had never discussed what to do in case of the present scenario. She had to try to read Ilya's mind from a distance. What would his strategy be, what would he try, what would he expect me to do? She was not very good at this.

As for Ilya, he read Katerinya's mind pretty accurately. He knew the lack of a message would put her in this anxious state. He still had a stash of African-spec phones hidden in his office at the University. He figured he could get one message to her before the communication would register with the eavesdroppers. There was no real need for a coded protocol. He would just say "I'm OK. Are you OK?" The content betrayed nothing about where she was, and the fact that he tried to contact her would tell Tarasov nothing that he didn't already know – except that Ilya had managed to get his hands on another phone. That would then soon be taken away as well. But if Katerinya replied with something like "I'm OK", Ilya would know that she had made it to Olena's undetected. That should help both of them endure this for a little longer.

So in mid-afternoon on the second day, Katerinya got a text message from an unknown number. It read "I'm OK. Are you OK?" Olena was reading the message with her. "It has to be Ilya!" Katerinya said, unable to hold her excitement. "They must have taken his phone! That's why he couldn't reach me!"

"Answer him, Katerinya! Before they take this one too."

In her time with Ilya, Katerinya had learned to be cautious about phone communications. Whatever you say or text, he would say, imagine that Tarasov is listening or watching. She was also aware that this might not be Ilya. Could be a trap. There was so much she wanted to say – and ask – but that would be dangerous if this was not Ilya. This newly cautious Katerinya decided that a simple "I'm OK" would tell Ilya she was safe, and it would not tell any non-Ilya anything at all. And it wouldn't tell Tarasov anything about her location either. So "I'm OK" it was.

This allowed both of them to get on with their days for a while. Ilya was waiting for Tarasov's "evidence" to materialize. Katerinya had no idea what she was waiting for. And that was a problem. As each day rolled into the next, her anxiety grew. She began to over-think the situation. Was it normal that Ilya did not try to contact her further? Was that really him the first time? Perhaps he was not OK. But why would they want her to think otherwise? To gain her confidence in hopes of getting her to spill information? But she hadn't. To get her to stay away, thinking he was OK when he really wasn't? What were they doing to him that they didn't want her to know about?

Olena had to work during the day, so Katerinya was home alone, with no one to talk to, and no one to keep her mind on a steady course. After a while, Katerinya's troubled mind began to blur the distinction between reasoning and desire. Reasoning said she should stick to the plan. Desire said she needed to be with Ilya. Desire influenced reasoning into preferring scenarios that she wanted to be true. She wanted to be with Ilya. She wanted to know that he really was OK. It was a losing battle for reasoning. Concern for her own safety had never been in the forefront. She was staying put out of deference to Ilya. The idea of taking action on her own pushed to the forefront. By the time Olena returned, she had already made up her mind.

Olena tried to dissuade her, but came hard up against the unquenchable desire for reunification. Olena understood this. She could relate to it. This was probably what she would have done herself. She could see that she was not going to talk Katerinya out of it, so she supported her friend, and went along with the plan. They packed some food and other essentials in Katerinya's backpack. Olena lent her a coat of hers that had a hood, so Katerinya would be able to make herself less visible in public. Olena had the foresight to ask about preserving the secrecy of her house as the hiding place. It might come in handy later. Katerinya could see the wisdom in that, so she altered her plan slightly to follow the clandestine route back to Tallinnskaya Street first. She would leave for the train station from there. Then she was off.

Now that the specter of waiting forever had been removed, Katerinya's confidence returned. She was taking action. She was in charge of her destiny. She had something to look forward to. The ever-resourceful Katerinya was now at her finest. At each station along the way – the woods, her apartment, the train station – she was preparing fictions to explain who she was and why she was going where she was going. She acted out the scenarios as she imagined them. She would not be caught off guard. It went surprisingly smoothly. Her backpack, and her youthful appearance – at least the part one could see under the hood – made her look vaguely student-ish. She fit right in on the train, walking the streets of Derazhne, and walking through the university. Then she had to make a decision. Should she go to Ilya's house, or to his office? Which would help her keep a lower profile? She realized now that her desire to see him had magnified her concerns about his safety. He could be just fine. She had no basis on which to decide, other than that she was already in the Quad, so it might as well be his office.

At 308 Dahlström Hall, she encountered an armed guard standing outside his door. His stance looked remarkably casual, as if he were bored. In a very student-like manner she said, "I'm here to see Professor Koskayin." The guard politely reached over and opened the door for her. That was guard-speak for "Go right in." When she entered, Ilya was alone at his desk. Katerinya had the presence of mind to turn and close the door before she let her emotions out. And the presence of mind not to speak too loudly. Ilya was in a similar state of mind. After a long, silent embrace, they each explained, in low tones, the situation from their own point of view. Ilya skipped any cautionary lecture about her staying out of reach at Olena's. He knew now that she would never follow such a plan without him there. The joy of having her at arm's length once again was tempered by the quandary of how to protect her in Derazhne. As each recounted the intervening events since their separation, and their personal ordeals living with the separation itself, there was a knock on the door.

They quickly separated, and Ilya preemptively went to the door, opening it to investigate. There he found Yulia Katyaevna waiting with the guard. Both were looking to him for the next move. Seeing the opportunity to provide a cover story for Katerinya, he looked at the guard, smiling, and said "Yet another student. Come on in." The guard, satisfied, returned to his post. Ilya closed the door after Yulia Katyaevna as she came in. The two women recognized each other immediately. They each vividly recalled their last meeting in this very office when the order of interruption was reversed. But that interruption had been quickly resolved without either one getting an introduction. Yulia Katyaevna felt obliged to be the one to bow out this time, but Ilya's behavior with the guard, and his immediate closing of the door let her know that there was something unusual going on. He motioned for her to take a seat in the overstuffed red leather chair, then put a finger over his mouth and pointed toward the door with his other hand. She got the message: "Talk softly so the guard doesn't overhear." Both women looked to Ilya to take the lead.

"This is Yulia Katyaevna, a student and advisee of mine. And this is Katerinya Emlynovna, a … friend of mine from Mariankursk. A very dear friend." Both women picked up on the fact that he had used the familiar forms of their names. Social formality could be dispensed with. It also encouraged each to regard the other as an insider, though they both wondered, "inside of what?"

Katerinya took the lead. "Please call me Katerinya."

Pleased to be welcomed into the fold, Yulia smiled and said "And you can call me Yulia." They both seemed happy about this. Yulia was determined to get right to the bottom of the mysterious circumstances. "Who is the soldier at the door? Are you being held prisoner or something?"

"No, that's just my bodyguard," Ilya answered, going along with the official story.

"Why do you need a bodyguard?"

At this point, Ilya could see that the circumstances already did not match the official story, so he decided to take Yulia into complete confidence. "You were right the first time, Yulia. I'm essentially under house arrest. There's a lot that you don't know about the political situation here in Derazhne. It's complicated, but the less you know at this point the better, for your own protection. Prince Tarasov wants me to be visibly working on a vaccine here in Derazhne."

"For the fake epidemic?" Yulia asked.

"You know about this?"

"Students talk. It doesn't make much sense. We're all skeptical."

"Well good for you! But don't let the guard hear you say that." She put a finger over her lips, smiling. Katerinya found this young student rather intriguing.

"Anyway, the Prince is afraid I will sneak back to Mariankursk to ... protect Katerinya. She was there, but now she's here. He doesn't know that." The more he tried to explain, the harder it was to make the key point. "He knows he can get to me by getting to Katerinya because ... " He searched for the proper words.

"Because she's your very dear friend." Yulia put her hand on his and said, "You don't have to say any more. I understand." She had always wondered who this previously unnamed woman was that she had met more than a month ago. Now she knew. She's very perceptive, Katerinya thought, watching Yulia. I like her.

Ilya was impressed too. "Katerinya was safe in Mariankursk. They forcibly brought me back here. Now that she's here, she's not so safe anymore. The guard apparently doesn't recognize her, but someone will eventually. I've got to find a place to hide her here in Derazhne until she can get back to Mariankursk."

"I'm not going back to Mariankursk, Ilya. I'm going to stay here with you." She said this as unemotionally as possible so it would not seem like begging, or pleading, or even asking. Just a fact. A foregone conclusion. Ilya got the point. She would not be going back to Mariankursk, at least not alone.

"Katerinya could stay with me! At my dorm. No one would think to look in the undergrad houses." She made a good point, both Katerinya and Ilya thought. As they were trying to compose the obligatory "Thank you, but we couldn't impose on you" response, Yulia kept going to sell the idea. "There's room. Many of the townies have gone home for the 'epidemic.' My roommate has. I came here with a lame excuse to 'procure essential services.' It's easy to get around on campus. Most of the soldiers don't even ask. Katerinya would fit right in."

She sold it. It so utterly solved the immediate problem of getting Katerinya out of the purview of the soldiers that they had to accept it. "But what about Ilya, I mean Professor Koskayin?" Yulia asked.

"'Ilya' is fine," the professor smiled. We're all comrades now."

"But what *about* you?" Katerinya asked. "How will you get past the guard?"

Ilya was about to say that it didn't matter. He could stay under house arrest as long as Katerinya was hidden away. But that meant, of course, that he couldn't see her again without the guard present. Then she would be exposed again. Two thoughts competed for his attention. He wanted to be with her, no matter what. And if he wasn't with her, she would just try to see him again anyway. Both thoughts implied the same conclusion. He had to hide out with her. "I'll ditch him later. I have a plan for that. Let's just get the two of you out of here now – nonchalantly."

After writing her house's room number on a piece of paper, Yulia stood up and said loudly enough for the guard to hear, "Come on, roomie. Let's get back to the dorm and study!" Katerinya smiled and got right into the performance. She opened the door, put her arm around Yulia, and walked with her down the hall making meaningless coed conversation. They even smiled and waved to the guard on their way out.

§

Ilya did indeed have an escape plan. He had been saving it for when he would try again to get back to Mariankursk. It was a good plan for eluding the guard, but he still hadn't figured out what to do about the trains. They would surely catch him there. So why not use the part of the plan that worked for the guard now? He wasn't trying to get to the train anymore.

The plan involved an alternate exit from the offsite synthesizing lab. Ilya didn't really have any reason to visit the lab yet for the actual vaccine work, but his "bodyguard" wouldn't know that. Because it related to the public vaccination effort, it was one of the sanctioned places he was allowed to go. At the end of the day, he went there with the guard in tow, carrying some meaningless lab paraphernalia that looked very research-y. Inside the lab, there was a series of underground mini rooms, full of apparatus, which were alternately used as cleanrooms and for conducting biohazardous operations. They had the appropriate warning signs on the outside, so it was easy for Ilya to convince his guard that this was the kind of place he should be going into alone. There was no obvious way out except for the entrance, so the guard agreed to wait outside. Unbeknownst to the guard, each minilab had a rear exit into a corridor that led to a stairway up to a ground level exit at the back of the facility. It was built for emergency exits, but there were no signs or alarms associated with these exits. Ironically, Ilya thought to himself, his escape would actually constitute an emergency exit.

He executed the plan without a hitch. Then he walked back to campus, through the Quad, and on to the undergraduate houses near the river, all the while avoiding soldiers. He was a Faculty Tutor at Yulia's house, so he had the appropriate keycard to gain access. His presence there fit the expectations of all who observed. This hadn't occurred to him when Yulia first hatched her plan, and it probably hadn't occurred to her either. But it was the perfect cover.

When Ilya arrived at Yulia's room, she and Katerinya were already negotiating sleeping arrangements for the night. Yulia's room was really a small suite, originally built for the sons and daughters of more wealthy parents. It was a corner room at the far end of the building. The interior consisted of a large main room with windows and built-in window seats on two of the walls, and a large fireplace between them. Off of the interior wall was a smaller bedroom. This was originally to house one student – one student who would be incented by the fineness and expansiveness of the suite, and the ornamental fireplace, to succeed in life so as to be able to afford such an accommodation later. Those were the old days. Although there were still many legacy students of wealthy alumni admitted to ensure a steady stream of donations, there were now many more scholarship students like Yulia. There were no more singles. The two roommates assigned to the room would decide between themselves who got the main room and who got the smaller bedroom. The tradeoff was lots of space versus privacy. The bathrooms were down the hall. Whoever had the smaller room had to pass through the larger room to get in and out of the suite. Yulia had chosen the smaller room and her roommate the larger. Now Yulia was offering to swap places, to give Katerinya and Ilya more privacy in the smaller bedroom. Katerinya looked around and had to agree, under the circumstances, and again credited her new roomie with a mature social awareness. It was a delicate little conversation.

There was, of course, some doubt about how or when or even whether Ilya would show up, since he hadn't disclosed his escape plan. Katerinya had been a little worried. Her first inclination was to run to him, now that they were safely in hiding together once again. They hadn't had a proper reunion yet. But she thought better of such a public display of affection in front of Yulia. She knew the nature of their relationship by now, but Katerinya could imagine this might be a little uncomfortable for her. It would be for her if she were in Yulia's place. They had procured the private bedroom, after all. There would be opportunity for that later.

Ilya had given tutorials before in the commons room at Yulia's house, but had never seen the interior of any of the rooms. He had heard about the "one person suites" as part of the University lore. The main room did seem opulent and refined, except for the single bed against one wall. They all sat around the large circular table in the middle of the room, finally able to decompress, and talk freely about the day's intrigue. Ilya asked Katerinya about her journey to Derazhne. She described the unexpected smoothness of it all. She was sure no one had recognized her, but was disturbed by the distant sights and sounds from East Derazhne. She had never encountered this kind of urban warfare before. She hoped it would not spread to Mariankursk.

Ilya suddenly remembered that Yulia was from the enclaves. "How are your parents doing?" he asked her.

"Not so good," she said somberly. "My father wanted to join Sokolov's militia, but my mother stopped him. He's not really a violent man. I don't understand how Sokolov influences people to do things like that." She looked over at Ilya, because she knew what his next question would be. "Yes, I'm through with Sokolov now. I'm never going back to that church. I'm a different person now. Or maybe I was always this person, but didn't realize it until I got away. You don't choose these sorts of things when you are a child, you know. You follow your parents' lead."

"And you were raised Orthodox, weren't you?"

"Yes, and now that's a problem. My parents live in the orthodox enclave. We had to go across town to Sokolov's church. Now their neighbors think they are Evangelical collaborators. They're not safe on either side. They have to lay low. I think that's how my mother convinced my father to stay away from Sokolov. I just don't understand how those people think, how they can follow orders to do such atrocious things in the name of Jossmit."

"They don't think," Ilya said. "That's the problem. They follow the leader. The leader thinks for them."

"But I know some of these people! They are not violent. They have individual moral consciences. Couldn't they all just stop? Stop obeying the orders. Then there would be no one left to fight. Let the two leaders destroy each other."

"It's a fact of human nature, I'm afraid. If everyone were rational, no one would follow leaders. Then tribes wouldn't be able to do things for the common good either, like distributing food and medicine to those who need it, building sewer and water systems, building railroads and schools. Right on the border of good and bad is banding together for a common defense. A defense against whom? Other tribes. Then the line between defense and offence gets a little blurred. It's not a rational act of mutual self-interest that binds tribes together, it's in-built, visceral emotions. Fear and loyalty. Fear of disobeying the leader, fear of being ostracized by your peers, loyalty to the leader, loyalty to 'your people', 'your kind.'"

"But I just don't understand that!" Yulia said.

"No, you just don't *feel* that. You are one of the odd ones, like me … and Katerinya." Katerinya was suddenly happy to be enfranchised. She hadn't thought about it like this, but she liked where it was going. "We somehow didn't get the tribal gene. We are not joiners. We don't feel the need to have a people, or a kind. We don't feel this emotional pull to be loyal to anything. But we do feel empathy. This is what you mean by the moral conscience, I think. We are fortunate, I suppose, that we don't have the fear and loyalty disposition to override it. The only way to understand this is to understand that we are different. We are not normal humans."

"Oh, that's so depressing!" Katerinya said. "How have humans survived this far if most of us are like that?"

"Ironically, it's why we *have* survived, and ended up dominating every other species. Large tribes that can act as one have a distinct advantage over unaligned individuals."

"I'm with Katerinya," Yulia said. "This is too depressing. Let's talk about something else. What do you do in Mariankursk, Katerinya? Are you a scientist too?"

Katerinya smiled, "No, I'm afraid science is not for me. I'm a professional translator. And an aspiring novelist."

"I used to think science was not for me too. I wanted to be an historian, but now I'm not so sure. I don't suppose I'm anything yet. I'm still an undergraduate."

"But you've been influenced by a certain professor we know, am I right?"

They both looked at Ilya, smiling. "I try," he said.

"He's having an effect on me too," Katerinya said. "I'm still a humanist, but I see science a little differently now."

The newly formed a-tribal tribe talked well into the evening until it became clear that all of them were hungry. The dining hall was closed, and they couldn't go out because two of them could not afford to be recognized. Yulia volunteered to get takeout. What did the group want? There was an immediate consensus: "African." As the evening wore on, Katerinya was happily reliving her undergraduate days. Yulia was still living hers, albeit with older roomies, and Ilya, as usual, couldn't remember anything about what that was like. But he could imagine it must have gone something like this.

When it came time to retire for the night, Katerinya and Ilya retreated to their private bedroom, and closed the door so they could discreetly resume their reunion. As Katerinya cuddled up, she said in a low voice, "I feel sorry for Yulia, Iliusha. She's such a nice girl. At first I thought she probably hated me, but she doesn't. She's taking it quite well."

"Taking what well?"

"Oh, surely you've noticed. She has a crush on you. Can't you see it? Well I can. I see the way she looks at you. I've been there. You don't expect it can go anywhere, but you can imagine, fantasize. Then I show up out of the blue, and now she has to sleep on the other side of the wall knowing we are in bed together. I feel for her, I really do."

"I thought it might be a possibility," he said. This kind of thing happens to me from time to time with bright young coeds. If I suspect it, I try not to engage them in eye contact very often, so as not to send any signals. I suppose that's why I didn't notice how she looks at me. You had the third-party perspective."

"Well, I saw it, and I feel so bad being the one to ruin her fantasy."

"Did anyone ever ruin your fantasy with the Karlsruhe professor?"

"No, not even an office visit. And certainly nothing like this."

§

The next morning, as they breakfasted over leftover African takeout, it was becoming clear to Ilya that the present arrangement was not sustainable. Yulia didn't know when her roommate might be returning. And the three of them looked a little out of place sharing a dorm room. He knew he could never get Katerinya to go back to Mariankursk on her own. But he couldn't go with her because of the train exposure. That's the first place Tarasov's men would be looking, and they would all know by now whom they were looking for.

Then he came up with a plan for hiding her out at Andzhelina Gullovna's house. She lived across the river in Solinovsk, so they would be reasonably removed from the University where the soldiers expected to find them. She also had plenty of space, and they would not appear out of place in her neighborhood, occasionally coming and going. First, though, he needed a way to contact her secretly. He couldn't do it by phone, even using Katerinya's, because it would be observed. He would do it by secure Internet email. The academic information flow on that channel was well protected cryptographically. He checked Yulia's Internet connection and found it more than secure, as expected. Undergraduates tended to be a little ahead of the curve on this technology. All you needed was a few computer science majors in your house and the technology spread pretty fast.

Ilya sent the query to Andzhelina Gullovna, then the group continued their discussions, waiting for a reply. Because the connection was secure, the message did not have to be short or cryptic, so Ilya laid out the whole scenario, from Tarasov to the fake epidemic, to Mariankursk, to Yulia's. He needed her to understand the entire context of the mission, and that she would possibly be a little exposed if they were caught. She should just pretend that she knew nothing about any of the context. Just that a colleague and friend had come by for an extended visit. She should delete the email after reading it.

It took some time for a reply, but when it came, Andzhelina Gullovna had accepted the challenge, and welcomed them to stay with her. She said soldiers only sparsely patrolled her neighborhood in Solinovsk, being upscale. Ilya and Katerinya's biggest exposure would be around the University and on the trams. Especially the trams. They should avoid them, and walk. That meant taking the long way east to the bridge, crossing over on the pedestrian walkway, then all the way back west to her place. She would leave the University early, by mid-afternoon, so she would be there when they arrived. Ilya and Katerinya said their goodbyes to Yulia, with Katerinya giving her a big hug and engaging in a brief, private conversation with her. They both seemed pleased by the outcome. Ilya didn't ask.

As they walked east through Derazhne along the river, Katerinya donned her hood and backpack ensemble. But Ilya was the one more likely to be recognized. He just steered them clear of any soldiers he picked up in his long-range vision. More people were out and about now than when martial law had first been declared. No one knew anyone who had succumbed to the "infection," and the soldiers had become pretty lax in enforcing the "procure essential services" requirement. No one seemed worried about a disease. Of more concern was what was happening in the East Derazhne neighborhoods. This helped Ilya and Katerinya blend in with groups of people not wearing uniforms.

There were more than the usual number of pedestrians crossing the bridge into Solinovsk. It seems that everyone was avoiding the trams. As Ilya and Katerinya started across the bridge, they saw two women with five small children between them. The women were busy talking to each other, and hadn't noticed that the children had drifted away toward the railing of the bridge. The first two boys were intently watching the water below them, and signaling for the other children to come see. When they realized the separation, one of the women hurried over to the railing to retrieve the children, all of them now watching the water and pointing. It was something of great interest to them. When the woman reached the children, she gasped in horror and covered the eyes of one of the girls. The girl broke free to get another look. By this time both woman were at the rail and abruptly turned the children around and herded them back toward the center of the bridge walkway. Katerinya was intrigued, and walked toward the railing with Ilya close behind. As he arrived, Katerinya had already turned and buried her face in his sabovar. He could see several human corpses floating with the eastbound current on their way to the sea. They were pale and bloated due to the gasses emitted by the bacteria in their chest and gut cavities. The skin on their hands was grotesquely wrinkled and peeling off. All were face down, sparing onlookers from the more grisly effects of their decomposing faces.

The scene didn't shock Ilya like it did Katerinya. It seemed to him that this is what you expect in times of war, as if he'd seen such things many times before. He couldn't recall any such memories, but he was beginning to be accustomed to these kinds of vague familiarities. He had lost the particular memories, but not the sense of having been there before. He helped Katerinya away from the railing back to the center of the walkway. She kept her eyes away from the water and straight ahead for the rest of the bridge crossing. She did not say a word. She did not know what to say. Ilya walked with his arm around her, realizing that this was probably her first dead body. He knew it would likely not be her last.

On the Solinovsk side of the river, they made their way back west toward Andzhelina's house. She lived in a quaint little neighborhood not far from the southern bank of the river. The pedestrian scene on the Solinovsk side of the river was a little different than that in Derazhne. More civilians, many fewer soldiers. The action was in Derazhne. This was a good choice, Ilya thought to himself. Andzhelina was waiting for them when they arrived. She and Katerinya had a very warm hug and welcoming mini-conversation, almost like two old friends. Andzhelina could tell something was off. Katerinya was a little unsteady. Ilya explained about the dead bodies in the river. "Oh, you poor thing!" Andzhelina said, re-hugging her. "Your first?"

Katerinya nodded silently, then said, "How do you get used to such a thing?"

"You don't. It's always awful to see."

"Have you seen them before?"

"Yes, a few. But only because I'm older and I live in a big city. You come to expect it in times like these, but you never get used to it." Ilya would like to have added some comforting wisdom, but he didn't have any. He couldn't answer such questions, and Andzhelina still did not know about his memory loss. He still had the cautionary sense that he should keep it that way.

Andzhelina showed the two around the house and where they would be sleeping. No negotiations necessary this time. They had their own private bedroom and bathroom in a guest suite on the ground floor. Andzhelina's bedroom was on the second floor. "Plenty of privacy," Andzhelina said, smiling in Katerinya's direction. Katerinya returned a grateful smile.

It turned out that Andzhelina loved to cook, as did Katerinya, so they soon became best chef-buddies. Ilya tried to help, but kept getting worked around as an accessory. He wanted to help. "Ilya, why don't you pick out the wine?" Andzhelina asked.

"Where?" he asked.

"Oh that's right. You've never been here. In the cellar."

"You have a wine cellar?"

"Oh, yes. Take those stairs," she said, pointing toward a door off the kitchen. Maybe he should have been here before, Ilya thought. But now he needed to see the full menu – how many courses, what's in each course. The women laid out their plan. He then went down to the cellar and selected three wines – a young Pinot Gris that would double as a warm-up wine for now and the appetizer wine at production time, a bold Cabernet Sauvignon with some respectable age on it for the main course, and a Sauternes which would serve as the dessert wine and the linger-after wine.

"Ooo, good choices," Andzhelina said.

"He's really into wine," Katerinya offered.

"I know. His reputation precedes him," Andzhelina informed her.

By the time they got to the lingering-after Sauternes, the conversation was in full swing. They had already covered the entire political intrigue, the outbreak in Mariankursk, the faux outbreak in Derazhne-Solinovsk, and enough of their improbable courtship to satisfy Andzhelina's curiosity without giving away anything that Katerinya and Ilya wanted to keep private. Inevitably, the discussion got around to dead bodies.

"I will never understand that," Andzhelina said. "How people who profess to be religious can do that to each other. Religion is about helping your neighbors, not killing them. I don't believe in Jossmit myself, but these people do. Isn't he supposed to be the champion of 'turn the other cheek?' Gentle Jossmit meek and mild!"

"Ilya says it all comes down to the tribal instinct in humans, something that had evolutionary advantage for getting us this far, but has unfortunate side-effects, like making you insensitive to people who are not in your tribe. Does that sound right, Ilya?" Katerinya asked.

Before he could answer, Andzhelina injected, "Why do you always have to *reduce* everything to biology, Ilya?"

"Because I'm in the explanation business."

"But why can't you just let the religious have their mysteries? Maybe they don't want an explanation for everything."

"But they do have an explanation. A bad one. Everything is attributed to the inscrutable will of some disembodied agency. If it's your tribe, God wanted you to do it. If it's the other tribe, the devil made them do it. It's that simple. They skip right over the fact that God doesn't seem to be winning most of these battles between good and evil. It virtually assures that these conflicts will just keep self-perpetuating. Good and evil can't reach a compromise."

"But aren't there some good religious mysteries as well, or at least some that are harmless?"

"Harmless is fine. But these spiritual non-explanations keep people from understanding how the world really works. And that can be harmful. Attributing the plague to the influence of evil spirits didn't help much, did it? People like me "reducing" those spirits to the predictable interactions of bacteria did help. Reducing explanations have the benefit of predictability. They enable us to do something about these mysteries."

"OK, I'll grant you disease and healing. These aren't mysteries anymore. I've been through this recently with S.K. Fedorov. He thinks all healing is really the miracle of God acting behind the scenes."

"Not a very useful explanation, is it?"

"No," Andzhelina smiled. "Not at all. But aren't there *some* things you don't want to reduce away? What about love? Isn't that real?"

Katerinya really wanted to hear his answer to this one. "Of course it's real!" he said. "Why does reductive explanation have to make things go *away*? Do me a favor, Andzhelina. Put your hand on the table and press. Press hard." She thought that sounded like a strange request. But she followed his instructions. "Now, why doesn't your hand pass straight through the table?"

An odd question, she thought. "Because the table is hard, and solid, and so is my hand."

"But you do know that both the table and your hand reduce to atoms, right?"

"Yes … "

"You probably didn't know that atoms are mostly empty space. If the nucleus of each atom were the size of a fly on this table, its nearest electrons would be about 4 or 5 houses away down the street. That's a lot of space between the subatomic particles. So when your hand atoms encounter the table atoms, the chance of any one of the particles colliding is pretty slim." He paused to let the thought settle in. "Your hand can't get through the table because of the summed up electromagnetic forces. Hardness and solidity are properties of the observable, macro world, not of its atomic reductions. Now, does that mean hard and solid are not *real*? Does the reduction explain them *away*?"

"No … "

"Exactly. The reduction tells us what hard and solid really are. Not that they don't exist. So if we can reduce love to the interactions of neurons and hormones, we learn what love is, not that it's imaginary."

Both women pondered this point for a moment. The three bottles of wine were also slowing down mental reactions. Andzhelina was the first to recover.

"So you don't believe in anything spiritual? Nothing immaterial that you can't see or touch, even with your instruments?"

"Well, I would say I believe in many more immaterial things that I can't see or touch than you do. The strong and weak nuclear forces, quantum gravity, quantum entanglement, dark matter and dark energy. The key difference between your spirits and my spirits is that mine can be measured. They have persistent states, and predictable behaviors. Both your spirits and my spirits are made out of immaterial stuff. But I can predict what my spirits are likely to do next. You have no idea what yours will do next. Am I right?"

Adding cosmological physics to the already entrenched effects of the wines made continuing this discussion a bridge too far. Andzhelina wasn't sure what she thought any more. Katerinya had never managed to get a position of her own started. And Ilya could see that the wine was preventing any further progress. Or perhaps it was the wine that had allowed them to get as far down this particular road as they had.

§

The next morning, Katerinya was not so surprised when she opened her eyes in yet another unfamiliar bedroom. She had been in several of these lately. She immediately reoriented to Andzhelina's guest suite. It was more colorful in full daylight than it had appeared at night. She appreciated the luxury of a private suite with its own bathroom. Almost like being in an upscale hotel. She felt like just staying in bed. She and Ilya had no place to go – no place they could go. They were in for the day. But then she remembered that Andzhelina would have a normal day at the University, and so might be up already. She would probably be preparing breakfast, and mindful of not disturbing the privacy of her guests. So Katerinya decided to get up and help with the breakfast, to break the uncertainty. They should really give Andzhelina a proper send off. There would be plenty of time to enjoy their private suite later.

At breakfast, Ilya privately toyed with the idea of taking Andzhelina aside, at some point, to see if she could convince Katerinya to return to Mariankursk – maybe go with her. But the opportunity for such a side discussion never arose, and the more Ilya thought it over, the more he realized it was not a very good idea. Katerinya would still not likely agree to leave without him, and he would have to interrupt Andzhelina's academic schedule to send her to some unknown location in Mariankursk.

After Andzhelina left for the University, Ilya and Katerinya eventually ran out of things with which to occupy their time. They returned to their private suite for the rest of the morning, made lunch, then confronted the "What now?" question. Katerinya had left her laptop with her novel and translation work at Olena's, and Ilya had no Internet connection. He himself had encouraged Andzhelina to password protect her home computer years ago, as he had encouraged all of his academic colleagues, so he could not get online, for news or vaccine work. They read a little from Andzhelina's library, and occasionally rehashed a little of the previous evening's discussion. Ilya had a lot of explaining to do.

When Andzhelina returned, in the late afternoon, she had some news. Sokolov and many of his deputies had been arrested. Coincidentally, the epidemic was now over, and martial law had been rescinded. "Imagine that," Ilya said. "What a coincidence."

"What does this mean, Ilya?" Katerinya asked. "Are you in the clear now?"

"I don't know. Seems like I should be. There may be hell to pay for skipping out on the Prince a second time, but it was harmless. It didn't interfere with his story line. They obviously don't know we are here. But we need to disassociate Andzhelina from the second escape somehow." He didn't have to think long. "Here's what we'll do. I will leave here, staying out of sight for a block or two. Then I'll start walking to Tarasov's palace, out in the open, waiting to be recognized."

"Are you sure that's a good idea, Ilya?" Katerinya asked with some concern.

"Well, I have to come to terms with Tarasov sooner or later, or he will always be looking for me. Looking for us. If I'm in the clear with Tarasov, I'll get my phone back and text Katerinya. If I text 'go,' Katerinya should inconspicuously leave here as well. One or two blocks. Just so no one sees you leaving here. Then walk to my place. Do you know the way from here?"

"Yes. Downriver, over the bridge, then upriver. I won't look in the water."

"And if you don't text?" Andzhelina asked.

"Then stay here. I'll have to come up with a different plan. Also, if I text 'stay,' same thing. If he lets me go, this will clear Andzhelina. We were never here."

"It sounds so risky, Ilya" Katerinya said.

"To keep hiding is even riskier. This is probably the best time to resurface."

With that, and a kiss and a hug, he departed for the palace. He had no problem clearing the vicinity of Andzhelina's house without being seen. Then he stopped being clandestine. He walked straight toward the palace, waiting to be apprehended again. To his surprise, no soldier stopped him, or even showed any interest in him. When he reached the palace, he realized that he didn't have a plan for getting to the Prince all on his own. He had expected to be escorted there. So he just walked right in. "Professor Koskayin to see the Prince," he announced. "Is he expecting you?" Isn't that rich, Ilya thought. "Yes," he said matter-of-factly. The guard disappeared into the inner sanctum for a while, then emerged to say, "Right this way." He was led into the Prince's private library, and Tarasov motioned for the guard to shut the door on the way out.

The Prince looked pleased, even smiling. Not his usual inscrutable self. "Ilya Erynovich!" he said, "You've saved me the trouble of fishing for you again. I knew this would be a cat and mouse affair. You play a pretty good mouse."

"A mouse does what he needs to survive."

"Indeed. So I gather the mouse heard the news."

"The mouse did. That's why he came to see the cat."

"And ... ?"

"And did you finally get your evidence against Sokolov?"

"Documentary evidence was hard to come by. I thought a lot about what you said last time – about how we did not need to make a case for the partisans on either side. We just needed something for a judge."

"And ... ?"

"And we shook the tree a little. Offered leniency for some lower down in the hierarchy to get them to turn on their superiors. This has a cascading effect up the tree. The first one to turn gets the best deal. The last one, well ... let's just say you do not want to be the last one. Now we have witnesses who will testify against Sokolov. The worst kind of evidence to actually prove anything, but the best kind of evidence in the public's eye."

"Will this help with the proxy war in the enclaves?"

"Not so much, I'm afraid. Osipov is not able to control his side's voluntary militia, and Sokolov's side, well now they have a martyr, so they are as entrenched as ever."

"Then what did you gain?"

"We cut off the head of the snake. The more professional of Sokolov's militia will now be crippled. We have most of their would-be commanders. The rest will slip out of town and join the guerrillas. I'm afraid this won't be so good for the outlying provinces for a while, but there will be no organized attacks on the two cities now. They are out of funding and out of supplies. Their hoped-for revolution is over. It's just a matter of time until they realize it."

"But if it's militia on militia now, even in the countryside, these true believers will never realize it. As long as they have fanatical leaders to exhort them, they will follow."

"I'm afraid you might be right, Ilya Erynovich. I'll just have to wait until the numbers are reduced enough, then send my own professional army to reinforce Osipov's irregulars – to finish off what's left of Sokolov's. The one I worry about is this commander Kuznetsov. He seems more professional than the others. His guerrillas will be the last to go. It's a flaw in human nature, don't you think Ilya Erynovich? This follow-the-leader thing. I certainly exploit it. To accomplish what I think are good things, I hope. But I don't think I will ever understand why it works. I would never follow one of these leaders. I would probably not even follow a leader like myself."

"Because you *are* one of the leaders, Koldan Sonvaevich. If everyone were like you – or me, for different reasons – this whole tribal organization regime would never work. This is not just *human* nature. We have perfected it, yes, but the follow-the-leader instinct goes all the way down the evolutionary line among social animals."

This piqued the Prince's interest. "Tell me more about this, Ilya Erynovich. Please."

"All social animals have pecking orders, a ranking of dominance in social interactions that usually has a single alpha male at the top. Aspiring alpha males will battle it out for the top position, but not for long. If too many are inclined to fight to the death, they would all kill each other, and the tribe is left with no leaders. So a lot of these battles for dominance are only virtual – ritual combat, if you will. There is a lot of posturing and threatening, baring of teeth and growling, with each player trying to assess which one is likely to win a real battle. The likely loser will typically concede before the killing starts."

"And these would-be leaders are relatively few, you're telling me?"

"Yes. If everyone had the leader instinct, there would be no tribes. Most individuals have to be naturally inclined to be followers. There are computer simulations that show the optimal balance between natural followers and natural leaders in a population to be about 80/20. That's where stable equilibrium tends to happen. Too many followers make the tribe leaderless, unable to act as a unit. Too many leaders leave the tribe perpetually fighting among themselves. When a population averages out around 80/20, you get successful tribes."

"And these leaders, the ones who end up on top. Do you think they all have a hero complex? Do they believe they are destined for this? That it is their birthright, or their divine right, or something?"

"I don't know. I suppose some do, and some don't. I can't relate to this instinct because I don't have it. I'm more of a non-follower than a leader."

"But you would make a good leader, Ilya Erynovich. You have that bearing. People are inclined to follow you. I've seen it."

"I think you're right. I've seen that too. Sometimes it comes in handy to get people moving. I'll sometimes step in when I see a group of people unable to get out of their own way. They will follow me. But it's not my calling. I abdicate the role as soon as I can. I would rather lead people to think for themselves, but I've come to realize that's an oxymoron."

"I'll let you in on a little secret. I don't have the hero complex either. I was born into my tribe – my family, my Principality – as its designated leader. I didn't choose this, or even aspire to it. But I do feel the tribal loyalty, the responsibility. I have a responsibility to lead my tribe. I have the skills and the disposition to do it, but not really the desire. I'm certainly unlike Osipov, or Sokolov, or even my immediate ancestors in believing that I have any intrinsic right to this. But unlike you, I don't have the luxury to indulge my doubt." Then he twirled the fourragere dangling under his left epaulet. "But I do like these things. The uniform befits me don't you think? Never speak of this outside this room, eh, Ilya Erynovich? Outside I am the supreme leader, confident in my station, regal in my bearing."

Ilya smiled, "The man who wouldn't be king. I suppose it helps that your tribe's succession is well-defined. You don't have to fight any rivals for your leadership. Otherwise you might not have."

"And what about your tribe, Ilya Erynovich? The science tribe. Isn't that a tribe just like every other social group?"

Ilya had to think about this. "I suppose it is. It has its rules and customs and peer expectations just like any other tribe. But no one is born into it. You have to choose to be a member. And there are no leaders! Yet we still manage to act as one and get things done." Ilya wanted to follow this line of inquiry even deeper – it was still not clear to him why the science tribe managed to pull this off – but he realized he had come here for a very different purpose. So he shifted gears.

"Am I free to go then? The 'epidemic' is over, right?"

"Yes, it is over," he smiled. "And you are free to go. But take care of yourself. These are dangerous times. And keep working on the vaccine. We may yet need it."

"Will I be able to board the trains now?"

"Ah, yes. That business. I'll have to put out an order to rescind the hold on your movement. It could take a day."

"I have a suggestion, Koldan Sonvaevich. Your men often don't know whom to believe when it comes to your orders. With the insecurity of texts on phones, it's easy for someone to impersonate you. How can your men be sure that your orders really come from you? I don't think Sokolov's men would have been capable of exploiting this. But I could have."

"And did you?"

"No. But I could have."

"And you have a solution for this?"

"Yes. Public key cryptography. The same thing we use on the Internet to sign and encrypt email. I could put an app on your phone that would allow you to digitally sign your communications using a private key that only you possess. You would then distribute its corresponding public key to everyone on your organization. When the message arrives, it will be indecipherable unless it can be decrypted with your public key. If it can be, that proves that the message had to have come from you – or someone in possession of your private key. You'll need to safeguard that private key."

"You mean memorize it?"

"No. It will be long and completely unreadable. It will be stored on your phone. You just need to protect your phone."

"And you can do this now?"

"Yes."

"Well then by all means do it! I like this idea. What would you like my order concerning you to say?"

"How about something like 'let this man pass.' And include my picture."

"Done."

"How about 'let this man, and all in his company, pass?'"

Prince Tarasov paused, smiling. "This means I will have to trust you."

"Do you trust me?"

"When we are at cross purposes, no. Not for a minute." He said nothing further for a while, eyeing Ilya. "But let's assume we have a common purpose from now on. I'm willing to be optimistic."

§

Once the app was installed, and instructions were given to Tarasov's lieutenants on how to distribute it down the hierarchy of the organization, Ilya got his phone back. He wasted no time texting "go" to Katerinya. There was joy at Andzhelina's house that day. The two women felt that a great weight had been lifted. They vowed to keep in touch, and Andzhelina slipped a Rioja from her collection in Katerinya's backpack. "Ilya will like this," she said. Katerinya gave her a hug. Then she followed the plan for a sneaky exit from Andzhelina's house, not knowing, of course, that this was probably no longer necessary.

Ilya took the tram home. It was too early for his pass from Tarasov to take effect, but he was interested in how strong the existing travel ban was among the troops. No one checked, no one asked. Consequently he arrived home before Katerinya did. She was on foot. The reunion, under no more constraints, lifted both of their moods. It had been a while since they could enjoy time together without something hanging over their heads. There was still a minor war in progress, but each of them felt a certain degree of freedom from its reach right now. Katerinya forgot about dead bodies. Ilya forgot about the need to protect Katerinya from Tarasov.

They decided to spend the rest of the week at Ilya's in Derazhne, then head back to Mariankursk for the weekend. Katerinya still had two suitcases here, after all. They no longer needed to escape to Mariankursk, they just had some loose ends to tie up there from their abrupt departure. It would also be nice to return to the country on a train they could freely travel on, and to a country house they could freely enjoy. Though Ilya was now thinking that Derazhne might be the safer place to sit out the remainder of the war. He remembered the Prince's prediction that it would finally be concluded in the provinces. He hoped it would not reach Mariankursk. Ilya proposed that since they were back to being city folks for a while, they should go out for dinner tonight to celebrate. Katerinya thought that might be a good idea. Then she showed him Andzhelina's gift. Suddenly Ilya had a better idea. Why don't they make their own dinner here? Katerinya thought that might be a better idea as well.

Over dinner, as he was explaining the cryptographic signature app to Katerinya – the one that would enable Tarasov to give them a system-wide pass – it occurred to him that he could do the same for himself and Katerinya. No need for a public key registry. This would be an encrypted channel for just the two of them, each holding their own private key and the other's public key. The public key could be used for privacy and the private key for authentication. They would then be able to text each other without anyone else knowing what they were saying, and they could be sure that the message had to have been sent by the other. "We could have used that at Olena's," Katerinya said. "Then I would have known that the message was really from you. And that you were really OK."

"But you probably would have come any way."

"Yes … I probably would have."

Chapter 8

GOD ON THEIR SIDE

The next day, at breakfast, they began reconstructing the threads of their lives that had been interrupted by the ominous events since the Crispness party. Although Katerinya hadn't worked much on her novel since then, she had to stop altogether once she left her laptop at Olena's. Ilya had done nominal work on the vaccine for Tarasov, though his heart was never in it, and he forgot about all of his other research work. Also, classes at the University had been suspended for the faux epidemic, and would now be resuming, so he would soon be back to teaching again. He had forgotten all about the Androsia project that he and Katerinya had abandoned when they were last in Mariankursk, when targeting his own DNA turned out to be a non-starter. He might have forgotten still if Katerinya had not just asked him about it. "That's right!" he remembered. "Well, I suppose I could have tried working on it back here when I was twiddling my thumbs under house arrest, but I forgot. I had other things on my mind." "Like me?" she asked. "Yes," he smiled. "Like you."

At this point, the enigma of the Androsia message came in two parts. The first, of course, was what the message would actually say. They had already decided that it was from Ilya, to Ilya. And that his past self had sent it to his future self because his past self knew his future self was about to forget something. He had certainly forgotten something. Something very big – his entire life history prior to 20 years ago. Although he would like to recover that, it was entirely too big to be the message itself, so there must have been some significant snippet from his past that was most important for him to recover in his present state. Or was it something about the near future that he needed to prepare for?

The second mystery was why the message had to be so secret. He had clearly gone to great pains to ensure that no one other than himself would decipher the message (perhaps too great, it seemed). Why? If this had just been about memory, like the "look in pocket" scenario from the train station, where the message simply recounted some of his missing past, why not simply say that! Why not just leave a note in plaintext in his office, or his house, that said "look in the file under …?" Then the target message could possibly have recounted his entire missing history. But the secrecy aspect put a different, ominous spin on the whole affair. He wasn't just recounting his past, he was warning about something from his past (for his eyes only) that would affect his future.

But at present, they had no new leads or ideas to pursue. Ilya could put in some real work on a vaccine back at his lab, but Katerinya would have no resources for her own work, so she would be stranded, cooling her heels in science-land. Realizing this, Ilya proposed that they spend the day in the twin cities, avoiding areas like the East Derazhne enclaves, and the river of course. There was still a noticeable presence of Tarasov's soldiers everywhere, but citizens now welcomed this as a visible security buffer against the troubles.

At Katerinya's request, they retraced their steps from Yaroslava's to Veronika's Fine Ladies's Apparel to the Kadnikov's mansion. Yaroslava's had not reopened for brunch yet, post-epidemic, so they had to lunch elsewhere in the Square. Veronika's was just starting to reopen. As they passed the window, the owner recognized them and waved. Then motioned for them to wait while she hurried out to meet them. She told Katerinya that her gown at the Kadnikov's had become the talk of the town. It was good for business. Every upscale woman wanted one of these now, though it did not fit most of them so well given its figure-hugging tailoring. It was also designed for someone with Katerinya's long, slender shape, so this limited its applicability as well. So Veronika had sold very few of these, but once in for a try-on, or a talking out of a try-on, she managed to convert many of the women to customers for other of her fashions. Katerinya was pleased by both aspects of the story — about being the talk of the town and the envy of high society ladies, and about being unique enough that few of them would own a replica of the gown. She would prefer that no one else had it, but that was probably asking too much. Veronika implored her that if ever she planned on attending another such affair in town, she would donate a gown of Katerinya's choosing if she were to model it for the world again.

Then they decided to head to the train station for a return to their home in the country. They would be back during the week, so Katerinya decided to just leave her suitcases, and their contents, at Ilya's house for now.

On the train, Katerinya thought about the novel that she had been neglecting. It had changed a bit since she first met Ilya, because her life had changed a lot. The main character, after all, was based on herself. It was fiction, so the character could have stayed the same even as its original basis did not. But she had a richer life now. It gave her source material she had not been familiar with before. The love interest was substantially different now, influenced by her own unexpected trajectory in these matters. She did not want this to be autobiographical, but the character seemed to keep updating herself, without first asking Katerinya's permission. And Katerinya was now consciously considering changing some of the plot to incorporate what she had experienced about war and high society. There was originally no character like Ilya. She had never imagined such a person. It would be a major change to introduce such a character now. And it would certainly change the direction of the love interest. She was still steadfastly resisting this, but at the rate at which the heroine was updating herself, it would only be a matter of time before an Ilya character began writing itself.

At Mariankursk, Ilya and Katerinya went straight to Olena's. She needed an update, and some overdue thanks, and Katerinya needed her laptop. They decided to celebrate their newfound freedom to walk about in public by going straight to Olena's front door. The Prince was once again on their side, and even so, the only eyes and ears that they needed to avoid on this walk were soldiers or Madam Zakharova. They saw neither. Olena had been worried during the information blackout, and was now so glad to see them whole and together again – and coming through the front door! That in itself spoke volumes. As their thank you gift to her, they treated Olena to dinner at Maxim's. It was unseasonably warm that evening, so they were able to sit outside. It was still winter by the calendar, but the unexpected weather served as the first portent of the spring that was to come.

That night, Ilya and Katerinya got into bed without their usual fires. It certainly felt like spring, both meteorologically and in terms of their prospects. Their pillow talk was about where they would be going and what they would be doing, not who would be chasing them and what they would have to avoid. There was still a little snow on the ground in the woodlot, and there would no doubt be a few more snows before it was all over, but for the first time since that fateful Crispness Eve, their landscape was clear.

§

As winter passed slowly into spring, the snows receded, seeds germinated, the daffodils, hyacinths, and bluefairies came out, animals entered their mating seasons, and the days gradually crossed over the vernal equinox heading for the summer solstice. And the affection between Ilya and Katerinya subtly changed its complexion as well. It had been born in the winter, during successive times of crisis. They had been drawn together by the need for protection, the need for shelter, the need for mutual comfort and support. Their time together had been constantly interrupted by forces trying to pull them apart. The war was not over, but it had not impinged upon them personally for months now. Their own experience of peace seemed like the new normal, so they were gradually settling into a new regime of peacetime affection. In this regime, they no longer needed protection, or shelter, or comfort from external physical forces, but they regularly retreated to the sanctuary of their private emotional space nonetheless. Not because they needed to escape, but because that was where the good stuff was.

Derazhne was still tinged with the effects of war, so the couple spent as much time as possible at their country home in Mariankursk. They could walk the streets freely, day or night, shopping, eating out, and people watching. They had occasional picnics in the park, and in the woods behind Tallinnskaya Street. The warmer days meant less need for fires, and thus less need for splitting firewood. Katerinya planted a small garden in the back at the edge of the woods to grow fresh vegetables and herbs – especially basil and rosemary. The evening sun lasted longer, and the morning sun arrived earlier, so Katerinya no longer tried to keep up with Ilya's waking with the sun routine. He was careful not to wake her by his movement, letting her awaken on her own schedule.

On one of these mornings in April, Ilya awoke with the sun at Tallinnskaya Street, as he usually did, but he did not fall back asleep. He watched the birds through the bedroom window playing out their mating rituals on the branches of trees still pale green with their cover of small, new leaves. He didn't know bird-speak, but from their behaviors it probably went like this.

"Hey, cardinal here, cardinal here. Check out these red feathers."

"Single brown male sparrow seeks single brown female sparrow for lifelong commitment."

"Hey baby, what's a nice bird like you doing in a tree like this?"

Then he watched Katerinya for a while, still sleeping next to him, her shallow breathing gently moving her chest. What struck him about their relationship in the earlier months was how much they were alike. As it had matured, he came to appreciate more of their differences. Aside from the expected male/female differences, there were still very few of these. He had a bit of melancholy in him. Between the highs of discovery and other victories, he could become pensive, a little sad, until something unexpected came along to lift his mood. Things that used to please him would no longer please him as much. He would have a sense of been-there, done-that. Ironically, it was a condition that he hadn't really noticed that much when he was single (well, as far as he could remember). It came to light in retrospect because Katerinya had mostly made it go away.

Her disposition was sunnier, or at least more consistently sunny than his own. This might be a male/female thing, he thought, but if so, that was a good thing – a good complement, like two puzzle pieces fitting together. She could be serious and resourceful when she needed to be, but her day-to-day disposition was playful, nurturing, inviting. She could often find a source of interest or delight in otherwise ordinary things. Things that he didn't notice. And although he didn't experience this delight directly, he could experience it vicariously through her. He realized now that this attracted him to her perhaps as much as her physical attributes. It was infectious. It bled over into him. His sometimes melancholy mood never managed to pull her down, but her brighter mood always pulled him up.

There was no other source of well-being in his life now that could match this, he thought. Other joys would come and go, without much staying power. But with Katerinya, there was always a next episode: the next day, the next morning, the next hour. The source never ran dry. Eventually, the source awoke of her own accord. A groggy smile spread slowly across her face. And so it begins, he thought to himself.

Ilya had a morning appointment with the young doctor at the Mariankursk hospital that day. There had been no cases of the plague since the first outbreak, but they still had not located its source. This was not a matter of imminent concern anymore, but they still wanted to be able to close the pathology book on this. It was the one part of the outbreak they still did not understand. After breakfast, when Ilya was about to depart, Katerinya said, "Now don't be too long, Iliusha. I have a surprise waiting for you when you come back." She liked to surprise him. He liked to be surprised by her. But he would never make it back for her waiting surprise. There was a different surprise waiting for him on this warm, spring day.

The hospital was on the southwest outskirts of the town, backing into woods on the south and west sides. The entrances were on the north and east sides where they connected to Mariankursk streets. Ilya entered through the main entrance on the north side as usual. At the end of his meeting, as he approached the north doors he could see an armed soldier blocking the north path on the outside. This was not one of Tarasov's men. He wore a semblance of a militia uniform, missing a few pieces, but in the colors of the Evangelicals. This can't be good, he thought. His hyperopia enabled him to see the soldier before he could recognize Ilya. So he turned and went quickly for the east exit. At the door, he saw a similar looking soldier blocking the external walkway there. There was no other way out. He would have to try passing them and hope for the best.

He looked straight ahead as he approached the soldier on the east, not making eye contact. The soldier glanced down at his phone, then up at Ilya. He waved to the soldier on the north who quickly began running in their direction. As expected, the east soldier stepped in front of Ilya, blocking his path. "Professor Koskayin?" "Yes?" Ilya answered expectantly. "You are to come with us." Ilya quickly looked north and south to assess his chances of making a run for it. His chances were not good. Two more armed militiamen emerged from the west and south woods to bring the total to four. They had made their point quite clearly. He was marched quickly to the south woods by the quartet, each glancing around nervously, anxious to get to the cover of the woods. There they had horses waiting. Four of them. They searched his pockets and confiscated his cellphone. Then they doubled him up on one of the horses with a soldier.

"May I ask what this is all about?"

The one who appeared to be the leader said, "You have been summoned by Commander Kuznetsov, in the name of God." They said no more.

§

The Kuznetsov encampment was more than a full day's ride from Mariankursk. The soldiers alternated between trotting and walking the horses so as not to overwork them. Ilya guessed from the position of the sun and the times of the day that they were heading consistently southwest. They alternated between roads, fields, and woods to stay away from other humans. One of the militiamen seemed to be guiding the others on the directions. He probably was once from the area, Ilya thought. They would pause at times on the roads when they could see signs of civilization ahead, and consult this man, who would then direct them into woods or fields. He also seemed to recognize landmarks on his own and would preemptively direct them off road. From Ilya's perspective, the longer it took to get where they were going the better because each successive mile put Kuznetsov another mile further away from Katerinya. No one that Ilya and Katerinya knew in Mariankursk was aware of Kuznetsov's proximity, so perhaps he was not nearby at all. This made it even more difficult to imagine what his interest in Ilya might be. Someone with Tarasov's network of agents would know he was in Mariankursk, but the mysterious Kuznetsov was a guerrilla commander from the countryside, without such a network. How he knew of Ilya, how he knew he was in Mariankursk, and even more vexing, why he cared, was a mystery.

The militiamen had food rations and camping gear for a multi-day journey, so they camped out in the woods on the first night. The April temperature made this bearable, but it was still uncomfortable sleeping on the ground. Ilya did not sleep well, dealing with both the ground and the intrigue. This was clearly not going to be a friendly social call. He had tried to engage the men in conversation around the campfire, but they would only talk among themselves. Ilya guessed this was due to prior orders.

At the end of the second day, they reached the militia encampment, deep in the woods. The soldiers escorted Ilya through makeshift rows of bivouac shelters to a central area where there were some larger tents housing the field infrastructure and the command center. Their arrival had been noticed by the camp, and as they approached the center, Ilya could make out a figure emerging from the central-most tent who appeared to be waiting for them. This, he guessed, was Commander Kuznetsov. As they got nearer, the figure waiting for them seemed oddly familiar to Ilya – like someone he had seen before. He had a noticeable limp, and a full beard, but neither of these features was part of the familiarity. It was something about his overall silhouette and the visible part of his face. Because of his hyperopia, Ilya was accustomed to recognizing people before they recognized him, but when he was close enough to determine who this was, he realized his adversary already knew him as well. It was Stepanov. Mitya Zhenyaevich Stepanov.

"Ilya Erynovich, please come inside," said Kuznetsov, né Stepanov. It seemed to Ilya that Kuznetsov had tried to suppress a smile for the greeting, preferring to seem unemotional. Was this for the benefit of his men, or did it reflect a change in the erstwhile Stepanov? When the two sat down in camp chairs inside, in private, he learned that it was closer to the latter. Through the beard, he could see several prominent scars on Kuznetsov's face. And his leg limp was very pronounced. The leg limp was probably from the bullet wound not properly healed, he surmised, and the facial scars probably from torture at the hands of Tarasov's men while being interrogated in prison. There would no doubt be scars on other, less visible parts of his body as well.

He was now a visibly changed man. Before, he had looked thoughtful, a man of responsibility trying to balance conflicting demands on his desired peaceful mission. He had evoked a sense of diplomacy then. Now he had the look of a military man on a wartime mission. He showed no emotion or accommodation. Soldiers can be like that, at least when they are in the field on a mission. They have empathy drummed out of them as part of their basic training. When they are in the field, they are supposed to feel nothing other than loyalty to their commanders. It makes them efficient cogs in the top-down military machine. They have a single purpose – follow orders. Stepanov was a professional military man, so he had both the basic training and the experience of a commander's reliance on discipline. Whatever empathy he may have had was probably beaten out of him by his recent inquisition. What was left was pure soldier. He was not a happy soldier of God, or even an angry soldier of God. He was just an inscrutable, focused soldier. This disposition certainly matched what one would have expected from reports of his alleged atrocities. Ilya waited for him to speak, hoping that the necessary introduction would open him up a little, reveal a little more about who he was now, but the silence lingered. So Ilya went first.

"When last we met, Mitya Zhenyaevich, you wanted to bring about a *peaceful* kingdom of God, as I recall."

"Mitya Zhenyaevich Stepanov is dead. He died in Tarasov's prison. You are now speaking to Commander Kuznetsov."

"Does this commander have a first name and a matronymic name?"

"No, he does not."

"And why has this Commander Kuznetsov summoned me all the way from Mariankursk?"

"I did not summon you, Ilya Erynovich. This is a time of war. I appropriated you. You are a resource to me, nothing more. When we first met, I believe I gave you my gun as a gesture of peace. You will notice where my gun is now." He pointed to his sidearm prominently visible in his holster.

"I believe you said we were both honorable men then as well."

"You may be. I only honor God now." Another silence. Ilya gave up initiating things. Now he would just wait. "I brought you here because I need your services. Let me get right to the point. When I escaped from prison, I inherited this army. They were amateurs, undisciplined. We had too little funding and too few resources. So I took them far to the west where I could teach them to be guerrillas. They are loyal, but some of them are crazy, and incompetent. I also inherited a foolhardy project to build a doomsday weapon. They were already working on it when I took over. This was originally Sokolov's hare-brained idea. If they were on their last legs, they planned to unleash it on Tarasov in the cities."

Now Ilya was on high alert. "Let me guess. It has something to do with the plague."

"Yes. They broke into one of the remote storage facilities that holds the legacy germs."

"*Yersinia pestis modernis?*"

"The one that caused the Great Dying."

"That's it."

"The men in charge of this are true believers that know very little about biology. They were helping with Mattson's theme park until they managed to break everything. Then he got rid of them. Sokolov moved them onto this project instead."

"I know the type, believe me."

"Personally, I'm not in favor of such a weapon. It is likely to kill everyone indiscriminately – including us. But I do like the idea of having it as a deterrent. The threat of using it may be a useful bargaining chip in a final negotiation. But I don't trust the idiots in charge to get it that far. I'm afraid they will kill all of us first. That's where you come in. I need your expertise to ride herd on them."

"You want me to be in charge of building a bioweapon?"

"I want you to babysit the fools who think they are building a bioweapon. I don't know how to undo it. Your job will be to make sure they don't annihilate all of us. Lead them astray a little. Secretly disable it if you can. Just make sure their fingers are not on the trigger. You see, Ilya Erynovich, you and I still have one goal in common. Don't you agree?"

"Where are they storing the bacteria?"

"I don't know. Does that matter?"

"Yes! Both the temperature and the containers matter a great deal. But I don't understand how they were planning to release it in a targeted area without infecting themselves."

"It gets worse. They had two plans. One was suicide delivery. Martyrs of God. The other was via remote-controlled drones. Are you familiar with these, Ilya Erynovich?"

"Yes, it's a very recent technology. Developed in Africa. I've done distributed cryptography work for them so that the control codes will not be compromised if the drone is lost. But what would Sokolov's guys know about drones?"

"Nothing. That's the problem. They've stolen a few and had already run a botched test near Mariankursk before I got here."

Then Ilya's red alert alarm went off. "Mariankursk! Those guys were responsible for the outbreak there? Did you know this when you first asked me about it?"

"No. No one on Tarasov's side knew about this. I only learned about it after I inherited these morons. They lost control of the drone. It flew northeast on its own and crashed in the woods near the Mariankursk hospital. Fortunately, there was a wind to the southwest that day, so most of the bacteria drifted away from Mariankursk."

Now the puzzle pieces started to fit together for Ilya. Most of the cases had come from people who lived near the hospital. Originally, he and the doctor thought the hospital itself might be the source, even though they had rigorously quarantined patients. The small outbreak could easily have been a major epidemic but for a favorable wind. But most concerning was that the infecting bacterium was a *mutation* of *Y. pestis modernis*. It had mutated since it was stolen from the legacy storage. It was a favorable mutation. The new bacterium was not as deadly as the parent, but its novelty left the human population without any medical defenses. This put a new urgency on his development of a vaccine for it. But it also indicated that he was being held here not just by Kuznetsov's gun, but by the possibility of a much larger calamity that perhaps only he could defuse.

"Take me to the team," he said.

With that, Kuznetsov escorted him out of the command tent and toward one of the other tents. He stopped first by one of the militiamen that had captured Ilya and asked him to search the professor. "We already did," the soldier replied. "He had this." The soldier handed Ilya's phone to Kuznetsov. It was locked, of course. "Unlock it," he demanded, handing it to Ilya. Everything of value on Ilya's phone was further encrypted once the phone was unlocked, so

Ilya saw no harm in letting Kuznetsov open the phone. But he had not considered Kuznetsov's unfamiliarity with the 'tracking on / tracking off' ruse. It had been off for a long time, but of course it said 'tracking on' in the settings, to fool officials in just such an inquiry. But now it had the opposite effect. When he saw the setting, Kuznetsov froze. Tarasov could have been tracking his location! He gave it back to the soldier, and told him to ride east for at least a day, then throw the phone in the nearest river. "Quickly!" he said. The soldier ran for his horse.

Then Kuznetsov summoned one of his commanders over and asked him to nominate a soldier under his command that he trusted. This would be the professor's full-time guard. Someone who would accompany him everywhere to prevent his escape. The commander thought about it for a moment, then looked around. "Shurupov! Get over here." The soldier came running.

"This man is your permanent prisoner. Do you understand? You go everywhere he goes. Do not let him escape. If he does, shoot him," Kuznetsov ordered. "Yes, sir!" the soldier saluted. "Go with him to the bioweapon tent. I'll be there shortly." With that, he went back into his tent.

When Ilya and the soldier were out of earshot, Ilya asked, "And what is your name, soldier?"

"Lavro. Lavro Mildaevich."

§

The bioweapon project was as Kuznetsov had described it – random bio-containers strewn around with no semblance of environmental control, a few stolen drone parts, and two "architects" who didn't know the difference between a virus and a bacterium. The original two were the geniuses fired by Aron Mattson for incompetence. Their commander at the time thought that it was a waste of scarce personnel to have two soldiers unavailable for field operations, so he rotated the two into combat. After one was killed, he relented and assigned the least combat-worthy soldier he could find to the mission as a replacement. It was the blind leading the blind.

After interviewing the two, and hearing their tales of the failed test at Mariankursk and the initial raid on the legacy storage facility, Ilya was appalled at the lax state of security that enabled that to happen. Asymmetrical warfare, the kind waged by small operators such as terrorists, used to be about bombs, and other such weapons of mass destruction. Now it was biological. Much more efficient and lower cost. You could kill just the people and leave the buildings standing. Only universities were capable of producing the technology, but their research was often funded by governments. It was mutually assured destruction pacts among governments that kept this kind of technology from being deployed, and it was mutual aid pacts among the universities that acted as the firewall. Both guarded against a doomsday vector falling into radical hands. But here it had already failed. If he ever got back alive, he would have to have the University and Tarasov up the security on the legacy storage of *Y. pestis modernis*.

Ilya got Kuznetsov to make it clear to the team that *he* was now in charge of the mission. No questions. Just follow orders. It helped that Lavro was permanently assigned to guard him. Lavro always had a weapon at the ready, and this sent a signal to the team. Kuznetsov employed the same fiction as Tarasov of the "bodyguard." This made it appear that Ilya was the commanding officer with an enforcer by his side. Kuznetsov didn't know it, but he no longer needed Lavro with a gun to keep Ilya here. Although he had been planning to escape at the first opportunity and find his way back to Katerinya, escaping before he managed to disable the weapon was now possibly equivalent to condemning everyone to death – he and Katerinya included. He had no choice but to fulfill Kuznetsov's mission – at least part one of that mission. For once, the scientist held the upper hand. It mattered what you knew and did not know. Only he would know when the bioweapon was no longer operational.

Lavro did indeed follow him everywhere, so he and Ilya had many conversations. There was, after all, a lot of non-work to do on the project. He sent the other two out for meaningless tasks while he tried to devise ways to disable the biological component of the device. Without any real lab equipment, this mostly amounted to sitting around, pretending to do "biological" things while he was busy thinking of possible ways out. The other two project members, now being functionally expendable, were rotated back into combat action. He and Lavro, not being expendable, were kept away from the front lines, always near the command center.

Lavro was still in his teens, and had never gone through the traditional basic training, so he had plenty of empathy left. He was apparently a good soldier nonetheless, having twice gone into action as the backup man, and having to pick up the rifle of his dead lead man to continue the engagement. His commanders liked him, but were a little wary of his youth and inexperience. His seemed to be a conscience buffeted by the winds of authority. He looked up to Ilya, and thus Ilya realized he could lead him as another authority figure. If Ilya did need to make a run for it someday, it was unclear whether Lavro would shoot at him. He would certainly be conflicted.

Ilya's immediate problem was how to even approach disabling the bacteria in the containers. He would, of course, know how to do this back in his own lab, but in the field he had to improvise in a most fundamental way. It was still not clear why the bacterium had mutated. Being a bacterium, the $Y.$ $pestis$ mutation rate was slower than that of a virus. Its replication could be retarded by extreme cold or warm temperatures, but like most pathogens its optimal environment for mutation was in host organisms during an outbreak. The more pressing issue was how to kill it. It could not survive ultraviolet irradiation, but you weren't going to find that in the woods. It probably couldn't survive more than a day or two exposed to direct sunlight, but he was not about to empty the containers on the ground and pray for two days of sun, with no rains and no winds. The only feasible course of action was to find a source of antibiotics.

Since he had time on his hands, Ilya took a long shot at obtaining an antibiotic from nature. The Penicillium genus of fungi is famous for producing – you guessed it – penicillin. He incubated bread crusts in plastic until the characteristic blue-green mold formed. To purify the penicillin from the spores he would need lots of chemicals that he did not have. It could be very detrimental to expose a human to the whole fungal growth because it consisted of several kinds of fungi, some of which produce antibiotics harmful to humans. But he wasn't applying this to humans. He was going after bacteria. So he simply introduced the whole spores to a sample of the bacteria in an improvised petri dish. The spores would secrete penicillin, and other things as well, directly on the bacterial culture. He was not optimistic, because penicillin was not effective in general on *Y. pestis*, but this was a genetic variant, so why not try. It had no effect.

Lavro watched this experiment over the course of several weeks, fascinated by this hidden power of nature and its orchestration by this equally fascinating scientist. He also didn't know that Ilya's purpose was to kill the bacteria, so he had no idea what the result of the experiment was. Ilya told him it was not successful, but didn't tell him what it was not successful at. He simply needed chemicals that are found in hospitals, not the woods, he said – leaving out the word 'antibiotic'. "Why don't we get them from a hospital?" Lavro asked.

"A hospital in the woods?"

"No, a hospital in a town. We sometimes take control of towns for provisions."

Ilya had not seen this kind of action yet. It had all been skirmishes with the Orthodox militia in rural areas so far. But the idea was planted. He consulted with Kuznetsov about adding an antibiotic appropriation mission to the next urban siege on a town with a hospital. With Kuznetsov, in private, he could say 'antibiotic'. Kuznetsov had no near term plans for this, but did tell him that the town of Prokomovsk was only a few hours ride on horseback from here. It was not controlled by either side, but it had a regional hospital. At this point, he sensed that he now had Ilya for the duration of his assigned mission, even without Lavro as a guard. So he suggested what would have been unthinkable only a few weeks ago. Why not send Ilya and Lavro on a smash-and-grab mission to the hospital? Desperate times called for desperate measures. The pair seemed to work well together. Lavro had the soldier skills, and Ilya had the mature judgment to keep them away from foolish schemes.

Lavro was thrilled by the news. He wanted to see action again. But Ilya prevailed on him, much as Kuznetsov had hoped, to take a more subtle approach. Lavro should dress as a civilian, hiding his sidearm in his coat when they approached the hospital. Then he should just follow Ilya's lead. They may be able to procure the necessary "hospital chemicals" without any violence at all. He was easy to influence. Ilya felt confident that he would be in control.

The next morning, Ilya and Lavro set out for Prokomovsk. When he was captured, Ilya was put on the back of another man's horse for the journey. He did not have to know how to ride. Now he was riding solo, and it came to him like riding a bicycle. He was actually quite good at it. It was another one of those muscle memory skills from deep in his cerebellum. He couldn't recall ever being on a horse, but clearly he had been. Many times. Neither he nor Lavro knew the town, so they hitched their horses to a tree in the woods at the edge of town and walked in like two civilians with a purpose. They asked the first passerby for directions to the hospital, which he freely gave. When they got to the hospital entrance, Ilya walked straight to the receptionist, with Lavro in tow. "I'm here to see the doctor in charge," he said, quite matter-of-factly.

"Is he expecting you?"

"No, but tell him I am Professor Koskayin, from Derazhne University, here to see him about an urgent matter."

The receptionist perked up, and immediately went into an adjacent room to inquire. Lavro was impressed with how Ilya could get people to do things like that so easily. The doctor emerged, and said "Professor Koskayin, please come in." Ilya looked at Lavro and said "Wait right here." Lavro obeyed without thinking.

Once in the privacy of the doctor's office, Ilya shut the door, and explained the situation to him. The doctor had indeed heard of him – and his association with the outbreak in Mariankursk. Ilya considered his options. Should he make up a cover story so as not to reveal his capture by Kuznetsov? But then he thought, why? If he didn't take the doctor into confidence, the news about him being in Prokomovsk would leak out with unknown consequences. So he decided to tell the doctor the whole story of his capture and the volatile bioweapon housed less than a day's ride from here. That got the doctor's attention, and a promise to keep the matter confidential. What did Ilya need? Antibiotics.

The doctor took him down the hall to the storage area. Ilya browsed the antibiotics. There weren't many. Eventually he located streptomycin and gentamicin, drugs known to work on *Yersinia pestis* in general. He asked the doctor if they had the antibiotic for *modernis* as well. Some, he said, but not much. How much did Ilya need? Ilya had to think about this. He didn't want to deplete the local stores. They would be needed in case of an outbreak. All he really needed was a small amount to test their efficacy on a sample of the bacterium – *if* he could view the results under a microscope. He explained this to the doctor. Did he have a microscope he could spare? They had only two. Then Ilya cast it as a trade-off between depleting the microscopes and depleting the antibiotics. With the microscope he would need very little of the antibiotics to test. Without it he would need a lot – enough that the results could be seen with the naked eye. The doctor saw his point, and also that the microscope would come in handy if the tests did not work – for future research attempts in the woods. So they had a deal.

As Ilya was about to rejoin Lavro with the supplies, he paused a moment at the doctor's door. Thoughts of Katerinya flooded his mind. Without his phone, he had no way to contact her – even just briefly to tell her was alive. He knew she would not be taking this well, and would try to find him again, if only she could. But she would have no clue where to look. As hard on her as this was, he saw the upside of her having to stay put, out of harm's way. If ever he could contact her, he should not disclose his location or circumstances. He had looked in vain for unguarded phones around Kuznetsov's camp. Kuznetsov had once been Tarasov's head of security, so he knew all about the dangers of tracking. Consequently he destroyed most phones he found anywhere in his encampment. His survival depended on Tarasov not knowing where his base was.

But the doctor would have a phone. What if he borrowed it for one brief message: 'I'm OK.'? He knew Katerinya's number by heart. But the call could likely be traced to Prokomovsk, he thought. Tarasov might then know Kuznetsov's approximate position. An attack on the camp might release the bacteria. Like it or not, he still had to protect Kuznetsov as long as the bioweapon was still viable. There was a brief struggle in his mind between reason and desire, with desire trying to convince reason that the probability of an attack was low. Think of poor Katerinya sitting, distraught, in Mariankursk. Reason won this time. He opened the door and left.

When they returned to Kuznetsov's encampment, Ilya immediately set up the trial. The notion of asking for a microscope had occurred to him on the spot, as a way to avoid taking too many of the antibiotics, but now he realized he should have been looking for this a while ago. It was his first real piece of lab equipment, and he could use more. Perhaps he could even return to Prokomovsk later, and do some work with the equipment there. He really needed to understand the circumstances of the mutation. And for that, he needed a real lab.

The cocktail of the three antibiotics did kill off some of the sample, but not all. He would never have known this without a microscope. The partial success indicated that not all of the cultured bacteria had mutated, at least in the samples he tested. To kill it all, unless it had mutated again, he would need the new variant antibiotic that he had developed in his own lab. But that was experimental and still only available at Derazhne.

§

As summer arrived, even with its fuller foliage cover among the trees, Kuznetsov was forced to move his camp. Successive engagements had enabled the other side to eventually triangulate his position. Ilya and Lavro's sedentary existence now shifted more toward the nomadic lifestyle. The importance of the bioweapon mission still kept them at some distance from the action, but they had to decamp more often now. Under-resourced from the start, Kuznetsov was now slowly losing by attrition, as Tarasov had predicted. The Orthodox militia was losing men at the same rate, so the overall balance of power remained the same, but Tarasov was not reinforcing the Orthodox forces with his own yet. This was probably also part of the plan. Osipov could not control them, so the fewer that remained when it came time for the endgame the better, from Tarasov's point of view. Although most engagements were fought in the fields and the woods, the small towns were growing weary of the constant cycle of occupation and reoccupation. Both sides wanted the same thing: supplies. This put a strain on the local economies for food and medicine. There was also a tit-for-tat retribution against perceived collaborators as each side retook the towns from each other. It was not a good time to be a small villager.

Ilya had been of a mind to return the borrowed microscope to Prokomovsk, as part of his plan to do his research there, but he had not anticipated the uprooting of Kuznetsov's base camp. It was hard to get a sense of the progress – or lack of it – of the war from the base camp, and Kuznetsov was not the type to share strategic information with Ilya. So for better or worse, he still had a microscope, though no longer a hope for access to a real lab.

At one point, Kuznetsov's raiders were able to appropriate a decent quantity of the traditional *modernis* vaccine from a hospital. Ilya had told them what to look for. It had posed a bit of a moral dilemma for him. By decreasing the local citizens' access to the vaccine, they would be more vulnerable in the case of an outbreak. But the only likely source of such an outbreak now was the bioweapon itself. An outbreak becomes an epidemic when it spreads quickly through a population without immunity. The unprotected population immediately surrounding the bioweapon was Kuznetsov's men. So Ilya weighed the consequences and decided to inoculate his new comrades first. Some of the samples still contained the original *Y. pestis modernis*, the architect of the Great Dying. Best to stop that deadly vector right here. Just in case.

During his inoculation campaign, it occurred to Ilya that he was naturally quite comfortable with needles, both for delivering the vaccine, and for blood draws. He knew how to find the muscle mass for a vaccine target, and how to find and deftly get in and out of veins without causing hematomas. He recalled his initial aversion to the blood draws at the Mariankursk hospital, but that was during the early stages of his memory recovery. This new skill, again of the muscle memory instead of cognitive memory variety, added to his growing inventory of prior skills now forgotten. He had forgotten where he learned this, but not how to do it.

After a few, very bloody engagements, he began to suspect that he had once been a doctor in his past life – the MD variety as opposed to the PhD variety. The troops generally didn't understand the difference between a doctor and a biologist, and they had very few actual doctors in camp, so they often came to him with wounds and other maladies, and the few actual doctors regarded him as a colleague. This pushed him closer to the front where he assisted in the triage operations – quickly deciding who was going to die from his wounds anyway and who was likely to be worth the limited resources for saving. Before long, he was performing the life-saving operations himself. He instinctively knew what to do. Since there was a distinct lack of sterilizing agents and antibiotics, the warfare had reverted to more historical norms where more soldiers died many days later from infections than from immediate physical trauma.

Because there was little artillery, most of the wounds were from small arms fire. These left pieces of clothing, small projectiles, and other environmental contaminants in the wounds, leading to bacterial infections, most often streptococcal. Without adequate sterilization and antibiotics, these wounds would lead to gangrene in the extremities, and sometimes to sepsis when the bacteria got into the bloodstream. Without the drugs, nothing could be done for sepsis. It was almost always fatal. Wounds to the chest or torso, which started out as gangrene, often took this course because there was nothing one could amputate. The most common survivable wounds were these to arms and legs. Once gangrene developed, the solution was to amputate the infected part to keep the infection from going system wide. So the most frequently used tool in the doctors' medical kit was the venerable bone saw. In the best case, there were anesthetics available. In other cases, you had the fully awake patient bite down hard on a wooden peg.

Ilya instinctively knew how to do all of this. He could certainly have learned about the infection problems from biology, and about the more primitive state of the battlefield from reading history, but this was not just intellectual knowledge he was now exhibiting. His accurate snap judgments on survivability during triage, and his familiarity with the technique of the bone saw was something that only could have come from having gone through this before in some previous portion of his life. It made no sense that he could have learned this in past centuries, so he reasoned that he must have been involved as a doctor in a wartime of similar antibiotic deprivation. It could have happened before if the conflict, like this one, was far from the reach of cities.

His comrades in arms had now fully adopted him as one of theirs. They gave him a medic's armband to wear in the combat zones to lessen the chance of the enemy taking him for a combatant, though he knew that the honoring of these conventions had long since died with the vicious, intertribal enmity that the horrific conditions promoted. He had the common sense not to rely on the armband for protection. He had to keep his head down and his eyes up, just like the real soldiers.

Kuznetsov's partisans may have adopted him into their tribe, but he had in no sense joined it. He had no enmity toward the opposing partisan tribe. He favored his own side only in a utilitarian sense — the greatest good for the greatest number. He would often approach the gravely wounded on the other side who looked like they had a chance of survival, if not left on the field to die. But he was always told to "leave them!" A command he had to obey to avoid the sanction of his own side. The circumstances, though, almost always favored the utilitarian calculation anyway. With the scarcity of proper medical resources, every enemy soldier he saved would mean one less saved from his side. And because of the militia's necessitated guerrilla mobility, Kuznetsov kept no prisoners of war. They did not have the infrastructure, the resources, or the will to do this. Even with the will, the other deficits meant that the stricken enemy casualty was going to die anyway.

Toward the end of the summer, the number of military engagements had lessened. There were more and longer lulls between the fighting. Both sides were now seriously depleted and fatigue had set in. Both the physical and the mental kind. Ilya could see that

Tarasov's plan was coming to fruition. How soon before the endgame, he wondered. He still had seen no opportunity to disable the mutated bacteria in the bioweapon, so he was no closer to shutting it down and escaping back to Mariankursk. At this point, he was suffering from his own mental fatigue. He was still holding up physically, though like many of the soldiers he had lost weight due to the scarcity of food rations. He took advantage of the lull to sit by a creek near the camp, in the middle of the afternoon. It would normally have been a pleasant experience in nature with the clear sky, the warm sun, and the sound of the flowing water. But now it was all suspended in a haze – a mental haze, part hunger, part exhaustion, part frustration. He had an innate ability to be stoic in circumstances like these. If he couldn't do anything about a predicament he was in, he would just resolve to endure it. This wasn't his occasional melancholy. This was a different state altogether. There would be no Katerinya to bring him out of it. It was a holding action until there would be a Katerinya once again. He missed her terribly, but he did not lapse into a state of pining, or self-pity. He just shut down to wait it out.

Over the summer, Lavro had evolved into Ilya's medical assistant. He still carried a rifle, which was now more for protecting Doctor Ilya during combat than for keeping him from escaping. He was a quick study, learning how to perform minor procedures and assist in major ones. He had often seen Ilya go to the temporary aid of enemy soldiers, and wondered why he wanted to help such evil men. He often let Ilya drift away from him now, not fearing an escape, but of course he couldn't let this happen for too long. So today he went looking for Ilya. When he located him by the stream, he sat down beside Ilya and popped the question that was on his mind.

"Doctor Ilya, why do you always want to help the enemy?"

"Why not? They're people, just like you and me."

"But they are evil people."

"What makes them evil – that doesn't also make us evil?"

Lavro was not used to answering questions such as these. He wanted to say 'because Pastor Sokolov said so,' but realized he didn't like the sound of that answer. He wasn't so sure about Sokolov anymore. "They killed my family, and my friends, and my comrades."

"I'll give you the comrades, but you've also killed their comrades. And from what you've told me, your own tribe killed your parents. And your friends effectively killed themselves trying to kill other people. All I see is people killing people. They're either all good or all evil." This was confounding to Lavro. He couldn't think of a next response. So Ilya prodded him some more. "Were the Evangelical militiamen who killed your parents evil?"

"No. They were good people who did an evil thing."

"And how does that happen?"

Some more thought. "They were confused. The Devil made them do it."

"Ah, the Devil!" To Ilya, this disembodied agent was even worse than the God agent that caused everything but explained nothing. This character was invoked to explain how evil existed in a world that the God agent could presumably prevent. It was said to be a conflict between *two* disembodied agents, much like war itself. But it had its own problems as an explanation. "So let me guess. God is on your side, and the Devil is on the Orthodox side?"

"Yes, that sounds about right."

"So these enemy soldiers that I'm willing to save are not inherently evil. They're good men that the Devil causes to do evil things?"

"Yes, that's it!" This was starting to work, Lavro thought.

"But your God is supposed to be omnipotent." Ilya quickly recognized that Lavro didn't know what this meant. "Your God is all-powerful. There is nothing he can't do, right?"

"Yes, that's right."

"Then in all of these battles between good and evil, between God and the Devil, why does the Devil so consistently win? Couldn't your God just put a stop to it and wipe out the Devil with one sweep of the hand? Why does there even have to be a battle?"

"But we *will* win this battle in the end! God is on our side!"

"I hate to break it to you Lavro, but your side is losing this war. It won't last much longer. You and the militia on the other side are killing each other off. When there are too few of either of you left, Prince Tarasov will swoop in and finish you off. If Tarasov is backed by the Devil, and you by God, the Devil will win. Again."

"But then we'll use the bioweapon, Doctor Ilya! That's why you're here, Kuznetsov says. God must have sent you!"

Now there's a fine irony, Ilya thought to himself.

§

By the fall, Kuznetsov's prospects had unexpectedly improved. His more professional military organizational techniques were beginning to give him an edge over the less well-organized Orthodox militia. The engagements had pushed his encampment further north into territory not quite as burnt over from previous hostilities. And this included towns that had not yet been plundered of their supplies.

One morning, when Kuznetsov ordered a small raiding party to scavenge for supplies in a nearby town to the north, Ilya volunteered to go along. It was not yet known who controlled the town – if anyone – or what resources might be found there. Ilya was hoping for a hospital, or a medical center of some sort, where he might get more antibiotics. He did not trust the raiders to know what to look for, nor to procure them without violence. Lavro, of course, accompanied him.

This northeast portion of the continent was known for its vivid fall colors, and the cold nights had contributed to a dazzling display this year. It was peak season with the maples going first in bright oranges and crimsons against the green of the other hardwoods that had not yet turned, and the softwoods that would stay evergreen. The party followed an unpaved roadway that their maps indicated would take them to the town. The landscape was wooded and rolling so visibility over each rise ahead was limited. They followed a classic patrol formation with a single point person at the front, and Ilya and Lavro at the rear. Of the two, only Lavro was armed, Ilya still wearing his medic's armband and carrying some medical triage supplies in a backpack.

About midday, a volley of rifle fire rang out from the cover of the woods on the left. It cut down the lead man, but hit no one else. As he ducked to the ground on the road for cover, Ilya was surprised at the partisans' poor aim. He had never been this close to the beginning of an engagement, so he had not really witnessed the actual fighting up close. He always came in later to mop up the bodies. The opposing soldiers ran out of the woods to continue firing on the run. This made their aim even worse. His own comrades returned fire from their positions on the roadway, but they were not very effective either. From very minimal cover behind rocks and fallen trees, both sides continued the random rifle fire back and forth. Still no one appeared to be hit. Ilya didn't understand either the poor marksmanship or the seeming lack of self-preservation from fighting with such scant cover, for both sides. Maybe the bad aim induced a false sense of security about being hit, he thought.

Lavro moved forward, firing, so Ilya took advantage of his cover fire to move forward and check on the felled point man. He was dead. The body itself provided a little cover for Ilya, who crouched on his stomach behind it as the enemy fired on his position. A few shots hit the body, but many of them scattered wide. These people just can't shoot straight, he thought. He grabbed the point man's rifle, and out of fairness, he tore off his medic's armband. Like it or not, he was now a combatant. Neither side was his side, in the tribal sense, but one side was going to try to kill him and the other side to protect him, so in a very pragmatic sense he had to join Kuznetsov's side. Following his own instincts for self-preservation, he rolled sideways into a ditch at the right side of the roadway, keeping his body as low as possible. At the first chance, he leapt up and scurried for the cover of the woods. He went deep into the woods at first, to catch his breath and to survey the field of battle. Hyperopia to the rescue once again. One of the enemy soldiers was firing from the edge of the right woods near the road. The others all had positions at the edge of the woods on the left side of the road. He saw his plan of action.

From his cover in the deeper part of the woods, he lay on the ground in the sharpshooter's prone position, wrapping the rifle strap around his left arm to steady it. He lined up the enemy soldier on the right through his gun sight, held his breath, and slowly squeezed the trigger. The shot struck him in the head, killing him instantly. As Ilya suspected, no one noticed. They had lost track of him and his position. He then ran forward in the woods to the north until the road took a bend. This enabled him to cross to the left side without being seen. Then he went deep into the woods on the left side and back toward the action. He took up a position about midway between the enemy soldiers from their back side. Then he dropped to the prone position again and took out each one with a single shot.

His comrades continued to fire at first until they realized there was no returning fire coming from the other side. Then one by one they began cautiously advancing to survey the enemy position. They were astounded to see only dead bodies. They hadn't realized they were such good shots! Ilya came forward slowly, with his hands and rifle raised so he would not be mistaken for the last of the enemy. When his men recognized Doctor Ilya, sans medic insignia, they were awestruck. Their aim hadn't suddenly improved, they realized. Someone else's had been extraordinarily accurate. They rallied around him, cheering and slapping him on the back. Ilya did not share in their sense of celebration. He had simply done what he had to do.

When they returned to camp, word quickly spread about the amazing marksmanship of the Doctor. Kuznetsov himself was intrigued by the story, and asked Ilya where he had learned how to do this. Ilya, of course, did not know. One more visceral skill from somewhere in his past. But Kuznetsov could not let it go. He wanted to find out more about this skill. He had his men set up a single bullseye, paper target on a post at standard firing range distance. The center ring of the bullseye was no larger than the diameter of a single bullet. He asked Ilya to shoot ten rounds at the target from the prone position. After the shooting, one of the soldiers fetched the target and brought it back to Kuznetsov. There was a single small hole about the size of a single bullet, with slightly irregular edges, at 2 o'clock in the third ring out from the center of the bullseye. Ten shots, all to the same location, but off-target.

Being a military man, and knowing about these things, Kuznetsov adjusted the gun sight down and to the left. This was not a sniper's scope, but a standard issue gun sight with a ring near the firing pin and one at the end of the barrel. The calibration of the sight was good enough for most soldiers, but its true accuracy could only be determined relative to the best marksman available. Then he had Ilya shoot again, this time using five rounds against a competition grade target – one with five separate bullseyes that would take one shot each. When the soldier brought back this target, it contained a single hole in each of the five bullseye centers. A perfect score. He was a natural sniper, even without a sniper's scope. What makes a good marksman is steady hands and body control, good breathing and trigger-squeezing technique, and exceptional long-range vision. The first and the third characteristics you are born with, but the second you learn. Ilya had learned this somewhere, and Kuznetsov naturally wanted to know where. Ilya couldn't answer, and didn't want to disclose his memory problem to Kuznetsov, so he just pleaded ignorance. The enigmas just keep piling up with this man, Kuznetsov thought. They were a source of both admiration and wariness. Who was this man?

Later, Lavro asked Ilya about this as well. He gave the same non-answer, but showed Lavro the learned-skill portions of the technique – breath control and trigger squeezing. It didn't help Lavro much with his own accuracy. Ilya surmised that the key skill he could not pass along was his hyperopia – you have it or you don't. But then he asked Lavro about the extreme inaccuracy of shooting he had observed in the skirmish – from both sides. "Is this common?" he asked Lavro. "Are soldiers mostly missing most of the time in battles?"

"I've never noticed. It happens so fast. You point your gun and shoot, and hope for the best. We didn't really have commanders today. When there are commanders, and a lot more soldiers on both sides, there is more charging at the enemy without cover. Then a lot more soldiers get hit. Was this your first action, Doctor Ilya? Today?"

Ilya was about to say, "As far as I can remember," but realized how improbable that would sound. Normal people don't forget such things. So he simply said, "Yes."

"Were you afraid? Don't worry, soldiers are usually afraid the first time."

"I never thought about it. I just reacted."

"But when you think you are about to die, doesn't it worry you that you will go to Hell?"

"No. Does it worry you?"

"Of course not. I will go to Heaven!"

"How would you know?"

Lavro hadn't thought that far. "The Scriptures say so."

"What do the Scriptures say?"

"That the righteous will go to Heaven."

"How do you know you are one of the righteous?"

Another uncomfortable pause. "Reverend Sokolov said so. We are the army of God."

"Don't you recall the Bible constantly warning you about false prophets?"

" ... yes ..."

"How do you know he is not a false prophet?"

He didn't. In fact he had lost a lot of respect for Sokolov since the bloodshed began. He reverted to an old standby. "I feel Jossmit, and his calling, in my heart."

"What did Jossmit actually tell you? Did he appear before you and speak to you? How would you recognize him if you saw him?"

"It wasn't like that. It was just a feeling."

"But the Orthodox soldiers report the same feeling. From the same Jossmit. The one that says 'Turn the other cheek'. Yet you somehow all got the same message, 'Kill the other guys'. Do you really think that if you were born and raised Orthodox you wouldn't have 'felt' the same message that they did? You have the ability to reason, Lavro. Think about it."

Lavro did not like to reason. He followed orders.

"Think about it, Lavro. Your God gave you the facility to reason and told you to avoid false prophets. If you are killed in battle, imagine what would happen on judgment day if you got this wrong. You are asked if you exercised good judgment in deciding whose orders to follow. No, you say, I took the word of the first leader-like person I encountered. What evidence of authority did he have? I didn't ask. Did you not see some of the inconsistencies in the Scriptures, some exhorting you to kill children and some to save them? I didn't really read the Scriptures myself."

Lavro did not like to think about these things. He changed the subject.

§

By the time the first snows of winter began to fall, Kuznetsov's prospects had begun to decline again. Sensing that the endgame was near, Tarasov had finally begun reinforcing the Orthodox troops with his own. That brought them more supplies, more weapons, more ammunition, and more discipline. Kuznetsov was now on the run, being pushed alternately west and north. Ilya's patience with his primary mission was beginning to wear thin as well. He needed a game changer – some way to get access to his own, custom antibiotic.

One day, he proposed to Kuznetsov that he take Lavro and attempt to get all the way back to the outskirts of Derazhne. Enough of his antibiotic would still be stored in the off-campus synthesis lab. They could run a below-the-radar mission there similar to what they had done in Prokomovsk – two horses, two plainclothed men, one able to peacefully extract the drugs. He saw no other way to finish off the doomsday device. In the summer, this would have been unthinkable for Kuznetsov. Having Ilya that close to Derazhne would have made it too easy for him to escape. Lavro would be easily overwhelmed. But he understood now that Ilya had just as much at stake in shutting down the bioweapon as he did. If he were going to leave before the device was inactivated, he would have left by now. He'd had plenty of opportunity in the last six months. As the endgame approached, Kuznetsov still hoped to use the threat of such a weapon as a bargaining chip, but an inert bargaining chip would work just as well, as long as the other side thought it was real. It wasn't clear that Lavro even mattered anymore. But the two worked together well, and Ilya would keep him under control. So he authorized the mission.

The two set out for Derazhne with three days' provisions, just in case. Derazhne was probably not that far away, but a lot could happen on the way. Kuznetsov had lost visibility into the eastern parts of the Principality from his encampment in the far west. Bivouacking in the snow was a little more familiar to Ilya now that he had been living outside for many months. He knew a lot more about it than Lavro, he noticed. Lavro was a city boy, so that made sense. Ilya, on the other hand was a ... person with an unknown past. As the city came into view from the west, Lavro felt a pang of homesickness for his old neighborhood. But it was tempered by the memory that all of his people were gone. He was a soldier living off the land, now. The neighborhood life seemed like a long time ago, much longer than the year he had been away.

The approach to the synthesis lab was as unremarkable as Ilya had hoped. They had left their horses well out of town and walked the rest of the way on foot. Because they did not have to enter the University proper, Ilya was not recognized until he went into the lab. There, of course, he was recognized. To the look of surprise on the receptionist's face, he put a finger over his lips to signal "Sshhh." He asked her quietly to get the lab director for him and ask him to act normal as well. The receptionist didn't really understand the circumstances, but she willingly followed the leader's order. He told Lavro to take a seat in the lobby and wait. No one would know who he was. When he got to the director's office, he explained as much of the situation as was feasible under the circumstances. It would be best if all parties to the conflict did not know about the true state of the bioweapon until he managed to kill the remainder of the bacteria. Then he would escape and inform Tarasov himself. The lab director also followed the leader, and went along with the scheme. Ilya took a little more of the antibiotic than he thought he needed to kill the remaining bacteria. Just in case. The supply here in Derazhne, even just for research purposes, was pretty good.

Before he left, Ilya could finally execute the action he had been waiting so many months to perform. He borrowed the director's phone – it was African-spec – turned off tracking, and sent Katerinya the simple message 'I'm OK.' He asked the director to leave tracking off for a day, so the source of the message couldn't be traced to any location in particular. Then he retrieved Lavro, and the two set off for the journey back west. All the way back, Ilya tried to imagine the scene when Katerinya would get the message. After all of these months, thinking perhaps he was dead, she must have been elated. It had to be soothing, welcome news, even though there wasn't much news. She would now have something to hold on to. No doubt others would have been asking her about his disappearance, right up to Tarasov himself. So the news would get out quickly, but the news would be minimal. No one had any basis for acting yet, and that's how he wanted it to stay until the doomsday threat was over.

Back at the encampment, Ilya had to manage expectations carefully. For Lavro, and the others connected to the project, he spun a story about a research project that would strengthen the bacteria. For once in his life, he was happy to be surrounded by ignorance of biology. As he painstakingly exterminated the remaining bacteria, they had no clue what he was doing. "There, that ought to make it more potent," he said. That Doctor Ilya, he really knows his biology, they thought. Aren't we fortunate that God sent him?

In his meeting with Kuznetsov the next morning, he reported the results as less definitive. Even though he was sure that they had not, he explained that the bacteria had mutated once again. Kuznetsov was a little more on the ball than the project team, but still pretty light on biology, so this improbable event was easy to sell. Ilya implied that he might be able to tweak his custom antibiotic to account for this (even though he could not), to buy a little time for "further study." He knew that once Kuznetsov knew the weapon was disabled, the game would change quickly, so he had to escape before that.

Kuznetsov was equally suspicious of Ilya, knowing that the professor had him at a disadvantage with respect to what he was reporting. He had no way to verify what he was being asked to believe. He watched Ilya for signs of a change in disposition, but he showed none. Neither man could read the other. They had had many conversations over these many months, mostly of the strategic, inscrutable variety, but Kuznetsov was gradually opening up, not really trusting Ilya, but seeing less and less downside to sharing information. He had provided much unexpected value to the tribe with his medical and sharpshooter skills. Kuznetsov knew this was not loyalty, but it made him feel differently about the professor than he had at first. He had become one of them in an extended sense.

Since this was perhaps their last conversation, Ilya decided to take a deep dive. "Will you use the weapon if you are on your last legs?"

Kuznetsov raised his eyebrows, sensing the incursion. "No. Even if it's still alive, I'll only threaten to use it."

"And if Tarasov calls you bluff?"

"No. I can't believe God would want that sort of mass destruction."

"But he rained it down on the whole of creation in the story of Noah."

"He told Noah he was going to do that. He told me no such thing."

"Does he talk to you, like he did to Noah?"

"No. Never. I have to make my own judgments."

"And you feel he would want you to spare the mass of humanity this time."

"Yes."

"Yet you've killed an awful lot of women and children, one at a time, with your sieges on towns."

"Those were necessary means to greater ends."

"But how do you know these ends were greater? How do you know they were justified?"

Kuznetsov pondered a long while on this one. "I don't, I suppose. I follow orders."

"But now you are giving the orders. You are deciding what others should do in the name of God. But you just told me that there are some things you will not order your soldiers to do. You have an individual conscience. Doesn't that supersede what some higher authority might have ordered you to do?"

Kuznetsov didn't answer.

"Do you remember the story of Isaac, from the Bible?"

"Yes."

"God tells Isaac to kill his own son, to prove that he will always follow orders, no matter how horrible they may seem. He was just kidding, of course, so he sent an angel to stay Isaac's hand just in the nick of time. But put yourself in Isaac's shoes. Also recall that you've been admonished, many times in the Bible, to beware of false prophets. How do you recognize false prophets other than that they command you to do heinous things? How do you know this is really God asking you to kill your son? Why would the real God do this? Is this not perhaps the false prophet speaking?"

"What are you asking of me, Ilya Erynovich? Why are you torturing me? What would you have me do?"

"I would have you think for yourself. Stop following perceived orders from unknown, unnamed, mystical authorities. You are pretty close to the top of the pecking order now. Make your own moral decisions."

After another thoughtful pause, Kuznetsov said, "You've given me a lot to think about, Ilya Erynovich. Now I have to get back to more practical matters. And you to your research."

"One more thing. Have you ever read the Biblical book Songs of Songs?"

"That's in the Bible?"

"Yes, in about the middle. I've just recently read it myself for the first time. If you ever get the chance, look at Chapter 16. Some Bibles subtitle it as 'The Story of Isaac'. It's another slant on that moral tale. You should look at it."

With that, the two men parted, one to prepare for the military endgame, and the other to make sure he was not around when the endgame finally came. Later that morning, when Lavro sheepishly reported to Kuznetsov that Doctor Ilya appeared to be missing, he was surprised by the commander's reaction. He expected he would come down hard on him. This was, after all, Lavro's primary responsibility. But Kuznetsov almost appeared to expect this. He was not surprised, but he sat for a minute adding up the situation. "What did he say when you last saw him?" Kuznetsov asked. "He said that if you asked, I should tell you that the bioweapon was now ready to be deployed." Kuznetsov fought back a half-smile. He knew what this meant. If Koskayin was gone, he had disabled the weapon. But on his way out, he had provided Kuznetsov with some credible cover for the troops, something he could use to sell the threat in a negotiation, all the while knowing the real doomsday threat was over.

"Take me to his tent," Kuznetsov ordered. At the tent, Lavro noted that very few things were missing. Kuznetsov looked at his things, various of them reminding him of conversations past. What was his plan? How did he intend to survive out there in the wild? He agreed with Lavro that it looked like he had taken very little. He picked up and examined a few biological-looking things. These might be useful even without Koskayin, he thought, so he stuffed them into his sabovar. The last item he picked up was a small, leather bound book. He opened it and thumbed through it. Then he opened to a random page:

So now I'm goin' back again
I got to get to her somehow
All the people we used to know
They're an illusion to me now
Some are mathematicians
Some are carpenters' wives
Don't know how it all got started
I don't know what they're doin' with their lives
But me, I'm still on the road
Headin' for another joint

We always did feel the same
We just saw it from a different point … of view
Tangled up in blue

"Poetry," he said to himself. "Not much use for that in times like these." He tossed the book aside into the snow.

§

For as long as Ilya could remember, he used to enjoy winter, but now he seemed less tolerant of it with each passing year, and particularly now that he was forced to survive outside in it. But on a morning such as this, with a clear sky and a bright sun, and a crisp layer of snow blanketing the forest, he could appreciate why it had always held a certain stoic pleasure for him. The sharp, crisp scents of blue spruce and bayberry against the clean, crisp, cold air. It was, he thought, a … what was the word he wanted? 'Bright'? No. 'Joyful'? No, that was not it. 'Merry'? Yes, that was it. It was a merry sort of crispness.

He had taken so little of his from the encampment because he had been hiding strategic items that he had taken from the camp inventory in a backpack that he had also purloined. It now contained wool blankets, a broken piece of a metal file, a small hand axe, a container of matches, a roll of binder twine, a jackknife, a cast iron Dutch oven, a small collection of first aid items, including some antibiotics, a stash of nanoprene, and an empty coffee tin. He took a sidearm and a rifle, and a small store of ammunition, in case he encountered hostilities. In his time living among them, he had noticed that the militiamen were not true woodsmen. They used kerosene and paper to start fires. They depended on raided stores for much of their food. Many slept in tents. This was not surprising, he thought. Many of them had been city boys before the war. They were not well adapted to living off the land autonomously. He, on the other hand, was. As he collected his strategic items and planned for his escape, he sensed yet more visceral skills that he could not recall learning. He could imagine building shelters and other small structures by lashing small pieces of saplings together. Wrap it thrice, frap it twice. Thus the hand axe and the binder twine. He could visualize the square lashing, starting with a clove hitch, pulling the frap tight around the wrap, and finishing with another clove hitch, but he could not visualize the events in which he learned this technique. He could imagine the entire progression of knots – he could see them being tied in his mind– from the figure eight to hold sheets in cleats, to the square knot, to the sheet bend for splicing two sections of rope, to the clove hitch for attaching to posts, to two half-hitches for tightening to a post, to the bowline for hauling or lifting great weight. He could flip a clove hitch over a post in less than a second by whipping together two loops. He could tie a bowline around his waist with one hand. He could hunt, fish, set traps, and build fires. He didn't have a compass but he could navigate by the position of the sun, approximately.

He estimated that he was roughly west northwest from Mariankursk based on what he was careful to observe on the ride back from Derazhne. It had taken him and Lavro two and a half days to cover the distance on horseback, so he knew he had a long journey ahead of him on foot. That's one of the reasons he did not bother to take much food. He couldn't take enough for the whole journey anyway, so he would hunt and forage for food on the way and save the space for other more essential items. He was hoping to eventually find railroad tracks. This would give him some sense of his north-south position in the railway network, and perhaps some sense of how much progress he was making. He would have to stay in the woods when trains approached because he had no idea which side controlled which trains.

After a day's walk, he set up camp in a sheltered part of the woods that would give him a good vantage point from which to see animals, human or otherwise, approaching. He ate from his stored food on the first night, and planned to hunt, fish, or forage in the days ahead once that was gone. Hunting took time, and required him to stay in one place, so he wanted to get as far on foot as he could with the prepared foodstuffs while they lasted. Distance from Kuznetsov was paramount at this point. Water was not a problem because of the snow pack. This would have been a much tougher proposition in the summer. He built a small lean-to structure for sleeping by cutting and trimming saplings with the hand axe and the knife. He used the binder twine to lash them together. One of the blankets served as the roof cover, in case of snow, the others he wrapped around himself for warmth. A fire at this point was not really needed. It wouldn't supply sleeping warmth. The only "natural" solution was conserving body heat with the blankets, but this is why he allowed himself one modern solution – nanoprene crystals crushed between the blankets. The old saw about building a fire to keep the wild animals away was a myth. The only predators in these woods were the timberwolves. Contrary to popular belief, he knew that wolves would rarely attack humans if not provoked. They are looking for easy prey to eat. We are too big and strange for that. Their natural instincts tell them "avoid that thing; look for some deer."

The next morning, to avoid being tracked by Kuznetsov's men, he broke down his lean-to, scattering the posts into the woods, and saving the binder twine from the lashings in his backpack. He would need these again each night. Once he started building campfires, to cook what he hunted, he would have to destroy and scatter the remains of these as well, but he was not there yet – though he had less than a day's rations left, he figured. By late afternoon, he decided it was time for the hunt. If he was near a stream, he would fish, but he wasn't. This left hunting for small game and foraging for tubers. It was not the season for nuts and berries and fruits. Digging in the snow for tubers was the only plant-based option. These would be hard, and need boiling. He knew how to clean and dress game animals for cooking, even large ones like deer, but he was after the small ones like squirrels and rabbits. He had no capacity for storing food. He had to eat what he killed within the same day. Hunting with the rifle would be easy for him, but he wanted to save the ammunition in case he encountered soldiers. He knew how to fashion a bow and arrows from small saplings and the binder twine, but he had no bird feathers for fletching the arrows. This would make them too inaccurate for hunting. So he built snares and traps for the small game, and foraged for tubers while he waited for a catch.

He got some of both – a small rabbit, and some edible roots. Tonight, he would have rabbit stew. After cleaning and dressing the foodstuffs, he was in the process of carrying the Dutch oven filled with snowmelt water to the fire pit for boiling. Its weight required both hands, so he was carrying the container of matches in the last two fingers of his right hand. Even the best of woodsman trip over the underbrush now and then, and for Ilya, it was now. In the fall, he lost the Dutch oven and the matches into the snow. Picking himself up, he could see that the matches had not only scattered into the snow, but had been drenched by the spilled water from the Dutch oven. They were now useless. The match container still had two dry ones, so he had to make these count. A lesser woodsman would have been stranded at this point, in winter without a source of fire, but Ilya had planned ahead.

After starting the cooking fire with the remaining matches, he refilled the Dutch oven and put it on to boil. Then he went looking in the woods for flint. Had he also been a geologist in a past life? He knew what to look for and found it – a small round flint stone. He cracked it in two with the back of the hand axe, yielding two pieces with sharp, jagged internal edges exposed. Next, he went searching among the reachable branches of the trees for abandoned birds' nests. Eventually he found one of those. He took his treasures back to the cooking fire to fashion the last piece of equipment he needed –

charred cloth. He took a linen handkerchief out of his sabovar pocket, pinched it between two sticks, and held it over the fire. As soon as the flames had covered the entire handkerchief, he dropped the whole flaming ensemble into the empty coffee tin and clamped its lid on tight to extinguish the flame. Then he opened the tin to let it cool. Inside was the thoroughly blackened handkerchief, now an irregular expanse of charred cloth. He delicately lifted it out, put the empty bird's nest in, put the cloth in the center of the bird's nest, followed by the two flints, and finally the fragment of the steel file he had scrounged from Kuznetsov's camp. This would be his flint and steel fire making kit – the source of all of his future fires.

After eight days of walking, Ilya had yet to find either a stream or a railroad track. Good thing it was winter, he thought. Otherwise he might have been dead from dehydration by now. He made better time by hunting, and thus eating, only every other day. Humans can survive a lot longer without food than without water. He had been avoiding roads to better avoid Kuznetsov's possible pursuit, but now eight days out, he figured that danger was probably over. He needed to seek out some semblance of civilization – a town, a person, a rail line – to figure out where he was on his journey. This started by following roads. Roads would lead to towns eventually. The trick was only to follow roads that were heading approximately east. Otherwise he would be moving away from his target.

Within the first half-day of following eastern roads, Ilya encountered his first human. He was an older man, walking along the roadside headed west. As usual, Ilya saw him before he saw Ilya. As he came into the other man's view, the man suddenly stopped. He turned and looked back east, then back again at Ilya. He appeared to be exhibiting the classic fight-or-flight behavior, except that being human, he had a third alternative – wait it out for more information. This appeared to be the state he was stuck in, clearly nervous and on guard. Why is he afraid of me? Ilya wondered. Then he remembered the very visible rifle he had slung over his shoulder. He took it off his shoulder, held it up toward the sky with his left hand, and raised his right hand, open palmed. Clearly a gesture of peace, he figured. The old man was anxious and confused. He turned and ran. Seeing that he had not gotten the intended message, Ilya fired one shot into the air. This got the man's attention. He suddenly froze, then turned around with both hands raised. This was not the way Ilya wanted to start a conversation, but it was the only means left at his disposal.

"Which militia are you?" the man asked.

"Neither. I'm a doctor." Ilya figured this would be easier to understand than being a professor. And apparently it was also true.

"Why the rifle, then."

"For protection … for hunting …" Neither sounded like a good explanation. "Look, I mean you no harm." He raised the rifle and his free hand again.

"Why did you shoot, then?"

"To get you to stop. I just want to ask you some questions. I think I'm lost."

The old man thought this over. "Put the rifle down and we'll talk."

Ilya did as requested. He even moved away from the rifle to make the point. The man then dropped his own hands and approached him, but still cautiously.

"Militiamen with guns have been a problem around here. You don't know who to trust anymore. Where are you trying to get to?"

"Mariankursk"

"Mariankursk? You *are* lost. That's a long way east of here."

"I know. I've been walking due east for eight days now."

"Well, that puts a different spin on it. You're a lot closer now I suppose."

"How close?"

"On foot?"

"Or train. Is there a rail line around here that would get me to Mariankursk?"

"Well, you're only about a day away from Pyatiskala on foot. You could get a train to Mariankursk there."

"Thank you. Do I just keep going east?"

"East? No, you gotta go south from here. You're well north of the western rail line."

"Southeast? Southwest?"

"Pretty much straight due south at this point."

"Thank you very much." With that, Ilya retrieved his rifle and left the road, heading due south. He now realized he had been going approximately east for eight days when he thought he was going east southeast. Without a compass, he hadn't done such a bad job of it, in retrospect. But now he was only a day away from Pyatiskala. The ordeal would be over soon.

When he built what he hoped would be his last fire at his camp for the night, he saw that he still had enough charred cloth for many more fires. The only two elements of his flint and steel fire kit that weren't reusable were the bird's nest and the charred cloth. He didn't need real birds' nests. He could fashion the same sort of structure out of dead, dry grass that stood above the snow in many fields. So each morning, he would build a new one to replace the old. If he had run out of charred cloth he would have had to burn something else made of cotton. So he always used small pieces – just enough to hold the spark. After setting up the tinder, the kindling and the logs for tonight's fire, he put a small piece of the charred cloth in today's artificial bird's nest. He put the nest on the bottom of the overturned coffee tin to keep it out of the snow. Then he knelt on one knee, striking the steel file against the sharp edge of the flint in a quick, downward motion. Sparks flew off the contact point, hissing, and fell into the charred cloth fragment in the nest. A few of these strikes produced a small red glow in the black cloth. Ilya immediately put down the flint and steel, picked up the nest, closing it over the cloth, and began to blow into it. The rush of oxygen spread the glow into a flame inside the nest. Ilya waited for the nest to be substantially flaming, then inserted it into the tinder. Behold Prometheus!

Chapter 9

THE STORY OF ISAAC

Yesterday was not a hunting day. If all went well today, Ilya had planned to be in Pyatiskala where he would once again be able to obtain civilized food. And warmth. And perhaps a bath. Living off the land had not seemed foreign to him. He might even have enjoyed it if he were not on a forced march in the middle of a war. And sleeping on the ground in the snow was definitely not something he envisioned ever being a part of his future. He was underweight again, like last summer, due to eating only every other day, but he was hoping that regimen would soon end. In his nine days out from Kuznetsov's encampment, he had not encountered a single soldier, nor seen or heard any evidence of the war. His time in the war had always been well to the west. He'd heard no news about Mariankursk or other points east, and thus assumed that this part of the country had escaped the hostilities so far. This was good for Katerinya, he thought. Worried as she might be for him, he did not have to worry about her safety.

By mid-morning he encountered his first railroad track. Now he had a decision to make. He had walked as due south as his sun-based orienteering would allow. It was not surprising that he hadn't struck Pyatiskala exactly. Finding the track first meant that he had overshot the town either to the east or to the west. If he assumed Pyatiskala was to the west, and was wrong, he would just keep getting further away from it. If he assumed it was to the east, and was wrong, he would eventually reach Mariankursk. That seemed like the better option, so he followed the track east.

Before long, he could see what appeared to be smoke rising from the horizon ahead. As he got closer, he could begin to see people, civilians not soldiers, walking next to the rail bed, headed in his direction. Some were on horseback. Some horses were pulling carts and wagons loaded with what appeared to be household belongings. It looked like an evacuation caravan. Having learned his lesson once, he exploited the brief interval between when he spotted them but before they spotted him to take his rifle off of his shoulder, and lay it in the woods at the side of the track. He still had the sidearm in his sabovar, in case he needed firepower, but this would be something he knew and they did not. As the convoy passed him, he inquired about where they were headed. He heard several accounts of militia taking over Pyatiskala. It had not been a voluntary occupation. There had been quite a bit of violence against those who tried to resist. Houses, stores and medical facilities had been forcibly occupied. Local government officials had been arrested. "Which militia was it?" Ilya inquired. No one was really sure. "Does it really matter?" someone said.

Somehow, the fighting had followed him east. Or had it been here all along? He didn't know. But now he had reason to worry about Katerinya in Mariankursk. No one he asked knew anything about what was happening in Mariankursk, but he did get the sense from their stories that this was the first siege on Pyatiskala.

Among the evacuees was a young girl, maybe 13 or 14, walking alone who had bloodstains on her dress and hands. Ilya's doctor instinct naturally led him to single her out. "Are you hurt?" he asked.

She seemed very anxious to keep moving, but paused to address his question. She looked at her hands and dress, and realized the source of Ilya's concern. "No, I'm alright. My father has been shot, and I'm trying to reach my uncle for help. My mother sent me. We don't know what else to do."

"Where is your uncle?"

"He works for the railroad. He has a house in the country near here."

Ilya quickly put two and two together. If there was one thing with which he was now thoroughly familiar, it was gunshot wounds. Her father could be losing blood. It didn't matter what the uncle might know. This poor girl had a doctor right in front of her with the necessary medical supplies. The course of action was clear. "I'm a doctor. I'll help you. Take me to him. Can you do that?"

She was stunned by her good fortune, but added a caution. "There are soldiers there."

"At your house, or just in the town?"

"In the town."

Her caution was well-timed. It reminded Ilya of his discarded rifle. He was likely to need that. He fetched it, put it over his shoulder once again, and followed the young girl back toward the east. Her name was Tatiana, he learned. Her father owned a small food market in Pyatiskala. When the militiamen stormed the town and had tried to steal his food stores, he resisted. They shot him and left him for dead. Her mother found him wounded, and helped him back to the house. She sent Tatiana to the local medical clinic for help, but there were armed soldiers preventing anyone from entering. When she returned home, her mother frantically sent her out to find her uncle.

When they got to the outskirts of Pyatiskala, Ilya could already see soldiers on patrol, but as usual, he saw them before they saw him and Tatiana. He realized that the presence of his rifle cut both ways. It was necessary for defense, but he would surely be challenged if one of the soldiers saw it. So they had to not be seen. Each time he saw a soldier from a distance, he asked Tatiana if she knew a less direct, but also less visible route to her house. She always did. She picked up on the plan immediately. Kid's got a good head on her shoulders, he thought. After a few such non-encounters with the militiamen, Ilya had seen enough of the uniforms to determine that these were the Evangelicals. Did they have more than one army? He had thought that Kuznetsov had all of the soldiers that were left after Sokolov's arrest. But he had been away from the east for a long time, with no visibility into what was happening here. Was this why it was taking Tarasov so long to finish this? Now he had new reasons to worry about Katerinya.

When they reached Tatiana's house by the back door, her mother let out a gasp at the sight of Ilya and the rifle. She thought at first that a soldier had captured her daughter and was returning to finish off the family. Tatiana sized up the situation pretty quickly. "It's alright Mamma! He's a doctor, not a soldier!"

Stunned, her mother asked, "Where did you find a doctor, Tatiana?"

"He found me," she said, smiling at Ilya.

The father's wound turned out to be in the leg. He had lost blood, but the bullet had missed the main arteries. Unlike on the battlefield, Ilya had this one under control. He had bandages, sterilization agents, local anesthetic, and sterile sutures. And if the wound got infected anyway, he had antibiotics. No more need for the bone saw.

Tatiana's grateful family treated Ilya to a warm bath, a change of clothes, and the best meal he had had in eight months. As they sat around the rustic dinner table under warm candlelight, Ilya told his long story, or at least as much of it as seemed wise. He left out the entire bioweapon intrigue, substituting instead that Kuznetsov had captured him because he needed a field doctor. The doctor parts of the story were much more salient anyway. He did include as much of the story of Katerinya as he could, so they could commiserate with his long odyssey, and his now urgent need to find her. As he spun his tale, he realized that his identity as a doctor didn't explain much about why Kuznetsov would come all the way to Mariankursk for one particular medical man, but no one asked. They had not had much visibility into the war from Pyatiskala, including the players and where they were located, so the tale seemed believable enough. This was the first brush with the war they had experienced, they said. That was good, Ilya thought. Good for Katerinya in Mariankursk. But where did these Evangelicals come from? He soon learned.

There was a pounding on the front door. Tatiana's whole family now knew that Ilya was a fugitive. Tatiana's mother turned to her and said in a low voice "Hide the doctor upstairs." Tatiana was right on it, leading Ilya up the back staircase. She glanced around, looking for the best hiding place. Then she took Ilya's hand and led him into her bedroom. She wasn't sure he would fit under her small bed, so she put him in her closet and closed the door. She stayed on the bed.

When her mother answered the door, a militiaman with a rifle asked, "Have you seen a doctor around here? A doctor named Koskayin?"

"No, we haven't seen any doctor."

"You're sure?"

"Yes, very sure."

The soldier considered leaving for a moment, then overruled himself. "I'm sorry, but I have to come in a look around. Just following orders." He seemed pleasant enough. Tatiana's mother glanced back at the dining room with her husband still sitting at the table, then opened the door for the soldier. She was a meticulous housekeeper, so she had cleaned up the blood from the wound as soon as it was dressed. After dinner, she had removed the plates and serving dishes from the table so they could listen to Ilya's stories. So there was no sign of blood, no sign of how many people had been at the table, and no sign of a wounded man, his pant leg covering the critical area. No visible signs of a doctor here.

The soldier looked around each room casually. Then he saw the stairs. "Mind if I check up here?" He asks permission? the mother thought. What kind of soldier is this?

"Yes, go on up if you must."

The soldier did a cursory check in each room. Nothing raised his suspicion. When he opened the door to Tatiana's bedroom, he was surprised to see her sitting on the bed with a book. He apologized for the intrusion. Tatiana also thought, "What kind of soldier is this?"

"Have you seen a doctor around the area recently? A doctor named Koskayin?"

"No. I haven't. Just doing my homework."

The soldier smiled, apologized for the intrusion again, and left. Now Ilya was doubly alarmed. It wasn't so much that the soldier knew his name. That only meant *someone* was looking for him. It was the sound of the soldier's voice that raised the stakes. He would know that voice anywhere. He had just spent eight months with him. It was Lavro.

How did he get to Pyatiskala so fast? He must have come on horseback. Perhaps Kuznetsov had sent him on a one-man mission. There was no way the entire army could have covered this much ground so fast. But there was also an Evangelical army here. How was Lavro associated with them? Where did they come from? After Lavro was gone for a good ten minutes or so, Ilya and Tatiana rejoined the family at the table. Ilya fleshed out the story a little further. He had already mentioned the Lavro character before. "That was him!" he told them. Suddenly the war stories that had seemed so far away earlier in the evening had come to their doorstep. "What does it mean?" the mother asked. "I don't know," Ilya answered, "but it's clear I can't stay here. You are all in danger as long as I'm here."

"But they've just checked here and didn't find you. They won't be looking for you here for awhile now. Isn't this the best place for you right now? You could stay with us tonight, and leave in the morning," Tatiana said, quite reasonably. Suddenly she reminded Ilya of Katerinya. She had that same resourcefulness.

Then there was a knock at the back door. Ilya and Tatiana instinctively got up and headed for the staircase. When Tatiana's mother got close enough to the door to see who it was through the glass, she said, "Tatiana, wait! It's your Uncle Vanya." Some of the refugees in the caravan had passed on Tatiana's story to him when they passed his house – the version that they overheard in her encounter with Ilya. He came as soon as he could, he said, trying to avoid soldiers. When he came in, he glanced at his brother who now seemed none the worse for wear, then at Ilya and Tatiana by the stair. "This must be the doctor," he said. "Yes, it is, Vanya, and he patched me up pretty good," her father said.

The extended family sat around the table once again for a round of bringing-Uncle-Vanya-up-to-speed storytelling. He was grateful that Tatiana had run into a real doctor before she got to him. He was a railroad man, not a doctor. Before that, he had a cherry orchard, but that was wiped out by the cherry blight of '35. He wasn't very good at things biological, it seemed. He wouldn't have known what to do. But trains he understood. And being a railroad man, he had answers for Ilya's perplexing questions. The Evangelical army had arrived by train from the west. Boxcar after boxcar of them, streaming into Pyatiskala Station. They poured out of the cars and took over the town. Tarasov had outflanked Kuznetsov to the west. He apparently didn't want him to be pushed completely out of the Principality because he would just reemerge later. He wanted to finish him off. So by outflanking him and driving him east, he hoped to catch him in a pincer move. But Kuznetsov still controlled the western railroads as he had all summer and fall. So he put his army on the trains and sent them east as far as he controlled the rails. That was the station immediately west of Pyatiskala. Now it was Pyatiskala itself.

So the facts now were these, both reported and inferred. There was only one army. It got here so fast by train. Kuznetsov and Lavro arrived together – today. They were one stop away from Mariankursk, so it made sense to sweep the town looking for Koskayin. Kuznetsov didn't know whether he was here or not, but he knew where he was headed. He probably used a lot more soldiers in the dragnet than just Lavro. So now what was Ilya to do? He certainly couldn't take the train to Mariankursk. Uncle Vanya, again knowing the railway system as a professional, had an idea. The western line out of Derazhne had born the brunt of the war in the far west. The northwestern line out of Derazhne had seen no hostilities. It was still firmly under civilian control. The nearest station on the northwestern line, Labivgrad, was only a day's ride from here. There was a man who lived near Uncle Vanya, a trader, who made a weekly round trip between Pyatiskala and Labivgrad using a two-horse wagon. He normally wouldn't be leaving for a few days, but, under the circumstances, there was no trading going on in Pyatiskala now, and a great need now for items from Labivgrad. He could probably be persuaded to leave for Labivgrad tomorrow morning. Ilya could hide in his wagon for the journey. Once at Labivgrad, Ilya could take the eastbound train to Derazhne, then switch to the western line out of Derazhne and come back to Mariankursk.

Ilya liked the plan. Uncle Vanya proposed that he and Ilya spend the night here, then in the morning he would take him to the trader's house and help plead his case for passage north. It was the least he could do, he said, for saving his brother. Doctor Ilya showed the family how to clean and change the dressing on the father's wound each day. If it should become red and swollen, he was to take the oral antibiotics that the doctor would leave with them.

§

Ilya and Uncle Vanya left early the next morning, just in case the trader had decided to make the journey today on his own. They took a wooded route, north of town, to avoid Kuznetsov's soldiers. The trader had not left for Labivgrad yet, but appeared a little skeptical when Uncle Vanya outlined the proposition. After some discussion, he agreed to the plan. Ilya suspected from watching the body language at a distance, that Uncle Vanya had traded something for the favor, though it was unclear what sealed the deal. The trader initially balked at Ilya's rifle, but Ilya explained that he would keep it out of sight in the wagon, and that having a rifle, and a marksman who knew how to use it, along for the ride provided an important level of security for the journey, given the proximity of the conflict. Put that way, the trader saw the wisdom of the arrangement. He would still prefer that both the doctor and the gun stay out of sight for the entire journey. He wanted to preserve his standing as a neutral party. This is what allowed him to trade between two towns. "No problem," Ilya said.

The trader was a loner, Ilya surmised. Even if he sat on the buckboard with him the whole way to Labivgrad, he probably would have said very little. So Ilya exploited the silence inside the wagon and napped often during the journey. Grain sacks provided a welcome alternative to the hard, cold ground of the forest floor. The journey transpired without incident. No one inquired. No one stopped, including the trader. He apparently preferred not to eat mid-journey. Ilya ate, when hungry, from the food Tatiana and her mother had prepared and packed in his backpack. It was almost like room service in a hotel. Breakfast in bed.

They reached Labivgrad by nightfall, too late for Ilya to get the last train east for Derazhne. The trader directed him toward the train station and Ilya set out for there on foot, determined to learn tomorrow's train schedules. Now that he was in a region without soldiers, and apparently a region unfamiliar with the conflict, he considered how he would appear in the station and on the train with his very visible rifle. It was not the kind of thing one could hide, except that he could store it in the overhead bin during train rides. He did not look like a soldier. His sabovar was his own. He had no vestiges of any uniform left. But his sabovar was tattered and exhibited a few dried bloodstains. It would be easier for passersby to categorize him if he did appear to be a soldier. That would explain the weapon, and most people would instinctively avoid him. He would have implied authority. But his appearance, it occurred to him, was ambiguous. He was a rough-hewn civilian who was armed and had clearly seen some action. What would they make of him?

In the train station, and at the guesthouse where he stayed overnight, he learned that people treated him with both curiosity and caution. Curious as to who he was, but cautious enough not to approach him to find out. That worked. He made it a point to smile at people when they got close. That helped too. Set them at ease. He would have stood out much more in Derazhne or Solinovsk, but in the rural regions, much closer to nature, his rough-hewn look was not that unusual.

The next morning on the train, once he had gotten through the station and into his seat next to a window, with his rifle in the overhead, he got no more looks or notices than any other passenger. He was back to being an ordinary citizen of the 41st century. Out the window, the view was mostly of hardwood forest with occasional open fields and rolling hills. The same kind of landscape he had lived in for the past eight months, except for the soldiers and the tents and the fortifications and the battlefield debris. It was the towns that were different. They were peaceful, normal, full of everyday citizens going about their everyday lives, not patrolled by soldiers under martial law, or burned over, or devastated, with occasional corpses hanging from trees as a warning to perceived enemy collaborators.

Was war the inevitable side effect of human nature, he wondered? With our innate disposition to form tribes and follow leaders? It enabled us to act as large wholes, to build civilizations and gain dominion over all of the other animals. But it had this nasty side effect. If there was more than one tribe, there would be an 'us' versus 'them.' There would be conflict. Was this like the pain of childbirth, an evolutionary side effect of perpetuating the species that is not strong enough to kill the mother? The pain survives because it doesn't prevent reproduction. We have learned to intervene in childbirth, to prevent the pain without disturbing the end process. Could we learn to intervene in the birth of civilizations, to prevent the wars, without disturbing the end process? He couldn't answer these questions. He wished he could.

Ilya could not recall ever having been on the northwest rail line. That didn't mean he hadn't, given his memory deficit, but he had no visual memories of the landmarks or towns he was passing by. Too bad, he thought. It's very pleasant looking country. He recognized the names of the station towns, but only because he had heard of them. All he knew was that they were towns in the northeast, not even that they had train stations. Sometime after leaving Kaliniyevka Station, the track crossed a river gorge on an elaborate trestle bridge. The river was not wide, but the water was fast moving in the gorge below, so it had not frozen. There was a picturesque meadow below at the side of the river from which one could see all the way up the gorge. A beautiful sight. He should come here sometime with Katerinya, he thought. A picnic maybe. About halfway across the bridge, he suddenly got that sense of déjà vu. This seemed like a place he had been before. He glanced backward to the west, forward to the east, and up the gorge to the north. The sense was still strong. There was no visual memory. No scene, no season. But a compelling similarity to something. The sense faded as the gorge moved out of view. He must have been here before, doing something with someone.

Trying to locate this memory would have consumed him all the way to Derazhne in the early days of his memory lapse – around the time he met Katerinya – but he was getting used to these episodes, particularly the déjà vu ones. He knew he couldn't retrieve the memory, so he stopped trying. The next stop, Yelangrad, was only one stop away from Derazhne. He had other things on his mind.

The train pulled into Derazhne station right on time. No more smoke rising from the neighborhoods like the last time. The military presence was minimal. It looked positively – normal. So the conflict must have spared the cities, as Tarasov had hoped, or perhaps had planned. He had so much to catch up on, so many people to see to reveal that he had survived, not the least of them the Prince himself. He needed to relay what he had learned about the bioweapon – that Kuznetsov might try to bargain with it, but it was inert now thanks to himself. All of these things would take time, and he didn't have time right now. He had taken the first train out of Labivgrad, which would give him time to make the last train back to Mariankursk if his stopover time was minimal. Everyone would learn everything in due time, but the overriding priority for today was to get back to Katerinya. The more time he spent in Derazhne, the more likely he would be recognized and drawn into something that would make him miss the last train. Tarasov would feel that Katerinya could wait one more day. Ilya, on the other hand, felt that Tarasov could wait one more day – at least.

The only thing preventing Ilya from just waiting in the station for the departure was the need to contact Katerinya. He didn't have a phone, but he had a stash of African-spec phones in his office. So he had one trip planned. To the office and back. Try to stay out of view and unrecognized. That would mean ditching the rifle. He put it in a storage locker at the station so as not to draw any attention, along with his backpack. Then he caught the tram to University Station, and carefully navigated the campus to avoid people. It seemed to him that he had been doing a lot of that the last time he was here, though now the reasons were reversed. Before, he didn't want his enemies to see him. Now he didn't want his friends to see him.

It worked. He got to his office without being recognized. The secure app that he had set up on his and Katerinya's phones was a pairwise protocol. It required each phone to hold its own private key and the other's public key. Since the phone on which he installed the keys for himself was now at the bottom of a river somewhere, the keys were effectively lost. They are very long bit strings, not the kind of things that humans can remember. He would have to rebuild the app on his new phone when he got to Katerinya's. That meant he could not communicate with her securely right now. Although the risk of being overheard by Tarasov was now minimal, Ilya was still eight months out of date on what had been going on with the politics. He did not even know if Katerinya was still in Mariankursk. So the message had to be text, it had to be brief, it had to be cryptic, and it had to allow for Katerinya to acknowledge.

So far, she knew he was "OK," whatever that meant, but nothing more. He remembered their old plaintext protocol to signal when he was coming to Mariankursk, but of course it would be a little different this time. So he sent, 'The first one now will later be last ... ', then ' ... train from Derazhne.' He waited. He hoped she had her phone on and with her. He waited some more. Then he got a message: "The times really are a changing ... '. Then: '... but the train times are the same!!!" That's my Katya, he smiled. He looked around the office quickly to see if there was anything he should take with him. No, just the phone. He put it in his pocket and headed out the door. If he were recognized on the way back to the station, he planned to just keep going. He had a singular mission now.

The train ride back to Mariankursk was a familiar one. A comfortable one. For more than a year now, when he took this route solo, it meant that he was returning to Katerinya. She would surely be waiting for him at the station at the other end. There were no known clouds on the horizon now, but that was just it. No *known* clouds.

They had made this assumption before and been wrong twice. And he didn't know what had transpired since he had been in the wilderness. So he tempered his optimism, and just concentrated on the singular fact that he knew. She would be there. The rest would take care of itself.

The waitress in the station café had not seen Dmitri for at least eight months. She feared something had happened to him, but didn't have the heart to compose a story about his demise. She saw Anna only occasionally now. Perhaps they had split up? But they seemed so happy when she saw them together last spring, back when they would take regular trips to and from Derazhne. The few times she had seen Anna at the station since, she did not appear to be happy. She always seemed worried. This is why she thought something must have happened to Dmitri. It was a sad ending. She didn't want to imagine that story.

But tonight, Anna had showed up at the station way earlier than usual. She was practically skipping, clearly happy about something. She waited impatiently on the passenger bench, trying to busy herself with reading, constantly looking up at the clock. But she kept smiling! She was overjoyed about something. When the last arrival from Derazhne was announced, she immediately rushed to the entrance for arriving passengers. She made sure she was at the front of line. Then the waitress saw why. It was Dmitri! He was the first one off the train. He was still alive! They hugged each other so long that the conductor had to move them out of the way of the other passengers. They were clearly in their own little world at this point. They just stayed in that embrace for the longest time. Other passengers noticed, but they did not notice other passengers.

Oh, it was so good to see Dmitri and Anna back together again. But poor Dmitri looked like he had been through a war or something. He had a rifle over his shoulder, and his sabovar looked tattered, and had what looked like bloodstains. And he looked a little wan, a little thinner in the face than she had remembered. But he was certainly a happy man now. The story lines began swirling in her head. Her imagination was ready to start up the saga again. What a nice couple they make, she thought. I'm glad it all worked out.

§

When they got back to Tallinnskaya Street, Katerinya sized up her rustic-looking man. When he set down the rifle and the backpack, she took off his sabovar and tossed it in the corner. "We'll have to get you a new one. You can't wear that." She wanted to burn it. Ilya was glad at that point that he had had at least one bath and a new set of ill-fitting clothes from Tatiana's house. As happy as she was to see him, Katerinya was a little concerned about how thin he looked. She took off his clothes, and drew him a hot bath. Then she got in the tub with him.

As she washed him, she noticed a few scars on his body, mostly minor, but one prominent one on his leg. It was healing, but it looked like it had been sutured. She touched it with concern. "Should we get you to a doctor, Iliusha?"

"Turns out I *am* a doctor," he said with a wry smile. That, of course, confused her, so he realized he had a lot of explaining to do. He narrated the story of his capture, the bioweapon, and his newfound skills as a horseman, a battlefield doctor, a marksman, and a survivalist. He left out the gorier details – like the bone saw. So much of the story was already a little shocking to her. He explained that the wound to his leg was the only one due to a bullet, and that was just a grazing. He left out a comparison to the more substantial wounds most soldiers endure (and the fact that many of them didn't endure).

"But how did you get wounded, if you were just a doctor?"

"Field doctors are always near the battle, usually behind the rear guard. You have to move forward sometimes to save the wounded."

"You didn't have to fight did you? I mean, you were just a doctor, right? Where did you get the rifle?"

Now, he supposed he had to relate the full story of his marksmanship. He had just told her the part about the targets in camp before. "I got it from a dead soldier ... that I tried to save. We were on a patrol and got ambushed. Then I had to fight."

She paused, wide-eyed. "You didn't have to kill anyone, did you?"

He appreciated that she said, '*have* to kill'. "Yes. Seven or eight men, I think."

She paused again, not sure she wanted to hear the details. "But you *had* to, right?"

"Yes, I had to. I had no other choice. I had no idea what poor shots these soldiers are, on both sides. They can't hit a thing. And it wasn't until then that I realized how good a shot I am. It wasn't really a fair fight, skill-wise. But if they all could shoot like me, I'd be dead now. None of them suffered. It was a single shot to the head for all of them."

Katerinya didn't want to hear any more of that story, which she signaled by grasping him around the shoulders and hugging tightly. She was just thankful he was alive. Ilya sensed this, so he changed the subject. "How did you make out here when I was gone?"

She looked up. "It was terrible. Not even knowing you were alive." Then she realized it was her turn. "You know me. I had to find out. Since you never came back from the hospital, I went there first. Some of the nurses saw what happened. The doctor recognized something about the uniforms. They were Evangelicals, he said. That's all I knew, for the longest time. I figured they must have taken your phone. I went to see Madam Zakharova, asking if she knew anything. She was surprised to find out we knew she was a spy. She denied it at first, but then told me she had heard nothing. I was so desperate, I even went to see Prince Tarasov."

"You went all the way to Solinovsk?"

"Yes. Straight to the palace."

"And they let you in?"

"I told the guard who I was, and why I had come, and then the Prince himself came out to meet me, and asked me please to come with him. '*Please*,' he said." Ilya was impressed. "He was as you described him. Authoritative and aloof. But once we were in private, he was very personable. He seemed genuinely concerned – for both of us! He apologized for having made our lives miserable. He apologized to me personally, for having put me through such distress earlier."

Ilya smiled. This was a good sign. "You have that effect on people Katya. People want to help you. Men especially."

"Why me?"

"Well, besides being very attractive – and that's a big part of it – you appear very honest, genuine. Tarasov is a good judge of character. That means he has some empathy – some capacity to feel what other people are feeling from observing their behavior. You had been just a name to him up to that point. But then you put a face on the name for him. He could now imagine how things had felt from your point of view. I think he genuinely was sorry."

"Well, I told him all I knew. That the Evangelical militiamen had taken you. This was alarming news for him. He said he would do everything he could do to find you, but wasn't sure what he could do at that point. Kuznetsov was way out west, he said. Why would he have sent men all the way to Mariankursk for you? I didn't know either. He said I would be under his protection from now on. I was welcome to stay at the palace if I thought I would be safer there. I thanked him, but said if you got away, you would be looking for me in Mariankursk, so that's where I needed to be. Then – get this – he told me he had a special agent in Mariankursk that I should call on if I needed help. 'You mean Madam Zakharova?' I said." Katerinya was particularly pleased with this part of the story. "You should have seen the look on his face. Then he smiled, shaking his head, and said 'I don't even want to know.'"

This made Ilya smile too.

"Then, two weeks ago, I got your 'I'm OK' text. And that's about it."

"Did you tell anyone?"

"Everyone! Right up to Tarasov. Everyone wanted to know. There wasn't much to tell, but at least they knew you were alive. Andzhelina spread the news around the University. I even got hold of Yulia. She was so relieved to hear the news."

Then Ilya realized he hadn't told Katerinya about the final escape from Pyatiskala, with Tatiana and Uncle Vanya. That would explain the ill-fitting clothes. Then he wondered, "Did you know that Kuznetsov is in Pyatiskala? That he controls the trains there?"

"No! That news hasn't reached here yet that I know of. If he's that close, are we safe here?" She was quite alarmed.

"I don't think so. He was looking for me there as soon as his troops pulled in on the train. He knows I was headed here. I think we should pack some things and head for Derazhne tomorrow, while the trains are still under civilian control."

§

The next morning, after awakening on clean sheets for the first time in eight months, Ilya had one more local trip to make before they took the train to Derazhne. After breakfast, while Katerinya did the packing, Ilya set out for the hospital. Now that he knew the cause of the Mariankursk outbreak, he wanted to pass that on to the doctor there. They may be able to recover the crashed drone, and learn something about the mutation. He hadn't planned to stay long. Just a quick in and out conference to pass along knowledge and outline a strategy. He had put the rifle in a closet at Katerinya's, figuring that they would leave it in Mariankursk, but he carried the sidearm with him, hidden in his sabovar.

Midway through the conference, an orderly burst into the room, panting. He had been running. He said soldiers had arrived at Mariankursk Station by train, boxcars full of them. "Which soldiers?" Ilya asked. He didn't know. They came from the west. From Pyatiskala. "Kuznetsov!" Ilya said. "It has to be." He had no time to explain. He bolted from the hospital, running toward Tallinnskaya Street. He could see militiamen coming toward the hospital, so he cut north and ducked into the woods. He continued running through the edge of the woods to the lot behind Katerinya's. He got there just in time to see two soldiers leading Katerinya away from the back stairs at gunpoint. She was frightened. He knew what was up. Kuznetsov probably sent them straight to her place as soon as they jumped off the train. They would use her as leverage to get him back. He had to act quickly.

The one closest to her was holding a pistol pointed at her. The other one had a rifle and was a little further ahead. The soldier with the pistol was older. Gruff looking. The rifleman was younger. About Lavro's age. The distance between Ilya and the gunman was not much more than that of a standard firing range. He pulled out his sidearm, and released the safety. He held it with both hands, finger on the trigger, then started walking slowly toward the gunman and Katerinya, with the pistol sight aimed squarely at the soldier's head. As soon as he was seen, he stopped and yelled, "Put down the weapon!" He didn't have a plan yet for the other soldier. He had to take care of the one threatening Katerinya first. The younger soldier was nervous. The older one wasn't. He reached out and grabbed Katerinya, holding her in front of him with his gun to her head. Classic hostage situation. "Drop your weapon, or I'll shoot her," he yelled. Ilya couldn't read him. Couldn't tell if he was bluffing. He might shoot her. The younger soldier now had his rifle aimed at Ilya.

In the cinema, this is the part where the hero puts down his weapon. Can't risk shooting and hitting his beloved instead. Everyone in the audience, and the hostage taker, knows this. Putting down the gun is the rational thing to do. But Ilya had a different thought. He was well within the range where he could put a bullet inside a circle no larger than the bullet itself, with a rifle from the prone position. He was standing with a pistol, so he wouldn't be quite as accurate, but he would be pretty close – maybe off by at most one bullet diameter. He was already in the marksman's position and had a bead on the middle of the gunman's head. Because of the soldier's pistol, the outer edge of Katerinya's head was at least 12 inches away. He couldn't possibly miss by that much. If the soldier had been smarter, he would have positioned his own head directly behind Katerinya's, but he wasn't smarter. Nobody in the movies expects a William Tell.

Ilya held his breath and squeezed the trigger. The bullet caught the gunman squarely between the eyes, knocking his head back violently and covering Katerinya's face and hair with the blood splatter. She was visibly shaken as the soldier fell backward into the snow. But Ilya didn't have a chance to see this yet. He had instinctively swiveled, and drew a bead on the rifleman's head. The younger soldier had instinctively turned his head toward the older one and Katerinya when he heard the shot. It was a fatal mistake. His rifle was still pointed at Ilya, but his eyes were not. In that split second, Ilya considered aiming lower, at a shoulder maybe. Perhaps he could just wound him. But the soldier's eyes quickly turned back, and his finger was still on the trigger. There was no time to adjust the aim. He fired, catching this soldier nearly between the eyes. His head was moving after all.

Now Ilya could attend to Katerinya. She was still standing in the same position, pale and trembling. She was in shock, he could see. He crammed the pistol into his sabovar and picked her up in his arms, then started running with her into the woods. It would have been difficult to keep up this posture for very long, even if he had been at full strength. He was now weaker, but also running on adrenaline, so he got about as far as he would have at full strength before he had to set her down for a breather. He could have carried her much farther slung over his shoulder, which he would have done if she were unconscious, but she was awake and in shock, so he wanted to see her face. He held her in a deep hug to keep her warm. It didn't take her long to respond. She was still trembling a little, but the color had returned to her face. Being Katerinya, her resourceful self kicked in, and she realized what a load this had been on Ilya. "Are you alright?" he puffed. "Can you walk?"

"Yes, I can," she assured him, though she was still a little unsteady. So they walked arm in arm, Ilya steadying her, and Katerinya fighting through the shock so that she wouldn't be such a burden. They followed the old clandestine path to Olena's house. There was no time to text ahead. When they reached Olena's back door, Olena was horrified at the sight of a blood-spattered Katerinya. Katerinya, closer to her resilient self now, picked up on this. "I'm alright, Olena! It's someone else's blood." Olena looked over at Ilya. "No, not his blood either. Someone else's." Olena didn't know what to think. Here was Ilya, alive and well after eight months – well, mostly well. He looked a little thin. And here was Katerinya, spattered in someone else's blood. And there were soldiers in the street, going from house to house.

"We'll explain everything later," Ilya said. "The soldiers are looking for us. Both of us. Is the attic hideout still operational?" That was explanation enough for Olena. She gave them both a hug, then escorted them up to the attic. She brought up warm water, towels and a sponge to clean up Katerinya. "It's probably better if you stay downstairs until the soldiers come to search the house," Ilya said. "They will be coming. We'll be OK up here for a while. Wait until they've come and gone before you come back." Olena understood the plan. She gave them both another hug, then went downstairs to play her role. Katerinya was fully recovered now – physically if not emotionally. The small bed looked like the clear place to wait this out for now, so she took off Ilya's sabovar and pushed him down on the bed. Then she joined him in a cuddle. This was just the therapy both of them needed right now. They drifted in and out of sleep while they waited.

They were awakened by a banging on Olena's front door. The soldiers had come. They could hear the voices from the attic. "We are looking for a doctor named Koskayin. Have you seen him, or any doctor?" Doctor? Olena thought. "He may be traveling with a woman. Name of Katerinya Emlynovna. Have you seen either of them?" "No, I don't know them. Haven't seen any doctor around here." (She thought that was probably true.) The soldiers insisted on searching the house anyway. They were not as polite as Lavro had been. They went room to room on the first and second floors, but had no clue about the attic stairs behind the linen closet shelf. It was fortunate that Olena had left the bloodstained cleanup items in the attic. "You live alone here?" one of the soldiers asked. "Yes," she answered. "Who sleeps in the bedroom upstairs?" "No one. It's a guest bedroom." The soldier asking the questions walked over to look out both the front and back windows, then turned to the other one and said something inaudible. With that, they left.

Olena followed the plan and waited a while. Then she checked the front window to make sure soldiers were nowhere in sight. With the coast clear, she came back to the couple in the attic. She had so many questions, she didn't know where to begin. So she didn't. She waited for Ilya and Katerinya to speak. Ilya suggested that they all go to the upstairs bedroom. This was halfway between the attic and the front door. That way, Olena wouldn't be caught leaving the attic in the case of another search request, and Ilya and Katerinya would have time to get back to the hiding place while Olena answered the door.

Katerinya started the story with their escape from Tallinnskaya Street – from her point of view. It did not have as much detail as Ilya's would have, but it explained the immediate issues of the blood and their sudden appearance at Olena's door. When she backed up in time to account for Ilya's disappearance, she decided to let Ilya tell that part of the story. There was a lot to tell, and parts that she didn't want to repeat. Ilya gave the executive summary, leaving out all of the gore. For Olena, it was still a riveting story.

It was unclear to Ilya why Kuznetsov still so desperately wanted to find him. He had fulfilled his original mission. The bioweapon was disabled. Perhaps he was afraid that with Ilya on the loose, this information would get to Tarasov, and Kuznetsov would lose his bargaining chip. He guessed that he had no interest in Katerinya other than as a route to himself. Kuznetsov would have known her name from his time with Tarasov, but he had no way to recognize her – only by name. This was good. Katerinya could walk the streets of Mariankursk unnoticed as long as she stayed away from 10 Tallinnskaya Street. The only witnesses to her appearance were now dead.

Ilya came up with a plan for how to wait out the siege of Mariankursk at Olena's. The couple should probably not spend any time on the first floor. Too easy to be seen through the windows. Too long to get to the attic quickly. They should definitely sleep in the attic. Olena should minimize her time in the attic. Extended time together should be on the second floor, like now. "But where will we eat?" Katerinya asked. "Yes, I have the same question," Olena seconded. "We need to fatten you up a bit, Ilya." He appreciated this. He did need to regain some weight. He proposed that Olena bring the food to the attic. There wouldn't be any evidence of a shared meal on the searchable floors that way. But it also meant Olena couldn't stay to eat with them. The women understood the need for caution.

§

Later that evening, as the three of them were sitting in the second floor bedroom, swapping tales of the times, a knock was heard at the front door. Ilya and Katerinya quickly made their way to the attic while Olena took her time descending the stairs to answer the door, to give them time. At the door were three soldiers, the two that had performed the first search and one more. He was an older looking man, with a very authoritative bearing. He had a stern but weary look about him. The soldier who had previously said the inaudible something or other to his companion explained that they were appropriating Olena's house as a temporary command center. They introduced the third man as Commander Kuznetsov. Overhearing this from the attic, Katerinya gasped. Ilya put his hand gently over her mouth. She recovered quickly – and silently.

Olena also recognized the name from the stories she had just heard, but she managed to suppress her surprise. "I'm sorry, but I didn't catch your name," Kuznetsov said. She hadn't given it, but was surprised by the politeness. "Zotova, Olena Anwynovna." "I apologize for the inconvenience, Ms. Zotova," he said. "My aide tells me that you have a lot of house for one person." He proceeded to lay out the plan whereby he and his aide would occupy the first floor. She could take the second floor bedroom. She would still have the run of the house, of course, as long as she didn't interfere. Interfere indeed, she thought to herself. She retreated to the upstairs bedroom without making any attempt at housekeeping for her new "guests." That was their problem. But now what? This would have happened anyway, despite her harboring Katerinya and Ilya. Just her luck. But she had to be careful not to contact them until the men were gone. Maybe they would leave and come back. But they didn't.

Ilya and Katerinya could hear it all from the attic. They too had to adopt a new diligence. They had to talk in whispers. They had to be careful when they moved not to bump anything, or step on squeaking floorboards. There was nothing to do for now but remain cuddled in their small bed. It was a convenient place for sleeping. They really didn't have to move. Olena did her best to move around a lot, and bump into things on the second floor, to give them some cover. If the soldiers got accustomed to hearing these noises, she reasoned, they wouldn't be able to pick out any made by the couple above her. Ilya noticed the sounds of her peripatetic behavior. "Why is she pacing about so much?" Katerinya whispered. "That's not like her." "I think she's giving us some cover," Ilya whispered back. "So we can make a little noise too." Katerinya smiled, grateful for her friend's thoughtfulness.

The aid left for a while, but the other soldier remained. Kuznetsov set up some maps on the desk in the main room, studying them. When the aid returned, Kuznetsov asked, "Any news on Koskayin?"

"Still no one has seen him since he left camp. Not in Pyatiskala, not here."

"And the girlfriend here?"

"No, nothing yet, sir."

"What about the party that went to her house?"

"They haven't reported back yet, sir."

He raised his eyebrows. "And you haven't checked?"

" … No, sir."

"Well send someone to check! No, you go and check yourself. Now!"

"Yes, sir!" And off he went.

Kuznetsov paced back and forth. This was clearly of great concern to him. He had a lot on his mind. He walked over to the bookshelf at the side of the room and began scanning the titles. He picked up Olena's Bible, then crossed the room and sat in a chair in front of the desk, facing the door. When the aid returned, he stood up and asked, "Well ...?"

"Both shot dead, sir. One bullet each. Right between the eyes."

Kuznetsov slumped into the chair. "Koskayin's here. No other human shoots like that."

Katerinya had been listening intently. "You *had* to, Iliusha," she whispered in Ilya's ear. He was grateful she understood this now.

"Any sign of her?"

"It looks from the tracks that they had her near the house. Three sets of footprints. One set of prints coming from the woods. Only one set of prints going back into the woods. No other prints. She's not in the house."

"She must be with him now. Tell the men we're looking for a couple. Any news from Pyatiskala?"

"Tarasov's forces have retaken it, sir."

"Have they all moved there?"

"No, sir. The main garrison is still in Derazhne. The field army is still just west of here."

"So we are surrounded," he said softly, looking into the distance. "We must find Koskayin now. He is here. We must find him, do you understand?"

"Yes, sir." The aid left again.

"Why do they need to find you?" Katerinya whispered. "I don't know," he whispered back. He really didn't. What role could he possibly play in the endgame now?

Kuznetsov sat in the chair for a long time, lost in thought. Then he opened Olena's Bible. He looked in the contents page for Songs of Songs. He turned to it. Then he flipped pages forward to Chapter 16. It was, as Ilya said it might be, subtitled Story of Isaac. He read to himself:

The door it opened slowly

My father he came in
I was nine years old
And he stood so tall above me
Blue eyes they were shining
And his voice was very cold

Said I've had a vision
And you know I'm strong and holy
I must do what I've been told
So we started up the mountain
I was running he was walking
And his axe was made of gold

Well the trees they got much smaller
The lake a lady's mirror
We stopped to drink some wine
Then he threw the bottle over
Broke a minute later
And he put his hand on mine

Thought I saw an eagle
But it might have been a vulture
I never could decide
Then my father built an altar
He looked once behind his shoulder
He knew I would not hide

You who build the altars now
To sacrifice these children
You must not do it anymore
A scheme is not a vision
You never have been tempted
By a demon or a god

And if you call me brother now
Forgive me if I inquire
Just according to whose plan
When it all comes down to dust
I will kill you if I must
I will help you if I can

When it all comes down to dust
I will help you if I must
I will kill you if I can
Have mercy on our uniform
Man of peace or man of war
The peacock spreads his fan

§

Ilya awoke with the sun, his usual ritual, the next morning. The single attic window was on the north wall, so the sunlight was not direct. Katerinya was still asleep, the two of them still huddled together in their clothes. He did not fall back asleep. He was fully awake, hatching a plan. He still had his new phone in his sabovar with his sidearm. He had already rebuilt the secure communication app for he and Katerinya, but that was now moot. Secure communication with her was just a whisper away. But he could use it to send secure messages to Tarasov, using the Prince's public key because he had set up that key in a public registry for the Prince's men. But security with the Prince was now mostly moot as well. Only Tarasov had the infrastructure for eavesdropping. Kuznetsov knew about the program, but he was now in the field with an amateur organization. What's more, Kuznetsov had no infrastructure for location tracking either. This was Tarasov's baby as well. In fact, tracking was now Ilya's friend. He could turn it on, and Tarasov would know just where to find him, even sitting right under Kuznetsov's nose – well, a little over his nose, to be precise.

But Ilya had to plan this just right to avoid collateral damage. What he had in mind was a special ops style mission – a search and rescue team to extract himself and Katerinya from the besieged Mariankursk, where the search part would be a foregone conclusion because of the cellphone tracking. But they had to be somewhere away from Olena's house so that she didn't get implicated. Her place had the perfect cover of being Kuznetsov's own headquarters. If the extraction took place somewhere else, there would be no way for Kuznetsov to tie her to it. When Katerinya awoke, he whispered the plan to her. When Kuznetsov and the soldiers left for the morning, they went down to consult with Olena.

Ilya called Tarasov on his private number: "Ilya Erynovich here. Note the new number."

"You're alive! And well, I hope?"

"Could be better. I'm here in Mariankursk with Katerinya Emlynovna."

"Mariankursk is under Kuznetsov's control!"

"Tell me about it. We're in hiding. He knows we're here, but not where. He's got men looking for us everywhere."

"How can I help you?"

"Can you get us out? Maybe a special ops team from Yelangrad?"

"Hold on. I'll put you in touch with the commander." There was a long pause. "Commander Repin here. Where are you in Mariankursk?"

"Believe it or not, were hiding in the attic of a house that Kuznetsov is using for a headquarters. Don't try to get us here."

"Where did you have in mind? We'll come on horseback from Yelangrad."

"Can you track my phone from the field?"

"Not ourselves. But we can have Solinovsk relay your coordinates to us in real time."

"OK. I'll turn on tracking when we get to a good spot in the northwest woods at the edge of Mariankursk. Text me when you are getting close, so we'll be on the lookout for you and I'll have your number."

"Got it. Should take about two hours to get to you. I'll send you a nonce message from my phone now so you'll have the number. Stay safe."

Katerinya and Olena were both crowding in over Ilya's shoulder listening to the call. Now they were elated. "You're going to be rescued by the Prince himself!" Olena said. "You must be pretty special!" "Oh we are," said Katerinya, smiling.

"We'll be far away from here when they come, so you never have to admit having seen us," Ilya told Olena. "Just shut up the attic and pretend it's not there. Now let's get out of here before the soldiers come back." They moved quickly. On the way out the back door, Katerinya hugged Olena. "Stay safe," she said, wishing she could take her with them.

Ilya and Katerinya's clandestine route between Olena's and Tallinnskaya Street already passed near the northwest woods Ilya had selected as the pickup point. They just had to go a little further north to where the woods ended in a large meadow. There was another stand of trees visible well to the north on the other side of the meadow. This is where Commander Repin and his men would be coming from. Ilya and Katerinya would wait just inside the woods on this side, to stay out of sight. Ilya turned on tracking. He was reluctant to do it until they got well away from Olena's. Tarasov was on his side now, but it still made sense to keep Olena out of all of this. Her place turned out to be a pretty good hideout, and the anonymity would keep it open as a future option.

It was a long two hours to wait. It was quiet and peaceful enough, but the soldiers were very close by, and the rescue mission had some risk. But neither could imagine anyone else they would rather kill two hours with. They just had to keep their talk low. At near the two-hour mark, Ilya got a text from Repin. The team was about 10 minutes away, and they had a positive location for Ilya's cell phone. Now the time seemed to pass even more slowly.

After a couple of minutes, Ilya's eagle-eyed vision spotted three militiamen to the east, on a patrol emerging from their side of the woods into the meadow. He crouched down and pulled Katerinya with him. He needed a new plan. Kuznetsov was probably scouting out the north now that he was hemmed in in the other three directions. These men were probably surveying an escape route. Should he move the pickup point further west? He decided it would be better to leave the decision to the professionals. He texted Repin: "3 Kuznetsov soldiers, on foot, heading your direction. Entering the meadow near us. They are visible, we are not." "Got it. Stay put," came back almost immediately.

Repin's team, three men and four horses, paused at the edge of woods on the north side of the meadow. They tied up their horses out of view, then spread out and began a slow creep across the meadow toward the patrol. They really look like professionals, Ilya thought. They wore white and blended in well with the snow. Kuznetsov's men had no such camouflage. They stood out against the snow. When Repin's men were in firing range, the shooting began. Both sides scrambled for cover in the open meadow, finding positions to fire from. Another sign of the professionalism of Repin's team is that they could shoot. This was not one of the endless fire and miss engagements Ilya had seen so many times in the west. Kuznetsov's militiamen missed, but Repin's were pretty accurate. They picked off two of the soldiers without sustaining any hits themselves. The remaining Evangelical had good cover behind a rock formation in the meadow, from which he continued to return fire.

At this point, it was clear to Ilya that the continued sound of rifle fire would alert Kuznetsov's men. More would be coming. They had to take out this last man quickly. He told Katerinya to stay down and wait for his signal. He slowly made his way east at the edge of the woods until he was directly behind the Evangelical. Then he slowly started walking toward him out into the meadow. He hoped Repin's men would correctly interpret the scene. They did. He could get off a clear shot from here, but this time he had an option. This wasn't a "had to" situation. He didn't have to kill him. He just needed to disable him. He aimed at his right shoulder, figuring a wound there would disable his trigger finger. He fired, hitting where he aimed. The soldier slumped forward dropping his rifle. Then Ilya motioned to Katerinya, yelling, "Run!" She started to run toward him. He quickly redirected her toward Repin's men. "Toward them!" She got the message. Repin's men rose and started moving toward her, keeping their eyes on the other two casualties, just in case. Ilya ran toward them as well, keeping his eye on his casualty. As he passed him, the soldier tried desperately to reach for his rifle with his left hand. Ilya pointed his sidearm directly at him and said, "Don't!" The soldier got the message. He would live to see another day.

Repin's men met them in the middle of the meadow and ran with them to the north woods where the horses were. Ilya helped Katerinya into the saddle of the fourth horse, then mounted in front of her. He was about to tell her to hold tight around him, but she figured that out on her own. At this point, Kuznetsov's soldiers were arriving in the meadow, following the gunshots. The men on foot would be no problem, but one of them was on horseback. He saw the Repin team take off to the north and pursued. Then two more horsemen emerged on either side of the meadow to join the pursuit. Two of Repin's men peeled of to engage them, leaving Repin, Ilya and Katerinya to deal with the first one. They might have been able to outrun him, but Ilya's horse was carrying a double load, so it was falling behind. They were still out of pistol range, but Ilya didn't like the thought of the pursuer gaining on them with Katerinya being the first target if he ever reached firing range. So he abruptly turned his horse around, shielding her, and charged straight toward the pursuer. This probably wouldn't be a fair fight either, he surmised. Both of their shooting accuracies would suffer, firing from horseback, but his was bound to be better. Here he really didn't have a kill/no-kill decision to make. He wouldn't be that accurate. He just aimed at the body in general and fired as soon as he thought he was in range. He wasn't yet, and this surprised his pursuer. He fired his own weapon, missing wildly. Ilya's second shot knocked him off his horse. Ilya couldn't tell where he was hit, and wasn't about to find out. He turned his mount around again and galloped north, meeting an amazed Repin. As they continued north toward Yelangrad, the other two commandos caught up with them. They had dispatched their pursuers as well.

After a while, the group slowed their horses to a trot. They were out of hostile territory now, and the horses needed some rest. Eventually they slowed to a walk. At Yelangrad, there were high-fives all around. Mission accomplished. Ilya and Katerinya thanked the team for rescuing them. Just part of the job, they said. "But the professor is a pretty good shot for a scientist," Repin said. The other men agreed. "No other human shoots like that," Katerinya said with a straight face. They looked at her, trying to figure out what to make of her comment. She made it harder on them. "Just ask Kuznetsov." Ilya just smiled, saying nothing. The three men really didn't know how to respond to that comment. So they just let it ride. That was the end of that conversation.

§

Repin's team was based in Solinovsk. They had come to Yelangrad from Solinovsk by train, then picked up the horses at a field office here. Now they were taking the train back to Solinovsk to report to the Prince. At the last minute, Ilya and Katerinya decided not to join them on the first available train, which was leaving soon. They said their goodbyes, then the couple went looking for a good restaurant in

Yelangrad. Katerinya had insisted. She needed to fatten up her underweight man as soon as possible, she said. Ilya did not resist.

Over lunch, they were again enjoying this feeling of relief, and the casting off of burdens. But there seemed to be a pattern to this. Each time they thought they were home free, some other unexpected event always seemed to intervene. So they were relieved, but wary. They were in the northwest country now, which had not been tinged by the war. Ilya wanted to show Katerinya some of the beauty of the region that he had seen from his recent trip from Labivgrad. But this desire was balanced by today's discovery that Kuznetsov might be scouting out an escape route to this untouched northern region. If he did bring the war this way, it wouldn't be lightning quick like it had come from Pyatiskala. His troops couldn't take a train this time – not because he didn't control the railroads, but because there *were* no railroads linking the west to the north. Staying in the region for a day would pose no risk.

So they decided to head west, at least as far as Kaliniyevka. Then they would reevaluate the day trip one station at a time. If they could not get all the way back to Derazhne after heading east again, they would stay overnight somewhere. Ilya resolved to adopt a new strategy for protecting Katerinya. No more stuffing her away in a hiding place while he went somewhere else. From now on, they would go everywhere together. At least until this war was over. She thought that was a wonderful idea. After lunch, they went to Yelangrad Station and purchased one-way fares to Kaliniyevka. That would be the pattern until they decided to return.

Just out of Yelangrad Station, they crossed the bridge over the river gorge going west. Katerinya remarked that it was just as Ilya had described it. The view up the gorge was spectacular, and the meadow below would be a wonderful place for a picnic – but not now. It was still winter, and the meadow was covered with snow. She asked Ilya how they would manage to get down to the meadow. His mind was elsewhere, trying to summon the previous sensation of déjà vu. He couldn't. It didn't happen the second time. He hadn't told Katerinya about that episode – just about the meadow – so he recounted it in retrospect. Knowing how this missing memory business weighed on him, she insisted, cheerfully, that it didn't really matter. The view was worth it anyway. In the back of her mind, she considered that it was possible he had spent some time here with someone else from his past. Maybe he even had a meadow picnic with her – or a him – no, most likely a her. It was just as well that he couldn't remember, she thought. Now she was determined to come back here with him to establish a new memory.

They got off the train in Kaliniyevka, walked around a little, then purchased another one-station, one-way fare west. They repeated the scheme at each station until they got to Labivgrad. Ilya knew his way around this little town, showing Katerinya the sights, and recounting his overnight stay here. They were now clearly out of range for getting back to Derazhne in the same day, so they took the last train east to Yelangrad, and spent the night there. They had a large room in a quaint little bed-and-breakfast near the station. It was quite an upgrade from their previous night spent in their clothes on top of the covers in Olena's little bed in the attic – afraid to move for fear of making any noise. Now they could enjoy the luxurious warmth of skin on skin – and noise was no longer an issue.

When they got back to Derazhne, they went straight to Ilya's house. It was a little musty, having been unoccupied for eight months except for the one night Katerinya had stayed there on her trip to see the Prince. Being Katerinya, she had changed the sheets then, and still being Katerinya, she insisted on changing the sheets again today. They aired out the house by selectively opening windows. It was still winter. Then they made the rounds at the University.

The first stop was at the Divinity School to see Diederick Brandt. Katerinya had not known him well enough to pass on the "I'm OK" message. He had gotten wind of it nonetheless, but was now very grateful to see Ilya alive again, and Katerinya with him. He had not seen her since the Crispness party last year. He noted, as everyone would today, that Ilya looked a little thin. "We're working on that," Katerinya said. The University, he said, had made out pretty well during the conflict. Prince Tarasov had kept it in the far west, so once the troubles in the neighborhoods died down, mostly because the erstwhile combatants had also gone west, Derazhne had remained calm.

Next, they went to Englund Hall to see Andzhelina. She was sooo glad to see them. Katerinya had kept her in the loop – with what little loop there was at the time – but now they were both here, walking around in the open like they owned the place. It was such a nice contrast to the circumstances of their last meeting, she said. Ilya asked if word had ever gotten out about their holing up at her house. "No," she said. "The hideout is still our little secret. And available if ever you should need it again." Ilya told her that they would likely not need to hide from Tarasov again. And that Katerinya was even invited to stay at the Palace now. Andzhelina was impressed. "You just walked right into the Palace without an invitation?" "I did what I had to. And now I'm even under his protection. Imagine that." She could imagine that. She could imagine the whole scene.

After Andzhelina's, Katerinya suggested that they try to visit Yulia. "She will surely want to know that you survived." Ilya thought that would be a good idea too. They found her in her undergraduate house around lunchtime. The hideout in her room seemed like such a long time ago, to all of them. Then Katerinya had an idea. She whispered something in Ilya's ear. He smiled, nodding his head. "I think that's a great idea." Then he turned to Yulia. "Do you have any plans for lunch?" "No," she said, "just the standard student dining hall kind of thing." "Would you like to go out with us? Our treat." How could she refuse that?

Katerinya's idea was to take her to Yaroslava's for the famous brunch. It was quite a revelation for her on her first visit. So she could only imagine how it would feel to a poor girl from the neighborhoods. And it was as she suspected. Yulia looked around, wide-eyed, at the traditional trappings and the upscale elegance. The bowing waiters and the sterling silver place settings. And the food! She kept glancing at Ilya. Katerinya noticed. "Yes, he's lost some weight. He had quite an ordeal." That was what Yulia was wondering about, but she didn't dare say it. Now that the subject was out, Ilya gave the executive summary of his ordeal again, leaving out almost all of the traumatic details. As he was learning, even sanitized, his time in the war made quite a tale for those unfamiliar with it.

Yulia said that she had decided to declare a major in biology. She was good at science and math in high school, but her school in the neighborhoods was not very good. Biology was glossed over as a method for classifying animals according to their appearances. Genomics did not come up much. She thought it was boring then, so she aimed toward the humanities like history and literature. She got good AP test scores in those subjects, but what enabled her to get a full ride at Derazhne, despite having a substandard science education, were her record aptitude test scores, and her admissions essay. Now she needed to take some remedial courses in science and math to support a biology major, but that was a good thing, she said. She was good at those things, and now she had an interest in them as well. She could see how it all fit together now. Ilya liked the sound of this, but urged her to stay general. Keep taking the humanities courses too. The best scholars in every discipline are the well-rounded ones, he said.

Just then, Ilya spotted Prince Tarasov coming toward their table from the private dining room. His aide, standing outside the private dining room door had spotted the trio and informed the Prince of their presence. He stopped at their table and said "Ilya Erynovich! Good to see you alive and well again. You do look a little thin, though." Ilya was getting tired of hearing this. "And Katerinya Emlynovna! Good to see you two back together again." "And who might this be?" he said, looking toward Yulia. Yulia had no idea how one was to address a Prince. He seemed downright friendly. Not what you would expect from the official portrait. Katerinya quickly stepped in, letting both parties know that we are all on a familiar name basis here. "This is Yulia Katyaevna. She's a student of Ilya's." The Prince did a slight courtesy bow. "And I suppose you know who I am," he asked. Of course she did. She had seen the pictures. "Yes," she answered meekly. "I suppose you have been missing your professor for the last eight months or so, eh?" Again a meek "Yes." The couple hadn't told her the part of the story about Katerinya going to the Palace, so this whole situation was quite overwhelming for her. Then turning to Ilya, the Prince said, "Repin tells me you are quite an amazing marksman, and horseman. Tell me, where does a professor learn these skills?" Ilya didn't know, of course. He responded with, "I'll tell you about it later." Again, Yulia was mystified. She hadn't heard those details either. "Then you will be coming to see me soon? At the Palace?" "Yes, that's next on our schedule." It hadn't been, but now it was. "Good, I'll be expecting you then." With that, he and his aides left through the front door.

The formal brunch at Yaroslava's would have made quite an impression on Yulia all by itself, but the unplanned audience with the Prince put it in a different dimension altogether. It was hard to imagine this was the same Prince they had been hiding from almost a year ago. Now Ilya and Katerinya were practically his pals. They talked to each other like close friends. What a tale she had to tell her roommate when she got back. No one would believe her, she thought. She wouldn't believe it if she heard it from someone else either. She was star struck.

Ilya and Katerinya had planned a few more visits at the University, but of course, their plans had been revised. They had planned to get to the Prince eventually, but now they would get to him right away. The guard at the Palace door already knew whom to expect. They were celebrities at the Palace now. The guard ushered them right in.

Ilya was prepared to disclose his memory problems to Tarasov. He had no other way to account for his skills. But to his surprise, Tarasov didn't ask a second time. The subject never came up. Ilya, of course, had to give some version of the whole eight months to the Prince, but with a different kind of editing. The gore would be no problem, it was his additional skills, like being a doctor, that he left out. That would expose another line of questioning that he couldn't answer, except by disclosing his memory problems. The main theme was the bioweapon. That just leveraged his scientific skills, which the Prince already knew about. The weapon would be news to Tarasov, and something he needed to know about. So Ilya related all of the details about this theme.

He told him about the test crash near Mariankursk hospital, which was the source of the outbreak. He told him Kuznetsov's account of how he inherited the project when he took over the command, how he captured Ilya to try to disable it, and how he planned to use it as a bargaining chip once inert. This surprised Tarasov — that the whole point of Ilya's capture was to disable the weapon. There were some things that Kuznetsov would not do, apparently. Ilya told the Prince that he'd had discussions with Kuznetsov all summer and fall. "He's a complex man, conflicted," Ilya told him. "He's a reluctant leader, like the two of us. He does not want to be God, like Sokolov. But he still thinks he's following orders from God, though I think I may have sown some doubt in his mind about that." This was a fascinating psychological profile of the man, Tarasov thought. Something that he could use if ever this conflict came to a negotiation. Though, of course, he would now know that Kuznetsov was bluffing about the bioweapon.

Tarasov's news for Ilya and Katerinya was that he had retaken Mariankursk from Kuznetsov. Repin's intel about the northern patrol made it clear that this was where Kuznetsov intended to retreat. So Tarasov's generals had split their southern army in two, sending one around to the north of Mariankursk, and then the other to retake the town. Kuznetsov was now surrounded to the north, unable to harass trains or towns. The trains were now clear from Solinovsk to the western borders of the Principality. Every train. Every line. The war would be over soon.

Katerinya breathed a sigh of relief. "Is it safe to go back to Mariankursk now? Was anything destroyed?" She, of course, had Olena's house in mind, but couldn't disclose that.

"From what I hear from my generals, Kuznetsov left the town intact. Not his usual occupation. They were already moving north when our forces arrived from the south. He could have made it much harder on the town if he had taken his last stand there. I think he knew the end was coming." He paused. "And what are your plans now? The two of you – once Ilya Erynovich recovers a little. Will you stay here? Will you go back to Mariankursk?" Katerinya looked at Ilya.

"We aren't sure yet, at least in detail. We have a new general plan, though. We are going to stay together, wherever we go. If either of us shows up here again, the other will be there too. At least until the war is over."

Tarasov smiled. "That's what I would do, if I were you. Let me know if I can help."

§

Before they left the Palace, Ilya advised Tarasov to reinforce the legacy storage facility where the *Y. pestis modernis* cultures were stored. This was a weakness that might get exploited by terrorists again. Someone had already thought of it. And humans like to copy other humans. The precedent had now been set. He also advised him to proactively vaccinate the population for *Y. pestis modernis* again, just as a precaution. With any luck, we shouldn't see the mutated strain again, he said. It had all been destroyed. So the new vaccine was no longer a priority.

The last stop for the day was to see Professor Ekholm. Ilya had been missing in action from the University for most of the year, so his courses had probably been reassigned to other professors. He needed to find out how and when he would fit back into the department. Ove Alfhildovich was, of course, glad to see him alive and well, though he was concerned with how thin he looked – but we won't go into that. Ilya was really tired of hearing this. He was also glad to see Katerinya. Since the Crispness party last year, everyone around the University had remembered them as a couple, so there was a lot of angst and sympathy for Katerinya when they would see her alone. Ove Alfhildovich recommended that Ilya take some time off. They had his courses and advisees covered through the end of the term. He was also due for a sabbatical this year, so this might be a good time to take it, he thought. "Take the time off, recover, come back in the fall," he said.

Ilya looked at Katerinya. She thought that was the most wonderful idea she could imagine. "Oh, Iliusha, let's do that." She dropped her usual decorum about public use of the diminutive and public displays of affection by reaching over to hug him and rest her head on his shoulder as she said it. Professor Ekholm didn't mind. He could see this would be good for the both of them. Without having said a thing, Ilya realized he had already agreed.

When they got back to Ilya's house, the question was where to spend his sabbatical. The obvious targets were here in Derazhne, or at Katerinya's in Mariankursk. With the war not yet over, Ilya wondered if it wouldn't be better to get farther away from the conflict. "Remember how many times we thought we were safe, only to get separated again?" Oh, did she remember! Then she had an idea. "Why don't we go to Karlsruhe? I still know some people there, at the University."

"And I have colleagues there at the University whom I've worked on government contracts with. Talk about escaping the war! That's on the other side of the continent."

"And it would almost be spring there. On the coast. I could write and translate, and you could do whatever it is you do – or nothing!"

"And Tarasov just said the trains are open all the way to the western border. That's it! We should go now, while the trains are still open. We should get past Mariankursk as soon as possible."

"You mean right now?"

He smiled. "No, tomorrow will do. We need to do some packing first, here and in Mariankursk. You'll need to get all your writing stuff, and we'll need to prep your apartment for a long absence. Can you pay the rent remotely?"

"Yes. I've done it before. Oh, Iliusha, we're really going to do this!"

They were really going to do this. Ilya's house had a red brick exterior and was well insulated. So his place needed very little prep for the absence. He did, however, need to pack a lot of clothes. Certainly more than the one set he had worn for the last eight months, but also substantially more than for his weekends in Mariankursk. He and Katerinya had distributed their wardrobes between here and Mariankursk a bit, but the piece you left in the other location was always just one train stop away. The western sabbatical would be for the long haul. They thought about taking the cellos, but they couldn't carry them and the luggage, and were reluctant to have them shipped. They would be here when they got back.

On their last night in Derazhne, on clean sheets, their pillow talk did not last as long as usual. Both were feeling the accumulated effects of the last several days. Adrenalin and foreign beds had kept them awake longer than their physical fatigue dictated. Now that they were in a familiar bed, and a familiar place, and once again had a sense that the future looked bright, the fatigue finally caught up to them. They drifted off to sleep in no time. Ilya did not go through his usual cycle of periodic awakenings. That meant he was having a long dream. He awoke from the dream suddenly. Suddenly enough to wake Katerinya. "Another dream, Iliusha?"

"Yes. A strange one, even by my standards."

"Tell me."

"It was a little incoherent. Themes blending into other themes."

"Aren't all your dreams like that?"

"Yes, but usually there is just one direction. One story line with improbable transitions. This time there were three distinct themes that kept transitioning into each other. All they had in common is that I was outside somewhere. I've probably already forgotten the start, but the farthest back I recall was that I was outside in the woods. Living off the land. I was the survivalist woodman!"

"You were probably reliving your escape from Kuznetsov, don't you think?

"Well, there were elements of that. The lean-to shelter for instance. But it was warm. Spring or summer. No snow. And there were others with me. We were all trying to survive."

"Survive what?"

"That was the second theme. A *Y. pestis* pandemic. We were all trying to outrun it in some sense. There were lots of dead bodies."

Katerinya didn't want to hear more of that story line, so she led him in a different direction. "What was the third theme?"

"Planting in my garden, here in Derazhne. Digging for root vegetables in the woods transitioned into digging in my garden. Not digging things up, but planting things. Then this would somehow get back to the woods and the pandemic. It's almost like it was meant to be one story, but the parts were sewn together pretty raggedly."

Katerinya had always wondered what was planted in his garden. She had meant to ask, but always thought of it in the winter, like now, when there was snow cover in the garden. They hadn't been in Derazhne long enough last spring to see anything come up before

Ilya disappeared. "What did you plant in your garden? I mean the real one, not the dream one?"

"I don't recall ever planting things there. It's just a bunch of very hardy perennials. Some previous owner must have done the planting."

"So that was it? Your dream, I mean."

"Well, there was a lot more to it, but those were the salient parts. The parts I most remember. We were trying to avoid other people. Afraid we would be infected. That's when I woke up."

It was a strange dream, she thought. But then all of his dreams are strange. At least he wasn't fish-flying in this one. The bacterium and surviving in the woods were clearly on his mind from recent events. She could understand those triggers. But what's that got to do with planting in his garden – which he had never done before, apparently? She lay with him in a cuddle for a few minutes. She knew from experience that that was all the longer it would take for him to fall back asleep. And she was right. She, on the other hand, would take much longer.

They caught the first train to Mariankursk the next morning. Their first stop was to see Olena, of course. Ilya stowed his suitcases with baggage claim at the station so that he wouldn't have to carry them all over town. Olena's house, as with much of the town, looked none the worse for wear. There were soldiers stationed all over the town, but the residents knew these were Tarasov's men, and were grateful for their presence now. Olena hadn't yet heard the outcome of the couple's great escape, so she was happy to see them whole again. In much better condition than the last time they knocked on her door. Katerinya told the story of the escape. Ilya thought that was appropriate because she would gloss over details that the two of them would find disturbing. Then she related the good news of the sabbatical out west. "You're going back to Karlsruhe? Oh, I still remember when you left for there the first time," she smiled. "You will come back, won't you?" she added, a little worried. "Oh, yes. In the fall. Don't worry." On balance, Olena thought this was probably for the better. The two of them needed to get far away from this war for a while. Despite the rumors of it being almost over, her own brief brush with the war left her wanting to get further away from it herself.

At 10 Tallinnskaya Street, Katerinya packed her things while Ilya shut and locked all the windows and doors. He also checked the plumbing to see if there were any water pipes exposed to possible freezing for the rest of the winter. Katerinya's house was wood framed clapboard, without insulation. Ilya adjusted the spigot for the bathtub to leave a small drip. This would keep water moving in the pipes so that they didn't freeze. He also closed all of the flues. As a precaution against losing her novel work in progress, he showed her how to maintain a copy of it on a server at Karlsruhe University. As long as she uploaded her laptop version whenever she had Internet connectivity, this would give her a backup if she ever lost the laptop. She had never thought of that. That would have been devastating. All of that work, gone! "Thank you, Ilya. Thank you, thank you, thank you!"

Their plan was to take the early evening train from Mariankursk as far west as it would go. With luck, that would be all the way to the western border of the Principality. After that, they would have spottier rail service until they reached the next national jurisdiction. Normally, these shared connections work smoothly, but with the war, and control of the railroads changing hands several times, they had to be prepared for some irregularities.

The waitress at the Mariankursk Station café had just started her evening shift when the couple arrived at the station. Oh look, she thought, it's Dmitri and Anna! He looked in much better shape than the last time. Clean sabovar, no rifle. Though he still looked a little thin. And they had so much luggage this time. And they were waiting on the westbound platform. Not going to Derazhne this time. She would have to start a new chapter in her head. Going west for the first time. Clearly staying a while – wherever it was. But still together. And looking happy. The possible story lines were unbounded.

As the train left the station, Katerinya asked, "Have you ever taken the train to Karlsruhe before?"

"Not that I can remember."

"But I thought you had been there before."

"I always took African Airlines. Much quicker that way."

"But isn't that rather expensive?"

"The government paid for it. Contract research."

This caused Katerinya to reflect once again on her first departure for Karlsruhe. The circumstances were so different now. Back then, she didn't know what the west looked like. Now she could play tour guide for Ilya, particularly the view from the train. Back then, she felt like she was escaping from her childhood home. Now she was a bit sad to be leaving her own home at Tallinnskaya Street. But she would be coming back. And back then, she was sad to be leaving her Derazhne ambitions permanently behind. Now she could fairly be said to have conquered Derazhne. She had become the talk of the town in high society, she was on a first name basis with her friend, the Prince, and she was absconding with perhaps U of D's most famous professor. Things were looking up.

They passed through the western railway towns as darkness was slowly descending. Starting with Pyatiskala, the towns had not fared as well in the war as Mariankursk. Each had a small garrison of Tarasov's troops now, to secure the railroads and help with reconstruction. This, of course, was not how Katerinya remembered it from her first journey. It was a sobering sight, and a reminder of how much she had grown up since the last time, how much more experience of the ways of the world she had now. Her novel-in-progress was also adapting to her new experiences. She hadn't written much during the period of Ilya's disappearance. She just couldn't. She was emotionally numbed by the experience, and the intractable waiting. Now she was in a better place. But her acquaintance with war and loss had grown by leaps and bounds. There was no way to keep this material out. Her heroine had changed, just as she had changed. And there was no way to keep an Ilya character out of the narrative now. It wasn't so different that she had to start again from scratch, but she had a lot of rewriting to do. This character had to emerge early on to make any sense. But she was no longer resisting this character. He was such an essential part of who the heroine had become. She wanted the world to know at least some of this story now.

Cell phone service got progressively worse as they approached the western end of the Principality. This was to be expected, even in times of peace. At the last station on the line, there was a small presence of Tarasov's soldiers, just in case, but the war had not reached this far. The town was still in good shape, like Katerinya had remembered it. The couple had bought tickets to the next station west, outside of the Principality. In times of peace, the westbound line would terminate there, under agreement with the government further to the west. The clerk at Mariankursk noted that it was a conditional ticket. They could not guarantee that the train would cross the border tonight. Ilya and Katerinya were prepared for this possibility, but to their surprise, the conductor re-boarded the train to tell them they would go on to Belfort, the next station beyond the border. They were the only passengers.

The town of Belfort was located in no government's jurisdiction. It was customary for principalities to have buffer areas between their claimed borders. Fewer disputes that way. So Belfort was in no man's land. No one's law applied there. Despite this, it was peaceful. It received extended services from both of its bordering governments, including police in times of need. There wasn't a lot there worth fighting over. And both sides depended on a smooth transition of the railways. That was easier to maintain than cooperative cell phone services. Here there were none.

Ilya and Katerinya found a comfortable overnight room right next to the Belfort station. Servicing train passengers was this small hamlet's main source of commerce, so they were good at it. As they settled in for the night, Ilya instinctively checked his phone, only to be reminded that there was no service here. They would be in an information blackout for a while. He wouldn't be able to track what was going on with the war. Katerinya thought that it was better this way.

Chapter 10

WHAT SQUIRRELS DON'T UNDERSTAND

Sixteen days earlier, when Ilya had first escaped from Kuznetsov's camp in the far west, Lavro was trying to keep a low profile. He had failed in his primary mission, and was wary about what might come next from Kuznetsov. The commander, on the other hand, figured that his ability to use the now inert bioweapon as a bargaining chip depended on it still seeming credible to all concerned. Thanks to Ilya's propaganda, the whole camp believed it was now ready to go. If Kuznetsov were to reassign Lavro, it might tip his hand about the viability of the weapon. So he decided to double down on appearances by reassigning the surviving architect of the mission, Luka Vladimirovich Shulyov, from the front back to bioweapon duty. What harm could it do? he reasoned.

What harm, indeed. Shulyov was anxious to do *something*, after he learned from Lavro that the duty mostly consisted of sitting around in the vicinity of the weapon doing nothing in particular. He still fancied himself a scientist, of the Aron Mattson variety, so after poking around a bit, he found the field microscope. A real scientist's tool! Lavro asked him if he was sure he knew what he was doing. Oh, yes, Shulyov assured him, how hard can it be? He found a slide that Ilya had prepared earlier lying on a table. He stuck it in and focused the lenses. He wasn't exactly sure what he was looking at, but these little bacteria were not moving. Shouldn't they be moving? Lavro did not know. "Doctor Ilya was the only one who worked on this," he said. Still sure of himself, Shulyov cavalierly opened one of the bio-containers and extracted a sample, prepared a slide, and looked again. Still no movement. A few more rounds of this and he delivered his conclusion to Lavro. "They're all dead!" "Can't be," Lavro said. "Doctor Ilya said they were primed and ready to go." "Well *something* happened," Shulyov said.

Realizing he had reached the end of what he thought was his knowledge on the subject, Shulyov reasoned that the only course of action was to replace the bacteria. When Lavro asked how he planned to do that, Shulyov explained that when he and his now dead comrade had broken into the legacy storage repository in Derazhne to steal the bacteria, they had taken more containers than they were able to carry on horseback. After dropping several, they decided to pare down their inventory to a more manageable number by burying the excess containers in the ground. They figured they could always retrieve them later, if necessary. Well it was now later, and it was now necessary. "Let's go tell Kuznetsov!" Lavro said. Shulyov thought that would be a good idea. This should raise his stature in Kuznetsov's eyes, he thought. What both of them didn't know, of course, was that it would have just the opposite effect.

When Kuznetsov heard the news, he was furious on the inside, but measured in his response on the outside. No, he said, they should under no circumstances take two horses and try to retrieve the buried containers. They should stay here. He was too busy to deal with this right now, he told them. But what he was really busy with was thinking of some credible excuse to keep them from going. For the time being, he would just rely on his authority. He made his decision quite clear and stern.

This made no sense to Shulyov. So he engaged in a little wishful thinking, as he was wont to do. The commander was busy right now, and he wasn't a scientist like himself, so he could not yet see how critical the second cache of containers was to the war effort. It was time for the scientist to take the initiative. Kuznetsov would thank him later, he thought. He couldn't go to Lavro with his mission because he had been present at Kuznetsov's explicit prohibition. But he knew a young lad named Sukin, about Lavro's age and temperament, whom he had befriended in his combat rotations. Sukin could be persuaded. So Shulyov laid out his original plan to Sukin, leaving out Kuznetsov's disapproval. He and Sukin were to leave at once. Sounded good to Sukin. So they got two horses and headed toward Derazhne. Same plan as with the original smash-and-grab – plainclothes. Only they didn't have to encounter any humans this time, or smash anything. The burial site was in the woods. If they were careful, and discreet, they could be in and out without anyone noticing.

The mission took a little longer this time. There were many of Tarasov's troops along the way east, so Shulyov and Sukin had to take evasive action. Before they could get back to Kuznetsov's encampment, the commander's forces had already been forced to break camp and retreat eastward. This is when Kuznetsov decided to use the railroads. It's also when Sukin and Shulyov's absence from camp was detected. Kuznetsov suspected that they had gone to retrieve the live bacteria. He didn't know much about this Sukin, but Shulyov was another matter. He never did trust him. Now he had a problem. He told his men to bring the containers of dead bacteria on the trains, to keep up the appearance of the threat, but to leave all of the rest of the equipment behind. He had two problems, really. He had to find the live bacteria containers, and he had to re-find Ilya to try to kill the actual threat one more time. So from Pyatiskala on, he ordered the troops to canvass the towns, door-to-door, looking for the professor. When they got to Mariankursk, look for the professor and the girlfriend. The second would lead you to the first. He sent a lone horse and rider east to look for Sukin and Shulyov. He wasn't optimistic about that search.

When Sukin and Shulyov returned to the abandoned camp, they were stumped as to what to do next. But Shulyov had an idea. For some reason he couldn't fathom, their comrades had taken the useless parts of the project with them, and left all of the still useful parts – like the stolen drones. These were still in their crates along with a batch of stolen cellphones. So Shulyov laid out his plan for Sukin. He explained that before Sukin had joined them, they had run a test of the drone delivery system near Mariankursk. It didn't go so well. They were unable to control the drone and it crashed. That's why they had stolen the cellphones. It was his idea, he proudly announced. He had come up with a scheme for controlling the drones with the cellphones. Each drone would have an onboard phone that could use its tracking facility to send its geolocation back to the controlling laptop. The fleet's position could then be adjusted in real time from the laptop, allowing the human controller to continuously adjust the fleet's trajectory until it reached the target area.

Sounded like a good idea to Sukin. Had Shulyov tested his system yet? No, but they could do that now. He proceeded to jury-rig the parts, using all of the containers and all of the drones. Shouldn't they just try one drone's worth first? Sukin asked. No, they had to use them all, Shulyov said, because he had to see if he could control the fleet as a whole from a single laptop. Sounded reasonable to Sukin. So they launched the whole fleet in a generally easterly direction, the direction they would use when they eventually launched the real attack on Derazhne and Solinovsk. Shulyov's plan was to get some experience with the fleet control system, then bring the fleet back. What could go wrong?

On the same day, north of Derazhne, Kuznetsov was preparing for the endgame. The professor had escaped again, with the girlfriend, on horseback a few days earlier. He had yet to find Sukin and Shulyov, and he was surrounded by Tarasov's forces with no access to trains. No point bluffing, because the real threat was now outstanding somewhere else. It was time for the killing to stop, he decided. Over the last week, he had been slowly transitioning from Kuznetsov back to Mitya Zhenyaevich Stepanov. The man who followed orders from actual superiors he could see and hear. He was done giving orders as though he had intuited them from some abstract deity that he couldn't identify. The right course of action was clear now. He should unconditionally surrender, explain the need to Tarasov to bring back the professor and find the outstanding bio-threat, before it got everyone killed. But before he could get the white flag hoisted, there was a problem back at his abandoned encampment.

The stolen cellphones were African-spec phones. They come from the factory with tracking set to 'off'. It is up to the user (in Africa), or the cellphone provider, to change this setting if they want to opt in. Shulyov didn't know this. He also hadn't taken into account the spotty cell tower service that he would encounter in the far west, but that was the least of his problems. With tracking off, a control system based on tracking is useless. As soon as the test fleet was launched, this became evident. The drones couldn't be controlled at all. They just kept heading east, though of course, Shulyov had no idea from the laptop where they were going. There was a strong west-to-east wind blowing that day, enough to keep the fleet from drifting apart and on a generally eastern route – toward Derazhne and Solinovsk. The drones were generally not designed to fly such long distances, so as they neared Derazhne and Solinovsk, their battery charge diminished, and they slowly lost altitude. All but one made it to the twin cities. The other one, the one at the southernmost part of the formation, got blown off course to the south toward Lirovo by a local wind at lower altitude. It crashed squarely into the roof of Noah's Ark in Aron Mattson's theme park. The rest of fleet crashed first into taller buildings, then into lower urban obstacles, spreading the live bacteria randomly over the population.

Humans often insist that everything happens for a reason. Often enough, what they mean by this is that everything happens for *someone's* reason – some agent, human or supernatural, brings about events by design to accomplish some purpose intended by the agent. In the case of wind direction, ancient peoples often attributed fateful weather conditions to the interactions and quarrels of gods. Monotheistic religions attribute them to the inscrutable will of one god. Weather forecasters, on the other hand, attribute these events to causes, not reasons. There are no agents involved, just atmospheric conditions. The difference is that the weather forecasters can predict what will happen based on the causes. The people who believe in the will of disembodied agents can't predict. They can only come up with a reason after the fact. Like Sokolov. He would no doubt have claimed to have foreseen this wind direction as God's retribution on Tarasov – after the fact, of course. But just fortuitously, the weather scientists would say, one of the drones just happened to crash into the prison where he was being confined. Was this perhaps God putting an exclamation point on his reasons?

§

When the sun rose the next morning, Katerinya and Ilya were asleep in their small guestroom in Belfort near the train station, unaware of the events that had transpired back east on the previous day. It was a clear winter day, but their bedroom window faced west, and was shaded by the thick forest, so there was no direct sunlight. This enabled Ilya to easily fall back asleep, and Katerinya to delay waking up. Eventually, they met in the middle. This was their first extended trip anywhere together, so there was a mood of adventure about the unfamiliar room. Places to see; things to do. There wasn't much to see or do in Belfort, it being just a remote rail stop, but they would soon be on their way to bigger places. Ilya unconsciously checked his phone again, and was reminded again of the lack of cell service. This also helped reinforce the mood. They were looking forward, to the west, not backward to the east. No one was pursuing them. Indeed, no one really could pursue them.

There was a communal breakfast at the guesthouse, timed to finish before the first train of the morning departed for the west. There were no trains definitely scheduled from or to the east right now, only one conditional arrival in the evening, depending on circumstances. That was the train they had come on last night. It returned to the Principality the same night, empty.

They sat at a table with an older couple and a solo female traveler. After the customary exchanging of names, they got to the customary "where are you from" and "what do you do" part of the conversation you have with such strangers. The older couple had been visiting their daughter who lived in Belfort, and were now on their way back west to Kievlynn. The solo traveler had just arrived last night from the west (not as far as Kievlynn, though) and was just sightseeing for the day. It didn't bother her that Belfort had no major attractions. The attraction for her was its very small, rural character. She liked peace and quiet. Ilya and Katerinya introduced themselves as a professor from Derazhne and a writer from Mariankursk, on their way to the west coast for a long stay. They kept the disclosure minimal. The reference to Derazhne, of course, raised questions from the others about the war that they had heard was raging there. Had they witnessed it personally? After a quick coordinating glance at each other, our favorite couple said no, they hadn't been affected personally. The actual story would have been too long and involved and just invite more incredulous questions about things they really wanted to leave behind for now. It was good to get away though, they said. That seemed to satisfy the curiosity.

After checking the routes and the timetables at the railway station, Ilya and Katerinya decided to book passage all the way to Zhivago via Kievlynn. They would stay overnight in Zhivago, then reassess the route the next morning. When they boarded the train, Katerinya took the window seat to relive her memories of her first journey out west. She had left Mariankursk in the fall then, and it was now winter, so the view would be a little different, though the first part of the journey would mostly be through woodlands. The difference, of course, was that the hardwoods would have no leaves now, so she could see a little more of the landscape. The color palette would be much smaller though – just white, browns and greens (from the fir trees). She had fully charged her laptop overnight in anticipation of doing some writing, but she had no thought of that now. Each time she saw something she remembered, she would relate her then and now experiences to Ilya.

As the train got nearer to Kievlynn, she could begin to see the shores of the great freshwater lake to the north. "Oh, Iliusha, have you ever seen this lake?"

He couldn't recall. "I know about it, and approximately where it is, but I haven't even seen it from the air, let alone the ground. It is quite large."

"I'm a little directionally challenged, so when I first saw it, years ago, I thought it was the ocean. It really looks like the ocean close up. If you stand on the shore, you can't see the other side. And the waves are just as large as the ocean. Unless you taste the water, you don't know that it's freshwater instead of saltwater. So I was really confused at first."

He was amused by this story. "But you were only a few days from the east coast. Didn't that give you a clue?"

"I was only 18," she pleaded, "and had never been very far from Mariankursk my whole life, so I didn't have a good sense of how large the continent was. A lot of the east coasters on their first trip west made the same mistake. Other passengers filled us in, of course."

"So did you taste it to make sure?" He was joking.

"No! If you're expecting ocean, you don't want to taste it. The real clue was the smell, and the color. The water is bluer than the ocean, and the smell is very different."

At Kievlynn, they got off the train during the stopover to check out the ocean that was really a lake, close up from the shoreline. Ilya could see her point. It looked for all the world like a blue, fresh-smelling ocean. He didn't taste it.

Back on the train and on their way to Zhivago, they had a substantially different set of fellow passengers. A lot of travelers got off and got on in Kievlynn. There would be another one of these huge lakes when they got to Zhivago, Katerinya told him. After a while they both noticed that they were discreetly staring at the same fellow passenger across the aisle. Katerinya leaned over to whisper in Ilya's ear. "Is it a man or a woman?"

"I had the same question," he whispered back. He realized that they didn't have to whisper. They just needed to talk softly. There was enough white noise from the train to cover their conversation. "My first impression was female. But he/she has some male features in the face. Just enough to make you unsure."

"What features are those?"

"The wide jaw. That's typically male. But now I think that's really the only male-like feature. If it is a man, that's one beautiful man. He/she is stunning."

Katerinya discreetly felt her own jaw. Nothing to worry about. "I think you're right. Too pretty to be a man. Are you attracted to her?"

"Yes! That's the strange thing. I think I'm a little homophobic, like most men. Women don't seem to have as much of a problem with this – judging other women as attractive, I mean. But men on men – we cringe a little. So if I thought this might be a man, my perception would change. But even now that I am unsure, my visceral sense wants me to believe this is a woman."

Now Katerinya was intrigued. "What makes her so beautiful – to you?"

He had to think about this. It's not something you typical analyze. It just strikes you. But it can be analyzed. So he tried. "High cheekbones. Balanced face. Well-defined eyebrows. Large eyes."

"Do I have those things?"

He looked at her with a smile. "Yes, you have all of those things. But you're different. I wouldn't call you stunning, per se."

"Why not?" She looked a little worried.

"Stunning is more of the femme fatale look. He/she has that look. A little bit unfriendly. A little too sure of herself. A sense that she knows how to deceive you, and that she might try to deceive you. She's beautiful in an objective sense, but she can't necessarily be trusted."

OK, that wasn't so bad. "But I can be trusted?"

"Yes! That's really what defines your beauty. It's part of your face. When I look at you – even when I first saw you – that's the most attractive aspect of your beauty to me. Your face has empathy, and honesty, and intelligence, and endearment written all over it. *Endearment!* That's the word I'm looking for. You have an endearing beauty, not a femme fatale beauty. I prefer your kind. What made you win over everyone at the Crispness party was that you were dressed like a femme fatale, and you had all of the classic features, but your face was endearing. A double whammy!"

Now she was feeling better about things. "But I could have been a good actress. I could have been deceiving you."

"Not for long. When you think no one is looking, you would revert to your natural demeanor. You couldn't keep it up forever." Now he was intrigued. "What attracted you to me?"

Now she had to think about it. Same as Ilya – it just happens. But you can try to analyze it. "Your eyes, I think. That's the first thing I noticed. They're very expressive, dark and deep-set. And you have great eyebrows. It gives you a look, a bearing. People naturally orient toward you. Your face says 'I know things'. 'I'm in charge'. People feel inclined to follow you, to ask you for advice. I suppose those are classic male features of authority. But your eyes, your face also have a choirboy aspect to them. A hint of vulnerability behind the stoic exterior. A touch of sadness sometimes. It makes me want to comfort you."

He laid his head on her shoulder. "You do. Believe me, you do."

She smiled. "Olena told me she thought you had bedroom eyes."

He'd never heard that before – well, as far as he could remember. "What does that mean?"

"I don't know exactly. But somehow it seems appropriate."

§

When they reached Zhivago, they had a decision to make. Katerinya disclosed that she had made a routing mistake on her first trip west. She thought Karlsruhe was straight west from Mariankursk. When she got to Zhivago, she discovered that the rail lines split into a northwest route toward Miniplus and a southwest route toward Sallewas. She had to choose one. She randomly chose the northwest route through Miniplus, not realizing that it would go all the way north to Sea Handle before it hit the west coast. Then she had to take the coastal railway back down south to St. Francisburg to get to Karlsruhe. The southwestern route through Sallewas would have been much shorter. She took that route on the way back. It was quicker, but once over the mountains, the landscape was much flatter, less interesting than the northwest landscape. In retrospect, she was glad she had taken the more northern route. They were in no rush to get to Karlsruhe, so Ilya suggested that they make the same mistake again – this time on purpose.

As Katerinya had said, Zhivago was situated on the shores of another one of those lakes that looks like an ocean. It was also very windy, perhaps because of the large lake. They spent most of their stopover there inside. It was a very blustery evening. On their trip northwest to Miniplus, the landscape became more rolling and more densely wooded. There were also many smaller lakes everywhere. And there were many fewer people. Miniplus looked like it had once been a great city before the Great Dying, but it was sparsely populated now. It was also much colder there than the winters on the east coast. Katerinya had last come in the fall, so she did not know this.

When they left Miniplus, they had planned to get as far as Montanasruhe up in the mountains. Katerinya remembered that there were wonderful tourist lodges up there with beautiful views of the rugged scenery. But to get to the mountains, the train first had to cross a wide prairie. A snowstorm across the prairie caused a delay for their train so that tracks could be cleared. This put the train seriously off schedule, so it could only get as far as a very small station town in the middle of the prairie, Piermont, by nightfall. The tracks ahead had yet to be cleared, so this was the destination for the night. Although grateful to be inside the warmth of the train, Katerinya and Ilya found the journey to the middle of the prairie to be visually arresting. The snow-covered landscape was cold, and flat, and desolate against the setting sun, stretching as far as the eye could see in every direction. There was nothing like this on the east coast.

There were fewer passengers on the train now. Those with alternatives, and an eye on weather reports, had taken those alternatives. Many decided to wait it out in Miniplus. That was the good news – fewer people to compete with for the few overnight accommodations in Piermont. The bad news was that Piermont was already critically small, not being a normal overnight destination on the route, so it had few public accommodations. There were no rooms available for Ilya and Katerinya by the time they inquired. This was a hazard of winter travel in these parts that neither of them was familiar with. It was not unfamiliar to the station manager. This kind of thing had happened before. He had a solution. He lived with his wife and daughter in a small house nearby. They had a spare bedroom. Eventually it was to hold a second child. They did not want to be in the bed and breakfast business, so they didn't make this publicly known. He did not extend this solution to every stranded traveling party, but he liked the looks of Katerinya and Ilya. They had the potential to be good company, he thought. If he hadn't, they would have been sleeping on the benches overnight in the station.

They each selected one suitcase to take with them on the short walk through the snow to his house. The station manager offered to carry Katerinya's, a standard chivalry gesture, but she declined. Ilya had already offered to pay for the overnight lodging and the station manager had declined, so she did not want to treat him like a porter for hire. They wanted to be gracious guests. At the house, the station manager introduced himself as Jasper Overa. This was his wife Emily and his daughter Ava. Now being outside of the northeast, Ilya and Katerinya switched to the first-name/last-name custom, introducing themselves as Ilya Koskayin and Katerinya Grigoreva. Katerinya knew this from her prior time in the west. Ilya knew it from his prior time in the world.

Mrs. Overa already knew the routine. Her husband only invited overnight guests when he thought they would make good company. Good company meant not just polite and well-mannered, but interesting. Living in the middle of the prairie, there wasn't much going on around them and very little access to news of the world. They had no Internet or cellphone service out here. So their only news of the world came from the stories of passengers traveling through. Mr. Overa thought that Ilya and Katerinya were likely to have good stories. If only he knew.

When they were shown the spare bedroom, the whole family came along. Indeed, the whole family came along with them everywhere. They were tonight's curiosity. The bedroom and the bed were small – a prospective child's bed. Mrs. Overa apologized for its size, but Katerinya assured her that they had recent experience with this kind of accommodation before – at Olena's. It was certainly preferable to sleeping on station benches. The reference to Olena's opened a peek into their stories. They wanted to know more. Katerinya assured Mrs. Overa that their stories were long and deep, but perhaps too long and deep to go into now. Maybe over dinner would be more appropriate. That worked, and bought them some private time in the room while the dinner was prepared. Their prior introduction as the writer and the professor from Derazhne/Solinovsk (Mariankursk was unknown to them) had already whetted the Overa's appetite for stories to come.

The Overa's little house was well insulated. Houses have to be, out here on the open prairie. Perhaps a little too well insulated for five people and a blazing fireplace at dinner. Ilya instinctively attended to the fire, spreading the wood to lower the blazing. Mr. Overa was surprised that a professor from the big city would know how to do this. "We have a place in the country – really a country town called Mariankursk," Katerinya explained. "Ilya splits wood and builds fires all the time there." This was the pattern of disclosure that they would follow all evening. The subjects to avoid would be any reference to Ilya's memory problems. That meant, by extension, that they had to avoid some of his surprising skills unless they could come up with a cover story. So the doctor skills, the shooting skills, the riding skills, the survival skills all had to be toned down to those a professor might have. Also, for Ava's benefit, there was minimal blood and gore. But once they got started, there wasn't much that they left out. The Overas listened wide-eyed to each episode, which only prompted more questions, which led to more episodes.

Mrs. Overa and Ava were particularly invested in the Crispness party, and the fashion show that led up to it. Mr. Overa found the whole saga of Ilya's capture, service and escape at the hands of Kuznetsov riveting. And the whole family was drawn into the story of their evolving relationship with the Prince. They were virtual celebrities, even more so to people who had lived their whole lives on the prairie. Mr. Overa's speculative investment in a news source had reaped returns that he never could have imagined.

Mr. Overa apologized for not having much news of his own to contribute. He had heard stories of the war back east from passing travelers, but nothing at the level of detail – nor the inside perspective – of what the professor and the writer could offer. They hadn't hosted sleepover guests for some time, but he had overheard recent conversations from passengers in the station. From what he could tell, there was some sort of epidemic raging there now. Someone had said that all of the governments bordering the Principality had suspended their railroad pass-through agreements with Tarasov – effectively a forced quarantine. You could enter the Principality, at your own risk, if you managed to get there without the trains, but you couldn't get back. No one from the Principality was permitted to enter neighboring jurisdictions.

This, of course, alarmed Ilya. "What sort of epidemic?"

"You're asking the wrong person, I'm afraid. All I heard was 'epidemic.' Is that bad?"

"Very bad. It has to be related to the outbreak I was dealing with when we were there. We must have gotten out just in time. You've heard of the Great Dying, right?"

"Yes."

"Well, it could potentially be that bad. How much further west until we can get Internet or phone service?"

"You're headed to Montanasruhe, I assume? Most people who pass through here are."

"Yes."

"Well, you won't find any there. You might have to get all the way to the coast before you get really reliable service."

§

The pillow talk that night, in their small bed, revolved around what they didn't know, but feared, was happening back home. The quarantine could just be an overreaction, Ilya said, or there could be a real epidemic. If the news had reached all the way to the bordering states, this was on a much bigger scale than the Mariankursk outbreak. And it was almost certainly some form of *Y. pestis*. But what form? Tarasov already had good supplies of the original *modernis* vaccine, or could quickly have them manufactured. And Ilya had killed off all of the new strain. Hadn't he? What could the source possibly be?

Imagining a real epidemic only raised their own concerns about friends back home and what it might do to them. But with no further information, that fear would just sit there, darkening the rest of their journey. Either way, being here was much better than being there. If the epidemic wasn't serious, they were on their way to a much-needed sabbatical. If it was, they were already well on their way to escaping it – together for once. Ilya had the ability to suppress worry about things over which he had no control – like this. Katerinya less so. But her knowledge of the ways of epidemics was shallow. She was nowhere near as aware of its horrors as Ilya. So he decided to keep it that way. They would focus on the good things in front of them until they could get more information. And that wasn't likely to happen until they got to Sea Handle.

The next day, the western prairie tracks had been cleared sufficiently for trains to resume running, so they were off to Montanasruhe. Katerinya somehow still managed not to project her current experience of snow onto her early fall memories of the mountain tourist lodges there, so she was looking forward to a different scene than the one they would eventually encounter. Ilya's expectations were a lot less specific: snow, lodge, scenery.

The rest of the journey across the prairie featured the same landscape with a different light – trailing, rising sun instead of forward, setting sun. The landscape only changed as they approached the mountains. The long, gradual ascent up the mountain range began to add more and varied natural landscapes, and more and varied railroad trajectories. As the elevations rose, the tracks began to wind around the sides of mountains, sometimes paralleling riverbeds, and sometimes creeping through tunnels bored into the rock. This is what Katerinya remembered, she said, minus the snow. At higher elevations, the train slipped through wooden snow sheds that were built over especially hard to clear sections of track. These had seemed oddly misplaced to Katerinya in the fall, without a hint of their true purpose. But now she understood.

They got to Montanasruhe by nightfall. They had no trouble finding sleeping accommodations this time. They went for the best room in the best lodge they could find. It was time for what passed as luxury in this part of the continent. The room was still pretty rustic, but upscale rustic. The bed was sized for two adults, and the bed linens had an impressive thread count. Katerinya especially liked that aspect. She had stayed at the other end of the scale when here as a student, when she wasn't really sensitive to things like thread count or room size. It was dark by the time they got to their room, so there wasn't much scenery to look at. That would happen the next morning, she said. Already though, she had made the necessary adjustment for snow. It would be a lot whiter this time.

In the morning, she was the first one up, going to their balcony windows for a look. "Look Iliusha!" she said, after dramatically drawing the curtains open. The view was sublime. A lake snaked around curves in a conifer-covered landscape with gentle rises. In the distance it reached a snow-covered mountain range. Water, evergreens, mountains. Why was that so special? The atmospheric colors! The lake was not frozen, so it reflected its surroundings like a shiny mirror. The dark green firs and the rocky rises were sprinkled with glistening white. A transparent morning mist was rising in dappled patches from land and water in the foreground. But in the background, the snowy peaks of the mountains changed from blue-white to bright, glowing pink right along the Earth's shadow line illuminated by the morning sunrise. Ilya was expecting white on white. They both stood at the balcony window and just watched for a while until the rising sun lost its pink wavelength, and the mist had dissipated. "Oh, it's so much prettier in the winter," Katerinya said. "So much more dramatic than the fall. At least the sunrise."

At breakfast in the lodge, most of the visitors were here for the outdoors. They had cross-country skis, and snowshoes, and backpacks, and sunglasses, and insulated parkas. All of the gear you needed to be outside in a place and season like this. The two urban east coasters, who had fled to the west, had none of these things. Katerinya explained that in the fall, she was able to go hiking, and take a tour boat up the lake. You didn't need any special equipment then. This was not a ski resort where you could rent these things. It was a train stop. If you wanted more than the view in the winter, you had to come prepared.

That was OK, they decided. The view was worth it. It was a pleasant lodge, and they had a nice comfortable room with a killer view. Besides, it was very cold outside. It was nice to watch the beauty of all that coldness without having to be outside in it. Even their balcony was covered with snow, so they had no incentive to slide the glass doors open to the outside. Their favorite activity turned out to be just sitting on the bed together with a view out the windows. Katerinya wrote a little. Ilya read a little. They talked a little.

During a lull in his reading, Ilya was watching a squirrel on the balcony alternately scurrying around and digging in the snow in vain for food. Each time it came up empty, it looked up, jerking its head around to survey its field of vision. Then it bounded to another spot and dug again in vain. If he were a squirrel, Ilya thought, he would have given up this routine a long time ago. But he wasn't a squirrel. That's what squirrels do. Search for food, store it or eat it, sleep, occasionally reproduce. That's their whole repertoire. He wondered if squirrels ever got bored doing this every day. He would. "I wonder if squirrels ever get bored," he said out loud.

Katerinya looked up from her writing. She had come to expect Ilya to ask strange questions like this from time to time. She thought about it. "I don't think so. Do any animals get bored?"

"I'm sure squirrels don't, but higher primates, like chimpanzees, must. Humans get bored so easily, so our nearest cousins must have some of that too."

"I think a lot of people don't get bored. Not like you and me. My parents, for instance. They were quite content living in the same place, doing the same things day after day. They saw it as their role in life, almost like the squirrels. They had no higher ambition."

"I suppose you're right. We're in the minority. Maybe that's what drives us to be academics."

"But I'm not an academic."

"You're an honorary academic. You have the same values. If you could make a living teaching creative writing, and still write your novel, you would do it, wouldn't you?"

"Yes, I suppose so." Now she had lost interest in her writing. She looked around the room. She wasn't bored. On the walls, there were four framed photographs of the same scene in a mountain meadow, presumably somewhere around here, one taken in each of the four seasons. Of the four, she liked the spring scene the best. There was a thick bloom of wildflowers, lilies, in the otherwise green meadow. The shape of the lily flowers reminded her of something. What? The fleur-de-lis! "Doesn't 'fleur-de-lis' mean 'lily' – in French, Iliusha?"

"Yes?"

"Show me your Androsia mark!"

"Why?"

"Just show me!" She knew where it was. She reached over and pulled up his left pant leg. "Look at the lily blooms in that picture. Now look at your tattoo. See the resemblance?"

He did. "What are you getting at?"

"Could the Androsia message be written in the molecules of a plant – a lily for instance?

Of course it could, he thought. Why hadn't this occurred to him before? "Are you sure you're not a scientist?" he smiled. "That's a great idea! I mean independent of the lily. Plant genomes can be huge. Much larger than human genomes. Also there is a lot of non-functional repetition in their DNA, a lot of DNA you could overwrite without hurting the plant."

"But it's not just any plant, Iliusha. The Androsia symbol *looks like* the lily flower. Maybe it's telling you to look at *lily* DNA for the message."

Again, scientist Katerinya to the rescue. "The genus *Lilium* would make a great target!" he said. "It's got one of the largest genomes among the plants – maybe twelve or thirteen times larger than the human genome. Maybe that's why I picked it. Lots of room to write!"

"Oh, this makes so much more sense now!," she said. "The fleur-de-lis wasn't just to throw other people off the meaning. It actually tells you where to look. All of its other connotations were to confuse others. Only the biologist would pick the right one!"

When they had last abandoned the search for the Androsia message, Ilya had not told her the detailed reason why – that large animal genomes, such as his own, can't practically be written into unless you edit the first embryonic cell at conception, so that the changed DNA will reach all subsequent cells through later reproduction. This would be impossible for him to do to himself. It would also be impractical to do this to any other animal whose original embrio you just happened to have. But this would be much more feasible with a plant. Because they are structurally so much simpler than animals, a whole, mature plant can often be regenerated from most of its mature single cells. Just take a small cutting, edit its DNA to add the message, then propagate it onto a new plant.

That was the good news. The bad news was that he only could have edited a specific lily plant. The lily's species as a whole would not be changed. There would just be this one, specific individual plant that carried the message. The reference genomes for all of the species of *Lilium* would not have his edits. So even when they reached Karlsruhe, where he would have Internet access to the reference sequences for all of the world's species of lilies, he would find no messages. There would have to have been one specific lily plant, somewhere once in his possession, that was the target.

He explained this to Katerinya – that if *Lilium* was the target, as she was proposing, they would have to look for some specific lily plant associated with his history. And since his history was pretty much limited to Derazhne and environs, given his memory limit, they couldn't follow up on this new lead until they got back east. Still, each new epiphany in the Androsia puzzle was exciting. Squirrels would never understand this. And the prime mover for most of these epiphanies was turning out to be Katerinya, the non-scientist. They made a good team.

§

The next morning, they boarded the train for Sea Handle. This would be a full day's journey across two mountain ranges to reach the west coast. The first range was the larger of the two, running broadly up and down the entire continent. The second was a narrower pre-coastal range, but it had a similar elevation around these parts. The snow would decrease and the temperature increase as they approached the coast because the west to east direction of the winds brought warmer air off of the ocean, making the land temperature more temperate than inland regions at the same latitude.

It would be another peaceful day of compelling scenery and marvels of railroad engineering, but they both were aware that their idyllic isolation from the troubles back east was about to end. Troubles always seemed to follow them just as they were getting comfortable together, only this time it could not impinge on them directly. No one was coming to separate them. But once they learned the inevitable news, there would be very little they could do about it. They would get cell and Internet service once again in Sea Handle, so by the end of the day, they could no longer pretend that nothing was happening. It did not dominate their mood. There were still a lot of pretty things to see. But it hung subliminally in the background nonetheless. Another thing that the squirrels just wouldn't understand.

When they were approaching the Sea Handle station, with Katerinya napping on his shoulder, Ilya figured that they must be in range of cell towers by now. He checked his phone. There was service. He tried calling Ekholm, he tried calling Diederick Brandt, he tried calling Andzhelina. He even tried Tarasov's private number. In each case, the call did not go through. At first he was alarmed. But as he thought about the situation, it occurred to him that transcontinental connections were unreliable even in the best of times. If Solinovsk/Derazhne was having a health emergency, that would disrupt the Principality's ability to reliably process the transfer handoffs. He would check again later.

When the train finally came to a halt at the station, Katerinya woke up, still in vacation/sabbatical mode. Ilya, of course, had already transitioned to what's-going-on-back-east mode. He let Katerinya take her time before the bubble burst, and discreetly tried all of the calls again, once they were off the train and in the station getting their luggage. Same result. That left the Internet. Surely there would be a connection when they got to their hotel.

There was. Ilya plugged in immediately. Katerinya was on the same page now. She had been since the train station when she saw Ilya checking his phone. He hadn't said anything, so she hadn't said anything. She pulled up a chair beside him to watch. The normally active academic intelligence network at Derazhne was noticeably inactive now. There were few recent postings and Ilya got no response for queries he posted on several threads. It was a little late on the east coast he realized, but he had never seen a level of inactivity like this before. There were always a few night owls prowling around. There was quite an active discussion on other academic networks however, particularly at Karlsruhe, concerning the situation at Derazhne. It did not look good. There was an out-of-control epidemic raging there, and the University had taken some big hits. Almost all of the discussion was second hand, though. There had been very little direct response from Derazhne-based colleagues.

For Katerinya, there wasn't much to watch, just Ilya's frustration with the lack of any direct information. He tried his phone one more time. No calls completed. He tried calling colleagues he knew at other universities in the mid-west and the south. He was able to reach both. That meant the telecom problem was in Tarasov's Principality. He stopped trying to reach there by phone.

That left email. It was asynchronous, but at least the Internet was up in Derazhne. His messages would get there. He would just have to wait for replies. He emailed Andzhelina, Diederick Brandt, Ekholm, and several others of his colleagues in the biology department – essentially everyone who had worked on either the antibiotic or vaccine with him. He also emailed the doctor at the hospital in Mariankursk. He thought about emailing the Prince, but thought better of it. Clearly, Ilya would be in demand back there, and he wanted to have a better understanding of where things stood before he got involved, or volunteered for anything.

When he and Katerinya checked out the next morning, he had only one reply – from the doctor in Mariankursk. Apparently the situation was pretty bad in Solinovsk/Derazhne, but Mariankursk had been spared so far. Katerinya breathed a sigh of relief at that news. All travel had been suspended and the whole Principality was under strict quarantine. He had sent the hospital's entire supply of the antibiotic and vaccine for *modernis*, plus Ilya's experimental antibiotic for the variant, to the University. There was much greater need for them there. He hadn't heard anything back yet specifically about the medications. Ilya and Katerinya would now be on the train all day, traveling down the coast to St. Francisburg, so that would be their last news for the day.

There was no escaping thoughts of the east now, but they tried. Katerinya felt a little better with the positive news about Mariankursk. Ilya adopted his there's-nothing-I-can-do-about-it-now attitude. The scenery from the train windows helped. The railroad ran through the valley between the pre-coastal and the coastal mountain ranges, so the views were of green valleys rather than the ocean. The change from snow-covered valleys to green valleys ushered them from winter into spring. That helped too. The farther south they got, the more the landscape of the valley floors and the nearby hillsides were devoted to vineyards. This was the primary wine-producing region for the continent. Now Ilya got to play tour guide. Katerinya had seen these views before (they were brown in the fall), but not being familiar with wine, she hadn't known what she was looking at. Ilya had seen all of them in his mind, and many of them in real life (that he could remember).

They both knew what to expect when they got to St. Francisburg. It was the premier city on the west coast, and only an hour or so north of Karlsruhe. It was a primary destination for tourists, many from other continents. It was *the* favorite travel destination for Africans, partially because they could afford it. Most tourists, however, make the same mistake on their first visit here. It is customary to take your vacations in the summer, at least in the northern hemisphere, and the west coast is well known for its sunny, dry climate. So most tourists end up in St. Francisburg in the summer – the worst season to visit if you are looking for warm, sunny weather. During the summer, the valleys east of the coastal range get very warm during the day, so a column of heat rises from the valley floor creating a barrier for the cooler, moist air coming in from the ocean. This causes the ocean air to curl back on itself and form a dense, cool layer of fog all along the coast. It stays stuck there until nightfall, when the cooling of the valleys allows it to flow eastward again. The only significant break in the coastal range is formed by the wide St. Francisburg Bay. So during the otherwise hot days of summer, a dense fog comes streaming into St. Francisburg from the Bay, blanketing it in cool white. It was now winter in St. Francisburg, though. The best time to visit for pleasant sunny days and no fog.

At their hotel, they checked the Internet once again. Andzhelina was fortunate. She had left Solinovsk to attend a conference at a university in the south the day before the epidemic hit. She never would have escaped otherwise. Now she couldn't go back, but from what she'd heard on the Internet, it was not a place you wanted to go back to right now anyway. She couldn't reach anyone there by phone. Diederick Brandt was holed up in his house in Derazhne, avoiding contact with other humans as much as possible. At least he wasn't infected – yet. Ekholm hadn't replied. The most senior member of his biology team also hadn't replied. But then he learned why from the other team members. He was dead. He had succumbed to the disease. They were all in lockdown, but they did have the inside view on the epidemic. Neither the *Y. pestis modernis* vaccine nor antibiotic was effective. And the experimental antibiotic against the new strain didn't work either. They did not know where the current bacterium had come from, but it must be a new variant. *Y. pestis modernis* must have mutated again. The bad news, as if the news wasn't bad enough already, was that, unlike the last variant from Mariankursk, this one was right up there with *modernis* in terms of ease of transmission, speed of disease progression, and rate of morbidity. This was like the Great Dying.

Ilya replied that if they could, they should try to sequence the new bacterium and send him the genome file. He also decided that it was time to email Prince Tarasov.

§

The next morning, Ilya and Katerinya embarked on the last leg of their journey, down the peninsula of St. Francisburg Bay to Karlsruhe. Ilya had often been to the University in short bursts. Katerinya, of course, had spent four years there. It was a familiar destination for both of them. Because the sabbatical had been a last-minute decision, they hadn't inquired much yet about where to stay in Karlsruhe. They had planned to stay at a hotel until they could find someplace to rent in town, or perhaps a little out of town closer to the coast. These plans were now pushed off the front burner by the epidemic back east. They stored their luggage at the train station and went straight to the biology department at the University. Ilya had colleagues there, and because of that, access to all of the research infrastructure that he had left behind in Derazhne.

They also had good Internet access, of course. Since last night, Ilya had received two email replies: one from his Derazhne team with the genome file, and one from Tarasov. From the Prince, he learned that Kuznetsov had surrendered the same day that the drones had crashed. He related the story of the second batch of the pathogen, as told by Kuznetsov. The politico-religious war was now over (Sokolov had died in prison), but the war with the new bacterium was just beginning. Human-maintained infrastructure was falling apart. They had no effective vaccine or antibiotic to treat it with. He knew he had no more physical leverage over Ilya, but appealed to his empathy for his fellow humans to aid in the battle as best he could. He had heard of the sabbatical, and figured it might be best that he work on the problem at a distance anyway. If he could spearhead an effort at Karlsruhe that would be much appreciated. The Prince even offered to fund the effort if the University was reluctant.

Armed with that, Ilya got the head of the biology department to call an emergency, all-hands-on-deck meeting of the researchers. Ilya explained the challenge in great detail and emphasized that it would soon not be just a problem in the east if the epidemic could not be brought under control soon. He related the details about how the new variant appeared to be as deadly as the one behind the Great Dying. This was the sobering exclamation point he needed to focus the common will. The chairman asked for volunteers to join Ilya in a team effort. He would work out the funding details later. Everyone volunteered. Too many for Ilya to handle. So he proposed that the team be headed up by his senior colleague on the staff there, Charles Hertzog. He would select and organize the team, and Ilya would be the consultant. Later that day, the chairman of the department reported back that the University had agreed to fund the entire effort – whatever it takes. Prince Tarasov's offer to fund it had impressed them. They wanted to do their part.

The team was assembled in short order, and Ilya gave them the initial briefing. He explained how he had cracked the code for the variant in Mariankursk, and that he now had a digital copy of the new variant's genome already in hand. It's possible that the same technique might give them a quick solution to a similarly sized mutation – assuming it was similarly sized, of course. It was a head start. Next they would need some live cultures of the bacterium for testing. There were plenty of these in Derazhne, of course. The problem would be in transporting them to the west coast. The other sovereign railway systems were no longer cooperating with the Principality. Ilya would work on this with the Prince, he told them. If they did come up with an antibiotic or a vaccine, there would be no political problems shipping that back to the east.

Katerinya watched all of this from a distance. She knew more about the ways of science, and the specifics of genomics, since she first met Ilya, but these were always explanations after the fact. Now she was seeing scientific intervention in a human crisis in real time. There was nothing like this in the humanities. No bickering, no turf wars, no endless committee meetings. Everyone was onboard, each person knew their role, and they acted immediately as a single unit. It wasn't a single leader who pulled them into line (though Ilya's quick focusing of the problem helped), it was the common set of facts that they all knew that pulled them into line. She had heard Ilya marvel about the effectiveness of this leaderless tribe before, but now she saw it happening. She still had no desire to be a scientist, but she was glad some people did.

After emailing Tarasov with the good news, and explaining that he needed to arrange for live cultures of the bacterium to get into the external railway system, Ilya and Katerinya reverted to their original mission – finding a place to stay. It didn't take long. A friend of Katerinya's, from her undergraduate days, put them in touch with a professor who had just started a sabbatical of his own. He was looking to rent his house in Karlsruhe during his absence, preferably to a visiting professor on sabbatical to Karlsruhe. The friend had the key, so they looked at the house the same day, even before retrieving their luggage. They both liked it. Deal! They could now skip the hotel and go straight to settling in.

When they set down the suitcases in the sunny, open entranceway of their new temporary home, they both immediately found a comfy chair to drop into. Silence. Calm. Rest. The journey here had been not so much physically taxing as mentally taxing. The ending featured a flurry of worry about things out of their control. But it had ended on an up note. The problems in the east were now linked to possible solutions in the west. Plans were set in motion. It no longer fell on just them now. They could possibly now even enjoy the sabbatical they had planned – though for Ilya it would be a working sabbatical.

Katerinya had planned to let her translation contracts atrophy as she finished them, so that she would eventually be able to work on her novel fulltime, but she got a call later that evening from her old creative writing mentor at Karlsruhe, Ian Corteja. He'd heard from her friend, the one that set up the house deal, that she was back in town for a while and had a job opportunity he wanted to discuss with her – something that combined translating and novel-writing. That seemed intriguing to her, so she arranged to meet him for lunch on the following day, with Ilya of course. That would give Ilya the morning to check on progress with the team at the University.

When Ilya checked in with his team the next morning, there was some good news. Prince Tarasov had arranged with the African consulate in Solinovsk to have African Airlines deliver the live cultures on a non-stop from Solinovsk to St. Francisburg overnight. The normal non-stop commercial flight had been suspended because of the quarantine, but AA was willing to do its part, with some financial assistance from the African Government. No other country on Earth could afford to send a virtually empty jetliner across the continent that quickly. News of the epidemic was getting around the world, and other countries were now invested in the need to keep this epidemic contained and ultimately brought under control. Extra precautions were taken for the flight. Only the minimum pre-quarantined crew with negative tests was on board. They would quarantine again in St. Francisburg before returning. The same protocol and route would be used to bring any vaccine or antibiotic back to Solinovsk. That whittled the Karlsruhe team's agenda down to just finding the biochemical solution. The synthesizing and dosing labs were already gearing up for large scale production once the specific science was in place.

So Ilya was in a good mood when he met Katerinya and Professor Corteja for lunch. He gave a brief report of the progress to

Katerinya, which was all she needed, and then a much longer one for the benefit of Corteja. Her old mentor didn't say so, but he marveled at the fact that Katerinya understood all of this as if she were a biologist. It was certainly over his head without the laymen's tutorial. She was still a cutie, he thought, even more so now. But something had changed. She didn't look quite so young now. It's not that she looked older so much as that she looked more confident now, more in charge. More worldly. That was it. She used to be a wide-eyed innocent, but now she had the bearing of someone who had been through much and survived, and was still none the worse for wear. She looked … wise.

It was a treat for Ilya and Katerinya to be having lunch outside in dappled sunshine in January. It's not that they were surprised, they had just forgotten. For Professor Corteja, this was just another day. Ilya was looking forward to getting reacquainted with the wines here in the heart of Chardonnay country. He preferred the west coast style, particularly the tradition of aging in the species of oak that was indigenous to his continent, with its less dense grain than the oak found on the other side of the world. On the east coast, it usually did no good to ask the waiter about the cooperage of the wines on the list because they usually didn't know. He expected more here. When the waiter came to take drink orders, the group agreed to share a bottle. Katerinya naturally looked to Ilya for the pick. Professor Corteja observed this dynamic carefully. Ilya asked the waiter about the cooperage of two of the Chardonnays on the wine list. He didn't know, but unlike on the east coast, he didn't try to fake it. He volunteered to ask the sommelier. Based on what he came back with, Ilya picked one of them. When the waiter returned for the approval tasting, Ilya was a little underwhelmed based on the description, but he didn't say so. He rarely did. If he was surprised to the upside, he would usually say that. But the point of the approval tasting was to weed out bad wines. This wasn't a bad wine, so he did his usual thoughtful smile and nod.

Corteja was still looking for his footing. After all three glasses were poured and tasted, he effusively praised Ilya's choice, looking toward Katerinya. This was a fine Chardonnay, he said. Ilya found this odd at first. It wasn't a fine Chardonnay. It was just OK. But then Ilya caught the drift. Corteja probably didn't know much about wines, but felt he had to keep up with Ilya in Katerinya's eyes. He took his cue, mistakenly, from Ilya's smile and nod. Goodness and badness in wine are, like the same qualities in literature and art and poetry, determined by veneration, Ilya would tell you. Experts with sufficient standing pronounce the initial judgment, and then others use this as a template for goodness and badness. Corteja took Ilya for an expert, and wanted to assure Katerinya that he too could see genius in winemaking when he tasted it. Only Ilya could see the humor in this. He kept it to himself.

As often happens with wine and good food, the conversation drifted around on many topics, none of them having to do with the initial purpose of the meeting. Katerinya had to give some accounting of her life since Karlsruhe, and since the most interesting parts occurred once she had met Ilya, those accounts dominated. Poor Professor Corteja was having a hopeless time competing with Ilya now. He had once been her older professor/mentor. The person she looked up to. Now it was clear that he had been completely replaced by Ilya. He found it particularly injurious that this scientist was now helping her with her writing. How does that work?

Katerinya was the one who finally got to the point of the meeting. "What was the job opportunity you wanted to talk to me about?"

"Oh yes, that!" They were already on their second bottle (the other Chardonnay this time). "I've been contacted by several foreign publishers who would like to get the novels they have published in their native languages translated for the market on this continent. Some of these novels are quite good. As you know, translating novels is not like translating instruction manuals. You need someone with a literary sensibility. I naturally thought of you."

"I've thought about that before, actually. And I'm pretty sure I don't want to do that."

This was not the response he was expecting. "Why not?"

"I translate to pay the bills. I write for personal fulfillment. These are very different goals."

"But why not combine them? You could pay the bills doing something fulfilling."

"But it wouldn't be fulfilling. For me, it would be agonizing. If these were just plot-driven thrillers or simple stories where he did this and she did that — very concrete, descriptive prose driven by short sentences and one-word adjectives — then yes, it would be like translating instruction manuals. You just have to get the denotations right, mostly. But stylistic prose, elaborate metaphors, sentence fragments strung together poetically to set a mood — these all require you to understand the connotations of whole phrases in the way the author intended, in the author's native language. Then you have to invent collections of words in the target language that would evoke the same mood to a native speaker in that language. You may be better or worse at this than the original author. You may unknowingly turn pedestrian phrases from the original into sublime phrases, or just as unknowingly destroy the original connotations because they struck you differently than the author intended. You are essentially writing a new novel from your own perspective, hoping that it does justice to the original."

"Sort of like translating verse, or song lyrics," Ilya injected.

"Yes! Because the words have to rhyme and fit the meter in the new language."

"And that's not a challenge you would want to take on?" Professor Corteja asked.

"No! Not if these are good novels in their native languages. I wouldn't want the responsibility. It would be harder than writing my own novel. I know what I want to say. I don't have to worry that I'm screwing up what someone else wants to say."

"She has a point, Ian," Ilya smiled. "The best way to combine her two goals is to monetize her personal fulfillment. She's working on it."

"I can see that," he said. There was still wine left, so the conversation drifted on in other directions.

That night, in their pillow talk conversation, Ilya related his take on the "fine Chardonnay" incident. He wasn't trying to ding Corteja, he said, he just found it humorous. Katerinya hadn't picked up on that, but she had picked up on the competition aspect in many other parts of the conversation. "You have to understand, Iliusha, you were mercilessly replacing him."

"Do you think he was jealous? Did he ever have a thing for you?"

"I don't know. I always assumed the crush was mine. I never acted on it. But he did pay a lot of attention to me. He encouraged it, as if he knew."

"But he never said anything?"

"No. But I don't think I was the only one. He had a reputation for that. We saw what we wanted to see, and I think he enjoyed that. He never acted on it."

"And if he had?"

She had to think about that. "That's a very good question. Now that I think about it, I think my crush was based on fantasy. It worked because I thought he would never act. It was safely in my imagination. If he had acted on it, I probably would have run away. That's the difference between you and him. I see it now. I thought he was attractive, but I didn't trust him. I trusted you the minute I saw you. I know you've said this before – about mutual trust – but now I see it. That's why we ended up together. He was the aggressor, or would have been. You were more passive. I initiated things. I *chose* you instead of capitulating to you."

"I prefer it that way," he smiled. "I wait for an invitation. Then I know you're in the mood."

She cuddled up to him. "I'm in the mood."

§

In the first few weeks with the team at Karlsruhe, Ilya was spending most of every day there. He walked them through everything that he had done back at Derazhne to modify the old *modernis* antibiotic, and what he had been working on for a vaccine. These were bright people, many of them senior scientists, and they picked it up quickly. Ilya realized that he might have gotten to the Mariankursk antibiotic more quickly if he had had a team like this at Derazhne.

With Ilya gone, Katerinya spent most of these days working on her novel. It was a little easier here. She alternated between writing at the house, taking her laptop to write in outdoor cafes, and sometimes just out in nature. The new and varied environments put her in a creative mood, and awakened old memories of the west coast that she could draw on for story ideas.

By early spring, both an antibiotic and a vaccine were ready for testing. Testing the antibiotic could be done on live cultures, which they had. Testing the vaccine required two phases: the first for safety and the second for efficacy. Efficacy could only be tested on people exposed to the disease, so that necessarily had to wait until the vaccine was shipped back east. But safety could be tested locally. Just had to make sure there were no unwanted side effects. The news of the epidemic and the University's pivotal role in combatting it had led to plenty of University volunteers. Once these tests were successfully completed, Karlsruhe could begin shipping the drugs east in bulk.

At this point, Ilya's day-to-day role had diminished to part-time consultant. Other people were in charge now, and he could always be reached by phone. So Ilya and Katerinya could now begin to actually enjoy the sabbatical they had come here for. Travel was on their minds. Katerinya had seen some of the sights in this part of the region as a student, but she was not into wine then, so she had never toured the famous wineries. Ilya, who was into wine, knew of many of these wineries, but had actually visited very few. There were so many. So they settled on a four day tour of three wine regions along the central coast – Ilya's suggestion, of course. First they would go up to Klaustohe where the warm, sunny valley produced grapes with high sugar content, which resulted in rich, bold wines. Chardonnay and Cabernet Sauvignon were the two ancient staples. Then they would head down the coast to Mt. Aery, a cooler, often foggy region right on the coast that was home to the best Pinot Noir vineyards. Then they would head well south to Pastorollay, a hilly, slightly inland region that produced a number of grape varieties with a distinct peppery terroir. Ilya's favorite varietal there was Zinfandel.

The next day, they were on the train to Klaustohe. Spring comes early on the west coast, and so do the first spring flowers. These were on vivid display as they moved through the inland valleys. First comes wild mustard, painting the meadows and hillside a bright yellow. Then come the poppies, brushing over the yellow with a golden orange. Finally come the bluefairies with their delicate deep blue. The mustard was in decline by now, the poppies were at their peak, and the bluefairies were just beginning to pop up. The mustard and the poppies were somewhat indigenous to the region. They grew elsewhere, but not in such abundance. Bluefairies, on the other hand, grew everywhere. They were very hardy and could thrive in most soils and climates. The blue blooms lasted into late spring, but the leaves did not die off in the summer as with other perennials. They remained green.

Katerinya had already learned a lot about wine from Ilya since they first met. She had learned how to smell and taste, and was developing a sense of her own palate – the varietals and styles she liked and didn't like. Now she was getting her education furthered in earnest, hearing it directly from the winemakers, and trying sample after sample in the tasting rooms. The couple repeated their experiment in gender-based wine ordering in at least one restaurant in each of their destinations. Sure enough, in Klaustohe and Mt. Aery, the staff got it wrong. They brought the approval tasting to Ilya, even though Katerinya had ordered the bottle. The gender of the waiter didn't seem to matter. In Klaustohe it was a male waiter; in Mt. Aery, it was a female. It wasn't until Pastorollay that they got it right. The waiter brought the bottle to Katerinya for approval. He got a good tip.

They had arrived in Pastorollay in the evening, and planned to tour the wineries the next day. The one Ilya was most interested in had a rather large estate. After doing the tasting room in the morning, they took advantage of a local concession for packing a picnic basket and blanket so that they could have a picnic lunch on the estate. They took their time searching out an inviting venue far away from anyone else. They found a remote, but picturesque spot where they set up their picnic, and imagined that it was their own private estate with its own private grounds. West coast gentility, they were. They had a bottle of wine in the basket, of course. Ilya had insisted that Katerinya pick it herself based on their tastings in the morning. They began the picnic with a toast of her wine.

"Do you think I picked a good wine, Iliusha? Tell me the truth now."

"Did you like it best of all the ones you tasted?"

"Yes."

"Then you picked a good wine."

"No. Really. Did I pick a wine that the experts would say is a good wine?"

"Who are these experts?"

"I don't know. You for instance."

"I thought all of the wines this morning were good, or good enough. There were no bad ones. I liked your pick second best."

"Why didn't you tell me?" she protested. "How am I to learn what the best ones are if you don't tell me?"

"Let's suppose you read three novels. The first you really didn't care for, the second was OK, and the third really appealed to you. So now you want to read more by the third author. Then you learned that the experts said the first one was the best – the publishers, the reviewers, the prize committee, the board that makes the list of the greatest novels of the 41st century all said the first one is pure genius. Would you like it any better then? Would you force yourself to read more books by this author in order to learn to recognize good novels?"

"No ..."

"Then you picked a good novel according to the only standard that matters – yours. And you picked a good wine according to the same standard."

"But aren't there classes people take to learn how to appreciate good wines? Don't sommeliers have to sit for these very detailed exams to prove they can recognize good wines?"

"They do. But what is being taught is how to recognize *venerated* wine. Goodness by consensus of influencers. If this consensus doesn't agree with your own palate, what's the point? The value of these classes is to learn how to taste what is venerated without looking at the label. Many people still can't do it. In a blind tasting they get it wrong more often than not."

"Then why bother?"

"To me, the value of wine education is to learn to recognize *characteristics* of wine – tannins, acidity, oak resin, dryness, grape varieties, aging – so you can determine which of these characteristics you like and don't like. Then you can pick out wines that are good according to your palate. Why drink wine otherwise?"

"But why does everyone want to follow the experts? Why would you drink a wine you don't particularly care for, just because the experts say you should?"

"That ... is the key question of veneration. Why indeed! I think what makes this system work is that people who follow the experts get pleasure from following them – from being judged by their peers as being able to recognize wine-making genius. The taste is secondary. It's an acquired taste, they say. The real pleasure comes from getting it right, or from being perceived by others as getting it right."

By now, the accumulation of wines (the morning's and the one recommended by Katerinya the expert) and the dappled sunshine were beginning to take their toll on the couple – in a good way. They were sitting on the blanket in a haze of happiness. Nowhere to go, nothing to do. Then Katerinya got that playful look in her eyes that Ilya knew so well.

"Iliusha, let's take our clothes off."

"Here?"

"Yes, why not? No one can see us. We're out in the middle of nature! Haven't you ever wanted to do that? To live like the animals, carefree and natural? We can enjoy our private space out here under the open sky. And it will still be private!"

"The birds and the squirrels will see us," he smiled.

She smiled too, still with that playful look. "They don't count. As long as other humans don't see us, it's just as private as being in our own bedroom. Don't you think?"

He liked the idea, but agreed that privacy was the key to this freedom. "I think we're still too close to civilization. There might be people walking the grounds. You don't want them to watch, do you?"

"No! And I guess I don't want to worry about that happening either. It would destroy the mood. Couldn't we go somewhere more remote? Farther away from here?"

Ilya looked around. "Well, the estate is large. And there don't appear to be any border fences into the hills. I suppose we could go further into the wilderness. It looks like the eastern hills just roll on and on without any sign of civilization."

"Let's go there, then!" She started eagerly packing up the picnic things and rolling up the blanket. Ilya helped. They trekked east, over several hills and into a secluded valley. They still had a sumptuous view of the landscape and an open sky. Since it was early spring, the grass was still green and the wildflowers were out. This particular valley was covered in bluefairies. This looked like the place. Katerinya was so eager to get started that she began undressing before Ilya had even put the picnic basket down. She reassembled the picnic scene with the blanket while Ilya undressed. Now they could resume where they left off. They toasted with the wine once more.

"Don't you just feel free, Iliusha?" To make her point, she jumped up and ran through the grass, waving her arms, then twirled with her arms out in a manner that reminded him of the first private fashion show she had done for him at Tallinnskaya Street – minus the dress, of course.

"Yes, I feel free. But pirouettes aren't my thing," he smiled. "I love watching you do them, though. I feel them vicariously through you. Like so many things." She knew that to be true. He often watched her do things that made her happy. And that made him happy by extension.

"Maybe we should make some natural clothes. Then we can go for a walk in nature." She returned to the blanket, fashioned a laurel wreath out of bluefairies and placed it on his head. It was a little too small, so he put it on her head instead.

Then he admired the vision. "I wish we had a mirror so you could see. It looks perfect on you." He then fashioned a simple bluefairy necklace, imitating the skill he had just learned from her. She put it on him. Then the two walked hand in hand, clad in their natural finest, through the valley of the bluefairies. Ilya was right. The squirrels were watching. But they didn't understand this either.

Chapter 11

THE PRESERVER OF LIFE

When spring finally came to the east coast, the spring rains came, ushering in the renewal of life. The rains fell on once dormant grass, rehydrating the crowns of the plants to allow them to grow new green shoots. The rains fell on trees, propagating a soothing background sound as the drops splattered through the still immature leaves sprouting and growing in their crowns. The rains formed puddles where mosquitos laid eggs to start the cycle of their next generation. And the rains fell on the dead body of Mrs. Stegnova, which lay slumped over the rotting concession stand, next to the grass, under the trees, near the puddles, in the ruins of Aron Mattson's theme park.

The day before she had succumbed to the plague, back in Lirovo, she had bought a cucumber, a jar of pickles, and some bread at the local market. For lunch she had eaten some of all three – stealing the life of the cucumber, the life of the bacteria that were themselves stealing the life of the pickled cucumbers more slowly, and the life of the yeast and what remained of the life of the wheat that foreshadowed the bread. Now that she had died, and her immune system had shut down, the bacteria, and the fungi, and to some degree the plants (decomposition adds nitrogen to the soil) were returning the favor, eating her, stealing what remained of her more complex life to make more versions of their much simpler lives. Animals joined the feast as well, with wolves and rats scavenging the corpse. Biological entropy.

The rains fell on the Ark, accelerating the dry rot of the wooden roof and the entry planks. These were human-made structures produced from the previous lives of trees, now being reclaimed by fungi. The sides of the Ark were spared because they were covered in pitch. More biological entropy.

The rains fell on the metal and plastic parts of the Parade of Animals, rusting their joints, cracking and discoloring their skins, and shorting the circuits in their exposed wiring. The rains fell on the metals of the tracks and cables that were built to pull the menagerie through its daily boarding and disembarking of the Ark, slowly decomposing them through oxidation. Mineral entropy.

The plague had come swiftly to Aron Mattson's theme park due to the direct hit by one of the drones. Its primary casualties of course were human. The bacterial population surged to life as the human population that it infected declined. The changing of the regimes was all the more rapid because of the concentrations of both people and airborne bacteria intermingling. With no immunity, natural or man-made, the bacteria had free rein of the human bodies, leaving their corpses strewn over the grounds, the venues, the exhibits, and the Ark, including inside, outside, and on the boarding planks. When the guides and the operators and the maintenance men succumbed, there was no one left to maintain the buildings and the wiring and the plumbing and the attractions. These were now showing signs of weathering and stress.

Inside the head house that contained the Parade of Animals, a dead operator had remained slumped over his console for several months, his corpse slowly decomposing. The closed circuit TV was still showing scenes of the slowly decomposing bodies inside the Ark for him to not look at. But about a week ago, his decomposing corpse had lost enough critical mass that gravity had pulled it off the console and chair and deposited it below on the long aluminum footboard. What had been designed, with the best of intentions, as a safety switch for stopping the parade due to an incapacitated operator releasing the footboard became a switch for starting the parade because an incapacitated operator was now pressing the footboard with what remained of his whole body. So the Parade of Animals had been running every day now for the past week – up into the Ark in the morning, and back out from the Ark in the evening – squeaking and grinding against the unlubricated tolerances between rusting track and cables.

With the insulation of their wires exposed and short-circuiting, and their rusting joints catching and snagging, some of the animals were malfunctioning a little. As the cable pulled the parade up the planks, the ostrich pair became entangled because the long leg of the male had snapped, sending him leaning into the female, whose long neck in turn wrapped around his. The preprogrammed motions of the necks, designed to move independently, were now colliding in a jumble of jerky motions that looked like either an elaborate mating dance, or a fight to the death. One of the elephant's trunks lost its ability to retract and became entangled in the rear legs of the zebra in front of it. The zebra now appeared to be bucking against the goosing of the trailing elephant. On the first few days of the parade, the robotic animals had to knife through human corpses covering the planks and pens, sometimes getting snarled until the motor driving the cable managed to push through, shedding the corpses like a snowplow. Now some of the animals were beginning to break off at their cable attachments and became new obstacles to be snagged or plowed away as the parade progressed. All the while, the robots of Noah and his wife stood at the top of the plank work, welcoming the disabled animals into the Ark with their coordinated sweeping gestures. "Welcome to the *Preserver of Life*," he said.

At 9:00 this morning, right on schedule, the parade sprang to life once again, creaking and grinding and plowing up the boarding planks. The designed sounds of the animals were now being drowned out by squealing shrieks of metal on metal. About halfway through the parade, the main cable finally snapped, sending the animals behind the rupture tumbling backward down the ramps, crashing into each other, breaking apart, and piling up in huge mound at the base of the Ark. Heads and limbs and necks and antlers and tusks and wings went flying in all directions. The animals ahead of the break first slid backward off of the cable until one of them became snagged and formed the new caboose of the train. This remaining train of animals was pulled into the Ark, bypassing the designed stopping point, and collapsing into each other like an accordion, squeaking, growling, bending, crushing into a mass of animal parts.

At the entrance to the Ark, where Noah and his wife were still cycling through their welcoming routine, a giraffe, one of the last animals ahead of the cable break, was jolted so violently that its long neck partially broke off of its body and swung wildly in a circle, just missing Noah, but severing Mrs. Noah at the waist. The upper portions of both the giraffe and Mrs. Noah splattered against the inner walls of the Ark, sending mechanical parts flying among the human corpses. As the one and a half giraffes were drawn crushing into the inner mass of animals, Noah somehow survived, still welcoming with his recorded phrase and sweeping gesture.

Then a transformer exploded with a deafening blast, sending a ball of flames skyward. The concussion from the explosion sent human and robot parts flying while the heat from the flames ignited the pitch on the Ark's surface. God's original instructions for covering the Ark with pitch were to preserve the wood from the coming floodwaters. But this Ark, of course, wasn't destined for a real flood. Mattson had insisted on a real pitch coating for authenticity. It did fortuitously protect the sides from dry rot, but had just the opposite effect in the presence of fire.

As the flames rapidly engulfed the Ark, accelerated by the pitch, Noah finally short-circuited, his movements becoming comically grotesque as he gestured through the empty portion of his half-missing wife repeating, "Welcome to the *Preserver of Life*, Welcome to the *Preserver of Life*." As the flames rose higher, tempered a bit by the spring rain, the frame of the Ark collapsed in on itself, leaving only a singular Noah and half his wife saying, "Welcome to the *Preserver of Life*, Welcome to the *Preserver of Life*, Wel ... *server of Life*, *of Life*, *Life*, *Life*, *Life*, ...

In Solinovsk and Derazhne though, the renewal of life was beginning in the opposite direction, if more slowly. The original bacterial hegemony had come from the skies, raining down on the humans below and decimating their numbers. But just as the bacteria and the fungi and the plants and the animals were gaining the upper hand, the seeds for a new hegemony were descending from the skies – in the form of African Airlines jets carrying vaccines and antibiotics. As these flowed into the hands of administrators and caregivers, then into the bodies of the remaining humans, one particular bacterium that had ruled the roost for months was suddenly being decimated. It was losing new hosts to infect, and being killed off in the ones already infected. Humans take a lot longer to reproduce than bacteria, so this event was not so much a renewal of life as a setting of the stage for a later renewal. But it did halt the decline of human lives. It was a preserver of what was left of life.

Chapter 12

A FAMILY OF ORPHANS

As spring turned into summer, and summer into fall, at their west coast home in Karlsruhe, Ilya and Katerinya watched the slow progression of encouraging news from the east. First the human trials were successful, then the mass inoculations began, then the new infection rate gradually approached zero, then the quarantine was lifted. People could travel in and out of the Principality once more, full rail service had resumed, and cell service was improving. The region had taken a big hit, though, and the reconstruction was just beginning. Their scheduled sabbatical was officially over, and it was now safe to return to the east coast once more. Tanned and rested, they boarded the train in St. Francisburg with their passage booked all the way across the continent to Mariankursk. It was now possible to do this once again. They took the shorter route back this time. They were no longer touring, they were returning to what was left of home.

The more southerly route east was as Katerinya had described it. Crossing the two mountain ranges was similar to the crossings in the north, except for the absence of snow.

The prairie was indeed flatter, and this being fall, dry and brown, not snow-covered. Once the forests were encountered, the scenes changed to deep greens. It was early fall and more southerly, so the leaves had not yet turned. But they would be turning by the time they reached the northeast, with the maples leading the way.

When Ilya and Katerinya finally reached the first few towns inside the Principality, the reds and oranges of the maples against the greens of the later-turning hardwoods provided a welcome relief from the memories of snow-covered destruction they had witnessed on the trip west. These were the towns hardest hit by the war, which destroyed buildings, but the least affected by the epidemic, which destroyed people. The quick shutdown of the railroads had confined the epidemic to the Derazhne/Solinovsk area (and Lirovo), so maintenance didn't suffer and reconstruction started earlier. Mariankursk was perhaps the luckiest of all of the towns on the line. It was just far enough west from the epidemic, and just far enough east from the war. So it managed to keep almost all of its buildings and its people. It looked remarkably the same to Ilya and Katerinya as the train pulled into Mariankursk Station.

The waitress in the station café had lost track of Anna and Dmitri since their departure to the west just before the epidemic hit last winter. She had other things to worry about. The epidemic had suspended rail traffic, and thus reduced the usual number of patrons for the station café. It still functioned as a lunchtime destination for locals, but was no longer profitable for the evenings. She got allotted some of the lunchtime hours, but it was not enough to earn a living, so she had taken other part-time work in town to get by. She had suspended her mental stories about Anna and Dmitri soon after they left, for lack of input. Then she had stopped her stories about passengers in general once there no longer were any. When the quarantine ended, and rail service resumed, and she could return to her evening shift full-time, she had begun to imagine passenger stories once more, but Anna and Dmitri had been long since forgotten.

Tonight, as she was serving coffee, a couple among the incoming passengers from the west caught her eye. What's this? Dmitri and Anna? Yes, it was them. With all of their luggage. They've come back! They looked good – tanned and healthy and in good spirits. I wonder where they've been. What they were doing. What they're up to now. The long dormant story thread suddenly reemerged. Ideas abounded.

The walk from the station back to Tallinnskaya Street was a homecoming for Katerinya, reminding her of her first return to Mariankursk from the west coast all those years ago. It was the same season – early fall. Ilya had never seen Mariankursk in the fall (as far as he could remember), so the red and orange against the green was a new scene. He knew this scene from the point of view of Derazhne, where the fall colors signaled the start of another academic year. Here it was more rural, and the color more intense because of the colder nights. He noticed the humidity in the air once again. When you live with it, you don't notice it. The west coast was more arid. He noticed the dryness when they first arrived there, but then became accustomed to it. A couple more days and the humidity here would seem normal again.

10 Tallinnskaya Street looked pretty much how they had left it. There were a lot of good memories associated with the rooms of the apartment upstairs, and a few negative ones associated with the area near the backstairs. But they had survived those, and now the area was associated with the woodshed and the need for Ilya to split more kindling. September is the warmest month of the year in Karlsruhe, but the start of the cold night season in Mariankursk. It was time for fires once again. Ilya split some kindling and started fires for the front room and the bedroom. Katerinya drew them a hot bath. Then they settled in for the night, back in their country home in the northeast once again.

§

After nine months on the west coast, far from the reach of the troubles that had stalked them here, Ilya and Katerinya no longer felt the need to go everywhere together. They still often did just because they preferred each other's company, but it wasn't a necessary precaution for Katerinya's safety anymore. So after breakfast on the next morning, they planned to visit Olena first, then Ilya would be off to the hospital to get up to speed on the epidemic while Katerinya stayed at Olena's for more detailed catching up. Mariankursk, as far as they knew, was still wholly intact. Tomorrow, they would embark on the much more arduous catching up in Derazhne where they already knew there would be missing persons.

Olena was sooo glad to see them. The couple had forgotten how emaciated Ilya looked when Olena last saw them, but Olena hadn't. "You both look so healthy now! And look at those tans. Did you spend every day at the beach out there?"

"You don't have to go to the beach," Ilya said. "The sun comes to you."

For once, Ilya and Katerinya didn't have harrowing stories to tell. They had had a normal, relaxed life for nine months, except for the worries about what was going on back here. Olena told them that after the brief occupation by Kuznetsov, things had been pretty normal in Mariankursk, though they were under a less restrictive quarantine for a while, waiting out the epidemic in Derazhne and Solinovsk. No one complained about that. The swapping of stories did seem a little anticlimactic after every other exchange since Ilya had arrived on the scene. They all agreed that this amounted to a net improvement. Then Ilya was off to the hospital.

Olena was still beaming as Katerinya related stories and details about their time out west. She was living vicariously through Katerinya. But when it came her turn to account for her time in Mariankursk, her mood changed. There wasn't much to tell, she said.

Katerinya picked up on this and asked if anything was wrong. "Nothing," was the answer. But Katerinya knew better.

"Olena, please tell me. One minute you're happy then the next you seem sad."

So Olena came out with it. "I'm so happy for you, that you've found someone like Ilya. He's perfect for you."

"But … ?"

"But I don't think I'm going to find someone."

"Oh, Olena, you'll find someone. I'm sure of it."

"Why are you so sure? I'm not like you. It was so much easier for you – not just because your prettier, but because you're more 'out there' – more of a risk taker. I just don't know how to get started."

"Me, a risk taker? Where did you get that idea? I always thought I was too passive – that all of my romances were in my imagination. I loved men vicariously through novels."

"But you had an affair as soon as you got to college – with the dreamy professor."

"No! There was no affair!"

"But your letters …"

"My letters were just more of my imagination. I told you about what I felt and wished for. But none of that ever happened…"

"Then, when was your first time?"

"With Ilya."

"You were a virgin?"

"Yes. Is that so surprising? It's a difficult business. I'm only less than two years ahead of you, Olena. You'll find someone. I know it."

Olena had to momentarily adjust her perception of her friend. "Was it what you expected?"

"No … it wasn't. It was very different from what I had imagined. I always thought that men chased women, and women played hard to get. You had to like him, of course, but if he was persistent enough, he would eventually wear you down until you gave in. Then you would accept him and ... and then all of your fantasies would come true. Isn't that silly? I don't think I ever believed that last part. But novels don't give you much more to go on. Living with a biologist, I've learned that this pretty much matches how it goes with all of the other animals – right up until the end. I don't think animals have fantasies. Humans have these extra dimensions to their love lives that we don't really understand very well."

"So neither of the professors chased you?"

"Corteja did. He took the initiative. I very much felt pursued. And I liked that at the time. I thought I was on the fast track. Fortunately, he never acted. He just persisted, waiting for me to surrender, I think. I didn't know how to do that. So nothing ever happened. I told Ilya this – that if Corteja had acted, I probably would have run away. That part of the scenario just didn't come naturally to me."

"And Ilya?"

"No. He never chased. And I never felt pursued. I was a little disappointed at first because this didn't match the script. But I could tell, in his own passive way, that he was attracted to me. It was a lot less exciting than with Corteja – but in a good way. I felt safe, all the way through the process. No one chased anyone. We just sort of started walking in the same direction at the same time."

Olena was anxiously waiting to hear the next stage of the story, but Katerinya appeared to believe she had given the full answer. So Olena skipped right to the end. "And then your fantasies came true?"

The question caused Katerinya to reflect for a moment. She wanted to get this right. "No. It has turned out differently than I imagined. I'm much more involved than I thought I would be. If one of us goes first, it's usually me. Ilya likes that, and now I do too. It's much friendlier that way."

Olena was certainly not expecting this. She was struggling to come up with a response, so Katerinya intervened.

"I know what you're wondering, Olena. A man who doesn't initiate? Perhaps I didn't say that right. Usually no one initiates. When you aren't wearing any clothes at bedtime, there's no preparation necessary. It just happens. It's the less usual times, in the middle of the day, where I'm usually the instigator. This is where we deviate from the other animals, I think. The male usually does something to the female. We don't do things *to* each other, we do things *with* each other. There's no conquering or capitulation."

Olena was still trying to digest this. "What about wooing? Isn't that the human way? You know, flowers and candy and all that?"

Katerinya smiled and reflected at the same time. "No ... no wooing I guess. Neither of us needs to be seduced or convinced or brought around to something we aren't already inclined to do. I guess we're just different. As I said, this never occurred in my fantasies. Reality is better."

"But what about the first time? Was he a virgin too? How did you know what to do?"

Katerinya smiled at this. "No, he most certainly wasn't a virgin. He knew exactly what to do. But it's pretty simple, Olena. There's not much to figure out."

"So he was the initiator the first time?"

Another pause for reflection. "No, I wouldn't say that. We had a strange courtship. It wasn't even a courtship, really. We both knew early on. I think each of us was waiting for the other to go first, but we both knew where we were going. Then suddenly the opportunity was there. He had to stay the night. The rest was easy."

§

The next day, as their train pulled into Derazhne Station, the damage that Katerinya and Ilya were afraid they would see was not that visible. Biological warfare is a clean sort of warfare. It silently destroys people, not buildings. This leaves an awful mess, but once the bodies are removed, everything looks normal again, if not quite as populous. Services and governmental infrastructures atrophy without the human maintainers, such as cell service, but this leaves no visible scars. If the maintenance comes back in a reasonable amount of time, the physical structures escape the ravages of entropy. And that's what happened here. Things were working again, and nothing physical got permanently broken. But many families and friends and associates and human psyches got permanently broken. It was a recovering place, but not a cheerful place. Ilya and Katerinya could sense this, just walking around the campus.

They had heard about some of the faces that would be missing before they arrived, and learned of others as they sat and talked with survivors. Ove Alfhildovich Ekholm, the chairman of Ilya's department, had perished, as had Ilya's most senior research associate. The biology department would have to be reorganized. Maksim Klavaevich Egorov, Ilya's co-lecturer from the history department, also didn't make it. That would be the end of the famous lecture series. And the Kadnikovs, both President Kadnikov and Mrs. Kadnikova, had died, putting an end to the annual Crispness party. It wasn't held last year because of the epidemic, and now, it appeared, it might never be offered again.

There was some good news. Andzhelina Gullovna had survived because she had fortuitously left Derazhne just before the drones hit. She was now back on campus, and looking into perhaps being the sponsor of the traditional Crispness party. Her place was too small, of course, but the Kadnikovs had willed their entire estate, including the mansion and grounds, to the University. So the original venue might still be a possibility. Everyone left was encouraging her to do it this year. It was just the sort of thing the community needed, they said.

And Diederick Brandt had survived. He had holed up in his house, managing to avoid human contact during the worst of it, but was infected right about the time the African Airlines jets were landing. The antibiotic from Karlsruhe saved him just in time.

Archbishop Osipov had survived. Pastor Sokolov had not. His entire set of co-conspirators perished with him in prison after it took a direct hit. His evangelical church had been taken over by a new pastor who was much more like a shepherd than a firebrand. The character of the congregation had changed too, not just because its prior leader had died, but also because so many of its more radical members had died too, either in the enclave conflicts or from the epidemic. Prince Tarasov had survived and was now leading the full-scale recovery effort. There seemed to be a general appreciation among the public now for how he handled both the war and the epidemic. For once, everyone seemed to prefer having someone competent in charge during a time of relative peace. Perhaps it was a new beginning.

The public vaccination effort was still continuing, with small pop-up clinics set up all over the two cities. There was a combination clinic and recruitment table set up in the Quad where passersby were urged to get a shot if they didn't have one already. Ilya and Katerinya didn't need this because they got their shots before they left Karlsruhe. Otherwise they might have approached the table. If they had, they would have recognized Yulia Katyaevna both recruiting for and administering the vaccine. She turned out to be one of the few people on campus, or in either of the cities really, with natural immunity to the bacterium. She learned this the hard way, as everyone around her was dying and she was not. So she had volunteered early on to aid the sick and the dying. It was grueling, and sometimes gruesome work. She could attend to patients that doctors could not, so she was often the only one present when they died. Her parents, many childhood friends, and several of her university classmates had succumbed to the disease. Yet she kept plugging along, putting in the long hours, resting when she could.

Because they didn't stop at her table, Ilya and Katerinya didn't see her, but when she looked up from finishing an injection and stamping the patient's card, she spotted them. At first she wasn't sure. She had not heard about the sabbatical, as everything at the University had come crashing down on the day they had left. She assumed that Ilya had died along with everyone else, since she had not seen or heard from him since. She had guessed Katerinya might be safe, living in Mariankursk. But this certainly looked like the two of them, right over there in the Quad. Her first inclination was to drop everything and run to them. But then she caught herself, and let her associate know that she would be right back. She walked, rather than ran, just fast enough to intercept them. It was a controlled walk by her body, masking the emotional chaos going on in her mind.

Katerinya was the first to recognize her. "Yulia! Look, Ilya, it's Yulia!" They both turned toward her as she stopped in front of them. She smiled at them, almost timidly, but something in her expression was off, they both thought. She looked careworn and weary – it made her look much older than they remembered. But she carried herself stoically, in charge, absorbed in the care of others while suppressing her own feelings. At first, she calmly related the story of her transformation into the caregiver role as everyone she knew was dying. She had been given a reprieve from death, and felt a responsibility to use this gift where it was most needed. This was clearly hard on her, both Ilya and Katerinya thought. The retched circumstances had caused her to grow up too fast. They sensed she was harboring a little survivor's guilt.

Then her stoic expression began to break down. Her lower lip quivered a little, then she threw her arms around Ilya, and embraced him as tightly as she could, sobbing uncontrollably. "I thought you were dead too, like everyone else." Ilya's response was involuntary. He held her tightly, comfortingly. Katerinya reacted to the drama before her without the slightest hint of jealousy. She was a senior stateswoman of love now, long past any insecurity about possible rivals. She knew Yulia had a thing for Ilya, and though there was likely an element of this in the mix of emotions, she could feel Yulia's profound grief, the dam breaking after holding it in for so long. Ilya was an emotional refuge for her, the only survivor of intimates from her happier days, a chance to drop her stoic exterior and surrender to her nascent vulnerability. Katerinya ached for her. She embraced them both in a three-way huddle and held on as tightly as she could as well. "I'm sorry," Yulia sobbed. "No, don't be sorry," Katerinya quickly consoled her. "Let it all out. Have a good cry. We are here for you."

And she meant 'we.' When Yulia's catharsis abated, Katerinya invited her to stay with them for a little while, at Ilya's place, even though she and Ilya had not even returned there themselves yet. This nuanced rescue endeared Katerinya to Ilya all the more. She had rescued them both. He did not know how he would have handled the situation, particularly with Katerinya, had she not been so thoroughly perceptive, and mature beyond her years. He was used to being Katerinya's guardian, her advisor, her tutor in the ways of the world. Now she was the grownup in the room. The caretaker. The emotional rock when others were struggling for a foothold.

Katerinya continued to take the lead. She didn't want Yulia to be forced to revert to her stoic role before she had a proper time to grieve. So she went to the vaccination table and asked Yulia's associate if she could take over for the rest of the day. Yulia had something urgent she needed to attend to right now, she said. In Katerinya's mind, she really did. It wasn't just an excuse. When she returned to Yulia and Ilya, she said, "I think now would be a good time to just go home for the day, don't you, Iliusha?" Ilya caught the drift. He went to retrieve the luggage they had left at Dahlström Hall while Katerinya took Yulia to their house.

Yulia was still pretty quiet when the two of them arrived at the house. Katerinya knew she had some work to do. She had to help her let down her guard and let her emotions run free for a while. She made some tea, then sat next to her and tried to approximate the role of big sister. They did have some things in common. Both had lost their parents while in college. Both had a crush on an older professor. Yulia was reticent to admit this, of course, but Katerinya encouraged her to let it out. She knew, she said. It was OK, perfectly natural. She understood. It had happened to Katerinya twice, she said. She opened up a little about the differences between Ilya and Corteja, and how in retrospect, Yulia had made a better first choice. Katerinya felt very big sisterly at that point, ready to recommend looking for the Ilya's of the world and avoiding the Cortejas, but then she thought better of it. This was Katerinya's own preference. Maybe it wouldn't generalize to Yulia. She should let her find her own path.

The therapy appeared to be working. Yulia opened up more and more. She never had a big sister. Is this what it was like? Katerinya told her that she didn't have one either. They were both only children. That added another layer to the bonding. Slowly, the involuntary smiles of a young undergraduate returned. She looked less burdened. She wasn't so utterly alone anymore. Nothing could undo what she had gone through. She was unalterably changed a little. But now it was more a little than a lot.

When Ilya arrived, Yulia made a point of embracing Katerinya, to show that she was equally grateful that she had survived too – and saying so. That was good therapy for Katerinya. She had never had a little sister. Was this what it was like? Later that night, during their pillow talk, Ilya remarked about the change he saw in Yulia after Katerinya's time with her. She was closer now to the Yulia they once knew. Katerinya agreed, and suggested they encourage her to stay with them, making her feel welcomed until Yulia herself volunteered it was time to go back to her dorm. It would be good therapy for all three of them.

§

There were still two more survivors that Ilya and Katerinya had intended to see before their day was cut short by the encounter with Yulia – Andzhelina and Diederick Brandt. Ilya suggested they pay back Andzhelina for hosting them during the hide-out phase by inviting her for dinner at their house. Andzhelina accepted immediately and suggested that she and Katerinya be the joint chefs again. She could come early in the afternoon. Since Katerinya did not know Diederick Brandt that well – he was more a fast friend of Ilya's – she suggested that Ilya visit with him solo in the afternoon while she and Andzhelina did the cooking. Sounded like a good plan to all concerned. Yulia had breakfast with them, then set off for a day of vaccination work. She would come back in time for dinner. Ilya and Katerinya thought this would be a good regimen, rotating her back into the world where she would feel useful, and then back to where she had the support of friends.

As Ilya walked through the Quad on his way to the Divinity School, he reflected once again, as he did every fall, on the irony of the academic calendar in the northern hemisphere. At the University, fall ushers in a new beginning. The color of the leaves and the cooler air are associated with seeing classmates and colleagues again after the diaspora of the summer. Classes are starting again, majors are being contemplated, new ideas and aspirations are being born. But from nature's point of view, this is the beginning of the dying season, the last hurrah before the colors and the leaves disappear, the greens turn to browns, including the ever-present bluefairy leaves, and most plants enter dormancy. Then in the spring, when nature is being reborn, the academic agendas are in their last hurrah. Courses are ending for the year, seniors are graduating, friends and classmates say goodbye, some for the last time in their lives. Even commencement, which means 'beginning' is more often thought to mean 'the ending', 'the last ceremony' before it's all over. This year there was a double irony. The worst of the dying had occurred in the early spring. Now the human community was being reborn, if not yet the bodies. At least the worst of it was now over.

Diederick Brandt was still recovering from the longer-term effects of the disease, but he was in his office. "Reading, writing, and contemplating," he pointed out, "are activities tailor-made for recovery. I guess I'm in the right profession. But you look good. Much better than I recall the last time you were here."

Ilya couldn't say the same about Diederick.

"Oh, go ahead and say it. I don't look so good as last time, eh?"

"Not as good, but still not bad, considering."

"That's very diplomatic. And how is your fair lady?"

"Tanned, like me," he smiled. "Will you be teaching this term?"

"No, I'm not quite there yet. I prefer being at the office after so much time cloistered at my house. I hope to be ready by the winter term. And you?"

"That's still being worked out. As you may have heard, my department took a pretty big hit. I suppose I should be thankful that the war is over and things are looking up again, but I can't help feeling that this is just a cycle. That it will happen again."

"Epidemics or wars?"

"Wars, mostly. Epidemics are relatively rare on their own. This one was a side effect of war. We can stop epidemics with vaccines and antibiotics. We don't have a cure for war."

"And I suppose my profession is responsible for a good many of them."

"Not all of them. There are plenty of secular wars as well. The root problem is human nature. Too many followers bound together in tribes with uncompromising leaders. Religion just makes it worse."

"And as I recall, you lay this all at the feet of evolution, am I right?"

"Yes, that's the most confounding thing about it. Tribalism has so much survival value for the species as a whole that we are defined by it. It makes it more likely that our species will survive, but not that we will enjoy the ride along the way."

"And you can't fix evolution?"

"We can. We've improved other parts of our nature by intervening. Starvation and malnutrition used to be much more common until we invented agriculture, for instance. My favorite intervention is language. Evolution gave us natural language. It's not very precise. We make mistakes and misunderstand each other all the time, but it's adequate. We can do so much more with it than without it. But then we used our brains and formalized language into mathematics and logic. Now we have completely precise and unambiguous formal languages that make science possible. Would that we could do the same sort of intervention with tribes."

"What would that look like?"

"I don't know … democracy, for instance. The Africans have it. Democracy is a man-made intervention in social organization. You still have tribes, but the leaders have to be elected by consent of the followers. Leaders can be removed by the consent of the followers. It forces more compromise. You have another way for achieving leadership change than by killing each other. But I'm afraid it's just as foreign to people as formal language. It doesn't come naturally. Some external force would need to put such a regime in place and enforce it. It would have to be set up initially by undemocratic means. That's the irony."

"Yes, I don't see that happening in religious tribes. The leaders are divine," he smiled.

"What if this is the necessary cost of being human? What if the only way for our species to survive is for us to be unhappy on average? I suppose we are the only species that has happiness, or at least unhappiness. So maybe this is a cost all surviving species have to bear. Other species don't know when they are unhappy. It's easier for them, I think. You have to be able to reflect back on the times you were happy and then compare that to what you are missing now You're frustrated by knowing life could be better."

"I suppose that's where we part ways, Ilya. I have the happiness of my faith to fall back on. You know, 'wishful thinking' as you call it.

§

Andzhelina arrived at the house soon after Ilya had left for the Divinity School, carrying two bags with the foodstuffs she and Katerinya had agreed on for tonight's dinner. She was surprised to learn that Ilya didn't have a wine cellar. That was so unlike him, she said. "He doesn't have *any* cellar, that's the problem," Katerinya explained. "But he always keeps some wines in a rack in the library." Andzhelina checked there and decided that the selection would be adequate for the dinner they had planned. Then they got to work.

Andzhelina had not yet heard the full story about Yulia, only the passing reference to her hosting the hideout prior to the one at Andzhelina's house. So Katerinya filled her in on both the pre-epidemic friendship story, the terrible trauma she had gone through during the epidemic, and the current rescue effort.

"So she's *staying* with you too? I thought you had just invited her for dinner."

"She's staying with us for as long as it takes. She's been through a lot, and has no one left. We're her family and her friends now. We're a family of orphans. We've adopted each other."

Andzhelina was unsure how to interpret this. "You mean literally? You and Ilya have both lost your parents?"

"Yes. I lost mine to a train accident when I was in college. Same age as Yulia."

"I'm so sorry! I didn't know. And Ilya?"

Suddenly Katerinya realized that they were in memory loss territory. Ilya did not want this to get out. Andzhelina was probably safe by now, but that was Ilya's call. So she tried to finesse the reply. "He lost his parents too. It's complicated. You'll have to ask him about it. On second thought, don't ask him. He doesn't like to talk about that." And all of this was true!

"Oh! OK." The orphan part had sidetracked Andzhelina's next question. Then she remembered where she was going. "What's that like – living with someone who still carries a torch for Ilya?"

"It's fine. Yulia opened up to me about it … well, after some coaxing. I'm like her big sister now." Then she thought to herself, if I'm her big sister, does that make Andzhelina my mother? Not *my* mother. She's nothing like that. But *a* mother? A mother figure? Nah, after a certain age, all adults are peers. And besides, Andzhelina was definitely not a mother figure. "I know what crushes on professors are like."

"But she is much younger than when you met Ilya."

"But the same age as when I met Corteja."

"You had a thing with Ian Corteja?"

"Just a crush. Not a thing. He had a reputation for pursuing young ingénues." The conversation with Olena was fresh in her mind. It had yielded some valuable insight about her relations with men, and Ilya in particular. But Olena was like a twin sister. Andzhelina was not. So she went for the summary. "Let's just say I made the right choice between him and Ilya."

"Ian Corteja ... I didn't know about this reputation."

"I think it was only local to Karlsruhe. Anyway, I think I understand what Yulia is going through with Ilya. I hope she meets someone like him someday."

"And you don't worry that she already has? Do you think Ilya might be attracted to her?"

"I'm sure he is. I'd be surprised if he wasn't. And that doesn't bother me at all. Neither of them are the kind of person that would act on attraction in a situation like this. I admit, I don't know Yulia all that well, but I do know Ilya. Very well. I'm completely safe."

Andzhelina didn't doubt it. Just then, Yulia arrived, so the conversation abruptly turned to something else. Yulia saw the preparations in progress and asked if she could help. "Of course!" was the reply. "Here, put on an apron and join in." Katerinya made the introductions, giving each of her companions a brief sketch of the other so they could place each other in the Derazhne universe. She worried a little that Andzhelina might start by asking Yulia about the epidemic. This would be the natural thing to do, but she wanted to keep Yulia off of that subject, if possible. But Yulia was a little closer to her original self now. She had always been good at sizing up a social context and finding a common thread to ask about. Looking at Andzhelina she said, "Professor Koskayin told me that you teach a course on the Bible as literature."

Katerinya jumped in to clear the air right from the start. "You can call him Ilya, if you want. We all do. I'm just 'Katerinya' and this is just 'Andzhelina'. We're all peers now."

"OK. Ilya told me that you teach a course on the Bible as literature."

They all smiled. "Yes, I do! Not this year, but every three years or so. Are you interested in that?"

"Yes! I had a religious upbringing, but I never learned about the true origin of the Bible until Prof ... Ilya told me about the Apocrypha and the Pseudepigrapha, and the Jesuit texts from Tacna."

"That was in a biology course?"

"No, I just saw the Apocrypha in his office once, and he told me all about it. I was reading from a book called 2nd Songs of Songs. I didn't even know there was a 1st Songs of Songs in the regular Bible. I never heard about that in church."

Both Andzhelina and Katerinya looked at each other with smiles and wide eyes. "Did you read any more of either of them?" Andzhelina asked.

"Yes! All of both of them. I was trying to figure out why one got into the Bible and the other didn't. They're very similar."

"And what did you think of them?" Andzhelina asked. This time it was a more open question than the one she once zinged Katerinya with.

"Well, they're kind of …"

"Erotic?" both women asked in unison.

"Yes, erotic." Suddenly Yulia felt enfranchised. She could tell that her two companions had discussed this before, and were welcoming her into the book club. She didn't know where this was going, but she was happy to be a part of it. "You don't hear anything, or at least anything good, about sex in Sunday school. And it's hardly ever mentioned in the Bible, so the Songs of Songs books surprised me. How did they get into the Bible? Well, one of them anyway. I can see why no one wanted to talk about this in church."

"I had the same Sunday school and the same reaction," Katerinya said. "They leave you to figure these things out later, on your own."

"Yes! I didn't understand until much later why Noah had to take two of every animal on the Ark. What was the second one for? A spare, just in case?" Both of the other women laughed at this story.

"Sex is in there, though," Andzhelina added. "You just have to decode the euphemisms. Carnal knowledge. There is a lot of 'knowing' going on in the Old Testament."

"Like 'Adam knew his wife and she conceived'" Yulia offered.

Then Katerinya jumped in. "I've heard that referred to as a euphemism, but as a translator, I disagree. I don't know ancient Hebrew, but the writers of these books, and we know there were many authors, used 'know' for a reason. This must have been the accepted usage of the times. Just as we have more than one sense for 'know' – to know that something is true versus knowing a person, being familiar with them – I think maybe they had a third sense. It's close to the knowing-a-person sense – *really* knowing a person. Think about it! It fits. It's like a conversation … a very deep, intimate, personal conversation." With smiles and silence, they both did think about it.

"I see where you're going," Andzhelina said. "I like that. But there must have been gradations. Like when Lot says 'I have two daughters that have not known man; let me, I pray you, bring them out unto you, and do ye to them as is good in your eyes.' That's the more familiar objectification of sex. The men are going to do something 'to them.' Not much interpersonal bonding going on there."

"Well, the word had to cover all the cases, I guess. But it could have been inspired by the better cases. It *must* have been inspired by the better cases. Why describe sex as a kind of familiarity between two people, if there is no 'getting to know you' sense about it?" Then she smiled. "I suppose that puts a whole new spin on 'I'd like to get to know you better.'"

The other two women laughed.

"You laugh, but think about it!" She was forced to laugh herself. "If you're attracted to someone, and you'd like to get to know them better, you're probably hoping that eventually you'll get to know them in the most intimate way possible. Just as love is on a continuum of affection, sex is on a continuum of familiarity. Wouldn't that be nice?"

They all thought so. Just then Ilya arrived. He had heard the giggling. "What were all you women talking about?"

They looked at each other. "Oh, nothing," they all said.

Whatever they had been talking about, Ilya could see that it had been a bonding exercise. And Yulia was now happily one of the gang.

§

Yulia stayed with her adopted family of orphans until the start of the fall term. This was her senior year, so she had the option of choosing a single room at her undergraduate house, but she opted instead for a suite with two other roommates. Ilya and Katerinya had encouraged her to stay with them for as long as she wished. Initially this was for much needed support, but she recovered quickly and continued her stay just because she wanted to. She had bonded with them. But the choice of a suite signaled her intention to form new undergraduate friendships. This was heartening for her adoptive parents, who were happy to see their fledgling ready to fly again.

As he was afraid might happen, the biology department offered Ilya the chairmanship. This was another instance of the kind of leadership he did not aspire to. At about the same time that he was diplomatically resisting the offer though, he received an offer from the University of Nairobi to be a distinguished visiting professor there for the following academic year. The upper tier universities liked to do these kinds of swaps because it raised both of their statures. Because he was still under contract to Derazhne for the next year, he had to get their consent. The timing was perfect. He agreed to the chairmanship on the condition that they agree to the visiting professorship. Done. Katerinya was thrilled by the news. She had always wanted to go to Africa.

By the start of the winter term, Diederick Brandt, as he had hoped, was well enough to return to teaching once again. Yulia reintegrated into the student life and only occasionally felt the need to visit her "parents." Though she did invite both suitemates to dinner once at her "home." And Andzhelina accepted the mantle of Crispness party sponsor at the Kadnikov's mansion, with funding from the University.

Katerinya took up the offer from the ladies at Veronika's Fine Ladies's Apparel to show off a new gown. The selection process took a lot longer this time. There were more interests involved now, and they had time to consider a wider range of candidates. What really slowed the process down were the conflicting goals of Katerinya and Veronika. Veronika had the expected anxiety of following her initial success with a felt need for an even more impressive second act. Katerinya, on the other hand, didn't want to eclipse the pinnacle of the Lady in Red. She was all for something dramatic, but she wanted her first act to be the one that everyone would remember. "There would never be another one quite like that," they should all be thinking. They settled on something substantially different from the first act – something that let Veronika extend her brand in a new direction, and that let Katerinya feel that the two acts would not compete.

To compensate for the loss of so many traditional invitees, Andzhelina prevailed on a couple she knew to invite a personal friend of theirs who had never been to the event before. It made the evening quite special when His Majesty Prince Koldan Sonvaevich Tarasov was announced.

At commencement, in the late spring, it was a tradition to have the class valedictorian give a brief speech. This year, everyone agreed, the honoree was quite special. Her name was Yulia Katyaevna Antonova. She gave a very moving speech about her personal experiences with the epidemic and the ultimate rebirth of the university community. After a standing ovation, the new university president presented her with a gift on behalf of the entire faculty and student body. This was not part of the tradition. It was a special token of appreciation prompted by extraordinary circumstances. Her "parents" were so proud of her.

Ms. Antonova had been accepted into the Ph.D. program in the Department of Biology at the University where she would be a Teaching Fellow in the fall. She would stay at Ilya and Katerinya's during the summer, both in Derazhne and Mariankursk, while they were preparing for their year abroad in the fall. When they were in

Africa for the year, she would continue to live at both houses as the fulltime caretaker. Pretty good digs for a first-year graduate student on a teaching fellow stipend.

And then there was the enigma of the Androsia message. Events had eclipsed it as a top-of-mind issue when Ilya and Katerinya had first returned to Derazhne. Eventually they remembered, so in the fall, Ilya and Katerinya diligently searched his house and office, and every other location around the University that he might have been associated with, looking for lily plants, potted or planted, symbolic or real, for sequencing. They found nothing meaningful in any of the DNA. They even checked everything growing in his home garden, at every season of the year, but there were no lilies to be found there.

So the enigma remained, waiting for a next clue.

Chapter 13

THE LAST OF THE ANDROSIANS

No one wakes up one day and suddenly realizes that they're old. Aging is a gradual process. The changes from day to day are not noticeable. Even the changes month to month are not noticeable. You need an external reference – some comparison of the way you look now versus the way you looked many years ago. You notice this at class reunions. Your previous classmates are 20 years older, but you remember them from school days. Sometimes the contrast is so great that you no longer recognize them without the nametags. If you age gracefully, some of your classmates might say something like "Oh you look exactly the same!" That's a compliment. It's often not true.

Katerinya was aging very gracefully, so she got this a lot at reunions. It just delayed the realization. Then one day she found a picture of herself and Ilya taken at the first Crispness party. It had been 20 years now since they had come back from Africa and she could see the difference. She already knew she had been hiding the gray hairs, but they appear one at a time. The picture clearly showed the difference between then and now. She had come a long way from that magic moment in the red gown. It seemed so long ago now. But she was not bothered by the change in her appearance. She was aging well. Rather, it was the image of Ilya beside her at the Kadnikov's that consumed her attention that day. Unlike her, he really did look exactly the same.

People often said this about Ilya, so he and Katerinya had become used to it. When you see each other every day, of course you look about the same. She had just assumed they were both aging well. But now that she could see the trajectory of her own well-aging, it became clear that Ilya's trajectory was something very different. He wasn't aging well, he just wasn't aging at all. He had always been of an indeterminate age. There was no known birthday to celebrate. But when she first met him, he had no gray hair. And now, 24 years later, he still had no gray hair. But she did.

His friend Diederick Brandt had retired. He was now clearly in his later years and rarely came into the office anymore. But Ilya was the same active professor of biology and mathematics, teaching, lecturing, discovering, and advising young students. He was exactly the same.

Andzhelina had also retired. She was now a Professor Emeritus who came into the office occasionally. She looked like a Professor Emeritus. She was no longer very active in the academic community, and needed help pulling off the Crispness party every year. She was about ready to hand it off to a more active sponsor. But Ilya was exactly the same.

Yulia was now the chair of the biology department at the University. As Katerinya had hoped, she had found someone like Ilya in the form of one of her graduate students when she first started teaching as a young assistant professor. Instead of reaching up across the age gap, she had reached down, or rather, he had reached up and she met him halfway. They had their own place in town, and would oftentimes have dinner with Ilya and Katerinya. But there was no mistaking the difference between the wide-eyed sophomore of 24 years ago, and the distinguished professor now teaching, lecturing, discovering, and advising young students. But Ilya was exactly the same.

Everyone, including Katerinya, had caught up to or surpassed him in apparent age while he just stayed the same. This had not been news to Katerinya, or Ilya, because it had happened so gradually, but today it was news to Katerinya. There was something clearly different about Ilya. The biological entropy that was slowly reclaiming everyone else couldn't lay a finger on Ilya. His lectures were famous for pointing out the inevitability of this process, but he had somehow dodged it entirely.

The revelation had come at mid-morning, in early summer, in their house in Derazhne, as Katerinya was doing some cleaning. That's when she had found the picture. Changing the bed linens was the next task, but she found herself unable to plow ahead with her planned agenda. She wandered around the house, lost in thought. She finally sat down in the library looking out through the French doors into the urban garden in the backyard. The planting beds between the red brick walkways were mostly cleared of the dying-in remains of the spring perennials. All that remained were the green leaves of the bluefairies because they don't die in like the rest of the perennials.

Ilya was at his office in Dahlström Hall today, working on the curriculum for the coming academic year with the department head, Professor Antonova (better known as Yulia to you). He would be back home later today. Katerinya's first thought was that she needed to confront him with this manifest evidence of his strangeness and ask for an explanation. But then it occurred to her that it was unlikely that he was harboring any secrets. She knew him too well for that. He wouldn't understand this any better than she did. It was nature she should be demanding an explanation from. How did this happen to Ilya? What was wrong with him – or perhaps put another way – what was right with him, and wrong with everyone else?

She sat right there for most of the rest of the day, turning the questions over in her mind. The more she reflected, the more she realized there had been clues. The dreams, for instance. He was always having dreams about other people and places and events that he could not recall in waking life. And these people, places, and events were often very detailed when he recounted the dreams, as if he had been there before. Perhaps he had been. And the skills he couldn't account for! The doctor, the woodsman, the marksman, the composer, the horseman, the survivalist, the extreme polyglot. There had been more, and no doubt others were lurking just below the surface yet to be discovered. How does one person acquire all of these skills in a single early lifetime?

He didn't know, of course, and that was the piece of the puzzle she just couldn't find a place to fit in. The whole memory loss thing. He had recovered about 20 years worth of his past early on, but then the improvements had plateaued. He hadn't made any significant progress since. There was this hard boundary he could not manage to push past. And all of the skills and the dreams were about times prior to that.

Katerinya eventually got back to her original agenda and changed the bed linens. When Ilya returned home, the subject was constantly on her mind, but she struggled to find the right way to bring it up. What was she going to ask him after all – why is he an alien? When they made use of the fresh clean sheets at bedtime, she finally let it out. She didn't ask any questions, she just showed him what she had discovered. Ilya liked the picture. The vision in red from so many years ago. He looked at it for several seconds, remembering the magic. Then he looked at her, still smiling.

"See the difference?" she asked.

"Well of course there's a difference. You were beautiful then. You're beautiful now. It's just a different kind of beauty. You haven't lost a thing."

She was, of course, very happy to hear this, but that was not the point. "Not in me, in you."

He looked at the picture again. "I don't see much difference in me. Do you?"

"No! None whatsoever! That's the point. You're exactly the same. Literally."

He couldn't see himself now, of course, but he was pretty sure she was right. And the difference in her from then to now drove home the point. There should have been a matching difference in him. And there wasn't.

She ran her fingers gently through his hair. "Look. Still no gray. Anywhere. But I have some. How does this happen – or not happen?"

The picture finally did for Ilya what it had done for Katerinya, only more so. He didn't look at himself much, but he was constantly looking at Katerinya. She had aged so gracefully that he had hardly noticed. Nothing stood out. She was still so endearingly beautiful. But the 24-year offset showed the change. They both had been blessed with good genes, exercised regularly, and ate well. This can slow the natural rate of cell senescence, postponing the effects of aging later into one's lifespan. But she was clearly senescing now, and he was not.

He tried to explain. "Humans go through three stages of life. First is development, from conception to about 20 – on average. In that phase we are getting bigger and more refined until the mature adult form is realized. Then for another 20 years or so – again, on average – we are in stasis. Every time entropy causes some part to wear out, our body has stem cells and proteins to repair or replace it. It's a standoff with entropy. It destroys, we recreate. We remain about the same. Then, for some reason, we enter the senescent phase where the repair and replace machinery is not quite so efficient anymore. It itself eventually wears out, so the accumulated damage to cells and organs begins to affect our functions. Entropy is slowly winning now."

"So I'm entering phase three, and you're still in phase two?"

"Well, that would explain what we are seeing."

"How is that even possible? Are there other people like this?"

"Not that I know of. But it is certainly possible. It would only take a few key mutations to keep the senescence clock from turning over. We don't know what those are yet, but someday we might. A lot of plants, like trees, don't senesce. They just keep growing until some environmental effect, like drought, or disease, or a windstorm kills them off. It looks like lobsters may be similarly immortal. They don't die by growing old."

"So you're immortal like that?"

"I could be. Or I could just have a much slower rate of senescence."

"Is that a good thing or a bad thing?"

"I hadn't really thought of that until now." He tried to think what that might mean for the two of them. And he didn't like what he came up with. "I don't want to be immortal, unless you can be too. I don't even want to senesce more slowly unless you can age at the same rate. We should be able to get to the end together – or not to the end together."

This was worrisome for her as well. "I think it's a bad thing. It would be so unfair to you. I don't want you to watch me grow old and unattractive while you stay in your prime. If we grow old together, we match. It's easier to handle that way."

He smiled. "Somehow I don't see that happening. You'll grow old, but I don't think you'll ever grow unattractive – to me."

She had simultaneous feelings of joy and sadness at that comment. She knew him well enough now to know that he was probably right. She would always be attractive in his eyes, even when not in the eyes of others. "But others won't see it that way. We'll be an odd looking couple."

"That will be their problem, won't it? Anyway, we may be worrying about nothing. Maybe I'm just a little bit slower than you, and eventually I'll catch up."

She liked that thought. Wishful thinking, Ilya called it. Believing what you want to be true. But that's what both of them chose to believe that night. Katerinya snuggled up and hugged him tightly, as if to prevent him from being carried off to the land of the immortals.

§

In the morning, they stayed between the fresh clean sheets for a long time. Last night's revelation was now unshakably on their minds. There wasn't much more to say. Their future would be different than they had imagined, or it wouldn't. It would take many more years to be sure which path they were on. There was nothing more to do about it in the here and now, except perhaps to cherish the here and now. So they stayed in bed for a while longer.

At breakfast, the mood was still subdued and thoughtful. Katerinya brought up the skills and the dreams. Didn't these seem to come down on the side of immortality, she asked? Ilya reconsidered them from the point of view of the new context and had to agree. They were both evidence of someone with a longer-than-normal past. But not necessarily an infinitely longer past, he said. He could still be just abnormally slow to age. He thought he was being scientifically fair. He wanted this to be true, of course. They both did. But it was no more or less probable than the immortality hypothesis. Scientifically speaking, it was a tie. There was no indication which belief was the true one, so they were entitled to choose. For now.

The key, of course, was his missing memory of the past. It was Saturday, so they had no place in particular to go today. Usually they would go to Mariankursk for the weekend. But the revelation had thrown them off their usual rhythm. Still, it was summer and they wanted to get outside, so they decided they would head there once again. There really wasn't much to pack because they had so many things at both places. They could just get up and go. But then Katerinya had an idea. Maybe they should try to go somewhere that might help trigger Ilya's memory. It didn't happen very often, but sometimes when he returned to a place he hadn't been for a while, brief memories popped up. It was a great idea in the abstract, he said. But where in particular? Where hadn't they been for a long time?

Then Katerinya suddenly had the perfect suggestion. "Remember the place on the rail line where the train crosses a bridge over a river gorge?"

"Between Kaliniyevka and Yelangrad on the northwest line?"

She was still a little directionally challenged, so the precise location didn't help. But what else could it be, if not that? "Yes! Remember you said we should come back there sometime in the summer and have a picnic by the river?"

"Yes," he smiled, now remembering that suggestion.

"We never did go there. But now it's summer. It's perfect! You had a memory there once. Maybe if we go there it will come back. And even if it doesn't, we'll have a wonderful picnic by the river. We always meant to do that!"

It was the perfect suggestion, he thought. Nothing but upside either way. So they quickly packed a picnic lunch and headed for the door.

"Wait," Katerinya said. "We'll need a wine. I'll select it, of course." She went to the wine rack and picked one she remembered favorably. There would be no second choice this time. These were all Ilya's wines.

The last time they had crossed the trestle bridge, Ilya had wondered how they would get down to the river. They asked when they got to Yelangrad Station and found out there was a footpath leading out of Yelangrad that took you right down there. It was only about a 15-minute walk. The train climbed the grade of the gorge from here. The path descended it. The site was as they remembered it, minus the snow. Now they could look up the gorge from the valley floor, and up at the trestle bridge in the distance. The summer sun was warm and, until the next train crossed the bridge, the valley was quiet and peaceful except for the natural sounds of birds and running water. Ilya experienced no new memories, but at this point they didn't care. They spread out the picnic blanket next to the river among the ever-present bluefairies. Ilya remarked that this would be an even more gorgeous sight in the spring when the bluefairies would be blooming. For now, they were a sea of dark green leaves.

Katerinya got into the playful mood again, and remembered their "natural" picnic all those years ago in Pastorollay. But looking around, it was clear that the privacy of nature would be interrupted every hour or so when a train crossed the bridge. Then they would be a part of the scenery for the passengers above. This would have to be a civilized picnic. But it was warm, so after a while they removed their shoes and sat on the riverbank, dangling their feet in the cool water. Ilya had to roll up his pant legs, but Katerinya was wearing a sundress, so no preparation necessary. They brought the wine with them.

And then it happened. Katerinya was sitting to the left of Ilya, so she could see his left ankle dipping in and out of the water. Ilya noticed some curious behavior. Katerinya kept alternating her gaze between his feet and the ground surrounding them.

"What is it, Katya?"

"Your Androsia mark. It's green. Now look at the green leaves of the bluefairies. See the resemblance?"

He did. The shape of the flowerless leaves matched the fleur-de-lis shape of the tattoo. And both were green. They had spent all of these years looking at flowers, expecting the mark to match some kind of lily bloom. But it was the shape, and color, of the bloomless leaves of the bluefairy plant. This is what bluefairies looked like for most of the year.

"Is that it?" she asked incredulously.

Ilya didn't answer right away. Instead, he pulled out his cellphone and checked for a signal. They were close enough to Yelangrad that he got one. Then he called Yulia. She answered. He asked her if there were any genome reference samples for the common bluefairy in the archives. She said she would check. No, there weren't. Then he asked her for an enormous favor. He would explain later. Could she please go outside and take a cutting from the first bluefairy she sees. They're all over campus. Then start up the sequencing machinery and send him the digital readout as soon as it finishes. That could take all day, she said. He knew that. That's why he was calling now. He and Katerinya were in a meadow up near Yelangrad right now, so he couldn't do it himself. But they would be on the next train home. They wouldn't get there until much later anyway. No problem, she said, and she was off.

Katerinya heard the conversation, of course, so she had her answer. On the train home, Ilya sought to temper their excitement with the memory of how many times their next great idea had come up empty. At this point, it was just a good guess worth checking out. They should be prepared for another dead end. Katerinya knew the drill.

When they got back to their house in Derazhne, Ilya was at his computer on the Internet before she could even put the picnic basket down. She pulled up a chair next to him to watch. The sequencing hadn't finished yet. But there was another avenue that Ilya wanted to try right away. He entered 'bluefairy' in a search query and hit enter.

And there it was. Hiding in plain sight. The title of the page said "Common Bluefairy." In the gutter sketch to the right there was a picture of the flowering plant in its characteristic blue color. Below that it said "Genus: Androsium." "Species: scientium."

They didn't bother reading any further, about how it was one of the hardiest and most adaptable of perennials, growing all over the world. It was also unusual in that its leaves remained green after the spring blooms dropped off. Instead, Ilya typed the search word 'Androsia' in a query, and hit enter. And as before, no search results. A difference between 'sia' and 'sium' had made all the difference in the world. His prior self must have known this. You had to be looking for bluefairies. Most people, himself included, did not know its scientific name. So Androsia would remain anonymous to anyone who could not connect his tattoo to the nonflowering bluefairy.

Now they had to wait for the genome file to finish the story. It was an interminable wait. They paced back and forth. They reminisced about all of their previous dead ends. They thought about making dinner, but they just couldn't. There was nothing else they could do, or even think about. This was the final answer. They just had to wait.

§

Later that evening, the file finally came. Ilya had changed his interpreted translation script to add a filter for stretches of non-words. The genome was likely to be very large, and much of it would carry no human readable message, so the script would just produce the parts that were readable. It turned out to be a *very* large message. It came in two distinct parts. The first was a brief history of the original Androsia project. It was, as Ragnar had said, a society of surviving scientists from the early days of the Great Dying. Only it wasn't a myth. They had banded together to record and preserve a summary of the scientific knowledge of their times, so that it would not be lost to future generations. The second, much larger part was the scientific summary, reflecting what was known as of the mid 21st century.

Once they had determined this two-part structure – described at the beginning of the history document – Ilya and Katerinya put the second part aside for a while. The human history was what they wanted to know about. The three founding members of the Androsians were Nick Glazer, George Kettleman, and Ilya McPherson. There were no other biographical details about them. The name 'Androsia' was derived from a science fiction story, popular at the time, about a place inhabited by androids that were indistinguishable from humans. The significance didn't go much deeper than that, other than that they viewed their version of Androsia as a virtual place where human knowledge would be stored for later recovery, if humans ever managed to survive the pandemic.

They were initially all scientists at the same university. As civilization was collapsing around them, they were spurred to found their mission when the science library at their university caught fire. The books that weren't destroyed by the fire were ruined by the automatic sprinkler system. This was their wakeup call to the possibility that paper books might not survive entropy if the pandemic went on too long. So they put out a call over the Internet to other universities around the world, asking for digital contributions to a knowledge repository that they were maintaining. A repository in this form would be tougher for entropy to kill, they reasoned. A lot of universities were already not responding, but for a while, those whose Internet connections remained live contributed. In many cases, they could just copy articles from collaborative sources like something called 'Wikipedia'. They made copies of their archive and pushed these back to other university sites for redundancy.

But slowly, the other universities began to drop offline as their Internet infrastructure collapsed. Several times the founders had to temporarily flee what was left of their own university to avoid infection. This is when it occurred to them that their project faced a threat they hadn't considered. At the current rate of failure, there would eventually be no more Internet. And if their digital assets could no longer be shared, eventually the access protocols would be forgotten. They needed a new way to beat entropy. That's when they hit on the biological solution. If they encoded their repository into the genome of a reproducing organism, each generation would copy the information into the next. They needed an organism with a large genome and plenty of non-functional DNA. Plants had those. They also needed a species that could survive in many climates and could easily reproduce. The best solution, they decided, was to make their own. They re-engineered some existing perennial species into an entirely new genus, custom made for their purpose. They called the genus *Androsium*. Since it had been invented de novo, it had only one species, which they dubbed *scientium* for its payload. Then they devoted what was left of their time to reducing their digital archive of knowledge to summary form so that it would safely fit in the non-functional regions of the plant's DNA.

This proved harder than they thought. Several collaborators who were still reachable online insisted on putting texts from the humanities in as well: the "great books," as it were. But no one could agree on what belonged on the list, particularly a short list. The running assumption had been that it would be up to future generations to decide what constituted great literature. They weren't really archiving "great science." Just essential science. Science was like that. If later generations disagreed, they could rerun the confirming experiments and decide for themselves. No one was choosing for them. The founders were just accelerating the rate of future recovery. In the end, it turned out not to matter. They ran out of space and time to even get all of the science in. So they left the humanities, including religion, to be reborn by natural means. If essential science survived, they reasoned, future civilizations would be able to reboot more quickly.

The Androsians' remaining days were devoted to spreading *A. scientium* as far and wide as possible. They were constantly on the run anyway, having to flee from infection after infection. The history recorded the eventual deaths of Nick Glazer and George Kettleman. The names of other remote collaborators were listed, but their fates were unknown after they ceased to respond. There was no mention of what happened to Ilya McPherson.

Ilya and Katerinya were stunned – both by what was in the message and what was not. They were expecting something about Ilya's memory, and more recently, something about his possible immortality. They did not expect this.

After some silence, Katerinya said, "Well, one of them was named Ilya. Maybe that was you? It didn't say he died, like the others."

"But that just means he was the last one to write about it. If he died later, no one would be left to write about his death. So we don't know much more than we did before. Maybe I'm this person; maybe I'm not. Why was it so important for me to find out about this?"

Then they took different approaches to the quandary. Katerinya decided to reread the history. Maybe they had missed something. Ilya decided to start reading the science summaries. Maybe there was something there. Ilya found the science part to be just what one would expect. In fact, some of the summaries read just like what one would find on the Internet today. So science had survived somewhat intact. We already knew that. Then suddenly he knew where he had to look. From plants to perennials to *Androsium scientium*. The summaries were well-organized. He got there quickly. The summary for *A. scientium* looked almost word for word like what he had previously seen on the Internet. So he queried for *A. scientium* again and compared the two texts side by side. They were identical – except at the very end. The genome version listed about 30 other 'known species' of *Androsium*. The first one on the list was *Androsium mcphersonii*. Hmm.

"I found something," he said. Katerinya looked over. He pointed out '*mcphersonii*'.

"That's almost like McPherson!" she said.

"It is McPherson," he said. That's how you form the Latin name of a species named after a person. It's the possessive. It means McPherson's Androsium."

"Well you should sequence that one then."

Ilya entered '*Androsium mcphersonii*' in a search query and hit enter. No results. "Hmm," he said. "The Internet doesn't know about that species. And I'm willing to bet it doesn't know about any of the others either. This is the one part of the bluefairy summaries that didn't make it onto the Internet – almost as if it were private somehow."

"Iliusha! Maybe it was meant just for you. What does that mean to you?"

"It means there are more species of bluefairies out there that no one knows about. How am I to find them? They're all over the world!"

Then Katerinya saw the connection. She got up, turned Ilya, still in his chair, around to face the French doors out into the garden. "There!" she pointed. "Almost everything growing out there right now is bluefairies."

She was right. They both went out into the garden for a look. The sun was nearly down now, so the light was dim. "But there are so many. Where do we start? It would take a year to sequence every one of these," he said.

Katerinya looked around. She saw again a pattern that she had noticed before many times but never asked him about. So she did now. "In the spring, when all of the flowers are blooming, most of the bluefairies are scattered about randomly among the other flowers. But this one bed right here has just bluefairies. Almost as if that was intentional. And they're neatly arranged in rows."

Ilya started counting them. He didn't even need to get to the end. About 30. Same number as the private list of species. "But which one is which?"

He went back in to look at the list of 'known species' again. Katerinya was right on his tail. He *had* missed something. A few words at the bottom of the section, just below the last species name. 'Left to right; top to bottom.'

As he was trying to infer a mapping from this, Katerinya said, "Look! The species names are not in alphabetical order. Wouldn't that be the normal way to list things?" She was right. That meant there was an implied order to the list. It started with McPherson's bluefairy for a reason.

"Katya, you've done it again. I think this is telling us that McPherson's bluefairy is the one at the top left of the bed. Let's take a cutting, and we'll go to the sequencing lab first thing tomorrow morning."

She couldn't wait. "Can't we go now? Don't you have a key to the lab?"

"But it will take all night. These are large genomes."

"Do you have to be there the whole time?"

"No ... I suppose we could go start it up now and come back in the morning."

"Then let's do that!"

Ilya had a better idea. "Let's take a cutting from all 30 and label them according to the species names we think they match. If we're right about McPherson, we can put number two in the sequencer before we leave. If we're wrong, the translation should tell us which one it really is and we can reorder on the fly."

Done.

§

Needless to say, sleep was hard to come by that night, even in their own bed in their own house. It was certainly more comfortable than sleeping in chairs at the lab. But their busy minds, spurred on by the expectation of results by morning, refused to let them drift off. They did sleep some, of course. It didn't seem that way to them because you are so aware of your restless waking state, and never notice the intervals of sleep. To make matters worse, this was early summer in the northeast when the sun comes up around 4:30 or so. They had to wait for the clock, not the sun.

When their alarm finally went off, and they were both awakened from actual sleep, they went straight to the lab. Their original guess had been right. The bluefairy that they sequenced was McPherson's. They loaded up the sequencing machine with the next in line, *A. millerii*, then started reading. The ordering of the species turned out to be a temporal ordering. They had been written in the order listed. At this point, they had already skipped two meals, but they were running on adrenaline. That wasn't sustainable. It would take them almost another week of continuous sequencing to get through them all, so they learned to pace themselves, and to remember to eat and sleep. But the slowly unfolding story they were reading was compelling and often caused them to forget, sometimes falling asleep from exhaustion in their chairs while reading late into the night. Their week's worth of reading turned out to be a private window into the past, chronicling what had happened to a single individual over the last 2000 years or so. They knew him as Koskayin, but others had known him by at least 30 different names, starting with McPherson.

McPherson's bluefairy held the longest message by far, because it chronicled the longest identity. The story began with the death of his colleagues and the disappearance of his remote associates. He had three missions at that point. The first was just to survive. So many hadn't. The second was to spread around the seeds of *A. scientium*, anticipating the worst case. The third was more optimistic. As long as he was still alive, he could put the digital repository on every Internet server he could find. If the Internet managed to survive, the knowledge would be available in human readable form. As the Internet continued to degrade, he himself became the repository. He kept several redundant copies of the archive on his laptop and a few external hard drives. He would always safeguard these, and always take them with him when he was forced to relocate.

Eventually the Internet went dark. Now it was just him, and of course *A. scientium*. The plant would survive him, but sequencing machines to read it would be somewhere way off in the future now. He and his laptop had been the only hope for a reboot in the near term. He had been using this resource to repair Internet connections and educate people whenever he found them. But electric power was now unreliable, and the chances for recharging laptop batteries were dwindling fast. So he had to regress from the digital age to the paper age and begin writing the repository down the old-fashioned way. His efforts seemed like a drop in the ocean at the time, but eventually the ocean started getting smaller. The remaining human survivors were now sparsely distributed – enough so that the bacterium had run out of adjacent hosts to infect. The scattered few who remained would now define the new human species.

He did not know he was an immortal at first. He had the same slow realization of his non-aging as the present day Ilya, but even more so because he had few socially stable reference points to compare with. Old friends weren't older, they were dead. It took until old friends began dying of old age before he realized he should have been in that cohort by now. And this gave him a fourth mission. Scientists in the mid-21st century were already close to figuring out how to stop senescence in humans. If he had managed to get there by random mutations at his birth, his own genome would be the template for which genes were likely responsible. It would cut through a lot of speculation and random testing. He was still on the fence about whether this was a good idea. It was so new, and hard to predict what this might do to humans. If the plague had not hit, he might have tried to keep this secret among his colleagues. There wasn't much chance of him getting sequenced now. But he discovered there were other downsides to being immortal in this new, more primitive world. Superstitions were rampant, and the presence of an immortal added fuel to the fire.

For a while, this wasn't much of an issue because there were so few people, and thus fewer people to remember him from many years ago. Eventually his generation was long gone, but he could still account for knowing so much about the pandemic and science and technology by pointing to his paper copies of the history. He could openly identify the Androsians, how they had preserved the scientific record and passed it down to him. He hadn't lived for centuries, he would say, the archive had. He could be the strange savant among them, who knew so many technologically advanced things, because he carried a surviving source of such information. This worked for a while. But as things began to stabilize, and civilization began to regenerate, with quite a bit of his help, there were more people. And more people to remember him. So he had to start relocating and adopting new identities as soon as he was in danger of someone noticing his non-aging. So one day, he set out across country and became Ilya Miller.

The original idea of writing his personal history, and then histories, was a simple side effect of his loneliness. He had a lot of time on his hands. He was careful to store these more circumspectly than the Androsium files, since they would give away his immortality. It turned out to be fortunate that he maintained these histories where he could easily read them. They were crucial to his recovery from his first memory loss episode. For the first eight hundred years or so, his memory had aged just like a normal mortal's. The further back in time, the less he could recall. The oldest memories got generalized and summarized, called up by one or two very salient events from the time, but the details were missing. He could still remember events from the onset of the pandemic because they had been memory-tagged with the fear and trauma of their times. But one day he woke up with the combined anterograde and retrograde amnesia that happened most recently in the Derazhne train station. As then, the anterograde amnesia was short lived, lasting only a few hours. Then the retrograde amnesia slowly recovered until it stopped out with a 20-30 year horizon. This cycle had repeated at periodic intervals ever since, every forty to sixty years or so. His theory was that the brain's memory capacity had a finite limit, even with generalizing and summarizing, so when he exceeded that limit — a sort of buffer overflow condition — a purging occurred. New capacity was created by pruning neural connections to the more distant past, making them available for overwriting with new memories. The temporary anterograde loss was probably a side effect of the reorganization.

Memories from before the horizon would periodically show up in dreams, but never in waking life, though he would sometimes have déjà vu experiences of these episodes when awake. Because his written histories were accessible to him at the time, he was able to read about his distant past, but could no longer recall it. This put a premium on continuing to write his personal histories, and leaving the sort of "look in pocket" prompts for quicker recovery from the purges.

It wasn't until the last century, when genome sequencing technology re-emerged, largely through his efforts, that he decided to stop keeping his past histories in plaintext. That's when he woke up to the fact that his fellow scientists would now be fully capable of comparing his immortal genome to the standard human reference. The whole point of *Androsium scientium* had been to make the past ideas *public*, so that they could be recovered faster. Now he had a need to keep his own history *private* — secret even. And this same artificial Androsium genus was the perfect target. That's when he came up with the idea of putting his histories in new species of *Androsium*, one for each of his past identities. They were each functionally identical to *A. scientium*, with just some of the non-functional DNA written over. He started a new bed in a new garden whenever he was forced by a new identity to move. So there were other locations where the 'known species' could be found.

Since he still needed a prompt to himself to look in the gardens, he got the matching tattoo on his ankle as the more cryptic 'look in pocket' mark. More recently, two groups had somehow connected the dots of past sightings, and learned about the mark. One was the Korihor people. Through their own twisted logic, they had equated him with the AntiJossmit immortal from 2nd Alma. There was something about the biblical religions that led them uniformly to assign immortals to the dark side. Not unlike the reception he got in the early Dark Ages. The Androsia copycats, like Ragnar, had seen this on him somewhere, at some point in their past, and it became part of their lore. They must have found *Androsia scientium* on the Internet, and made the connection with the flowerless bluefairy. That part was public, after all. Immortality was not part of the public story, so they were harmless. But if they found him, it made it more likely that the Korihrians would. So then he had two groups to avoid. Once they started stalking him, he started planting fleur-de-lis denotations wherever he encountered them to send them on a wild goose chase. He had never intended to make it so hard on himself.

§

In the McPherson text, Ilya had finally found his parents. He still could not remember them, but his former self told him his mother's name was Rene Applewhite and his father was George McPherson. In the beginning, he was Ilya McPherson, because his mother had liked the sound of the name 'Ilya'. He inferred that he had no siblings because Ilya McPherson hadn't mentioned any. Why name your parents and not your siblings if you had some? So this made him a bona fide only child, like Katerinya and Yulia, but it looked like he no longer qualified as an orphan. Their deaths weren't mentioned, from which he inferred that they had died of natural causes. Outliving your parents doesn't make you an orphan.

He was born in a place called California, but there was no mention of his childhood. As he moved from one life to the next through the centuries, he had adopted new surnames, and much later, novel matronymics, to blend in with the customs of the times. He had been, at various times Carlson, and Atkins, and Garcia, and Thibault, and Ganser, and Kirsanov, and Tsiolkovsky, and many others. Each time, he had taken pains to choose an actual name drawn from the surrounding cultural milieu, familiar sounding enough to blend in, but not familiar enough to invite inquiries into his ancestry. In the early years, he kept his first name as 'Ilya.' But as the population grew, having a long string of successive 'Ilya's made it easier for people to trace him through property records, so he began using new first names as well.

The present Ilya could not remember planting his *Androsium* garden because he had last added to it two lives ago when he was Krasimir Jannaevich Vetochkin. The last bluefairy species in the bed was *A. vetochkinii*. Historical Ilya had first come to Derazhne around 350 years ago with some associates on a mission to rebuild a university from the ruins of a prior one here. The northeast was one of the last regions to recover and repopulate. That's when he first started planting the garden at his house. He liked Derazhne, and the new university, so much that he alternated between here and other locations every other life. When his immortality was in danger of being discovered and it came time to leave, he would deed the house to the new identity living elsewhere. When that identity had to move, he would in turn deed the house back to the next identity taking up residence in Derazhne again. That way he could keep the garden. Ilya recalled from the deed search at Katerinya's years ago that his previous identity must have been Kevin Telmans from Ariona. That meant there was an *A. telmansii* growing somewhere in a garden in Ariona. He would need to find it and bring back seeds to plant here.

Without the Telmans history, Ilya assumed that the name his mother had given him must have been available for use once again. Thus he had become Ilya Erynovich Koskayin. Now he also knew that his mother's name was not Eryn.

His various identities over the last two millennia had been scientists, musicians, doctors, artists, historians, novelists, composers, philosophers, architects, inventors – but always scientists. He was the keeper of the Androsia repository, after all, and was largely responsible for gradually transferring it back to the new Internet, once that came back, under pseudonyms or anonymously.

Katerinya found it particularly illuminating that he had been both Jespersen, the composer of the famous cello nocturne that had started his memory recovery, and Krayevsky, one of his favorite novelists. It made sense that he would like his own novels, even if he didn't know he was the author, she thought. He must have liked the manuscripts he had sent off to publishers all those years ago when he wrote them. And he was the same person with the same tastes now.

The Jespersen story hit home for her. When he had written the nocturne, he played it often, and discovered that for some reason it acted as a memory trigger when he went through his purging episodes. It was so therapeutic that he destroyed all of his other cello compositions when he stopped being Jespersen, so this would be the one piece that he or other people played.

She also noticed that after his first stint as a novelist, the prose style of the histories of his personal lives became more nuanced, and very moving when he described the social costs of his immortality. He had had many past loves, and several children, all of them daughters. None of them inherited his immortality. He knew this because he had to watch most of them die, many years after having watched their mothers die. He had anguished over dying spouses, and disappearing to avoid dying spouses. Neither was better, he wrote. This was particularly hard on him before he had his first memory purge, because he always knew what was coming. And he was carrying so many sad memories forward. She wondered if this might be the cause of his present background melancholia – being vaguely sad for no reason.

She didn't know if Ilya would agree, but she thought his life may have been better with the memory purges. Between the time of a purge and the later time when he re-found the *Androsium* histories, he was essentially a new, normal person. He could fall in love expecting that he and his soul mate would be able to walk through their lives in sync. She felt fortunate that they had met right after a purge, and it had taken some 24 years to discover his immortality. And even now, reading about the sad stories of his past, these were not memories for him anymore than they were for her. That had to be better than actually having the memories. Yes, the memory purges probably made this bearable, she decided. She was heartened to see that through all of those centuries he was a serial monogamist. She would have expected that after knowing him all these years. That's who he was. But it came at a steep cost for him, she thought. He would have fared much better if he were the love-em-and-leave-em type.

Katerinya eventually found the significance of the river gorge déjà vu. Ilya had been there with a past love. They had gone there to plant the bluefairies that now cover the valley. Ilya had really turned a phrase on this one. The story broke her heart. This was someone whom he found when he already knew his immortality. There was no grace period. He tried to talk her out of it, knowing how it would end, but she wore him down. They had to live her whole life knowing. Who had it better, she wondered, me or her? I think I did, she decided. Would I have tried to wear him down? I probably would have.

§

About 10 years ago, Ilya and Katerinya had bought the house at 10 Tallinnskaya Street in Mariankursk to ensure they would always have access to it. They rented out the downstairs apartment and kept the upstairs pretty much how it had been when they first met. It was convenient for weekend escapes and even day trips. But recently they had looked for something more remote – a place of ultimate privacy at the cost of being not so convenient to get to. They bought a small island about 4 hours up the coast by train in the rural northeast. The island had one expansive house that they paid to remodel and bring up to building code. It could only be reached by boat from the small village nearby, but they had a boat and the crossing was short and well protected from the larger waves of the open ocean. The view from the eastern exposures was dramatic, all ocean with occasional small uninhabited islands. From the widow's walk, you had an uninterrupted, 360-degree view of the coast.

After learning of Ilya's past, and still grappling with what it would mean for their future, they decided now would be a good time to go there. It was still summer, their obligations in Derazhne were minimal until the fall, and this seemed like a good place to take time out and reflect. They had been there before, but only for brief periods. It was not the best place to visit in the winter. But this time they settled in and acquainted themselves with every inch of their house and their island. The quiet and the privacy were such a luxury. There were no people to observe them. There weren't even any squirrels to observe them.

Katerinya was still adjusting to the notion of Ilya being all of those historical people, and having been in love with all of those past women. She kept wanting to ask him about them before she would realize again that he knew no more about them than she did. He had no memories of them. They were just characters in stories for both of them.

One warm afternoon, as they were sitting on their front porch facing the bay, she got the urge again, before catching herself. She so wanted to hear more about these women. How was she like or not like them? So she tried a different tack.

"Iliusha, do you think we will turn out just like your past loves? I mean the ones with the same timeline. The ones where you met them before you knew."

"Well, I don't remember any of them, of course, but I suppose *I'm* the same person. My inclinations would probably have been the same then as now. But you weren't any of them, so we don't know if any of them would have your inclinations. Or maybe you're all different, and it turns out differently every time."

She thought about that for a moment. "At the level of detail in which you told all of the stories, they all did seem similar. And similar to me. Maybe you have a type. And I'm that type. But maybe it's because you didn't go into enough detail."

He smiled. "We'll never know. I have no memory of them to compare. Lucky me. I don't have to compare you with anyone. For all practical purposes, I am what I can remember. So you are the first true love I've ever had."

She liked that thought. He was certainly hers. "Iliusha! You could be a novelist again in this life! You have 2000 years of life experience to draw on. All the places you've been, all the things you've seen, all the things you've felt. Your well would never run dry. I would kill for that kind of resource."

He smiled at her. "Katya, my dear, you already have the same resource. These are no longer experiences for me, they're just things that I've read. We both just read what amounts to 30 very interesting novels about a protagonist from the past."

"Ah … I suppose you're right. Other authors' novels are a standard resource for one's own ideas. The only advantage we have is that no one else got to read them."

"You could use them for ideas – as long as you didn't disclose my immortality."

"I'm not sure I could. The immortality angle is the main storyline in all of them. What about your own published novels? The Krayevsky novels? Were any of those inspired by your past lives?"

He had to think about that. "Good point. I don't know. I don't remember when I last read them. I should make it a point to reread them from my current point of view."

"Do you think you might have cheated a little with your own novels? You wrote that it wasn't cheating to preserve scientific literature, because everything could be re-verified later. But you left out things like novels because this might prejudice future expectations of greatness. Do you think you might have played a role in preserving your own novels?"

"Preserve, no. I didn't start publishing novels until there was an established publishing industry again. So mine had the same chance as every other novel written at the time."

"What about Zimmerman? You must have liked his works in the 21st century. Might you have had a hand in their survival?"

"Well, it's not in any of the bluefairy archives. I suppose I could have kept a copy on my ancient computers, then put it on the new Internet when that came back. I don't know. I just assumed Zimmerman was lucky. His works just happened to survive where others didn't. Who knows how many works considered great in their times were lost. You know – "the first one now will later be last?""

She smiled at that. "I know you can't remember any of it. But there is a difference between you and me when we read your history. You *were* all of those distinguished people. Don't you feel some sort of kinship with them?"

"I suppose I ought to if I was a normal person. But I don't have that tribal sense that so many do, where they identify with their ancestors and feel bound to the heritage of the tribe, even though they never knew any of these people. And I *was* these people, but still don't feel the need to celebrate them. And I clearly was part of a tribe, the Androsians. We had a mythical past, and we accelerated the recovery of civilization. Ragnar's people, who are not connected to the real Androsians, feel pride. Yet I still don't."

"But you felt the need to chronicle them. You are still preserving their history."

"But that's for me – nobody else."

§

Later that evening, Ilya pulled out the histories and began randomly reading from them again, trying to imagine himself being there. He had been there, of course, so it was not hard to imagine this, but he was hoping to get closer to identifying with his prior self, just as he gradually got closer to feeling like Koskayin when he was first learning about himself from others in Mariankursk. In his famous lecture series with Egorov, he had always covered the genetic bottleneck of humans – the biology – and left the ideas part to Egorov. But what made the Great Dying so unique was that it was the Earth's first bottleneck of ideas.

He hadn't thought much about this from an evolutionary perspective. Only humans have this element of parallel evolution, where their collective ideas, written down or remembered, are inherited by the next generation of ideas. Each generation is derived from the last. There is a continuity to it. But these otherwise smooth evolutions can also be disrupted by near extinction events, like in biology. And they recover in different ways. He was the only human alive today to have witnessed such a bottleneck of ideas.

What was true would still be true. The speed of light would still be the limiting velocity of the universe; the atomic elements would still decay at the same rates; the Earth's tectonic plates would contract and expand in the same way. The new people would eventually discover these truths again.

But what is beautiful, or sublime, or genius is not so stable. It will change with the extinction of most of the previous art, and literature, and music, and drama. The few works that survive this bottleneck, due to random environmental accidents, will be the founding population of new generations to be passed down, as if the original works had never existed.

And what is holy, that supernatural beacon that broadcasts personal revelation to believers, is particularly volatile. It will suddenly switch sources, like the Earth periodically switches magnetic poles. And then the most amazing thing will happen. All of the believers in unison, like so many magnets, will reorient to point to the new pole, and begin to feel the divine revelation from a different source.

When they got into bed later that night, it was still very warm. So they slept without a top sheet on. After both of them had drifted off to sleep, Ilya had a virtual thunderstorm of dreams from his past. His previous lives emerged and intermixed with each other in many and varied ways. The scenes were very colorful, and freighted with past emotions. He eventually awakened with a start, but not enough to wake Katerinya. He couldn't get back to sleep. So he quietly got up, so as not to wake her, and went into the hallway where he continued to replay snippets of the dreams that he could still remember.

Then the man who never felt tribal pride was overcome with an emotion that was new to him – a sense of belonging. He knew who he was now, and felt an urge to disclose this to the world. The mythical tribal lore of past heroes and ancestral identity had been passed down through the ages to him in one uninterrupted transmission – from himself to himself. He walked up the stairs and out onto the widow's walk. He stood, stark naked, and looked out over the bay. It was still a warm night. Then he raised his arms as if in triumph under the full moon and declared to the universe at large: "I am Ilya Reneevich, first and last of the Androsians!" The sound of his testimony carried outward and upward, borne on the compression wave that encoded its meaning, propagating on into the upper atmosphere, attenuating as it spread, dissipating into nothingness.

Chapter 14

THE DYING OF THE LIGHT

A s the years passed, and it became more evident that Ilya was out of step with his age cohort around the University, it became time for him to retire the Koskayin identity. Andzhelina and Diederick had passed away, leaving very few associates who knew him from the beginning of that identity. But later acquaintances were beginning to notice. He resigned from the University and moved permanently, he said, to his private island with Katerinya. There she could age, and he not age, in private, so no one would see the growing gap between their apparent ages. They still held the other two houses in Derazhne and Mariankursk. Ilya had found the Kevin Telmans house and garden in Ariona. The Telmans identity had deeded it to the Koskayin identity before he returned to Derazhne. Ilya recovered *A. telmansii* for planting in his Derazhne garden, then sold the Ariona house. He and Katerinya had planted a replica of the Derazhne garden bed in back of 10 Tallinnskaya Street and on their island, to add to the redundancy.

Yulia's partner had died before his time from an incurable disease soon after the move to the island, so Ilya and Katerinya invited her to move in with them again, permanently this time. She also resigned her position from the University. Because they had stayed in touch, she had already suspected that Ilya was not aging, so when they took her into the fold, and let her in on the secret, she was not completely surprised. It was a calculated risk on Ilya's part. Yulia was an eminent scientist now and would know just what to do with his genome. He guessed that she would not act on this knowledge, and she pledged not to. Now he needed to wait out an entire generation here before going back to Derazhne as someone else, or move away and transfer the deed in the generation-skipping routine. He decided to put off that decision until much later. He did not like contemplating the death of Katerinya or Yulia.

He was now approaching the forty-sixty year range for his next memory purge, so he had to begin thinking about writing Koskayin's bluefairy and committing it to the gardens. But with Yulia and Katerinya still around, it was not necessary yet. They could always fill him in, if the purge happened on their watch.

With no more inland obligations, they could all travel wherever and whenever they wanted, using the island as their home base. Their brief stays among strangers in foreign places would yield nothing about their differential rates of aging. And they always made it a point to take along *Androsium scientium* seeds for random scattering.

Both Ilya and Katerinya had read about dealing with the differential aging of a lover in the bluefairy chronicles, but now they were experiencing it. It's strange for the one growing older, Katerinya found, because you feel less adequate and you feel guilty about letting your partner down. It helped both of them that Katerinya was still aging very gracefully. She let her hair go gray, and cut it short so that it framed her face. She managed to keep her slim figure intact. She was still quite stunning. And this was not just Ilya's opinion. She regularly got these compliments from strangers on their travels. She needed that. It told her this was not just Ilya being blind or kind.

§

On a warm, windless, summer day on a small island off the northeast coast, about 4 hours north of Derazhne by train, a pair of seagulls was hunting for mussels at low tide. They possessed a skill that biologists sometimes call the extended phenotype – a skill, like beavers building dams, or birds building nests, that is inherited through genes, even though there may be a learned component derived from imitating others. On first observing the seagulls' behavior, a human might find it odd. What are they doing? They repeatedly landed on the exposed shoreline at low tide, picked up a mussel shell in their beaks, flew up to a great height, then dropped it. Can't they hold on to it, a human might wonder? But this is a skill, not an incompetence. They drop the shell hoping that it will hit something solid, like a rock, and crack the shell. Then they can have lunch.

The seagulls occasionally saw humans from both their flying and walking perspectives, though in both cases, the humans were usually on the ground. It was rare to see them up so high this time, they thought, though they didn't think much. They were thinking about lunch. The humans, up on their high perch on the widow's walk of a large house, had already finished their lunch, and were now in the conversation and wine phase of the ritual. There were three of them. Two of them were engaged in a very animated discussion about science (though the gulls knew nothing about this) when the third one interrupted.

"You know, I never imagined that someday I would end up in a household of scientists."

"Are we boring you?" Yulia asked.

"No, not at all! It's just ironic, that's all. I've always had great respect for science, but it was never something that I aspired to myself. I didn't really have the skills, or what's more important, I didn't have the patience. I thought that the reward only comes at the end, when you can finally demonstrate something. On the way, I imagined it would be frustrating, sterile, colorless, no emotional joy. No wishful thinking, as Ilya says."

"I notice you're using the past tense. Do you still feel that way?" Ilya asked.

"About it not being for me? Yes. But I've changed my mind about the colors. I've learned from you, Iliusha, that you don't have the patience to wait until the end either. But you get something rewarding along the way. You have your own colors – and not just your synesthetic colors. When you explain how things work, it's not like reading from a textbook. I think textbooks give science a bad name among non-scientists. They're pretty dry. But you explain it almost like a fantasy novel. There are epiphanies, and surprises, and magical things that are actually real."

"So science is no longer sterile and colorless for you?" Yulia asked.

"Not when I hear you two talk about it. It has color for me now. Colors I didn't see before. And as I've learned from both of you – how birds can see many more colors than humans – I think maybe you two see colors that I can't even imagine."

Yulia smiled. "I used to think about science like you did, when I was in high school. I didn't see the colors until I met Ilya. But I had the skills, I suppose, so I jumped right in. But I went straight from religion to science, jumping right over philosophy. Ilya explained to me at the time that that was the natural progression of human belief. Philosophy grew out of religion, and science grew out of philosophy."

"I don't remember it quite that way," Ilya recalled. "I was just comparing the tribal rules of the three belief systems. How they differed. I didn't mean to imply that there was a natural progression."

"That's funny. I remember it as a *required* progression. That religion had to come first and philosophy second. Maybe that was my own spin. But think about it! It was language that made us modern humans. And what did language first give us?"

"A way to encode useful truths that could be passed on to others," Ilya said.

"No! A way to encode useful falsehoods! Think about it. Most animal beliefs *have* to be true. They are simple generalizations of actual experience. You can't experience false things. It takes language to formulate elaborate beliefs about things you can never directly experience — gods, for instance. Chimps have no way of conceptualizing a disembodied super-chimp that rules over them all from a different realm. So language made widespread falsehood possible! I'm not talking about lying here. Religion used the abstract thoughts of language to come up with the first cosmologies."

"So the first religions were just bad scientists?" Ilya asked.

"Not really bad — for their times. There was just nothing to constrain their hypotheses. And as you say, tribal authority took over, so people weren't allowed to challenge these beliefs when the evidence got better. Then the philosophy tribe came along to allow challenges by reasoning, and finally the science tribe came along to require evidence to settle arguments."

Ilya smiled. "I like that. Language first gave us useful falsehoods. Then the science tribe refined them into truths. I'll have to write that down in Koskayin's Bluefairy."

"I always meant to ask you about that — the notion that the science tribe succeeds because it's full of a-tribal people," Yulia said. "I thought that at first. But over the course of my career, I've come to realize that science is chock full of tribal people, just like every other human social organization. I've seen plenty of leaders and followers, plenty of veneration, plenty of tribal pride and competition."

"You're right. Science doesn't succeed because it's full of a-tribal people. It *is* full of people with an exceptional skill set, but on average, they're just as tribal as anyone else. It succeeds because of its tribal *rules*. And in the absence of a supreme leader, and without the veneration of "great scientists," the rules are what keep it operating as a single unit."

"But science venerates great scientists," Katerinya injected "You have Newton and Darwin and Einstein and all the others."

"But those are just names," Ilya said. "If the Androsians hadn't preserved the names, they could just as easily been Smith or Jones or Taylor. It was their *theories* that counted. Yes, there's a little bit of veneration of long held theories that makes them harder to overturn than less famous ones. But the tribal rules give you an even bigger reward if you manage to overturn one of the venerated ones. There is a premium on proving things false. This tends to suppress inertia. And the requirement of replication tends to suppress cheaters. So if science is just your day job, because, let's say, you just happen to be good at math, but your overriding goal in life is to be accepted by your peers, and avoid being ostracized by your peers, than your slavish adherence to the tribal rules to chase these goals makes for good science. Isn't that remarkable? It's tribalism that makes science possible."

"Make sure you write that down in Koskayin's Bluefairy too," Yulia smiled.

"But how did science get these rules to begin with?" Katerinya asked. "Who started all of this if there were no leaders?"

"Ah, a few a-tribal people. It doesn't require many. Just a few of them in the right place at the right time to get it started. I think democracy has the same problem. It's not really a natural tribal organization. It just has an extraordinary set of rules. The Africans have it and we don't because a few special people were in the right place at the right time there. They set up the rules, and now the state enforces the rules. But I'm afraid it's not stable."

"Oh, I remember our year in Africa very fondly. Don't you Iliusha?"

"The cultural parts, yes. And the wealth, the technology, the creature comforts, and the entrepreneurial spirit. The 'can do' attitude. Those were all good. But we stayed with good people. There were parts of the country where we would not have been so welcome."

"You mean the Black Supremacist regions."

"Yes."

"But they are in the minority. Isn't democracy a safeguard against that rising to the national level?"

"I don't know. I used to think that, but now I'm not so sure. I don't think the designers of democracy ever contemplated political parties. There was this naïve notion of rational individuals voting in their own self-interest. What could be more fair? But very few individuals are primarily rational. People don't like to think very hard – certainly not about government policies. So tribes in the form of political parties fill the void with pre-formed positions and reasoning. You just have to decide which party you are in, then follow whatever the party says. This puts huge blocks of voters under the control of a few party leaders. So you're back to warring tribes, just without the wars. The elections become proxies for the wars. But there's the same animus, the same vilification of the other tribes."

"Better than wars, isn't it?" Yulia opined.

"I suppose so," Ilya said, not sounding very convinced.

"This is too depressing," Katerinya said. "Let's talk about something else."

Yulia made an attempt to shift to another topic. "Have you decided what to do with the Koskayin identity yet?"

"No, not really," Ilya replied.

"What is there to decide?" Katerinya asked.

"I think she's referring to my immortality. Yulia and I have had a few discussions about that. I face this decision every time I change identities. Is it still worth the cost to me and those I love to keep this a secret? This is the first time I've discussed this with a biologist who knows my secret. She's given me a different perspective."

"Why do you have to keep it a secret?" Katerinya asked. "I mean besides keeping people from chasing you. If you went public, and published your genome, and worked on the cure for senescence, there would be more of you."

"That's just it. I'm not convinced that would be a good thing. Everyone would want it, whether it was good for them or not. Look at Africa where so many people are obese — because people want sugar and salt and fat and convenience, and venture capital funded businesses are more than happy to give it to them. If nobody dies anymore, except by environmental causes, the planet will eventually run out of resources, unless we restrict new births. That wouldn't be a good thing."

"Think what it would do for religion — or rather, *to* religion," Yulia said. "They're the ones currently selling immortality, but you have to buy into it on faith and follow their rules. If you were sure you could live forever without the rules, they would lose their franchise."

"I think you are suffering the most, Iliusha," Katerinya said. "By holding the secret, you are always condemned to outlive your partners. But if anybody could choose immortality, couples could make their own decisions. They could choose to senesce together, or stay the same together. Oh, Iliusha, if I had the choice I would have taken it. Then we wouldn't be in this sad state we are now."

"She has a point, Ilya. You might even have the option of ending your immortality. If a molecular intervention can be inferred from your genes, the reverse intervention could turn off your genes. Then you could be like everyone else."

"But only the wealthy would have the option," he said.

"At first. But once the technology reached economies of scale, it could be available to everyone."

"As long as everyone didn't get on the immortality bus and stay there. I've always believed it's better to know than to not know. I don't believe in suppressing knowledge. But this is a gray area. It's not really knowledge yet. It's possible knowledge. And I have no obligation to publish my own genome. So it's not suppression. I'm not taking any overt action. I just don't want to be the one who invents something that turns out badly. I don't have enough confidence that it won't."

"I think you are being too noble, Iliusha. The only person we are sure is hurt by this is you." Then Katerinya had a disturbing thought. "You wouldn't consider suicide, would you?"

"No," he smiled. "I've thought about that. But it's harder than you think. Someone could dig up my corpse and still get my DNA. I'd have to be cremated, but the bones and teeth would still contain DNA. I'd have to have these ground down and the whole pile of ashes scattered in the ocean or something. And I couldn't count on this. I'd have to depend on the executor of my will."

"Katerinya and I would have to do it."

"Oh, Yulia, don't say that! We could never do that!"

"I don't think you have to worry," Ilya said. "That's just not me."

From then on, Katerinya could be sure that Ilya would outlive her. But she could never be sure what the two biologists might decide to do after that.

§

Katerinya finally published her much-revised novel titled *The Lady in Red*. She had, in effect, written many almost-novels, each chronicling a slice of the person she eventually became. It was the discovery of

Ilya's immortality that finally made her confront the finiteness of her own life and bring the revisions to a close. It became a bestseller and a critical success. One critic marveled at the extraordinary imagination of Ms. Grigoreva because no one could have experienced all these things in a single lifetime. More than one critic noted that the male character bore a striking resemblance to the Dmitri character in Anna Yartseva's beloved book of short stories titled *At the Station.* That book, also a bestseller, had been published years earlier by a first-time author with no formal education who had once been a waitress at a train station café.

Eventually, Ilya made his decision. He and Yulia had discussed the options between themselves first, but then decided Katerinya had a right to be part of the decision as well. So they all three sat together one evening and went over the plan. Katerinya was happy that they made the right choice this time. She put her hand gently on Yulia's and said, "Take care of him when I'm gone, will you?" Then reflecting on the reality that Yulia had already well surpassed Ilya in biological age, she revised her dying wish to "Let him take care of you."

As her days wound down toward the inevitable end, Katerinya adopted the advice of the ancient poet, resolving not to go gentle into that good night. Her disposition then seemed to grow brighter, at odds with the trajectory of her path. And as the great Reaper strode across her corporeal landscape, extinguishing her small internal fires, she died as she thought she would, gently raging at the dying of the light.

Made in United States
North Haven, CT
07 December 2025